"YOU ARE LIKE THE MAN IN MY DREAMS," SHE SAID . . .

"Was he a real man, this girlish romance of yours?" he asked.

She nodded. "Oh more real than life. A tall man with dancing blue eyes that caught mine—and set me dreaming." She laughed softly. "Such dreams die slowly. When I was in London I searched every face, every passing carriage."

"And did you ever find him?"

"Only once in a dream."

Antoine groaned. He took her by the shoulders and twisted her body so that her gaze had to meet his. "Julie, Julie," he whispered. "Look into my eyes."

"You," she moaned, softening with desire. "You!" And she raised her lips to his . . .

A ROMANCE OF OLD WORLD INTRIGUE AND A PASSION THAT FIRES A BOLD NEW LAND!

ALEXIS HILL

PASSION'S SLAVE

j

A JOVE BOOK

Printed in the United States of America

Library of Congress Catalog Card Number: 79-84074

First Jove edition published August 1979

10 9 8 7 6 5 4 3 2 1

Jove Books are published by Jove Publications, Inc.,
200 Madison Avenue, New York, N.Y. 10016

TABLE OF PARTS AND CALENDAR

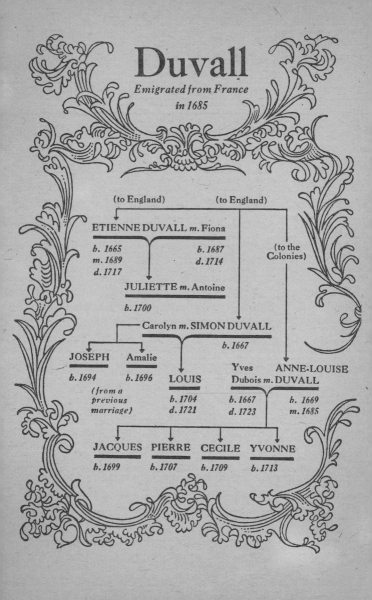

Duvall

Emigrated from France in 1685

(to England) (to England)

ETIENNE DUVALL *m.* Fiona

b. 1665   b. 1687
m. 1689   d. 1714
d. 1717

(to the Colonies)

JULIETTE *m.* Antoine

b. 1700

Carolyn *m.* SIMON DUVALL

b. 1667

JOSEPH   Amalie   LOUIS   Yves   ANNE-LOUISE
                                    Dubois *m.* DUVALL

b. 1694   b. 1696   b. 1704   b. 1667   b. 1669
                         d. 1721   d. 1723   m. 1685
(from a
previous
marriage)

JACQUES   PIERRE   CECILE   YVONNE

b. 1699   b. 1707   b. 1709   b. 1713

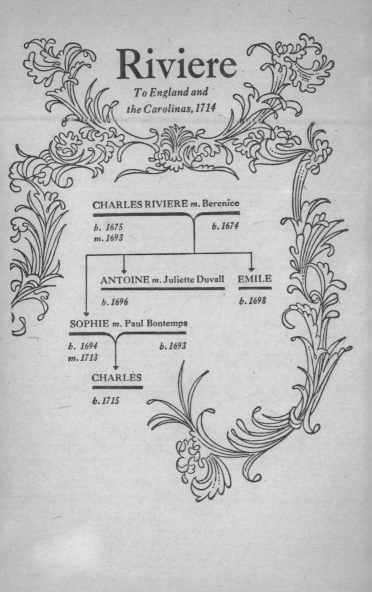

Riviere

*To England and
the Carolinas, 1714*

CHARLES RIVIERE *m.* Berenice

b. 1675   *b. 1674*
m. 1693

ANTOINE *m.* Juliette Duvall   EMILE

b. 1696   *b. 1698*

SOPHIE *m.* Paul Bontemps

b. 1694   *b. 1693*
m. 1713

CHARLES

b. 1715

PASSION'S SLAVE

PART I
THE GREEN YEARS
July, 1714-November, 1721

Chapter One

Julie Duvall could not have put a date to that memory, not what day of the week it was, nor even what month it was for sure. What came back to her like the pressing of a blazing brand on tender flesh was the terror she felt when she was first roused by love.

Falling in love was no astonishment, every girl dreams of that. Falling in love was a natural part of growing up, like being able to wear one's hair up and sleeping in a room without a governess. Falling in love was fun to anticipate, but there was nothing terrifying about it.

But the feeling that had flowed along Julie's limbs like molten gold, weakening her grip on her mare's bridle and causing mysterious, instant changes in her young body was truly terrifying.

As the coachman's blue eyes had held hers, and as he had leaned, smiling, towards her, she felt herself straining towards him as if her body was a gift that she would freely offer. In that moment, she would have died for the pressure of his lips against hers, the weight of his broad chest upon her own slenderness. Without will or pride, she had become, at his brazen glance, the helpless slave of her own passion.

The coach had passed. Only a stirring of dust motes in the sunlit air and the distant cadence of the horse's hooves remained of its passing but Julie still trembled from the fear that her own emotions had roused in her. The young man beside her turned with sudden concern.

"Julie?" Giles asked softly. "What is it? What is wrong?"

She shook her head as if to free it from the strands of madness that had bound her. "Nothing, Giles," she stammered. "The coach—" Her voice trailed off.

Giles's eyes glistened with delight. "Did you ever see such horses? Such a carriage? The queen herself would ride in a coach such as that. Matched horses," he repeated shaking his head, "eight of them matched like patterns stamped from the same piece of metal." Then, glancing at Julie, his voice fell, suddenly contrite, "Are you sure you're all right?"

13

Julie realized that a weakness had followed the surge of passion through her body. She swayed, and braced herself against Giles's chest with an outstretched hand. Startled at her touch, he slid his arm about her tentatively and pulled her close. Playfully, as he had since they were children, he slid his lips along the line of her cheek until they found her mouth.

Giles's kiss began as all his previous caresses had, as a fleet brushing of her lips by his. It was Julie who made this embrace different. Stirred by her unspent passions from the coachman's passing, she clasped her arms about Giles, pressing her full breasts against him as she opened her lips for the exploration of his tongue.

It was Giles who pulled away, dishevelled and stiff. His color was high and he plucked at his clothing, breathing unevenly. "Good God, Julie," he said angrily. "What in hell are you trying to do to me?"

Julie's hands flew to her lips, which felt bruised and thickened from the fury of the kiss. She stared back at Giles, her golden eyes wide with dismay. Then her glance dropped from him, and she blushed deeply.

"I'm sorry, Giles," she said, honestly penitent. "I just don't know what made me act like that."

He glared at her before turning away, pretending to do something with the bridle of his horse. She heard his labored efforts to control his breathing. She studied the smooth line of his cheek and the glow of his tawny hair in the sunlight, Giles was dear to her. For a long time she had entertained herself with dreams of them grown up together, her dark head beside his fair one. She knew that his father was dreaming the same, that he hoped for his son to marry the only child of the wealthy merchant Duvall. But she was only fourteen and he was going on twenty. She was still a girl at home, and he would be going up to Oxford in the fall. And now she had made him angry with her because of that wild spell that had seized her at the coachman's passing.

"I am so sorry, Giles," she repeated softly, pleading with her voice and her eyes for him to look at her.

When he did look up, he smiled crookedly. "I'm sorry I cursed at you, Julie," he admitted. Then his manner grew purposefully playful. "You may be only a half-grown brat, Julie Duvall, but you have more wiles than any woman

14

needs. You caught me off guard—maybe we should return to the house."

"Not yet," she pleaded. "We came to watch for my father's return."

He shook his head. "I don't know how you can be so sure he will come today, Julie. How long has he been gone, two months? Three? Yet you are certain that he will come up that road today."

"We had a message," she told him. "Papa's banker friend sent a message that papa's ship would be docking three days ago and that he would come up to the country today."

The road they were watching lay at the foot of the long, yew-lined drive that curved up to the Duvall estate. A deep triple planting of trees shielded the house from view from the road. There, in the shadow of the roadside trees, Giles had tied his horse and Julie's mare while they waited. Having submitted to her pleading, Giles located two flat stones and offered one to Julie with a courtly gesture. When she sat on the stone, the blue of her dress spilled in a wide, colorful circle on the grass.

"I know your mother will be happy to have him come back," Giles said thoughtfully, staring through the trees. He had heard common talk in the village that Julie's mother, Fiona Duvall, was cursed with some strange illness with the child she was carrying. She had lost two sons in childbed since Julie, and there was much clucking of tongues about her condition.

Julie nodded, her eyes darkening with concern. "She will be fine once papa is home," she said firmly. "When he is here, everything is fine."

The sun's shadows changed in the woods as they waited. Julie, a restless energy tingling her to motion, gathered wild stems which she plaited as they talked. Giles was full of his plans of college and the horse and the gear he would take. She nodded idly as she half-listened, trying to keep her mind from straying back to the blue-eyed coachman.

Suddenly, his voice stilled and he grinned at her. "A coach," he announced, "I feel the vibration of a coach along the road."

"Maybe it's papa," she cried with delight as they both jumped to their feet to look. Then Giles shook his head.

"It's coming from the wrong way," he pointed out. "And

15

anyway it's not a regular coach, just some great shabby thing with spavined horses clumping along."

Julie strained forward to look and then turned towards Giles with a groan. "Oh, I know that trap. It is my uncle's. That means we will have to put up with him and his brood."

Giles stared at her disapprovingly. "What kind of a way is that to speak of your father's brother?"

"Oh, stop trying to raise me, Giles," Julie said crossly. "I'm not a child you know. And as for what kind of way that is to speak, it is only honesty. Uncle Simon is a great clod of a man who eats too much and drinks too much and spins wild schemes like a great bloated spider."

"Julie," Giles cried. The genuine shock in his voice brought a peal of laughter to Julie's lips. Giles reached towards her as if to reproach her, but she slid away from his grasp.

"And his wife is a great untidy shrew who leaves an evil smell in the room when she passes," Julie added, taunting him from just beyond arm's reach.

"Julie," Giles repeated, grabbing for her arm. "You really must watch your tongue. . . ."

She scrambled for safety, her dimples deep with mischief. She looked around at him from behind a tree. "And my uncle's stepson is a great, wet-mouthed lout that his mother thinks I should marry."

Giles was almost upon her as she finished the final taunt. The merriment drained from his face at her words, and his face turned suddenly pale. When he caught at her arm, his grasp brought a quick cry to her lips.

"Never," he said firmly, chilling Julie with the intensity in his voice. "No man will ever marry you but me. Do you understand?"

He caught her in his arms, pulling her close but making no attempt to reach her lips.

With her head against his chest, Julie listened to the tumult of his heart, smelled the fresh scent of his flesh, and felt her body soften against him. When she did not reply, he shook her gently. "Promise me, Julie. Promise."

She nodded against Giles's chest to soothe him, but a sadness heavied her lips. She would marry Giles Urban; she was as sure of that as anything in her world. She only wished she could not so vividly remember the coach passing in the road. She could still see the flash of gold and white paint on

16

the carriage's body, the postillion in his fine flared coat with buttons that caught the sun's light.

But it was the coachman who dominated her mind's eye. She had noted the glint of the sun on the queue of his powdered wig, the way his long, fine legs swelled the satin breeches which were gartered with rosettes beneath the knee. But all of that was just ornament. It was the man himself who had taught her to fear her own emotions, that full, half-laughing mouth and the blue eyes so brilliant that it seemed that the sky itself was shining through them.

She would marry Giles, she told herself silently. But she shivered a little in his arms, knowing that her marriage with Giles, with anyone else in the world, had been shadowed forever by that chance passing between the coachman's eyes and her own.

Chapter Two

As the Linton carriage worked its labored way over the rutted road back to London, the footman, Antoine Riviere held the image of the young couple at the roadside in his mind. God, what a beauty that child had been, with the promise of voluptuousness swelling against her bodice, those golden eyes staring at him from a face like a flower. Her companion reminded Antoine of himself before his bulk caught up with his growth, when his beard was newly rising even as his voice deepened.

The heat of the sun forced rivulets of sweat to flow under the footman's heavy jacket, but Antoine, unheeding, sniffed the warm air like an animal with hunger. How could he have forgotten the intoxicating scent of new-mown hay without the mustiness of the stable or the dust of the fields bedded in it?

To be young and to be in the country, as he had been the summer he had been fifteen and having holiday in Provence. Those fields had been mounded with such hay, and the larks had sung all the nights through. But that had been the summer to end all seasons, a mare in her prime, the best falcon he ever had to wrist, and in the fragrance of a sunlit field, his first lesson in love.

Madame LeFevre, his mother's trusted friend, her dark eyes laughing, had spread her round limbs for his sweating, fumbling efforts. Such a woman, plunging him from ecstasy to anguish with a glance, drowning his guilty resolves with moist lips opened for his exploration.

Antoine laughed aloud at the memory, and a passing laborer, in a thick smock stiff with cow dung, stared at him with stupid astonishment, as if laughter itself had become a hanging offense on the highroad.

London would seem newly miserable after this trip through the countryside to Bath and back. His servant Titus was luckier. Titus's part of their bargain was to keep the gamekeeper's cottage Antoine had found in the woods of Essex. When he and Titus had fled France six months before, there was just enough gold to secure the cottage and provide food for a few months.

Antoine himself had suggested that the post of a footman would supply enough money to tide them over.

"You as a servant, sir?" Titus had asked, peering at him with his good eye.

"Come now, Titus," Antoine had jested to the old dwarf. "If you have done it all these years, surely I can do it for a year or two."

"No question of that," Titus responded, "but you're a gentleman."

"The belly of a king and a commoner sing the same tune," Antoine reminded him. "And if I should try to make my way in London, I would need clothes and chambers and a carriage. As a footman I will have my back and my bed covered and something in my purse as well."

"You'll find the few pounds a servant makes in a year no quick way to fortune," Titus warned.

Antoine nodded with a smile. "There are fortunes to be made in London. You hear of them all about Europe. What better place to study the opportunities of London than from the back of a fancy carriage on her streets?"

Titus fell silent, knowing, as no other man did but Antoine, how great that fortune needed to be for Antoine to buy himself free with honor.

Antoine thought smugly that his own decision had been canny. But even after two months on the back of the carriage, he had made no sure decision as to his course. He saw

18

the fortunes of the merchant traders rise as great ships plied their triangles of trade. Woolens, spices, tea, coffee, and tobacco flowed into the hands of investors and owners alike. But the trading business was slow. A man could lose his youth before his profits came.

And in truth, it was all a gamble of a sort. With the coasts prickling with privateers and the high seas with pirates, with taxes and the fury of the sea itself to contend with, a man might as easily win himself a tarpaulin shroud as a balance in the Bank of England.

There were quick gambles and slow gambles, he told himself with a secret smile, and he was not a patient man.

As Antoine brooded, the countryside changed. Wide green fields became less frequent, and scars of the city began to appear along the highroad. Villages were pressed tighter together, like huddled men fearing the night. At a crossroads, he watched a swarm of black flies rise humming from the corpse of a highwayman rotting in a hanging metal cage to warn new offenders. Then the skyline of London loomed ahead, darkened by the floating curse of dense smoke as London's numberless coal fires fouled the evening air.

The horses snorted with impatience as the carriage's progress slowed to a crawl among the costermongers and ragged children that crowded the streets. Pickpockets and thieves with their pox-spoiled faces seemed to swirl about the carriage wheels in a soiled human brew. But only the hordes of prostitutes raised their eyes to meet Antoine's. They were a motley crew, from the painted harridans to the brazen young girls who seemed no older than the child he had stared at back in the country. No wonder Londoners die young, he thought ruefully. And no wonder they were such stunted and sad-mouthed people. To breathe the stench of London with its diseased multitude was to woo death in life.

On an ordinary night, a ride like this would depress him, but this night nothing could spoil his good humor. For in his belt, laced firmly against his belly, he could feel the heaviness of gold for the first time since he reached these shores. Gold, warmed by his own flesh and secret to himself alone. For the hundredth time, he thought back over the events of the past days, puzzling this unexpected bounty which had come so suddenly and without his own seeking.

The trip to Bath had seemed an ordinary enough journey

at the first. The master Linton was sending the carriage to bring back his mistress from a few weeks of taking the waters for her health. Of course, the talk below stairs had given a different face on that. The cook and the parlormaid, gossiping over tea, reported that the mistress, a familiar with the queen's court, went not for a stiffness in her joints which the baths would relieve, but to heal the fevers of her passion for gaming, a disease well treated at the handsome tables of that city.

Antoine had paid their gossip little heed. Mistress Linton, an aging, high-voiced harridan whose face was almost totally concealed by patches and paint, seemed as unlikely as a gambler as she did as a bedmate to him. The marvel of the trip for him was the way it had fattened his purse and brought to his life a new level of mystery and puzzlement.

Upon their arrival in Bath, the mistress Linton had protested her unwillingness to leave. The postillion and Antoine had been told to amuse themselves in the city while she readied herself for her reluctant return home. Those had been entertaining days. Antoine was often behind the tables studying the play. Accustomed to the more brilliant guests in his father's home in France, he was often amused by the careless, witless play he saw and the money changing hands through witlessness instead of skill.

That last night in Bath, Antoine had lingered over a fat roasted hen and a tankard of the dark, rich cider of that region until the night was nearly spent. Still unready for sleep, he wandered into a gaming house to stroll among the tables and to watch the play. A fever for gold seemed to hang in the clouds of tobacco smoke that layered the air. If men ever were levelled, Antoine thought with a grin, it was at gaming. Laborers and squires, fine ladies and whores breathed shoulder to shoulder and elbow to elbow along the gaming boards.

Near midnight a messenger elbowed his way through the crowd to Antoine's side. Antoine protested as the man thrust a small leather bag at him.

"You have mistaken me for another," Antoine told him, shrugging the man away.

The boy shook his head determinedly. "You was pointed out to me," he insisted. "I was to make you take it, will y'or no."

"But I have no friends here," Antoine said, suspicious of any gift offered in that gold-fevered room.

"Not that you are knowing of maybe," the boy suggested with a leering smile. Then thrusting the bag into Antoine's hand, he disappeared into the crowd. Finding a deserted place along the wall where the candlelight flickered near, Antoine loosed the leather cord that bound the bag. Along with a quantity of coin, he found a note scrawled on crisp paper and folded twice. The script was obviously that of a woman, but the letters were formed boldly, with straight up and down strokes that suggested great strength. The message was simple enough and gave no clues about its author.

"The game is to the brave," it said simply. "Try your luck."

Antoine counted the coins into his hand. Five guineas. He searched the room with his eyes, but it was like trying to fix on a hare when the hounds were running. The crowd milled from table to table, so that after a few moment's search he despaired of setting even one of their faces firmly in his mind. As he had told the messenger, he had no friend at Bath, unless one chose to count the postillion who Antoine knew was rutting a milkmaid in the rooms above the inn's carriage house.

It was strange how much the feel of the guineas in his grasp made the play more attractive. He began to study the play at the tables more seriously, fingering his unsought bounty with thoughtful fingers.

Earlier in the evening, there had been more fools than drunks about the tables. Now the numbers were evenly matched. As he slipped into an empty chair, Antoine glanced down the table only once before entering the play. Idlers love winners as Antoine well knew, and he felt the small group of watchers gathering at his back. When his take had swelled to fifty guineas, he heard a wag call out to the others, "Look now, this will be another footman who will be ordering his master to mount." Not all the raillery was kind. A sweating squire who lost with a recklessness that smelt to Antoine of despair took no pains to conceal his rising fury as Antoine's winnings neared a hundred pounds.

"What would a French clout like you spend all that gold on?" he goaded, his tone growing ugly.

21

Antoine rose, towering above the man who swayed unsteadily on drunken legs.

"Spend it on mounting English whores," he said brusquely, pushing himself free of the man's grasp in a burst of ribald laughter.

As the rattle of the carriage shuddered to a stop at the Linton house, Antoine leaped to his tasks with alacrity. The sooner through for the night, the sooner he would be free to seek his own barren room above the carriage house. There would be a pint of ale and some cheese and maybe, when her evening work was done, the parlormaid Meg would come across the courtyard bundled in a dark mantle to creep in beside him and warm his bed.

One hundred pounds, he reminded himself with amazement. But who had been his mysterious benefactor, and how would that debt be recalled?

Chapter Three

After leaving her mare with the stableboy and releasing her dog Bonbon to race off into the fields to celebrate his freedom, Julie circled the house and entered through the servants' door. The kitchen was heavy with steam scented with the strong odors of boiling vegetables. The room was so hot that Julie wondered if the great fire would be necessary to cook the joint that spit and crackled on the hearth. The cook herself turned towards Julie without stopping her spoon. "There you are, miss," she said with some relief. "Miss Mary's been here a couple of times looking for you already."

"I was riding with Master Giles," Julie explained.

"The master's brother is here," the cook told her, turning back to her brew. "With his family too. Miss Mary had us make hot water for your bath."

"Thank you," Julie said. "If someone can send it up now, I'll go dress."

As she slipped almost soundlessly up the back stairs, Julie could hear the rumble of voices from the great room at the front of the house. Her uncle's loud, harsh voice and the higher querulous voices of her aunt and cousin Amalie were

22

muffled only slightly by the walls between. Only Louis's voice was missing.

Naturally, she wouldn't hear Louis through the floorboards. He was only a child really, nine going on ten, and a quiet, well-mannered child at that. Her papa thought him sickly, but Julie would hear none of that. He was her pet, her own beloved pet. She liked to imagine that she could remember him from birth, but that was unlikely since she was still under four when he came. But she could remember his baby softness in her arms and carrying him about when he was old enough to walk alone. As for the others, they would go jump for all of her.

She waited in her wrapper until she heard the maid finish filling her tub and setting out towels and oil and that light floral perfume that her father had brought her on his last return from the east. She pondered how brothers could be so unalike and wondered passingly which one her Aunt Anne-Louise would most resemble. She shuddered as her uncle's laughter sounded faintly in her room joined by the high-pitched giggle of Amalie. They were like swans among swine in her father's house. I hate them all, she told herself fiercely. No matter how Giles rebukes me, I hate them all except Louis.

Hearing the maid shut the door behind herself and the clatter of her steps down the stairs, Julie stood and let her wrapper drop to the floor. Then, on impulse, she walked into the sun that sent pale shafts of light through her window. Her flesh warmed in the light, and she laughed softly as a ray of sun touched one small, high breast paling the pink of the nipple almost to the whiteness of her skin. With her lip caught between her teeth, Julie studied her naked body thoughtfully.

Her body these past months seemed to have taken on some new mysterious life of its own, independent of her. The small, hard breasts had thrust themselves forward, and without losing her slenderness, the line of her waist and hips had changed, leaving her waist so narrow that buttons had to be sewn over on her fitted gowns. That this new shaping of her own flesh spoke to other people was just becoming clear to her. Giles's open admiration and his stumbling surliness were somehow linked to it. For Giles to attend her like this filled her with happy warmth, but then Giles was a squire's son and a gentleman. Her stepcousin Joseph was something else.

23

When he looked at her, the brightness and greed in his mean eyes made her feel somehow soiled. And when he spoke with his moist mouth close to her, she felt dizzy and sick.

Absorbed in her thoughts, Julie did not hear approaching steps until her maid Mary opened the door. With a startled cry, Julie took her wrapper from the floor and held it before herself in an untidy bunch.

"Well, I should think," Mary said brusquely, looking sternly at this child whom she had served first as nurse, then as governess, and now as maid. "What kind of a lady are you to stand like that in front of a window for the world to see."

"The world," Julie giggled. "Not even a sparrow has come to pry, Mary."

"Never mind that," Mary said. "Into your bath. You must be the one to entertain the guests with your mother not up to rising."

Julie sighed. "But I do love the sun, Mary. I love the feel of the sun on me."

A smile tugged at the corner of the older woman's mouth. From her tone of forced fatigue, Julie knew that Mary's rebuke was coming only in jest. "I know all about you and your loves, Julie Duvall. You love the sun on you and the wind ruining your hair and you love racing that great mare of yours and a pudding with fruit in it. . . ." She paused to catch her breath as she tested Julie's bath water with a careful finger.

"And you, Mary," Julie said softly. "I love you and maman and papa and my cousin Louis and Bonbon. . . ."

"And being clean," Mary finished sternly, nudging her charge towards the tub. "So let's be about it."

With practiced hands, Mary caught Julie's mass of dark curls and twisted them into a topknot secured by a ribbon. Then upon her knees, the old woman soaped the slender young body vigorously until Julie's skin glowed from the heat and the pressure of the cloth.

"Do you think that papa will get here today?" Julie asked dreamily, raising first one arm and then the other at Mary's silent direction. Mary studied the child as she bathed her. There was sadness in seeing how like her mother Fiona this Julie had grown to be, almost as if it was God's will that Fiona, in the fullness of her youth, would be replaced by a younger copy of herself. The same fine features and high cheekbones beneath those haunting yellow eyes.

"You didn't answer me," Julie said almost crossly. "Does that mean you don't think he will come?"

"I do think he'll come," Mary said swiftly. "I was dreaming and my ears missed your words. He will come tomorrow if not today, and high time it is too."

"Why do you say 'high time'?" Julie asked quickly. "Is it something about maman? How is she today?"

"Turn your head now," Mary said officiously, plunging the cloth into the water to make a stream down Julie's chest. "Your mother is not feeling the best," she said levelly when she knew that Julie could no longer see the concern in her eyes. She was like a witch this child. She could scent a lie or read a mind with the merest glance at your face. It would profit nothing to tell her that Fiona was better, for the very sight of that feverish face would betray the truth. But neither was there any reason to upset her by telling her of the swelling in her mother's limbs that grew more painful by the hour.

"She will be better when my father is come home," Julie said hopefully. "She loves him as I do, and he has been gone too long from us."

Mary nodded. "It is a long journey to Levant," she agreed. "And the Lord be thanked that he is back in England safe after such a long sea voyage."

"Will he find me changed?" Julie asked as Mary towelled her dry.

"Taller, I ween," Mary said thoughtfully, then hiding a grin, "and vainer and more impudent I might say."

"He likes my impudence," Julie giggled. "He told me himself that he did not choose maman for a wife because she was a suet pudding."

Not until her dress was buttoned and her hair pulled back under a freshly ribboned hat did Mary mention the guests downstairs again. "Lunch will be ready before we are finished at this rate," Mary fussed, pulling a few stray curls from under the cap to fall loosely on Julie's neck.

Julie, her eyes fixed on the window did not even realize Mary was speaking. "Do you believe that love can come in a first glance of someone, Mary?" she asked suddenly.

25

Mary's hands stopped, and she stared at the child with amazement. "What is it to you about love, you are a child."

"Maman was young when she and papa were married," Julie said slyly. "How old was maman when I was born, Mary?"

"I don't recall right off," Mary said crossly. "But that was not love at first glance. They were friends for years. . . ." Suddenly the maid's voice trailed off, realizing. "If it is that Giles Urban you are thinking of, he is only a squire's son and beneath your station."

"For heavens sake," Julie said, flushing under Mary's eyes. It had not been Giles of whom she had been thinking but the handsome footman with the clear, blue eyes who had sent her to Giles in a rush of passion. Then she almost giggled. What would Mary shout if she knew she was dreaming of a footman.

"Love at first glance is rare," Mary mused thoughtfully. "I recall how when Mary the Queen was betrothed to William of Orange, to be King William later, the child wept her heart out. For two solid weeks she did nothing but weep, and her eyes were as red as berries when the vows were said. But later they loved one another deeply and truly."

"But she was a queen and a woman," Julie objected.

"Not such a woman," Mary contradicted her. "A little past fifteen was all."

Julie's tawny eyes widened as she stared at her companion.

"That's little older than I," she said.

"Don't set yourself to dreaming, Julie," Mary warned. "Your father will not let just any man take his bird from the nest."

"I shall marry for love as my maman did." Julie said suddenly. "Whether papa will or not, I shall marry for love." Mary glanced back at the child with surprise and a small twinge of fear. She wondered if Etienne Duvall might not live to rue the day he had trained this child up with such independence of spirit. Julie, unconscious of her maid's studious glance, clasped herself in her arms remembering with a return of that warmth that had flooded her before. He is the handsomest man in the world, she told herself secretly, and only such a man can I ever love.

26

Chapter Four

In his rough room above the Linton carriage house, Antoine Riviere chose a book from the small store he had brought with him from France. Stretching his long frame across his bed, he lay half-reading, half-dreaming while the candle burned down in its socket. For a while he listened for the rustle of the wench Meg's mantle on his stairs, but soon even she drifted from his mind. The excitement of his gambling win and the long sunlit drive back through the open countryside had lulled him into a drowsy content.

It was from this torpor that he was startled to his feet by a sudden, imperative step on the stair leading to his chambers. He rose silently and listened to the heavy steps reach the top and pause. This was no light, woman's step, but the tread of a man who was heavy and sure of himself. With his slender knife secreted in his hand, Antoine flattened himself against the wall just inside the door and waited.

When the ill-built wall behind him trembled from his visitor's fist, Antoine chuckled to himself. At least the fellow was not intending to take him by surprise. It was not unlikely that the man's blows against the door could be heard from the street.

"Who goes?" Antoine challenged when the tumult stopped.

"A message for Antoine Riviere," the reply came. From his voice, Antoine judged the man to be in midlife, a man of some hulk from the resonance of his tone, and by God, the accent was French.

"Slide it under the door," Antoine ordered.

"It requires an answer," the man countered.

"After I have read it, we will discuss an answer," Antoine insisted.

The peak of paper widened to a folded sheet sealed with a single, hurried drop of wax. With the note to the light, Antoine at once recognized the script, and he smiled at the bold vertical hand of his mysterious benefactor, his angel of Bath who had sent him gold for his gaming.

The message was at once coquettish and cryptic. Like the first, it bore no signature.

"If you would like to thank me prettily, my man will bring you in safety."

A rebuke and a promise, the mingled scent of adventure and danger. For surely even this bold woman knew that men did not lightly travel the streets of London at these hours of darkness. After a moment of hesitation, Antoine shrugged and threw open the door.

The man leaning against Antoine's wall was a type that Antoine knew well. He was typical of those sturdy men who labored in his father's fields in France. Thick of neck and heavy of torso, his short, thick legs were rooted like old trees on the wood of the stair and his hands hung at his side like tools at rest.

He returned Antoine's stare with a studied insolence in his broad, flat face.

Damned truculent bastard, Antoine told himself with secret amusement. If indeed, as his father said, the king and his court were the lifeblood of France, then men such as this were her bones and sinew. The man's dark eyes gleamed at him without expression from under his disordered nest of heavy brows. Antoine was sure that the man had guessed him as accurately as Antoine himself had assessed the peasant.

"You expect a reply," Antoine said.

The man did not answer with the obsequious haste of most English servants. Instead, he nodded his head gravely, shifted a wad of something from one cheek to another, and then spoke.

"You would come or you wouldn't," he said flatly. "Either way it is a reply."

"I come," Antoine said. When the man did not acknowledge his words, Antoine went on. "If you would like to come in from the night air, be welcome."

The man shrugged but did not move or reply except to stare with a mild disinterest into the dark of the courtyard.

Even when Antoine pulled the door of his room behind him and joined the man on the stair, the peasant had no comment. He only set off down the stairs with his heavy shoes wide apart, setting up a shiver of sound from the weight of his tread. It was only as they reached the street that the man acknowledged Antoine's presence at his side.

"You are armed?" he asked tersely.

When Antoine touched the knife at his belt, the man nodded, tapped the sword at his hip, and set off. Shortening his stride to match the man's brisk, graceless pace, Antoine followed through the twisting maze of London side streets. Occasional sounds of revelry came from ale houses beyond his view, and the distant howl of dogs echoed hollowly along the streets. Aside from the watches who patrolled their streets with lethargic tread or leaned against walls in drunken sleep, the life of the city was shadow upon shadow, a furtive figure stirring beyond the light, the pip and rustle of vermin in the alleys with the green of their eyes flashing from a mass of rubble.

His companion stopped to hail a watch in a brick-lined street, and Antoine looked about with interest. This was a street whose shops were all dedicated to the trappings of women. Along the street level and below the stairs were millinery and dressmaking shops, signs for fine silk and baubles, a specialist in fine perfume. Antoine knew of the area as one where men of some substance kept their women with rare elegance of style. The buildings were all brick as this area had been taken to the earth in the Great Fire. The door which was held open for Antoine was finely appointed and of heavy, polished wood of good price.

The man left Antoine to wait in a small, delicately appointed entry as he disappeared into darkness. Looking about, Antoine realized that the room seemed known to him. Perhaps it was the deep bowl of blue cornflowers arranged in the French style with masses of white daisies reflected in the gleam of a shining tabletop. Such was his mother's taste and those women who were her friends.

The room beyond the hall was lit so dimly that when the peasant left him at the door, Antoine did not at once realize that a woman was watching him from the far wall. Beyond the broad, red oriental rug, her figure blended into the fullness of the tapestry like another in the series of statues that ornamented the room. A low fire burned silently, and Antoine, stilled by the tension he felt in the room, stood immobile in the doorway, waiting for the woman to turn to him.

Even from the door, he could trace the slender line of her body with his eyes and the piled abundance of pale hair above her face that was hidden from him. The silence was broken by the woman's slow, warm laugh. Even as Antoine started with recognition of that sound, she turned to him, only her dark eyes visible above a fluted fan.

"This is cruel of me, my dear Antoine," she said with relish, "but I admit to loving the advantage."

He nodded with a slight bow, puzzling the voice which, even more than the laughter, stirred his memory teasingly.

"But I shall be crushed if you do not remember me, Antoine Riviere," she went on all in a breathless rush. With the fan still before her face, she began pacing lightly back and forth along the richly covered wall, speaking swiftly with a bantering tone.

"It is well known to us all that a woman never forgets her first lover. Dare I presume that the same can be said of a man?"

She had not finished her question before Antoine moved towards her with a shout of laughter starting from his throat. "Madame LeFevre," he cried out gaily. "Upon my life it is you." Her fan dropped to the floor as he seized both her hands and pressed them to his lips. God, even her scent was the same, a headiness of lilac and rose that had mingled with the sweetness of hay and the musky odor of his own seed. But she was old to me then, he realized in wonder, staring at her with delight. "And you are still beautiful."

· She threw back her head with laughter, and a glint of scarlet glowed in the light from the circlet of rubies at her throat. "It has not been that long, you tactless boy," she reproached him.

Wordlessly he studied this woman who had been so deeply embedded in his life. Her dark, dancing eyes were the same, the curve of her throat into which he had buried his child's head in bliss, but the mouth which had taught him passion in slow, searching skill had a sense of sadness in it, a certain forcing of its curves, as if beneath the smile lay a great reservoir of tears.

"How hungry I am for news of you," she said, leaning towards him, "of your life and why you—you of all people—are serving as a footman. Antoine," she chattered on, "I was helpless with laughter when I saw you at Bath. A footman of all things. The son of Charles and Berenice Riviere posted on a carriage back like a token, a trained monkey

30

for all of your master's friends to envy and admire. It would be the scandal of Paris if this were told."

How much he had forgotten of her, but the memories came swiftly in her presence. Her torrent of quick, jesting words had always seemed to spring from a store of energy so vast that excitement entered every room in the wake of her quick steps. Words fell from her lips steadily as she led him to a chair and sat down directly across from him, knee to knee, like two children readying for a game.

"I cannot wait," he said suddenly reaching for her as she leaned toward him, her face dimpling with pleasure.

She caught his face in his hands and drew his lips to her own. "For old time's sake," she murmured, "only for that, Antoine."

As her lips softened under his, the sudden surge of his old importunate desire for her swelled against his breeches. She pulled away with rueful laughter.

"So this is how you greet old friends? You rake," she scolded. "First we must talk."

"Talk," he told her with despair. "With a woman like you this near, I am expected to talk?"

"I must hear how you came out at Bath. From where I watched, that seemed a goodly amount of gold you won."

"A hundred pounds," he told her. "And I have still not thanked you prettily, as you suggested in the note. I never even saw you in that room."

"I was careful with my fan," she told him. "I had seen you the day before and thought I was dreaming. But a little discreet inquiry confirmed it was truly you. That night I came with the money and the note, and you were nowhere. I was in despair until you finally came, walking among the tables like a giant dauphin in disguise," she laughed softly. "I have always heard that when one wants a gentleman's attention, send gold."

Antoine was only partially distracted by the creamy abundance of her breasts above the low throat of her gown; his mind raced past her anecdotes to the questions of her life. Where was Monsieur LeFevre? What was she doing in this place, in London with only the peasant servant at her bidding.

It was not an easy story for her to tell. Finally she took Antoine's hand in her own and studied it, turning it in her own as she talked. He had known that her marriage with the old man LeFevre had been arranged by her family. He had not known that her childlessness had been due to the old man's impotence which reduced monsieur to rages of accusation and vituperation. "At last it was too much," she told Antoine, raising her eyes to his to plead for understanding. "When his only joy came from seeing me suffer and the whip marks bleed across my back, I ran away."

"Alone?" Antoine asked.

She shook her head. "I had a friend at court, a wise, good man whose only fault is a temper of such wildness that his mind leaves him without warning. Our love had grown slowly, without any contact between us." She stopped and gripped her own hands intensely together, struggling for words. Then she raised her eyes to Antoine. "There are such loves, Antoine," she said wistfully. "Loves that are at once blessing and curse, joy and horror. These loves are meant to be, like morning, or death."

She paused, and Antoine waited before asking, "And this friend, where is he now?"

She spread her hands in despair. "Who knows? That same violence I spoke of rose in a conversation in a coffee house. There was the challenge and Jean, who brought you here, was his second at dawn. The other man died."

"Is your friend in prison then?" Antoine asked with some confusion. "They call it manslaughter here, and for a man with property it is only a short term."

She looked at him aghast. "Oh, Antoine, there is no way my friend who is so wild and free would spend one night with the world barred away from him." Then she leaned towards Antoine as her voice grew intense. "You may name me as mad, Antoine, but I have ever had small sights of what is to come. Long before we left together, I was able to take all manner of brutality because I knew that life would bring me to his arms. Now, even with no word, for he got cleanly away, I know he lives and I know that he dreams only of his return to me."

A stillness lay in the room when her voice ceased, and Antoine, with a sense of chill upon him, felt a stab of envy for the love that this woman bore her nameless "friend."

The same chill seemed to touch Madame LeFevre, for she shivered slightly and reached out for Antoine's arms. "Hold me, dear Antoine," she asked gently. "Memories give me a chilling of the blood."

Not even his knowledge of her passion for her friend could chill the lust that came when she fitted into his arms. When their lips separated, she rose and took him by the hand. "Come," she said softly. "We are both homesick for the hay-fields of Provence."

Her firm, beautiful legs, released from the hoops and petti-coats, were as delicious as he remembered. He slid his hand gently between her thighs, stroking that silken firmness with impatience. "You didn't used to take so long," he complained softly. She laughed and lifted her final garment over her head with a sleek movement. Her slender belly was still firm and appealing with pale moss shadowing her skin.

As she slid into his arms she sighed, "That time I feared you might take flight from me." She grasped him with her hand and laughed, "This time I do not fear."

Antoine roused her passion with gentle hands, with the probing insistence of his tongue. Was it pride that prompted hm to use every skill he possessed to bring her to that moaning pitch of ardor? Pride or no, when he finally thrust himself into her arched and writhing body, a slow cry of ecstasy escaped her lips, and her fine, strong legs gripped him hungrily.

The pumping of his seed into her belly was met by a rush of warm pressure that informed him that her satisfaction was equal to his own. As he relaxed, sliding the heaviness of his body from her, he felt the low, bubbling laughter start deep in her throat. With a start, he realized that this joy of loving was been Madame LeFevre's great gift to his manhood. He had lost count many times over of the women since her, but their lovemaking had never ended like this. Guilt or snoring or a vanity that sought a thousand thanks, but never a fine-bodied woman dripping his seed and laughing with the sheer joy of satisfied lust.

When his passion renewed itself so swiftly she teased him, stroking his distended veins to bring the blood coursing in giant throbs.

"Something must be done for the serving class," she teased solemnly. "Pity the poor footman whose starvation cannot be satisfied."

She brought him brandy warmed by her hand and, pulling a mutual cover about them, piled up beside him in the bed.

33

"I have a confession, Antoine," she said soberly. "I did not bring you here for lovemaking nor for the sake of our old friendship. I have a plan and I need a partner."

"What kind of a plan can you have that an impoverished footman could help you with?"

"A daring plan," she said brightly. "But one with some pleasure in it too. You see, because I loved my friend and did not fear his desertion, I have been an unselfish mistress. I have smuggled away no extra gold for a private hoard. What moneys he gave, I spent to please him, so that now, with him gone from me, I am near destitute."

"But this house, the servant, must be costly to maintain."

She nodded. "That is my problem. But I cannot leave. I must be here when he finds his way back to me. For that I need money. Even as you need money, Antoine."

He stiffened at her words. What did she know of his own need for gold? She laughed lightly at his change of expression. "Oh, don't worry about me. I am not going to pry. Only I have heard the gossip of Paris these past months, of how the family of Charles Riviere flew apart of a sudden, like leaves in the wind, how you and Sophia were gone at once without warning. And of the strange coincidence that a young duke who was heavily in debt and unable to buy his freedom disappeared too. I do not wish to know where the missing duke or your lovely sister have gone, but I see you here in London as a footman. The son of Charles Riviere does not brace himself as a footman unless he needs a bed and a roof and money. Am I right?"

"I need money," Antoine admitted.

"And Titus the great deformed dwarf, is he with you?"

At Antoine's nod, she sighed with satisfaction. "Inside that miserable body is trapped a great and wise man. I hope he had not been lost in the storm."

"You speak of plans and then chatter gossip," he accused her lightly.

"I have some money and will have credit for a time. I remember your skill at gaming from the salons in our circle at home, your mother's friends and mine. If I should put up the money and you the skill and we should split the winnings, we would both be rich in time."

Antoine stared at her thoughtfully. "But where there is money to win there is money to lose," he reminded her.

34

She shook her head. "Only for fools," she told him. "The Engish are fevered for gaming. They gamble with their heads on their laps and their purses hanging free. Sure, there would be losses, but I swear to you, the gains would outstrip them."

He shook his head. "I know little of their sports beside a few games."

"Jean knows them all," she assured him. "He knows which cocks have the cruellest spurs and what horses can break out from the mudded tracks they set them on. He knows the underbelly of this city like his own hand." She paused then added, "And there is always my gift for seeing ahead. I knew you would win at Bath, Antoine, I knew it as I wrote that note to you."

He slid his hand about her neck and down over a smooth breast which had escaped the covering. "I like you as a partner," he said softly.

But she shrugged herself free and shook her head. "For old time's sake, remember?" Then, with a winning smile, she lifted her brandy to his. "And if we are to be partners, don't you think you could learn to call me Mignon?"

Chapter Five

The moon was invisible beyond the smoke clouds that hung over London as Mignon LeFevre's servant led Antoine back to his carriage house. But in the country north of London, the moon rose clear and fragile, silvering the tops of the yews along the Duvall drive and gathering small pools of light on the carefully tended lawn. The house itself lay dark and sleeping except for Julie who stood at her window watching the shadows change along the curved drive.

There had been too much excitement in her day for her eyes to close meekly in sleep at Mary's command. If there had only been that marvelous morning ride with Giles, she would have been excited. But having her father come rattling up the drive at teatime had made the day too precious to release to sleep.

How lean and tanned he was. How springily he had bound-ed up the stairs to seek out Fiona who had not felt well enough all day to join their guests.

Torn between his duties as host to his brother and brother's family and his desire to be with his beloved Fiona, the handsome man, with Julie tagging along, had wrapped his wife in a dark velvet mantle and carried her down to the great room where she was placed by his side. When the tea things had been cleared and the men fell into conversation, Julie observed her father's constant distraction with his wife, the absent yet tender way he held her hand in his, stroking the pulse inside her wrist and bending her slim fingers about his own.

Amalie and her mother were nattering away at each other about a woman of their church but Julie felt no interest in their talk. She leaned against her father's knee and drew pictures for Louis while she listened to the men talk. Joseph, sulky and disgusting as usual, sat by the fire cracking nuts and throwing the shells into the hearth fire and only occasionally turning to stare at Julie with that mean, sullen leer.

There was nothing new in the argument between her father and his brother. They discussed a disagreement that she had heard them go through many times over the years. But she listened anyway, enjoying the sound of her father's voice in the room after all these months, happy to have them all together again at last.

Her Uncle Simon seemed more intent than ever before on persuading his brother to lend him money for the South Seas Company which, according to him, was making fortunes for every man who had gone in for the stocks.

"Every man tells of his successes," her father said lazily. "Few men boast of their mistakes."

"The mistakes are being made by those who hang back," her uncle said forcefully. "Look where you would be now if you had bought into the East India Company when it was newly commissioned."

"The East India Company is a different thing," Etienne reminded him. "As indeed I am willing to concede that the one South Seas Company may be. But all about it are springing up these overnight mushrooms which poison the taster."

"Then you think the men crowding 'Change Alley for those stocks are all fools," his brother challenged. "Because you have had success in your own trade, doesn't give you any expertize in other men's projects."

"You sound as if you had come to my side, brother," he laughed. "Since I know my own business, and it makes me rich, why should I dabble with things I know naught of? And Walpole himself is issuing warning about those projects—"

"What projects are these that you keep mentioning?" Fiona asked quietly from her husband's side. "Is it the same trading in spices and Cyprus wool and tea?"

"Not on your life," Julie's father replied with a laugh. "To see those notices would send you to fits of laughter. How about a proposal to turn salt water to sweet? Or a machine that runs forever with only one start? There is even one soliciting money for a project too secret to be told—Can you imagine an author not able to dream up a new pipe dream and starting that?"

Simon, his brow dark with fury, bolted his ale and refilled his tankard. "If I had but five hundred pounds," he grumbled, "you'd see me double it within six months."

Julie wondered at her father's patience with his brother. How many hundreds of pounds he had extended to this man, to cover gambling debts, to meet tax payments, or simply to keep his family in meat; but always the great gains he was after came to some mischance. "God gives and God takes away," Julie had heard her Aunt Carolyn say with resignation. Only it seemed to Julie that in her Uncle Simon's case, it was her father who gave and her uncle who threw away.

"None of my pounds will go into those companies, Simon," Etienne said firmly, "and that is a final answer." He laid a hand gently on his wife's swollen belly. "There is Julie and perhaps a son within a month or two. All my gold is kept firm for their welfare."

Simon's muttered curse did not escape his brother's ears. Etienne paled as if with anger and rose. "I think my bird droops with the night," he said, reaching down to lift Fiona into his arms. "And I myself have a long day's business behind me. We will to bed, but make yourself comfortable as long as you will."

Julie leaped up to go with her parents, unwilling even for the sake of Louis to spend any more time in the room with Joseph, whose loutish stares were making her flesh creep.

As she slipped into her bed, she heard her father's voice

37

laughing with his wife off in their shared room. It was no good, she could not sleep with such joy in her heart. For a long time she stood at the window, wriggling her feet against the cold of the floor and thinking of love and marriage. She thought of Giles and her father, but most of all she remembered the strange magic in the footman's glance. The queen herself, she remembered with surprise, had been only fifteen when she was wed.

Finally chilled to her bed, Julie drifted to sleep only lightly. There was a strangeness in the house, a sense of omen that stirred her rest with vagrant fluttering dreams. Then she wakened suddenly, her heart pounding. It was more than a dream. Something was amiss in the house. She was suddenly sorry that she had insisted so firmly that her companion Mary be given a room in the other wing of the house. "I am too old to have a nurse at my bedside," she had protested. Now she wished Mary near, with her flat, brusque voice calming her fears. She listened intently, hearing the sounds of doors opening and closing. Then she heard the sound of a horse being driven swiftly along the drive, and the great front door slammed as if in haste.

Groping into her dressing gown, Julie crept to her door with her long hair still atumble around her shoulders. She was astonished to find the hall ablaze with light, candles flickering in all the sconces as if for a party. Then she saw her father leaning against the wall outside the room he shared with her mother, his head buried in his hands.

She fled to her father, but before she could reach him she was startled by a wail of agony, more like the cry of a tortured animal than a human. She threw her arms about her father, "Maman?" she asked him, tears already coursing down her face.

He buried his face in her hair, gripping her so tightly about her shoulders that she feared she might cry out with pain.

"The child is coming," he said brokenly. "The midwife is with your mother."

"But it is too soon," Julie cried, trying to shut out the sounds of her mother's agony.

"Pray," her father told her sternly. "Pray for your mother." Then his voice broke like a child's. "For the child it is too late, pray for Fiona."

There was no one for Julie to turn to. Her own maid Mary was within the room with the midwife and the others. Seizing her mantle, she crept down the stairs. It was halfway down, crouched against the rail, that she found Louis. Clad only in a shirt and breeches, he had rolled himself into a ball with his hands clasped on his head and his thin arms tight against his ears.

Julie stooped and put her arms about him even as her father had done to her. He began to sob helplessly, pressing close to her warm, murmuring voice.

"I'm afraid, Julie," he sobbed. "I am afraid."

"Come and pray with me," she said, pulling him to his feet.

He shook his head. "I cannot live with those cries." He curled his arms over his head again, his small, thin face contorted with grief.

"Come," she insisted, dragging him along with her.

She led Louis out of the house and across the moon-pooled lawn to the summer house beneath the yews. There, with only the night bird's cries for company, she wrapped the child and herself in her mantle to ward off the chill.

Julie murmured endearments to Louis and caressed his smooth face until his sobbing finally stopped. Then he stirred in her arms, tightening his arms about her neck.

"When I am a man, Julie, I want you to be my wife."

"You are too much younger than I, Louis," she told him. "Why, you are only a child and anyway you are my cousin."

"Joseph is your cousin too," he said with a tone of accusation.

"What has that to do with anything?" she asked sharply.

"They talk of it all the time at home, my parents and Amalie. How you will be married to Joseph and the family will have fine fortunes again."

Julie told him hotly. "He is an ugly, nasty beast, and I hate him worse than any boy in the world."

"But he's not a boy," Louis said. "He is soon to be twenty."

"Even if he were my own age and clothed with gold and crowned with riches I would not marry him." Julie said firmly. "And you can just tell your parents and Amalie that for me too."

"Oh," Louis said in a small voice. "I wouldn't dare do

39

that." But strangely, at her words, his small body relaxed. Like a young animal, he burrowed his head in Julie's neck and fell asleep.

Julie was afraid to move lest she disturb him, but she lay watching the moonlight on his face for a long time, his delicate features, the dark brush of lashes on his cheeks. Finally, even her consciousness of her mother's ordeal was buried in drowsiness, and she slept.

It was her stepcousin Joseph who wakened Julie, jerking her from Louis's arms and dragging her to her feet roughly. Dawn was touching the skyline behind the house, and Julie's teeth chattered with chill as Joseph thrust himself against her, his rough hands groping along her back. His face, so close that his breath stank in her mouth, looked like that of an old cowherd that often passed along the highway. His eyes were mean and small like his mother's, and the scent of him made her nauseated.

"Wake up," he kept shouting at her, shaking her this way and back, his hands busy on her body. As Julie struggled and screamed against his grasp, Louis wakened with a cry. He clawed at his stepbrother until Joseph threw him away with the back of his fist.

"You can lie all night with that brat," he told Julie angrily, "but if I lay a hand on you you scream like a shrew!" Louis picked himself up and ran towards the house, crying and stumbling through the half-darkness.

"Better shut your trap," Joseph called after him. "They've no time for your tales tonight. The old woman and the brat are both dead."

Julie froze in his grasp, her mind only dimly perceiving his words. Something in her stunned gaze at him made Joseph draw back from her. Stiffly, with the cold of the earth seeming to move upwards through her body like rising fog, Julie walked to the house, her dry eyes more anguished than tears.

Chapter Six

The bells of the village kirk tolled all day for the death of the stillborn son of Etienne Duvall and for his wife Fiona who was loved throughout the countryside for her beauty, her good works, and the glancing charm of her wit. Within that same month the bells of London tolled their measured score for the death of Queen Anne, the last of the Stuarts who was known for her hatred of Whigs, the dullness of her court, and a lamentable weakness for backstairs intrigue.

But all the bells after Fiona's fell on Etienne Duvall's deaf ears. Past the loss of his wife, there was no name for grief. He walked the rooms of the house he had built for the woman he had been able to love for only a brief time. Unable to face the living pattern of his passion in his daughter Julie, he fled to commerce as a refuge. Months passed and then years. The Hanoverian George came to the English throne with his dumpy German mistresses and his sullen mistrust of the people he ruled. Winters blew and summers bloomed as Julie spent her days in study, needlework, and racing her mare with the hound Bonbon at her side. Sometimes when Giles Urban was down from Oxford, Julie, warmed by his devoted attention, wondered if this great affection might one day grow into a love large enough to fulfill her life.

Etienne Duvall returned from one journey only to embark on another. Julie, who had once been hungry for his presence, began to think of him as a heartbreaking pilgrim who only carried grief to his table.

Through those years Julie felt herself blessed to have three good friends: her good maid Mary, her young cousin Louis, and her father's banker Henry Furlong who alone had the power to shield her from the persistent meddling of her Uncle Simon and his family. Like rats making wary sallies into a granary, her Uncle Simon and Aunt Carolyn made furtive efforts to intrude on the peaceful loneliness of her life.

First it was her Aunt Carolyn's pity for the "griefstruck

child Julie" that prompted the woman to insist that young Julie come and make her home with her own blood relatives.

"It is unseemly," her aunt insisted, "to leave a young girl in the charge of a great house with uncaring servants."

Henry Furlong greeted this proposal with indignant resentment. Stretching himself to his most magnificent height, which was barely past the topknot of Julie's curls, he turned on the woman angrily.

"Madame," he said, "this is the home of Etienne Duvall, and this child is his heir. This child, this hearth, this home is all the poor man has to return to. Would you deny him this?"

Tearful with gratitude, Julie thanked Henry Furlong when they were alone together. The aging banker, his face still flushed with rage, patted her arm awkwardly.

"I will do all I can for you, my dear," he assured her. Then he shook his head with a concerned frown. "But I do wish your father would set his affairs in order."

"Affairs in order," Julie wailed. "But father is young. You frighten me when you say things like that."

"Never a better time than when young," he reminded her. But when he took his leave, Julie noticed he was still frowning a little and mumbling to himself.

It was to Julie alone that her Aunt Carolyn made the second suggestion.

"Your father's dear brother has suffered great reverses," she told Julie with a long face. "A word from you, my dear, and your Uncle Simon and his family could join you here in this great wasted house, bringing you company and help."

Julie dropped her eyes from her aunt's, horrified at the thought of sharing a roof with Joseph and Amalie and their parents.

"I cannot do that," she told her aunt. "After all, this is my father's house, and I cannot make free with it without consulting him."

"Your wishes are your father's wishes," her aunt assured her, smiling through the garish paint and patches which she seemed to add in direct proportion to the passing years.

"I shall speak to Mr. Furlong about it," Julie finally said, knowing full well how greatly her aunt feared the banker.

"You must not do that," her aunt protested hastily. "But if you yourself should decide, we could just make the move and surprise your father on his next return home."

The third and most obscene suggestion came to Julie from an unexpected source. Henry Furlong was up from London in celebration of her seventeenth birthday. She and the maid Mary and the cook had all worked to make a very special tea, small cakes crusted with sugar, an apple tart flowing with melted caramel, and a pudding of fruit and nuts which Julie had gathered in the woods and picked from the shell herself

Mr. Furlong, wiping his lips carefully to avoid her eyes, had broached the subject with obvious timidity.

"Your uncle has been to London to see me," he began.

"Oh?" Julie waited warily.

Mr. Furlong stirred uneasily in his seat. "He tells me the happy news that you are much in love."

At her confused frown, he went on hastily. "He asked me to contact your father and discuss a marriage agreement between your stepcousin Joseph and yourself."

His sentence was never properly finished. Julie leaped to her feet so swiftly that her tea dish went flying. She was wild with rage, wanting to seize her friend and force his words back into his throat.

"Lies. Lies. Lies," she shouted. "In love with that lout? That nasty miserable beast? Marry Joseph? I swear as God is in heaven I would kill him first."

"Julie. Julie, my dear," Mr. Furlong's face swelled with amazement. "I had no idea. The man came to me and told me quite convincingly that this was your wish. I admit I was surprised, but one never knows with the young." His voice trailed off as he reached for her hands. "Believe me, child, I meant no ill. How was I to know?"

"Lies," she said more calmly. "And whatever you do, no word of this must get to my father until I can speak with him myself. But mark this. I will not bed with that beast. I will marry for love as my father did."

"Sit, Julie," Mr. Furlong coaxed. "Marry for love? Is there another?"

Julie hesitated. "Not really," she admitted. "There is the squire's son Giles whom I love like a brother." She hoped that Mr. Furlong would not detect the hotness that that lie brought to her cheeks. "But there is such a man that I could love, Mr. Furlong, and until I meet him, I shall remain unwed."

43

He laid his hand on her arm, "Dear Julie, you are a beautiful child. I never thought to say this to anyone, but you are even more beautiful than your mother Fiona. No man could resist your love brought openly to him."

She laid her own hand on his and smiled. "Thank you, dear friend." Then she added softly, "And please no word of that dreadful idea to my father. Being so far, he might take it for truth."

He nodded, observing mildly that he was expecting Etienne to return to England within the month. "Then the two of you can talk of these things," he said. "And with luck I can persuade him to get his affairs in better order before he leaves again."

"You mention that so often. Does it concern you so much?"

He nodded with a frown. "The property settlement is one he made shortly after he and his brother came from France. I think from the arrangements that your uncle had not—" he paused and groped for words, "revealed himself to his full extent at that time."

"What does that mean?" Julie asked.

Mr. Furlong shrugged. "Your father planned that one third of his property be settled between your uncle and your aunt in the colonies."

"Anne-Louise," Julie nodded.

"The other two thirds would be for his wife and heirs, if such existed, with the manangement of the property to be in his wife's hands until the children attained the age of twenty-one, at which time it could be distributed."

"But in the absence of a wife still living?" Julie asked.

"His brother Simon would have full control of those assets until the children came of age."

Julie shook her head. "I can't imagine father having done that. He knows what a gambler my uncle is. A wastrel—I have heard papa use the word myself."

Mr. Furlong nodded. "As I implied, that wisdom came later. For these reasons, I carry high concern that Etienne's testament be changed to a wiser plan without delay."

Etienne Duvall was never to return from that last trading voyage. A fever he had contracted in Ceylon grew worse once his ship left port. When his burial at sea was announced

44

in England, the bells tolled again in the village kirk, this time for Etienne Duvall's memory and to the end of Julie's childhood.

Chapter Seven

Antoine Riviere loathed to admit, even to himself, what great store he set by the counsel of the old dwarf Titus who had been with him since childhood. As he pondered the proposal that Mignon LeFevre had made, he felt a growing desire to hear Titus's reaction to the plan. Deciding that the safekeeping of his winning at Bath was reason enough for the journey to Essex, he rode north at his first opportunity.

"There is an element of risk," Titus warned when Antoine had related his adventure to the old man. "There is always her protector to think of."

"But he is gone from England," Antoine reminded him.

"Ships sail both ways," Titus said. "A man who duels and kills in a fit of temper will not lightly take this friendship between his woman and a footman. Will you take quarters with her?"

Antoine shook his head. "We agreed that is best left as it is. It is safer and more discreet."

Titus chuckled. "Discreet is a strange word for you to use." Then he fell silent, cocking his head so that his one good eye gazed wistfully at the coals on the hearth. "And you say that she is still beautiful?"

Antoine thumped him with a roar of laughter. "You old roué. Then you remember too. She is more beautiful by half and cleverer too."

"Let us hope that she is not too clever for her own neck," Titus grumbled, poking at the fire. "And yours, I could add."

Antoine rose with a laugh. "The two of you would make a pair. She claims some second sight that sees the future, but from what I see, it is only the fretting of a woman's fears." As he spoke, he undid the purse laced beneath his coat. "We need to hide this hereabouts. I fear its safety in those miserable chambers of mine."

Titus held the bag a moment and then nodded his head.

45

He scuttled across the hearth to the left of the fire, where the stonework ended and the wainscoting began. Laying his hand gingerly along the edge of the wood, he pressed and pushed about, frowning with concentration.

To Antoine's astonishment, a section of the wall swung free silently, exposing an aperture large enough for a crouched man to pass freely.

"A priest's hole," Titus explained. "The man who once owned this house was a Papist. The rumors said that he and his family were killed for their faith, but I never dreamed of such as this."

"How did you come upon it?" Antoine asked, peering into the darkness beyond the wall at the clever joining of the spring in the wooden work.

"Awkwardly," Titus told him, "by dropping a piece of wood against it when my hands were chilled. And the devil of a time I had locating the catch that second time."

With the leather pouch stored in the aperture, he turned back, closing the secret place silently behind him.

"Good enough," Antoine nodded. "When I have a thousand pounds to my credit I will open an account at the Bank of England. In the meantime, with the priest seekers gone these many years, it should be safer than in a church."

On his way back to London, Antoine whistled merrily. What had the man at Bath said on the night of his winning? "Another footman who will be telling his master to mount?"

To Titus's undisguised astonishment and Antoine's delight, the gambling partnership between himself and Mignon LeFevre was successful from the first.

Antoine was quick to admit that much of this "luck" was due to Mignon's careful management and her servant Jean's complete grasp of the underworld of the city. It was Mignon and Jean who chose what games to frequent, what fighting cocks to lay their bets on, and what horses ran best in the cloying mud of an English track. It was Mignon who counted their take, dividing it fairly among the three of them, with an extra guinea or more when Jean had taken a hard knock in a street fight in Antoine's defense.

Mignon also insisted that Antoine not let his true name be known in the familiar fields of London after dark.

"It is easy enough to do," she said brightly. "Just use a different name in every gaming house. With that accent of yours, the name will have to be French, but that is the limit to your restrictions. How about kings? Think of the possibilities: Charles, Robert, Philip, Henri, even Louis, if you want to stay in fashion! And when you run out of kings," she giggled happily, "why, then you could use the names of some knaves. We both know a few of them in France."

Laughing at her volubility, Antoine followed her counsel for no better reason than that it was an entertainment for himself and Jean to remember to pause at the door of a tavern and try to remember what name he was known by at its tables.

With Jean always at his side, Antoine, with the string of names trailing behind him, came only to be known as the French Footman, who was the first to have his money down and the most apt to walk off with another man's gold. He was a gambler's gambler, as ready to risk a thousand pounds on a hand of hazard as to bet ten guineas in a game of quinze. His tall figure was known from the fancy houses in Pall Mall to the cockfighting pits in Dartmouth Street near Westminster.

When he lost, which was sometimes the case, he paid up with an insouciance that inspired the less fortunate to spin romantic tales about him. He was a member of the French court sent to spy upon the shipping of London. He was the bastard son of a noble Flemish line whose inexhaustible funds were brought privately to Dover by night.

But even as his fortunes rose, his spirits flagged.

"My soul is shrunk to a miser's wad," he complained to Titus, only half in jest. "I watch my accounts rise like an old man slavering at the lifting of a petticoat."

"The more gained, the sooner freed," Titus reminded him with some concern. As his master's gaiety had bled off, a restless moodiness came in its place. A sadness and loneliness behind Antoine's blue eyes heightened the scent of danger that Titus still sensed in the enterprise.

"Has aught been heard of the madame's friend?" he would ask gingerly as the months and years passed.

"What concern is that to me?" Antoine shrugged. "Jean grows rich, and I deposit towards my debt, and she keeps her bed warm for his return."

"I do care," he added thoughtfully, after a moment of consideration. "But only for Mignon herself. She loves that man

47

with such pain that his absence is a living death to her. Fugitive or not, such a man is truly blessed."

It was strange how Antoine's respect for that love had weaned him of passion for her. The parlormaid Meg had trailed off to the country with a Yorkshireman in tow and, the new parlormaid followed the same path across the yard to his rooms. And sometimes in the Strand he found a fresh-faced girl who suited him for dalliance for a month or two. But lonely he was and lonely he would be until the last of the debt was set away.

For the time, mean as it was to scrabble for money night after night, that was his life.

While the gaming houses of London and Bath and Tur-bridge Wells knew the French Footman as a figure for romance, his anonymity stopped at the Bank of London. Antoine Riviere was a name to be respected, an investor whose swelling account earned him fawning attention.

He and Jean, with a camaraderie born of time and shared adventures, became loyal and mutually respectful friends. Antoine could sense from the flicker of a lash in the old peasant's eye, which way to leap to escape danger.

It was early in the spring of 1718 that Mignon began her small nattering of worried concern. Antoine shrugged it off at first.

"You are having the vapors," he kidded her. "Your faith rises and falls with the weather."

She shook her head soberly, struggling to convince him. "I have that feeling, Antoine," she insisted. "Perhaps we should stop all at once and you go off from here."

He stared at her. How much did she guess about his need for this money? He had told her only that it was a debt of honor and no more than that.

"You are so near," she insisted. "You must be near the end of what you need."

He nodded. "Very near," he conceded. "But it must be paid to the penny, not a nippet less."

She even began dividing the winning differently. She set aside Jean's share and piled all the rest before Antoine without even counting it.

"What of you?" he asked with amazement.

"I want it over," she said fretfully. "I want it all over before some dread thing happens."

48

"Have you any idea what is pricking your mistress?" Antoine asked Jean.

Jean shook his head slowly, "Not to be sure. But I mind her concerns. She is right more than wrong about things."

"But she hasn't talked to you?" Antoine pressed.

Jean's mouth jerked in a half-grin. "She don't need to tell me. I take her food back uneaten and hear her wake at night with dreaming to walk and cry."

"Does she think or feel that her friend is dead?" Antoine asked on impulse.

Jean stopped in his tread, and his mouth gaped at the thought. "The master. I had not thought of that." Then he started off again, nodding as he walked. "That would bring such sadness to her heart. Aye. That would be a cause for her strangeness."

Spring turned to summer, and yet she wore always a shawl about her shoulders as if cold.

"I am chilled," she explained, her eyes accusing him. "I have dreamed that I will not be warm again on this earth."

Instead of pondering her words, Antoine only feared again that somehow the great love she bore her friend had given her a secret knowledge of his death.

"You are a remarkable woman," he told her tenderly. "One hour with you across the room is better than a mile of virgins laid tail to tail for my pleasure."

"Such a foul mouth," she laughed.

"Such a fortunate man who has your love," he told her.

Startled by the unexpected sincerity in his voice, Mignon raised her eyes to his. "Unfortunate and fortunate at once," she said intensely. "Oh Antoine, he is such a strange, troubled man whose blood runs too wildly hot for his head, but he is all my love. He is truly mine as I am his, but yet I have strange fears. This shadow that seems to follow me, chilling me in the fullest sun. Antoine, can his love for me have turned to hate?"

How could he comfort her? Like Jean, he felt that if indeed some unknown truth troubled her, it was that her friend had somehow met death.

"I am afraid, Antoine," she whispered into his thoughtfulness. "I am terribly, terribly afraid."

Antoine shook his head brusquely. "I dislike that talk, Mignon," he said firmly. "I cannot abide talk of Gypsy fore-telling and superstition."

Sudden tears rose in her eyes. "This is more than superstition," she exclaimed. "Everything about me changes, and the changes all are threatening."

"Mignon," he rebuked her.

"Ask Jean," she flared with sudden anger. "Jean too must be aware. Surely he has noticed that the watch has been changed on our street after so many years of the same old man. Ask him about this new watch who comes with his face and form hidden in a great dark mantle no matter how bright the day. Ask him of the bearded monger who cries his wares through the day. He comes and cries and although no one buys, he keeps coming. And always his eyes are on this house, my windows. Tell me then, would a vendor cry on a street where he never made a penny?"

"Fantasies," he told her. "All fantasies. You need a rest, to get away. Why, my Mistress Linton has three weeks been off to the country for the summer. How about a week in Bath for you? Jean and I will keep accounts and come and see you while you are there. Brighton?"

She shook her head with despair. "I cannot escape by flying," she said with a tone of defeat.

Strangely enough, Jean did confirm some of her tales.

"Perhaps the old man fell ill and died," Antoine argued. "Watches are mortal like other men, you know. And there is not yet a law that the watch cannot be changed on a given street."

"We have never seen the new man's face," Jean said flatly. "I myself walked right up to him only to have him turn away with a gesture for me to pass."

"So he may not be a man for loose talk."

Jean grumbled with impatience but fell silent.

That August night began like any other summer night. The luck ran better than usual. The crowd at the Button House was half-distracted by an argument at one of the tables, and Antoine, taking advantage of divided minds, swelled his winnings to a thousand pounds before midnight. Rather than be a witness to the inevitable fight that would ensue from the argument, he and Jean drifted out onto the street to start for home.

A high wind had for once swept the sky above London

clean. A scattering of stars challenged a finely honed moon curved above the East India House and the air was remarkably free of stench.

As they turned into Mignon's street, Jean grunted with surprise. Following his eyes, Antoine realized that the watch was not at his post. His eyes searched the street, annoyed that the guard should be lowered on such a street as this. Still seeing no sign, Antoine quickened his steps beside Jean's to climb the stairs to Mignon's chambers.

Once inside the entry, a shiver of warning moved along Antoine's spine. Conscious of the unnatural silence of the place, he motioned Jean to follow. As he turned, he was momentarily stunned to see a look of shocked horror twisting Jean's usually placid face.

Though he turned with a spin, Antoine did not see Jean's assailant until the peasant had leaped at him, sword bared, his wide legs braced for battle.

Past the two men whose clashing swords rang in the narrow hall, Antoine sped to Mignon's bedroom. He found it in darkness, but a sickness struck him at the scent of the room. Above the mingled scent of rose and lilac that was Mignon's favorite, he caught the unmistakable stench of blood. He threw the drapes back from the window so that the pale moonlight could illuminate the room.

"God in heaven," he cried softly. Mignon, clad only in the sheer nightdress that she affected on summer nights, lay in a lake of her own blood. No wizard could determine which blow had killed her. Her face, her breasts, the round, firm grace of her shapely belly, all had been slashed to ribbons by the sword of a madman.

Breathing shallowly with horror, Antoine shut the drapes slowly, leaving the wide, staring eyes of his friend to the mercy of darkness. Only then did he realize that the sounds of battle beyond the door had ceased. In that stillness he was conscious of the rustle of vermin within the walls, the cricking of leaves against the window of the room. Then a slow change in the light alerted him that the door to the room was opening stealthily, one careful measure at a time. Drawing himself close to the curtains of Mignon's bed, Antoine waited, his knife against his wrist, for the intruder to be recognizable. He dared not cry out lest it not be Jean whose shadowy figure still moved furtively into the room.

When the figure stopped, Antoine tightened his breath, fearing the sound of his heartbeat would betray his position. Into that silence came one heartbroken, hoarse cry, like an animal in pain, as Jean, his sword clattering to the floor, saw his mistress's butchered body in the dim light from the hall.

"Jean," Antoine spoke to him curtly. "Stiffen yourself, man. What happened below?"

Jean only wailed between his hands until Antoine seized him roughly and pulled him to his feet. "Naught can be done for her," he said roughly. "What of the man below? We must go for the watch, the constable."

But Jean's head was wildly shaking back and forth. "No, no," he cried. "It is the master. This is his house."

Antoine paused then shook the peasant again. "And is he dead?"

He shook his head again, turning his face from the bed with his mouth twisted with grief. "Only stunned from the wall against his head."

"Stunned," Antoine said. Then hastily, "Jean, there is no time. If this is your master, he will cry an alarm and we are doomed. We are intruders, not he. Your stores?"

"I have nothing here," Jean said, his wit returning slowly. "A horse," he said. "I have a horse."

They were at the door when they heard the clamor below in the street. With a curse, Antoine realized that the sounds of the sword fight would have started an alarm by now.

"The back way," Jean said swiftly. "There are no stairs but a window is low."

Antoine's slim frame passed the window in ease, but Jean's thick torso came through only after grunting and scraping by which time the sounds from the street came louder and a pounding on the locked door to Mignon's chambers revealed that a timber had been brought to batter it down.

Moving carefully in the shadows, Jean led Antoine to the carriage house which opened on a pathway behind the building. Antoine watched with impatience as the peasant's broad fingers fumbled in the dark to harness the huge, black gelding who had whinnied softly at his master's coming.

Jean would have gone back for his sword, as he noticed it missing, but Antoine cursed him softly. "Your sword or your head, you fool," he warned.

With Antoine behind him, Jean slapped the horse into an

52

easy trot along the pathway and onto a narrow street. From this distance, they could see the lights of flares and still could hear the clamor of their pursuers.

As Jean guided their mount onto the brighter-lit street, Antoine saw that the coat of his companion was drenched with blood from his battle. The watch, starting at the sight of him, cried out with alarm, "Halt, who goes there?"

He grabbed for the reins of Jean's horse, brandishing his sword. Antoine leaned forward and sliced at the man's hand with his knife. But as the watch fell back, the tip of his sword sliced down the length of Antoine's leg, splitting the breeches open and releasing a fountain of blood.

"Ride, Jean. Ride," Antoine cried fiercely, gripping his thigh with his hand to try to stanch the flow of blood. "If you ever raced a horse, man, do it now."

With the canniness that Antoine had grown to expect, Jean veered the horse through streets deserted of revellers and night people. After what seemed an hour of the jerking agony of this flight, Jean pulled the horse to a stop outside the city gate.

Antoine, weakened by loss of blood, did not protest as Jean, holding the sturdy fabric in his broad, stained teeth, tore his own bloody jacket into ribbons to bind Antoine's leg.

"Now can you ride?" Jean asked, peering into his face.

Antoine nodded. "But what of you? You have no mount."

Jean smiled. "I need no mount. You have friends? The dwarf you told me of?"

When Antoine nodded, Jean stared at him a moment. Then he pulled a leather pouch from his inner belt. "She gave me this for you," he said numbly.

Antoine turned the pouch in his hands studying Jean's face.

"She said I'd know when to give it to you," he explained. "She was right, you know. We were fools not to listen. It must have been the master in the watch's cape. That monger with the beard she complained of, a tall, thin man in disguise." Jean nodded, his expression bitter. "I should have known he would come back like that, boiling with fury and seeking betrayal. Sweet Jesus," he said, shaking his head to rid it of the sight his mind could not contain.

"But you, Jean," Antoine protested. "What of you. Have you gold?"

53

The peasant laughed. "More than ever in my life, and in safekeeping too. You are sure you can ride? It isn't safe to tarry here."

Antoine nodded, holding the peasant's square, thick shape in his eyes. "Good hunting, Jean," he said quietly.

"Good hunting, master," Jean replied, nodding his head jerkily. Antoine prodded the horse a few short yards and then wheeled and turned back.

"One thing, Jean," he asked, overtaking the plodding walk of his friend. "When did she give you this pouch for me?"

The moonlight was full on the man's broad face as he pondered the question. "A month away maybe, at least that."

With his throat choked, Antoine wheeled the horse and began his long, painful ride to the woods of Essex.

Titus was wakened by the unfamiliar sound of a horse's whinny beyond the window of his room. He spied a long time between the heavy crossbars of wood that guarded the door before he could fix his one good eye on the rider. Then, with a curse, he unbolted the door and half-dragged his near-unconscious master's body off the gelding and across the clearing into the cottage. When he had stripped him and bathed him of his blood, and had dressed the sword wound that ran the length of his master's thigh, the dwarf somehow got him into Titus's own bed. Clucking and hissing, he tore the footman's uniform into small shreds and fed it into the fire.

When he found the leather pouch, he shook his head. Then, pressing carefully against the wainscoting, he opened the priest's hole, threw the pouch into that darkness, and squatted before the fire waiting for dawn.

Chapter Eight

The summer that blazed unmercifully on the brick of London shone no more charitably on the woods of Essex. The massive trees closed their leaves like guarding hands against that unremitting sun. Even at midday only dapples of golden light found their way to the forest floor, surprising wild flowers into bloom and glinting on the stream that ran near the gamekeeper's cottage.

Titus, hopping along with his uneven gait, scoured the forest like some mythic creature seeking potions for enchantment. Garnering berries from the bushes, he made fragrant jams. The plums from gnarled trees were imprisoned in tarts crisp with sugar. Rabbit and mushroom simmered together in dark gravy flavored by wild herbs.

Titus's efforts were all wasted on Antoine Riviere. With his great body sprawling listlessly on the bed, he only prodded at the food before turning away, the blackness of his thoughts too dense a barrier for his natural appetites.

The wound itself healed slowly but well. The raw of flesh renewed, leaving only a purpled line of scar as testament to the madman's sword, but the injury to Antoine's spirit seemed past healing. Titus, his one good eye cocked at an inquisitive angle like that of a small bird inspecting food, watched the summer flow past his master with growing despair.

Titus had too few hours in his day now. Along with his ordinary chores and the care of the sick man, he tended the black gelding which had brought his master home. With a woven leash of great length he walked the horse daily to keep it in trim. He groomed its coat to a shine, as the beast dropped its head down to nuzzle him with affection. It was to this beast that Titus poured out his concern over Antoine's melancholia.

The sun's heat waned, and in among the green, bright colors stained the forest. Fall winds brought showers of nuts which Titus shovelled into baskets, crawling, leaping across the leaf-matted forest floor. The first white of frost had dusted the roof before Titus, seeking a cool storage spot for the forest's bounty of apples, remembered the dark passage behind the wainscoting by the hearth.

Grunting with effort, Titus labored the fruit back into that clean, dark place and rose with a sigh. Only when he glanced back, did he notice the dark leather pouch he had thrown in there the night of his master's return.

Titus emptied the pouch to find a quantity of gold coins and a circlet of perfect rubies in a setting of fine gold. Chuckling with delight, he held the bauble in the sun's ray, watching the jewels splash his hands and doublet with blood red light.

Titus did not notice the small folded paper until he was refilling the pouch. The paper had been carefully sealed and folded again and again to fit in that small space.

Titus stared at it a long time, wondering if wisdom did not lie in leaving it there with that forgotten hoard. Finally, he made the hard decision. His distorted face was tight with concern when he entered his master's bedroom and waited silently for Antoine's attention.

Antoine, his eyes fixed on the moving leaves in the forest beyond his window, did not at first acknowledge his servant's presence. When he turned, Titus sensed his irritation at being interrupted. His voice betrayed the low, seething anger which had seemed to lie just below the surface of Antoine's control since the night of his return.

"What is it now, Titus? Would you stuff me with food again with the morning only half-spent? Or did you come to nag at me like a slattern to be up and about whether I feel it or no?"

Titus waited for his ire to be spent before he answered. "I have found a letter for you," he began. Then he hesitated. "It has been here all the time and I only just now——"

Antoine pulled himself up on his elbows, a puzzled frown on his face. "A letter? A long time? What's in your head, man, what are you saying?"

"I was storing apples," Titus began uneasily, "and I opened the priest's hole there by the hearth. You remember the priest's hole, sir?"

"God's blood, man," Antoine shouted at him. "Stop that nattering. No more about apples and priest's holes. What letter? From where?"

Drawing the letter from behind his back, Titus handed it to his master then drew back quickly. Already he regretted ever taking it from the pouch. As Antoine stared at the script on the note, his face emptied of color. Then, as suddenly, the blood rushed back. Gripping the letter in both hands, he shouted at Titus.

"About your business, man, *go.*"

Titus fled, shutting the door firmly behind him, then leaning against it with a faint exhalation of despair. He had been

56

wrong. He had scraped up raw flesh on an old wound that was healing albeit slowly.

Disconsolate, he pulled a shawl from a peg and made his way to the stable. As the gelding whinnied softly in welcome, Titus laid his head against the horse's warm, twitching flank. After a bit, he roused and began to groom the horse methodically, seeking by the familiar retreat of labor to distract his mind from Antoine's anguish.

The horse's coat was gleaming from the brush when Titus felt the beast's muscles tighten under his hand as the horse stiffened and turned to stare behind him. Turning, Titus saw Antoine's tall, spare frame braced against the open door of the stable. Sweat shone on his face, dripping onto the ungroomed beard that had grown during his convalescence. Exhaustion showed in his eyes as he struggled a little for breath, clinging to the sides of the door frame with one hand while he leaned heavily on a broken branch that he held like a cane.

Antoine forced a smile, but his tone was bitter. "I have become an old woman in that bed, Titus," he said. "I must even rest now before I return."

Titus overturned a low barrel and dusted its bottom for Antoine to sit.

"Go on with your grooming," Antoine said, letting his weight down slowly. "That is a fine beast you have there."

"Indeed he is," Titus agreed. "Strong and wise."

Antoine chuckled softly. "This is who you have been courting during my illness then?"

Titus kept his face concealed from Antoine's eyes as he replied. "The time was to come when you would need a mount," he explained. "It seemed well to keep this one in trim."

"The time is come, Titus," Antoine told him.

"Then you have plans?" Titus tried not to let his eye wander to the injured leg extended stiffly before his master.

"I have plans," Antoine confirmed. Then he laughed, a short, bitter laugh that rose shallowly from his throat. "One does not live by choice in this world but because the breath comes and goes. And breathing, I have my debt to pay. Less than a thousand pounds there is to raise now, Titus. I have totalled my numbers, and we are near the end."

Titus remembered the leather pouch with its small store of

gold that still lay in the priest's hole but dared not mention it.

"Gaming is through for me," Antoine went on thoughtfully. "I dare not risk my face in London even though I am nameless there. Mignon's 'friend'," his voice rasped with bitterness, "has obviously bought a pardon from his duelling offense. I dare not risk his naming me as the butcher of his own foul deeds. If he lives, that is," he added thoughtfully. "I would to God he was dead of slow wounds that festered and tormented."

Listening, Titus slowed his strokes along the horse's coat. The gelding snorted softly, stamping with pleasure at his touch.

"Fast money," Antoine said slowly. "Only with fast money can I free myself from my debt and this cursed England."

"Speed and safety are seldom wedded," Titus told himself silently.

The barrel rolled on its side as Antoine heaved to his feet. "But first to get my strength back," he sighed. With his rude stick rustling in the crisp leaves, he started his tortuous trek back to the cottage.

Titus did not press Antoine about his plans. Instead, he watched with silent apprehension. As the chill moved deeper into the ground, Antoine drove his body rudely back into condition. He ran alongside the gelding on the cold paths of the woods, startling the bleached winter hares from their warrens. He raced the great beast along the byways, crouched on his back so that the two of them blended into a single dark mass moving like a storm-driven wind. The food that was ignored before was now devoured with lusty appetite, so that Antoine's spare body heavied with the graceful smoothness of hard flesh and muscle.

Antoine, in all this time, never spoke more of his plans. Soon enough, he would be submitted to Titus's stares of disapproval, his dire predictions of doom. The less the old dwarf knew, the longer Antoine's peace.

But Titus added his master's hours and found a sum of concern without being told. He heard his master off in the wood firing the blue-nosed pistol for long hours, practicing his skill against the moving game among the trees. Partridges and grouse and young fat hares came back on the gelding's saddle, but Titus found them bitter eating because of their source. With the cottage bolted and boarded against the night, Titus watched Antoine labor over carefully drawn maps, drawing and discarding and starting out again when one sheet after another flamed up in the fire. This was a life as long and hard as winter, hard, punishing days and long, cold, solitary nights, with only the cry of the night owl for company.

"I am booomo a monk," Antoine groaned to himself when a sweet dream of penetration wakened him distended and racked with lust. On such nights of waking, he would bring a candle and unfold again the well-worn letter from Mignon.

Her face would come alive again in the edges of the light, and her laughter, muted by his own body pressed against her, echoed in the call of nightbirds outside the window. Except for the phantoms that rose at the sight of her script, he did not need to read the letter at all. Her words were committed to his memory like the copy-book prayers of his childhood.

Toni, my love,

I feel my friend nearing, with the heat of his fury scourging me, but still I cannot flee him. How can I flee my own heart's blood? I wait for love or death at his choosing. If it is death, you must not blame him, Toni. We knew, he and I, from the first, that a flame such as ours would have no easy drowning.

My prayer for you, Toni. Keep love on the outside of your body like the skin of a reptile which can be slipped off and dropped away. This other love is an agony of the heart and bowels that I would have you spared of. My love, dear Toni and a last farewell.

Mignon.

With the acrid scent of the fresh-snuffed candle still in his room, Antoine would stare at the moving shadows of the forest beyond his window. Mignon had known. Her Gypsy wisdom had been wholly right. But she would never know how her blood had stained him. The horror of love, its hidden springs of anguish that he had only glimpsed in his sister's despairing face had become a rushing river with Mignon's death.

"Have no fear, gentle teacher," he spoke to her memory bitterly. "No woman born will touch my heart again. Only a fool drinks the same poison more than once."

59

With the fine full moon of March, Titus's poorly concealed fears were realized. The highroads whose ruts had been frozen to a stiffness during the deep of winter began to soften into great swamps of mud which slowed the swiftest coach to a racking crawl. Lumbering from side to side, the carriages overturned in ditches, piling passengers and luggage alike into the sea of slime. Axles broke and horses fell lame. Travellers took their lives and their fortunes in their hands to venture forth. Their helplessness made them the easy prey for the rapacity of the highwaymen, and no number of miscreants hanging along the route seemed to discourage this roving band of vultures.

Antoine, his pistol in his belt, wearing a mask as black as his full and curling beard, rode forth on the gelding at the moon's rise. Titus turned away without a sign, unable to watch him melt into the forest darkness.

Cantering through the lanes of Epping Wood, Antoine held his map within his mind. He felt the first fine surge of high excitement since those early gambling days with Jean and Mignon. How deep his debt to Mignon was. Even as she had sent him into the games sober and prepared, she had trained him for winning. Unlike the common highwaymen who ranged along the roads with random ferocity, he approached this night prepared in every way. Thank God for once, that England was so primitive a land. In France the *maréchaussée* would threaten his adventure, but here there was a fortune on the road but for the taking.

One thing about a life this empty of joy: it became a bauble to risk without a qualm!

Chapter Nine

Giles Urban urged his mount off the great road before he reached the entry to the Duvall drive. Guiding the mare through masses of underbrush and twisting between small trees, he was able to stay under cover of the yew trees so that his approach was not visible from the house. Once clear of the brush, he released the mare to an easy canter, kneeing her towards a plum grove beyond the knoll. The August earth was spongey from summer rains, and a cidery tang of fallen fruit perfumed the air.

As he neared the grove, Giles searched for Julie in the shadows. Surely she would be there. He had sent her the message by post in plenty of time. It was seldom enough that he had a day free to come up from London, and with all due apology to his own parents, it was only for these brief moments with Julie Duvall that he welcomed each chance to come.

With the earth's softness muffling the roan's hoofbeats, Julie did not at once discern his approach. A hard thrust of passion roused him when he saw her slender figure leaning pensively against a tree. Her head was bent over a blossom whose petals she was tossing away one by one. Her dark curls were crowned with a snippet of lace bound with blue ribbons. Thank God she had finally abandoned the somber mourning she had worn so long after her father's death. The deep-cut throat of her blue dress revealed her welling breasts, and the fullness of the voluminous lace-trimmed sleeves only accented the smallness of her waist.

How strangely fortunes fell, Giles mused. The same years which had marked Julie for loss and mourning had only brightened his own promise. After his two years at Oxford, his father, enriched by having bought some surrounding land, had bought Giles into the moiety of a petit chamber, and he had been admitted to the Middle Temple. These has been exciting and hard-working years for Giles, dispatching year-books and attending the sessions of the queen's court and common pleas as a spectator. Only a couple of years more and he could perform his moots and begin his own practice at law.

Then his long years of waiting would be through. Even though Julie was French, his father had already indicated that he would not put obstacles in the path of a marriage with Julie Duvall. There would be no end to their expectations. House of Commons, Justice of the Assize, Lord Chief Justice? Who could name the end of his hopes with Julie at his side and her handsome fortune available for their pleasure?

Then he would make up to her for the anguish of these years under her uncle's guardianship. How startled he had been to discover that her long-ago criticism of Simon Duvall was fully justified. How mean and cunning the old man had shown himself to be when he once got Julie's property under his guardianship. He had dismissed all her staff except her old companion-maid Mary and replaced her trusted domestics with his own spies so that Julie had neither privacy nor joy in her own home. It was because of her Uncle Simon's hirelings that Julie insisted that their meetings be held secret and apart like a common cowherd and his wench.

The greyhound Bonbon returned from a searching run to his mistress's side. He barked in alarm as he saw Giles crossing the field, alerting Julie. Glancing up, Julie dropped her flowers, and even as Giles watched, seemed to change from a pensive woman to a delighted child again. Careless of the brush that tugged at her dress, she ran towards him, her arms outstretched and her mouth curved with delight. Reining his mount, he waited until she drew near. Leaning, he caught her by her slim waist and lifted her up beside him, her lightness an astonishment in his arms.

As his mouth ached to possess hers, Julie seized him in a tight embrace like a child, circling him with her arms and pressing her fine, firm breasts hard against him. Then, burying her head in his neck so that her fragrant hair massed about his face, she snuggled like a puppy against him. "Oh, Giles, Giles," she murmured against his flesh. "How lovely to see you. How lovely of you to come."

"I couldn't stay away, you know that," he told her, loosening her arms so that he could stare hungrily at the smooth perfection of her face, those glowing, golden eyes that haunted him so mercilessly when they were apart.

"How beautiful you are," he breathed softly, startled, as he always was, that her perfection outstripped his extravagant memories of her.

She smiled, so that her dimple came fleetingly in her cheek. "It is you who are beautiful," she corrected him, arching her brows haughtily. She touched the ruffle of his cuff and ran a finger lightly down the embroidery that trimmed his rose red jacket. "Such a fop you have become, Giles. Even red high heels!"

He shook her gently. "A gentleman must look the part," he reminded her. But he grinned himself. "In all truth I do get very amused by what peacocks we men have become. The brass snuffbox," he tapped his pocket elegantly, "and the gleaming walking stick which you will note I did not trouble with. At least I have not affected a stemmed looking glass. Although, if it could make me see you plainer, I would even stoop to that."

"It's all very beautiful," she admitted, "But can you sit on a fallen tree with me in that plumage?"

After swinging her to the ground, Giles dropped the mare's reins on the grass where she had already begun to crop lazily.

As he reached for Julie, she caught him by the hand and led him, half-running into the edge of the woods.

"But where is my kiss for greeting?" he protested. "Surely after so many weeks?"

Plumped on the log, she patted the flat place beside her, urging him to sit.

"Have you forgotten?" she goaded. "When I kiss you, you rebuke me."

He groaned as he spread the flaring tail of his jacket and joined her on the log. "Will you never let me forget that day?"

"Never," she said with a laugh, leaning into his embrace. The touch of her soft lips under his renewed the thrust of passion that he had fought so hard to control. Forgetting himself, he bent her slender back, letting his lips taste the soft flesh of her neck, the hard, firm heat of her exposed breasts.

"Giles, Giles," she insisted, flattening her hands against his chest to force him away.

Regaining his breath with difficulty, he held the small of her back lightly with careful hands, content for that moment to feel the warmth of her flesh under his hands with only the sheer of her light clothes between them. "You don't realize how hard I have tried to forget that kiss," he told her honestly. "Come on, Julie. You have never kissed me like that again."

She shook herself away determinedly. She laid her hand by his throat gently, her eyes suddenly pensive. Her other hand strayed to Bonbon, stroking the hound's silken coat. "The devil touched me that day," she decided aloud.

"When we are married, Julie, we will invite the devil to our bedding," Giles whispered, his lips against the coolness of her ear.

She shivered and pulled away. "Giles. What kind of a here-

63

tic have you become with your red heels and your brave talk of challenging demons?"

"A man as much in love as I," Giles told her, "has much confusion about his worshipping."

Soft, sudden laughter parted her lips. "I do forget how much fun you are to banter with. I swear, Giles, lawyers are the world's most entertaining company."

Catching her hand, Giles traced the line of a wedding band on her finger. "Please be sure to keep that passion for a lawyer's conversation, Julie. I intend for you to spend your life making fine, mocking fun of me even as you always have."

As always when he spoke of marriage, Julie led the conversation swiftly away, inquiring of his parents's health, of his life away from her. Only after sharing all his adventures with her did he shake his head firmly. "Enough of me, Julie, how does it go with you here?"

A darkness shadowed her eyes, and her small figure drooped a little unconsciously. "It is as ever," she said in a bored tone. "Not worth putting words on really." Giles cursed inwardly. How different her life could have been if only Fiona and Etienne Duvall had been spared.

"When will you come into your estate, Julie?" he asked, boldly enough. "At twenty-one?"

She nodded. "Only a little more than a year. Anyone can survive a little more than year, can't they, Giles?" Contrite at the complaining tone of her voice she smiled purposefully. "It's not all that bad, you know. I still have Mary to talk to, and sometimes my young cousin Louis and my father's banker Mr. Furlong."

At her own words, her mood changed swiftly. "I had forgotten about my most wonderful news. The excitement of your coming sent it flying right out of my head. Mr. Furlong and his wife have invited me to London to visit them this fall. Isn't that exciting? Mary will stay here to run the house, and I will get to travel by coach and see all of London as their guest. I have not been to London since my father—" her voice trailed off. Then her dimple flashed again with happiness. "As mean as my uncle is with me about my own money I have cajoled from him some fine new clothes, a new mantle with a hood and gowns for dancing and promenading."

"How marvelous for you," he said, trying to hide the apprehension her news had brought to him.

"How marvelous," she mimicked with her mouth pursed. "You don't sound as if you think my holiday is all that marvelous."

"Well, think of my side of it," he pointed out. "One look at you and all of London will go to its knees. You will be feted and courted until you are completely spoiled. Promise me that every time a fop kisses your hand you will remind yourself that you belong to Giles Urban, the man of your future."

She laughed merrily. "I have a better idea. The moment he touches me I shall shout it and startle him off his high heels into disorder."

Laughing in spite of himself, Giles asked, "Will you spend the season in London then?" His concern was only a little eased by her jesting.

"Oh, no," she shook her head. "The Furlongs are leaving for a sojourn in France very soon. They have their licenses to sail in late September." Then she grinned wickedly, her eyes glinting at his discomfort. "That will give the gallants of London less than a month to win my heart from you."

Glancing at the sky, Julie started. "How quickly time passes when we are together, Giles," she sighed. "I must go back before some knave is sent to search for me. It is only by riding each morning at these hours that I have made any time at all for myself away from those rough hirelings of Uncle Simon's."

Even knowing the discomfort that would plague his ride all the way home, Giles spoke softly. "Only let me hold you a little time, Julie, so that I can hear your heartbeat against mine. God knows when we can be this near again."

"I am too hopelessly affectionate with those I cherish," she said softly. She fitted into his arms, her head fragrant about his mouth, and he clung to her for a long minute. Then Julie pulled away with a sigh.

Giles left the grove first because she wished it so. The last time he looked back, she seemed unreal, like a small, perfect porcelain figurine of a girl with a hound. Her sleeve fell back at her gesture of farewell, and he was at once pained and delighted to imagine that her golden eyes glistened with tears.

Even as her precious minutes with Giles were wont to pass

too quickly, Julie's days in London sped quickly into weeks. Mistress Furlong, in spite of her great age and her round figure that even stringent corseting could not conceal, was a fount of boundless energy. Her seemingly inexhaustible list of things that must be done before she left England kept Julie and herself flying from shop to shop, from milliner to dressmaker to perfumery. Their days and their nights were breathlessly full. Julie, accustomed to the loneliness of her country estate, loved all London's pleasures the same—the small, gay parties at which she was feted, the walks along the avenue for shopping, promenading in the mall at Saint James park where the deer and cattle grazed on green turf between the avenues crowded with fashionable men and women.

Her pleasures were so various and the days so fleeting that Julie could not bear to spend an extra hour in sleep. Mistress Furlong lingered late in bed of morning, having her chocolate and roll with a paper to read before dressing for the day. Spurning the assistance of the maid the Furlongs had provided for her, Julie wakened and dressed with the first sounds of the city. Then she hastened to have breakfast with Mr. Furlong who, like herself, was an early and amiable riser.

Their morning talks covered the widest range of topics, for this bright, cordial man, like Julie herself, was curious about everything in the city that reached his attention. Together they laughed at the extravagant fashions of the time. He shared with her the coffee house gossip about "that German king" as he called King George. He had seen Handel's opera *Rinaldo*, and he described the settings to her in glowing detail. She asked him about Tyburn, having seen a festive procession winding past Saint Sepulchre's Church. The chained man had ridden in a cart with his own coffin and as he passed, flowers and blossoms showered him from the hands of the mob that ran alongside.

Mr. Furlong nodded wisely. "A curious hunger in a common man seeks a hero who is braver than himself. The man who breaks the law springs into legend. There is even now one of these legends growing in the countryside." With his eyeglasses poised on his nose he pulled a paper close and read to her. "Now listen. 'It has been reported by Lord Cranburnely that he and his party were accosted on their return to London on Sunday last. The highwayman relieved His Lordship of some quantity of gold, two watches, and some jewelled baubles which belonged to the ladies of the party. His Lordship believes his accoster to have been the Blue-eyed Giant from his appearance. He sported a terrifying beard and was of giant proportion, but he kept a remarkable civil tongue in his head while stripping the coach.' " Mr. Furlong rustled a moment more in his papers, "More about this same chap. This from the *London News Gazette*. 'The Blue-eyed Giant who has been harrying travellers from Aldgate to Cilchester stopped a coach and took off a bride's dower plate along with some jewels. He did spare the unfortunate mistress her wedding band which he saluted with a tossed kiss. This giant bearded man is said to be more daring than John Collington, more dashing than Dick Adams, and as determined for booty as old Moll Cutpurse herself.' "

He set the paper away and smiled at Julie. "He will not last," he assured her. "They all swing at Tyburn in the end. Unless they have the gold to buy their freedom. But in any case they are gone, for the only freedom they can buy is for transport to the colonies. This man in particular has little chance to stay free for long with a double bounty on his head."

"A double bounty?" Julie asked, confused.

"There is a prize of forty pounds for thief-taking if the thief is a proved highwayman," he explained. "For the Blue-eyed Giant the bounty has been matched by some man of substance whom he apparently offended. Many a soul in London would consider they had come into a fortune with eighty pounds."

Immersed as he was in his city, Mr. Furlong seemed to forget that his companion was a simple girl of nineteen. He regaled her with tales of success and failure by merchants of the city, clucking with despair over the highly inflated stock of the South Seas Company. "It has become a positive mania along 'Change Alley," he explained. "The price of a one-hundred-pound share has risen to well above a thousand, and men have indentured their whole estates against some future profit."

"My father shared your opinion of such ventures," Julie remembered aloud. "How he laughed at Uncle Simon for trying to borrow money for those 'wild schemes,' as papa called them."

67

"Your father was a wiser man than many of his peers," Mr. Furlong nodded.

He lifted the coffeepot and then froze with a look of startled dismay on his face. "I hope—" he began, then his voice stopped.

When he paused, Julie leaned towards him. "You hope what, sir?" she asked.

He shook his head with irritation. "I was only going to say that I hope your uncle has not invested any of your property in such wild schemes. But I have no reason to think that might be true."

"If he had, would you not know of it, sir?" Julie asked.

He wiped his mouth with a frown. "Not necessarily. He could make commitments against your accounts and your estates, and we at the bank would know naught of them until they came up for collection." Then seeing her concern, he smiled with forced joviality. "Look at us, borrowing trouble like a housemaid against her wages." He pushed a jam pot towards her. "Have some of this good plum butter to brighten your smile."

Julie smiled happily. "That is the plum butter I sent you and your mistress Christmas last, from the plums of our own hedges."

He nodded. "And we have tasted it with much pleasure." Then, as often when they talked, his expression turned suddenly quite sad and his tone very maudlin. Laying a hand on Julie's, he shook his head. "If God had blessed my wife and me with children, Julie, I could only hope they would have been such as you. Not only are you skilled in household ways beyond your station, but there is a depth below your beauty which will stand you in good stead long after your youth has fled."

"I hope you are right, sir," Julie told him, half-dismayed but wholly touched by his words.

Mr. Furlong surprised her one morning with the gift of a collection of Spectator papers. She was delighted to find in these pages mention of the coffee houses she knew by sight, the parks she had walked, even puppet shows she had lingered by during her stay.

Giles, she discovered, had been only a little wrong about the men of London. Julie was cynical enough to wonder whether it was her appearance or the fact that she was only seen in the company of an officer of the bank that brought so many young men to court her so gallantly. The Furlong house received a steady stream of these young men who came to pay their respects and conduct silly, airy talk with Julie while they stared at her through eyeglasses held aloft on stems.

"Giles need not have feared these peacocks," Julie told herself, repressing a giggle. They were all as alike as cornflowers in a meadow and less entertaining. But as little as she cared for the gallants of society, Julie was not averse to looking about at the men of the city. As she moved about in carriage and sedan chair, she studied the faces she saw. Beggars, dandies, merchants, and Newgate prisoners, marching two by two, passed before her eyes. And she always turned with a swift curiosity unbecoming to a lady when a white coach passed by.

Sometimes by carelessness, she even caught the eye of a footman and was forced to retreat behind the fan that Mistress Furlong insisted she carry.

I invented him, she told herself at last. I invented that footman out of the wild, romantic dreams of a very young girl. Yet she searched the city still for the firm lines of that tall, fair body and the blazing impudence of those blue eyes.

Chapter Ten

Julie watched wistfully as the maid folded her gay London clothes back into the brass-ribbed trunk. Julie had been persuaded to extend her visit with the Furlongs to the last possible moment. When they saw her safely onto the coach for home, their own carriage would take them directly to Dover for their long stay abroad.

"Why didn't we plan to take Julie with us?" Mistress Furlong sighed as they watched Julie's chest being hoisted onto the coach. "It has been like turning young again to have you with us, my dear."

"When we return, we shall simply steal her away," Mr. Furlong told his wife. "Now that we know how to bring every gay young blade in London to our bidding, we will use this information. By charging half a crown to every smitten young bachelor who wishes to call, we would shortly launch a fleet of ships financed by love alone." He winked broadly at Julie, kissed her damply on the cheek, and waved farewell as the driver whipped the horses into action.

Only when the rolling fields of Middlesex lay beyond her window, did Julie feel the least anticipation about returning to her own estate. Her dear Mary would be there, she reminded herself. Mary would be anxious for all word of London, where she had lived as a child and where she would return when her days of service were through. There would be Bonbon, writhing with happiness, running his ecstasy in swift circles about her. She pushed a sudden urge to self-pity from her mind lest it stain her homecoming.

But no effort would have saved that arrival. She felt an alien strangeness in her house the moment she entered. Mary greeted her effusively but in spite of her obvious efforts to conceal it, Julie was struck by a look of tragedy in the older woman's eyes.

Even the servants with whom her uncle had replaced her own staff seemed more withdrawn and sullen than she remembered. After an indifferent meal that was rudely served, Julie at last lost patience with the sense of secret sorrow that seemed to hang like an invisible pall over the house.

"Whatever is going on in this house?" she asked with more impatience than she ever showed to Mary. "This place feels like a new death."

To her astonishment Mary, who prided herself on being a woman who did not turn easily to tears, buried her head in her arms and began to wail.

Julie went to her swiftly, patting the old woman's shoulder and apologizing over and over. "I am sorry, Mary. Please forgive my crossness. I have lost patience without cause. I know that if anything were wrong you would tell me."

When her words only evoked a fresh storm of tears, Julie drew back and waited, apprehension moving like a chill along her spine.

"Lost," Mary said finally in a voice heavy with tears. "I thought to wait until tomorrow to tell you—when the sun might be shining. But it is lost—all lost."

"What is lost? What are you talking about?" Julie asked, her patience strained towards breaking.

Mary waved her hands widely as if that movement might encompass the world. "The house, the lands, the stock," she said grimly. "Even the horses that tilled these fields."

"How can that be?" Julie cried.

"They were pledged," Mary said numbly. "All pledged for stock which is now worth nothing at all. Your uncle with his grand plans for making millions of pounds from thousands has lost it all to thieves who have disappeared with the money and left only the paper in his hands."

"He can't have done that. It was my father's property, and my own," But even as Julie spoke, she knew that indeed he could have, and in some secret place in her mind she accepted that this danger had moved in her understanding since her talk with Mr. Furlong early in August.

A sudden, harsh voice spoke from the door. "Wouldn't you know," her Aunt Carolyn's high voice broke in. "Wouldn't you just know that the fancy lady in her London clothes would be blaming my poor dear husband when he tried his best to make an increase of her goods?" She swept into the room as if she had suddenly become mistress of the house. "God gives and God takes away," she added piously.

Turning to Mary, she spoke briskly. "We pledged to give over when the mistress returned and now she is here. She will go back with us to our home tonight."

"But my things," Julie cried. "My furniture, my horse, my trappings—"

Her aunt eyed the brass-ribbed trunk with greedy eyes. "Only what you had with you in London has not been counted," she told Julie. "I will have the man throw in on the trap. It is late enough to set out as it is."

"Bonbon," Julie cried softly, remembering.

Her aunt sneered. "You can tie the beast on behind if you think it's worth it. If he can live with his belly full of the mud he'll get on the way home, it's all right with me."

When she swept from the room to shout orders to the servants below, Julie went into Mary's arms.

"My love, my bird," Mary crooned softly into her hair.

"Don't worry about me," Julie told her, pulling back to see Mary's face. "What about you, Mary? Where will you go? What will you do?"

"London," Mary said quietly. Then she went to the desk and scribbled swiftly on a slip of paper. "This is the lodging of my sister Margaret. If you ever have need, Julie, seek us out." Dropping her eyes with embarrassment she added, "When her master of many years died, he left her a settlement. With care it will sustain us both."

"Oh Mary," Julie cried with a fresh stab of despair. "If only my father had known. How handsomely he would have provided for you. How much I would give for only enough to make you independent again."

Mary sniffed before belatedly drawing her apron to her reddened nose. "We had good, rich years together, Julie, and now we are come down together. May God keep you in that strange house."

"I have a few guineas," Julie remembered suddenly. "It is left from the money I took along to London. Let me get them for you."

Mary shook her head firmly. "I have my fare and some small savings from the years. You keep your guineas well hidden for an unknown need."

In the grief of that leave-taking Julie did not at once realize that only her aunt and her stepcousin Joseph had come for her. Her uncle and Louis were not in the rude farm wagon that waited at the end of the drive. When Joseph piled her trunk in the back, he grudgingly agreed that she might keep Bonbon beside her "if she didn't care about vermin crawling about on her." Their old carriage, mean as it was, had apparently gone the way of all else. Heavy tilling horses drew the cart along the rutted roads that led to her uncle's home. The rolling and tilting of the cart made the heavy chest slide against Julie and Bonbon, nearly crushing them at turns of the road.

Bonbon twitched nervously in Julie's arms at the fearsome sounds of the night countryside. At a crossroads, three limp bodies, stripped of what clothing they had boasted, hung from the scaffolds, a testament to the perils of the road and the industry of the thief-takers.

The nightmare into which Julie had been plunged seemed to have raised a wall of separation between herself and the life into which she had been disinherited. Voices seemed to come from afar, and a numbness in her heart made her impervious to the jeers and insults that her aunt and stepcousin aimed at her. She performed unaccustomed tasks with the dogged persistence of a sleepwalking machine. Even her hands became strange to her, spotted with burns from the spit, with hard, sore calluses from the tools she was handed to work with.

When, after some weeks, her uncle had still not returned, Julie forgot about him. She feared to ask anything of her termagant aunt so she put him from her mind like she had so many things since her return from London. In all this time of trial, there was only Louis to comfort her. He was taller than she now by a great deal but frail and sickly, afflicted with a cough that she heard racking during the night through the ill-built walls of the house. His skin was as white as her own, and beneath his dark hair, bold spots of color often stained his cheeks.

"We could be taken for brother and sister," he told her, lifting a lock of her hair from her face as she bent over a tub of soiled clothes.

"It is the same," she smiled at him. "You are closer than any other human to me—all the family I own."

"And I shall protect you," he pledged, "I'll always protect you."

Julie smiled at him, but inside she shivered. Each day that passed Joseph grew more bold with her, and his mother paid no attention to her great, loutish son. More than once she was able to fight her way free of him by sheer luck or the agility of her small body. Once she struck him hard across the face for his wanton fondling, and he stepped back with a twisted smile.

"I can wait for you, slut," he told her with a sneer. "There'll be nobody else to have you after this, you know. Who knows, even I might not want in your cunt with your fine feathers gone. You're lucky to have anybody look at you twice."

Like Julie, Bonbon changed with the new circumstances. He was no longer a young dog, and what food Julie was able to reserve for him was not enough to flesh his great body. He quivered with chill as the autumn days turned shorter, and when he rose to walk he stumbled like an old, sick man.

With the first frost, Julie began to take him to her room with her at night. Folding her mantle by her bed to keep the chill of the floor from his bones, she soothed him to sleep with her hand, reassured by his steady heartbeat under her palm.

73

Winter's first storm howled in on a bitter wind in the late afternoon. A fine dust of snow piled like sugar against the bushes and trees. Louis, his deep, dry cough made worse by the penetrating chill, helped her fill the woodboxes against the chill of night. The clothes which had served so well for the London summer did not protect Julie from the chill of the big, poorly sealed house. With supper over and the table cleared, Julie went to her room to huddle beneath her covers beside Bonbon as the winds drove at the house with unabating fury.

Two months had passed since her return from London and her arrival at this place. She thought of the Furlongs enjoying their long sojourn in Paris and Nice. She thought of Giles and that last morning together there in the plum gove. But what profit did it do to think of friends of other times? Joseph goaded her that girls without fortunes were girls without hope. These people whom she had loved and shared happy times were now a world removed. She might have married Giles and had a good life with him. But she would have brought to that marriage enough property to make up for the coolness of her passion for him. As a pauper, even if he sought her out, which was unlikely enough, she could not wed him. She would be exploiting him even as her Uncle Simon had exploited his wife when he married her for her land and then despoiled it.

"I cannot go on like this," she realized. It was as if the wind that howled behind the wall was clearing her mind of cobwebs. "There is a better way and I must find it for myself."

It was only then that she remembered Mary's plain, impassioned face raised to her own. "Come to me if you have need," she had said.

Startled by her sudden clarity of thought, Julie sat straight up in the darkness, clutching the coverlet about her bare shoulders. "It need not be charity I ask for," she told herself with excitement. She had seen the needlework in all the fine London shops and had known that her own work was better and more carefully done. "I can do needlework and keep accounts," she told herself with surprise. "I can spin and weave and make fine jellies and conserves."

She plumped down into the bed again, warmed by the hopes she had discovered for herself. She would run away and go to London, she decided. Her hidden guineas would pay the fare, and Mary would help her to begin. Soothed by the thought of this release, she fell asleep smiling for the first time in weeks.

At first she thought it was the howl of the wind that had wakened her, and she only nestled a little deeper into the nest of her covers. Then she realized with a start that the slow, steady rumble was Bonbon, his head alert in warning at her side. She sat up and stared into the darkness of the room. Bonbon was on his feet now, and she gripped the back of his slender neck, shushing his rising growls. He tried to wrest loose from her as he bared his fangs and stared at the door.

Frightened, she tugged her comforter from the bed and slid down on the floor to crouch beside him. It was only then that she realized that they were not alone in the room. She recognized Joseph without being able to make out his thick figure. She smelled the sick scent of ale which always hung about his soiled tunic. As he stood there, immobile in her doorway, she rose to her feet, still gripping Bonbon.

"Get out of my room, Joseph," she hissed, not wanting to alarm Louis and his mother and Amalie who slept down the hall.

"When I am damned good and ready," he said. "What's that filthy beast doing in here?"

"Guarding me," she said sharply. "Now get out of here before I scream."

He laughed rudely and took a step towards her. "Hell of a lot of good it would do to scream. Who do you think would hear you above this gale?" From the slur in his voice she realized that he was drunk. As he took another stumbling step towards her she backed away, still gripping the dog. Her move had been a mistake. The paleness of her low-cut gown caught what light there was, revealing her position to him.

Then with startling swiftness, Joseph lunged for Bonbon whose back was arched against Julie's restraining hand. The dog slashed at Joseph's hand, his teeth ripping the flesh along the wrist. Joseph, with a curse, wadded his great fist and slammed the dog against the side of his head. With a moan, Bonbon went limp, his fine legs twitching against Julie's ankles.

"You beast," Julie screamed. "You miserable, drunken

75

beast." She clawed at his face and beat on his head with her fists, but he only caught her to him, tearing her nightdress from her chilling body. With his thick thigh thrust between her legs he forced her backwards onto the bed. As she fought and clawed, he caught her loose hair with his hand and jerked her head back, the hard knot of his lust pressed against her naked belly.

"Oh God," she cried. She tried to scream, but his stinking mouth covered hers, shutting off even her breath. His thick tongue gouged her throat as he tried with his free hand to force entry into her writhing body. Waves of nausea racked her, and her back coursed with pain as he pressed his weight on her slenderness.

She did not hear the first low growl as Bonbon staggered to his feet shaking his head from the numbing blow. With the second growl, the dog was upon Joseph, diving on his bared back, his great teeth shaking and tearing at bleeding flesh. Joseph flailed at the animal, screaming with rage and pain.

Freed from his weight, Julie slid to the floor and fled to Louis's room, sobs tearing through her bruised throat.

Without pausing, she opened the door and shook Louis awake. Not until his startled eyes swept her body did she even realize that only the shred of her gown hung from her shoulder.

Louis was instantly alert. "Joseph, Bonbon," she gasped. Louis, his fine face darkening, seized the poker from the cold hearth in the room and rushed past her down the hall.

As she turned to follow him, she heard the high, anguished cry of an animal in agony. Her shock and pain closed in on her in darkening waves, and she slumped to the floor just inside Louis's door.

It was Louis who helped her dig a grave for Bonbon in the half-frozen soil beyond the cattle stalls. Joseph did not show his face in the house all that day. When Julie tried to press Louis for what happened between the brothers after she fainted, he only shook his head. "It's over now, Julie," he said firmly, suddenly seeming to be the older and the stronger. "It's over."

"But it's not over," Julie cried, tears starting to her eyes. "He will try again—and again."

"And when he does, I shall kill him," Louis said flatly.

76

She stared at her beloved cousin with thoughtful eyes. Then she slipped her hand through his arm.

"I will tell you a secret, Louis. I am going to run away."

He stopped in the path and stared at her stupidly.

"To London," she nodded. "I have a friend. You remember my maid Mary? I will go to her. Will you help me?"

He pursed his lips in thought.

"Our father is in London," he confided. "In a debtor's prison. God knows when he will be released."

"I could never go to him." Julie said, "Not even if he were free."

Louis nodded thoughtfully. "How will you travel?"

"By night," Julie whispered as they were nearing the house. "I would stay off the roads as much as I could. I have a little money for food, but not enough for an inn. Once in London, Mary would protect me."

"Terrible things could happen to you," he warned.

She looked at him, her golden eyes compelling his own to honesty. "Terrible things happen to me here, Louis," she reminded him.

When the house grew still except for the ticking of cold in the walls, Louis came secretly to her room. She was astonished at the sudden fullness of his figure in the light of her candle.

"All my clothes," he explained. "And you must do the same. Put on all the clothes you have, one upon another, and your great mantle over the top. We will put some soot from the hearth about your face to spoil your beauty. That way we will be both warm and safe."

"What do you mean with that 'we'?" she asked, staring at him.

His low laugh ended in a long, painful cough, then he grinned at her.

"It means I am going with you, little sister." Then he pulled back his cloak and showed her the pistol strapped to his belt. "A half-hour is all you should need to dress," he told her with his new authority. "Meet me in the kitchen hall in half an hour."

When she reached the hall, Louis was already outside in the dooryard. Fine steam floated about his head from his breath as he turned to her.

77

"I was afraid my hacking would waken them," he explained, taking her arm in his with a reassuring smile. It was a clear, cold night with the earth frozen so firm that it left no mark of their passing.

PART II
THE KNIGHT OF
THE ROAD
November, 1721–May, 1722

Chapter Eleven

With the wind driving the snow against his face like icy
spittle, Antoine cursed himself for venturing out on such a
day. But the raging storm just past had set his teeth on edge
so that he could not stand the tight cottage and Titus's company for another hour. Experience had taught him that most
of the men who scavenged along these highroads were indolent fellows who would spend such a day as this with a whore
and a bottle in some stinking den in London.

From his post in the thicket just above the roadway he
commanded a view of the road in both directions. Even in
the snow, he should be able to hear the approach of the carriage he was waiting for. He had watched the driver load at
an inn near London. He guessed the man to be a Yorkshire
landowner who had been caught by the early storm while
transporting his wife and her trappings back into the drear
north. Because the boot of the carriage had been piled high
with luggage, Antoine knew there would be no footman to
contend with, only the portly driver and the couple themselves along with a dour-faced maid with a pinched nose and
stiff mouth.

His horse stirred restlessly, stamping one foot and tossing
his head with impatience. With a pat from Antoine's hand, he
was reassured and dropped his head to nudge the snow from
a frozen clump of wild grass beneath the tree.

The Yorkshireman's booty had damned well be worth this
wait, Antoine thought bitterly as the snow swirled and eddied
along the ruts of the empty road.

The horse heard the approaching wheels first, tensing his
ears and staring blindly into the curtain of falling snow. Antoine reached for his mask and then thought better of it. Although the approaching vehicle was not yet in view, Antoine
recognized the slow, waggling rhythm of a coach. While other
bandits beseiged the coaches constantly, Antoine felt it to be
as unprofitable as it was dangerous. Not only did coach passengers seldom carry much that was worth stealing, but too
often some young buck on board, eager to appear a hero to

his doxy, pulled a gun and added risk to the heist. Apprenticed as he had been to gambling, Antoine was not one to double his odds for half a profit.

The coach and six emerged from the snow like drunken ghosts reeling along the road. The horses's heads were circled in clouds of translucent steam which streamed past the driver who was huddled like a frozen statue on his box. The glass coach itself, even being tugged along at this easy pace, moved awkwardly on its rough wheels, swaying and tilting under the mountain of luggage piled on its roof. Antoine smiled to think of the unexpected intimacy that its hapless passengers were enjoying as the springless coach tossed them together like dice in a closed hand.

From his post above the road, Antoine stared idly down at the untidy luggage, bundles and chests strapped indiscriminately together in a snow-covered mound. Only when the coach was full abreast did Antoine notice the dark shape of something unsecured in among the chests and trunks. He leaned forward to stare at the mass which was strangely free of snow cover. It couldn't be a passenger, he told himself, not in a storm like this. He knew that coach drivers took passengers on coachtop for whatever coins a peasant could dredge up for a fare. But surely not in such a storm.

But he was wrong, by God. There were peasants huddled in that mass of dark fabric. Poor devils. He could make out two figures clinging to each other and taking the brunt of the storm full face.

"Miserable creatures," he shivered at their plight. The mantle that sheltered them both appeared to be of sturdy, fine stuff, and the movement of the two shook the snow from its folds. Even as he stared, he realized that within that wrapping a struggle was going on. With a sudden lurch, the cloth fell back exposing a young man's face raised to the sky. Dark eyes blazed from a face of singular beauty. The cheeks were stained as scarlet as a painted woman's, and the boy's mouth was open in what appeared as a burst of laughter. Or song. The boy was struggling to free himself of his companion, not realizing as Antoine did, that a chance careless motion would plunge him from the swaying coachtop.

Mad, Antoine decided glumly. The boy was clearly mad and his companion was hard put to keep him on the coach's top at all. "That's all that London needs," he told himself wryly. "Another crazy beggar in her streets, another desperate peasant lured to town to fight like a rat for life along its alleys."

As suddenly as the coach had emerged from the snow it was gone, and the sounds of its departure were muffled by the snow. But the memory of the young madman's face clung to his mind as he held his post, hugging his own body for warmth.

He gave himself one more hour to wait when a peasant passed. He was young and truculent, kicking the flanks of his mean mount like a cricketer. He was muffled to the eyes, which were small and darting as if he sought a quarry in the roadside brush. Antoine pressed his hand flat against his horse's neck to caution for silence. The youth looked too stupid even to be a thief-taker, but he was searching for something along the road, and Antoine was not hungry to be noticed. Athwart his saddle, the young man carried a cudgel that Antoine himself would not be eager to have swung at him.

Antoine tortured himself through that last hour with thoughts of the Yorkshireman stopping in an inn, swilling ale by a deep fire while fat hens turned on the spit. "Only a little more," he promised his mount. As if his reassurance were a signal, he heard the labored breathing of approaching horses and the squeak of the carriage's wheels along the ruts.

With the Yorkshireman's silver-plate and jewelled trifles packed away, Antoine left his victims standing by the roadside. They needed to see him gallop off towards London so that any report they gave would lead pursuers astray. Only a few miles down the road he would take a path through open fields and double back to reach Epping Woods.

Antoine stored his mask and bound his face in a muffler. The beard that served to terrorize travellers was all too memorable a feature at other times.

Freed of the numbing vigil, the horse took to the road briskly. The snow needled Antoine's face as he bent to his mount's steaming neck. He was only a mile from his turning-off place when he was startled by a clamor in the road ahead. Over the whistling wind and his own horse's hoofbeats, he heard the neighing of horses and the shrill squeals of women's voices. Reining his mount to a dancing halt, Antoine listened, then nudged his horse off the road and in behind a row of trees. Under cover of the trees, he drew stealthily close to the fray and then was barely unable to control a shout of laughter.

The scene was like a Hogarth drawing. The great glass coach lay on its side like a giant beetle, its thick wheels helpless in the air. The hubbub was immense as the horses, trapped in harness, squealled their rage and struggled for footing. The driver screamed curses as he struggled to right the trap with the aid of several grunting male passengers. The screams of the women from inside the upended coach only added a little flavor to the din. The luggage, which had been bound so cavalierly on the coach's top, had been thrown like careless dice across the field beyond the ditch.

The luggage reminded Antoine of the peasants who had been struggling among those chests and boxes. What of the mad boy and his companion under the dark cloth?

He circled the mass of luggage carefully and only by chance looked back across the field to a darkness glimpsed from the corner of his eye.

There were not two figures but three. As he cantered up, Antoine realized that a woman, or a child perhaps, was crouched on the frozen earth trying to shield a figure on the ground beside her. Above her, wielding his great cudgel with murderous swings stood the peasant who had passed him earlier along the road.

"Good Christ." Antoine muttered, his stomach churning at the violence in the man's face. This animal fury was none of his damned business, but the helpless cries of the woman were more than Antoine could ignore.

"Hold up," Antoine shouted at the peasant. "Let them be."

The peasant turned his mean eyes to Antoine and snarled. "Be off. This is none of your mind."

Conscious of the gun at his belt, Antoine stayed his hand. There was nothing for him to gain here and everything to lose, but the sight of the man's face sickened his sight.

"I say hold off," Antoine repeated, dancing his mount towards the peasant threateningly.

Wordlessly the peasant turned and swung his cudgel in a wide arc. Only his split-second agility saved Antoine from a broken head. Fury flamed in his chest. Sliding swiftly from

84

his saddle, he grabbed the end of the clod's stick and braced his boot against it.

"You meddling bastard," the peasant shouted, struggling to regain his control of the weapon. "I'll show you what to hold."

The snow spun about them, making the packed earth treacherous underfoot as Antoine struggled to separate the man from his weapon. What a rock of a man he was, but his brain was as weak as his body was strong. With a sudden feint, Antoine tricked him off balance so that he fell sliding on his backside, leaving the cudgel in Antoine's grasp.

"Move and I'll open your head," Antoine warned. The man edged backward on an elbow, and Antoine raised the cudgel. "You want your brains on your tunic?" he asked mildly.

Keeping the man in careful view, Antoine studied the peasant's victims. The mad young man was dead. His face, still wearing that exhultant smile, stared sightlessly at the sky. Blood still bubbled through the snow that clung to his dark hair. The woman huddled over him, moaning softly. Antoine caught the briefest glimpse of her matted hair and filth-streaked face as she glanced up at him and then returned to her keening.

"It is too late," he told her. "The boy is dead."

With her face still darkly muffled, she turned to look at him. Her eyes held that glazed, unknowing peasant stare that gave his flesh frisson, but their color was magnificent, a clear, tawny gold that glistened between dark, tear-stained lashes. One of those leaps of memory that had plagued him so many times during these lonely months arched in his mind. Somewhere, back in his memory's depths, there had been such golden eyes as these. They were wedded in his memory to joy and sunlight and the scent of the open countryside.

"He is dead," Antoine repeated, groping for her understanding. A furtive movement by the peasant on the ground brought Antoine about with a menacing step. The peasant cringed, and his voice dropped to a whine.

"She is mine," he told Antoine.

"He lies," the girl's voice was vibrant with hate.

"She's mine," the peasant screamed. "No man can have her."

Antoine felt laughter bubble to his lips. My God, the slavery of man to lust. This miserable, bulky-shaped creature with her filthy face and matted hair, and still this beast was slavering after her.

"He lies," the girl repeated. Then she wilted, pressing herself against the dead boy, sobs tearing through her throat.

Antoine paused with indecision. He could heardly leave her here at the mercy of that crude clod, yet how could it be better for her in London, if indeed the coach was righted for travel again?

"You go to London?" he asked, his eyes wary on the peasant still on his backside on the frozen ground.

She nodded.

"I'll find you there, you miserable slut," the peasant shouted. "I'll seek you out wherever you are." The man's tirade was peppered with obscenity, and his eyes narrowed with cunning. "I'll tell them how he died, that miserable weakling. About how you dragged him out into the storm with his bloody cough. There's laws against kidnapping, even for such as Louis."

Antoine watched her fine eyes widen with horror. Then, as she struggled with the mass of mantle about her and tried to rise, he held out his hand to her. That moment of inattention was all that the peasant had waited for. Antoine saw the peasant's arm rise and the shadow of the clutched stone, and he ducked.

The stone which was aimed at Antoine struck the girl aslant her head. She fell, wilting smoothly like flowing water, falling onto the body of her murdered companion.

"You slimy beast," Antoine snarled, turning on the peasant. Fury boiled in his bowels. Time weaved and plaited in the whitened air. The image of those golden eyes closing and Mignon's white body reddened by a madman's blows blended together to feed the rage that scalded up in his throat.

As Antoine approached with the cudgel in his hands, the peasant scuttled backward, dragging his cold butt like a crab and pleading for mercy. It was no use. Antoine layed the man with a crushing blow, and then another for good measure, while the peasant, covering his head, begged for life.

"You're not worth hanging for," Antoine told him with a

86

final kick and turned away, his stomach gripped with sudden sharp pain.

The girl still lived. The faintest fluttering stirred her lashes when Antoine lifted her head. Beyond him, he could see the wounded peasant furtively dragging himself to the shelter of the far woods.

"Go, bastard. Go," Antoine called after him. "I've saved you for the gallows."

But sweet Jesus, what to do with this unconscious slut? He couldn't leave her to die in the open fields where even the cattle could not survive the winter.

He would find a place along the road to leave her. An inn perhaps. A parish house.

Strangely, for all her bulk she felt light as he lifted her in his arms. Setting her like a doll against his chest, he circled the coach, now righted and being dug from the mire, and cantered down the road.

Chapter Twelve

Like a runner who has gained his second wind, the storm rose with a new ferocity as the day turned towards twilight. Chilled by the wind at his back, Antoine huddled over the warmth of the silent girl who rocked in his arms. Sometimes her head rolled back a little, and snow flakes caught in the dark fringe of her lashes. Poor miserable slut. What brains she might have had, had surely been mashed by the stone's force against her frail skull.

The villages he passed were shuttered tight against the storm. He saw no life along their streets, and the churches, unlit, with snow piled against their sealed doors, looked least likely places to leave a wounded body.

Only when he entered Epping Woods did the storm seem to abate. He could still hear the howling of the wind in the tops of the great trees, but there, on the forest floor, the snow came gently, drifting in a steady blanket that covered brush and stone and disguised the paths that Antoine was accustomed to follow.

Inside the cottage, Titus fretted anxiously as darkness filled the forest. He scuttled to the window to peer from his stool through the high, small windows that looked into the forest. Salt beef and onion simmered in the iron pot over the grate, and the flatbread had long been warmed against Antoine's coming, but still Titus saw only the occasional shadow of a dark-winged bird in flight against the massed snow outside. When a branch dropped its burden of snow upon the roof, Titus startled in alarm.

When he heard the sound of hoofbeats outside the door, Titus scurried to unbar it. He danced backward as his master filled the doorway with the great dark mass he was carrying. Antoine stamped impatiently to shake the snow from his legs.

"Stand back, man," he ordered roughly. "I can't see the bloody floor over this creature."

Silenced by his confusion, Titus watched as his master carried his burden down the hall in great strides and disappeared into a low chamber on the right of the hallway. Clots of snow marked Antoine's passage down the hall. Before Titus could retreat, Antoine, empty handed, returned to shed his outer clothes and tighten his shoulders before the fire.

"Mash me up some tea, Titus," Antoine told him brusquely. "I will empty the traps while you take care of that slut back there."

Titus poured the boiling water onto the wad of leaves in the bowl and challenged Antoine, "You'd go for the traps in this storm?"

"It may be the last fresh meat until spring," Antoine said. "This is no storm, but a blizzard and showing no sign of letting off."

"So you brought yourself a woman to warm your bed," Titus said angrily, no longer able to contain his anxiety over the silent burden Antoine had carried past him.

Antoine handed the dwarf his empty bowl with a roar of laughter. "It's not likely my bed would be that cold," he told the dwarf. "It's some miserable wad of a peasant that was about to be killed. She can stay here until she's on her feet again. Or dies," he added thoughtfully. "She could die, I suppose with that wound of the head. But it's better to sink her in the forest than let her freeze out there where I found her."

Titus snorted with disbelief. "You're sure she's not a trap they set? With the bounty they've set on your head, it would be worth some rascal's time."

"Not a chance," Antoine shook his head. "I almost didn't see the baggage after she was thrown from a coach spill. Ease your head and see what's up with her."

Instead of obeying, Titus stood stubbornly by the fire while Antoine muffled himself for his return to the storm. "She has a head wound," Antoine called back to him from the door. "It might need cleaning."

Head wound. Titus started for a bowl of warmed water then paused. "Best to see first," he told himself. "Fool's trick to bring anyone here."

The candle he set in the wall sconce flickered weakly in the airless, boarded-up room. The girl was only a great heap of dark fabric on the bed where Antoine had laid her..

Working gently, scarcely breathing, Titus unwound the scarf from about the girl's face. He winced as he pulled it loose from her blood-matted hair, but the girl herself made no sign. With careful fingers, he untied the mantle and laid the hood back from her head. Once her face was exposed with the dark mass of curls spread out upon the bed, Titus withdrew his hand quickly. His breath came irregularly and he moaned softly to himself.

What madness was this? A filthy peasant slut? The face before him was finely, delicately boned with fine, high cheekbones and a dainty nose whose nostrils flared sensually above rich, full lips. The cleft in her chin was like the shadow of a small jewel.

Gingerly, lest she waken and be startled, Titus parted the strands of hair and studied her wound. Just above her temple, a mound of bruised tissue showed the source of the dried blood that matted her hair and cheek.

Titus froze as she sighed, but from her pallor he was sure that this was no simple sleep from which she would easily waken.

Moaning and chattering by turn, Titus cleaned the wound and sponged the blood from her hair. When he bathed the filth from her face, revealing the glowing perfection of her skin, he could hardly contain himself. What mischance was this for such a girl to fall into Antoine's hands? This was not a maiden who could disappear and not be missed. Titus fretted and groaned as each act he performed for her fortified his certainty that the sleeping girl somehow spelled doom to his master and himself.

When the woolen mantle was folded away, Titus lifted her like a child and slipped off the coarse peasant smock which she wore under it. To his astonishment, he found yet another warm winter dress, this one of fine style and a rich, dark color, fastened with small, hand-painted buttons. He nodded in understanding. She had been in flight and had worn all the clothing she could put on rather than leave it. But who was seeking her even now? The final dress was of soft blue, a silken frock designed for her alone. Ornate lace was craftily sewn at the throat, exposing the fine, high abundance of her breasts. The bodice was carefully tailored to cling to a waist no wider than Titus's hand, he saw as he lifted her to loosen the garment.

Antoine made his way through the snow-filled forest carefully, moving from trap to trap, watchful lest he be lost in the vast, anonymous whiteness of the place. It was well that he knew these woods like his own hand, what a hellish night to be abroad and lost. He chuckled as he added the last fat hare to the bounty on his back, remembering Titus's face as he had left. For once he had shocked the old dwarf into silence. That was a trick that would never last. Antoine knew to expect the dire predictions, the muttered warnings that Titus would badger him with before the girl was gone.

But fret as he might, the old dwarf had a heart like warmed cheese. Antoine knew that if any hand, short of a surgeon's, could mend her wound, it would be Titus's. And slut though she be, Titus would treat her as gently as if she were the handsomest lady of the land.

With the fresh game strung to a peg, Antoine fed and watered his gelding and closed the stable door against the drifting snow. The lines between master and servant had been well nigh rubbed away since their flight from France. There was no sense for Titus to flounder in drifts on a night of chill.

The warm, rich scent of cooked meat filled Antoine with ravening hunger as Titus unbolted the door for him. "Good God, let's eat," Antoine cried, throwing his soaked cloak on a bench. "I've gone this day long without a bite in my mouth."

Titus leaped to serve him with a strange look about his mouth which did not escape Antoine's notice. When Titus did not at once mention the wench, Antoine held his questions. Let the dwarf have it his own way. It was only after he had devoured his second great bowl of stew and wiped his broth away with folded bread that he leaned back with a groan of satisfaction.

"There'll be no more trips to the road for a while," he said, reaching for his pipe. "This storm stretches from here to London town, it's too cold to travel and too easy to be tracked in."

Titus, his face secret against his master, moved about his tasks without comment. Finally, half-exasperated at losing the game, Antoine asked.

"Was the wound deep?"

Titus, with a strangely devious look, only shrugged. "You might want to see for yourself."

"I trust your word," Antoine said curtly.

"If she wakens, she lives," Titus predicted.

"If she wakens," Antoine repeated in astonishment. "Then she's still not come around?"

Titus shook his head. "But her breath is coming evener now, as if she is nearer sleep. But a fever comes with it," he added, almost as a warning.

Antoine studied the old man a moment before knocking his pipe out against the grate. Titus had something extra in his head. What could have set such a pall of silence on that jabbery old man? Antoine rose stiffly, stretching his long body nearly to the low beams of the cottage roof. "I might as well see how she fares," he said, feeling not so much concern as curiosity. How had that dazed girl managed to eat his own dwarf's tongue?

"You might leave the kettle on the hob in case she would waken hungry," he suggested.

The cottage had been built for smaller men. Antoine had to lower his head to enter the extra chamber where he had set down the wench. The single candle on the wall darted and flickered at his body's movement in the small room. The bed, which was set against a cloth-hung wall, was almost as narrow as a bench, and Titus had drawn its rude curtains shut to shelter her face from the light. Lifting the candle from its socket, Antoine pushed back to curtains to look in.

Titus had laid the girl to bed gently. The light of the candle only showed him dark masses of tendrilled hair above a woolen coverlet. Her face was turned away from him in

91

shadow. Replacing the candle in its socket, Antoine lifted back the cover with both hands.

A low, incredulous oath escaped his lips. This could not be the wench that he had carried. The girl was small, not much larger than a child. Her perfect body curled against the linen was clad in only the filmiest silken gown. His eyes followed the curve of her rounded throat to the fine separation of her high, full breasts whose nipples gleamed rose under the sheer fabric of her covering. The curve of her waist and hips, the fine, soft moss just barely visible at the base of her rounded belly brought a bold rush of passion to his loins.

Perhaps the chill wind reached her consciousness. She stirred, moving her head restlessly on the pillow so that her lips parted in sleep and a fluttering tugged at her lashes. Her legs shifted in position, baring the creamy flesh of her inner thigh. Antoine pulled back as if she had struck him.

"Jesus," he whispered fiercely.

Titus's tone was acid from the door. "If that is a peasant pudding, you have the taste of kings."

"Good God, Titus," Antoine shook his head. "Believe me, she stunk of the fields and was thick as a shoat in my arms."

Titus nodded and then hopped across the room. "Here is that answer." He showed Antoine the stack of clothing several feet high. "Silks," Titus said, "handwoven woolens of the most precious kind, two aprons of the finest Cyprus wool, and that mantle is lined with fine skins. And this ball gown?" Titus showed the edge of the lace-trimmed blue gown, and his voice rose in a question.

"She has stolen all this from her mistress," Antoine decided flatly.

Titus shook his head. "They were made for her. Look how the gown is fitted to her form."

Antoine did not need to look. The memory of that seductive body was blazoned in his mind.

Antoine nodded. "Then she is some fine gentleman's doxy. But what was she doing riding on a coach in a freezing storm with that young madman?"

"She was running away," Titus said certainly. "But it still makes little sense. Look at her hands."

When Antoine leaned over the bed, the fragrance from the girl's body rose, filling him with a renewed passion. The flesh of her arm was like silk but burning with heat. As Titus watched, Antoine lifted her hand into the light. The graceful fingers which curled about his own were harsh to his touch.

"Calluses," Titus pointed out. "And burn scars. The flesh of her hands is rougher than my own."

Antoine could not pull his eyes from the sleeping girl. He let his hand stray along her smooth hip then gently slid his hand in between the blazing warmth of her thighs. She stirred, and something like a growl sounded from Titus's throat.

"She blazes with fever," Titus rebuked him.

Antoine eased his hand away, angry at the power of his lust for the child-woman before him.

"Some envious wife has driven her out," Antoine decided aloud. "So what is there to mourn? She's safe here and probably healing. Was the wound bad?"

"The wound itself is not bad," Titus said. "It is only in a dangerous place. She will either live or die."

"She'll live," Antoine said stubbornly. What better way to spend a snowbound winter than romping in bed with a discarded doxy whose gratitude he would be happy to accept.

Chapter Thirteen

Julie felt herself floating beneath a drumbeat of pain. When she stirred, lifting her hand to her anguished head, a hand caught her own and held it away in a gentle grasp.

"Nay," the voice said softly. "Keep your hand away." It was too dark in the room to see what face bent over her own. Julie submitted, her exhaustion was too great for her to fight whoever nursed her.

"Louis?" she thought to ask into the darkness, struggling to call her cousin's name with hope.

"Sleep now," the voice came. "You are safe."

Safe. Julie stirred in the warmth of the bed. The muffled darkness of the room spoke to her of different places, distant times, being carried, bundled in a cloak in her father's arms. But her father was dead. She cried out softly, and a hand lifted her head. The cup of her lips was filled with warm, sweet tea.

Too weak to bring her hands from under the covers, she let herself be fed like a child. With her thirst slaked by the flood of sweet warmth, she drowsed again into that half-sleep in which she had floated for so long. She felt the coverlet being drawn close about her throat, and she smiled. Mary. Never mind how, her governess Mary was there with her, and she was indeed safe.

Julie's next consciousness came in a dream of fire. She felt the flames course about her, burning her flesh to agony. The fire was peopled by phantoms, her mother, running down the wide stairs at Essex, flinging herself into her father's arms, Julie herself with Louis by her side fleeing the fury of Joseph, dodging the great stick that rose again and again over their helpless heads. She screamed and forced the coverlet from her blazing body. She ran screaming towards the glint of light that shone against one wall. She battered against the closed door, begging to be released from the flames she felt about her.

When the door opened, she was blinded by light. The strength that had come with her terror deserted her. With one arm across her eyes to shield her from that blinding light, she fell forward.

Strong arms like her father's caught her, lifting her as lightly as when she was a child. She clung to her savior, winding her arms about his neck, sobbing in the rough, matted hair of his bare chest.

"She is mad with fever," Titus murmured to Antoine. "She must be cooled or her brain will be burned with fever."

Antoine, from his post against the wall, watched as Titus bathed the girl's face and arms with cool water. The handsome man clenched his fists as he watched the dwarf's hands slide the cool cloth along the girl's smooth hips. Unable to bear the sight of those gnarled hands against the girl's smooth flesh, he pushed the dwarf aside and finished the bathing himself, letting his hands linger only fleetingly on the smooth flesh that cooled under his ministrations. Finally, her cries of anguish abated, and a soft, tentative smile replaced her sobbing. She stirred languidly and then wilted into a deep normal sleep.

Antoine stood up and tossed the cloths back into the bowl that Titus held, studying the delicate body sprawled across his own bed where he had laid her after her flight into the hall.

"Is she all right now?" Antoine asked.

"For a while at least," Titus replied. "The fever could return, or the sleep could heal her."

"We'll leave her be," Antoine decided aloud. "I don't want to start that screaming and caterwauling again."

Titus, without meeting Antoine's eyes, smoothed his master's pillow under the girl's head, lifting back the heavy mass of curls so that she could not turn on them if she stirred. Then, at the door, he looked back at Antoine, his one good eye half-closed in a squint, "Will there be more for you?" he asked.

"Not unless she goes daft on us again," Antoine replied crossly. "I'll watch a while to be sure."

For a long time Antoine stood in the darkness watching the girl sleep. The snow outside the window endowed the room with a glint of brilliance in which Antoine could trace with his eyes the rounded delicate curves of her body in his bed, the changing perfection of her face as it stirred with dreams. The lust which had come with his first sight of her had not abated. But it was not this girl who set him afire, he told himself. Any decently shaped woman would have affected him the same. After all, he had had no woman since Mignon, and the passion that had slept in him, rearing itself only in dreams and nightmares, had only been brought to life by this shapely strumpet.

He smiled. There would be time. The fever would go, but the long nights of winter lay ahead. The exhaustion of his day fell upon him in that silence. Careful of disturbing her, he eased himself down on the free side of the bed and lay staring into her sleeping face.

Antoine finally dozed, only to be wakened by soft murmurings from his bed companion. Her fever was rising, small circles of color glowed in her cheeks, and she stirred restlessly, as if in alarm. Suddenly, without warning, her dream grew cruel, and with a sharp cry of anguish she reached out to him, pressing her flaming flesh against him. When Antoine attempted to disentangle her firm arms from his neck, she only clung tighter, moaning.

"I'm no Goddamned martyr," he told himself furiously, folding her eager body in his arms. It took all the strength he had to slow his haste with her. Savoring the softness of her belly against him, he slid his hand on that small mound of fur and was past containment.

When he parted her thighs she only writhed a little against him. When he thrust himself into her, he was startled by the blazing heat and the resistance. Her body flinched with pain, and he withdrew feeling the warmth of her blood on him. Astonishment brought a curse to his lips. What kind of mystery was this, that a virgin should fall into his bed like a bundle of rags?

She returned his stare with wide-open, yellow eyes. Then, remarkably, she smiled, a dimple fleeting in and out of her cheek. Reaching up, she prisoned his face in her hands and cried with delight, "It's you!" Her voice was vibrant with disbelief. "I have waited so long. It is you."

He covered her parted lips with his own and explored the sweetness of her mouth as he thrust himself again between her thighs. With a delicious stirring of motion, she rose to him, thrusting that round mound against him even as he muffled a cry of delight as he pumped ecstasy into that eager body. Then he felt her go limp in his arms.

Rebuking himself as mad, Antoine fondled her gently, cupping her breasts in his hands, tasting the salty sweetness of her flesh with his tongue. Again and again he penetrated her, lifting her feverish body against him. At last he slid her inert form into the curve of his body.

Her fever continued to rise. She clung to him, nestling closer as if with affection, her heat like a burning brand against him. Suddenly, he felt her body begin to vibrate. As she clung to him, laughter bubbled from her lips with that same joy of passion that Mignon had always expressed when the lovemaking was through.

He did not intend to throw her free of himself so fiercely, but he tore her from his arms and leaped to the floor.

Mignon. But this child was no informed woman of the world, she was a virgin and guileless. Her flesh even though unperfumed was fragrant to his lips. He remembered Mignon and her slavery to love that had earned her death. Not Antoine, he told the darkened room fiercely. I have not risked life to be free of the slavery of debt to fall bondage to any woman. Let her take her beauty and her laughter and her wide, haunting, yellow eyes into some other man's soul.

96

But even as he looked down at her, his lust for her stirred again. He lurched across the narrow hall to stretch himself on the narrow bed and sought sleep.

Chapter Fourteen

The fever which had broken so briefly that first night returned to Julie with renewed vigor. For days on end she lay in a raging delirium, sometimes crying out at the phantoms that haunted her dreams, sometimes lying by the hour with her glazed eyes staring silently at nothing. Titus nursed her like a child, cooling her fevered limbs with moist linen and forcing liquid through her unknowing lips to keep her lifeblood flowing. Often he was awakened from exhausted sleep by her anguished cries. Then he would pin her flailing body to its bed with his own to keep her from injuring herself or from fleeing into the bitter cold which had settled on the forest in the wake of the snowstorm. And all the time he dealt with Julie with tender solicitude, he harbored a low, seething fury towards his master Antoine.

When he had returned to her at dawn that first morning, her fever was already high. Upon finding her alone in his master's bed, he had uncovered her to cool her fever. It was then that he saw the delicate shift thrown aside and the blood-spotted sheets that betrayed both her purity and his master's insatiable lust in seducing the helpless, fever-maddened girl.

Word never passed between them of what Titus had seen, but in a pattern long established by their years together, each man reacted to the other in kind. Sensing Titus's anger, Antoine retaliated with a matching fury. Peace was gone from the hearth as Titus scuttled about his tasks with silent resentment while Antoine, kept from his roadway by the ease of tracking him in the fresh snow, sat and drank or smoked in sullen silence, always painfully conscious of Julie struggling for life in her old, low-beamed room down the hall. For Titus, having found her despoiled in Antoine's bed, had removed her to that darkened small room to tend to her needs.

He told himself that he had moved her there to protect her

97

from his master's insatiable lust, but he knew this to be less than half the truth. For one thing, Antoine had not looked at the girl nor inquired of her even one time since that fatal night. But the important thing, the truth that Titus could just barely admit to himself, was Titus's own fear. She was young and firm, and Titus believed that the fever would safely pass. But he both hoped for and dreaded the day when those yellow eyes would clear of the fevered glaze.

There, in the dark of that room with the mist of delirium before her eyes, Julie did not flinch from him. She moved to his touch with trusting affection, obeying his smallest command with a gentle patience. Most often, she called him "Mary" and chattered to him of food and games and a gentle river. She talked to him of her hound Bonbon and of a child she loved named Louis. She had spun about his voice an unseen world in which Titus moved with wistful joy. He showered on her the same mute passion which he had previously been able to give only to dumb animals who would not flinch nor look aside from his great knobby face with its twisted smile and single staring eye.

At last, inflamed by his long captivity, Antoine took to the highway again, and Titus was left with long days to spend freely with his slowly healing charge. He bathed her perfect body, cooing and moaning like a child over her smooth slenderness that seem to shrink daily as he watched. The burns on her hands and wrists healed to pale pink stains, and the flesh on her hands grew as soft and smooth as her cheeks.

Titus washed her long, fine hair in melted snow and brushed it to shining loveliness. Then, even as he had the black gelding, he plaited her hair into long braids that fell almost to her waist before they exploded into masses of curls from under the tendons of leather he bound them with.

When the lord's messenger came to the cottage seeking game from his gamekeeper, Titus bolted the door of her room and scurried to meet the man outside the cottage. When Titus handed him the frozen rabbits and the young hind that had been dressed for his coming, the man nodded with approval. "It's a marvel that your traps weren't all lost in that storm. Not only traps, but men were lost, you know." He glanced past Titus at the glowing hearth as if to suggest that a bowl of something warm would be welcome, but Titus made no sign of welcome.

The man shrugged and hung the game across his saddle, preparing to depart. "There are many hoofmarks about this place," the man noticed with a frown as he turned his horse. "You have had visitors?"

Titus forced a cackle. "They have wandered through these woods like the game," he said. "It has been a rare day that not one or more lost souls have come banging at the door seeking directions."

The yeoman laughed in reply. "I came near making some wrong turns myself," he admitted. "As well as I know these trails."

The first day of strong sunlight wrought an almost magical change in the forest. The tops of the drifts melted and became glazed with brilliance. The roof water chimed from the eaves, and the frozen river crackled and sang with thaw.

Antoine, having wakened early and bolted a lusty breakfast of bread and cheese, had long ago galloped off on the gelding through a forest blazing with reflected light. Finding his charge still sleeping, Titus wrapped himself in a shawl and honed his knife to a razor edge. Making his way unsteadily across the melted drifts, he went to the great tree where Antoine had hung the dressed deer in the upper branches to keep the frozen meat safe from the wolves. He climbed the wet, slick limbs with difficulty and began to butcher patiently at the hard flesh.

Julie wakened to the stillness of the cottage and stared about with amazement. The sun streamed through the narrow opening of her door revealing the room she was in as a narrow, boarded cell with a single bed with curtains and a low, crude bench. Her first attempt to sit upright brought a great dizziness so that she sat a long time waiting for the frantic beating of her heart to subside. She felt her face damp with her exertion, and when she wiped it with her hand, she was astonished to find her own hands healed, as if by miracle, of their scars and burns.

Where was she? What was this place? Her clothing was all neatly folded on the bench against the wall, and a basin of water steaming slightly in the cool air showed that someone had been in the room within the hour.

Louis. She shut her eyes tightly to rid them of the memory of Louis, his mouth flecked with blood from his racking cough. He had kept stumbling, and the cough had grown worse with every mile. Then the coach had come, and the driver had taken the last of her coins to let them ride.

Past that the memories jumbled together. There was the chill of the wind and Louis's fever sending him into a laughing madness that nearly drove him from the top of the coach into the road below. And Joseph. She shook her head helplessly. How had she come to this place, and what place was it?

Moving carefully, lest her unsteadiness betray her, she labored into clothes, the petticoats, the blue dress, and finally, with supreme effort, she managed the buckles on her shoes. She stood, bracing herself against the wall with a sense of triumph. Unfamiliar braids bound her hair down to her waist, but she only shrugged and wrapped them about her head, securing them with a ribbon pulled from the sleeve of her dress. But it was cold, and the only sound was a slow, rhythmic chiming like a muffled bell. She pulled her mantle from the stack of clothes and pulled it about her and walked out into the hall. Prickles like needles moved up her ankles and her face was damp with effort, but each step gave her a sense of added strength.

She stood a long time staring at the great room that surrounded the crackling hearth. The room cried of comfort like the kitchen of her old home. The great fireplace was flanked by wainscoting. A pot simmered on its trivet, and the smoke-darkened bellows stood at hand. Tables, benches, a desk piled with books and papers, neat rushes on the floor. There was no sign of woman anywhere, no spinning wheel, no basket of wool.

By standing on tiptoe, she could see into the clearing outside the cottage. The giant trees with the sun-slanted shadows brought her instant fears from childhood, tales of elves and small people, of gnomes and werewolves. But the glistening of the snow and the blazing light on the iced twigs dispelled her fear.

Fastening the hood of her mantle tightly, she nudged open the heavy door a crack and stared into the woods. Once her eyes adjusted to the blaze of light, she nodded with understanding. This was a gamekeeper's cottage, such as those she had often seen when hunting with her father. Traps hung along the rude stable at the back of the cottage, and the drying pelts of rabbits and hind and one huge dark wolfskin almost covered the length of one outer wall. When a movement in the woods caught her eyes, she shaded them to see better.

Something moved in the branches of a giant tree beyond the stable. She caught the glint of a knife rising and falling as the creature labored on the large, high branch. Then she was able to distinguish the carcass of a deer trembling from the blows of the knife. She heard a grunt of satisfaction as a great chunk of the frozen meat fell free to bury itself in the drift beneath the tree.

Still hidden, Julie watched a creature dismount the tree like a giant spider, its great arms wrapped in a shawl and its face half-hidden by a pointed hunter's cap. Once on the ground, the creature leaped up and down about the meat, working it loose from the snow, and then hoisted it on the hump of his back and started for the cottage in a rocking, uneven gait that was strangely threatening.

Julie stood frozen, feeling her heart tight in her throat. The face of the dwarf was too hideous for her mind to accept. She leaned against the lintel of the door moaning softly. All the dread tales of her childhood returned at once, witches and ogres, giants and dwarves pitting their evil against man. When she forced her eyes open again he was drawing nearer. He grunted under the weight of his burden, and he kept his single eye down to be wary of his footing. But even as she backed away from the door and pulled it quietly shut behind her, she heard his crooning.

The dwarf, between his grunts and sighs, was crooning a soft, low song that she recognized as the soothing rhythm of her long dream just past. Her fears and terrors, her coolness and hopes of the past days or weeks were bound to that same crooning.

"No," she cried silently. "No." Not even knowing what she was denying, she fled down the hall to the room in which she had wakened. With her mantle drawn tight about her, she flung herself across the bed and waited, her chest tightened with terror but helpless to guess what would happen next.

She heard the door flung open and the thud of the heavy object thrown upon the floor. But the crooning went on, fading and growing louder against a series of household sounds. Finally, after what seemed an eternity, she heard soft steps along the hall and felt, rather then knew, that the dwarf was peering in at her from the open door to the hall.

With her fists tight against her cheeks, Julie waited.

"Ah, my little mistress," the voice said softly. "Then you are up and dressed." There was a sad finality in the tone, as if the act had been both a joy and a despair to him. But it was not the words, but the voice that brought an instant surge of recognition to Julie's heart.

This was the voice which she had dreamed was Mary's roughened by pain and darkness, the voice of the hands which had bathed and healed her and fed her with loving, coaxed life through her fevered lips. With her heart thumping, Julie pushed herself up to turn and face the creature at her door.

The light at his back cast Titus's face into shadow. Although not more than half the door's height, his broad arms and shoulders almost filled its width. His cap was gone from the long, gray matted hair that hung alongside his face. Julie felt her breath enter her lungs with a sharp pain as the single eye fixed on her. There were tears in the dwarf's eye. Had the outdoor cold brought this streaming of tears to the dwarf's hideous face?

Carefully, with her fists clenched beneath the mantle, Julie forced herself to speak softly.

"Good morning, sir," she said. "I know your voice."

Titus shifted his weight from his shorter leg to his longer one in a sort of hopping dance of relief. She had not screamed with alarm. But then perhaps it was too dark for her to see his face.

"You usually call me Mary," he said, after a minute.

She laughed softly. "I'm sure you go by a different name than that. Forgive my fevered madness."

The light was full on Julie's face now, and the lips which had been so restlessly appealing in illness, were now, in health, smiling, irresistable. Titus moaned softly in fear.

"I am called Titus," he told her. "Titus the Gamekeeper."

"Titus," she repeated quietly. "Yours is the voice that led me through my sickness. And yours the hands," she added thoughtfully.

She could sense his waiting like a coiled snake in the doorway. What did he wish from her? Why did his voice, which had only held gentleness before, have the harshness of fear now?

Then she remembered the shiver of revulsion which had

102

passed over her when she first glimpsed his deformed face from her post by the cottage door. If she had met him without warning she could not have repressed a grimace or possible a cry of alarm. It was this rejection that he waited for.

The hard knot of tension moved uneasily under her ribs as she rose from the bed. Looking directly into Titus's miserable face, she smiled the widest, warmest smile that her lips could muster.

"Titus," she forced a teasing lightness into her tone. "Can you believe that after all you have done for me that I would dare to ask for more?"

He frowned, staring at her, not understanding. Then she reached for his hand which was rough and hard to her touch.

"I wakened with great thirst," she told him quietly. "Could I ask for a bowl of tea from your hearth?"

It was as if she had liberated him from an enchantment. He shifted his weight swiftly and exploded into instant movement. He started down the hall, turned, and came back to motion her to follow, then shot off again, chattering all the time. "Forgive me. Of course. Anything you wish. And hungry too, I ween. Fine tea. Hyson," he added with some pride. "And sugar for softening it. Come sit. Come. Come."

Overwhelmed with relief, Titus was helpless to please her enough. "For you there should be a chair," he mourned, hopping to the hearth to pull a bench at a good angle. His hand trembled as he tilted the boiling water into the bowl with its precious handful of tea leaves.

Titus carried the bowl of tea to Julie with both hands. As she reached for it, he raised his eye to her face in the full light of the sun-filled room. Under the dark crown of her wound braids, her yellow eyes returned his gaze serenely. Then her lips parted with a surprised smile, and she admonished herself.

"My fevered dreams have been unfair to you, Titus," she told him. "You are taller than I thought, and even kinder."

There had been no flinching when her eyes met his. He would have sensed it if there had been. Not since Antoine as a child had explored the rough ridges of his great deformed face had any human accepted him thus, without flinching. What small corner of himself Titus had reserved from her was now totally gone.

He kept adding sugar to the bowl of tea until she stayed

his hand with laughter. Then, with the blue skirt in a bright pool about her on the floor, she drank the tea and ate hungrily of his flatbread spread with a gooseberry paste from the summer harvest.

"Dreams," she told him. "Such dreams I have had." She raised her eyes to him questioningly. "Was it you who brought me here, Titus? How did I come?"

When he turned back to answer her questions, she leaned her head back against the wall drowsily. The warm tea and the sunlight, along with her unaccustomed activity, had left her drained of energy. "The coach," she tried to remind him, her voice heavied with exhaustion. "Louis and I bought our way on top of the coach—"

When her voice faded, Titus watched her head droop in sleep. Removing the last crust of bread from her hand, he carried her back to the darkened room. She only stirred a little as he settled her between the coverlets. As he drew the door shut, he could hear the sweet, even rhythm of natural sleep.

Chapter Fifteen

The glare of the sunset was staining the drifts with color before Antoine reined in at the gamekeeper's cottage. The anger and shame that had seethed in him the past days rose again at the sight of the cottage snug against the coming dark with a pillar of fragrant smoke fingering its way skyward through the trees. He should have left that damned old dwarf in France to fend for himself the best he could. His father could have obtained no proof that Titus was part of the conspiracy that robbed him of gold and daughter and son in one sudden reaping. But the old man would have guessed, Antoine corrected himself in fairness, and if he had not guessed, his fury at not getting his way would have struck out blindly at anything related to Antoine. As close as the father and Titus had been throughout Antoine's childhood, Titus would have been a mote in the old man's eyes that he would have cleaned with murderous dispatch.

But having brought him to England, Titus was still a servant, though it was seldom enough that the dwarf saw fit to remember it. What business was it of Titus's whose maidenhood Antoine spilt on the sheets? Antoine's annoyance roughed his hand on the gelding so that the beast whinnied his discomfort at the stall gate.

The scent of food cooking reached Antoine before he crossed the clearing. With an oily cooking tool in his hand, Titus loosened the bars and swung the door open. The smell of the venison crackling and browning on the spit brought a rush of moisture into Antoine's mouth.

A glance down the hall revealed the door to the girl's room still closed. Titus had been wrong, Antoine thought with irritation. He had said that the girl would either live or die. The wench did neither. Instead, she lay in that endless, dream-haunted sleep, poised between death and life, torturing him with her inaccessibility.

With his outer clothing off and a bowl of tea between his hands, Antoine watched Titus carve great succulent slices from the joint of hind. Was this an apology of sorts, he wondered, seeing the polished apples in a bowl, the flatbread soaking in butter in the warming pan? When Titus dipped a bowl of fragrant onions and potatoes to set alongside the meat, Antoine raised an eyebrow at him. Indeed, the dwarf's expression was lightsome.

"Something happen here today?" Antoine asked, his pride overcome by curiosity.

Titus angled his eye off towards the ceiling beam thoughtfully before replying. "The lord's man came for game," he said, nodding, "and inquired of the hoofmarks in the snow."

At Antoine's frown, he hastened on. "I told him that many travellers had been lost and had inquired here for directions."

Blowing on the steaming vegetables, Antoine nodded. "And that story went down with him?"

"He had come close to losing the way himself," Titus explained.

At Antoine's nod of satisfaction, Titus pulled his shawl from his peg and scuttled out to groom and bed the gelding.

Antoine ate with lusty appetite. These long days of travel without food had become a burden to him. But the great beard that he had grown during his illness kept him from stopping in public places for meat and drink. With the bounties growing for the capture of the blue-eyed, bearded giant,

105

he dared not risk being seen in any public house. Perhaps he should shave away the beard now, he thought idly. Many a highwayman dealt in disguises. He knew their tricks and scoffed at many of them. But now, having made his own beard a trademark that struck terror into the travellers he stopped, he could return to his own clean face again. A false beard would fit his belt as well as his mask did.

Immersed as he was in thought, he heard no sound at all. It was only as he turned to refill his bowl of tea that he saw her standing there. He sloshed the boiling liquid on his hand and muttered a startled curse.

There was terror on her face as she stepped back. "Titus?" she asked, her voice breathless. "Where is Titus?"

"Good God, woman," he said, wiping his injured hand. "I have no intent to eat you. You startled me, that's all." Then he paused. "Titus is out at the stable. He will be back soon."

Furious at himself for staring, Antoine watched her sigh of relief tighten the well-fitted bodice of her gown. Her eyes caught his in rebuke, and she said tartly, "I hoped you were a friend of Titus's."

"A friend of Titus, is it?" Sudden laughter replaced his anger. What a little spitfire this yellow-eyed child was shaping into. "And if I am not a friend to Titus?" he asked. "But instead an enemy?"

Fear widened her eyes again, and she stepped back from him another careful step. With the movement, a spring of curl escaped her ribboned hair and danced along her cheek.

He would have reassured her but Titus was there in the door, stamping the snow. She flew to the dwarf and stood beside him, staring back at Antoine.

Titus looked from one of them to the other as he shut the heavy door and drew the bolt. "She asked if I was a friend of yours, good Titus," Antoine said mockingly. "What should I tell her?"

Titus shifted from one leg to the other uncomfortably. "More than a friend and less," he finally replied.

"And the same could be said for enemies?" Antoine goaded him.

Not understanding, but sensing their hidden combat, Julie moved a step nearer the dwarf, her shoulders squared combatively.

Antoine, unable to bear it longer, burst into laughter, great

106

belly laughs that brought him to his feet to tower over them both. With one step, he crossed the room and took her reluctant hand in his. Pulling her towards the fire, he still chuckled.

"You silly wench. Of course he is my friend. And Titus has no enemies but his own body. Now come over here and warm your naked flesh. I didn't drag you from a bloody snowfield to freeze by my own hearth. My God, Titus, she's as thin as a rail. We'll have to fatten her somehow."

"But at least you have your head back together," he said motioning her towards a seat. When she still stood, poised as if to fly, his anger rose swiftly. "Good God, woman. Don't stand there like a statue, sit down."

With her eyes wary on him, she sidled onto the bench. He noticed the rounded elegance of her arms as she folded her hands into her lap demurely. Even without looking at her, he could feel the sleek line of her body arched there on the low stool, the narrowness of her waist, the regal grace of her neck supporting that wild, dark abundance of hair.

"Have you eaten?" he asked, in a purposefully milder tone.

She nodded. "I had some bread and tea," then suddenly, as if surprised by her own confusion, she turned to Titus. The cleft in her chin caught the light as she turned her profile towards Antoine. "Maybe Titus remembers. I ate and don't remember anything after that. But it has all been confused. The sleeping and dreaming and waking in flame." She paused. "But I did have bread and tea with Titus today. Do you understand?" Her head cocked at Antoine as she asked.

Jesus. The wench. She had better bet her life that he understood. She had risen from the dead to torment him with every movement of her body. She had turned his own servant against him, Titus, whose loyalty had been stronger than any nobleman's bond. Now she baited him with innocent-sounding questions while her swelling breasts tempted him beyond endurance.

"I understand that a good hot meal could do you no harm after such adventures," he said, controlling his urge to lash out at her for the discomfort she was causing him.

With a serving of Titus's food before her, Julie ate with gusto. As the rich broth warmed her, it brought a new surge of strength and courage. She burned from the bearded giant's lustful eyes on her, but she could not resist studying him cov-

107

ertly as she ate. He was indeed a giant compared to Titus and herself, but his long limbs were elegantly formed, and the turn of his fine head was appealing to her, rousing a half-memory that she could not pin down. His vibrant masculinity overpowered the small room. His beard was a curling bounty beneath those brazen blue eyes. This man, who was more and less than a friend to Titus, held the secret keys to her confusion. He must know the story of those anguished hours and days that her illness had sponged from her memory. But the force of his vitality and the undisguised hunger of his eyes on her, stilled her questions.

"Since you have been our guest this long," Antoine suggested, "Perhaps it is fitting that Titus and I should know your name."

"Julie," she told him quickly. "Julie Duvall."

"And I am Antoine Riviere," he said with a chuckle. "How does it come that two Frenchmen like ourselves meet in a snowy English field, Julie?" Then he paused. "But you have no accent."

"My mother was Irish," she explained. "And my father a Huguenot who fled here long ago."

"Was?" Antoine asked. "Then he is not living?"

"Nor my mother," she replied quietly. "I am alone except for an aunt who lives in the colonies."

"And except for Titus," he added mockingly.

She raised her clear yellow eyes to his, annoyed by his mocking tone. Then she lifted her head imperiously, straightening that fine, slim back whose silken skin his hands still remembered. "Except for Titus," she affirmed challengingly.

From the corner of his eye, Antoine saw the old dwarf's body vibrate with silent laughter at the girl's sauciness. What kind of a witch was this Julie Duvall? Tart-tongued women were not to his taste, yet she could not move an eyelash nor stir her body without imperative desire stirring along his loins. Irritation at his own lack of self-control stiffened his mind and his tongue against her. It was only fair that he give her the same discomfiture that she so deliberately fed him.

"You do have a good friend in Titus," he said softly. "After all, it was Titus who wiped the blood from your hair and healed your wound. It was he who stripped that sweet body and cleansed it with loving care, bathing your nakedness, tend-

108

ing your fine hair, and holding you to your bed when you were raging—"

Her face burned with humiliation for both Titus and herself. Titus hopped in his corner, his face contorted with anger, but she leaped to her feet. Even on tiptoe, she barely reached Antoine's shoulder but her fury was giant.

"And gave me life," she shouted at Antoine. "Don't forget that, Antoine Riviere. It is one thing to haul a body from that snowy field you mentioned, and I thank you for that. But it was Titus whose hands tended my illness, who breathed life into me when I was burning with pain—" Her voice was caught in a helpless sob. She conquered her tears within seconds. Drawing herself stiffly, formally straight, she turned from Antoine with a swish of her skirts. "If you will excuse me, Titus, I think I will retire."

By the time Antoine caught his breath, he saw that Titus, too, had left his accustomed place and the room was empty. The hearth seemed curiously barren, but the storm of conflicting emotions that Julie had begun in him made sleep impossible.

He stretched his long legs before the fire and lit a pipe from a gleaming coal. Why had he let his passion make him so splenetic? After all, she had come to his arms unspoiled. The memory of her flesh, the soft, protesting cry as he had rent her bathed him with sweat. It was only his body's hunger, he assured himself, that made her fill his mind day and night since her coming. But how was he to rid himself of this burning obsession?

And he must be free. Even after paying the exorbitant fees of the receivors, his months on the highway had accumulated nearly the fortune he needed to replenish what he had taken from his father's store. He was nearly free to make a life for himself, free of debt and entanglements. The thought of being enslaved by passion for this girl when his goals were so near met filled him with fury.

The fire had slumped to embers by the time she came back. The chill was moving into the room, spilling along the window edges and moving in cold drafts about his ankles on the fender. He knew she had come before she spoke. Wrapped in her mantle against the chill of the house, she stood as before just inside the room as if poised for flight.

"Master Riviere," she said humbly.

109

"Yes, mademoiselle," he replied, not lifting his eyes from the hearth.

"My guilt at my ingratitude has kept me from sleep," she told him quietly.

It was obvious that her words came with difficulty. Antoine nodded, trying to control his inclination to leap to her side.

"I do appreciate that I would have died if you had not drawn me from that snowy field," she went on. It was strange, he thought, how she repeated that expression the same each time as if it was a lesson she had learned and no part of her own past. "I know that if you had not saved me then, that all of Titus's tender ministrations would not have brought me to life." When he still did not reply, she went on softly. "Forgive my rudeness to you. And thank you, Mr. Riviere, for my life."

No longer able to resist the pleading in her voice, he looked up at her. She had drawn very near, and her face shone from within the hood of the mantle with the glowing purity of ivory. Her clear, gold eyes were intent on him, and her lips parted in supplication.

"I deserved the snap of your tongue, Julie Duvall," he said quietly. "Come and sit by the warmth of the fire. I only hope that the life I saved for you does not turn out to be a burden in time to come."

She studied him briefly with her eyes, and then obeyed.

He pulled up a stool beside himself in front of the fire, but she shook her head and went down upon the rushes, sitting a little apart from him so that the glow from the freshly stirred embers lit the angle of her face and chin, teasing his memory of the throat and breast that lay hidden.

"You say 'that snowy field' as if by rote," he said, after a moment. "Don't you remember more of that day than that?"

She shook her head. "I heard those words from you. I only remember being on the coach with Louis raving with fever—"

"Louis?" he asked, his voice suddenly harsh. "That was the young man with you, your brother?"

"Like a brother," she said quietly. "He was only a cousin but I loved him dearly. And he was very sick."

"Go on," he pressed. "Why were you and this Louis on the coach in that raging storm?"

She shrugged. "I had only a few guineas. We were running away to London, and Louis coughed so much."

110

"Together?" he asked, pressing it on her understanding.

A flush rose to her cheeks. "It wasn't like that at all. I had to run away to save myself from his brother. He went with me, to protect me." she paused. "We have been best of friends since we were both children."

He nodded. "And then the coach was overturned."

He saw a shiver move along her arms, and she leaned forward to stare into the embers, as if remembering. "Ah, yes," she said softly. "It reeled and staggered and finally went over throwing Louis and me a long way in the deep snow. Then suddenly Joseph was there." She shivered again, drawing the mantle closer about herself.

Antoine slid from his bench to take a place on the rush floor beside her. "Tell me about Joseph."

"He is the son of my uncle's wife," she said slowly, "and Louis's half-brother. He is cruel and vicious and terrifying." She paused and tightened her lips in concentration. "Perhaps I dreamed that Joseph followed us. That he was beating on us both with that great stick he always carries. He was cursing Louis, and I tried to protect him, but Joseph is strong like an animal—" She shuddered at the thought.

"That was not a dream," Antoine told her gently.

She stared at him. "Louis?" she asked tensely.

He nodded and took her hand in his. "He was dead before I got there."

"No," she cried suddenly. "Oh, no. No. No." She buried her face in her hands and rocked back and forth with grief. Antoine laid his hand on her back to comfort her. Her hair, which she had released from Titus's braids, fell silken across his hand. The scene of it in his nostrils brought a groan to his lips.

She swayed against him, unconscious of his anguish. "I killed Louis," she said miserably. "I killed him by letting him go away with me. He could not bear the cold and the wind, not with that cough that brought blood to his lips."

Antoine took her firmly in his arms, his voice almost harsh against her hair. "Listen to me, Julie," he insisted, "listen closely. You did not kill Louis. It was the blows from Joseph's cudgel. And even if he had not been along with you, he would not have lived. If there was blood in his cough, he had only a little time. The fever and the cough had killed him already, there was only the actual dying left."

111

Pulling herself a little away from him, she stared earnestly into his eyes. "You swear this is true?"

"You must have guessed," he rebuked her.

She nodded, "I tried to pretend to myself because I loved him. But Joseph." Then her eyes widened in wonder. "You were there, on a black horse, and you fought Joseph."

He nodded and pulled her head down to rest on his chest for fear he startle her by seizing her mouth with his own.

"And you brought me here with you, to Titus. Why?"

"God knows," he laughed. "To torture myself, I suppose. I thought you were some grubby little country wench who would surely be killed by that great lout. And you were unconscious from a stone he threw at me that caught your skull instead."

She lifted her hand to the remembered pain on her head. "And after that came the dreaming."

Julie was conscious of his warm protecting arms about her, the strength of his hands against her back, but she had no fear. She should move away. What kind of a girl had she become to let this great bearded stranger shelter her in his arms like a baby?

Yet it seemed that his nearness was as right as destiny. Louis was gone. She had known it in her heart, and her mind had rebelled at facing that truth. Now she was truly friendless, with only her dreams.

" 'Most parfit gentile knight,' " she murmured softly.

When he puzzled her words, she laughed softly. "That is a phrase I once read. It is strange that you should have saved me, Antoine Riveire, for you are so very like the man whom I have always had in my silly girlish dreams."

She stirred into the hollow of his arms so that he could not see her face. "Women are all like this," she explained gently. "My governess Mary has told me about it. They see a face and fix on it in their dreams. Only the reality of love will ever replace that dream." She turned to him with a half-apologetic smile. "Forgive me but you are very like the image I carried."

"Was he a real man, this girlish romance of yours?" he asked.

She nodded vigorously. "Oh realer than life," she said with sudden enthusiasm. "I was a child by the roadway with my friend, and a coach came by. To me, a country child, the

112

coach was unbelievable, gold and white and glistening. Then there was the footman, a great, tall man like yourself with dancing blue eyes that caught mine and set me dreaming." She laughed softly. "Such dreams die slowly. When I was in London I searched every face, every passing carriage. A footman, can you imagine?"

Antoine caught his breath hard. The road from Bath in full sunlight, the freshly mowed fields and the angelic child with the clear yellow eyes.

"And did you ever find him?" he asked quietly.

As her eyes clouded over, a faint blush rose to her cheeks. Suddenly she dropped her eyes. "Only once in a dream," she replied, her voice very low and subdued.

Antoine groaned to remember that fevered night, her eyes wide on his and her lips curved with delight, crying, "It is you. It is really you."

He took her by the shoulders and twisted her body so that her eyes had to meet his own. "Julie, Julie," he whispered intensely. "Look into my eyes, look at my face. Remember me as I remember you."

The mantle fell back as she stared at him. Her throat and breast glowed above the thin shift, gilded by firelight. Then her hands rose and she caught his face between her hands as she had that first night.

"You," she whispered huskily, her lips softening with desire. He saw her nipples firm against the sheer shift, and he slid his arm inside the mantle, cupping her throbbing breast in his hand, tracing the delicate cage of her ribs, then tangling his fingers gently in the soft hair at the base of her belly.

"You," she moaned softly as she raised her lips to his. The thickness of her lashes half-hid the gold of her eyes as her body reared against his hand, bathing it with creamy warmth.

"Julie, Julie," as her smooth thighs opened for his entry, Antoine covered her mouth with his own, abandoning himself to her passion.

Chapter Sixteen

In the quiet of the cottage after the departure of Antoine, Titus busied himself about the hearth. He set a fresh pot of water to boil against Julie's wakening and grunted about in the apples he had stored in the priest's hole until he found crisp ones which would polish to brightness with a handful of snow. Only when the sun angled its clear light halfway across the room did he became concerned that Julie slept so long and grow disturbed that her fever might have returned from too much activity the night before.

After passing through that door for so many weeks without hesitation, it was strange to knock timorously at the closed door of the small room. When no answer came, Titus rapped louder before finally pushing it open with a slow creak. The bed was empty, its coverlet thrown aside on the floor. Squinting about in the gloom he saw that Julie's mantle was also gone, and he gave a low moan of despair, rocking back and forth on his heels with a keening cry.

He had been wrong about Julie. She had fled from his own ugliness and his master's rudeness. She had fled into the woods where wolves ranged their winter hunger. And beyond the woods lay the village. Titus shuddered, wiping a stream of moisture from his face. Better she should fall prey to the ravening wolves than the scoundrels of that village, this girl who knew less than nothing of men and the world.

With the open door behind him, Titus pierced the air with his wail of grief. His cry died in his throat as he heard Julie's call of alarm.

"Titus," he heard her wail. "Oh, Titus, what is wrong?"

He turned to see her in the door of his master's room with her mantle drawn hastily about her white shift. Her eyes were wide with fear, and when he turned, she ran to him and clasped her bare arms about his neck. "Titus," she begged wildly. "Are you all right? Are you in pain?"

He shook his head, unable to speak. Drawing back from him, she flattened her hand gently against his face, wiping

114

away the stream of tears that coursed from his eye. "Tell me, Titus," she insisted. "Why did you mourn?"

"I thought you were gone," he said finally, in a low, choked voice.

She wilted with contrition. "Oh, Titus," she said gently. "I am so sorry." When she tried to find words, none came, and her face reddened under his gaze. After a minute she finally whispered, "I was with your master."

Titus stared at her, unable to separate in himself the conflicting strands of emotion that assailed him. Rage and pain and sorrow warred in his heart, twisting his face into fearful grimaces. He ducked his head and pulled free of her, hopping away down the hall, leaving her standing on bare, chilled feet staring after him.

After one stunned moment of realization, Julie fled back into Antoine's room and threw herself miserably across the rumpled linen. When her agony of sobbing ceased, she curled in her mantle and stared out at the winter birds that flickered in the tree beyond the window. What had happened to her? What insanity had stirred through her soul and drawn her lips and her body to Antoine in that raging hunger for his touch, for him to possess her wholly as he had done? She remembered Giles, drawing back from her embrace that first time she had exchanged glances with Antoine disguised as a footman, and shuddered with shame.

"He is a fever in me," she told herself with wonder. "I weep for Titus and his loathing of me. I weep for the lost purity of my girlhood, and yet if Antoine should walk through that door and lay his hand upon me, I would rise to his touch with the lust of a strumpet." The scent of his flesh was still on the bedcovers and she rested her hand in the indentation left by his sleeping form, and even those ungraspable things were dear and exciting to her.

When Titus's rustling ceased in the room beyond, she heard the sound of the great door closing behind him. From the window, she watched his uneven passage across the snow, head bent, swaying from side to side and muttering to the frozen clumps of bushes between the great trees whitened on one side by the driven snow. She watched him leap again and again until he loosened the traps from the stable wall. Then he disappeared into the darkness of the forest.

The long day passed heavily. She barred the door as she

115

had seen Titus do and dressed and arranged her hair and ate an apple by the fire. Once she heard horsemen pass quite near. Concealing herself by the window, she watched them pass, a great red-bearded man on a bay mare and a smaller, thinner man who seemed to be talking steadily as he rode. She saw his hands gesturing forcibly, while the bigger man only nodded in acknowledgement.

When they came abreast the cottage, the thin man fell silent and slowed his horse to stare intently at the cottage. Her heart fluttering wildly, Julie drew back into the shadows, fearful that she had been seen. When she next looked, they had passed without stopping, but still they looked back with the darting glances of men plagued by suspicion or fear.

She meant to tell Titus about the horsemen, but when he returned with his face still white with despair, she forgot about the strangers in her concern for his unhappiness.

In the slow days of working by his side, Julie at last won back Titus's friendship. But the dark shadow in his eye never wholly left. Sometimes she caught his worried glance on her by chance, but he always glanced quickly away, his single eye loath to meet her own.

There was too little to occupy her time. One afternoon when Titus returned with a full harvest of game, Julie chose a knife from the shelf and sat on the rush floor beside him.

She felt his eye on her as she slit the carcass of the hare, breathless with fear that she might have forgotten the skill her father had taught her when she was a child begging to help him with his game. When the pelt was free and she started to slip her knife into the animal's belly, Titus took it from her to finish the cleaning himself.

"This is a strange skill for a lady," he told her.

"I hunted with my father when I was a child," she told him.

"And your mother?" he asked.

"She grew faint at the sight of blood," Julie said. "I think I was eager to learn because her faintness amused him and I did not want him ever to laugh at me."

"You do not miss your family?" he asked.

"There is no one left," she said simply. "I was used to being alone."

"Where will you go from here?" he asked suddenly.

116

Her hands paused only a moment before beginning again, quickly, as if to conceal that moment of weakness.

"I do not know, Titus," she replied quietly. "Would you like me to go?"

He shook his head wordlessly then rose to prod the fire, slamming the poker vehemenently against the hanging pot.

With her hands idle and so many hours of waiting, Julie managed to think of many small mysteries about their life. The days were ritual. Both men rose early. Titus, clad in his shawl, scurried forth to run the circuit of his gaming traps. Antoine stayed by the fire until his return, when, with a nod, he saddled the black gelding and set off through the woods with empty saddlebags beneath his mantle.

The books on Antoine's desk were all in French. With the stumbling, school-girl French she had learned before her father's death, Julie labored until her head spun. She mended clothes for Titus and Antoine. The tunics Titus wore were small and wide, not long enough to fit a child in length. Antoine's garments could not have offered more contrast. The finest lace and hand-sewn ruffles trimmed his cuffs. Julie fought a stabbing jealousy as she mended this work. What loving hand had made that row of stitches or painfully laid color by color to trim the velvet vest? Sometimes she laid down her needles from being blinded by jealous tears. But then she would remind herself of Antoine's lips against her flesh and blush with confidence and ardor. The long ritual days and the breathless nights spent in Antoine's arms spun out like beads on a chain that led time into spring.

The snow cleared to dark patches, green appeared in low places, and the river sang all night beyond the windows. The mysteries that Julie had pondered through the winter faded from her attention with spring. She gloried in the growing beauty of the woods beyond the cottage, and only once in a great while did she sense any element of peril in their lives. Casual conversation held carefully away from her hearing intrigued her as well as the great pains that Titus went to to conceal her presence in the cottage.

When the lord's man came for the game, Titus not only asked her to stay within her room in silence but bolted it behind her until the man was gone.

"But why?" she pressed. These imprisonments came so

117

much oftener with winter broken, and the room was stale and dark.

"He must not see you or know you are here," Titus told her.

"Gamekeepers have wives and even children," she told him. "Suppose you took a wife, would you hide her too?"

Titus exploded into laughter, then his face twisted painfully. "Such a woman as would have me I would not have to hide," he said bluntly, turning away to still her questions.

Now the windows could be left ajar through the warmth of the day, and Julie lightly let all worries slip from her mind, not even remembering to ask herself that hard question that she had pondered with winter. How would this all end?

Chapter Seventeen

In deference to Titus's obvious terror of her being harmed in the forest, Julie stayed near him and the cottage, seldom venturing farther than the stable or the clearing that surrounded the house. It was by chance that she found the faint path that led from the clearing along a high knoll some distance from the clearing. On the crest of that knoll, the sun penetrated the trees and brought masses of wild violets into bloom. No matter how often she went to pick them, they seemed to bloom again in renewed vigor.

One morning, kneeling to pluck the flowers, she was startled by the sound of horse's hooves very near. She forced herself flat on the new grass, terrified that she might be observed, for it was only then that she realized that the knoll led along a cliff that overhung the public road.

Holding her breath for fear of attracting his attention, she saw the red-bearded horseman pass a second time. Seen that close, he was a massive man with untidy hair and small, half-closed eyes as if he had trouble in seeing. The slim, voluble man was not with him this time. Instead, he was accompanied by a thick-bodied peasant like himself with whom he was engaged in earnest conversation.

Julie wondered later if it had been the bright ribbons in her hair that caught the man's attention. Suddenly she heard a soft curse and the sound of a horse being reined to a sudden stop.

"Look there," the red-bearded man whispered tensely. "There's a wench in the grass."

Julie, scuttling back down the slope into the concealment of the far side of the knoll, could not distinguish the words of the other man's muffled reply.

"A pox on your insults," the red-bearded man shouted. "I ain't that blind that I don't know a wench when one lies before me. Come for the proof."

Julie, numb with terror at his words, heard the scramble of the horse mounting the cliff. With her hood pulled tight and her mantle flying behind her, she leaped to her feet and ran breathlessly for the cottage. She heard their shouts in pursuit.

"There she goes, the slut," the red-bearded man shouted with excitement. The snap of his whip on the horse's flank cracked in the air.

"Stop wench," he shouted, attempting a softer tone as he called after her.

Julie fled madly, never looking back, spilling the violets all along the path. As she entered the clearing, she saw Titus motioning to her frantically from the stable door. She veered and ran towards him, tears coursing down her cheeks and her lungs threatening to burst with pain. Even as she heard the horses crashing through the brush alongside the clearing, Titus was at her side. He jerked her into the stable and roughly pulled the mantle off her head and back. Hopping sideways, he swept the straw from the stable floor and tugged up a wooden trapdoor that was concealed in the floor.

"In there," he whispered, "and make no sound."

She let herself swiftly down into the dark aperture. Even as she saw Titus lower the trap in place, she realized that he had drawn her mantle about him and had the hood half-pulled over his gnarled head.

Curled into the dark passage, she heard the scrape of Titus's feet replacing the straw and the shouts of the riders as near as her own breath.

Once he had concealed the trapdoor in the floor, Titus pulled a stout staff from against the wall and waited just inside the door for the horsemen's challenge.

He had not long to wait. The horses slid to a neighing stop

in the newly thawed mud of the stableyard, and the red-bearded man dismounted with a cry of triumph.

"In there," he shouted to his companion. "We have the wench trapped in there."

In the dark of the stable, Titus waited until the man's huge body filled the open doorway. Then he stepped forward, the staff in hand and a fierce look on his face.

"Stand back, man," Titus shouted. "Unarmed I run from you but armed I hold my ground."

With a look of stunned disbelief, the red-bearded man stared at the distorted face of the dwarf, at the brawny arms coming from beneath the velvet mantle, at the stout stick in position to joust.

"Stand back and name yourselves," Titus commanded harshly.

The red-bearded man stepped back. "A maid," he said uncertainly, his mouth suddenly slack. "I saw a maid run in here, in such a cloak." He stared at Titus's hooded head.

Titus advanced on him one slow step at a time, until the light shone full on his upturned face. "A maid am I? Is there a maid such as I that you would run for?" His high, raucous cackle filled the clearing. "Are you blind, man, or sick with lust? Has spring got into your eyes as well as your cock? Stand back or I'll show you what this maid is good for."

The other rider, still astride his horse, saw his companion backing out the stable door. Then he saw Titus's yellowed face with astonishment and collapsed in a gale of laughter.

"Sweet Jesus," he shouted. "What manner of maid is this?" He struggled for words but could not manage his breath for merriment. His companion, his face as scarlet as his beard, glared angrily at both of them.

"I swear I saw a maid," he said ominously. "And by God, a maid I'll have."

Titus turned his single eye to the man's companion and cackled again. "Shall I make that bargain with him? That he can lay with my blessing any maid he finds in this stable—aside from me?"

"And if there be two like you, gamekeeper, he may have mine too," the other man laughed.

The red-bearded man, his eyes blazing with fury, stalked to the door of the stable and glanced in. He entered, staring about furiously. He tapped his whip against the stanchion

120

and climbed up to peer into the almost empty loft. Titus watched him, lounging against the open door.

"Don't grieve too much," Titus told him after the inspection was through. "Many a man has chased me by mistake. And by God, a man such as I must always run. I would have been shot for a bear more than once if it were not for my heels."

The red beard nodded at him, mollified by his amiable tone. "I ween you are no taller than a maid, even if you be thicker. And surely that's a maid's mantle you wear."

Titus nodded. "And in such a cloak, how could a man be sure from a distance?" Then, as if suddenly caught by thought, Titus leaned forward threateningly. "What business had you in these woods anyway? Milord is not generous to poachers. Nor do I know your face as a local man."

"Not poachers," his companion spoke up swiftly. "We're after a richer game than what you keep."

"Richer than hind?" Titus asked with an amazed stare.

"There's a great bounty out for the bearded highwayman, the Blue-eyed Giant they call him. Word has it that he's been seen in these parts."

"That so?" Titus asked, affecting a quickening of interest. "Here in Epping Wood? Have you seen him yet?"

"Not yet," the man admitted. "But it's only a matter of time now." He swung back onto his mount. "Eighty pounds is worth a man's time to set watch for."

"Eighty pounds!" Titus whistled softly. Then he broke into a sudden cackle. "Why, you could buy a better maid than me with that much gold."

"Better wenches than him," the companion repeated with a shout of laughter.

"I should hope to God," the red-bearded man agreed, turning his mount towards the road. "Sorry we ran you like a hare, gamekeeper."

Titus watched his visitors to the road and beyond, listening with a cocked head to their distant hoofbeats fade into silence. Then, muttering and chattering with relief, he pushed aside the straw and lifted the rude wooden trap.

Julie, crouched in that fetid place, stared back at him with wide, yellow eyes. She reminded Titus of hares trapped by a spring as he let down his hand to her.

She shook her head. "Titus," she whispered fiercely. "Look about me."

121

"Come now, Julie," he coaxed, dancing back and forth with dismay. "The earth is cold down there and you will take a chill."

"Titus," she cried. "You know. You know about this bounty down here." She took his hand and sprang up beside him. When he lowered the trap, she kicked viciously at the rotten straw that covered it. "Silver plate and watches, bags of gold and fine rings. Antoine—a highwayman." Her eyes blazed with fury. "A rotten thug robs the roads like a vulture. Why, Titus? Why does he do this?" She seized the dwarf by the shoulders and clung fiercely. "Tell me why, Titus?"

He turned his head fretfully, refusing to meet her eyes. "For a man's reasons," he blurted out. "His own reasons."

She stared at him. The chill was still on her from her cold hiding place. The wind, riding across the clearing, cut through her thin dress like a knife. Titus hastily wrapped the mantle about her shivering body. Then she turned and walked, head down, across the clearing and back to the door of the cottage.

She remembered the wheeling birds of carrion circling above the rotting corpses hung along the road, the naked bodies swaying in the wind, their heads drooping helplessly like broken flowers. Antoine. She saw the cages where the cries of the starving men plagued the traveller's ears for a mile or more. Antoine. The Blue-eyed Giant. She remembered Henry Furlong's voice above the faint clatter of china and the rustle of newspapers. Plum jam and the scent of rich coffee in an elegant London breakfast room. "His days are numbered." How many were left. Oh, God, how many days did Antoine have left?

Slumped by the fire, staring at the coals, listening to the faint hissing of the evening meal simmering in the pot, she heard Titus enter and hang his shawl on the peg by the door.

"Those men were here before," she told him dully.

"Before?" He tensed like an animal. "When?"

"Some weeks ago," she told him. "They only drove by and stared. You were out with the traps."

"Was it morning or evening?" he asked urgently.

She stared at him, trying to remember. "Late morning," she decided aloud. "Closer to noon perhaps. Does it matter?"

"It matters," he said shortly. Then he stood silently, staring at the fire and the fuel supply.

"Those are thief-takers searching for Antoine?" she asked, the words painful in her throat.

"Aye," he replied, still immersed in thought.

"Can you warn him?" she asked timorously.

Only then did he turn his eye to her. He chewed painfully on his lip and then replied. "Aye," this time in a dolorous tone.

She did not bother him again, sensing that his mind was fully engaged in some mystery of its own. When he finally turned to her, it was with a plan.

"I must bolt the door from within," he told her. "I will return or he and I will return together, but the door must not be opened to any voice but ours." He paused. "There is fuel for warmth and there is enough food."

Then he shook his head and frowned. "Better than that, they must think that I am gone from here. I'll build up the fire now, but when it fails, don't build it up again. Seal the windows after I am gone and use the bed for warmth."

Julie had never been beyond the door of the hall cranny where Titus slept. It was under the eaves, a hiding place not much larger than a man's form. A pallet lay on the floor and a folded pile of rough tunics served as a pillow. Titus unsealed a small window leading out under the eaves. He showed her how the boards fitted back in from the inside to conceal the passage. Then he stared at her reflectively.

"Did that same father who taught you to dress a hare teach you to shoot?"

She nodded. "I was slow at loading but my aim was straight."

He scrambled down the hall and returned with a thick-nosed gun which he laid gingerly in her hand.

"Have care of this," he warned. "It is loaded."

She watched as he wrestled his hump through the small aperture and disappeared into the dark. She sealed the hole with trembling fingers when she heard the faint thump of his body striking earth and the sound of whisper-light footsteps receding.

Darkness fell about Julie in the empty cottage. She yearned for a single candle against the gathering gloom but stayed her hand. Soon there was no light left in the room except the desultory flicker of the dying fire. Once, above the cry of the owls in the clearing, she was sure she heard the muffled nicker of a horse off in the woods. Pressing herself alongside

123

the barred window, she could see a slit of darkened forest but nothing more. Behind the restless scudding of clouds, the moon came and went, making shadows that stirred like the wind.

The cooling house ticked and creaked. She wrapped her mantle tighter and curled on the warmed stones of the hearth. A heaviness of grief lay at the base of her throat so that she could not swallow. At great length, she drifted into troubled sleep.

Chapter Eighteen

The sound that startled Julie awake was less a knocking than a gentle tapping, repeated again and again like a loose board troubled by a persistent wind. She listened for a long time with her heart racing before she realized that along with the tapping was the low sibilance of a human voice. She rose stiffly from the hearth and pressed her head to the door to listen. Titus's whisper was a steady crooning, her own name over and over as he begged for entry.

As she unbolted and swung open the heavy door, Titus staggered into the room, his shawl caked with mud and his face ashen. Behind him in the wood, faint trails of mist moved tenuously through the trees, promising dawn.

With the door bolted behind him, Julie tried to revive the fire without success. After leaning a few moments against the lintel of the door, the dwarf came and squatted beside her. Although his gnarled hands were scarlet with cold, he finally coaxed the fire to flame.

Julie restrained herself until she could bear it no longer. "Where is Antoine?" she asked finally.

"He is safe," Titus replied without meeting her eyes. "It may be some days before we see him, but he is safe."

Through the lonely days and nights that followed, Julie watched Titus come and go, setting his traps and bringing in the game to clean and dress against the coming of the lord's servant. She watched him make flatbread and cook it on the pan above his carefully timed coals, turn meat on the spit until it was browned and dripping with flavor. His face was

124

empty of expression as she studied him, but she sensed in the jerkiness of his movements and an almost animal alertness in his eyes that the fear he denied grew in him like the length of the spring days.

She slept in Antoine's bed, pressing her head against his pillow because of the scent of his flesh that clung there. She slept only fitfully in the empty bed, often being alarmed awake by the call of a night bird or the movement of some beast in the thickets beyond her window.

When Antoine finally returned to her, she did not at once realize that he was really there. Too many nights she had dreamt of his fine, long legs tangled with her own, only to waken chilled and alone with the pillow damp with night tears.

When she felt the warmth of his thigh against her own, she wakened with a soft cry, turning to him with outstretched arms. But his face against her own was strange, smooth and beardless.

When she rose on an elbow to stare at him in disbelief, his blue eyes danced at her impudently.

"What have you done?" she cried.

He only grinned at her with a wicked smile and rubbed his cheek against hers. Then with a quick, expert gesture he seized the hem of her shift and pulled it up and off to throw it in a pale arc across the room. With the thrust of his desire pressed against her, he laid her back upon the bed.

"I might have lost my head coming back to you, woman," he whispered with his lips close to her own. "I am lucky only to be rid of that bush of a beard."

It was nearly dawn before he finally released her into the hollow of his arm. As he lay staring at her, she felt a warmth of laughter uncoil in her belly and chest, and she wriggled with the delicious animal joy of their love.

When she wakened again, the bed beside her was empty. She knew that night and the nights with Antoine that were to follow were snatched from the growing peril that shadowed Titus's eyes. More and more, her fear for him and her aching desire for his return lightened her slumber. On one such restless night, she stirred awake in a spasm of fear. There was a different sound in the cabin. Moving silently to the door, she was able to distinguish the low, conspiratorial voices of Titus and Antoine in the room beyond.

"There is no answer," Antoine said. "She has no wit for the world and no protectors except us."

She could not distinguish Titus's reply, but she heard Antoine's snort of frustrated annoyance.

"Her maid! Good God, man. What makes you think a spavined old governess is equipped to guard a creature like that? Her body is her doom. She could disfigure herself, smear herself with dung, or be pitted with the pox, and still she would draw men like carrion does flies. Look at me, swearing to keep my freedom, swearing by all holy to shake the dust of England from me forever once my debts in France are paid. And what happened? She has me snared like a hare in a spring. I court death for the dance of those bewitched yellow eyes." His words ended in a groan of despair.

Julie crept back to their bed, her heart torn by conflict. The anguish in his voice brought tears to her eyes even as his testament of love flooded her with delight.

It was less than a fortnight later that a late spring storm darkened the sky ominously in late afternoon. The wind rose and gusted about the clearing rattling at the shuttered windows and moaning in the tops of the surrounding trees.

As a low rumbling of thunder drew nearer, Titus, wrapped in his dark shawl, went forth into the storm to secure the traps and the stable against the coming storm.

Julie heard the pelt of the rain begin before he returned to the fireside. She craned at the windows to watch the shafts of lightning glow among the distant trees. The rain struck the ground of the clearing with such force that it splashed back into the air, making the air ring with sound. Then, to her astonishment, she noticed a mass of unfamiliar shapes dimly lit by the lightning. As she watched, she realized that two horsemen, abreast, were pulling their nervously dancing horses into the clearing outside her door.

Pressing herself against the window frame, Julie trembled with terror. She did not dare bolt the door and lock Titus outside with the intruders. Just as the first horseman swung from his horse, she saw Titus hobbling towards him from the stable path.

"Halloa," she heard Titus call. "What business have you in the lord's woods at this hour?"

The first man stood in the shadow of his horse so that Julie could not see his face, but the large, red-bearded man stood

126

forth boldly. His face looked loose and fleshy at this near view, and his lips were wide and dark in the sudden flash of light illumining the clearing.

"We came for your visitor, gamekeeper," the man said roughly. "We have tracked the highwayman here, and we mean to take what we came for."

Julie backed off from the window and fled to her room. Had Antoine really led them to the cottage? She couldn't guess, but she knew that Titus was no match for the two men. She looked about her room frantically, seeking a place to hide. She grabbed the folded pile of her clothes and thrust it under the coverlet on the bed. Then she slid in behind the tapstry above the bed and flattened her hands against the wall, hoping that the uneven draping of the fabric would conceal her presence.

With sinking heart, she heard the scrape of the great door opening. Thunder crashed quite near, and even in the muffled air of her hiding place she could hear the splash and drip of the storm while the door stood ajar. Heavy feet sounded in the room beyond, and she heard furniture being rudely shoved about.

The sounds of search grew nearer as she heard the men going through Antoine's room across the hall. When the heavy breath of one of the men sounded in her own room she found herself holding her breath with terror. The bench was thrown across the room and she heard the bedclothing being pulled from the bed. She recognized the voice of the redbearded man as he roared with frustrated fury.

"Keep your sword on that miserable dwarf," he shouted to his companion, "but get me a light in here."

There was a scraping along the hall, and she heard him mutter, "By God we'll have that blue-eyed bastard if we burn this place down around his ears."

Satisfied that the room was empty, he seized the curtains of the bed and jerked hard. When the aging cloth ripped in his hands, he seized a larger handful and tugged like a madman. The whole of the curtaining pulled loose at once, filling the air with a cloud of choking dust and exposing Julie to his startled gaze.

For a moment, he paused in startled silence. Then his voice fell to a purr like a mating tomcat. "Oh ho," he said wisely, edging towards her across the mass of fallen fabric.

127

"It's the highwayman's wench we have now. The giant's whore, and what a fair one she is."

As he circled towards her, Julie slid away and darted along the wall trying for the door. He was too quick for her. He caught her by the arm and pulled her against his heavy body roughly.

Clawing and twisting, Julie fought against his grasp on her. It seemed like the nightmare of Joseph's attack on her, and she cursed him silently as she clawed at his face.

"You thorny bitch," he snarled angrily as her nails streamed blood across his face. "I'll have your ass for that trick." Then he hurled her down hard on the uneven mass of bedding and clothes and curtaining littering the floor. Catching the front of her dress with one hand, he ripped it apart exposing her breasts and belly in one swift move. He was groping at his trousers with one hand as he pressed her down, his foul mouth open and searching for her own.

With one last, desperate burst of strength, she arched her body hard against his weight and pulled her mouth free of his slobbering. "Antoine," she screamed. "Oh God, Antoine."

Only as the beast in her face smiled with a satisfied leer, did she realize her mistake. "That's a good wench," he purred, pressing his hard cock against her thigh. "Bring on your highwayman. Come on, tart, scream for your man. That way I'll have both the game and the gold."

Her eyes widened with horror. "Oh please God," she prayed silently. "Let Antoine be miles from this place. And let the crashing thunder have muffled my cry if he was near." She clamped her lips and glared at the man with silent fury.

"Scream," he whispered fiercely, thrusting her legs apart and plunging himself deep into her body with such brutal force that she could scarce restrain a cry of pain. His ferocious rutting knocked the breath from her lungs and brought tears to her eyes, but she wept in silence.

She felt the pumping of his hideous warmth fill her, and he groaned softly before he attacked her again. "Scream, you bitch," he ordered fiercely. He grasped her bare breast in his hand and twisted it hard, bringing tears to Julie's eyes. "Call for your rogue," he insisted, "or I'll slit your Goddamned body from neck to crotch." His fury was mounting as he seized her hair and jerked her head back, his finger clawing between her legs, but still she moaned almost silently.

128

Then he muffled a curse and braced his knee on her belly to hold her still as he tugged at his belt. "I'll slit you like a hog," she heard him say. She saw the flash of a dagger's edge as he drew it from his waist.

Julie braced herself to bear the pain she knew was coming. But his voice died in his throat with a strange, wet gurgle. His hand on her hair loosened. Instead she heard a hollow sound like something moist being struck by stone. The man's beard suddenly scraped along her face, and his slack mouth swam past her eyes. Above his limp body she saw Antoine, his blue eyes blazing and a bloody staff still raised in his hand. He kicked the man aside and reached for her. Even as he drew her against him, she was pleading, "Fly, my love, fly," she pleaded. But he only held her closer to his warmth, his face buried in her hair. "Oh please, Antoine," she begged, giving way to the sobbing that she had fought so long. "My very love, run for your life."

When he only held her, stroking her hair, she tried to pull away. "Save yourself, Antoine."

"You are myself," he said firmly and silenced her lips with his own.

"And Titus?" she asked with sudden fear.

He shook his head towards the room beyond. "There's no time. Dress swiftly, bring little, we three must fly."

With trembling fingers, Julie searched the mess of the room for clothing. We three. What chance would a girl and a dwarf and a great man like Antoine have in hiding? As she struggled with her buttons, she heard the whinny of a horse outside and Titus's uneven steps along the hall. Then, with sinking heart, she heard what sounded like the voices of many men through the rain, sounds beyond the window.

"Titus," she called, dragging her mantle behind her into the great room. Antoine was nowhere to be seen. The red-bearded man's companion lay on his face just inside the door, and Titus was struggling to get the massive bolt in place standing on the man's silent form.

A glimpse through the window confirmed her worst fears. The clearing was full of horsemen and these were no casual thief-catchers. Her eyes caught the glint of metal buttons and the blaze of red as she recognized the crown's men dancing their horses in the uneven, jaggd light.

Wide-eyed, Julie watched Titus hop from the door to the

wainscoted wall beside the fireplace. His back was to her as he fingered the wood carefully as if time had stopped in the clearing outside.

"Antoine," she moaned aloud to herself.

"The black horse is swift," Titus said quietly. "Come, Julie."

The scent of apples filled the air with a sudden fragrance as Titus slid back the hidden door that led to the priest's hole. Titus caught Julie's hand and shoved her towards the dark opening. "In there," he said swiftly. "You must stay in there until there is only silence for many, many hours."

Julie crouched to enter the passageway. The shouts outside were worsening, and a heavy, rhythmic thunder began to vibrate the very walls of the room as the soldiers wielded a battering ram against the heavy door. Julie heard the splintering of wood and the metallic rattle as the hinges loosed their hold.

Titus knelt outside the opening and groped on the moist earth beside Julie. Finding what he sought, he caught her hand and pressed a small leather pouch into it. "Take this," he told her. "It is yours to use as you need."

"Titus," she pleaded. He shook his great deformed head as if the battering of the door and the rending of the wood was of a different world. He extended his hand towards her face. With tears streaming from his single eye, he let his hand move softly down her cheek in the gentlest of caresses. Then, swiftly, he pushed the concealing door shut, and only the memory of his anguished face hung in her mind, like a glow of sun when shadow comes swiftly.

Behind her somewhere, rats clawed along the passage and disappeared into the earth. With her head bent between her knees, she tried to shut out the sounds of the room beyond, the shouts of the men as the great door gave way, the tumult of their boots on the hearth, and a faint, muffled cry that caught at her heart like a sharpened hook. The sounds of the soldier's feet, the breaking of crockery, even the tramp of feet were finally replaced by the distant sounds of horses, and then only the rain and the faint, far, diminishing rumbles of thunder.

"Antoine," she whispered silently to herself, "my God, my God, if only Antoine—"

PART III
THE CIRCLET OF RUBIES
RUBIES
May, 1722-August, 1722

Chapter Nineteen

Julie remembered struggling for enough air to breathe in the closeness of her dark hiding place. She remembered black waves of exhaustion that came oftener and oftener as she waited for the din of battle to stop. Then she remembered nothing. The painful chill that pierced to her bones stirred her to consciousness. Her body ached and the raw open wounds from her attacker's hands blazed with pain. The apples which had seemed so fragrant when Titus opened the secret door now filled her head with a rotten sweetness. At her slightest movement, a scurry of protest skittered away with the rats which had drawn near again, emboldened by her stillness.

There was no hairline of light to tell her if it was night or day. When she strained to listen, she thought she heard the faint, muffled cry of a small bird. She shook her head in confusion. Such a sound could be only another part of the dizzying sickness that spun in her head.

Titus had told her to stay. He had not told her how to escape this place when it had been, as he had said, "quiet for a long time."

Fearful that she might lose the leather pouch in the darkness, she tucked it into the bosom of her dress to free her hands. The secret had to lie in the door itself. Slowly, like a child playing at blindfold, she felt along the surface of the door from one side to the other. Outside in the room, the wooden door had been smooth, sanded to a sleek finish, with carefully mitred joints. The inside was splintery and rough, pricking at her fingers with sharp splinters of raw wood. She explored its surface carefully, seeking some hinge. Nothing. Only after her hands had made their painful pilgrimage the third time over the entire surface of the door, did a fluttering of panic begin in her throat. Was there indeed a way out from the inside?

Childhood terrors returned to her. She remembered the whispered stories of dark skeletons found prisoned in tunnels and niches, the bones of the unblessed dead found clawing at the bricked-up doors of old turrets. In her own father's house there had been that storage room under the west wing that had lay empty because no servant could be forced to enter its confines. They protested that the black moths that fluttered about its recesses bore the souls of two men who had been barricaded into that chamber and left to die.

As her terror increased, she found it increasingly harder to breathe. Gasping for air, she fought back tears as she forced her fingers, now raw from the rough wood, to make their careful circuit of the wooden door one more time.

When nothing stirred, she slumped against the door in defeat, giving way to her terror and despair. Triggered by her weight against the left panel, the door swung open at once with a faint screech of complaint. She tumbled into the room beyond which was bathed in the gray, chill duskiness that comes just before the dawn.

In the shock of her release, she did not at first realize that her fall had been cushioned by the body of Titus. He lay on the floor beneath her, his skull smashed to shards that stained the rushes of the floor about him. His single eye stared forlornly into the darkness of the roof.

Julie moaned and slid away from him, covering her eyes to shut out the agony of his face, but the stench of death in the room could not be shut out. She recognized the dead man over by the great door as the smaller, gray-haired man who had accompanied the red-bearded monster to the clearing before. He was curled in death like a great worm withdrawing from touch. His arms clutched at the hilt of a sword buried in his belly. She knew without doubt that the red-bearded man himself must still lie where Antoine had caught him in the act of trying to mutilate her.

"My God, my God," she murmured despairingly, just as a morning bird began its first tentative trill from a tree beyond the splintered door.

They would be back, she realized with sudden panic. If for nothing else, they would be back to bury their own dead. And what about Titus?

She had seen the humiliations that the king's men had wreaked on highwaymen, dead men turned to carrion in their cages along the great road, the severed heads posted at the crossroads to stare eyeless from among the circling crows.

How could she think they would be more gentle with Titus who had sheltered a highwayman wanted by the king?

But burial was impossible. There was not time for her to scratch even a shallow grave from the rain-soaked earth which was tightly webbed with the tangled roots of those great trees.

Titus had said that the black horse ran swiftly. He must have meant that Antoine had gotten away. But even if they found their prey flown, in fact, as soon as they admitted his escape, they would return. She must not be found there. But neither must Titus.

Avoiding even a passing glance at the room across the hall, she struggled to get the great woolen coverlet off Antoine's bed. After spreading it as smoothly as she could inside the hole behind the door, she dragged and pushed Titus's body back into her own hiding place. She shuddered at the touch of his cold, doughlike flesh against her own, but with her lips caught painfully between her teeth, she at last managed to lay him inside the priest's hole. She crossed his yellowed hands on his chest and covered him with such tenderness as he had shown her during the tormented weeks of her own illness.

She tried vainly to remember what words the cleric had said over her own dead mother, but the words had flown.

"God love you, Titus," she whispered. "God love you, Titus, my friend."

As she swung the door shut and felt it click tightly under her hands, she felt the great grief stir in her heart. She stared at the innocent panel of smooth wood that hid a friend she would treasure to her own last breath.

It was perhaps fortunate that the heaviness of her grief for Titus dulled her senses. She made her own preparations to leave the cabin in a plodding, methodical way. She would need her clothes of course, and money. Her fingers strayed to the leather pouch still hidden inside her dress. The gold coins felt cold and forbidding to her touch, but the circlet of rubies caught the first rays of dawn coming through the open door, splashing the room with blood red motes of light.

But how was she to find her way? Six months had passed since she had been brought senseless to this place. In all that time she had barely put her foot outside the clearing. She knew east and west from the passage of the sun. Beyond that, she knew nothing.

With her clothes bound together and her hair wound neatly about her head, she stared at the disarray of the room. Maps. There had been careful, hand-drawn maps in among the French books on the shelf on the far wall.

The shelf was down and the books, some broken from their spines, were scattered in the mess of broken furniture on the floor. She searched among the rubble while dawn came rosily through the trees and the clearing began to throb with birdsong.

She was dismayed to find the maps were all in French. She could identify the cabin and a number of trails that led away from it to join different roads beyond the edges of the forest. West and south of the cabin was a crudely sketched gate marked London. Along the roads that led to that gate were squares marked *auberge*. She pondered the word before suddenly remembering her father's voice recounting some humorous story of an innkeeper. "Aubergist," he had called the man, only to have her mother laughingly correct his lapse into French.

The coaches to London would stop at such inns, she knew. With the crisply folded map in the inside packet of her mantle, she left the cabin.

The nearest road was the one along which she had seen the red-bearded man ride that first time. It was a temptation to start along it rather than plunge into the forest to follow an ill-marked trail. But she shook her head. Along that road would come the king's men returning for their dead. She set off along the wooded trail without looking back.

The trail strayed like a wandering animal. Run-off streams from the rain of the night before coursed along in twisting rivulets. She wished for the pattens she had learned to wear in London to keep herself dry from the wetness underfoot.

The way seemed long, but her mood lifted steadily as she left the cabin farther and farther behind. Antoine had gotten away. She was sure in her heart that somewhere he was safe. No hardship was too much to face until she could slip into the warmth of his arms again. A sense of excitement at this challenge quickened her steps. She was amused at her own bravado in choosing the danger of the forest over the safety of the wide road. From an open and forthright girl, she had become wily. It was for Antoine.

She ceased to startle at the sounds of small animals in the

136

brush and stood enchanted as a stag crossed her way in great
bounding leaps. Its wide eyes betrayed its fear to be greater
than her own. When the sun had passed the top of the sky,
she grew slow with exhaustion. The wounds on her thighs
plagued her at every step until she gave in at last. Finding a
smooth stone against a great tree, she sat to rest, leaning her
head against the rough, wet bark of the tree. The humming
of insects and the industrious carolling of the birds lulled her
into exhausted sleep.

She wakened in terror to the unmistakable whinny of a
horse very near. She scrambled to her feet preparing to flee
into the woods to hide before she realized that the horse
stood literally above her. Even though it was caked with
mud, she could see that its color was a solid, gleaming black.
With one foot poised delicately on the tip of the hoof, the
massive animal stared at her curiously from gentle, dark eyes.

He was riderless, but mud-caked reins dragged in the grass
alongside him. She watched him warily a moment before
kneeling to pick a handfull of pale spring grass. When she
held it out to him he first shook his head wilfully, then
plucked it from her hand with careful lips.

Running her hand down the creature's neck, she studied
him. There was no mark of color on him anywhere. Titus
had called Antoine's mount "the great black beast." But if
this were Antoine's horse straying riderless in the forest, she
would have to believe that he had fallen into the hands of his
enemies.

But no! If he had found sanctuary, he would slap the horse
free for fear it betray his hiding place to his enemies.

Catching her breath with fear, Julie tugged the animal to a
near stone and clambered upon him like a schoolboy onto a
pony. At the tap of the reins on his neck, the horse ducked
his head and then started along the trail at an easy canter.

The creak of wheels and a muffled hubbub of voices soon
warned Julie that they were nearing the great road that led to
London. Without her signalling him, the horse slowed his gait
to stand hidden in the edge of the woods. A farm cart passed,
and after it a trading wagon loaded with provender and a
stout country couple laden with baskets. Only after they disappeared from view did Julie cluck the horse from his cover
and onto the great road.

Soon they reached a scattering of houses surrounding a

church spire. At the crossroads ahead, she saw the great wooden board of an inn clanking on its chain against the wind that had risen with the late afternoon.

She was reining in at the inn when she heard the rattle and crunch of a coach approaching from the north. Just as she dismounted, the coach came to a shuddering stop in the muddy street, disgorging its passengers into a noisy rabble of small boys and dogs who had appeared from nowhere as the coach reached the village street.

The hostler leaped to the coach horses quickly enough, but Julie saw him eyeing her strangely as he worked. She saw him grumble something to his helper so that the other man turned to stare at her with the same eager insolence.

She turned from him, pretending interest in the passengers of the coach. She watched an oversized gentleman help his wife from the coach with a gallant hand. Then a cleric, clutching a small valise, grimaced as he set his shoe in the muck of the street.

But the hostler's helper had left the coach to approach her. He was a small, wiry man with searching eyes which only slid uneasily away when she returned his stare.

"What of the horse?" he asked.

"He will need food and water," she ordered firmly.

"What horse is that?" he asked, without moving to take the reins. "That is a horse I have seen before."

"It is a common enough horse," Julie said levelly, noticing that the coach passengers were lingering to listen to their exchange. "He will need both food and water," she repeated.

"How did you come by that horse?" the man asked, his tone nearly threatening.

The assurance in the man's tone frightened Julie. She felt her heart racing and tried to disguise her fear with the signs of anger.

"How does anyone get a horse?" she challenged tartly. "One raises it or buys it. My uncle bought this one only a few hours past."

The man laughed wryly. "A few hours ago," he scoffed. "And him caked with mud and you travelling alone without a saddle even—"

"I'm not travelling alone," Julie lied fiercely, seeing the new interest with which the coach passengers were studying her.

The portly gentleman and his wife had edged very near, and Julie caught the woman studying the quality of Julie's mantle speculatively. "If he is not already here, my uncle will arrive within a hour. I am travelling to London with him by the next coach."

"Your uncle, is it?" the hostler leered. Then he reached for the horse's bridle. The beast shied away showing a warning of white about his eyes. The hostler stepped back swiftly from the horse's dancing hooves. "If I wasn't sure before, I am now." he said angrily. "That is the horse of the giant high-wayman and none other. A mean beast he is too, never letting a stranger within touch of his flesh."

A babble of excited talk stirred the crowd. Julie was about to lash back in anger but thought better of it. She forced a quick laugh and turned to the crowd about her. "A mean horse this one is indeed. My uncle and I were coming this way together when the horse we shared was lamed by a fall. There came along a lad, a boy not more than ten or twelve, leading this horse. Would a mean horse of a highwayman be led along a road by a tad like that?"

"And tell us where this uncle of yours is now," the hostler challenged, a little put back by the laughter of the crowd.

"He led his good horse back home," Julie explained carefully. "She is a mare with foal and too valuable a beast to abandon with only a small limp."

"And if he does not get here in time for the coach?" the man asked slyly.

"Of course he will," Julie said stoutly. "But if he did not I would journey on alone. His wife has great need of care, and I would go to her direct."

To Julie's relief, the portly gentleman from the coach stepped forward with an officious air. "Look here," he said to the hostler gruffly. "Her Ladyship has been deucedly patient with your claptrap. Get on with the horse and mind your tongue with gentlefolk."

The hostler grumbled and eyed Julie hotly, but a murmur from the other passengers decided him to turn away. He led the black horse towards the stable, keeping a wary distance between the hooves of the beast and his own backsides.

"Thank you so much, sir," Julie said, turning to the man and his wife gratefully. "Do you suppose that boy really sold my uncle a highwayman's horse?"

139

"Aye, 'tis possible," a voice spoke from the group now entering the inn. "There was a great chase last night for the highwayman they call the Blue-eyed Giant."

"Is he then in custody?" Julie asked.

"Not the last I heard," someone spoke up. "But there were soldiers in Epping Wood this last night and a great chase to the north that went the night through."

Once inside the inn, the dumpy woman at her side laid a gentle hand on Julie's arm. "Come and have a pint with Willum and me, my dear," she said. "Unless of course your uncle is here already and he'd be welcome too."

Julie made a great show of searching the room with her eyes. Then she sighed.

"Indeed he is not, and I'd appreciate your hospitality." Then she giggled. "Wait until I tell him what manner of horse he put me onto."

The woman shook her head. "You're a brave one for so young," she added, settling herself on a bench with a wide spread of skirts almost filling the space left to Julie. "And do you really mean to go on to London alone if your uncle is somehow delayed?"

"I have no choice," Julie said. "My aunt needs me."

"We'll watch over you if it comes to that," the woman said with a motherly pat. "We like young people, Willum and I do."

Julie supped the ale slowly, wishing the woman would not press her face quite so near. She felt guilty, after they had been so good to her, to be repelled by the flaccid flesh of the woman whose face was so powdered and painted and marked by patches that she seemed struck by some disfiguring pox.

Julie learned at once that while the woman's name was Dorothy, that her Willum called her Doll, a questionable pet name for a creature of such significant bulk. And Doll was one to talk so that Julie was free to rest her tiredness in silence while the innkeeper brought a joint and some vegetables on a steaming platter.

Julie was even relieved of further lying about her condition. Doll at once presumed that Julie's aunt was with child and nearing term. While Julie and Willum devoured the thick wedges of beef and the rich gravy that bathed the bread, Doll launched into a long and gory recital of all of her own childbed woes. When their glances passed, Willum winked jovial at Julie, seeming not at all disturbed not to have a chance to put in a single word.

Only when they were at the pudding, did Doll leave her doleful recital to fix her attention on Julie again.

She dropped her voice to a sibilant whisper and leaned even nearer to Julie. "If it pleases you, my dear, Willum will have the innkeeper put you in a room next to ours. You can't have missed the looks you've been getting from some of the men hereabout—pretty as you are and all, and travelling alone."

"I would be much indebted," Julie said swiftly, dropping her eyes to her plate lest she again meet the bold eyes of one of the diners at a near table. "And indeed I am tired enough for an early night's sleep."

"Even as we are," she told Willum, nodding.

After leaving a message for her "uncle" Julie was shown upstairs by the young tavern maid who identified herself as Maggie.

"You're a brave one to be travelling alone after what happened last night," she told Julie as she turned the bed back. Julie turned from brushing her hair to stare at the girl. She was not as young as she looked at first glance. Julie guessed her in her thirties though still trim. A faint dusting of spice-colored freckles shone across her nose as she leaned towards Julie. Her eyes were wide with excitement.

"The witch and the dwarf," the girl explained. "Has no one told you of the witch and the dwarf?"

"I have been travelling all this day," Julie told her honestly enough.

"It was the raid in Epping Wood," the girl whispered. "And a bonnie fray it was. Two thief-catchers and one of the king's men killed. It is said there was a witch there too, and a dwarf."

Julie turned back to her brushing for fear the girl might notice the way her hands had begun to tremble. "Highwaymen are everywhere," Julie said. "But this talk of witches and dwarves is something different. How did it end?"

In the glass, Julie could see Maggie fingering the fabric of Julie's nightdress thoughtfully as she spoke. "The highwayman scaped the trap somehow, and the others, they disappeared."

"Disappeared?" Julie asked feigning disbelief.

141

"The witch was there, a dying thief-catcher swore to it himself. But the dwarf was killed by the king's men and by the time they got in the witch had hidden herself in another form or gone up in smoke. In any case she disappeared."

Julie stared at her. This then explained the way the cabin had been all pulled apart with not a crock left unturned.

"And the dwarf who lay in his blood had melted away to a few bloodspots on the rushes by the time they got back just a little before dawn." Maggie paused, her eyes narrowing at Julie's back. "Where was it you said you got that horse again?"

"My uncle and I were passing Epping Wood," Julie said, "when our horse went down. This boy came along and offered it for sale."

"Then perhaps the highwayman was witched away too," Maggie said thoughtfully.

At a cry from the hall, she started for the door quickly. "Sleep well," she called after she passed into the hall, with one quick look back into the room.

Julie readied herself for bed with a light heart. "He lives," she whispered to herself for the thrill of the words echoing in her mind. "They lost him in the woods—he lives."

Accustomed as she was to the endless silence of the deep woods about the cabin, Julie slept lightly. She kept stirring awake, conscious of the laughter of the men in the common room below, the stamp of horses from the street. But in spite of her lightness of sleep, the intruders were in the room and almost upon her before she sensed their presence.

"Take her now," she heard a hoarse voice whisper as she felt hands groping for her throat.

Slipping away like an eel, Julie eluded the shadowy figure and let out a fearful scream. "Help," she cried. "Thieves. Help!" Even as she screamed, she brought her knee up hard against the softness of flesh. The room was suddenly alive with sound, muffled curses, and an anguished, high groan.

Within seconds the room was filled with people. The innkeeper was shouting wildly. Hot wax dripped from his candle which he held up high to light the room and expose the hostler cringing against the wall whimpering, "She led me to it, she led me to do it." The writhing form on the floor was the maid Maggie who rolled about clutching her belly and screaming blasphemy at them all.

142

Doll and Willum, hastily put together with cloaks over their nightclothes, came swiftly to Julie's side. With a glare at the crowd of men staring from the hall, Doll engulfed Julie's nearly bare figure in her mantle pulled from a chair.

"Poor dear," she cried, staring at the bawd on the floor. "To have a young lady treated so. You come along with me, dearie. Willum and I will see you safe to London."

Within a few moments, the hostler and his wench were led away, and Julie's things were packed off to be put near a cot in the room with Doll and Willum.

While Doll sent Willum off for a glass of brandy to settle "the poor ladie's nerves," Julie slipped the leather pouch from its hiding place. She took the ruby necklace out and secreted it separately from the gold. That had been too close a call. With only the coins hidden on her person, she sipped the brandy with her protectors before slipping into a deep, phantom-haunted sleep.

Chapter Twenty

Morning came with a great clamor at the inn. By the time Julie sorted out the sounds that assailed her, the crow of the cock and the rough voices from the stable and the clatter of pans in the kitchen below, she realized that Doll was struggling into her clothes. Willum, who had dressed and slipped out early, had left Julie with the task of bracing herself against Doll's reluctant lacings. When at last Doll's ample pink flesh was forced into a fashionable shaping and her paint and patches all in place, Julie herself was combed and packed for the day's journey. Julie's head still spun a little from the brandy of the night before as she nodded and smiled at Doll.

The woman's tongue was like a bell clapper, beating away at one topic after another until Julie's head was dizzied by the sound. Only when they were both readied to join the others at the innkeeper's table, did Doll's stream of talk turn personal enough that Julie needed to reply thoughtfully.

Doll placed a pudgy hand, quite brilliant with rings, on Juile's arm. "Don't be taking this in any wrong way," she pleaded. "But Willum and me have travelled a great deal. There's a bit of advice I'd like to offer if you won't offend with it."

"Good heavens—" Julie protested. "How could I take your advice amiss? Where would I be even now without your helpfulness? I would be grateful for any counsel you could give."

"It's the problem of thieving and robbing," Doll said, her voice turning confidential. "There's no way to tell an honest man by his sweet talk and his fine feathers. Thieving eyes will be watching each time money is exchanged, for the bit of breakfast you'll have, a few pence for lunch along the road, and the shillings you give to the coachman for fare. The lightest fingers in all of England ride these coaches."

"What should I do?" Julie asked.

"If I was you, I would count out my fare and what will be needed for the food and maybe even what a carriage might cost to get you to your aunt's once you are in London town. Then I would keep the bulk of my money hid in some secret place that no one could guess, not even to be reached for when there were quick eyes about."

"That's excellent advice," Julie said. "You must know how grateful I am to you and your husband." Doll turned away as Julie withdrew the leather pouch from the hidden pocket in her mantle and counted out the coins, setting out a little extra for passage in the city as Doll had suggested.

"How lucky I was to have met you," Julie said, putting the pouch safely away and tucking her arm through Doll's. Julie thought a strange look passed the woman's face at her words, but they were starting down the wooden stairs and Doll, unsure of her footing, might just have been concerned lest she fall.

"Willum and I like young people," was all the response she made.

After a breakfast, made more confusing by the absence of Maggie from among the help, Julie was wedged between Doll and Willum in the rocketing coach. She was only able to see the rim of the window and a small patch of clouded sky. Numbed by the swaying of the coach and the warmth of the tight enclosure, she drowsed and sometimes slept soundly through the length of the journey. From this half-consciousness she was roused to the great clatter and turmoil of the coach's arrival in London. Even Doll and Willum seemed infused with the haste of the city. They were out of the coach and gone in the crowd before Julie even had a chance to thank them again for their protection.

Grateful for Doll's advice and that small experience she had gained visiting the Furlongs in London, she hailed a conveyance and told the man the address of her old maid Mary.

The fare he quoted to her seemed outrageously high. She felt the coins in her hand and realized she needed threepence more to meet his price. Only then did she slide her hand inside her mantle to get out her leather pouch of gold. She searched the pocket again before she could accept that her store of money was gone. She gasped and looked about wildly. Doll. It had to have been Doll or Willum who had robbed her while she was crowded between them in the coach. But the driver was still glaring at her with a challenging look. She tossed her head haughtily.

"Do you take me for some country wench that will be robbed blind by your greed?" she asked him crossly. "Take five pence off your fare and you have a rider."

"Five pence," the man bawled, his face reddening with anger and surprise.

Julie, her heart pounding furiously, tightened her arm on her bundle and started to walk away.

"I'll cut it by tuppence but not a mite more," he called after her sulkily. "You'd have a man starve."

Starving was the last threat over him, Julie decided, noting the great soft belly that rode above his breeches. She pretended to hesitate before turning back to him.

"Oh very well," she said in a resigned voice. "I'd not want a lean, hungry person like yourself to go without supping because of me."

The wryness of her tone escaped him, but he did have the decency to avoid her eyes as they set out.

"Thank God for that circlet of rubies," Julie told herself earnestly, feeling its weight in the breast of her gown. In spite of the precariousness of her position, she fought back a ripple of laughter. What a gull she had been to accept Doll and her Willum so freely. Doll had been so furious with the maid and the hostler. No wonder about that. She had feared that the scurvy pair would get to Julie's property before Doll secured it for herself. I am learning in a costly school, Julie admitted to herself.

The traffic along the streets made progress very slow. The light had begun to fade above the haze of coal dust that hung above the city. A lamplighter moved along the street as Julie dismounted and laid the last of her coins in the driver's hand.

How good it would be to feel safe again. Now that she would be with Mary, her days of lying and deceiving could be past. Only her love for Antoine must be kept hidden inside her heart.

People scurried past the house, which was near Fleet Market, with dour and unsmiling faces. Julie turned from them to pull on the bell rope again, standing close beneath the overhanging second story of the building.

In time, the door inched open to reveal a young girl staring out at Julie. The heavy smell of stewing mutton flowed through the passage, and from inside Julie could hear the yapping of what sounded to be a small dog.

"I have come to see Mistress Mary Curlew," Julie said plainly, hoping that the girl's ears were as eager as her eyes which searched Julie steadily through the crack of open door.

The door swung wide open so suddenly that Julie stepped back in surprise. The girl stared at her a moment then turned and ran to the back of the house. "Gar," she said in a sepulchral tone as she ran.

The girl had barely disappeared through the door than it was open again. Julie watched a stout, older woman sail down the hall towards her bearing a single candle aloft. A dog accompanied her, a small, flat-faced animal who was so ludicrously fat that he seemed to skate along on his tiny inadequate feet.

The woman was dressed entirely in black which accented the heaviness of her face and jowls. Unconsciously, Julie's hand flew to her chest at the shock of seeing that face, Mary's face, changed a little by time and a certain extra width between the eyes. This must be Mary's sister, she realized from the startling likeness.

When the woman drew near enough to see Julie's face, she stopped still a moment. Flapping her hand at the dog to caution him to silence, she nodded to Julie to come in. Then she made a quick gesture of caution with her finger against her lips and turned and closed the door she had left open behind her.

Mystified, Julie watched her return with swift steps and

146

reach for Julie's hands with a strange expression on her face. Her words, a carefully sibilant whisper, startled Julie with their directness. "You are the Duvall child?" she hissed.

At Julie's nod, the woman smiled. "Welcome, my dear," she said, still in that careful whisper. "My dear sister Mary expected you these many months. Welcome, my dear. I am Margaret Curlew."

Julie would have spoken, but Margaret shook her head again. Then with a conspiratorial nod, she took Juile's hand and began to speak in a loud tone, obviously for listening ears beyond the kitchen door.

"I am so glad to meet you, my dear. I will take you up myself. Come along and be fresh before we have tea."

Julie followed Margaret up the wooden stairs with great confusion. The gentle harshness in her voice was like the same tone in Mary's speech, but Mary had certainly never been given to signals and silent grimaces as this woman was. Nor would Mary have been able to abide the dog which, snuffling and grunting, labored painfully up the stairs after them, maneuvering only a step at a time as he hauled his sausage body onto each riser.

At the top, Margaret Curlew turned and smiled back at Julie. "You might just give Thump a lift there at the top. He's not the young dog he once was."

Julie hefted the beast by its round belly and set it on the floor of the hall. Without a glance at her, he tacked towards his mistress and posted himself against her stiff, black skirt.

The room Margaret Curlew showed Julie into was tidy and welcoming in spite of its simplicity. A plump comforter was folded neatly across the foot of the bed, and the wardrobe that dominated the wall of the room glowed from careful polishing. A small sewing chair was poised on the finely woven rushes of the floor with a side table bearing a basket of bright wools. The basket was one that Julie remembered. The room itself felt like her maid Mary. Julie turned to the woman who was setting the candle on a small shelf beneath a looking glass.

Margaret Curlew read Julie's mind through her eyes and nodded, her own dark eyes getting moist at once with the threat of tears.

"These three months past," she affirmed. "God rest her."

At Julie's gasp of dismay, Margaret spoke swiftly. "It was

a good death. She died with a smile on her lips. I found her like that—smiling. It had been a cough that went into her lungs and her breath simply stopped. Smiling."

"Mary," Julie whispered aloud to herself. "My dear, good Mary." Before she realized her tears were coming, she found herself in Margaret's arms, being comforted against the stiffly laced bosom of her new friend.

"There, there," Margaret whispered into her hair. "She loved you, my dear. Yes, how she loved and grieved for you."

Then she took Julie away gently and looked at her. "I must confess that I doubted my own sister. I thought it was only love blinding her, that no child could be as lovely as her words painted you."

She lifted a tendril of Julie's hair and let it spring back onto the soft curve of her cheek. "Those golden eyes, that mouth," Margaret shook her head. "You have been richly blessed, Julie Duvall. And you must know that you are welcome here—and safe."

"Oh, I cannot accept your hospitality," Julie said. "Mary told me—"

Margaret nodded. "She told me of your condition and that she had urged that you come. She expected you long ago. And as for staying here, I have no chick of my own, no more than Mary had. I was given a generous settlement when the last of my charges were grown, and I have income too. I only grieve for your safety."

"You keep mentioning safety," Julie asked, her clear eyes studious of Margaret's face.

"You must know that you are sought," Margaret said with astonishment.

"Me? Sought?" Julie asked with amazement.

Margaret nodded. "That is why I was taking such care below the stairs. No one must know your name or that you are here. In fact we must go down soon before gossip starts in the kitchen."

"But what am I sought for?" Julie asked.

"Murder and kidnap," Margaret replied angrily. "They came in late fall seeking you, a constable along with a great, gross harridan claiming to be your aunt. They came again and again, certain that we were sheltering a criminal here."

"But I didn't kill anyone," Julie wailed.

"Mary knew that, and I believed too," Margaret said crossly. "But Mary was terrified lest they find you before we did."

"Louis insisted on running away with me—"

"Later," Margaret held up her hand. "For now we need a tale of you and a new name. My Kit in the scullery has a tongue hinged on both ends. Shall we say that you are a friend from the country? No, better make that a niece, some blood kinship makes it more convincing. Yes, and you have been governess to a fine family who went abroad." Margaret's forehead was lined with the efforts of this tale she was weaving. "The governess is good because that might help explain your fine clothes and way of speaking. But you still need a name. A servant's name would be most convincing. First and last," she pressed Julie.

Julie shook her head wildly, "Poll?" she asked.

Margaret grinned suddenly, looking the life of Mary in the turn of that smile. "That's what I have been called many times, maybe another name."

"Sukey," Julie decided aloud. There had been a Sukey in her father's house, a plain girl whom Julie had loved for the merriment of her laughter filtering up from the kitchen when she worked there.

"And the last name?" Margaret pressed her.

The name came to Julie's lips unbidden. "Titus," she said firmly.

"Well enough. You need not talk much about your past. Only be wary of that Kit who has more passion than brain." Margaret rose and turned to the door. With a moan of complaint, the dog Trump heaved onto his legs and started after her. "Come for tea as soon as you feel ready." She laid a gentle finger on Julie's cheek. "Your tears for Mary are not to be worried over. The Thames in flood would not wash the beauty from that face."

Julie adjusted the candle to arrange her travel-worn hair in the small mirror. "Sukey Titus" she whispered to herself. Back into deceit again. Would it ever end? Only when she was with Antoine, she thought ruefully. Antoine. As always, the sound of his name echoed in her mind flooded her with mingled joy and pain. Simply by drifting her eyelids shut, she could feel the hard warmth of his arms tightening about her, the gentle persistence of his lips moving along her throat.

Where was he? What fugitive hole did he huddle in? She shook her head and forced her trembling hands to arrange her hair. Would that he were in this safe, prim room with her. Safe.

Not since she rolled from the priest's hole had there really been such a moment to reflect. The warmth of Margaret's concern for her had flowed over her and weakened her. The scenes of the past days flickered in her mind like glimpses caught from the back of a racing horse: the coarse beard of the rapist above her face, Antoine's body pressed against the fresh wounds of her attacker, and Titus turned to cold dough in the blood-fouled room.

Her face in the mirror wavered before her eyes then disappeared in her torrent of tears. It was there, with her head down on her arms, exhausted by weeping, that Margaret found her and led her off like a child to have tea.

Chapter Twenty-One

It was like being a child again in the kitchen of her father's home. The great room smelled of the mutton and spices and coal smoke which had darkened the ceiling to a rich, even hue. Overall was the rich scent that rose from a steaming tea crock ready for dipping.

Margaret made excuses for Julie's lateness, explaining that the shock of hearing of Mary's death had overwhelmed her. In the manner of people freshly reminded of death, the girl and the young man at the table acknowledged the introductions in hushed tones.

The girl whom Julie had startled so thoroughly at the door was introduced as Kit. There in the well-lit kitchen, Julie could see that she was exceptionally pretty. Warmth from the cooking fire had brought a deep apricot glow to her cheeks. Her hair was a rich brown that glinted with red lights as she turned to nod briskly at Julie. The blue of her eyes appeared almost startling between lashes so thick and black they looked painted on. Only her mouth spoiled the effect. Kit's lips were full and ripe enough with color, but the sulkiness in her expression would have spoiled a much less comely face. Her tone, as she mumbled, "How do, Sukey," told Julie at once that not only did this Kit have (as Margaret had said) a tongue hinged on both ends, but a temper that was set on a very shakey trivet.

Julie guessed the young man in his early twenties. If he had not been taller than Margaret by several inches, she would have set his age much younger. He clattered to his feet awkwardly as they entered the room, his face and neck turning a deep, painful red as he looked at Julie.

Julie fought the grin that twitched at the corner of her mouth. Mark Hatter, as Margaret had introduced him, was appealing in the same heart-tugging way that her hound Bonbon had been as a half-grown pup. Poor fellow, nothing seemed to match or fit together properly for him. His dark, shabby coat was short of sleeve so that a great knob of wrist was exposed as he reached out to steady the table he had set rocking by his awkwardness. His limbs seemed indifferently joined to his long, thin body giving him a nervous, insubstantial air.

His shyness was too great to let Julie catch his eyes for more than a second, but that glimpse was enough to win her interest. How amazing in this terrified young man's face to find dark eyes gleaming with intelligence and warmth. Although his linen was as shabby as his coat and breeches, it was as tidy as it was threadbare.

"Mark is apprenticed to a silversmith," Margaret told her proudly, setting a tray of buttered bread closer to her guest's hand. "And a fine artist he is too, you'll see some of his drawings, I'm sure."

As Margaret settled herself at the table, the dog Trump posted himself beside her right knee and set up a low, steady whine of complaint that continued throughout the meal.

Margaret's affection for the young man was obvious. As she served tea, she elaborated on his importance to her. "And it's not only what he does at the smith's that is great, Sukey," she went on, stressing the strange name as if to set it firmer in her own mind. "He does a hundred things hereabout for Kit and me that we would be hard put to get done on our own."

Mark flushed even deeper at her praise, ducking his head self-consciously with a grateful glance at Margaret. Whether it was his obvious embarrassment or the way the tea danced in the bowls when Mark shook the table again, Julie couldn't tell, but something about his manner enraged Kit. She drew in her breath sharply and stared fiercely at him with her bright eyes half-closed.

Anger became Kit, Julie decided with a rush of something almost like envy. The girl's shapely body seemed alive with emotion, from the faint tapping of her foot to the full rosy breasts which seemed poised to leap from the low, ruffled neckline of her dress. She was rapping a spoon crossly on the table. Where her sleeve fell back, her well-formed hands joined with a wrist as small and soft skinned as a child's. Mark could do worse, Julie told herself with an inner ripple of amusement. It was obvious that Kit would give full agreement to that.

During the flurry of tea, Julie studied the room about her. There was more to see in this room than in the kitchens she was used to. Along one wall hung a row of shelves that were crowded with pots and baskets of dried grasses and seeds. Above the hearth, where they had apparently been hung for drying, were several sheaths of vegetation bound with sturdy thongs.

The tea, while not the treasured hyssop that Titus had brewed for her, was strong and fragrant. After apologizing for a lack of sugar, Margaret had spooned a glowing dollop of honey into Julie's bowl, which gave the tea a fragrance like a blooming garden.

The conversation limped along awkwardly. Mark stammered out something about the weather, a topic which was soon exhausted. Margaret, raising her voice a little to be heard over the complaint of the dog, prattled on about a child of the neighborhood who had been run down by a runaway carriage in the street. Julie listened, finding herself less distracted by the talk than by Kit's obvious growing tension across the table. The girl seemed about to explode with annoyance, yet when she did speak, her voice was level and controlled.

"Did you only come to London today then?" Kit asked, staring at Julie unsmiling.

"This afternoon," Julie replied. "By coach."

"From where?" Kit asked.

"Up near Epping," Julie replied quickly. "I can't tell you

152

exactly what village because it was such a long ride with so many changes."

"You would think you might know where you started," Kit said, still staring at her.

Her rudeness made Mark forget his shyness. "You came by coach alone?" he said, obviously startled.

Julie hesitated. What a great excitement her story of her adventures at the inn and the robbery following would make at this table. She thought better of it. "I rode with an elderly couple who were very watchful of me," she told him wryly. "A woman named Doll and her husband Willum."

"And how did you come to know Mistress Mary so well?" Kit challenged.

"My goodness, Kit," Margaret broke in with a forced laugh. "Mary has known Sukey here all the child's life."

"How can that be when your sister was in service with that French family all those years?" Kit pressed.

"Mary always found time for her family and friends—and their children," Margaret's rebuking tone forced the girl to retreat to a sullen silence.

"What are all the leaves and seeds and rushes for, Aunt Margaret?" Julie asked, as much to change the subject from herself as to satisfy her curiosity.

"I have a fancy for doing simple cures," Margaret replied.

"Simple cures indeed!" Mark cried, his shyness totally forgotten in his indignation. "Margaret here is the finest healer in all of London town. Wait until you see what fine people make their way here to ask her help. Just this weekend past the magistrate's son was afflicted with a cough that kept the child from food or sleep. And where did they come for an elixir?"

Margaret shook her head quickly but Julie saw the faint blush of pleasure brighten her face. " 'Twas a simple enough brew of horehound and honey with a little resin in to break the thickness in his throat."

That little boiling kettle of a Kit was obviously ready to explode again. What an uncomfortable sort of person to live about, Julie thought with amazement as Kit leaned forward and banged her spoon loudly on the table.

"All this chatter doesn't get the work done," she said crossly. "There's no coal for the morrow, and the tea things still to be done up."

Mark glanced at the girl and then at the coal bucket with surprise. At a glance from Margaret, Mark shrugged and rose. Kit herself flounced out of the room as if on urgent business.

"She must have planned to go gossip with her friend Trudy after tea," Mark suggested, starting off with the bucket.

Margaret shook her head after them. "Mark guessed wrong about Kit. Any talk of healing makes her like that. I brought her here to save her from Bedlam. She was perfectly mad, poor child, clawing at herself and laughing to set the damned to dancing. They would have put her behind bars for life, however long that would be."

Julie stared at her in amazement. "And you healed her?"

"Not such a hard case," Margaret admitted. "It was Saint Anthony's Fire, a madness that comes from eating too much of a certain dark bread that has been badly made. The affects pass in time, and I could not bear to see that lovely child be prisoned."

Julie shook her head. "Now she seems fine except for a certain quickness of spleen."

Margaret glanced at her and laughed. "Well you might say that, but her spleen is more her fiery nature than any illness that I can cure. Poor gamecock that she is, she has taken a great fancy to Mark."

"But doesn't he ever see how lovely she is?" Julie asked.

Margaret shook her head. "He remembers those long weeks when she was tied like a beast to restrain her violence." Then she smiled. "Mark has a great store of loyalty. He cannot forget the cruelties she tried to inflict on me during her madness."

"Is it then your custom to take in the helpless, Margaret, like me?"

The woman's eyes grew serious. "Mark's mother was in service with me—a lovely girl but rather more dreamy and suggestible than is good for a girl in service. I think the master would have been fair with the girl but Her Ladyship—" Margaret shrugged. "I was fortunate to be able to take him in when his mother disappeared."

"I think you are wonderful," Julie said, catching the old woman's hands in her own. "You—and your gift of healing." Unbidden, Titus came to her mind, his knowing, his gentle hands.

154

Margaret pressed Julie's fingers hard. "The wonder is that you made it here safe. It was my dear Mary's constant fear that you came to some harsh end."

Mark's arrival at the door startled the dog into a shrill agony of alarm. Margaret rose swiftly to admit him with his burden of coal.

In spite of her pleas, Margaret refused to let Julie assist with the cleaning up. "Later," she said. "When you are rested." Kit, who had returned with no more explanation than she had made at her departure, tossed her head to show how little she approved of Margaret's pampering of this stranger.

Julie was in her gown, with her hair brushed loose about her shoulders when she heard Margaret's voice outside her door. She had already spent a guilty hour trying to decide how much of the truth to tell this good woman. It was not possible to look into that face that was so much like her own Mary's and confess to that long idyll in the woods with a man with a price on his head. Yet Margaret must have some explanation of the half-year just past since Louis's death and her escape from her uncle's house.

When Julie opened the door, she found Margaret balancing a small tray bearing a decanter of berry wine and two glasses.

"I am not much for spirits," she told Julie as she entered and set the tray on the small table, "but this is a special night to have my Mary's dove safe in this nest."

With her voice quiet against the dimness of the room, Julie told of the drear and terrifying times at her uncle's house and of Louis's insistence that he escape with her. For the most part Margaret listened in sympathetic silence, only nodding now and then to indicate understanding. It was when Julie began to recount the details of her flight that Margaret asked several thoughtful questions.

"Did anyone see the two of you thrown from the top of that coach, anyone whose name you know or who could be found?" she asked.

When Julie shook her head Margaret signalled for her to continue her story.

Then again she interrupted. "And did no one turn from the road to see this battle between you two and Joseph?"

"It was too far," Julie explained. "The snow hung like a tapestry between us and the road."

"And the gentleman who came to your rescue, could he be reached to give witness in a court of law?"

Julie stared at her bleakly, finally understanding the intent of these questions. Then she shook her head. "He is gone from these parts," she said vaguely. "It was his going that brought me into London."

"Then he is the one who took you to his home for his wife to heal you?"

"He had no wife," Julie replied. Too late did she realize how cleverly Margaret was drawing at the real story she was striving to conceal. "It was his servant who cared for me," she added boldly, letting Margaret guess what she would about the nature of this servant.

Margaret's eyes were careful on Julie's face.

"And you do not know how to reach him now?"

"No idea at all," Julie replied, hoping that the wavering light of the single candle would conceal the rapid beating of her heart under her sheer gown.

"And the servant?" Margaret asked.

"Dead," Julie said numbly.

In that moment of silence, Julie felt Margaret's waiting settle on her like a cloak. The cry of the watch from the street finally broke the spell, and Margaret sighed.

When Margaret spoke again her voice was lighter, almost bantering. "So if he is gone we did not tell too much of a lie to poor Kit downstairs. Now we must turn our thoughts to your safety. If it were not for the kidnap and murder charges against you you would be safe here forever, but as it is—"

"Oh, I would never impose on you like that," Julie protested.

Margaret's voice roughened. "There will be no talk of imposing," she ordered. "It is my privilege. If I did not do it for yourself, I would do it for our dear Mary. What of family? Didn't Mary tell me that you had some family already abroad in the new world?"

Julie nodded. "My father's only sister fled to the Carolinas from France when my own father and uncle came here."

"Would you know how to find her there?"

"I know the name of the town and the river nearby."

"That should be enough," Margaret conceded. "That is

156

said to be a rough, hard place with savages still making war upon the settlements."

"That would be better than being a fugitive for a murder I did not cause," Julie reminded her. "Thanks to the quick fingers of Doll and her Willum I have no gold, but I do have one piece of fine jewelry. Could that be sold to buy my passage to America?"

Margaret nodded thoughtfully. "A man could do it and get an honest price; for a woman it would be riskier." She paused and glanced up at Julie. "Surely you know someone who is both trustworthy and friendly to you."

Julie shook her head bleakly.

"There was a squire's son," Margaret mused aloud. "A lad from your neighborhood that Mary told me was greatly smitten with you."

Julie's eyes widened in astonishment. Giles Urban. How long had she gone without a thought of Giles even passing through her head. But at Margaret's words, he was full in her memory, the almost-golden beauty of his coloring, his fine head bent to her in supplication. Then she shook her head. He would be well into the law by now and making the fine life his father had planned for him. A quick twinge of pain came as she admitted the truth to Margaret. "He was smitten, true enough, but the blow was not enough to survive my change of fortune."

"Like that," Margaret said wryly, lifting the decanter to Julie's glass. Then she paused, the decanter still in her hand. "Your father's banker," she announced with delight. "Mary spoke of him with such admiration. He showed so much concern for you when your aunt sought you there. Could he give us guidance with this problem?"

Julie jumped with excitement. "Of course, Henry Furlong. Why didn't I think of that? I shall go straight to him."

Margaret shook her head warningly. "That would be unwise, my dear. After the constables sought you here, they went to him. He sent a message to Mary telling her to warn you to take great care lest you fall into their hands."

"It was brave of them to face Henry Furlong," Julie said with a wicked grin. "They were both a little wary of him."

"But we could send a message to him safely," Margaret added thoughtfully. "My master left my own affairs in the hands of that bank, and I often send Mark to do business."

157

She rose and set the empty glasses on the tray. "Even if Mark were watched, as we all might be, there could be no suspicion in his taking in a small deposit, seeing Mr. Furlong, and returning with a message for you."

Julie stared at Margaret. "Is it that bad, Margaret? Am I in such danger that we must think of spies and betrayals?"

Margaret hesitated only a minute, then she nodded. "They are people driven by some great fury for revenge. Hate is a harder goad even than greed. Murderers go to Tyburn tree, my dearheart. We cannot be too careful."

When Margaret left the kitchen bearing the decanter of wine on the tray, Kit stared after her speculatively. She stared at the distaff in her hand and frowned a moment at the fire. "Wouldn't you give a penny now to know what those two will be jawing about upstairs?" she asked Mark.

He was laboring over a design on his lap. He added a careful line and didn't even look at her.

"It's no concern of mine or yours," he said mildly.

"So who cares of concern?" Kit said, looking over at him. "I'd still like to know what they are up to. That's no country maid that she's trying to pass off on us, you know."

Mark's head came up with a jerk. He stared at her. "What kind of a fool are you to go spinning tales? The less you know, the more your mouth runs."

"So who's the fool?" she teased, a small smile beginning to play about her mouth. "How can you hope to be a smith when you are blind? Why, that dress she wears costs what a governess would lay by in a year. And the way she speaks! Where is that funny *a* they put in their talk? She's a lady and she's in hiding for somewhat or other. And while I'm about it, she's a bit of a snob, with that witch-eyed, yellow stare of hers flicking here and there and not missing a corner."

"Hiding," Mark exploded with annoyance. "Why should a lady come hiding to such a place as this. Tell me that."

Kit, delighted to have his gaze full upon her, straightened her slim back and leaned closer as if to share a confidence.

"How about if something went wrong? Like her being with child and with no husband? Margaret is such a healer, you say. Why, she could tend to that so easy. Milady takes a sojourn to London—" In a mocking falsetto, Kit mimicked a lady's voice.

"Have you heard now that our dear daughter, down to

158

London with friends is come back with a fever. Poor dear, it struck her right there in the season—"

Mark, goaded to fury by her apery, shoved hard at her bared shoulder which was now pressed against his own.

"You foul-mouthed slut," he said fiercely. "How dare you lay such a tale on poor Miss Sukey."

Poor Miss Sukey indeed. Kit recoiled and spat at him, rubbing the shoulder he had lunged against. "Her name is no more Sukey than mine is Good Queen Ann. She's in hiding, she is, and Margaret up there is a party to it. They're up there plotting something this blessed minute."

"Shut your foul mouth," Mark hissed at the girl. His impulse to strike her was only halted by remembering the pain when he had tried to lay hands on her before.

"I'll make you a wager," she whispered coaxingly, her blue eyes sparkling with mischief. "A farthing says that if you was to stand outside that door and listen, you'd get yourself such an earful you couldn't hold your head up. A farthing," she repeated with a lilt, to tempt him.

"Bitch, bitch, bitch," he growled, his voice intense with loathing. "Because you are a rotten slut does not mean that all women are the same. I thought your raving madness was better healed than this. You slide a foot towards that door to listen, and I'll break the leg it hangs from."

As always, the reference to Kit's madness set her temper to blazing. Narrowing her eyes, she leaned towards him, her voice bitter and taunting. "Look at the little prentice," she cooed. "If he hasn't set his own crotch on fire by lusting for a lady. Fool, maudlin, simpering fool."

Mark, unable to abide the sound of her voice, leaped to his feet to glare down at her. The breathtaking innocence of Sukey's face filled his mind. Pursing her lips, Kit let her glance openly stare at the fit of his breeches. To his horror, he felt the faint swelling start, pressing the cloth. He reddened with fury at his own body's betrayal.

"One more word of such talk and I'll beat your pate back into the addle it once was," he threatened her. "And don't think you can go gossiping and lying to your scullery friends without my finding out, either. Keep your mouth off Sukey or I'll give you reason to wish you had."

The pots along the wall clattered from the banging he gave the door. Kit stared after him, sick at heart. That had been just a tease about his lusting after that skinny, yellow-eyed bitch. Damn if she hadn't hit on the truth.

She glared about the room furiously. Finding nothing else to vent her wrath on, she grabbed his sketch from his bench and threw it on the last coals of the fire. She watched the blackened edges curl towards the center, like grasping hands, before the whole of it exploded into flame.

"Burn," she hissed bitterly. "Burn, witch, burn."

Chapter Twenty-Two

Julie spent the better half of the next day mulling over the message she would send to Henry Furlong. She had written few enough letters in her life anyway, a few notes to her father when he was abroad, some lines of appreciation to a hostess who had entertained her. When she finally finished with the words in a style that was pleasing to her, she found herself with a tabletop covered with half-started notes and scratched-through lines. She swept her mistakes into the bin by her table and was sealing her letter when she heard Margaret's voice at the door.

"I wondered how it was coming along," Margaret asked, with a glance at the neat desk.

"You can't believe how many mistakes I made before I got it right," Juile laughed, motioning at the half-filled wastebin.

Margaret's horrified look filled Julie with remorse. "Oh, I never thought," she apologized quickly. "All that fine paper of yours that I have wasted."

Margaret shook her head and leaned over to fish out the scratched-out notes. "It's not the paper, my dear. Don't give that a thought." When she had retrieved the last of the sheets, she made them into a twist that fit into her apron pocket. "Kit may not be a student of any fame but the poor creature can spell out a few lines of type. We cannot take a chance."

Julie shook her head. "I am afraid I am a poor conspirator," she said. "I never thought."

"It is an ugly thing to learn," Margaret conceded, "But it would be even uglier to have your affairs noised about the neighbor's kitchens. Never mind about these, I shall burn them myself. And is that the finished letter?"

At Julie's nod, Margaret slipped it into her other apron pocket. "I have spoken to Mark about the errand at the bank, and he is happy to do it for me in the morrow."

Excitement wakened Julie at the first cries of the hawkers in the street. Careful at the window, she watched the milkmaid pass, swinging her pails jauntily among the fruit pedlars and the other mongers who swarmed the street. It was not long before Julie heard a door bang below her in the house. Then she saw Mark's slender figure making its swift, jerking progress down the street and out of sight.

That day was heavy with waiting. Julie bathed and tidied her clothes and then sat a long time embroidering a small tapestry that Mary had left unfinished. Each time she was below stairs she tried to woo the girl Kit into friendliness, but it was no use. The girl only tossed her cap at Julie's efforts and answered the gentlest questions with a rude, sullen quip. By the time dark finally fell and Margaret was setting out a tea of rich, dark bread with a steaming leek soup on the hob, Julie felt the strain of the waiting like a band drawn too tightly about her head.

Although they did not speak of it, Julie knew that Margaret was scarcely less eager than herself. At the sound of Mark's foot at the door, Margaret ordered Kit to finish up brewing the tea for her. Ignoring the girl's outraged stare, she signalled Mark into the parlor and closed the door carefully after him.

"Tell me how it went, Mark," she said directly, not even bothering to light a candle in the dim room.

"I took the deposit in just as you said," Mark reported dutifully. "But when I asked to see Mr. Furlong the young man there said it was impossible. He said that Mr. Furlong was a very important man and I should send my business along to him and not put on airs."

Margaret grimaced. "And so?"

"I told him that I was to deliver this message in person and to take your name into his master." Mark stopped a moment before going on. "The minute he did that, I was taken in at once."

Mark's dark eyes searched her face. He was impressed, Margaret realized, that an officer in the largest bank in Lon-

161

don would leave his business at the sound of her name. Mark was also curious.

"We have known each other for a long time," she told him, hoping the half-truth would allay his curiosity.

"I handed the note only into his hand as you said," Mark went on. "He read the letter and then read it again. He seemed mixed about what he read somehow. He got to his feet and marched back and forth a good deal before he even looked at me. Then he blew his nose a time or two and sat down and stared past me, beating a little tune on his desk with his finger."

Margaret nodded. This was what she needed to know, that Henry Furlong was as concerned over Julie's plight as she was herself.

"Then he gave me the message," Mark said, looking at Margaret very directly.

Impatience sharpened her voice in spite of herself. "The message, Mark, where is it?"

"He did not write it down," Mark explained. "He said three things to me. After each sentence he made me repeat it over to him. Then he told me to repeat all three of them to him two more times, all the way through, to be sure that I would remember them."

"And do you?" Margaret asked, leaning closer.

She saw the quick, nervous flick of his tongue on his lips and the fine sheen of sweat across his brow. "All day long I have been saying them over to myself," he said. "I know them like my name."

"Yes?" she pressed.

Mark spoke slowly and carefully, as if he were trying to bring to the simple phrases more meaning than his puzzled mind had been able to find in them. "The first was 'GOD BE PRAISED'."

Margaret muttered a silent "amen" into her collar.

"Then he said, 'THE FIRE IS STILL BLAZING'."

Margaret waited.

"Then only, 'WORD WILL COME'."

Margaret sighed. "Would you say them all over again for me, dear friend."

Mark grinned shyly, the flush of his embarrassment acknowledging her words. "GOD BE PRAISED. THE FIRE IS STILL BLAZING. WORD WILL COME." Mark's face was suddenly dark with misgiving. He blurted the question at her in a pained whisper. "You aren't mixed up in some awful political plot, are you mistress?" His voice was pleading.

Margaret's eyes widened in wonder.

He stumbled on awkwardly. "The Whigs and Torys, you know. The streets are full of how men are risking treason by their attempts to get a Stuart back on the throne."

Her peal of merry laughter rang through the house. Julie, tense by the kitchen fire, startled at the sound.

Margaret laid her hand on the young man's arm. "Bless you, Mark. I am past politics. Which ape wears the crown no longer troubles me."

Mark's jaw dropped, and a look of fear came into his eyes. "With that kind of talk you risk treason too."

Margaret fixed him with a sudden, serious stare. "I am safe in what I say before you, am I not?"

For only a moment was he dumbfounded. Then his voice choked as he tried to speak. "I would die before I betrayed you," he said solemnly.

"Now that is a pledge I certainly never intend to collect," she said, her voice suddenly lighter. "But if great discretion were needed, I could depend on you, couldn't I, Mark?"

"With my life," he said simply.

Julie's golden eyes darkened at the message. "Then he too is afraid," she said quietly.

"Afraid for you, my dear," Margaret amended.

"Then what is there for me to do?" Julie asked.

"Wait with good grace," Margaret admitted. "Only that."

"But I cannot stay on with you, eating your food," Julie began.

Margaret interrupted her in that loving, cross voice which was so like Mary's. "You can finish that tapestry that my sister started. We will find many things to keep your hands busy." She lifted Julie's chin with a single finger and waited for Julie to bring a wistful smile to her. "You will wait with good grace," she told the girl gently. "Never fear."

The first few days were the hardest. Julie was unable to think of anything but Henry Furlong's "word." She pondered on how the message would come. She wished that he might bring it in person. She imagined watching a carriage stop and

163

seeing his fine, round, portly form step out, brave with ruffles. But that was impossible.

A messenger, perhaps he could send a messenger. The watch for this unknown messenger laid a great strain on her days. Many strangers came to Dame Curlew's door. They came to ask counsel, to buy cures, or to beg her to come with them to heal a loved one. Julie searched each face and turned away with despair.

But even as Julie sought an escape from this danger that England held for her, she dreaded the thought of going so far from Antoine. "If only the two of us could flee to the colonies together," she thought. "There would be money enough and to spare if the gems in the ruby circlet are as well cut as they appear." They could find some simple place, she thought, remembering that winter in the gamekeeper's cottage like a glowing dream from which she had wakened to anguish and pain.

Every day confirmed her discovery that London itself was simply a gossipy village grown large and dirty. Her ears were filled with the "news" of the place. Each visitor that came for Margaret's help, each evening of talk by the fire brought new chatter of who was pilloried and who was freed, who had lost money on the 'change and who was being cuckolded by his handsome wife. She knew that Antoine must still be free, for nowhere had she heard that the Blue-eyed Giant had been taken for his price. All of her dreams were of Antoine, but dreams pass in minutes while days passed only in slow aching hours.

Margaret, pained by Julie's distress, did all she could to divert the girl. She encouraged Julie's interest in the simple cures that were Margaret's stock in trade. She taught her the names of the herbs and roots, where they could be found and what were their uses. One day, under Margaret's careful eyes, Julie weighed and measured and brewed a clear, perfect bottle of cure for dropsy.

Margaret, proud of her pupil, turned to her in jest. "In another time we would be burned for witches for this work," she told her. "Aren't you afraid to learn the work of witches?"

"I only wish to learn the arts of healing," Julie admitted. "After that, who cares what they are called?"

Kit, flouncing about the kitchen, glared at Julie as she

hung over the pot with Margaret, but Kit dared not let her tongue fly against the girl when Margaret was about. She only grumbled and tossed her head and muttered fiercely under her breath at the thought of this precious Sukey who had spoiled the fine peace of their home.

It was Mark, under the spell of his growing worship of Julie who unwittingly made trouble for her at every turn.

Margaret put Mark's problem into words first. Julie and Margaret were sewing peacefully with Kit on an errand. Margaret peered over at Julie with a curious glance. "Do you realize that you have bewitched my Mark, Julie?" she asked.

Julie laughed. "Hardly bewitched," she said. A warm smile stayed on Julie's face, deepening the dimple in her left cheek. "How could anyone wish harm to such a great, lovely creature as Mark?" She caught a thread between her teeth, snipped it, and laughed. "In fact, how could anyone do otherwise than love him?"

"But like a toy or a pet," Margaret suggested.

"Like that," Julie said. "And tenderly for his gentleness."

"Are you blind that his love for you is different from that?" Margaret asked soberly.

Julie sighed. In the beginning, she had absently flirted with Mark, even as she had always flirted—with her own father, with Giles, with the foppish bucks of London and then with Antoine. Only lately had she been concerned that his lightsome touch was not a game but dead serious with him. "I have been a little worried about that," she confessed to Margaret. "It cannot be serious, you know. It is just that I am new and strange to him. When I go away—"

"He does not accept that you will go away," Margaret said quietly. "He has asked for my consent to court you."

Julie's work fell to the floor. Her eyes widened with shock. "Oh no, Margaret," she cried. "What can we do? I will not have him hurt, yet I cannot marry him or any—"

Margaret's eyes were flat on Julie's face as the girl caught her words unfinished.

"You were about to say that you could not marry him or any other man. Are you pledged?"

Julie tightened her lips against her teeth in anguish.

"I am not pledged," she said quietly.

"Are you wedded?"

"I am not wedded," Julie replied. Even as she spoke the

165

words, a storm of denial raged inside her. "I am wedded," she wanted to scream. "I am bedded and wedded and pledged and married all in one with a love that makes other marriage a game of charades."

When she raised her eyes to Margaret, she read the understanding in the older woman's eyes. Wordlessly, Margaret laid her work aside and took Julie against her breast. Julie heard the steady, warming drumming of the old woman's heart, felt the gentle hands stroking her hair. "I will tell Mark only that it is too soon. I do not have the heart to tell him that you are not for him—not now or ever."

"Couldn't you help him to notice Kit a little?" Julie asked meekly. "How can he be blind to her worship of him?"

"He is blind to everything in the world except you," Margaret told her. "But oh my dear, I do wish that you had grown up in a harsher school. It is all very well to dwell on the beauty and excitement of love—don't protest, I can read this all in your eyes. But we are women, Julie, and the name of a woman is victim. A little time in the real world would soon teach you that to give away your heart is to threaten your own life."

"Is this true for Mark too?" Julie asked, not quite understanding.

Margaret shook her head. "Not Mark," she said stiffly. "Mark had the good fortune to be born a man."

If Julie had been slow to realize Mark's growing passion for her, Kit had not. Her shining eyes narrowed to a slit of fury each time Mark's glance even strayed toward Julie.

When Julie expressed interest in his drawings, he brought a sheaf of them to her. "Keep what you will," he offered. "Keep them all if you have any desire to, I can do others."

Julie stared at the sketches with delight. Many of the pages were covered with designs suitable for a pot or a salver. These were lovely enough, but the other pages caught her heart. Mark had sketched small, perfect scenes of the city, as near and real as a heartbeat. There was the face of a starving child raised in supplication, an old woman pushing a barrow of oysters with the exhaustion of age alive in the lines he had drawn.

"You are an artist," Julie cried.

The crimson that rose from his collar went clear to his eyebrows. "Perhaps some day," he said. "There is a fellow here in London now, a man called Hogarth. You should see the scenes he does, Sukey. And he was once a silversmith like myself."

"I say you are an artist now," Julie said happily, choosing a picture to keep for herself. Then she handed it back. "Please sign it for me, Mark, that I may one day boast of it among my friends."

Margaret's mouth twitched with gentle humor, Mark nearly exploded with pleasure, but Kit ripped her shawl from a chair and slammed out of the room with a muffled curse.

Two weeks had passed since Henry Furlong had gotten Julie's message. Each day set a new heaviness on Julie's heart. He was afraid, she decided. He had forgotten. Something dire had happened to him and she no longer had a friend in the world outside this humble room.

Not understanding the source of her sadness but desperate to have her happy, Mark took to bringing small treasures home to her. One day it was a great, perfect orange that the hawker had sworn was only that day off a boat from Barbados. Again it was a small, carved ape that was jointed to dance if you pulled a cord from his head. Kit fumed and snorted, but no one paid her any mind. Most nights Kit slipped away after the work was done and went to hobnob with her friend Gertrude down the street. Those evenings Mark and Julie would talk by the fire while Margaret dozed in her chair or plied her needle between yawns.

It was a nosegay of fresh roses that loosed the roiling fury of Kit's jealousy. Mark had concealed them under his coat and only laid them by Julie's plate when all were seated for tea.

"How lovely," Julie said, burying her face in their fragrance. "I have never seen such dainty, yellow roses before."

"They are the color of your eyes," Mark said, then ducked his head in an agony of embarrassment. Kit snorted and rose to her feet abruptly, spilling the bowl of tea before her. She went to the cupboard and took a cloth for the widening spill. By the time she spread the wet cloth by the fire to dry, she seemed to have become composed again. "Shall I add more hot water to the tea, mistress?" she asked Margaret in a calm, level voice.

167

Margaret, still distracted by the scene just past, raised her brows with surprise and said, "Why yes, Kit, thank you."

It was made to seem like an accident the way Kit's foot caught in the rushes. The stream of boiling water arched across the bench where Julie sat, bathing her in scalding fluid. Julie leaped up and then fell backwards with a cry of pain.

"You stupid, careless wench," Mark shouted, leaping from his seat to kneel by Julie. "Oh Sukey," he cried softly, "Are you in pain? Are you all right?"

"Get away from that bitch," Kit screamed, her voice breaking with hysteria.

"Shut up," Mark shouted without looking back. "Sukey, Sukey."

It was Margaret's high shriek that made Mark turn, and barely in time. Kit, her eyes blazing and her breasts heaving with fury, had lifted the warming pan to bring it down on Mark's head.

Mark dodged and slid away. Swiftly on his feet, he seized her wrists and twisted her hands loose as she howled with pain.

"You bait of Bedlam," he shouted, twisting her wrists with his great, strong hands. "How dare you wreak your venom on Sukey? You are not fit to touch the hem of her dress. Apologize—" his voice rose with a fury equal to Kit's own, and she quailed before it. "Ask her pardon, you miserable, mad bitch." Still holding her wrists, he forced her down to her knees on the rushes, then farther until her head was pressed on the floor by Julie's feet.

"No," Julie cried between her teeth. "No, Mark. No." The pain was making her giddy. She clutched at the table for support, still crying, "No," both to Mark and to the waves of pain that flooded her limbs from the scalding water.

Margaret was swift to her aid. "Mark," she ordered in that harsh, sudden voice. "Take Sukey to her bed upstairs and lay her there. Then come directly back and brew the strongest tea you can, a rich infusion for her burns."

Kit, whimpering, was staggering to her feet.

"And you, missy," Margaret turned to her. "Get you to your room and don't let a foot stray from it. If your choler is not cured by morning, we will find a new restraint for it."

"The whip," Mark muttered, darting venomous glances at her. "Let it be a whip, and I myself will wield it."

"Upstairs," Margaret ordered crossly. "Get Sukey on up-stairs." She was filling her apron with ointments as she spoke, and she started up the stairs before Mark.

Julie, swooning from the pain, barely remembered the trip to the upstairs room or even her clothes being stripped from her. She first roused to the cooling moistness of linen being pressed along her burned thigh and leg. At her soft moan, Margaret spoke.

" 'Tis tea, my child. Tea cools a burn."

"And later the ointment," Julie said, without opening her eyes, "the ointment of mutton tallow that we made those few days ago?"

"The same," Margaret told her gently, lifting the wet dressing to add new moisture to it.

"You will not punish the girl harshly," Julie asked plead-ingly.

Margaret spoke without stopping the ministrations of her hands. She only sighed. "I could not find it in my heart to punish her harshly, Julie," she admitted. "Your beauty is like a curse, Julie. How can I blame Mark for coveting you, or that ignorant girl for blazing with jealousy? You have a face and a body that other women would die for." She paused. "And some men would kill for."

Julie lay silent, hearing again that other voice in that dis-tant room. "Her body is her doom," Antoine had said. "She could disfigure herself, be pitted with pox, or smeared with dung, and still she would draw men like a carrion does flies."

It should have made her happy to remember the passion in Antoine's voice. Instead, tears welled from her eyes.

"Oh love," Margaret cried with instant contrition, "Pay no attention to an old woman's babbling. I am just bewitched myself and am careless of tongue."

Margaret fell silent, her hands gentle along Julie's thigh. The watch cried in the street below, and a great wave of sadness suddenly moved onto Julie's heart. She cried out from the sudden desolation of it. "Margaret," she cried. "I want to die. I want to die."

Margaret looked at her with disbelief.

"My child," she pleaded. "Do not tempt God with words such as those. It is only the pain. By morning the pain will begin to pass away. Then you will remember how much you love life."

Chapter Twenty-Three

Margaret was right about the pain from the burn. By the next morning, thanks to the tender care she had received, the pain from the burn was much relieved. But the heaviness that had settled on Julie's heart was unchanged. Each word she spoke seemed to be drawn past a great lump of grief deep in her throat.

Within another day, Julie found herself able to walk without even limping. She concealed what discomfort she felt because of Mark. His frantic concern for her was so watchful that it was frightening. If she showed the slightest sign of distress he grew livid with fury and commenced to rail anew at Kit.

Margaret seemed sunk in some withdrawn silence that was puzzling to Julie. Her answer came when Margaret herself came to Julie's room bearing a great bundle of clothing. Julie watched curiously as Margaret unwrapped her burden onto Julie's bed—a full, coarse blue dress and a capacious white apron, a white cap innocent of lace on its ruffles, and dark stockings with rude pattens.

"Not exactly a wardrobe fit for a princess," Margaret said, "but do you think you could abide dressing like this?"

Julie lifted the dress and shrugged. "What is in your mind, Margaret?"

"The same as ever," Margaret admitted. "Your safety."

Julie was astonished to catch a glint of tears in the older woman's eyes. Margaret whisked them away quickly with a brush of her hand raised as if to smooth her hair, but Julie was not fooled.

"Mark is gone the day long every day," Margaret explained. "I cannot find it in my heart to put Kit out into the streets where she would only come to the worst of ends. But neither do I dare leave you to be prey to her murderous passions."

Julie waited thoughtfully. Margaret's tone fell into one of petition.

"You have become greatly skilled in the small arts of

170

healing, Julie. If you were dressed humbly as a disguise and came along with me as an assistant, it would serve both your safety and my work." She waved her hand at the humble clothes. "It is a cruel thing to suggest to one of your station—to go about dressed like a peasant—"

Julie shook her head swiftly but Margaret went on. "If you have a better idea, my dear, do speak it at once. If you would feel disgraced to be seen in such attire—but after all, it is only for this waiting time until your friend gets word to us."

"I am not worried about the clothes, Margaret," Julie told her quickly. "I am only struck dumb with your confidence in me. I am speechless with thanks to have this chance to learn more of this business of healing. I could wear rags with pride if I were wearing them as your assistant."

Margaret's shoulders slumped with relief, and she let herself down heavily on the side of the bed. Then, at the sound of Trump's whine outside the door, she started to rise again. Julie noticed for the first time a heaviness in her friend's movement as she started to raise herself up.

"I'll get him," Julie said, swiftly rising to open the door. Trump, after a snuffle of reproach at Julie, waddled over to flop by his mistress.

"Are you unwell, Margaret?" Julie asked with sudden concern. "There is a paleness in your face, and you have begun to look thin to me of late."

Margaret shook her head and laughed. "Sometimes I find myself overwhelmed with years," she admitted. "No more than that." Then she added brightly, "Think how much strength it will save me to have you along as my helper. I really need you," she admitted, then added with a smile, "as well as wanting your company."

Seeing Julie dressed in clothes even plainer than her own and with that abundance of glowing dark hair almost wholly hidden by the plain servant's cap, mollified Kit somewhat. Mark, his heart relieved of the same concern Margaret had felt about Julie's safety, grew less tense, ceasing his attacks on Kit. Instead, he acted as if the girl simply did not exist, ignoring her presence in the room as if she were no more substantial than the motes of dust that spun in the summer air.

Sleeping or waking, peace seemed to have flown from Julie's life. She could not breathe without that heaviness of

171

grief catching at her chest. Her nights were tormented with terrifying dreams in which Antoine was submitted to suffering and abuse. She dare not let her mind move to Henry Furlong lest she be driven to admit that her old friend had truly abandoned her to her fate.

From all these things, she escaped into her work with Margaret. These weeks were times of great learning for her. Those bright, golden eyes, half-concealed by the ruffles of a servant's cap, studied London like it was a great, soiled book.

She clapped along on her pattens beside Margaret, learning to dodge the night soil thrown from chamber pots at the windows along the streets. She grew quick to tighten her skirts against the grasping hands of diseased beggars clawing at her. She explored the seamy underbelly of the city that she had barely glimpsed as a guest in a fine banker's house.

She found excitement as well as disgust at the rowdy lustiness of the city. She marvelled at the shops on Fleet Bridge where the mingled smells of gingerbread and nuts and oysters reminded her of Christmas and baking day and an open cesspool all at once. Skipping a little to stay abreast of Margaret's determined stride, she plied her friend with questions.

"What is all this about cheap weddings?" she asked Margaret, pointing at the cluster of signs that advertised Cheap Weddings While You Wait, or No One Weds For Less.

Margaret snorted. "Another dodge about the law, my dear," she said. "The law says that a married woman cannot be prisoned for debt but that her husband must serve for her. From this law a new trade has risen. For ten shillings, any wench with a constable on her tail can buy a husband. Of course he gives a false name and she sees his heels the moment the vows are spoken, but she goes off free to become indebted again. Not a bad bargain."

Not only husbands, but also truth could be had at a price. She asked Margaret about the idlers lounging about the court street with wisps of straw sticking from their freshly polished shoes.

"Straw men," Margaret explained. "That bit of straw is like a signboard. If you need a witness to swear you were playing at cricket in Essex when you were actually robbing some knave in Gravesend, there is your man. He will swear to anything for a price."

172

"But surely the judges recognize these fellows after a time," Julie protested.

"Once in a while perhaps," Margaret shrugged. "But when a proven murderer can buy his life by being transported to the colonies, don't you imagine that every judge has his price too?"

As she learned of London and the ways of men and women, Julie learned the ways of the sick and the troubled and added this knowledge to the heaviness in her heart. Only the healing of the sick brought her any joy at all.

When Margaret was called to attend a child stricken with pox, she was distraught. "What shall I do with you this day?" she asked Julie, wringing her hands. "I cannot take you into that place of pestilence. With that lovely, unscarred face I know that pox would come on you within a fortnight. It is rare enough that you have come to this great age without falling afoul of it."

"They thought I had it once when I was very young," Julie confessed. "Somehow it stopped as it started." She pushed back her sleeve to show three small, fair pits in the hollow of one wrist.

Margaret peered at the spots with high attention. "And what had you been doing when these came?" she asked.

Julie grinned with embarrassment, deepening the dimple in her cheek and making her golden eyes dance. "You must promise not to laugh," she warned. "Your Mary was very angry with me about this."

Margaret waited, only half-smiling.

"We had a milkmaid named Lolly," Julie confessed. "I loved the stable and the great beasts they kept there. When no one else was about, she let me take the stool and tug at the great warm teats of the cow. I loved it, feeling the stream of milk move under my fingers, hearing it sing into the pail."

"Aha," Margaret nodded. To Julie's amazement, Margaret handed her her shawl and rose to start on the journey across town.

"God has been good to you, you know," the older woman said as she strode briskly along. "That is the spot that often comes on a milkmaid's hand. It saves them from a pox. Thank God that you were such a wilful and troublesome child."

Ever after that day, the thought of pox came to Julie's

173

mind in a flood of red light. She herself hung the windows of the child's room with red-dyed cloth, shutting all light out except what dull reddish glow made its way through the weave of the cloth. Together she and Margaret swaddled the child in deep red cloth, keeping all light from him except about his eyes and a little of his mouth that he might breathe.

"This will lessen the ravages of scarring on his skin," Margaret told her. "That is, if he outlives the fever, as few enough do."

Certain of these healing missions left scars of their own on Julie's understanding. There was a filthy place Margaret had been called to in a dreary section of the town. She had been told that a young girl was grievously afflicted with sores.

The man who opened the door for them was so unlike their surroundings that Margaret and Julie exchanged a startled glance. He was dressed like every dandy that Julie had watched parade in the mall with a fashionable lady tucked beneath his arm. His high wig was fantastically curled, and the linen exploded from under his scarlet waistcoat in a foam of ruffles. His hands were so burdened with rings that Julie thought it a wonder that he could open the door without help. He met Julie's eyes boldly and seemed to forget the reason these two women had come.

"What have we here?" he asked softly, a gentle smile baring his teeth. "Can beauty be cased in such simple cloth?" He extended a finger toward Julie's cap and would have pulled it off to free her hair if Margaret had not broken in brusquely.

"We have come to heal," she said sternly. "Take us to the sick girl and leave my wench alone."

The man shrugged and turned to lead them down a short hall that was rank with old dirt and stale food odors. Even as he walked, he kept darting his glance back to Julie as if he were weighing her for some hidden intent.

Julie heard the sick girl's cries before the door was open. The cries were like those of a small, helpless animal who had abandoned hope. When they entered, they only saw a slimness under a soiled sheet and dark terrified eyes staring from the pillow.

Margaret threw the cover back to expose the wholly nude body of a young girl. Not even the lacing of scarlet wounds across the girl's breast and thighs could conceal her loveliness. Julie judged her to be little more than a child with the fine, high firm breasts of a girl of twelve or thirteen. Although the girl's eyes were swollen with weeping, they turned to Julie and Margaret from a lovely, heart-shaped face that touched Julie with its expression of betrayed innocence.

"Help me," she pleaded, her lips thickened with pain.

Julie fought back her own tears as she lifted the girl's head and eased water into her parched mouth. Margaret cleansed the wounds with warmed water, and Julie, her hands deft from anguish for the girl's pain, dried them gently and smoothed on the ointment that would first ease the pain and then help heal the broken flesh. By the time they had packed their things to leave, the child had drifted into sleep, her fair face peaceful against the dirty pillow.

While Margaret was storing away her medicines, the dandy slid into the room to stand close to Julie. He was so near that she could see the pock marks beneath the paint on his face and smell the mingled odor of soiled linen and musky perfume. His hand's touch was as soft as a girl's on her own, and she pulled away in disgust.

"Get rid of the hag, my love," he whispered to you. "Come back without her. I can see the beauty hidden in there." He motioned at her coarse dress.

"Let go of me," Julie hissed, backing away.

"But there is money, my dear," he crooned. "Whatever that witch pays you, I will give you twice." He picked at the shawl Julie had pulled tightly about her bare throat. "And lovely clothes we would have for you, suitable for such a lovely body as yours."

Margaret broke into his crooning with a harsh cry. "Would you clothe her in lashes like that one?" she asked bitterly. "Take your hands off my girl and reach for your purse. Quickly," she ordered, as his glance lingered lovingly on Julie.

Margaret drew Julie from the place with a flurry of skirts, her face set in anger.

"What happened to her?" Julie asked. "How did she get so terribly hurt?"

"Bridewell," Margaret said bitterly. "She was taken for a whore to Bridewell and punished with lashes. It is the law of men. And fine women and men go to watch this sport as an amusement. That loathsome parody of a man!"

175

"But at least he wanted to help her," Julie said. "He called for you to heal her."

Margaret stopped in her tracks and stared at Julie. "I never forget that you are a lady, my dear, but I do forget how little you know of the world. He is only having her mended because she is still young and brings a high price. It was he himself who sent her out whoring even as he wishes to send you. Mark me, the only reason he pays for her healing is to speed the time until she can hold the weight of a rutting man again."

After such days as that, Julie did not wonder that Margaret seemed to grow lean and gaunt before her very eyes. She only wondered that the old woman could smile at all with such knowledge lodging behind her fine eyes.

But as Mark had told her at the first, Margaret had patrons from the finest houses in London too. Late one afternoon, a great hammering at the door startled Margaret and Julie from their chairs. When she had read the note that the tiny black page handed her, Margaret reached for her cap and shawl. Then she turned and stared at Julie thoughtfully.

"I don't know, my dear, if you should come along for this." In the silence of her thought, came the loud banging of Kit slamming about in the kitchen preparing tea. At the sound, Margaret shook her head. "What is to do must be done," she said dryly. "Get your cap and shawl and come along. Never mind the pattens, we will travel in style tonight."

When they had been seated in an ornate carriage, the driver whipped the horses to a lather. As he cursed the beasts through the darkning streets, Margaret spoke softly to Julie.

"We go to the childbed of Her Grace, the viscountess," she explained. "This is the fifth time she had been brought to bed with child and only two survive—both girls. Two boys were born still, the first with a drunken doctor and the second with a midwife so filthy that if the child had drawn breath he might well have expired from the fumes. I don't do this as a regular thing, but the viscount is a friend of my old master's son, and I long ago promised to try to save a son for him."

Julie struggled to breathe in the close air of the bouncing carriage. Against the clattering of the carriage, she heard another medly of noises, the anguished cries of her mother that strange night, the rush of feet along the hall and stairs, and

176

finally, the crude voice of Joseph as he shook her awake. "The old woman and her brat are both dead." Dead. Dead. Dead.

She and Margaret were received into the grand house not as servants but as saviors. The viscount himself, a slender young man in immaculate white breeches with scarlet rosettes at his knees, met Margaret in the hall and took her hands in his with great emotion.

"God speed with you, Dame Curlew," he said. "I depend on you for more than life."

Julie was blinded at the scene in the room beyond. Candles blazed in great profusion along the walls. Great masses of flowers perfumed the air, and the glint of silver and crystal was everywhere about the room. The viscount's guests stood like poised dancers in a tableau. One of the older men spoke to his companion in a voice that carried easily to where Julie stood.

"Look at the wench there," he advised his companion. "If she is as clever as she is appealing, an estate will be secured this night."

The other man stared over the rim of his glass. "The old dame is famed for her skill. God pray it is enough or Edward stands fair to be ruined."

Confused by this talk, Julie fled after Margaret up a great, curved stairway, past the austere faces of lords and ladies staring blindly at each other across the blaze of light. Passing a door in the hall, Julie noticed it was ajar. Two small faces peered out at her. As she paused, the taller child, a girl of about six, stepped forth and caught Julie by the skirt. Her small face was reddened from weeping and her lips trembled as she whispered to Julie, "You will save maman, will you not?"

Julie knelt and laid her hands on the child's arms. She felt the child's flesh tremble through the sheer sleeves of her nightdress.

"We will do all that we can," Julie promised. "And for the child too."

"Of course," the girl said dully, "for the child too." Then she pulled herself away and returned to her sister.

The woman stirring on the white, ruffled bed looked much older than her husband. Her face was creased with pain and Julie felt a dull animal flatness as the viscountess turned her

177

eyes to them. As Margaret moved about, giving swift orders to the servants who milled about the room, Julie drew near the woman and reached for her hands.

Sweat stood in rounded drops on the woman's face. A great contortion, like a massive fist gripping her invisibly, moved the mountain of her belly. The woman gripped Julie's hand like a metal vise. "Help me," she breathed, when the vast contortion was passed. "Oh God, help me and my son."

Julie could not have spoken had her life depended on it. Instead, she touched her hands with a fragrant oil and began to press the woman's throat and shoulders with those fine, strong movements that Margaret had taught her. Julie felt the woman's muscles loosen under her grasp. The pregnant woman closed her eyes. Julie watched the viscountess's tears seep down from under the closed lids and become mingled with the sweat that streamed along her neck. Margaret directed Julie as the labor grew more violent and its pains were coming closer together. Julie bared her arms and rubbed the woman's legs with all her strength to loosen the muscles that jerked and quivered from the pressure of the coming child. Then the viscountess gave that cry that was more a shriek than a human sound. Julie saw the child burst from her body in a storm of blood. Julie had to turn away as Margaret seized the child. Her heart was frantically assaulted by mingled joy and anguish.

There was a silence as if all breath had stopped in the room. The mother fixed her terrified gaze on Margaret. No person moved until the sound came, a small, pitiable rasp that grew suddenly lustier until it filled the room, like the cry of an enraged cat.

The pain seemed forgotten. The viscountess's face contorted with joy. "It lives," she moaned. "The babe lives."

Then Margaret drew near, holding the infant up for the mother to see. "He lives," she corrected softly. "And a bonny strong boy he is too."

"Thank God," the mother moaned. "We are saved."

When it was over, Margaret and Julie were drawn into the parlor and begged to toast the new heir. The viscount himself seemed unable to believe his fine success. "A son," he repeated with delight. "A living male heir." He pressed Julie into a fine brocade chair and handed her a glass of port that glowed as red as his wife's blood.

"What day is this?" he asked, stupid with joy. "We shall toast this day and my son."

Julie held the glass to her lips only to find that she could not swallow. The word had passed along the street, and the bell rang furiously as neighbors and friends came to congratulate the new father. Julie, silent in her chair, heard their laughter and talk numbly, remembering only the anguish of the woman upstairs and the agony with which this celebration had been bought.

"I must away within the hour," she heard the new father tell a friend in a confidential tone.

"Surely not this night," his friend protested.

"But she is expecting me," the viscount insisted.

"Caution advises that you send a messenger with an apology," his friend said wryly. "To hear tales of your sojourn tonight would not loosen your father-in-law's purse strings, I wager."

The viscount cursed softly in agreement and turned to move among his other guests.

There was talk of the market and a ship lost in a storm off the Irish coast; someone inquired of a new coffee house and another reported a record profit on a shipment of slaves to the colony of Virginia. Then a man wearing ice blue and leaning against the fireplace spoke up. "Is tomorrow the day that the Blue-eyed Giant comes to trial?"

"I hope so," another man sighed. "I am sick to death of hearing about him. My wife and her friends go daily to throw flowers to him in the press yard. A fine figure of a stud he must be."

"When was he brought in?" someone asked. "I was out in the country and only just heard he was nabbed at last."

"Four weeks ago this night they carried him into Newgate in chains," the man in blue replied.

Their voices faded to a soft buzzing in Julie's ears. She clung to the stem of her glass fiercely, afraid that it would fall from her hand. "Four weeks ago this night."

She heard Margaret's voice and roused to find her friend's hand on her arm.

"You must excuse us now," she heard Margaret tell the viscount. "This is the first birth my helper has assisted with, and I think it has taken a heavy toll of her."

179

Julie felt herself being wrapped in her shawl and led dumbly from the house to the carriage.

"You came home in style," Mark commented, watching at the door as they were helped from the carriage.

"It is in thanks for many things," Margaret said mildly. "A fine woman will not be put aside for failing to secure sons, a viscount will hold his entail into another generation, and just incidentally, a child is born."

Margaret stayed to help Julie undress and insisted on brushing her hair loose for the night. When Julie lay quietly on her pillow, Margaret apologized again, with great contrition.

"I had no idea how much of a strain this would be on you dear child. You will forgive me?"

Julie shook her head. "It is not that, Margaret," she insisted. "I am glad I was there. I am only tired this night." Then she asked softly, "Tell me, Margaret, how long since I was burned?"

"It was four weeks ago this very evening," Margaret said.

Julie nodded and turned her head away, feeling the heaviness in her chest stir at the movement. So this grief had come to her the very night that Antoine had been borne in chains to Newgate.

"I should have known," she whispered to the empty room. "I should have known."

Chapter Twenty-Four

As the weeks passed Margaret found herself caught in a painful inner conflict about Julie. She could see the girl's hopes failing steadily with each day of disappointment, she could hear through the bedroom wall the muted rhythm of Julie's nightime grief. Yet as earnestly as Margaret wished for Julie's happiness, she secretly dreaded the day when she would lose the companionship and help of the lovely girl.

For Julie had unfolded in Margaret's understanding like a slow convoluted flower that revealed new shades of color with each opening petal. In the beginning, Margaret had accepted her for what she seemed to be, a surpassingly beautiful young lady who had fallen on hard times through no fault of her own. The girl's clevernesses could be laid to good early training. A girl of her estate needed to acquire good needle skills, and some authority with numbers, a mastery of the arts of the kitchen, and the ability to organize her time. All these aptitudes were important for the day she would become mistress of a great house.

But how could one explain her aptitude with the sick, and her interest in the healing of disease, her almost truculent courage in attacking the filthiest problems of the healer with impassive gentleness?

Margaret well knew that most girls of Julie's class would have swooned or grown hysterical at many of the tasks that Julie had helped her perform with only a quiet word of encouragement to the patient.

But there were darker mysteries too. Julie seemed unconscious of the fact that even gowned like a common drab her passage turned heads from one end of London to the other. Only a woman whose heart was fully abandoned to love would fail even to notice the open flirtations of such various men.

Yet she had said that she was neither pledged nor married. Margaret was most of all concerned by the secret knowledge that had come to her by the chance of Julie's being burned by Kit. That night, as Margaret had bared Julie's body to minister to her painful burns, she had been aghast. There was only one way to explain the deep, raw wounds that were barely beginning to heal along the girl's thighs and belly. They were the unmistakable claw marks of a violent man, as were the bruises on her fine, full breasts and the marks of teeth along her shoulder.

As this mysterious and unhappy girl abandoned her hope of help from her old friend, Margaret decided to take unto herself the role of provider. She began to lay aside a store of money in a special place for Julie. It was not a gift, she told herself. Julie earned every guinea of it with her unflagging service by Margaret's side. Margaret alone knew how many extra shillings had been added to her fee in gratitude for the skill of her gentle assistant.

By late June, when Margaret and Julie, by some unspoken mutual agreement, had ceased even to mention the possibility of help, word finally came from Henry Furlong.

181

Margaret and Julie were returning from a long afternoon of calls about the city. Margaret, whose strength had visibly failed during the past weeks, nodded her thanks as Julie took the key and unlocked the front door for her. Trump, as always, set up a great yapping when he heard them enter. But in that moment between the opening of the door and the sound of his sharp bark, a strange sound had come from the kitchen. Margaret and Julie stopped in the doorway to exchange puzzled glances.

Kit's rippling laughter had been unmistakably set against the deeper, stronger laughter of a man's voice.

Without stopping to remove her hat, Margaret dumped her packet of cures on a chair and sailed towards the kitchen with Julie close behind. Trump, who had been waddling to meet her, was spun about by her skirts and sent rolling into a corner with a sharp yelp.

As Margaret reached the kitchen door, a young man scraped to his feet hastily, nodding vigorously. Kit, her face flushed with pleasure, also jumped to her feet with a guilty start.

"He's from the butcher, mistress," Kit said breathlessly. "He comes with a goose for you."

The young man, still nodding, lifted a great goose from the table and thrust it at Margaret like a peace offering.

"I ordered no goose," Margaret said sharply, eyeing the well-bled, white flesh of the bird and gauging what price such a fine fowl would command.

"A gentleman ordered it for you," the butcher's boy explained. "He picked it out himself, special. He said he was 'debted' to you and wanted nothing but the best to send you as a gift."

Margaret relaxed visibly and Julie laughed. "Something new in the style of a grateful patient gift," she said.

"And did this gentleman leave his name with you?" Margaret asked.

The boy shook his head and laid the goose back down on the table where he and Kit had been sharing tea. "He most specially sent this note, ma'am. That's why I stayed on, you see." He slid a glance at Kit. "I was told not to leave the goose until I could put this note into your very hand." He fished in his pocket and withdrew a square of paper much the worse for having been pressed inside his breeches.

Margaret studied the unbroken seal on the note and then slid it into her own pocket. "Your master will be wondering what has got you," she said more genially. "Here's a penny for your pains." Then she added wryly, with a glance at the table. "I hope the time did not lie heavy on your hands."

"Oh no, mistress," he said hastily, backing towards the door. Then he flushed and looked over at Kit again. "Quite to the contrary," he said. "To the contrary."

As Kit followed the young man to fasten the door behind him, Margaret drew the note from her pocket. After studying the seal for a moment, she broke it and began to read the words slowly, her lips moving silently as her eyes moved along the lines. Julie conscious of the gratitude that followed Margaret's ministrations, smiled fondly at her and then went along to her room. She was hanging up her street clothes when Margaret came to the door.

When she turned to see her friend's face, Julie knew at once that something was amiss. She watched as Margaret closed the door behind her with great care and then sank into the chair as if to compose herself.

Margaret looked suddenly older and tired.

"Is something wrong?" Julie asked.

"Quite to the contrary, as Kit's young man would say," Margaret mustered a weak smile. "That goose was a very clever dodge. Your friend the banker sent word of his plan by that innocent little ruse."

Julie stared at her in disbelief. "Henry Furlong?" she asked, shaking her head. "I had given up hope—"

Margaret nodded. "As had I, but we both misjudged him. He has been abroad and dared not trust your need to anyone else. Here, read his message for yourself."

The heavy paper crackled as Julie spread it open. A faint sadness came at the sight of his handwriting. Such simple notes she had once received written by that hand. "My good wife and I are so grateful for the gift of the berry jam." Such as that. However this was not a note but a carefully written letter.

Greetings, My Good Madame,

Urgent business across the water has kept me from London this month past. I fear that you and our friend have lost faith in me by not hearing. I have risked that

183

misadventure rather than put this business into other hands.

The merchant named below is famed for his honest dealings and a discreet tongue. He avoids all pawned property and stolen goods and can be trusted in all. He has been told that a lady of high birth has a family piece to sell. He often performs such services for gentlefolk. The trinket is to be taken to him this night at his shop. He will appraise it on sight and give its honest price in gold to your messenger.

The country woman and her son are still about. Choose your messenger carefully.

My wife and I send dearest wishes to you and our friend. Godspeed.

Below, in careful script, was the merchant's name and the place where his shop was to be found.

"Tonight," Julie breathed, feeling a suddenness of shock at the thought.

Margaret nodded absently.

"Could I go?" Julie asked.

Margaret shook her head vigorously. "It is clear that he still fears greatly for you. He must know best."

Julie started to ask what messenger but the words were unnecessary. Margaret shrugged and asked. "Who else but our Mark?"

Julie sighed. Poor Mark. It was always Mark that came to her aid and defense. And to what end? There was no way she could either reward or repay the painful devotion that he yielded to her with every glance.

"It isn't fair," she said quietly.

"Fair is an exception, not a rule," Margaret told her.

From the back of the big wall cupboard, Julie drew out a heavy woolen gown she had not worn since her flight to London. With Margaret watching, she slit the fine line of stitches along the hem of the dress and withdrew the ruby circlet. She spilled the gold-linked chain of fine stones into Margaret's hand without a word.

"God's blood," Margaret cried, staring down at the jewels. "This is not a trinket but a king's ransom. When you said you had some jewelry I had no idea—"

184

"Then it will be enough to buy me passage to the Carolinas?"

Margaret laughed softly. "And back again and there again and the return. A thousand pounds would be my guess, a thousand pounds at the least." Then with a strange grimace she held up her hand in warning.

Margaret rose swiftly and moved towards the door. Julie closed her fist tightly about the jewels that Margaret thrust at her. With a quick wrist, Margaret flung the door open to find Kit's face near pressed against her own.

The girl jumped back with a frightened cry.

"What carrying on is this?" Margaret challenged the girl. "What brings you to skulk at doors and burrow at keyholes?" Then, as suddenly as her anger had flared, it seemed to flow away into a chuckle. She laid her hand on the terrified girl's shoulder and caressed it. "My Lord what a fright you gave me appearing at the door before my face. Forgive my shouting at you. I must be overtired to have so short a temper."

Then she turned towards Julie with a smile. "Sukey and I were sitting here gossiping about the man who sent the goose. A viscount he is, with clothes that would set a peacock to envy. And that house of his. I was just telling Sukey here that I wager he has spent a fortune on furnishing alone—a thousand pounds at least, that's what I would wager. A thousand pounds at least."

Kit's eyes slid from Margaret to Julie suspiciously. Then Margaret caught the girl's arm with her own. "I expect you came to get some help with tea." Then she turned back to Julie.

"Kit and I will go down together. Do get yourself dressed and come along. We must celebrate that great goose that His Lordship has sent to our table."

As their footsteps faded on the stair, Julie let herself down with a great sigh of relief. Had it worked? Had Margaret fooled the girl with her false tales of their conversation? Or had Kit heard too much to be put off by such a ruse?

Mark ate with his usual meager appetite, sipping his tea absently, drawing more sustenance from Julie's face than from the plate before him.

Julie herself was fidgety. She felt that Kit was only partly

185

fooled if at all. There was a slyness in Kit's face, and she seemed uncommonly quiet as she watched first Margaret's face and then Julie's with a speculative stare.

Mark did show some proper respect for the size and excellence of the goose. He listened with nodding interest to Margaret's tale of the birth of the viscount's son and how the house was so handsomely furnished. Caught by her friend's fever to be convincing, Julie herself leaped to describe the cradle they had prepared for the child, how it had been draped with the finest French lace and woven with ribbons. Kit remained as silent as ever, only staring at them with that strange look that belied the words.

"Our Kit here made a conquest today," Margaret said with a teasing laugh. "We returned to find a butcher's boy tongue-tied with ardor over herself here."

A faint smile twitched at Kit's mouth. Then she tossed her head with a sly look at Julie. "There are some about who like the red-headed wenches," she said with a haughty laugh.

At Mark's snort of derision, she sank again into her sullen, watchful silence.

Julie insisted on helping Kit clear and clean up in order that Margaret might be able to speak to Mark alone. Kit accepted this help with such poor grace that Julie's apron was sodden with splashed water by the time Mark returned to the kitchen.

Kit was quick to note the sober expression on his face. "What's up with you?" she asked. "You look the death."

"The death indeed," he said hotly. "I only forgot an errand and must go out when I would rather stay here at home."

"I'll go with you for company," Kit offered swiftly.

"I wouldn't walk with you in the kennel," he told her curtly.

"And I wouldn't go to court with you, if you must know," Kit said, wiping her hands. "I've a promise of my own to keep tonight in any case."

"The butcher boy?" Mark sneered.

"And so if it is?" Kit asked. "He's a red-blooded buck who's not mooning above his station." Even as she spoke, she tugged her shawl from the hook and was at the door. "Tell mistress I will be back early enough."

"You best tell her yourself," Mark called after her. But she was gone, disappeared into the dark that lay beyond the single lantern outside the door.

"Feisty wench," he muttered, with an apologetic glance at Julie. "She's in a great hurry to come to some bad end."

Chapter Twenty-Five

With Kit gone from the house and Julie off in her own room upstairs, Margaret drew Mark into the small parlor. She checked carefully that no gap in the drapery might allow a view into the room from the outside.

"Give me your right shoe," she said, holding out her hand.

Mark watched her cut a careful slit into the wide flap of his shoe just above the buckle. Frowning intently, she worked her finger into the opening until it was wide and deep enough to contain the whole of her finger. Then she smiled up at him, "Make no mind about the damage, Mark. You will have new shoes for letting me do this. It is only for security."

Mark never saw what was in the packet. He did not even see from what place she produced it. He only knew that suddenly Margaret was holding a small packet of what appeared to be silk in her hand. In the next moment, the packet had disappeared into the flap of his shoe which she handed back to him.

"There," she said. "See how that fits."

He slid his foot into the shoe gingerly. The contents of the package lodged in behind the buckle, pressing a little on the top of his foot.

"I feel it there," he told her.

"Enough that you would limp when walking?" Margaret asked.

He tried his weight on the shoe again, stamping his foot lightly. Then he shook his head. "I would not like to go all across London this way," he admitted. "But for an hour or so it would be fine."

Margaret nodded with satisfaction and rose. "It will be far less time than that," she assured him. "But limping would give away to a careful watcher that you had somewhat hidden there."

"My stride will be even," he assured her.

Looking at him, she was afflicted with a sudden rush of painful emotion. "Do take care, dear boy," she said in a voice with a hint of tears behind it. "You have told me you would be discreet for me?"

"You could trust me with your life." He felt his own throat pained from the conflict he read in her face.

He read the address she had written out for him. "I know that lane," he told her.

"And you can repeat the man's name to me again?" Margaret asked.

He said the name carefully, remembering the morning at the bank when Mr. Furlong had asked him to do the same kind of thing.

"You are only to say that this is the package that your lady had sent. You are not to give him your name or let him ask any more of you. If he presses, or is a man who bandies words about to pass the time, you must play the dolt and know nothing." She paused. "A lot of *milady's* tossed into a talk can make any lad sound stupid," she advised with a grin. "I have no doubt you have already learned the uses of appearing stupid."

Mark nodded, and then his face split in a sudden mischievous grin. "Yes milady, I'm sure, milady," he said in the dull, flat tone of a witless street urchin.

It seemed to Mark that her laugh was overmerry for his jest. It was as if her senses were tuned to such a fine pitch that the smallest thing might tilt her on into hysteria.

"We'll have a glass of port together when you return," she promised. Then she turned. "I was near to forgetting this," she exclaimed. She handed him a dark, cloth money belt with laces for fastening it at both ends. "On your return, Mark, you will be carrying more gold than either of us has ever seen in a lifetime. Godspeed."

"You trust me with this errand but not its cause," he reproached her gently, pausing at the door. The pressing of the packet against his foot had already started a small throbbing that rose to his ankle and moved towards his knee.

She laid her hand on his arm. "It is not mine to tell," she confessed.

Sukey, he told himself as he let himself out into the street and saluted the old watch on the corner. What made him think such disloyal things? It was that bitch Kit who had put all manner of suspicions into his head. Without her snake tongue he would never have thought of Sukey as mysterious or be troubled to see in her style and carriage that difference in station that Kit had suggested. If it was for Sukey that he was making this strange night errand, the pain in his foot would be precious to him.

He slid his tongue along his lips and breathed deeply of the foul night air. He was no artist in silver, but only a poor finisher learning to engrave a little, but he could limn in his eye every angle of Sukey's face, how the softness of her cheek turned into a gentle curve that held a pool of shadow at the base of her throat. His mouth imagined the flavor of her warm mouth under his own. Sweet Jesus, perhaps after this night—if the errand had something to do with Sukey, it might mean that Margaret might listen to him about his great desires to court the girl.

He speeded his steps, lighthearted, only to remember his errand. He adjusted his pace to resemble that of an apprentice returning late in order that no footpad would waste an attack on him, figuring that there was not the price of a pint on him from Saturday to Saturday.

When he turned into the lane, the watch rose from his stool, raising his light. Mark nodded to him curtly.

"Milady sends a message." He named the merchant's name clearly in a bold, strong voice. The watch peered at him, shrugged off the hope of a coin, and grumbled back onto his stool.

The shop was down a little hall from the street. A manservant with a broad, flat face left Mark in a plain waiting room that held only a square table with two chairs and a tall candelabra with only one taper lit. Mark waited where he was left, trying not to look about him in case he was being watched. He only stood, staring steadily at the wall in order to be the dolt of a messenger that Margaret had suggested.

At a shuffling sound behind him, Mark turned to face the merchant. From the look of him, one would think that Cromwell still wore his head. The man's clothes were altogether dark. Even his gaiters were black, even though they seemed woven of the finest stuff. Instead of the shoes Mark expected, the man's thin, slightly bowed legs disappeared into woolen slippers that whispered on the floor when he moved.

The keen expression in the man's eyes, and the unsmiling seriousness of his glance belied his old-fashioned, sleepy stance.

"Milady instructed that I bring this to you," Mark said, startled to hear his voice break a little in tone like an unbearded boy. The old man watched silently as Mark removed his shoe and fished the packet from within its lining with trembling fingers. As Mark held the silken pouch in his hand, he was startled by its heaviness. It felt like something loose and disjointed with a series of small heavy knobs. He felt his heart begin to race for no reason, and he handed the packet to the old man swiftly, as if the silk covering was hot to his touch.

The old man nodded and turned away. "Wait here," he said in a gruff voice.

"Where did your lady get this bauble?" the old man asked suddenly, his voice surprisingly cordial. The merchant had moved outside of Mark's line of vision. Feeling that it would be unseemly to turn and watch him, Mark held his stance. By straining his eyes, he could see the old man's figure bent over something red that seemed to glow in his hand in the light of the candle.

"I have no thought of that," Mark admitted in a dull uninterested voice. "Milady only said I should bring it here and take back to her what you would send."

"And do you know how long your lady had had this bauble?" the old man pressed, his voice positively larded with feigned friendliness. Something in the man's tone started a shiver of apprehension along Mark's spine.

"I have no thought of that," Mark repeated dully. "Milady only—"

This time the man broke in. "Yes, yes, I see," he said ,the warmth gone from his voice as suddenly as it had come.

"You wait here until I return," the man said, after a minute. "You might sit if you wish," he added almost grudgingly.

Mark nodded but declined the chair. Instead, he stood in the same spot. After a while he felt himself stirring restlessly from one foot to another. An undefinable sense of peril stirred at him. He had heard the shuffle of the man's slippers down the hall and the muted noise of a servant's call bell. Then a silence too deep to be normal.

That sense of danger stirred Mark from his post. He moved silently to the door and looked down the long hall. He saw a door ajar into a well-lit room. Framed against the light, he saw the old man's figure move towards the hall, motioning silence to someone beyond Mark's line of vision.

With his hands flat against the wall to lighten the weight from the floor lest it creak, Mark slid along the hall towards the outside door. He had eased the door open with only the slightest creak before the old man looked out and saw him. Then the old man's voice was sudden in the hall, strident with command.

"Stop, thief," he shouted. The servant plunged into the hall as Mark slid through the door and slammed it behind him. He was down the stairs and onto the street before the watch could get to his feet. He wielded his stick and started after Mark, but was no match for Mark's speed. As he turned the corner, Mark heard the hue and cry begin. "Thief. Stolen Goods," the old merchant was shouting. "Run for a constable. Citizens, hold that man."

Windows slammed along the streets. A pair of old bawds posted at a corner caught at Mark with their outstretched hands. He felt a sharp pain and heard his clothing rip as he pulled himself free. Running footsteps seemed to be everywhere. His only thought was that he must not lead his pursuers back to Margaret and Sukey.

Into an alley and across a lane he went, then around a strange corner doubling back. He had run a long time before he thought it was safe to slow his pace. His lungs ached from the race, and the scratches where the harridan had clawed at his cheek stung with dried blood. Slowing to a walk, he wiped his face clean and took his bearings. Then he turned and headed toward home, assuming the awkward half-trot of a man late for supper and wanting to be by his own fire.

Only after passing two watches who did not even rise at his steps, did he begin to feel secure enough again to return to Margaret's house without keeping a constant watch about him.

From the corner, he was amazed to see the house ablaze with light. He paused and stared at it thoughtfully. She had said she would wait up and have a glass of port with him when he returned. She expected him to bring gold. There was no gold in the belt about his waist, and why was the house lit

191

like a festival? Perhaps it was because he had been gone so overlong that she was concerned about his safe return and gold she thought he carried.

Even with these assuring thoughts, Mark did not approach the house in his usual direct way. Instead, he circled about and moved carefully along the back wall to swing the back door open into the kitchen.

He did not enter. Instead, he stood outside in the dark listening to the rumble of voices from the room beyond. Then he pushed the door shut and faded back into the dark of the alley.

Chapter Twenty-Six

Once Mark was on his way with the ruby circlet hidden inside his shoe, a pall of waiting seemed to settle upon the house. At Margaret's suggestion, Julie had gone off to her room while Margaret gave Mark his final instructions about the delivery of the jewelry. He would not be gone long, Margaret had assured Julie. An hour perhaps, the older woman had said, maybe a little longer.

Julie tried to force her mind to the handiwork in her lap. She loved the design, which showed a sinuous dragon of red and gold which wound itself through a glade of riotous spring flowers. She tried very hard to concentrate on the work, even to the point of setting herself a certain goal. She picked a special wreath of flowers and told herself that she would have them finished, with the last knot tied, by the time Mark had finished his errand and returned home.

It was no use. She could not keep her mind on the swirling leaves of the climbing vine or trace with her whole mind the curl of the flower petals. When she had made two mistakes and had to withdraw the silk threads, she laid the work aside.

Henry Furlong was a wise and careful man. If this plan had not been the best one, he would have chosen another. Julie dug in the pocket of her apron and took out his letter to read again.

She tried to imagine his voice reading the words, his careful tones describing the strategy for selling the jewels without her name or face being seen. It would go well, she promised herself. It would go so well that there would be enough money for her to buy Antoine's freedom from Newgate. Once that was done, the two of them could go to the colonies together. Margaret herself had said that every judge had a price. And even if the judge would not release him for money, he need only ask to be transported, she would either pay his fare or pay the bondsman's fee on the other shore.

She set the candle high and sat down before the small glass. Absently, she loosed her hair and began to comb it for the night. As it fell on her bare shoulders, she shivered. Antoine had liked to catch his hands in the fullness of her hair, gently pulling her head back until her throat was exposed to his searching lips. She bit her lips painfully at the surge of painful desire that possessed her. Her passion for Antoine was like that dragon that moved so tenuousley through the flowered wood. No matter how far she was from him, that burning hunger for his nearness moved like a flame through her hours.

He was still at Newgate. The heaviness in her heart convinced her that he had not been freed. As for his sentencing, the hangings on Tyburn Hill were too loudly noised about the city for her to have missed word of the hanging of a highwayman. That event gathered great crowds who went with chairs and lunches and waited many hours to have the best view. He had to be still in Newgate, and she envied the young women of the town who could come and go freely instead of skulking about in disguise as she did. They went with baskets and flowers to Newgate, passing their gifts through the bars of the press yard or getting entry where they could even dine and sup with the prisoners. What she would not give just to see Antoine, even from afar. Just to see his face and know that he fared well and remembered her with longing.

The sound of Margaret's restless steps pacing the rooms below broke into her revery. Once in a while, Thump would complain vigorously of the steady traversing of the rooms, unable to rest when his mistress kept going from window to window searching for Mark among the passersby on the street. The least I can do is share this lonely vigil, Julie thought guiltily.

Fearing that Mark might return suddenly and find her im-

193

modestly dressed, Julie pulled the coarse blue dress over her delicate underthings. While her hair was still loose on her shoulders and her slippers in her hand, she ran down to find her dear friend Margaret.

The older woman did not hear her approach in her stockinged feet. As Julie reached the door of the kitchen, she saw Margaret stop and lean against the door lintel as if for support. Her face was twisted with pain. As Julie watched, the older woman pressed hard on her lower belly with a white hand as if to crush some gnawing viper that tormented her.

"Margaret," Julie asked in quick concern. "What is giving you such pain?"

The forced smile and the shrug with which Margaret straightened did not fool Julie. "I must have eaten overmuch," Margaret told her lightly. "My food lies heavy in me."

Julie crossed to her.

"I would not challenge your word lightly, Margaret, but I think it is more than that."

Margaret stared at Julie with that hard, straight look that Julie remembered from Mary's face.

"What will you do now?" Margaret asked with no hint of warmth in her face. "Will you throw me down like a calf and examine? Is the helper to a healer become a healer herself?"

Julie dropped her eyes and froze where she stood.

"Forgive me," she said quietly. Then she looked up at the thinness of Margaret's face, the way the sleeves of her dress hung loosely about the prominent bones of her older friend's wrists. "It seems to me that you would not speak so harshly to one who loves you if you did not have something you wished to turn me away from."

"Fah," Margaret snorted, turning towards the hearth so that Julie could not see her face. "I am cross-tongued because of those young people. Mark might have been delayed by any wild thing in the streets, a band of Mohawks, a crowd of ruffians. Or even a fire. But where is that wench Kit? She knows better than to jabber by another fire this late. And she also knows that I will not send you battering on kitchen doors for her as I might send Mark."

"They will both be along," Julie assured her, her mind still puzzling the pain that her friend was so valiantly trying to hide. "Have you a warmth like fever? Is there a swelling?"

"We will brew tea to pass the time," Margaret said calmly. "I will tell you how it is to be old, to have pains in the belly and shoulder and shortness of breath. To have a body that you have worn in carelessness begins to collect its debts. The disease is time itself, Julie and time alone cures it."

"At least let me handle the hot water," Julie insisted, taking the heavy kettle from her friend. She filled the pot and was turning to replace the kettle on the hob when the hammering came at the front door.

Even with a cloud of steam about her face Julie noted the look of raw fear that changed her friend's face. "You finish with that," she told Julie hastily. "I'll see what ruffian has the gall to bang at a decent person's door at this hour."

Through the open door, Julie caught the glimpse of the uniform beyond Margaret. The constable was facing Margaret on her own threshold, and she saw Margaret brace her arm across the doorway to forbid him passage. Then she saw that the constable was not alone. Another figure was behind him, a slender man in dark clothing whose wig seemed hastily donned. She saw the light angle on the wide buckles of his shoes as he leaned forward.

"We are seeking one Mark Hatter of this house."

"There is no Mark Hatter here," Margaret said flatly.

"We know that to be false," the constable said in a tired voice. "We know that he lives here with one Margaret Curlew, that he is apprenticed to a silversmith and was abroad this night."

"He may live here," Margaret said sharply. "I never said he didn't. But there is no Mark Hatter here now."

The older man frowned at the constable. "From the speed he left my shop he could have been here and back twice."

"Then you must come back another time to see him," Margaret said, trying to shut the door.

The constable would have none of it. "I have no charge against the young man," he assured her. "This gentleman needs to ask him some questions, that's all."

"He is not here," Margaret repeated. "If there is no charge, I suggest your companion return in the daylight and ask his questions sensibly."

"We have only her word that he is not here," the man reminded the constable.

A quick flare of anger flushed Margaret's face. She threw

195

the door wide. "Come in then. Look for yourself. Search every room if you wish. There is no young man here."

The constable was undaunted by her tone and entered stolidly.

Julie caught her breath sharply. The constable mounted the stairs into the upper rooms, leaving the rooms lit as he left them. Julie stood in the doorway afraid to look about or move. She was sure that she had heard the furtive opening and closing of the door behind her. "Please let Mark have heard enough to hide," she thought desperately.

Then the constable was moving down the hall towards her. She stepped aside to let him pass. He stopped when he drew abreast of her and stared at her with something like astonishment as he swept her with his eyes. Julie's hand flew involuntarily to her hair loose upon her shoulders and breast and remembered with sudden embarrassment that her slippers lay forgotten by the fire in the kitchen.

"My girl was about to prepare for sleep when you disturbed us," Margaret said acidly.

The constable flushed and stamped on into the kitchen where he lit every corner before turning back.

Julie was conscious that the darkly attired man had studied her with his full attention ever since entering the house. When the constable returned to the hall, the other man spoke to Julie for the first time.

"Is this milady?" he asked with a wry tone to his voice.

Margaret glared at him, edging closer to the girl.

"What kind of a question is that?" she challenged hotly. "This is a child from the country who has been making her home here with me. Milady indeed! What kind of a lady would be hobnobbing in the kitchen with the likes of me—and half-barefoot too?"

"Stranger things," the man muttered, his eyes still shrewd on Julie's face. "Enough of this babble with women, constable. Let us to the fact of stolen goods."

The phrase even caught Margaret off guard. "Stolen goods!" she exclaimed. "What is this of stolen goods. Not Mark—"

Seeing her weave a little for support, Julie moved swiftly to her side and slid an arm beneath her elbow.

"My friend is not well," Julie said sternly. "Mark Hatter is not here. Please state your business and be gone."

196

The old man broke into a short, dry fit of laughing.

"Did you hear this, constable? Is this then the way a child from the country talks, to take such a tone and with such an accent and to her betters too? What do you think of the style of this country girl, constable?"

The constable was clearly confused. He looked from Julie to the merchant and back, at a loss as to how to begin.

"The girl is right," Margaret said tiredly. "State your business and be gone."

"The business is a neck circlet of fine rubies," the old man said, his eyes careful on her face. "These stones are joined by hand-crafted links of the finest gold. There are seventeen rubies in the piece, and each of the links of chain is etched with a fine design like small tongues of flame."

"So?" Margaret asked, her face unreadable.

"This necklace, which I have described in such detail that you might know that there would not be more than one like it in all of England, has been listed on the slate of stolen goods for a very long time. Most owners would have abandoned hope by now, but the owner of this piece is persistent. Each year the reward has been increased for the apprehension of the person who tries to sell it."

Julie dared not breath lest she betray her own thoughts. Stolen. Why hadn't she thought of that? My God, the gold and the jewels must be from a robbery Antoine had made on the highroad.

She opened her lips to speak, but Margaret was too quick for her.

"God help me," Margaret cried. "That I have been taken for such a fool! Do you mean that vicious little man had the gall to pay for my services with stolen jewels? What evil there is in this world. What ruffians."

The old man stared at her. "Then you admit that you were the one who sent that piece to me to be sold?"

"Admit it? Why should I be ashamed?" Margaret challenged him. "Ask any man along these streets. Ask in the coffee houses where the doctors try to sell their wares, ask them who is the healer. There came to me a young man whose wife was heavy with child. Pains came on her while she was in this town, but it was not yet time. They sent her to me that the child might be saved. I cared for her, and she went away still with child."

"And thereby came the jewels?" the constable asked.

Margaret nodded. "He pleaded that he was far from home and had little gold but would pay with that bauble."

"Then you had better be able to name that man and bring him before the magistrate, Sukey Titus, for the jewelry was stolen when murder was done. Whoever sells it is suspect of murder."

"And a natural for the Tyburn tree," the old man added lightly.

Margaret's mouth had dropped at his words. Before she could recover, Julie stepped forward to correct her. "She is not Sukey Titus," Julie said gently. "That is my name, and the necklace is mine. It was given to me by a friend," her voice faltered, "for favors."

The two men exchanged a glance. "This is the story we thought to hear," the old man said, nodding. "And what is all this about the stranger with wife and child?"

"A good woman's attempt to shield me," Julie said.

"Pay no attention to her," Margaret said sternly. "Can't you see that she is giddy and given to lies?"

The men ignored her ruthlessly. The old man's eyes swept Julie again with a look of distaste, from the loose bounty of her hair to her slender stockinged feet. "I suppose you can easily name this man to whom you gave favors."

Julie flushed at his tone and only held her head stiffer. "It would do no good," she told him. "He is dead these many months."

"In that case, you would lead us to his grave," the old man suggested, "and swear on forty Bibles that it was he who gave you this priceless jewel."

"On four hundred Bibles if need be," Julie said firmly.

"Well," the old man was clearly amused. "We have our choice of tales. Fortunately, that is not all we have. We have also the wench who sent us here, who gave us the names of this pack of mysterious folk. Maybe she can clear up whose ruby circlet the prentice brought to my shop."

"What girl is this?" Margaret asked quickly.

The merchant shrugged. "Some red-headed wench who appeared on the street before the prentice was out of sight." He smiled. "A fortunate young woman she is too, for she will be given a handsome award for her pains."

"Kit," Margaret hissed, realizing the game in the instant.

Kit had indeed heard more at the door of Julie's room than she should have. And she had not been fooled by the attempts Margaret had made to cover the story. Instead of lolling by Gertrude's hearth with her usual bundle of gossip, she had followed Mark. She felt her head swelling with fury. Traitor, she thought wildly. Great rivers of blood seemed to course behind her forehead, and she felt herself grow giddy and faint.

"The girl here is trying to protect me," Margaret said weakly. "I am the person you seek."

The constable shook his head. "The Sukey Titus we seek was named as being about twenty, slim of body and dark of hair." He paused and shifted his shoulders a little nervously. "With eyes as yellow as a witch." He turned to Julie. "You'll come along with me, Sukey Titus. The magistrate will hear you in the morning."

Margaret, with her head pumping painfully, managed to struggle to her feet. "But you cannot take her away. You cannot put this child in jail on the ravings of another wench gone mad with jealousy. Leave her in my care and I will swear to have her there at what hour you name."

The old man laughed. "We have already heard what an easy tongue you have for lying, mistress. And besides, there is a reward for the seller of the necklace. One hundred pounds. Are you prepare to put that bond on yourself to bring her in?"

Margaret pulled herself stubbornly erect. Julie saw the quick darting of her hand towards her pained belly, and then her equally swift withdrawal of that sign of weakness. With slow dignity Margaret turned from them and mounted the stairs.

"You might just get yourself shod before we leave," the old man told Julie. "Those dainty green hose of yours will not be improved by the soil of the streets you will walk."

By the time Julie retrieved her slippers from the kitchen, Margaret was descending the stair. She had made a bundle of her apron which hung heavily before her and clinked as she made her way from stair to stair.

She crossed to the old man and dumped a pile of coins into the chair beside him. "There," she said. "Count them. You keep a watch too, constable, and I will write a receipt for you to sign."

"This is irregular," the old man said, his eyes drawn to the gold.

"It was your own suggestion, sir," the constable reminded him. "It was you that named the bond. And after all, you still have the jewels themselves. Even if this wench should flee, you should have twice the hundred pounds for your pains."

The old man shook his head. "Nay. The reward is not for the necklace but for the deliverance of the seller."

"It was yourself that set the bond," the constable said stubbornly. "Count it out and I will see you back to your shop with it."

As the door closed behind them, Julie found herself even unable to thank Margaret for this incredible act of ransom. She simply moved into the older woman's arms to stand silent and anguished against that welcoming breast.

"My child," Margaret said softly, stroking her hair gently. "Do not grieve. You have simply been betrayed by the giver of that gift. You need only to name him, pet, and it will be over."

Then Julie's tears came. "I spoke truly, Margaret," she said, her voice choked with tears. "He is dead. And there is no grave. No grave at all."

Margaret stared at her dumbstruck. When she raised her head, it was to see Mark standing in the doorway, his face twisted with anguish, his great fists knotted at his sides.

"It was Kit wasn't it?" he asked Margaret. "It was Kit who betrayed her."

Margaret sighed and nodded assent.

"It is all my fault," Mark raged. "What a great fool I am. I kept imagining strange shadows moving along the streets. I put it down to my own cowardice. It was that bitch, that mad debased spawn of a whore. I shall kill her. You know that, don't you Margaret? If aught harm comes to Sukey there, I shall kill that bitch with my own bare hands."

PART IV
THE DARK
STRANGER
August, 1722-September, 1722

Chapter Twenty-Seven

During that long night, Julie heard each round of the watch, each stirring among the small birds that nested in the eaves of the house. When dawn showed as a murky glow beyond her window, she abandoned hope of sleep. She could not make her mind accept the day that faced her. Numbly, she bathed herself and, wearing only a sheer, white chemise, stared vacantly at the cupboard where her clothes were stored.

She heard the whining complaint of Trump hauling himself up the stairs and then Margaret's voice at the door calling for her to "open."

"You need a little warmth in you," Margaret explained, entering with a tray balanced carefully on both hands. The pot of strong tea that perfumed the air was accompanied by thick warmed slices of Margaret's whitest bread spread with peach conserve.

With the tray safely on the table, Margaret eased herself into her usual chair. "What had you thought to wear today?" Her voice was matter-of-fact, almost blunt. Julie was grateful for the firmness of her tone, fearing that the faintest hint of sympathy might loose the fluttering in her breast into panic.

"Have you a suggestion?" Julie asked, for all in the world as if they were discussing a party she planned to attend.

"It will be a hard choice," Margaret said mildly. "You must be careful to dress the part of a simple country girl. Yet the more prosperous you appear, the better you will be treated."

Julie turned to her with a wry smile.

"Perhaps I could manage to go both ways at once," she suggested. "That is the way I feel inside."

"Would you like to run away from this?" Margaret asked in a low tone.

"And cause you to lose that great fortune you poured into that man's hands?" Julie was incensed. "Not a chance. I have done nothing criminal. I accepted the circlet in good faith and I do not see how they can dare punish me severely for that."

"It is as well that you feel that way," Margaret admitted. "There have been guards posted on the house all night to prevent you from flying."

"Fools!" Julie snorted, turning again to the closet to rustle angrily among her things. "I have this plain blue gown," she said after a minute. "Perhaps if I wore it with an apron of white and a cap with simple trimmings?"

Margaret nodded. "And it might be well to pull back that fine hair of yours a little more tightly than usual—to give a look of demureness."

With the blue dress dropped over her head, Julie backed up to Margaret for her buttons to be fastened. "Will they let me come back home?" she asked in a small voice.

"God knows," Margaret said glumly. "But we must prepare for any event. If you should be bound over for the Grand Jury, they will put you into Newgate directly."

Julie stood frozen, letting the terror of that word move through her. Newgate Prison. She had thought of little else through the long night, but hearing the word said out plainly like that was a bath of ice to her flesh.

"In the event of the last," Margaret went on stolidly, "you will need an entry fee and some food."

"Food?" Julie asked turning in surprise.

Margaret nodded. "There are three great perils to Newgate," she explained soberly. "The first is the danger of violence from those other depraved souls who will nest there with you. The second is the threat of jail fever which is brought on by filth and the rotten food and foul water of that place."

"And the third?" Julie asked when Margaret's voice trailed off.

"It is the giving way," Margaret said. "You must not let the horror of the place nor the treatment you get enter into your heart and make it dismal. Hope has saved more lives in Newgate than any barrister. You must keep reminding yourself that Mark and I will be doing all we can from the outside. Mark will bring you food and some water to drink and keep yourself clean with. Myself, I dare not come. As inured as this old heart is to pain and suffering, I know that to see

204

you in such a place would be more than I could bear." Her voice broke briefly before she regained her usual firm tone.

"I will send fresh changes of clothes for you. Jail fever is filth fever. Never lift your hands to your lips without washing them, never let anything from that place enter your mouth."

Then Margaret slapped her knee smartly and rose. "Enough talking of the worst. Drink up your tea and eat. Time moves away from us."

Then at the door, with her back to Julie, she spoke quietly. "There will be many questions, my dear. Those men will not let you off as lightly as I did. There are great empty places in your story, and I have left them there out of delicacy. You must have a sturdy tale, easy to remember so that you cannot be tripped up in a lie. Never think of what you are hiding, for it will bring a hesitation to your lips. Your purpose is to survive, to be free to return to us who love you. But think, Julie, think on your story and try to give it more life."

The streets were already raucous with sound when the constable came to the door and called for Julie. The manacles hung loosely from his hand as if he were ashamed to be bearing them. At Margaret's disdainful stare, he thrust them at his companion saying, "There will be no need of these."

For a man of his girth, the constable walked swiftly. Julie found herself growing breathless in her attempt to keep pace with him. The curious stares of the mongers followed them along the street, and a band of small boys, playing at grenadier, shouted and waved their swords and followed them a street or two before losing interest.

After the bright vitality of the street, the dark hall that led to the courtroom was a plunge into night. Julie groped along between her guards to settle into the seat they indicated. There was sound enough here, the drone of low talk from among the lawyers and the rattling of papers and benches as case after case brought new faces out of the great room to approach the bench.

Julie searched the judge's face for hope and found none. His great, florid face was punctuated with heavy, dark brows. Under the white curls of his mammoth white wig, his lips were pulled down in such a disdainful expression that Julie wondered if such a mouth could manage to smile if it wished.

There were so many people, manacled prisoners, and dap-

205

per young barristers, weeping young women with babes at their hips, and stiff-backed merchants scowling impatiently that Julie could not at once absorb the scene. Then her eye fell upon the merchant who had accused her. He stared at her unwinking with an expression of pious triumph about his mouth. Beside him, wriggling self-consciously, was Kit. Her flaming hair was carefully arranged and dabbings of powder had paled the usually rosy contours of her face and throat. Julie dropped her gaze to her lap only to realize that her hands, unbidden, had been pleating the fabric of her apron frantically in a fever of terror.

After what seemed an eternity, Julie heard the name Sukey Titus intoned from the front of the room.

A dapper young barrister leaped to the bench and read the charge against her. A whispering hush fell on the room when he produced the ruby circlet and held it to the light. He stated the facts of the case in the most dramatic manner possible: how the necklace had been stolen from the murdered Frenchwoman Mignon LeFevre, how the messenger of Sukey Titus had attempted to sell it to an honest and innocent merchant who had tracked her down by the aid of an informer.

When Kit was called forward she gave her testimony with her hand on an open Bible, but her eyes strayed to Sukey in triumph.

"And I listened beyond the door to see what was up," she told the court breathlessly. "They was whispering a lot but I heard the words 'a thousand pounds' as clear as you please. That's when I knew for sure there was some mischief afoot.

"Then that Mark Hatter, the prentice that lived there too, was off in the other room for some more whispering, then he made a big to-do about an errand he had to do. I was putting two and two together and decided I'd see for myself what was to be. I just slipped out and waited and glad I am that I did. I was tired of that place anyway, with that Sukey putting on airs and Mark himself mooning around her."

"Then you followed the apprentice clear to his destination?" the attorney prodded her.

She nodded vigorously. "Until he went to that house and stayed in there a long time. The watch kept looking at me, and I was almost to giving up and taking off home when the ruckus started. There was shouting and the cries for the constable, and Mark Hatter came running out and took off, and I just stayed."

Julie closed her mind against the girl's tattling. She vaguely heard the constable's voice testify that the accused, "said Sukey Titus" had admitted the necklace had been hers and she had sent it to be sold.

"There seems little to judge here," the justice commented tiredly. "You have the necklace, the girl admits she had it. Bring the defendent forth."

Julie was grateful for the hand of the guard under her elbow as she approached the bar. The judge's eyebrows rose slightly in something like astonishment as she raised her eyes to his. His question was curt.

"What do you plead?"

"I sent the necklace to be sold," she said.

"Then you plead guilty."

"I did not know that the necklace was stolen goods," she told him. "It was a gift to me and I needed to sell it."

"That is a gift of some value." His tone was sarcastic. "Who was this benefactor of yours."

"A friend," Julie replied.

"And his name?"

Julie paused. "He went by the name Titus."

"The same as your own?"

"Yes, sir."

"And was this Titus a relative of yours?"

"No sir."

"And how did he come to give you this necklace?"

"I was alone, wishing to go to the colonies. He was near death. He gave me this necklace and some gold coins to provide for my welfare."

"And could you tell the court where this man called Titus is buried to support your story?"

"No sir," Julie's voice weakened in spite of her firm resolve.

The judge stared off above her head. "It is passing strange to me that after a man has given you a gift of such value, you would not trouble yourself even to mourn at his services." A titter of appreciation passed among the lawyers gathered near the bench. One man stepped from among them and passed a slip of paper to the justice. He prodded spectacles onto his nose and stared at the paper a moment.

"You are to describe the man Titus to the court."

Julie paused, startled at the order. "He was short of stature," she said, "with light hair, a man of great age. He had been lamed so that he walked unevenly." She raised her eyes to the judge, pleading for his understanding. "He was a gentle man but not handsome to look upon."

The judge turned to the attorney who had passed him the paper. After a whispered exchange, the judge motioned for the attorney to speak.

The attorney bent near Julie with a mocking smile on his lips. Julie's senses were assailed by the heaviness of his perfume. His wig was immaculate, and as he waved the paper in his hand, she caught the glint of jewels on his fingers. She drew back a little from the nearness of his face to her own.

"The man who invaded the home of Mignon LeFevre, who slashed her to ribbons with a sword and escaped taking the ruby circlet from her neck was a tall man. He was a dark-haired man with a courtly bearing. His eyes were blue, and he was known commonly about London as the French Gambler. Do you wish to change your testimony?"

The sense of his words set Julie to trembling. She clasped her hands together tightly to steel herself. Antoine. He was describing Antoine. Not once had it occurred to her that the necklace had been anything but the fruit of his robbery along the highroads. Madame LeFevre . . . the necklace from her throat. Julie's hand flew to her own throat. Finding her voice gone, she shook her head numbly.

The attorney smiled. "It seems she is reminded of some error in her testimony."

Julie shook her head frantically, forcing the words from her anguished throat. "There is no error," she insisted.

"The man who gave me the necklace was short—shorter than I even. He had a limp as I said and fair hair—an ugly man without courtly bearing."

"She lies," the attorney shouted, his face still near her own. "She lies under oath which is a sin in the sight of God and this court." He reached for the Bible and thrust it into her hands again. "Look to your mortal soul, Sukey Titus, and tell us again that this man who gave the necklace to you was a dwarf."

Julie clutched the Bible and raised her eyes to the justice. "Indeed he was a dwarf, your honor, if you would choose

208

that word. I swear by all that is holy that it was he who gave me the necklace and now he is dead."

The bench creaked as the judge shifted his frame.

"She seems very sure of this tale," he told the attorney mildly. "Have you other evidence that she has cause to be held?"

"We have the word of these two," the attorney said. "The merchant to whom the jewels were offered and the constable who heard her admit she sent them for sale. Is it not enough that she had the jewels? She has been caught and admitted to trying to sell property that had been listed as stolen."

When the judge's expression did not change, the attorney grew conciliatory. "I am willing to accept that she did not know the jewels are stolen, but I am unwilling to accept this babble about a dwarf. If she goes free, the last chance to find the brutal murderer of Mignon LeFevre goes with her. Is possible that being confined until the session, under the charge of selling stolen property, her memory might be improved so that the name of that foul fiend would be available to the court?"

The judge frowned and considered a spot on the wall to the left of Julie's head. A fly droned by and lit on the fullness of the judge's white wig. It cleaned its body with its legs, a dark wriggling spot in the sea of pale curls.

When the judge stirred, the fly flew straight up with a whir of complaint. The judge frowned at the attorney and then at Julie.

"Very well, commit her. Next case." His tone was heavy with ennui.

Chapter Twenty-Eight

"Commit her." The judge's words were like a dark hood being lowered over Julie's life. Everything changed. The attendant shoved her roughly back to her place on the bench. The constable's delicacy about the manacles disappeared as he chained her to a heavy, old costermonger who scratched and muttered by her side until the court was dismissed. By the time she heard the gates of Newgate Prison clang shut behind her, her ankles were raw from the rubbing of chains against her tender flesh.

The day that had only been murky with overcast seemed to turn into a festering darkness inside the walls of the prison. Julie and her companion were prodded along dark halls and thrust into a great stone room that seethed with life.

Before the scene even took shape in her mind, Julie felt her throat tighten towards gagging at the stench of the place. The odors of human waste, rotted food, and stale drink struck her all at once along with the sweet, sickly smell that she had learned to associate with a fevered illness.

A room full of eyes turned to her. Once unchained, an old woman scrambled away hailing greetings to someone in the far end of the room. Women of all ages, some of them great with child, a boy who seemed barely past childhood, and a group of men laughing roughly among themselves all stared at Julie who was standing inside the doorway alone and apart.

A man of great age, his face ridged with wrinkles and yellowed with filth, scrambled towards her in a crablike gait. He cackled at her from a gaping mouth in which only a few dark teeth were set like mileposts.

"Chummage," he croaked, motioning for the others to follow. "Such a fine lady. Welcome. Chummage."

Julie, repelled by his nearness, stepped back only to find herself pressed against the wet surface of the stone wall.

"Ow there," a girl called out. "She don't know what you're after. Leave her be. Give her some time."

The old man cackled, louder this time. "Time is what the court gives. We want chummage." He prodded Julie with his finger. "Pay or strip," he ordered.

The girl scrambled to her feet from a straw pallet and approached them. Julie watched her fascinated. She moved like a small, healthy animal. There was a flash of fine, rounded calves as the girl hopped up to stand, her mouth a little agape, to stare at Julie. Julie was astounded at the vibrant color that the girl seemed to radiate about her. Her nose was tip-tilted above a merry mouth, and her dark eyes danced under a cloud of untidy, dark hair. With her fists on her hips, she examined Julie from cap to slipper and then laughed.

"Ow. Ain't you a proper one now? What did they bag such a one as you for?"

Her intense curiosity was disturbed by the old man's jostling at her side. She turned swiftly and laid a hard crack on the old man's head. "Lay off her now, you old boozer," she said curtly. "Give the lady a bit to catch a breath." Then she laughed again, a low ripple that set her full bosoms bobbing above the low neck of her shabby dress. "Not that there's air worth the breathing in this hellhole."

"We've a rule of the house here," she told Julie in a confiding tone. "When you come new, you have to cough up, you either give us your money or we strip you bare. Garnish we call it, or chummage."

Julie opened her palm to show the coins she had left after paying the entry fee. Her voice seemed to come from some unfamiliar place, tight and constrained with terror. "This is all I have," she told the girl. "You are welcome to it."

The old man clawed towards her hand, but the girl slapped him away. "Get your filthy paws off her," she ordered. Then she tapped Julie's hand from underneath so that the coins flew every which way, rolling into hiding under the matted straw of the floor. A great scramble ensued as the prisoners leaped into the fray to retrieve the coins.

The old man, content with one coin, sped to the door and set up a shout. "Brandy. Bring brandy."

"Pretty, ain't it?" the girl asked Julie with an engaging smile. "I'm Ellie, what are you called?"

"Sukey," Julie remembered numbly. "Thank you, Ellie."

Ellie shrugged elaborately. "So for what?" she asked. Then her eyes narrowed with curiosity. "And what's in the packet there?" She eyed the dark cloth purse that Margaret had slid over Julie's arm as the constable led her away.

"I think it's food," Julie said hesitantly. "I haven't looked."

"Then at least you've a friend out there," Ellie said. "Good enough for you." Then she grinned again. "I myself have few enough friends outside this place. My friends took to dancing young and are no more."

At Julie's confused look, the girl explained, "Dancing on a rope, that is being hung on Tyburn Tree." Then with a twinkle of mischief, she rose on tiptoe and assumed a dainty pose.

"Oh ring the bell for Dirty Ellie
Make a posy just for me.

211

From rotten Newgate, foul and smelly,
I shall fly to Tyburn Tree.

"Now tell me that I shouldn't be trodding the boards with my name out front as an actress!"

Her grin was infectious. "Here," she said, shoving the straw about to make a place by herself. "Stay near me now and don't be wandering about." She angled her head towards the group of men who were eying Julie and talking roughly among themselves. "With luck we'll keep them beasts off you."

Turning her back to the room she showed Julie the hilt of a small knife tucked into her waist sash.

"They know that I'll not stand back from changing a cock to a hen with my silver finger here."

The stink of the cheap, raw brandy that her money had bought soon overwhelmed the other smells of the place. The sounds of revelry rose and then finally lessened as the prisoners went from roaring drunkeness into sleep. It was black behind the high, wire-covered window, and Julie, exhausted by the day, slumped on the pallet beside Ellie and closed her eyes.

She was wakeneed from sleep by Ellie's urgent whisper. "Hey there, Suke," she urged. "It's you they want, get up before you be dragged."

Still stumbling from sleep, Julie was seized by the guard and pulled from the room without explanation.

She was shunted along dark halls, past an exercise yard filled with men who stared curiously at her passing. At last she was thrust wordlessly into a small, dark room whose damp walls were partly covered by a sodden drape. A man with his back to her sat at a table playing at cards. The decanter of red wine at his side glowed with the same rich red as his ornate coat. He did not turn nor acknowledge her presence until the guard left, banging the door tight behind him.

Then the man moved suddenly, rising with such alacrity that his bench tumbled over in a great clatter on the floor. He crossed the room in swift steps and seized her arms with both his own.

"Julie," he cried, his voice heavy with emotion. "My God, my God, Julie."

She stared at him, at the snowy mound of elaborate ruffles at his throat, and at the clear, fine eyes. Her legs went suddenly limp beneath her, and she fell into his arms with a strangled cry of disbelief.

Giles. Giles Urban. And he was holding her close even as he had when they were children, his head buried in the fragrance of her hair and his voice murmuring endearments against the flesh of her throat.

Chapter Twenty-Nine

This is a world within a world, Julie thought as she watched Giles transform the room before her eyes. After a discreet rap, two men entered bearing fresh linen for the table. Before they left, both hot and cold food brightened the table which was brilliant with tapers. There were sweet red-skinned plums and bunches of juicy grapes, a well-browned capon whose crisp skin covered succulent, white flesh which had been delicately seasoned with onion and sage. The carafe of wine was refilled, and a fat loaf with cheeses waited the knife.

Giles placed her on the bench beside himself and chose the choicest morsels for her plate. Having not tasted food since dawn, Julie ate with a good appetite. Gile's appetite seemed less for the food than for her as he sat as if bewitched, devouring her with his eyes, unable to keep his hands from her person, lifting a curl with a hesitant finger, laying his jewelled hand over hers with great tenderness.

"Julie, my love," he murmured. "I thought to die when you were brought into the court this morning. My first fear was that those miserable Duvall people—" Then remembering, he was hasty to apologize. "Forgive me that she and that lout go by your name. But I feared that they had found you and brought you to to trial for murder." He shook his head. "I told myself that I was dreaming. That by some chance of fate two faces had become that beautiful, two sets of eyes could glow with that glint of pure gold. I waited trembling beyond the room to hear your case. Can you imagine what my thoughts were when you answered to that other name?"

Julie had to laugh. "Because of those miserable Duvalls as you call them, I am forced to hide under new identity."

He nodded. "And wise it was too because all the court has grown to know that name. The father, your uncle, is in the debtor's prison on Fleet Street, and they stay nearby in some of those miserable hovels that debtor's families use. But how my heart dropped, thinking they had succeeded in bringing you to trial. How did that murder accusation come to be?"

Julie, warmed by the wine and strengthened by the warm meal, looked up at him with a smile. It was as if they were home again, young and carefree with Bonbon at their side, and surrounded by the sweet smells of meadow flowers instead of the rank stench of the gaol. She grinned with such mischief that the dimple came swiftly in her cheek.

"Did I not tell you what beasts those people were, Giles Urban? And did you not lecture me like a cleric for my pains?"

He caught her hand and bent her fingers inward to form a cup which he lifted to his lips and kissed tenderly. "You told me and I was soon to learn, my dear," he admitted ruefully. "Too soon to learn."

At his insistance, she told the whole story. She remembered him only as going up to Oxford with law in view. Now he was altogether the lawyer, a sober listener and quick when the question was needed. Oftentimes as she spoke, a furious, dark shadow crossed his face, and she heard a muffled curse beneath his breath.

It was only when she came to tell him of her rescue from Joseph's wrath, that her words faltered. His eyes were swift and searching on hers

"And who was this that drew you from the snow?" he asked.

"A stranger," she replied.

"But not a stranger forever, surely Julie," he rebuked her.

"Let me tell the story my own way," she pleaded.

He shook his head. "That will not be good enough I fear. Since this morning I have been busy all the day with your affairs. I have looked into the case of the necklace that you are accused of trying to sell. How much of the story of Mignon LeFevre do you know, my dove?"

"Only bits and pieces," she confessed, relieved that he was

214

so distracted by fondling her hand that he did not see the flush of color rise to her cheeks.

Releasing her, he strode back and forth across the narrow room, sometimes pausing to make a point to her with a fine gesture, sometimes deep in thought with his hand at his own forehead. How distracting it was to watch him. This was her Giles, her own dear, dear Giles who had once made such sport of the fops of London. How richly he was dressed. How professional and wise he seemed as he told the story to her, now and then darting a searching glance at her face.

"After a long and bitter marriage to the nobleman LeFevre, she fled France with her lover. They settled in England where all went well for a time. Then her lover, who is known as a man of great rages, fell afoul of English law by duelling. He left her alone with only a manservant and fled the country to escape a prison term. For a long time she waited like a virgin, but then there came a man."

"How do you know all this?" Julie asked, wishing not to believe all the details he threw into the story.

"I told you," he reminded her impatiently. "I have done nothing else but search out this story since you were taken from the courtroom." He waited, and when she stayed silent, he went on.

"Her lover returned to England, but he did not make himself known. It is said that his jealousy of Mignon was as great as his passion for her. He spied on the house and was rewarded by seeing a tall, young man come and go at all the strange hours of night. He discovered this young man to be a famous gambler who wreaked havoc among the gaming tables of the city with his devilish luck at cards. The night he chose to confront them with their guilt, the gambler turned violent. He murdered the woman with a broadsword and left with her jewels, escaping with the aid of the manservant."

"That is a long time ago now, Julie. But his rage still burns like a new-lit fire. He wants blood. He would prefer the blood of the young man who put horns on his head and then robbed him of his love, but lacking that, he will settle for your death."

"Why?" Julie asked. "Why me?"

Giles leaned towards her, his eyes studious of her face. "He thinks, in fact he swears, that you are the love of that blue-eyed gambler. Only you can lead him to that man."

215

"The man who gave me the necklace is dead," Julie said quietly.

Giles threw up his hands in frustration. "Ah, such a woman. But this is not a game we play now, Julie. It is life and death—your life or your death. I have seen you play games, Julie my love, and I have not forgotten one moment of the hours and days I have spent with you. This is some game you play. I sensed it in your face and in your voice when you gave that careful reply to the questions at court. I know you well enough to know that you could not have sworn that holy oath and lied—your mother's Irish ghost would have reached from the grave and caught at your throat. But I know you are not telling but a half of what you know. You know who that blue-eyed gambler is, and you are foolishly protecting him. For your loyalty, I would kill him myself. But you must think, Julie, think!"

It was foolish of him to tell her to think when Antoine was so full in her mind already. Giles's face was near her own, his earnest eyes holding hers, the warmth of his breath against her own. But the warmth of the wine somehow glazed her eyes so that Giles's face softened and fused and changed into Antoine's. It was Antoine's breath that was warm upon her mouth, and she felt again that fine tingling of passion course along her limbs as Antoine lowered his warm flesh against her own.

Into that moment, a harsh clamoring sounded outside the window. Julie felt the weight of the clapper as if it struck within her own head. She cried out and clung to Giles who held her close, stroking her tenderly until her heart slowed its racing.

"That is the clerk of Saint Sepulchre," he said quietly. "This is his second visit here today. He stands beneath the windows of those condemned to die on the morrow. You cannot hear his words for the noise of his bell, but he is warning those wretches of the eternal flames of hell that await them unless they repent and make peace with God."

Julie thought of Antoine who was somewhere in this foul place along with herself. Was that bell for him? Was he among the wretched ones who would ride the cart to Tyburn in the morning? Her chest ached with anguished fear as she clung to Giles.

Misunderstanding her silence, he spoke softly to her. "Let

216

me tell you how it could be, my dove. Instead of Tyburn you could be free of this charge. I know a place, fine, warm rooms that overlook a garden where sweet birds sing. Those rooms would blossom to your taste. You could have a woman with you to care for you and tend your needs and be your companion. I would dress you in the fine silks that your beauty deserves. What a gentle life we would have, Julie— safe from your relatives, freed of this miserable bondage."

Julie frowned with confusion, drawing apart to stare at him. "You would marry me? A woman who has been brought to court for selling stolen goods? You would risk your great career and all your privileges by marrying a woman without dowry and with such a burden of shame?"

He flushed under her gaze. "Marry I could not, Julie," he told her with difficulty. "I have already a wife and a fine son who is upon his feet to walk by now—"

She wrenched herself from his arms. "Beast!" she cried. "You would have me betray the man who befriended me that you might gain me for your whore?" She was on her feet, stamping in helpless rage. "Courtesan. Mistress. Where is your mind, Giles Urban? Do the circumstances of money stolen and a change of fate change me from a lady to a strumpet for you? Beast. Monster. Beast."

He had risen too and stood watching her with a rising gleam in his eye. Finally he could contain his laughter no longer.

"Ah, Julie," he said gently. "The old Irish fire still warms that French blood of yours. God knows this is not as I wished it to be, but time and circumstances have twisted our lives like a growing stem. It is the way of the world that I had to make a loveless marriage for position and property. I do not even rue that because it is that same position and property that would now allow us the freedom to share some of our lives together.

"And since your answer has set the question to me, I shall quite plainly answer. Yes. Yes, I would have you betray the man who befriended you. Yes, I would have you do any act, say any word that would save your life, Julie Duvall." He seized her hands and drew her to him. "I could make you happy, Julie. I have never loved any woman but you. Your face swims between me and any other woman's graces. Please Julie, consider."

217

His tone was so beseeching and the tenderness of his love so moving that Julie's anger drained away, leaving her limp. She felt suddenly chilled and slipped herself into his arms as if to warm herself.

"Time and circumstance you say," she repeated sadly. "What kind of a master is this justice that you serve? What kind of justice will let the revenge of a cuckold destroy a life that is innocent of the crime?"

Giles was silent for a long moment, only holding her closely. "We are all the same, Julie," he told her. "The simplest apprentice and a man like me. We accept a master without knowing his failings or reading what is hidden in the heart. And having pledged ourselves, we turn our eyes aside to protect us from our own grieving. But woman does not understand this discipline—yours is a different kind of life."

She stared past his shoulder into the darkness of the prison room. A different kind of life. Was this true? But she had a master, a true master who had enslaved her. There had been no apprenticeship in her service, and there was no day at which she would be set free to depart and never look back. Giles had a master called justice. Hers was named Passion, and for Antoine she had lied and deceived and suffered humiliation and was like to die. Yet, without that master, life was not worth the breath it took to sustain it.

"The name," he prompted her. "Only the name."

"The man who gave me the necklace is dead," she repeated dully.

He drew back and considered her. "I could have you sent back to that pit that you were brought from," he said mildly. "Think on that place. The fever is there, Julie. We lost a fine man, a judge who had been on the bench many years. He did not go near Newgate Prison. The disease was carried to him across a bar as he questioned a prisoner. And those spotted faces among that rabble—you must know what those spots are. In polite society they are covered with patches, but the disease is the same and the spots carry the madness from one life to another."

She shuddered at his words. The French Disease they called it, the sickness that came from lust, to rot the body, scar the skin, and eat away the mind.

"But I cannot send you back to that hellhole, Julie. I need not do it. You will reconsider. The cost of this special room

218

is no great burden to me and I will know that clean, warm water and decent food may keep you safe. One day you will repay me with the name of the man who butchered Mignon LeFevre."

Julie studied the young man she had known since childhood. He had been wrong to remind her of how well he remembered her childhood games, how easily he could tell her mind. Well, she remembered too. She rememberd when the power had been with her instead of in his hands. She remembered her compassion for him when he anguished with jealousy or longing. Had she been kind or had she used him to her own ends as he wished to use her now?

She had been gentle with him because she loved him in that special way that she still did, in spite of his patronizing words. The Irish blood he loved to remind her of flamed at his attitude. The new Julie, who had chosen the hard trail through the woods away from the cabin, who had battled the hostler about Antoine's stallion, stilled her tongue. It was the way of the world—she hated that phrase. If he would seek to use her, she would use them by the same token.

For as long as Antoine lived, there was still hope. Her own life would mean nothing if that bell tolled for Antoine. If that day came, God forbid, she would speak his name to Giles and be welcome.

She lowered her eyes so he could not read the yellow gleam of perfidy in them.

"It is wrong for me to accept this from you, Giles," she demurred.

His voice glowed with delight, and he took her into his arms tenderly. "Thank you for your sweet reason, Julie. How could I sleep, knowing you were suffering?"

"But what if I should go mad here alone, with only the beetles on the walls and the cries of the wretches for company?"

He paused, startled at her thought. "Perhaps there is someone you could have come and share this space with you—when I am not here," he added hastily.

She concealed her smile. "There is one person I can think of," she said slowly. "She is only a street girl, but she befriended me in that dungeon. She offered to protect me with her knife. From the men of that place who are like ravening

219

beasts." She added the last with a sly glance that he did not catch.

"Bless her," he said with honest fervor, reaching for the bell rope. "Then it is agreed?"

He drew her to him and held her close with a new familiarity. His tongue pressed her lips apart and probed her mouth hungrily. His lean leg pressed her thighs apart, and she felt the surge of passion start in him.

Then the jailer's step was heard beyond the door, and Giles released her with a sigh. "There will be other hours," he said softly, as if aloud to himself. "You say she is called Ellie? The guard will bring her along." He glanced about the room. "I will have pallets brought, and a mirror for my beauty."

Then he turned to the guard, issued a number of crisp orders, pressed money into the man's open hand, and was gone.

Chapter Thirty

Alone in the room with the sudden silence that followed Giles's departure, Julie sat very still. A world within a world she had thought when she first entered this room. Now she knew that it was a prison within a prison that she had chosen for herself. The wet stones of the wall glistened in the light of the lantern, and a faint clicking sound came from behind the drapes where beetles stirred among the stones. Distant sounds of the revelry of drunken prisoners filtered through her high window. From somewhere came the high keening of maniacal despair.

Pushing the remains of the meal aside, she buried her head in her arms. "My fine words," she told herself bitterly. "I am become a whore in spite of it all. What will Margaret and Mark think to find me here? Never mind that," she rebuked herself fiercely. "I am alive and Antoine is alive. Margaret herself said that the giving in to despair was the worst thing of all."

It had seemed whimsey that made her press her good luck to ask that Ellie be with her. Later she felt that she had been inspired to ask for the merry girl to share her days.

The fowl was still warm on the table when Ellie, shouting

and cursing her protest, was shoved along the hall and tumbled into the room. She caught her balance and stared at Julie silently before looking warily about her.

"Ow now, what have we here?" she cried with a wide, delighted smile. She walked around, gingerly lifting the drape with a knowing hand and staring at the bone lantern to gauge its value for pawning.

"And food." Her eyes widened with excitement as she leaned over the table. Her moist tongue slid along her lips hungrily as she stared at the generous portions still waiting on the table.

"Sit. Eat. Be my guest," Julie said. "I made very free to have you sent here without your leave. You don't mind, do you?"

Ellie, with her legs straight before her like a man, was already into the food. She seized a joint of the capon and tore it loose from the carcass, disdaining the knife. With both hands greasy to the wrist, she rammed the food into her mouth with small moans of delight.

"Mind. Mind," she mimicked, when she had emptied her mouth with a great swallow of wine. "Should I mind being treated like the queen herself, and without having to bed with a fat German to boot? It's as if we were in the Tower itself instead of this filthy hole. How did you come into this?" she asked suddenly. "Not as I would have done I wager, by lifting my skirts for it." Her glance on Julie was too keen to miss the flush of red that rose in her cheeks.

"Like that," she said. Then she shrugged. "Never mind, lovey. It's better to be rutted and live than to lie alone and rot."

"Oh, Ellie," Julie protested. "It is only that he wants something from me that he thinks he can get this way. He is willing to pay some price for it."

"So what did I say?" Ellie challenged her. "It's the way of the world, it is." She tore off a great piece of cheese and laid it on a wedge of bread. She handed it to Julie with a mimicry of a courtly gesture. "Do come now and eat with me. I have always been loathe to dine alone."

In spite of herself, Julie giggled. Curling on the bench, she nibbled at the cheese and bread with Ellie and drank the rest of the wine that Giles had left in his glass.

Ellie was like a chipmunk, full of curiosity and life. It was she who found that by shoving the bench to a certain position, they could stand on tiptoe and watch the prisoners in the exercise yard below. It was Ellie who told her about the condemned prisoners for whom the death bell had been ringing.

"There are four men and a woman this time," Ellie informed her. "There is a prentice to a bricklayer who laid open his own master's head with a brick. Then there is a woman who was taken for stealing bread for her children."

"They can't hang a woman for stealing bread," Julie cried.

"Oh, just can't they now?" Ellie said, astonished that Julie should speak that way. "Then there is a counterfeiter of coins. They say his richness is like that of a lord but he will dance all the same. There's some mystery to why he has not bought himself free since he is clearly able." She shrugged. "Then there is a pickpocket like me only a man and a highwayman. There's always a highwayman every hanging day."

"A highwayman," Julie repeated. "What is he like?"

"A sniveling coward most of all," Ellie said. "That great wailing and caterwauling last night was him." Ellie was too busy to notice the eagerness of Julie's attention. She was slipping grapes from a cluster one at a time until she had a great handful which she crammed into her mouth with the flat of her hand. Then she shook her head.

"He's not much a man to look at, this one. Small, he is and swarthy with little, mean eyes. He might have been somewhat better to look on before he lost his hair with the pox. His pate shines like a spring apple, and him with no wig to be hung in."

Not Antoine, Julie breathed with relief. Then a sudden pang of compassion coursed through her. All those lives . . . and one for stealing bread.

"You can't do that, Sukey," Ellie warned quietly. "You can't let the hurting of other deaths into your feelings. You take each day, each morsel." She waggled the fowl's thighbone at Julie. "You live," she hissed. "Every minute you breathe you must live and not look about you. Eh?"

Julie nodded and set down her wineglass. "We live," she agreed quietly.

True to her word, Margaret did not come to Newgate. Mark entered, looking askance at Ellie and bringing fresh water and clean linen for Julie.

Concern ridged his young face, "Is there nothing more we can do for you, Sukey. Anything at all?"

She shook her head and laid her hand on his arm.

"Dear, dear Mark," she said, not meaning to bring that rush of agonized color to his face. "Already you do too much. And Margaret is right to stay away. She must fear leading the others to me that I would have murder charged to me too." She phrased her words carefully with a timid glance towards Ellie.

"That is the reason she gives," he admits, "that and her softness of heart to see you thus." Then he frowned. "She does not do well, Sukey. She grows too tired, and her face shows pain that she will not admit to. I do all that I can, but with Kit gone there is much labor."

"She is ill," Julie told him glumly.

"She gets angry when I say that to her," Mark said.

Julie smiled at him. "She shouted at me when I did too," she confessed. "She would not even let me know her symptoms."

"She is an angel," he said quietly. "But I fear for her."

After handing her a note from Margaret, he was gone.

"Tell me," Ellie said slyly. "Are there more? There is the young lord in the fancy wig who has set us up in such style here. Then this soft-voiced prentice comes. How many heads dangle on this Sukey's ribbon?"

Laughing her words aside, Julie curled up to read the note from Margaret.

Mark has made many inquiries of the state of your case, my dear. I have done the same among my friends and patients. All agree that if you would give the court the name it seeks that you would go free. Consider, my jewel. Your life is sun to us all.

Always the same, Julie thought, crumpling the note in her hand. What can I give to Antoine now but my loyalty? And even if I did not love him with this painful passion, I would still owe him my own life from that day in the field.

"If we had time enough," Ellie said wistfully. "I would

223

wish you to teach me to read. And maybe make writing that could be read."

Many weeks were to pass before the new sessions would be held. The days came and went like flights of pale gulls that brightened the window and then were gone. Ellie worked with the letters that Julie wrote for her and learned, with grand pride, to form her own name. She taught Julie some games of cards and then beat her soundly at them. Julie taught Ellie to make fine stitches on the work that Margaret sent. They ate and drank the wine that Giles had sent and walked in the exercise yards with the catcalls of less fortunate prisoners following their steps.

When Giles came, Ellie was sent away. With the lantern hooded, Giles made gentle love to Julie and afterwards would lie for a long time sheltering her in his arms like a child. She lay with his firm, young body against her own, feeling a gentleness towards him, raising her hand to stroke the fine, tawny hair that still curled and ducktailed like a spaniel when his great wig was laid aside.

"The name," he pleaded, when his passion was spent. "Tell me the name so that this hellish game can be over. Tell me the name that I can put you in a worthier place, without fear."

"I promised you nothing, Giles," she reminded him. "I thank you with my heart." She paused. "And with my body which would surely have fallen to disease by now except for you. But it is you who say I know what name to tell."

So he would sigh and rise and dress and go away, lulled by her lovemaking to be gentle in his demands about the name of the mysterious, blue-eyed murderer.

As if there was not anguish enough in her life, another small mystery came during those days. It was Ellie who first noticed the dark man who was always watching from the street outside when they walked in the exercise yard.

"Look at him," Ellie whispered. "He's here every day, and it is you that he is always looking at."

When Julie looked his way his eyes caught hers at once. Even with his back to the sun, his eyes glittered with malice. Looking at him, Julie was seized by a sudden weakness in her limbs, as if she had stepped suddenly to the very rim of hell and might not be strong enough to pull herself back. Trying to conceal the terror she felt, she only shook her head. "He comes to see someone else," she told Ellie. "I have never seen that man before in all of my days."

"It is you he seeks," Ellie insisted stubbornly. "And he's a mean-looking one, that bounder."

Even aside from his terrible eyes, the stranger had a frightening mein. In spite of her will not to look, Julie found her gaze drawn to him. He was taller by a third than the ordinary Londoner, and his flesh was darker in color. He wore fine clothes, and the cane he carried had a gold tip that winked in the sun. She could not tell whether the dark curls that lay on his collar were his own hair or a wig, but his eyes upon her, under those dark, brooding brows, set such a trembling in her that she professed to be cold and asked that Ellie return with her to their quarters.

Some great impatience in the court stirred them to bring Julie again and again before the justice. She had thought she would have peace until the sessions. Instead, they took her over and over. There would be a great hemming and hawing and threats to her life if she did not do as they wished. Margaret had indeed been right. She knew at last that there was nothing wanted of her but the name of the murderer. They framed their questions a dozen ways to try to trick that name from her lips.

Ellie, whose fine nose for gossip missed nothing, sniffed out the story and grew quite cross with her.

"Tell them, for God's sake. If you don't wish to tell the truth, make up some name and pass it off with a fine tale." Her face brightened with mischief. "I have an even better idea. Think of some bounder whose guts you hate and name him. They only want a neck to put the rope on. Give them the neck and go free."

Then she leaned forward and her voice grew wistful. "It is only another form of lying, but I like to make up stories of what could be. Would you like to hear the fine one I thought up while making those stitches this morning?"

Unaccustomed to any shyness in Ellie's tone, Julie looked up with a smile. "Tell me your story, Ellie," she urged.

The girl's eyes sparkled with excitement and she unconsciously clasped her hands together, almost as if she were praying. But her lips could hardly speak for smiling as she spoke. "We take the case that they somehow let you free. You could hold out for some cash from your fine bucko and buy

225

me free alongside. I would steal and you would save it until we had passage." Her face blouded. "If worse came to worse, we could always go indentured, but the other would be better. My, how I would steal—such plate and fine linens and pocket watches and soon we would get us on board with fat hens and cheeses for the trip."

She stopped and looked at Julie triumphantly.

"That is a fine tale," Julie laughed, "But how does it end?"

"In the colonies, of course," Ellie replied. "How I would like to see that place with its rosy Indians and fine fields of tobacco. You would be the lady and I would be your maid, and we would cut a swath that all London would get ear of. You might even have a small black boy of your own to fan you when the wind blows hot, like fine ladies have here."

Julie laughed merrily at this picture of herself with one of those poor, overdressed black children staggering under the weight of a great fan. "I would be more apt to pull him onto my lap and give him comfits," she confessed.

Ellie's expression grew very stern. "Ow now, that must not be. If I can force myself to be a well-mannered maid without a *damn* or a *bloody* in my talk, then you must learn to behave like a lady yourself. To bring honor on our great school of Newgate Prison."

Then Ellie's expression grew sober. "You have only to tell them the name," she reminded Julie.

Julie shook her head. She had to say the words the same way every time so that her tongue would not be tripped by despair or fatigue. "The man who gave me the necklace is dead."

Such moments of lightheartedness were few. Giles's arms about her tightened with fear. Mark's face grew ever longer as the weeks passed. Over and over, Julie heard the bell of the clerk from Saint Sepulchre tolling, morning and night, and then the great church bell itself tolled the cart that rolled to Tyburn. The shouts of the crowds and the sound of the bell made great knots of pain in Julie's stomach.

Mark's news from Margaret was ever more somber. "Her strength fails by the day," Mark told her. "She protested at first, but now I carry her up the stairs at night and down in morning."

"She needs me," Julie wails. "Why am I here when my dear friend needs me?"

226

"Because you will not say the name," Ellie said flatly.

In time, Mark did not even protest the impudence in Ellie's tone. His silent reproach weighed even heavier on Julie's heart than Ellie's cross canting at her. And when they walked in the yard, the dark stranger dimmed what sun there was with the dark implacable hatred in his eyes on Julie.

Little by little, Julie lost hold of the world about her. She retreated into her mind where Antoine could be with her, his smile only a glance away, his hand warm on her arm. With her needlework idle in her lap, she relived those gentle days with Titus and the passionate nights with Antoine in the deep woods of Epping. Sometimes she lifted her head, thinking she heard a lark sing, only to realize it was the screech of a prisoner's chain from beyond the window.

She knew that Antoine still lived, for word of the blue-eyed highwayman had come through the gossip to Ellie's clever ears. He was said to be a great, unsmiling man who bore his imprisonment like a caged beast. They were only wanting one witness to hang him, but they would not let him go for that lack. Julie thought of the straw men she had seen lounging in the street and prayed that no man would buy a false witness against him.

Bored by her inactivity, Ellie spent the day hopping up and down from the bench to watch the courtyard below. That morning, she let out a great screech that caught Julie's startled attention.

"It's him. It had got to be him now," the girl cried, hopping madly on the bench so that it danced dangerously. "There is the man I would be a woman for."

"Then you've found a treasure down there," Julie said, wetting the thread with her lips to thread a fresh needle.

"My God, such fine thighs, such great fine legs, and a back like a soldier." Ellie sighed and turned from the window. "I am too long without a man, dear Sukey, that I would grow damp between the thighs at the sight of a felon I have never before seen."

"You are simply a wanton little strumpet," Julie said indulgently. "This passion will pass in time for you to be greedy for dinner."

Ellie giggled. "You are probably right." She chose an apple from the bowl and sunk her teeth deeply into its crisp flesh. "But it is a waste that I would lie here when that fine figure

227

of a man and I could be rolling together in the hay of his cell."

"Then you would leave my company and warm water brought daily for a bath and warm food and bright wine for that man in the press yard?" Julie asked her slyly.

"For a night I would," Ellie confessed. "For one good romping night I would."

Her curiosity finally roused, Julie set aside her work and climbed up on the bench herself. She could not at once get into position to see the man Ellie was moaning over. Then a figure moved from the shadow and walked briskly across the yard. She stayed so silent that Ellie stopped her chatter in puzzlement. Antoine, clean-shaven, as she had seen him last. He was dressed simply in a dark coat that she remembered mending when its sleeve had been rent by an overhanging branch in the wood. He was pacing swiftly back and forth like a caged animal. She could see the tightening of the muscles of his thighs as he turned to retrace his frantic steps. His shapely head that she had cradled so often on her breast was bowed in somber thought. When he turned so that she saw the fine line of his face that second time, she felt her head begin to swim. She groped for balance before tumbling off the bench in a sickening swoon.

"Whatever came over you?" Ellie pressed, when she had brought Julie around with a press of cold water to her head and throat.

"I grew dizzy of a sudden," Julie said, lifting her arm to her aching head. "All went strange for me and I fell."

"You ain't bleeding, are you?" Ellie asked. "Has that fine lawyer set a babe in you?"

Julie shook her head. "It was only a little dizziness." She forced herself to her feet. "See? I am fine now."

After that day, Julie was quick to the window when she heard steps in the yard below. How she yearned to send word to him, to call through the high, slatted bars and let him know that she was there, that the terror that shadowed him also hung over her own head. It was no use. He never lifted his eyes from the ground or looked up, not even when fine women of society called to him from the fence and threw flowers to him on the dark earth of the yard.

During those months that she had been with Margaret, she had often lain awake whole nights nursing the pain of her

228

loneliness for Antoine. Over and over she had told herself that if she could only see him, know that he was still alive and well that she would be happy.

Now that she could mount the bench almost daily and hold him in her eyes, she was more griefstruck than before. Her nights were plagued with dreams that she wakened from crying. Ellie, her eyes bright with speculation, only watched her and said nothing.

Chapter Thirty-One

Each of those nameless days that blazed and dimmed beyond the window of Julie's prison room moved faster than the last as the time for the sessions neared. An indefinable tension stirred in the room, filling both Julie and Ellie with restlessness.

Sometimes Julie wondered if Ellie were not part witch. That girl knew every snippet of gossip that passed within the walls of Newgate. The very stones seemed to breathe rumor into Ellie's head, all of which she freely passed on to Julie. And all these tales were related in the vulgar street talk that Julie had grown so accustomed to that she would, on occasion, use it herself to Ellie's raucous delight

Of course, the girl moved about the prison in a way that Julie never did. Ellie was oftener and oftener taken back to their old cells while Giles spent his precious hours in Julie's arms. Once the pattern of these visits became established, Julie noticed Ellie doing a strange thing. Ellie had made a small corner of the room where she stored her clothes. Julie saw her slip a half-cheese, or a part of a loaf into those rags as if to hide them from Julie herself. Astonished and half-irritated at this squirrelling away, Julie spoke crossly to her.

"There is no need of that, Ellie," she said, catching the girl in the act. "We need not fear being without food or drink as long as they are trying to wring that unknown name from me."

Ellie flushed, more at being caught than at her sneakiness Julie decided.

"It's not for us," Ellie admitted. "It's for them." She

waggled her head towards the old cell where she and Julie had met. "The guards only take this back to their quarters and make merry of your bucko's money. They've only the rottenest slop to eat in that cell and that only once a day. It's no harm to the men, they've the strength for it but those wenches with babes—"

"What will happen to them when the sessions come?" Julie asked, ever conscious of the nearness of that dreaded day.

"Some will stay and some will swing," Ellie shrugged. "Those wot has great bellies by now will be let to live until the babe comes. Them wot has pleaded their bellies and aren't showing a child yet is done for." She shrugged again. "It's all chance—like the big highwayman. Who knows until the day is come if they've found another witness against him? It's hold or hang, and who's to know ahead? But as for your food, you can send it back with them bastards if you've a mind to."

"For heaven's sake no, Ellie," Julie protested. "Take all there is and be welcome. I just didn't understand your hiding it away like that. You could have asked from the first."

Ellie grinned that wicked grin that set her eyes dancing. "It comes more natural to me to steal than to ask," she admitted. "Likely nothing will reform this baggage but a dose of hemp rope."

"Don't say that," Julie cried, running to her and clasping her in her arms. "I can't bear the thought. How could I have borne these weeks without you?"

Ellie squirmed away with embarrassment. "You've no business holding onto a street scum like me," she said crossly. "And as for me being a help—it ain't my name you cry at night when you twist and moan there on that pallet."

Julie froze. Ellie did not meet her eyes but tossed her head and turned away. "That's all I'm saying now," she said archly. "But mark my words I say it only to you—now." She paused and then added in a low, fierce tone, "But I've this to say, that if they set you to hang, I'll go banging on that door and calling that name to every ear in London, I will. You'll not dance on Tyburn for any man that breathes, not while I can speak his name."

"You couldn't," Julie whispered, dumbfounded at the girl's words. "You wouldn't take advantage of my friendship—my love for you." Her voice broke.

230

Ellie kicked furiously at the rushes on the floor. "Lay off me now," she said angrily. "You're like all the rest of them at heart. You all think that only quality can hurt from love. Hurt is hurt," she said bitterly. "Kennel or castle, hurt is hurt."

"If you love me you will not betray me," Julie told her softly, touched by the passion in her voice.

"Ow," Ellie wailed in a strange, high tone. Then she fled to the corner where her clothes were stored and curled there with her back to Julie. When Julie went to her, Ellie thrust her away with a stiff arm, but the shaking of her shoulders betrayed to Julie that her friend was weeping silently like a crouched and beaten animal.

Concerned as she was by the nearness of session day and distracted by her hours of watching Antoine from the window, Julie did not really notice the change that came in their days.

It was Ellie who fretfully brought it to her notice. "Where's that grand prentice of yours?" she asked crossly. It's been days since he came bumbling in here with his great bald hands and his face coming red like a bad-lit coal."

Julie stared at her. "Mark," she cried in astonishment. "Why Mark hasn't been here for ever so long."

"Five days," Ellie told her. "Five whole days."

"He must be very busy," Julie mused. "With the maid gone and only him to tend Margaret in her illness."

"Well that's not proper cause for him to neglect us," Ellie grumbled.

Us. Julie glanced at Ellie thoughtfully. Then a twitch of a smile played about her mouth. "Did she dare tease Ellie about Mark? Just a little tease?"

"Perhaps he has found a girl outside who is better than the birds of Newgate," Julie suggested lightly.

Ellie whirled on her. "Not by half," she said. "That's not a man to chase every cleft that prances along the street. More apt something fearful has come to him. Maybe some drunken Mohawk has busted his head or he'd be along here to us. He could be lying dead."

As well as she knew Ellie's talent for making large and fearsome tales to fit her emotions, the words frightened Julie. When he did not come that day or the next, Julie called for the jailer and had pen and paper brought for a letter.

She had not written a proper letter to anyone but Margaret

these many weeks. The last careful letter she had written had been to Henry Furlong asking for his help. The irony of that thought stayed her hand for some minutes. Then she wrote:

Dear Mark,
If you do not come before my next trip to justice, and if my life not be spared this coming time, please do this one favor for me. Come to Ellie and be kind to her. Her crime is mild, and she would be released on promise of transport. Make her plead for that transport; tell her she would serve some brief years and then be free. Make her do this for me. I would die happy knowing she would still live.
To Margaret and to yourself, this comes with love.

She had formed the *J* of her signature before she remembered. She scratched it over and signed *Sukey* in bold letters.

It was the last day before session when Mark finally came. Julie leaped up from her bench when she saw it was Mark whose form filled the jailroom door. She ran towards him with outstretched arms. Then she stopped short of him. His face was haggard with exhaustion and his usually clear eyes were veined with red. Her voice trailed off into silence as he crossed the room to set down his package with the tired steps of an old man.

It was Ellie who went swiftly to him and urged him to be seated. Julie was at once beside him.

"Margaret," she ordered. "Tell me about Margaret."

"She fails," Mark said dully. "Forgive me, dear Sukey, but I could not leave her side until now. Only because the doctor is there could I slip away."

"The doctor!" Julie cried. "Oh, Mark. Do not let them bleed her. I learned from her that it is dangerous to be bled. I pray you did not let that doctor bleed her."

Mark looked up at her sadly. The suffering in his face brought a rush of tears behind her eyes. He took her hands imploringly.

"Sukey, Sukey," he pleaded. "What other could I do? She was hot to the touch and her mind flying away into madness. I did all I knew and nothing helped. She screamed with pain and I sent for the doctor."

232

She buried her head in her hands and wept. He rose and patted her shoulder with his great, awkward hands.

"The hearing is on the morrow?" he asked.

She nodded. "Oh, Mark, I must hear how she gets on."

"I will come if I can, but I leave her only sleeping. A woman of the street comes by day and tends her. I will slip away early to you if it is possible for me. God's blessing on you, Sukey," he said gently. Then, raising his eyes above her head, he looked over to Ellie. "And God's blessing on you too, Ellie, and my thanks for your great goodness to my friend."

At the door, Julie pressed her note into Mark's hand then rose and kissed him lightly on the cheek. Something rather like a strangled cry came from his throat, and he moved hastily off along the hall away from her.

Ellie sat very still with her eyes on her lap and her bright face twisted with pain.

"She is dying," Julie told her friend dully. "She is dying and what the disease cannot do to hasten it, the doctors will. And I am penned here by fools."

When the storm of tears was spent, she leaned back with her head against the cold, wet stones. "What else can happen, Ellie? Dear God, what else can happen?"

"You can put your mind to other things," Ellie said briskly, having recovered her control in that sturdy way she had. She tugged at Julie's hand. "Come, walk. Come to the window and see the sunlight. Put it all from your head and live the minute. Hope is left."

Hope. That had been Margaret's counsel. Rather than let herself dwell on Margaret, Julie let herself be led to the window where the last colors of sunset were fading beyond the grim outline of the prison. Pigeons with breasts like bowling balls stamped along the roof crooning in their throats and fluttering crisply for balance. The exercise yard was nearly empty. Only two or three men lounged along the wall catching the last few minutes of light in the warm outside air. Then, as Julie watched, a guard moved briskly across her angle of view. He clattered at the gate with his key and swung the wide gate open.

The woman who entered seemed smaller than life. She was clothed all in black with dark, trailing scarves that flowed gracefully in the air as she walked. Her face was wholly

233

veiled, but the smallness of her waist and the delicacy of her swift steps showed her to be young and lovely even from that distance.

She was barely inside the courtyard when a figure moved from the shadows towards her.

Julie gripped the edge of the window, digging her fingernails into the stone for support. Antoine.

He seized the woman hungrily in his arms and clasped her so tightly that her slippers were lifted free of the ground. He buried his head in her neck like a child, and then, letting her free, he threw back the veil and lifted her face to his.

The violence of his hand loosened her cap and veil, which fell unheeded to the earth. It also loosened whatever restraint the woman had set upon her hair. As Antoine's face met hers, a cascade of hair the color of burnished copper spilled down the girl's back in a great rippling of color that shone in the dying light.

"Ow," Ellie cried at Julie's side. "God strike me for my envious lust." She struck her forehead with her palm and leaped off the bench to pour herself a great glass of wine which she downed in one gulp.

Julie did not move. Like a stone maiden in the King's Park she stood without breath or life to watch the two figures in the yard below. After a while, Antoine knelt and handed the girl her headpiece. Her upraised arms, as she set her cap and veils in place, showed the fine, high line of her generous breasts. Her waist was only a hand's width above the billowing of her voluminous skirt. When her cap was in place, Antoine knelt to kiss her again, full on the mouth as before, and then she dropped the veil.

When the last light of day died, they were still walking back and forth across the courtyard close enough to each other that they seemed to be a single moving shadow. Antoine's head was bent over hers in intent conversation, and he carried her small gloved hand tenderly inside his arm, covered protectively by his own.

Margaret was lost to her. And now Antoine.

Julie threw herself, fully clothed, on her pallet and turned her face to the wall. Ellie's lilting song, a little off-key from the wine, faltered and then stopped altogether. She stood staring at Julie a long time, her face twisted by anguish. Then

234

she kicked off her own slippers, stripped her clothes off, and threw them into the corner.

"Whoreson," she spat as she pulled the cover over her nakedness. "God may he dance. God may he dance."

Chapter Thirty-Two

The morning of the sessions was strange from the start. Julie woke light-headed, as if the air in the room was not rich enough to sustain her breath. She bathed in the warm water that was brought daily at Giles's command. She tried not to recognize the faint melody of the heartbreaking tune that Ellie hummed under her breath as Julie pulled her clothes on. It was the same melody that Ellie had sung to her that first day, and God help her, the words were imprinted in Julie's brain.

Oh ring the bells for Dirty Ellie
Make up posies just for me.
From rotten Newgate, foul and smelly,
I shall fly to Tyburn Tree.

When she had dressed, the anguish of the waiting settled her primly on the bench with her hands in her lap. Only the footsteps in the hall brought her to her feet. She prayed that it be Mark with news of Margaret.

Instead, it was Giles who entered, his fine face etched with pain. He seized her hands and kissed the palms lingeringly, seemingly unconscious of Ellie watching from across the room.

"It is now or never, my love," he warned her. "Live, love. Speak the name and live. For me, if not for yourself, love, live for me."

"Who would choose death?" Julie asked, forcing a smile to brighten his face. She lifted her arms to his neck and smiled into his face. "Giles, my dear, you have done far too much for this lost cause. You have made it possible these weeks for me to exist with moments of pleasure in spite of my pain. For that I bless you with all my heart. But, Giles, the man who

235

gave me the necklace is dead. He is dead, Giles, as he has been since long before this whole thing began."

Anger twisted his face and he seized her shoulders and shook her roughly. "God in heaven, woman. Have you taken leave of your senses? You will die. There is no law that they have to believe the testimony of a prisoner at the bar. They can merely accept the evidence you have given in admitting the jewels were yours. You can die. What can I say to convince you that the man you are sheltering is not worth your life? If it were his life instead of yours what would he do? I ask you. Would he ride that cart to Tyburn to save your life? Never."

Julie's tears came in spite of her resolve. She shook her head.

"Games. Always clever games," His voice turned from disgust to sternness. "I will be there in court and I will be watching you. I command you to speak the *whole* truth when the moment comes."

She bowed her head as he left.

"He's right," Ellie said quietly. "You know he's right."

"Shut up," Julie told her fiercely. "Shut up. Shut up. Shut up."

That cascade of copper-colored hair shone in Julie's memory, the hunger of Antoine's mouth searching for those other lips. "If it were his life instead of yours, what would he do?"

God help her, she knew. The weight of that knowing was a stone between her breasts.

The justice stared at her as before only a little more boldly.

"Has your memory improved, Sukey Titus?" he asked, his eyes travelling insolently past her eyes to her lips and then to that soft cleft where her breasts began.

"My memory holds only the truth," Julie said, dropping her eyes to avoid having to watch the sickening way his tongue probed over his teeth as he stared down at her.

"And you are prepared to die for the marketing of this stolen property?"

"I did not know the jewels were stolen," she repeated as before.

Something stirred across the room. She glanced aside to see Giles standing, splendid in his full wig and the panoply of his

236

office. His eyes shone on her with that same fullness of love that she remembered from those green years of their shared childhoods. With Giles she could have safety and comfort and the endless gentleness of his love for her.

With Giles she would have time, and in that time his love might dim the memory of Antoine's body reaching for that other woman with such passionate eagerness.

For that one moment that she faltered, the judge leaned forward expectantly.

But would she forget? Could she forget? Her fate had been linked to Antoine's from that first day when their eyes had caught and held as the gold and white coach rattled by towards London. A recklessness flooded her. She lifted her breasts and tossed her head back. Did she really want a life, however pleasant on the surface, when her knowledge of Antoine's betrayal would rankle like a worm in her heart forever?

The judge's voice urged the question softly.

Into her mind, half-crazed by despair, that little melody of Ellie's came singing—only a little changed.

> Bring the bell for Pretty Julie
> Make up posies just for me.
> From rotten Newgate, foul and smelly
> I shall dance on Tyburn's Tree.

"The man who gave me the jewels is dead." She said it loudly, startling the judge. Because she knew it was the truth and because life without Antoine would be no life at all, she found herself suddenly laughing.

The judge's face darkened with fury. He screamed at her with such force that the heavy jowls that hung by his mouth like saddlebags waggled wildly.

"Take her out of my sight," he shouted. "I want this woman out of my sight. The sentence is death."

In a great flurry, the shackles which had bound her to the prisoner by her side were loosed. Two stout guards, who seemed overzealous in their task, dragged her from the room and down the hallway towards the street. This was irregular. It registered in her mind that the pattern had been broken by the judge's loss of control. She felt like a bundle of some merchandise being hastily handled with no concern for its safety or welfare.

When it was over, she tried to reconstruct those few minutes, but they remained hazy in her mind. They had been dragging her along the hallway and there was no escape from their brutal hands. A crowd which had been waiting outside cheered as they emerged from the door into the brilliance of sunlight.

Then there was a carriage there, and the door stood open. Horses stamped restlessly, and she felt the lewd grasp of a guard's hands on her buttocks as he lifted her. She heard a muttered whisper and the clink of coins, and she was thrown into the darkness of the carriage.

As the door slammed and the horses were loosed, she heard a woman's scream. At the forward surge of the horses, a strong hand caught at her and set her upright in the seat.

Blinded by the sun outside, she tried to see the man who had set her beside him. There was darkness only, with a dim shape that spoke in a low, strong voice filled with fury.

"Now we will learn how you came by those jewels, you spawn of the devil," he laughed softly. "Now you will speak."

She started to scream, but the sound of the rattling coach drowned out her cries. Then a corner was turned, and she was thrown against her companion, still screaming.

"Shut your rotten mouth," he hissed, and he clapped a hand on her face. She clawed at his hands and managed to sink her teeth into the side of his hand.

He cursed and flung her free of him. She heard as well as felt the thud of her head against the wooden wide of the carriage. A multitude of spinning lights whirled about her. Then she felt herself slipping, and there was nothing for her gripping hands to catch.

Chapter Thirty-Three

Mark sat in the low chair pulled close to Margaret's bed. He gauged it to be nearly dawn by the sudden chill that sent a shiver through him. Since the chair was too small for his frame, he perched on the edge with his elbows on his knees and his head supported on his hands. There were two separate rhythms in the room, like two instruments playing against each other, the hoarse snuffling of Trump's healthy sleep against the shallow breath of his mistress.

The doctor had shaken his head dolefully when Mark returned from his visit with Julie. Mark had not moved from the room since, staying near Margaret as if his living presence would ward off the coming of death. Instead of responding to the doctor's ministrations, Margaret had grown steadily weaker since his leaving.

Perhaps it was as well that Sukey could not see her, Mark thought morosely. Margaret had grown so thin these past weeks that the flesh was barely stretched over the bones of her face. The growth that swelled in her belly stood out under the cover like a coming child.

When the watch called the hour in the street below, Margaret stirred. Mark watched her struggle to raise her eyelids without success. As her lips vibrated helplessly, struggling for sound, he leaned very near her face.

"Mistress?" he whispered.

A shadow of a smile twitched at her yellowed lips at the sound of his voice. "Mark," she managed to say. "Dear, dear Mark."

"I am here," he reassured her. "Is there somewhat I can get for you? Tea? A bite of food?"

The smile tried again, and her head rolled from side to side on the pillow. "Time," she managed to say. "I want time."

Mark could see the pain coming as she braced her waning strength against its fury. Sweat leaped out on her brow and across her upper lip. He laid a cloth on her face and was sick to feel the heat of her flesh burn through the fabric as he wiped her skin dry.

With the passing of the pain, a trembling came. Finally, he realized it was a grand effort that she was making. Great muscles stood out on her neck, and her lips struggled for sound.

"Mark," she finally said, and the words tumbled out after like water poured from a broken ewer. "Julie," she said. "The banker Furlong. Help Julie. Save Julie."

But I don't understand, his mind rebelled wildly. Her eyes opened and were intense on his. "Swear," she insisted. Her voice was a hollow force in the room.

"I swear, mistress," he said helplessly. "On God's name, I swear."

As her eyes fluttered shut, she tried to raise her hand. Mark caught it in his own, and the bony fingers tightened on his hand with a sudden brutal force, "Bless you, Mark, dear Mark."

Then as it had come, the pressure failed. Her hand dropped away from his to lie, palm up, on the coverlet. He saw a fan of moisture form on the sheet that covered her as her body emptied itself of fluid. The hollow exhalation of her breath rustled like the scrape of dry leaves across bare ground.

"Oh God, oh God," he cried, burying his head on her chest. Beside him, the dog Thump wrestled himself free of the young man's weight and set up a howl of misery that bore no resemblance to his ordinary complaint.

Mark heard the rap of the neighbor woman at the door downstairs then her tread upon the stairs. He had no need to tell her what had happened. At the sight of his face, she threw her apron over her head and began to wail.

"She is with God," Mark rebuked her.

The old woman, her face contorted with tears, patted him awkwardly. "I'll watch with her," she sobbed. "Get you to the coroner for a writ."

Only because Margaret's sister Mary had died that brief time ago did Mark know what steps to take. By the time he had notified the authorities, and summoned the women with their cloths and basins, and been to the coffin maker's and by the church, the morning was half-spent.

Then, for the first time, Mark stopped and asked himself what must be done next.

Sukey. Dear, anguished Sukey must be told. His heart pulled him towards Newgate, to the one human soul whose grief at Margaret's passing would be equal to his own. But there was the matter of his deathbed pledge to Margaret.

Julie. He pondered this name that Margaret had repeated again and again to him. Who was this Julie that he had made a deathbed promise to save?

Perhaps, since she had mentioned their names together, the banker Henry Furlong would be able to clear his mind on this. Brushing his shabby clothes which managed to appear even more disreputable with his mourning linen, Mark set off for the Bank of London.

The clerk apparently remembered his face for Mark was admitted immediately into Mr. Furlong's private room. The banker nodded his clerk away and reached for Mark's hand.

"You bring me news?" he asked, his face closed to expression.

Mark nodded then battled his emotions as he told of Margaret's death.

"Did she sent any message to me?" Mr. Furlong asked, after a suitable silence had passed.

Mark shook his head. "She was weak beyond speaking many words," he explained. "She mentioned your name to me along with another, a name I had not heard her speak before."

Mark changed his position in the chair, suddenly restless at the weight of his promise. "She said the name *Julie* over and again. She bade me swear to help this Julie—to save her." He raised his eyes to the banker's face. "I could not deny her though I knew not what she was referring to."

Mr. Furlong tapped his quill a few moments on the desk. Then he rang the bell for his clerk. After a whispered consultation with the young assistant, he turned back to Mark.

"What has become of the girl Sukey who was there in the house with you?" he asked as if straying from the subject at hand.

"She was to sessions this morning," Mark said.

"And how did that go?"

Mark shook his head. "I have no way to know. I was busy with the affairs of my mistress."

"How did you consider her chances of being freed?"

"I have no idea," Mark admitted. "She has sworn that the man who gave her the jewels was named Titus and that now he is dead, yet they continue to bring her back for questioning." Mark paused. "I believe she fears for her life since she sent me a special letter asking that I take pains for a girl she has befriended there at Newgate."

A soft smile moved across Henry Furlong's face just as the clerk tapped at the door. He handed Mr. Furlong a thick sheath of papers before letting himself out silently again.

From his drawer, Mr. Furlong fished a pair of spectacles

which he balanced precariously on the bulb of his nose. He shuffled among the papers and drew one forth.

"I have here the last testament of one Margaret Curlew," he said quietly. "In it she leaves her property, the annuity that her late master put on deposit in her name, her desposits of moneys which she has earned in her trade of healing, her linens, her plate, and various household goods to Mark Hatter." He leaned closer to read the words with exactness. "'That he might free himself of his apprenticeship and pursue that life of comfort and industry to which his goodness and gentleness have entitled him.'"

Mark stared aghast at the banker, his hands gripping the arms of his chair. "But that is not possible."

"It is possible and it has come to pass," Mr. Furlong corrected him. Then he stared soberly at Mark. "This bequest brings you hope and opportunity. Your deathbed promise is quite apart from this and a different thing. Your pledge is not in writing, you know. You have no obligation under the law to be responsible for it."

Mark was startled from his shock by the inference. He stiffened in his chair and his words came out more boldly than he intended. "The obligation of my pledge to my mistress is as binding as that document in your hand," he said angrily.

Mr. Furlong nodded. "Then we need to speak seriously and at some length." There was a lightness of relief in his voice.

It was more than an hour later that Mark emerged from the bank with his head whirling. Mr. Furlong's words had been too much for him to absorb all at once. But he knew now that the bitch Kit had been right all the time. Sukey was indeed a lady. Julie. He tried the name on his lips and savored its sweetness. Juliette Duvall, commonly known as Julie, the daughter of Fiona and Etienne Duvall.

That had been a strange speech that Henry Furlong had made with his fingers pressed tightly together and his forehead ridged with thought. "There is a fateful balance in this world, Mark Hatter. To some, much is given that the eye can see, but in that person often much is missing. My good wife and I have talked on this many times, on how a man is given wit and handsomeness and along with it, a tawdry soul given to avarice and cruelty. We see often those of plain, even ugly demeanor whose saintly spirit makes a mockery of physical

242

beauty. Julie has ever been one in which the balance is strange. She is beautiful and bright and gentle of spirit. We pondered, when she was yet a child, what lack there was in that child to make this delicate balance in which we both believe. Time has shown us what fate was planned for this seemingly overblessed creature. She has been deprived of loving parents, had her property stolen, been betrayed and defamed by those who should have cherished her. Somehow this pattern has been repeated again in the matter of this necklace. Her beauty and gentleness are her own doom."

Mark speeded his steps towards Newgate. Margaret, had she been given time and life, would have provided for Julie, saved her, as it were, in Margaret's own words. Now it was his responsibility, more than that, his precious privilege.

The room at Newgate was empty.

"But where are they?" Mark pressed the guard who led him to the chamber with a careless shrug. "Where are the women who were here?"

The guard noted the shabbiness of the prentice's clothing and shrugged. The jailer probed at his gums with a splinter of wood. Then he spat. "The slut Ellie is below where she'll bide until she hangs. As for the other, God knows."

"Take me to Ellie," Mark ordered.

The guard stared at him. "Who are you to shout me about like that?"

Mark was suddenly grateful that Mr. Furlong had pressed on him an advance against his inheritance. He slid a guinea from his pocket and tossed it in his hand, staring the man down.

"Take me to Ellie," he ordered again in the same tone. He hoped that his face would not betray the temerity he felt at this new role he was assuming.

The guard's face changed subtly. He pocketed the coin and turned on his heel sharply.

Ellie did not even lift her head as he entered. It was only as he stood over her and spoke her name that she realized anyone came. She scrambled to her feet, her eyes streaming tears as she rose. "They got her," she wailed. "Oh my God, someone has got her."

She landed against his chest like a child. He patted her back awkwardly before setting her away.

243

"Get hold of yourself, girl," he admonished. "Who has got her? What do you mean?"

Ellie shook her head, unable to stop the flow of tears. Then she sniffed loudly and would have wiped her paw across her nose if Mark had not quickly thrust his kerchief into her hand.

"I got it from the others," she sobbed, "being as I was still in the court when it came about. She made the judge angry with her tart words, and he swelled up like a toad and screamed at her. Then he had her cut loose and taken out of the court." Her eyes narrowed at a thought. "Could it be that the judge was bought to have it happen like that? The guards had been bought—there was money seen to change hands. Sukey was grabbed onto the street and pushed in to a dark carriage with the curtains all drawn shut so none could see inside. The horses went off like the Bible says, ranting and snorting, and leaving a fishmonger lying in her blood in their path."

"But who took her?" Mark pressed. "Whose carriage was it?"

"Ow," Ellie squalled, spouting a freshet of new tears. "God knows. God knows."

"You will stop this yowling and listen to me," Mark said sternly, catching her by the shoulder and giving her a sound shake. She was shocked enough to draw a deep breath and stare at him.

"Better," he nodded with approval. "Now listen to what I say. I will find her. If she lives, I will find her and keep her safe. But you must help me."

She nodded, holding her breath in an effort to stop her sobbing.

"You must find out everything you can about that man who paid for that room for the two of you. Listen to all the talk and report it to me. You must ask again and again about the carriage that stole her since some bit of fact often comes in some talk that is not aired at the first." He paused and his voice grew gentler. "And there is one thing more."

She eyed him warily.

"I am making the plea that your sentence be commuted. I am paying the fines that are assessed against you and your score in this place. In return for this, you must agree to be transported. You will go as a freewoman but with no fortune

244

to make a new start. But you will be free and a colonist. Do you understand?"

Her simple face was like a mirrored pool. Disbelief and delight and wonder crossed it like ripples then left it smooth again, blank with shock.

Then she began to tremble. She dropped to the floor and clasped him about the knees. "Oh holy Jesus," she whispered. "Oh holy Jesus, God have mercy."

He pulled her to her feet.

"This was her wish for you," he explained. "Thank her, not me. But you must help me find her."

"Not a rat will screech in this place that I do not hear," she promised. "She lives—tell me that she lives."

"We have to believe that," Mark told her. "The two of us."

Chapter Thirty-Four

When consciousness returned to Julie, she was careful not to stir. She felt the rattle of the coach in her pained head and felt the furious beat of the horse's feet as they carried the vehicle forward. Then there was the harsh scrape of the carriage braking and a driver's voice whoaing the beasts who brought the coach to a shuddering halt.

Her closed eyes registered a brief blaze of brilliant light before she was enfolded in something smooth. Then she felt herself being lifted like a child and borne through a door that creaked on its hinges then up a flight of stairs.

It was the pain that made her submissive. Her body ached from the tumbling she had received. The sudden brutality of her abductor numbed her into fear of facing this madman again.

Her eyes were still tightly closed when she felt herself thrown onto a soft bed to roll like a doll against a mound of pillows.

"Pierre," she heard a cold voice shout. "Come and tend this whore."

She felt herself to be alone. Without moving, she opened her eyes to the room that contained her. She knew at once that it was a woman's room from the scent of mingled lilac

245

and rose that came from the bed curtains behind her. The walls were decorated with a bright pattern of pale blue with gold. The drapes at the windows, like the curtains of the bed, were of some soft gold that deepened into an amber tone at the folds. A trim, white fireplace framed by curlicues of wood was covered by a painted fan that portrayed ivory fauns gamboling against a field of bright leaves.

She was not the only woman in the room. Staring at her from above the fireplace was a full length portrait of a lovely, young blonde girl. Her mound of pale hair seemed to catch the light in the room and beam it forth like a new sun. Her dark eyes were startling against the ivory perfection of her face. Her gown was pale gold with panniers of a deeper gold against which one hand held a careless nosegay of cornflowers and white daisies.

But it was not the careless grace nor the compelling beauty of the girl that brought a gasp to Julie's lips. Circling her smooth neck, with a pale curl falling across the stones, was that circlet of rubies which the painter's skill had made to twinkle with glowing light.

She heard Giles's voice, reciting the story to her, Mignon LeFevre's story which had become so inextricably wound into her own life. Was this the woman whose lover had been exiled only to return to find himself cuckolded by a dashing, blue-eyed gambler? Was this the woman whom Antoine had loved and murdered and robbed of the ruby necklace that Titus had pressed into her hands?

Her last sight of Antoine, his intimate pose with the copper-haired girl in the prison yard, brought a groan of anguish to her lips. How many chances had she had to betray him to his enemies? And now she was herself in the hands of Mignon LeFevre's lover—he could be no one else. Better to dance at Tyburn, as Ellie put it, than to face this girl of the portrait and and know that Antoine's passionate hungers had been fed here too.

The voice from the doorway was rough with fury. "The slut observes the queen," it sneered.

As she turned to the voice, her hand flew to her lips in shock. The man in the doorway, arms crossed against his chest, legs spread wide apart as if in triumph, stared back at her with those same gleaming, dark eyes of implacable hatred that had filled her with such terror at Newgate.

"You recognize me then." Some bitter parody of a smile twisted his mouth. He crossed the room and thrust his gold-tipped cane at the portrait. "My rubies," he told her fiercely. "One drop of blood red ruby for every year I waited to have her for my own. And now she is dead." He paused as if the word had struck the breath from him. "Dead," he repeated. "Even as you will be unless you reveal the name of the beast who robbed me of her."

Then, as if unable to bear the sight of her further, he spun on his heel. She heard his boots clatter as he descended the stairs.

The man Pierre who replaced him at the doorway was a squat man, heavy of body and flat of face. He was simple, she decided with a sudden clutch of fear. He grinned at her stupidly and then began to nod and motion her to follow. "Come," he said in a thick, unsure voice. When she did not at once respond, he scowled crossly like a child and started towards her threateningly.

She leaped from the bed only to stand wavering from dizziness. Her hand flew to her head to steady it. His small eyes watched as she gained her balance and did his bidding. He walked ahead of her down the hall, glancing back constantly. In his blue smock and routh pants, he resembled a shepherd leading a balky sheep to slaughter.

The small room where he led her was hazy with steam. A curved tub breathed fragrance into the air from its contents of heated water. Piles of blue and gold blankets, the shades of the room she had left, had been set by the tub. Pierre said some curt words to her in French, too rapidly and too strangely accented for her to understand. At her look of confusion, he pantomimed that she should remove her clothes. She felt herself flush scarlet as she shook her head violently.

He started towards her and she backed away, eyeing him warily. His bulk made him awkward, and after a few flat-footed feints at her he bawled for help in French.

His master was instantly at the door. Their quick exchange was beyond Julie's childhood French, but she stood with her arms crossed glaring at them both.

"Bitch," the dark-eyed man muttered, crossing to her with swift steps. There was no eluding him. He caught her by the hair and with his other hand caught the neck of her dress and ripped it off her in one swift, painful motion. The cloth

247

scraped at her arms as he ripped the sleeves off and threw the tatters of cloth away. He glanced at the sheer undergarment which was all she had left. "Get the rest off or have it torn off," he told her fiercely. "I want the foul scent of Newgate out of my chambers."

Inwardly raging, Julie turned her back to Pierre and slid off her stockings and slippers and finally the white chemise. He caught them from her hands and bundled them phlegmatically with the rest of her torn clothes.

Because it at least offered a respite from Pierre's staring, she slid into the tub voluntarily and began a furious sudsing to provide more cover from his eyes.

When her body was tingling from the hot scrubbing, and her freshly washed hair was bound in a blue turban, Pierre again said the only English word he seemed to have at his command.

"Come!" he ordered, motioning her into the hall.

She hesitated a moment and then caught a dry cloth and draped it around herself. He pushed her ahead of him along the hall and down the polished stairs.

Not even the humiliation of her near nakedness nor the fear of what lay ahead could blind her to the beauty of the quarters she found herself in. The graceful steps ended in a hallway where fresh flowers were reflected in an ornate, gold-and-white-framed mirror. A giant, hand-carved clock spoke softly to itself from the opposite wall, as Pierre flung open the drawing room doors.

The long, elegant room was again dressed in tones of gold and white, with touches of blue. The statuary, the arrangements of fine furniture, the glow of elegantly polished wood made a startling background for the great spiderlike shape of the dark man leaning against the mantel of the fireplace with a half-filled glass of red wine in his hand.

With barely a glance at her, he spoke to Pierre. With a single strong jerk the servant whipped the covering from her body, leaving her to stand naked and shivering, her bare feet still damp against the pattern of the rug. Without haste, the man set down his wineglass, pulled a packet from his pocket, and came towards her with the ruby circlet gleaming in his hand. She flinched as his hand touched her, and he stopped, his eyes narrowed in fury.

"You will not move away from me, slut," he told her

fiercely. "I have bought you at great cost and I will be served as I say."

"I am no slave," Julie said. "I may be a prisoner, but I am no slave to serve you."

He did not seem to hear her words. Instead, he frowned as he hooked the delicate catch of the circlet and adjusted it against the flesh of her throat. Then he stood back and smiled bitterly.

"There, Pierre," he said cordially. "Is that not a comely little whore? We grant that the murderer who has gained her mistaken loyalty has a delicate taste for female flesh."

Then, reaching forward, he tugged the towel from her head so that the mass of half-dried curls tumbled in ringlets onto her shoulders and down her back.

"Fah," he spat with a gesture of loathing. "She has the hair of a savage. Bring me the shears."

"No," Julie cried, aghast.

Fury darkened his face. He caught her bare arm and twisted it up behind her back until she bit her lips to hold back a scream. "You do not say that word to me, slut," he told her. "Now, hold her, Pierre."

With the hard arms of the stocky peasant pinning her arms close, the master whacked at her hair which fell in mounds about her on the carpet. Then he surveyed his work and handed the shears back to Pierre.

"Shaving would be better I expect," he mused, "but this will at least enable you to keep a wig in place." He kicked at the curls about his feet and turned away. "I like my women fair," he explained mildly. Then he motioned to a chair by the fire. "Sit and drink with me."

Forcing herself to forget her nudity, and struggling to control the trembling that racked her body, she poised on the edge of the chair and stared back at him. If he were not a mad, cruel beast, he might be a personable human. Indeed, she was going mad herself even to consider that. But he was tall and hard of body with a chiselled line to his bones that bespoke good blood. Only the glittering fury of his eyes and the cruel expression on his lips destroyed what might have been an imposing face.

"When I bid you to drink, you drink." he commanded. She lifted the goblet as he hissed at her. "Yes master," he prompted. "When I speak to you, the reply is 'Yes master.' "

She raised her eyes to his with the most scathing expression she knew how to assume and said, simperingly, "Yes, master." Then she emptied the goblet all at once as she had seen Ellie do. She coughed from the flow of sudden heat through her chilled throat.

"The woman you replace could outdrink a musketeer and still pass a pretty jest," he told her tauntingly. "Tell me your name."

"Sukey Titus," she replied.

The flat of his hand caught her across the face, knocking her from her uneasy perch on the chair. The goblet shattered into glistening shards among the strands of hair still piled on the carpet.

"Tell me your real name," he hissed. "I am not a lecherous old judge content to ogle and be cajoled. I am not a fop of a young attorney to be drawn yapping by the smell of a yellow-eyed bitch. Your true name."

"My name is Juliette Duvall, master," she said numbly.

"I sense a first lesson in truth," he said approvingly. "Where did you get the necklace?"

The hum in her head and the pain along her jaw fused into a trembling terror that she could not control. "The man who gave me the necklace is dead," she began, but he struck her again before the words were finished. This time she did not rise.

Chapter Thirty-Five

How many days and nights passed while he vented his fury on her with his questions and blows, his insults and humiliations, Julie could not gauge. Only the numbness of the repeated mistreatment saved her. She grew able to sit stark naked in the elegant dining room, wearing only the ruby circlet and an elaborate, curled wig of pale hair, and pretend to eat across the table from her master.

She learned to stand and stare back at him with her golden eyes and a perfectly impassive face as he raged and insulted and threatened her.

"The worst he can do is kill me," she reassured herself.

"Or perhaps that is the best and that is why he doesn't get on with that."

She was never alone. Every minute of the day and night one or the other of the men was with her. When she stirred to wakefulness at night, it was always to find her master sitting silently beside her watching her sleep.

She remembered Ellie's threats about the name that she had called out in her sleep and grew afraid. She dug her nails into her palms to keep herself wakeful. She spilled the wine she was served to keep herself sober. She learned to hide behind a bland, unchanging expression lest some change of mood in her face would give him fresh clues in his frantic search.

It was this last, this training her face to impassivity, that made her think of home. The gardener at her father's house had kept a small shed full of tools and potting aids. Once Bonbon had run free of her and chased something into that small hut. She had followed to find that he had trapped a young hare back in a corner where the dog's paw could not pull it forth. Squatting in the dimness, she had studied the tiny animal. Its ears were traced with rose, like the shells her father brought her from far shores. Its eyes shone like polished slate, and she could see, through the thick, soft fur of his side, the tumult of his terrified heart banging against his ribs. But still, he had sat unchanging, as if the very act of concealing fear and foregoing flight made him invisible to her eyes.

Hiding behind the secret, serene face she had learned to assume only made her tormenter's fury more frantic, but she felt secure. And as a hunted animal knows the ways of a hunter better than the hunger knows his quarry, she studied her master in the interest of survival. The glittering madness that had so terrified her at first became at last cause for her pity.

This was not true madness, she decided. This was the great grief of his lost love that had burned away his stable thought. How could she blame him for this? Hadn't her own dear Giles called her mad for clinging to her private "game" when a simple word would save her life? Would she not have clawed her way through stone walls and bare fingers if it would mean that she and Antoine would be back together

251

sharing life and love? If this were madness, then she sickened of the same illness.

His brutal fury with her was something else. His anger flamed with such heat that she could not believe that any man had energy enough for this emotion. Yet he never had the normal energy that she had learned to expect from a man. If he had ravished her brutally or made of her what he always called her—whore, slut, prostitute—then she would understand. It is unlike a man of some youth and great strength to live like a priest when he is constantly exposed to a woman he can command, she decided.

Then she began to notice that his most brutal attacks on her, his cruellest blows came only when he had exhibited what to her were the signs of a man's rising passion. He was unable to perform the act of a man, she decided. Somehow, without a knife, the death of Mignon had made of him a castrato.

These things she decided and kept secretly in her heart. But the third rush of truth about her master came upon her with such suddenness that she made the great error of speaking out.

Sometimes by night, when he thought her sleeping, she saw him turn and stare at Mignon's figure above the mantel. This did not startle Julie, for she herself was barely able to keep her eyes from that lovely face, even with the painful jealousy that it evoked in her.

But there came a night when the moonlight was strong on her master's face as he turned to stare at the girl whose pale hair gleamed with light from the flat surface of the canvas. She saw his expression clearly and was astonished to see that the dark eyes did not glow with tenderness. Instead, his gaze on Mignon was one of such furious loathing that Julie gasped in astonishment. The truth struck her like one of his own blows across the side of her head.

Caution forgotten, she sat upright in the bed and accused him. "Murderer," she whispered. "You are the murderer." Her voice rose as she spoke. "*He* did not butcher Mignon. You did it yourself. I know it. I know it."

He was stunned for only a moment. Then he leaped from the chair with a great animal cry of rage and threw himself at her. She clambered away to escape him even as he groped at his side for a sword that was not there. With a strangled cry and hands like claws, he started for her throat.

The bloodcurdling shriek that had torn from her throat brought Pierre. The exchange between the men was fearsome to watch, but Pierre's thick voice, chattering rapidly in that crude, peasant French, cooled the madman's brain. She curled in the corner on the floor as Pierre led her master away, as stone silent as a dead man.

After that night it was as if a sea change had come over him. He chose a new attack in his long war against her will. He rapped at her door (a decency which he had never before shown). At her reply, he stood in the doorway quietly.

"You will bathe and dress yourself for a venture in the city," he announced in a quiet voice. Then, with a false brightness, he added, "You might enjoy seeing some of your old friends again. I understand there is to be a hanging."

She was grateful that he turned away quickly. What did he know? Was it Ellie? Was it Antoine? She had been locked away this long time from the real world. God only knew what had taken place in the world outside her private hell. She hugged the covers, fighting back tears of terror until Pierre, scowling and motioning and mumbling "come," came to get her.

She knew without asking that the clothes that were laid out for her were Mignon's. She had finally grown accustomed to wearing the dead girl's wigs which her master insisted on because of their pale color. But to draw the pale blue stockings of the dead woman over her own warm flesh made her cringe.

The dress was of a heavily woven silk that fitted tightly about her waist. Its bodice was pointed in the shape of a *V* over her flat stomach. Full side panels in the overskirt emphasized the smallness of her waist, and her breasts rose quite daringly from a nest of fine ruffles. The matching cap was set back on the blonde wig, with its ribbons tumbling down to her bare shoulders. The ruby circlet, which he never let her remove except for bathing, gleamed above the pale colors of her dress.

She saw the line of white strain come along her master's jaw as she came down the stairs towards him, but he turned away quickly with a sneer.

"It was clever for me to think of this expedition," he com-

253

mended himself as he took her gloved hand into his own steel grip. "A little sunshine can only improve your complexion, which is as pale and as distasteful to me as the belly of a raw pike."

The carriage which had brought her at such a breakneck pace went leisurely along the streets with the curtains caught back to expose its occupants. So great a crowd had gathered at Oxford Street that it was impossible for the carriage to get through. Pierre stopped the carriage, and the master bid her dismount. Holding her hand tightly in his own, he sauntered along among the rabble that comprised the crowd. The grip on her hand and arm was so cruel that Julie was strained to keep her tears from beginning to flow.

When the bells of Saint Sepulchre set up their grim tolling, a great cheer went up from the crowd. All manner of objects were hurled at the passing cart, onions and dead animals and flowers bound in bright ribands and eggs too long past their season. Julie, her fine skirts, swaying among the ragtag crowd, felt terribly conspicuous. A gentleman whose face was strange to her paused to stare so intently into her face that her master's hand tightened on her arm.

"A friend of yours, no doubt?" he asked. As the gentleman caught the master's eyes, the stranger gave a brisk bow and hurried off.

"I have no friends here," she replied, praying that she spoke the truth.

"Then perhaps that man could become one," he suggested pleasantly. "What price would a whore like you bring in such a market as this? I could set you on a cart and have the crowd bid for your favors." His tone turned threatening. "Perhaps that 'he' that you mentioned last night might step forth and claim you for a few handfuls of coin."

She stared at him. So that was it. In her astonishment and great relief that it had been he and not Antoine who had murdered Mignon, she had made a slip of the tongue. He now knew from her thoughtless remark that there was a "he" who had not committed the murder that he had done himself.

"There but for my kindness, you might be riding," he pointed out as the cart passed near them. The wretches on it were dodging the offal that was being thrown. Julie winced to see, crouched in despair, the old woman to whom she had been chained on her first trip to Newgate. But the faces she

254

most dreaded to see were missing from the cart: Ellie was not there, nor was Antoine.

"The highwayman," she heard the crowd shout. "The highwayman." She schooled herself to show no greater interest. Still she felt a weakness of relief come over her as a small, bright-haired man rose to his feet in the cart and held his manacled arms aloft in a gesture of triumph before falling back among his chained companions.

They turned away a little short of the nevergreen tree itself. Julie sighed with relief, not feeling able to bear the sight of such wanton destruction of life. It was as they were working their way back to where Pierre waited with the carriage, that Julie felt rather than saw the young man staring at her. The intensity of his gaze brought a flush to her cheeks, and she quickened her steps at her master's side. It was to no avail. She saw the young man making his way through the crowd only a few feet away, keeping abreast of her with his eyes intent upon her as if she were the first Indian or a rare species of pet ape.

There were so many people of the city who might know her. There were the many patients she had served at Margaret's side and the merchants where they had shopped along the streets. Even, pray God that it not occur, there were her relatives, Joseph and her aunt. But the young man who stared at her so intently was none of these. She would have remembered that broad face dusted with freckles, the gap-toothed grin that was empty of wit or humor. Her steps must have lagged because her master jerked her along cruelly, making an ache begin in her wrist that was to keep her wakeful all that night.

That single slip of her tongue changed everything about her life. It gave her master new hope that he would indeed outwit her. He no longer insisted that she be humiliated by spending her hours in ridiculous nudity. Instead, he set out fine costumes for her and looked at her with approval. He stated his own hope boldly, and it set a chill to her heart.

He swallowed a bite of beef and washed it down with that red, French wine he was partial to. "This will work, you stubborn wench. There is no way it will not work. As little as I find you to my taste, I am sure that the bastard who lost you is wanting you back.

"If he or his friends are free upon the streets of London, I

255

shall parade you in their eyes. Then, when he attempts to come for his own, he will meet this." With a quick gesture, he swept a gleaming stiletto from his person and turned it in the candlelight of the table.

At her leap of terror, he laughed softly.

"We will traverse the city. Does he like cockfights or the bullpens? Will he pass along 'Change Alley or walk in the mall? We will chance upon this mysterious 'he' of yours, and your tight-lipped stubbornness will all be for naught."

"The man who gave me the jewels is dead," she repeated even knowing what would follow. After he struck her, he rose and stamped from the room, cursing her as she scrambled back to her feet.

"Give him a name," Ellie had pleaded. "Say any name." In this time that had passed, had Antoine made his fatal journey to Tyburn? She burned with anguish at the thought. If only she knew, then how boldly she would spit the name at him. Then the master would kill her. She was sure that in the end he would kill her and put the anguish of this torture behind her.

Through the day, as they had ridden through the streets of the city she had thought of that small, trapped hare again. She had thought of how it stayed silent and impassive until the moment for freedom had come, when Bonbon, distracted by some other happening, removed his attention to a few feet away. Then she had seen the swift, white length of the hare's darting in a zigzag back and forth into the cover of the thick woods.

She had told herself that she would bide her time in that same silent way, waiting for the chance moment that she might leap free of her master to bury herself in the crowds that teemed London's streets.

But seeing the slim knife had changed that. No distraction could come to give her escape time from a man whose motions were so swift, whose intent was so murderous.

That night she wept in her sleep. When the dampness of her pillow chilled her awake, she raised her eyes to his dark eyes staring back at her. Waiting. Always waiting for the moment her tongue might slip again and betray Antoine.

Chapter Thirty-Six

Henry Furlong watched young Mark Hatter enter the room. These weeks just past had been a revelation to the old banker. "That prentice has become a new man," he told his wife more than once during that time. "Having become a man of some property, being inspired to fulfill that deathbed pledge, he has grown in stature. He is impressive, my dear, I say that out directly. He is an impressive young man and has turned into something like a gentleman without knowing it."

"If only he can save dear Julie," she said back to him. "I would honor him as a ragman if he could bring that girl to some safety."

But the girl had disappeared. It was as if the dark carriage that snatched her from the door of the court had rattled off to hell to be buried in the bowels of the earth somewhere.

Seeing the shadow of despair still dark on Mark's brow, Henry Furlong nodded him into his chair. "No news then?"

Mark shrugged and sighed. "Not of Julie, I fear. But other things have been managed somewhat. My plea on behalf of the girl Ellie has been approved. She will be released on the stipulation of her transport. I have located a merchant ship which is leaving for the colonies within the fortnight. I have even made arrangements for her supplies on the journey. But there is no word of Julie, not even from the picture."

Henry Furlong dropped his eyes. This had been a mad scheme of Mark's from the first, but Mark had not been able to see it thus. When some days and a week had passed without word of Julie anywhere, when all their leads had trailed to dead ends, when it was established that neither the girl's odious kin nor the infatuated young Giles Urban was behind her abduction, Mark had clutched at this wild scheme.

Mark first came and slid a drawing across the desk to Henry Furlong. The face in the sketch took Henry Furlong's breath away. It was Julie to the hair, a little older by the year or so since he saw her, but no more than time would have set upon her since their last meeting. But that face, so like Fiona's had been, with the wide, fine forehead and the arch of perfect brows. The eyes stared back at him glinting with that rare gold, framed by the sweep of lashes. The same delicately formed nose above the ripe warm lips.

"My God," Mr. Furlong had cried. "Your skill would challenge Hogarth."

"But is it Julie as you remember her?" Mark asked. "Would a stranger recognize that face?"

"In a minute, less than a minute," Mr. Furlong assured him. "It is not like nature to create two perfect molds that fine."

Mark smiled with delight.

"Then here is my plan. Every prentice in this city shall see this picture. There will be a handsome reward, a full pound, a fortune to any prentice such as I myself was a few weeks ago. A pound shall be paid to the man who sees this face and tells me where the girl can be found."

"This is madness," Mr. Furlong protested. "It would take you a year to reach every prentice in this city. They are like the rats in the kennels, the fish in the Thames, too numerous to count."

"Aha," Mark cried. "That is the idea. Like the rats and the fish they have a community of their own. The noise of this reward will spread among them like pox. They will come to me in armies seeking to see the face. They will seek out that girl though she be hidden in the veriest side lane of London."

"Mark, Mark," Henry Furlong said sadly. "I know what property the goodwife Margaret left you. I know how charitably it has so far been spent. If this wild scheme should help you to find Julie and you spirit her off to the colonies to join her aunt, then what will you have left?"

"My health," Mark replied, "my skill with silver, and a pure soul."

"For the sake of a deathbed wish you are mortgaging your future and your chance to rise in the world. Is that not too much to risk?"

"For the deathbed wish alone, perhaps it is," Mark agreed. "But I think that what I say to you now is not a surprise. Seldom is it given to a man to love as purely as I adored Julie when I knew her only as Sukey Titus. Seldom is it given to be able to serve such a love without hope or chance or reward."

"You do not delude yourself that the world will honor or reward you for this kind of unselfish giving, do you?"

"If I free Julie to the hope of a new life, and the same for this foul-mouthed but great-hearted Ellie, I shall have reward enough." Then he grinned. "Who knows? I may indenture myself one day and end up a smith of some fame on those same shores."

Henry Furlong sighed and would have spoken, but Mark held up his hand.

"One moment, sir. There is one more thing I would say on this subject of rewards. I would exact a promise of you that whatever transpires, Julie is never to know where the resources came from that saved her. She is to think they came directly from Mistress Margaret herself."

"That is not a fair thing to require of me," Mr. Furlong protested. "The girl has a right to know to whom she is indebted."

"I ask you this as a pledge of honor, sir, as one man to another." Mark held out his hand.

"This is a rum go," Henry Furlong protested, then he paused a moment. "While we are on the subject of confidences, I have a confession to make to you. My own good wife whom you have never met is a woman of stout constitution and heart to match. She has been painfully fond of dear Julie since the girl was only a babe. She has not let me dine or rest in peace since Julie's arrest. She berates me night and morn for my 'stupidity' in handling the whole affair."

He paused and cleared his throat with embarrassment. "More to get her mind on something positive than otherwise, I have told her of each step in this great search for Julie. This has kept her out of mischief for the most part, but she did take one strange turn. She went to a Gypsy teller and paid the woman a handsome fee to look into the future."

Mark was tense on the edge of his chair.

"You and I know this is all nonsense," Mr. Furlong reminded him, "but the woman was convincing."

"So what was she told?" Mark pressed.

Mr. Furlong cleared his throat. "You know how those women are, those swarthy Gypsy wenches. They say ever the same thing but in such a way that a gullible woman will swallow it like a shrimp on a hook."

"What was she told?" Mark asked more firmly.

"That the girl she sought would take a long sea journey," Mr. Furlong sighed. "And that she would find a great love and would find him in widow's weeds."

Mark frowned. "The long sea voyage sounds promising, and surely the great love possible." He had the misfortune to flush deeply at his own words. "But what is this of widow's weeds?"

"My wife read the signs just as you have, but she seized on the last with great fervor."

"How is that?"

Mr. Furlong sighed. "She has gathered together the trinkets and comfits that a lady would need for that long voyage. She has also had full widow's weeds made for dear Julie. She claims, in her woman's logic, that Julie will be much grieved at the news of goodwife Margaret—and that such a costume, with the heavy veils and darkening effect, will do much to protect the girl from the unwelcome attentions of the men aboard whatever ship she travels on."

Mark's face glowed with delight. "What a clever wife you have, Mr. Furlong."

The banker groaned. "What I have is a great store of shipboard provisions and an eager wife nagging at me to produce a girl to fit into that wardrobe she has assembled."

"It is an act of faith," Mark said. "I take it as a good omen."

"As you will," Mr. Furlong sighed. "But do keep us abreast of every small thing that happens. Such tidbits of news are all that keep my life at home from becoming insufferable."

The lodgings on Fleet Street were somber indeed with only himself and Trump rattling about in the rooms. As soon as the search for Julie was successful, Mark would let the place go. Each night as he turned the corner a fresh wave of loneliness struck him. He remembered how it had been when they were all there, Kit banging furiously in the kitchen, Margaret nodding in her chair, and Sukey (would he ever learn to think of her otherwise?) rising to meet him with that smile that churned his heart with painful desire.

But now the house's blind eyes stared bleakly into the street. He did not even glance down at the darkness on the

260

stoop until he had his latchkey in hand. A fellow scrambled to his feet from the shadows and smiled at Mark.

"I have been waiting for you, sir," he said. "I must have napped off a bit there."

"Waiting for me?" Mark asked. "For what reason?"

The boy looked about nervously. "Could I come inside and then we would talk?"

Mark, alert against a trick, looked about. "Are you alone?"

The boy nodded furiously and then whispered. "It's about the picture, sir. The picture of the girl."

The girl. Mark's hand faltered with the familiar key, jiggling it wildly in the slot before he could make it set right.

"Come, come," he urged the boy. "Come on back here."

He set a candle to light in the kitchen and blew the flame up under the kettle that the char had left on the hob. He was afraid to let the boy speak for fear it might be another of the false runs that he had encountered since the word got about.

"Now about the picture."

Mark gauged the boy to be in his late teens, a small, ill-shaped young man with a broad face darkened by freckles. His smile could best be described as stupidly amiable.

"It's about her hair, sir," the boy stammered. "The girl wot I see is like yours to the line except for the hair. What color was the hair again, sir, that I might see if it is the girl who is worth a pound to you?"

"Dark," Mark said. "Almost as black as the ravens who walk by Saint Paul's."

The boy frowned and hopped back and forth from one foot to the other. "They be twins then," he decided aloud. "They be twins and the one I see has fair, almost white, hair. But the faces is the same and this one so sad."

"And where do you see her?"

"The first time on Oxford Street," the boy said eagerly. "Because the hair was different, I made cause to watch some more. She got into a dark carriage with all black horses."

"And tell me about the carriage?"

"Black it was with only a flip of silver trim."

"And was she alone?"

"Oh no sir, she never is. Not that time or the next or the time after that."

Mark struck his forehead with dismay. "My God, you have seen her these three times without coming to me."

"I thought to be laughed at," the boy confessed. "With her hair so white and all."

"Tell me. Would you know a wig if you saw one?"

The boy's mouth fell agape. "On a man I can tell. I never much think of that with women."

Mark sighed. "And who is with her since she is never alone?"

"A gentleman," the boy said quickly. "A tall gentleman with a streak of mean in his face. Mean eyes," the boy added. "And never smiling."

Ellie's words: "There was a man, the dark stranger we called him. Every day he stood beyond the fence and stared at Sukey. Not speaking, not smiling. Eyes like a drawn sword he had, looking hate at her to make her shiver in the bright of noon."

"And have you ever stayed after this carriage long enough to see where it gets to?"

"Close but not exact," the boy confessed. "It always gets away from me on Leicester Square—into one of those lanes that lead off."

"Sweet Jesus," Mark cried.

The boy stared at him.

"Nothing, nothing," Mark said. His own apprenticeship had been in Cranbourn Alley just off there.

"If it be she will I have a pound, sir, or is that a story I heard?"

"You'll have the pound with my blessing," Mark said. "Leave me your name and where you can be reached. If I find her as you said, you'll have a pound to steam."

He was letting the boy out when he turned and smiled that silly grin again. "There was another thing I meant to tell," he said to Mark. "This girl, the fair one, has a bright set of beads around her neck that are the prettiest red I ever seen. Like blood they are, that red."

Chapter Thirty-Seven

Fatigue and hunger forgotten, Mark banked the fire again, spilled a mess of food out for Trump, and went into the night once more, with his stout stick in hand and the lightest heart he could remember for a long time.

The easiest way to gather a crowd of prentices, Mark thought with a grin, was to call them out for a pint and tell them you're buying.

"Ten or twelve sturdy boys could stall a carriage," he reminded the silversmith prentices as they leaned together over the table. "It's too busy a street for the horses to get away—particularly if someone was to grab the reins at the first cry."

"And what if the wrong carriage was got?" someone asked.

Mark shrugged. "What's to care, just so the right one is got alongside. The one we want is a big black one with some flocks of silver along the side, nothing fancy."

"Then what's to be done?" a nervous voice asked. Mark recognized him as Tim, a rabbity sort, who flinched at the cast of his own shadow.

"Nothing you all ain't done a hundred times," Mark reminded them. "Just plunge about in the street and topple the gentry and keep the shout up. A few 'There he goes,' 'I see him', 'Grab the bounder,' that sort of thing. I would like a man to stand up for the holding of the reins if you'd please."

"I'm for that," a man named Bob spoke up. "I do like the feel of lively beasts under hand."

"And how long so you need with this carriage?" a sober voice asked.

"Two, three minutes," Mark hesitated, "maybe five"

"No constable gets there that fast," someone scoffed.

"That's the idea," Mark grinned. "By the time he comes, it's all over and another pickpocket has made a lift and got away clean."

"And when will this lark come off?"

"As soon as tomorrow but who's to know? I'll stay about and loiter until the right time. But keep the ears cocked, say?"

263

"I'm for the lark for sure," one of the fellows laughed. "I wanted the pound, but I'll settle for the play."

"Your plan makes me uncommonly edgy," Mr. Furlong protested. "What if the dark man is armed or his driver a fighter?"

"In the confusion of twenty howling prentices, a kingdom could go down," Mark reminded him.

"I for one shall breathe easier when it is done. And you say you'll have a hired carriage waiting to whisk the girl into?"

"Every day from tomorrow on," Mark assured him.

"Well, I'll bless the Norman law and shake your hand if you bring it off, lad," Mr Furlong sighed, rising to shake Mark's hand for luck. "And let us know, son. Let my good wife and me know the minute that the girl is safe."

For three days, Mark moped along the shops around the square watching for the dark carriage that the flat-faced boy had described. For three days, he paid off the carriage he had hired whose driver had sat all day scratching himself and grumbling but was happy enough to have full fare with no work at each day's end.

The fourth day came with a weak sun barely glowing through the great haze of coal dust that London wore like an old hat. It was bearing on noon when Mark saw the dark carriage roll forth from Newport Lane. The fair-haired girl sat stiffly on the seat, her bright face blank and unsmiling. A riot of pink ribbons floated from a high, ruffled cap, but the face under the mass of frosty curls was Julie's. Mark recognized the tilt of her fine nose, her tawny eyes sad and unsmiling. Behind her like a shadow of doom loomed the figure of a man. One glimpse and the carriage was gone, leaving Mark hard put to control the wild drumming of his heart.

Forcing himself to walk calmly along the street, Mark passed the word to the key prentices. He checked that his own hired carriage was in such a spot that no amount of confusion would prevent the man from making a quick departure. The day droned endlessly as fear hardened in Mark's belly like a bad fish. The day wore towards sundown, and still there was only the ordinary traffic along the street. What if the carriage would not return? What if they had left with luggage in the boot for a trip to Bath or a sojourn in the country? There was no surety that every carriage that rolled forth would roll back. What if the prentices were gone for the night when the dark carriage came spinning back towards its lane?

In the midst of his panic, he heard, among the cries of the hawkers, the rumbling of a new carriage. Sedan carriers leaped aside as the dark horses came along the street, heedless of the traffic in the way.

Mark pitched into the full of a crowd, bumped heavily against a woman carrying a great armload of silver, and then let out a great cry of alarm.

"Pickpocket, pickpocket," he howled at the top of his lungs. "After that man, I've been robbed." Pointing wildly into the crowd in the path of the oncoming carriage he continued his howling. "Hue and cry. After that man."

That excellent law, the good Norman law as Henry Furlong had called it, galvanized the street. From every shop and coffeehouse the people came pouring to pursue the fleeing criminal.

The teeming crowd which clotted the street forced the dark horses to a bucking halt. The carriage, caught just at a turn, waggled back and forth dangerously. The street was an anthill of apprentices, all whooping and shouting and toppling sober citizens from their pins. From the corner of his eye, Mark saw his friend catch the reins of the horses as the driver, screaming French blasphemy, whaled at him with a stout cudgel.

As he raced quickly towards the carriage, Mark noticed a stout woman of some considerable age. Instead of fleeing to the safety of the walk as other women had done, she was bearing down on the carriage with the dignity of a flagship. She cut through the crowd of howling apprentices like a knife, leaving them gasping in her wake. Go back, he wanted to scream at her, but the carriage was keeling his way and he leaped to the opportunity.

It was Mark's hope that the man inside would come toppling forth with the opening of the door. Instead, as Mark swung the door back, the man was framed above him. His face was twisted in a snarl with a lean, shining blade poised above Mark's head.

"Hey now," a voice came behind Mark, as did a cry of "heave to." At the signal a group of the prentices threw themselves heavily against the carriage causing it to keel the other way and throw the man off his balance.

My God, he would slice Julie with that dagger, Mark thought in panic. Mark doubled himself and threw himself into the carriage directly against the lean legs of the man inside. He felt the strength of the man's legs like trees against his shoulders as he struck them. But the trees were felled by his weight and the two of them went rolling, past the seats, through the open door on the other side and out into the street.

The dark stranger had gone down like a stone. He strove to raise himself once and then, with a great groan, lay back. Mark struggled to his feet to search for that blonde head along the street. The cry of "constable" was noised along the way and the swarm of prentices dispersed, disappearing into shops along lanes and down the way. She was gone from the coach, but where was she?

Mark studied the crowds that lined the street. He saw the driver leap to his master's aid and half-lift him into the seat of the carriage. Only when Mark had glanced into every shop and searched every lane did the enormity of his failure hit him.

Something like sickness came over him. He buried his head in his hands for a moment then made his way to the hired carriage he had so hopefully supplied.

"Where to now, sir?" the driver asked.

"To hell," Mark said defeatedly, counting out the driver's fee and pressing it into the man's hand.

"Tomorrow again?" the man asked hopefully.

"Never," Mark said dully. The word echoed in his own head like a funeral knoll. He had failed. God only knew where Julie had got to now. It was lost. All was lost.

Chapter Thirty-Eight

Julie concealed the relief she felt when she heard her master direct Pierre to return home. The long day had become increasingly insufferable to her. As little peace as she was able to find in that blue and gold prison, its quiet was still preferable to the "entertainments' she had seen submitted to this day.

She stared stright ahead, trying to blot from her mind the scenes of the hours just past. When his plan to expose her in London until he chanced upon the haunts of the man whose name she protected failed to produce any success, he grew frantic with desperation. A frenzy for blood had been upon him all the day long. He had led her to a series of scenes more brutal than her mind could have conjured in its wildest delirium.

The scent of blood hung in her head from the frightful carnage at the bear pit, the cockfights, and the unequal battle between a chained mastiff and a group of ravenous dogs.

Withdrawn behind her impassive face as was her wont, she did not even heed what streets they passed as Pierre whipped the horses towards home. The carriage was starting into its turn off Leicester Square when a muffled curse at her side roused her from her revery. She was struck painfully in the ribs by her master's elbow as he struggled at his waist for the dagger he always carried there. She looked about her in astonishment. The usually peaceful street was alive with rabble. The din was deafening. Above the shouting of many voices, she heard the terrified whinnying of the carriage horses. The carriage rocked wildly as the horses were jerked to a stop.

It was then that she heard that single phrase through the window, a phrase out of her past understanding.

"Get him," strange voices cried. "Hue and cry."

Mark's voice in the warm coziness of Margaret's kitchen. The four of them at tea with Thump complaining in his corner and conversation knitting them together in warmth and gentle affection. Mark's tale of the thief who had raced from his master's shop carrying silver plate, his amusement that she had not heard of that old Norman law which forced every man into the streets in pursuit of the criminal. Hue and cry with pandemonium was often more helpful to the thief than a quiet intense chase might be.

The carriage was rocking wildly from side to side throwing her now against her master's back and then against her own door.

A sense of danger quickened her heartbeat. Her mind reached for the unthinkable word—escape. She was the hare

267

in the garden shed, and the dog's attention had wandered. She had only half-phrased the idea in her own mind when a draft of air told her that her master's door had been flung open. He leaped to his feet. His back was to her and she saw the flitter of the knife poised above his head in self-defense.

She was concious of the sudden warmth of tears on her own face and was puzzled at them. She was not afraid, but an intolerable excitement trembled in her limbs. "Courage," it flashed in her mind, "is what comes when you have nothing left to lose." The small voice inside herself overpowered the din of the streets and the wild neighing of the horses.

"Fly."

She seized the handle of the door and threw her whole weight against it.

"Fly," the voice prodded imperiously. "Fly."

The moment that she rolled out of the open door into the street, the carriage began to rock even more wildly. Her hands smarted from striking the rough stones of the street. With her palms stinging painfully, she tucked up the heavy silk skirt of her gown and scrambled to her feet. Even as she rose, she tugged the great blonde wig from her head to throw behind her under the wheels of the carriage. Her head felt light, almost giddy with only her short curls about her face.

"Fly," the voice commanded over and again.

She could not run. People were packed along the street like pickles in a crock. She ducked her head and began to shove and dive her way among them, wriggling and poking to put distance, any amount of distance, between herself and the angry roar of her master's voice behind her.

Strange bodies were warm against her, her nose was assailed by the mingled stench of sweat and perfume. Hands caught at her, and she wrestled free of them. Then the corner was turned and the crowd, still moving towards the turmoil, was streaming away from her. She slowed to a walk, feeling the harshness of the street through her dainty slippers as a solid and profitable pain. She was almost free of the last of the crowd when she heard, high and shrill and beseeching the sound of her own name.

"Julie," the syllables hung in the air. "Julie Duvall."

Her heart seemed to stop. That voice. She stopped stockstill to stare back. The woman bearing down on her was dishevelled. A great wig was cocked awry and her mouth was open, gasping for breath like a fish on a stream bank. She was carrying a large bundle which she used like a weapon to batter her way towards Julie.

"Stand back," she shouted, more like a fishmonger than the lady that she was.

Julie felt the fresh rush of tears come as the woman reached her, caught at her arms, and folded her against her ample bosom in a frantic embrace.

"Julie," Madame Furlong gasped. "My dear. My very dear."

"Mistress Furlong," Julie cried, feeling her legs grow weak with relief.

"Up, up," Mistress Furlong ordered, her face beaming with delight. "This way, run quickly. Follow me."

There was no need for Julie to follow. Mrs. Furlong had seized her hand and was dragging her along almost roughly towards the familiar carriage that waited on the street. The driver Jack had the door open at their approach, and, in spite of her bulk and breathlessness, Madame Furlong climbed smartly into the seat and pulled Julie up behind her.

"Home," she called to the driver. "And a bottle of porter if you can make it in half-time."

Mistress Furlong struggled with the ties on her bundle and drew forth a mass of black. "Quickly, put that on," she ordered, "in case someone follows."

The widow's cap had rich, flowing veils that fell to Julie's shoulders, completely concealing her face and the mass of riotous curls that it covered. Julie sighed with blessed peace as she felt the privacy of that half-darkness circle her face.

"Dear one," Mistress Furlong cried, seizing her again in a fervent embrace. "It is done. At last you are safe. A Gypsy told me."

Julie tried to sort out the breathless story from Mistress Furlong's chatter. It was no use. Some things were repeated over and over: "the Gypsy" and then the phrase "that great Mark Hatter." There was something about a picture and "poor dear Margaret" over and again. But in between every breathless sentence came that same note of high triumph.

"I told Henry what the Gypsy told me and he only laughed."

Julie leaned her head back tiredly against the soft cushions of the carriage.

"Whatever this all means, I thank you, oh God. How I thank you."

"Mark." Mistress Furlong fairly exploded his name. "The poor boy must be frantic not knowing you are safe. And this is all his doing, you know, his and the Gypsy's."

Julie nodded numbly. Mark Hatter and a Gypsy. She tried understanding and settled for acceptance. "Mark and the Gypsy," she repeated, her voice husky with gratitude.

The handsome house on Pall Mall was as Julie remembered it. The same clock chimed in the elegantly dressed parlor, and in its cage by the window, Mistress Furlong's linnet slept with its head covered by its wing.

Mr. Furlong, in dressing gown and slippers, with his wig laid aside and his sparse gray hair caught back in a queue, leapt from his chair with astonishment.

"Julie," he cried. "Mistress. My God it is done." Then he frowned. "But where is Mark? Is he not with you?"

His wife was suddenly so distracted by the task of removing her gloves that she could not meet his eyes. "We haven't seen the dear boy, my dear," she said quickly. "But then I would not know him if I had seen him." This last was was an obvious reproach.

With his hands still on Julie's arms, Henry Furlong turned to his wife. Such a brilliant rush of color came to his cheeks, and his eyes bulged so alarmingly that Julie was for a moment terrified that he was threatened with a seizure. He had some difficulty speaking, and when his words did start, they popped out with explosive force.

"What—What have you been up to, my lady?" His tone was anything but gentle. "What mischief have you been making?"

Julie was hard pressed to contain her giggles when she saw the mock astonishment and innocence come to Mistress Furlong's face. "Me? Mischief?" she asked. "'My dear Henry."

"Don't you 'Dear Henry' me," her husband almost shouted.

"I happened to be in Leicester Square," she began.

"Happened, happened," he groaned, seizing his head in his hands.

"And there was a great to-do about a pickpocket—"

"Oh fool," he groaned. "I am wedded to such a fool."

"And this carriage was overturning at the corner, and who should tumble out but Julie here—our dear lost Julie." Mistress Furlong let her eyes stray to Julie, then her arch control was gone as it had come, into swift penitence.

"Oh my dear Henry," her voice was pleading. "I was so dreadfully afraid that something would go amiss with Mark's plan. And it did, it truly did. The man with Julie was armed with a knife and he attacked Mark." Her husband's groan did not slow the tumble of words. "While they were wrestling for the weapon, I saw Julie come tumbling out of that rocking carriage like a bundle of laundry. Then she was up and off down the street like a shot." Mistress Furlong pressed her hand against her heart, her eyes pleading for her husband's sympathy. "Never did I think I could make these old legs pump that fast."

"But she did run," Julie put in with a giggle that she could not suppress. "She flew after me at such a pace that I was way around the corner when she caught up with me."

"Thank God for that," Henry Furlong seemed a little mollified. "But what of Mark? What of that great Mark? How did he fare in this knife fight? Does he know that our Julie is safe?"

His wife's voice was brisk with efficiency. "I have sent Jack to Margaret's house in Fleet Street to find him. I told him to wait the night through if need be. I promised him an extra bottle of porter for this," she added in an aside. "Mark will have to go back there. Where else has he to go?"

Where else did Mark have to go? Through the busy hours that followed, Julie pondered that question. She knew the violence that seethed beneath the dark exterior of her former master's control; she knew without a shadow of her own doubt that he had killed his own beloved in a fit of passionate jealousy. How would gentle Mark have fared at his hand?

She was cosseted with fresh, strong coffee with clotted cream floating in golden baubles in the cup. There were sandwiches of the breast of a turkey sliced thin and an apple cake with caramel topping still warm from the oven. Yet Mark did not come.

She was told the sad tale of Margaret's last hours and of her interment in a grave near her own dear sister as she had carefully outlined in her last testament. Julie wept for the goodness and powers that had passed with her friend and for the bleakness of her own world knowing that Margaret was absent from it. And yet Mark did not come.

When the clock tolled eleven, Mr. Furlong, his face slack with fatigue, finally made the decision. "You two are to go to bed," he ordered. "If anything is heard of Mark you will be knocked up directly. There is no sense in stealing your strength from the morrow."

Julie, in a gown that she could fold about herself twice, heard the rattle of the carriage in the drive and then the low voice of the bell sounding in the house below. Mistress Furlong had folded a rose-colored robe across Julie's bed. By the time the servant's step was heard on the stair, Julie was wrapped into the robe and out into the hall.

The draperies in the parlor had been drawn for the night. Only a single small candle lit the capacious room. Mark stood very straight in the center of the room with his cap held diffidently in his large hands. Since he did not hear her quiet feet on the stair, Julie took advantage of that brief moment to cherish him with her eyes. He was no longer a lad, she realized. He had become a man over these weeks. What had appeared to be ungainly and awkward in his stance had become a manly solidity.

She called to him softly, eager to hear his voice.

"Mark," she said. "Is it indeed you?"

"Sukey," His voice broke with the word. "Sukey, Julie. Thank God. Thank God."

Without hesitation, she flew to him and wrapped her arms tightly about his neck. "They have told me," she confided. "They have told me that it was you who cleverly found where I was being hidden. That it was you who planned that brilliant escape from my tormenter. Oh, Mark, you are my greatest friend."

His body was so tense in her arms that she pulled back to stare up into his face.

"How can I ever thank you, Mark? How can I repay my great debt to you?"

She could not understand what a cruel temptation came to Mark. She only knew that for a moment, his fine, open face was twisted with anguish. He shuddered as if some inner struggle had brought a shock of physical pain to his body. Then he bowed his head a little and his words were little more than a whisper.

"It was Margaret's doing," he told her slowly. "I have only acted in her stead."

At the mention of her friend's name, the fresh ache of her loss returned to Julie. She leaned against Mark's breast in grief. Somehow, the steady thunder of his heart beneath her head was comforting to her.

Then the others were down, and fresh candles were set in the sconces. Wine was served all around, and a feeling of holiday even wakened the linnet to hesitant song.

There was much retelling of the tale of Julie's escape, from everyone's point of view. Each of them had a host of questions that must be answered instantly.

"I must know where you have been all these hours," Julie told Mark. "I died for your wounds so many times since the darkness of night came."

Mark hesitated and then answered soberly. "I went along the river to the bridge," he confessed," and stared a long time down at that swirling current."

"Mark," Julie cried, chilled at the implication in his words.

"There seemed little to live for after my failure," he told her.

"Then what brought you back?" Mistress Furlong asked. "Was it some second sense that Julie had indeed been saved?"

"Or the fear of the eternal damnation that is visited on suicides?" Henry Furlong put in with a pompous glare of reproach at his wife.

Mark looked very thoughtful for a moment. Then his face flushed in that old way that brought a smile of gentle affection to Julie's lips. "I may as well confess it," he said, his own face breaking into a wide grin. "I came back because of the dog Trump. He stinks something fierce and is never without a complaint. He is cross and unpleasant and even surly with his food. But he would have starved if I had not come back to care for him." He raised his eyes to Julie with an apologetic smile. "You remember, our mistress was able to love him, and I have learned it from her."

The laughter that followed his words eased the tension in the room, and soon their talk turned towards the future.

"In only a few days, a ship readies for the trip to the colonies," Mark told Julie, exchanging a mysterious glance with Henry Furlong. "This craft is set for Charles Town. Would you be able to reach your aunt's colonial home from that place?"

Julie nodded. "She lives near Charles Town," she replied, "very near as I understand that land." Her words came from some strange place outside herself. Antoine. How could she leave England with Antoine in chains? "Very near" she heard herself repeat.

"Then it would be acceptable for you to have your passage arranged on this ship?" Mr. Furlong asked, his eyes thoughtful on her face.

She dropped her eyes that no one might be privy to the agony of this decision. "I will take passage and feel fortunate to have escaped the perils of the past months." Then she frowned. "But what of the cost of all this? It must cost many pounds to send a person all that way. Into whose debt am I falling?"

Mark's reply was overquick. "Mistress Margaret left much property for a woman in service," he explained. "Her last dear wish was that you be saved."

Julie missed the exchange of rueful glances between Mr. Furlong and his wife.

"Tomorrow I will show you the stores I have got together for your passage," Mistress Furlong said with excitement in her voice.

"And Mark has even made arrangements for a young woman to travel with you as a companion," Henry Furlong put in.

Julie stared from one to the other of them in disbelief. "How could you have been so sure I could be found?" she asked. "When I myself had given up hope of any release short of death, how could you have possibly known that all this would come about?"

"A Gypsy told me," Mistress Furlong said with a triumphant shake of her head at her husband.

PART V
FAIR SEAS AND FOUL
September, 1722–Last of October, 1722

Chapter Thirty-Nine

Coming from imprisonment to freedom, from the darkness of her master's loathing to the warmth and affection which surrounded her at the house on Pall Mall, Julie fell into a state something akin to shock. She was able to perform all that was expected of her, but a sense of detachment gave her the eery feeling that she was watching this person—this Julie Duvall—while she herself stood a little apart, a ghost at her own joyful feast.

Mark regaled her with details of the *Tilbury Belle*, the ship which was already nearly ready for its crossing, and of the ship's captain, a man named Douglas who had come highly recommended.

"It's not the fanciest of ships," Mark told her, "but it is seaworthy. It plies that triangle of trade: England to the colonies with manufactured goods, then on to the West Indies with grains and lumber, and then back home with sugar and molasess. The trip will be lonely since there will be no passengers aboard except you and your companion. Good luck and fair winds will see you in Charles Town in seven or eight weeks, safe with your father's sister."

Because he so clearly wished for her to be happy with his arrangements, and because she felt such a surge of fondness for him, she smiled approval while her heart ached at the thought of leaving Antoine.

With a great groan, Mistress Furlong let herself down on her knees to show Julie the clothing and trinkets that she had prepared for her. The scent of dried lavendar rose from the neatly folded garments in the sea chest, and Mistress Furlong challenged her to find the carefully concealed locked drawer where money and jewels could be hidden.

Fearing that her dark master might apprehend her if she dared to be abroad in London, Mark had arranged that she not board the ship until it left its head on the Thames and moved out towards the sea.

With each day that brought her closer to that journey to

Gravesend, Julie found it harder to lay aside her inner conflict and respond to the pleasantries of those about her.

She thought of Newgate with longing. If she were only able to see Ellie and know that she was all right. Mark had informed her that the girl was willing and planning to plead for transport, but Julie needed reassurance. Secretly she thought that she might even catch a glimpse of Antoine, his fine, straight figure marching its brisk, tortured passages back and forth in the exercise yard. Even to hold him with her eyes from afar would ease this not knowing that gnawed at her like a sickness.

How could she leave on a fair wind while he was in chains with the gallows still shadowing his life? Why was she facing this perilous journey for a life that was meaningless without him?

Sleepless, she stood at the window of the bedroom at night. The wind that stirred the trees beyond her window spoke of Epping and the massive forest that had held that cabin in its heart. When small birds twitched in the branches outside, she shut her eyes, trying to believe that Titus was hopping along the path in the clearing and the great horse was bringing Antoine from his night's adventure back to her arms.

"It is the not knowing," she whispered aloud to herself. "Perhaps if I knew that it was all over for him I might begin to heal—" But at the very thought of his death, she would collapse into tears, unable to bear the thought of a world that did not somewhere hold his face and his voice and the strong, fine intent of his eyes meeting her own.

The Furlongs, watching her labor under the stress of this great anguish, pondered her distress in private.

"Never mind that her father was French and her dear mother from Ireland, that girl is English. To the bone she is," Mr. Furlong insisted. "She is grieving at the thought of leaving this great country behind. And as I think on it, I fear that I would be the same if I were forced to leave my king and country forever."

"I think it is simply fear," Mistress Furlong argued. "Think of that crude life she will face, Indians and blackamoors and huts hacked out of trees and all manner of wild beasts roving beyond the door."

"Good grief, wife," her husband rebuked her gently. "This is 1722. Charles Town is a booming little city. Many of its citizens are French like her father. I assure you that they have lovely homes and good, safe streets to walk upon. It is a city that is growing famous for commerce. Why there are twenty thousand people there if you choose to count the black slaves. The rice from those marshes is as fine as any in the world. Our Julie is not being dropped into a wilderness of savages."

"I'd like to know how you can be so sure about that," his wife fretted unhappily. "What kind of a woman is this aunt of hers? What if she turns out to be as cruel and stupid as her own brother was?"

"Show me some faith, woman," Henry Furlong bellowed, more concerned than he wished to admit. "Pluck up your courage and put a bright face upon this change lest you infect her with your own fears and only make her doubts stronger."

"Mark could cheer her with only a few words," Mistress Furlong fussed. "Why doesn't he tell her that her companion on ship will be her friend from Newgate? That would at least give her somewhat to look forward to."

Her husband shook his head. "That Mark knows what he is about. He feels that Julie's distress at leaving her own grand country will be eased by the surprise of finding that she has that bright-faced girl for company. We can only honor his wishes on this."

The barrels and crates and bundles of stores were finally piled into a separate carriage for Gravesend. Julie's head was stuffed as tight as that carriage with the advice of everyone about her.

"Keep your veils down and your mantle about you when moving about the ship," Mark counselled. "It is well known that men at sea are a rough sort with a poor hold on their passions. They would be tempted to dangerous acts with a face and form like yours."

The maid Nellie who daily clucked over Julie's crisp, short curls, and tried to shape them into the pattern of fashion, spoke of sea travel with great authority. "My own brother is a mate in the navy," she confided to Julie. "He has the belief that one must eat living green to stave off sickness. You make yourself a garden," she advised Julie confidentially. "Set turnips with the tops up in the lightest place, and eat the green wot grows." She nodded wisely. "Saves you from sea fever."

Mistress Furlong herself had cast her mind on past the journey itself and advised Julie on the "great decision of a woman's life" as she called it.

"Marry yourself a man of business," she said firmly. "Once a man falls under the sway of money, his natural fevers cool and he will ever be faithful to what is at hand."

At Julie's astonished look, the older woman flushed. "It's my own way of thinking," her friend explained. "It's better for me to have sometimes ennui than ever heartbreak."

"Sometimes ennui." The phrase stayed in Julie's mind as she was tucked into the carriage between Mistress Furlong and Mark. What could life be except ennui without Antoine, not sometimes ennui, but an endless life of it stretching ahead?

It was late afternoon when Julie's chests and packages had all been hauled aboard the *Tilbury Belle* and stored in her stateroom. Caught in the melee of the crowd, Julie clung to Mark's arm, unused to the half-blindness of the widow's veiling that concealed her face and darkened her view of her surroundings.

Having never been aboard ship, Julie stared curiously about at the room which had been provided for the months ahead. The stateroom looked to be the height of a man and about half again. Trim beds were fitted against the opposing walls, and under the beds were the stores that been been brought aboard. A small table with two neat chairs completed the furnishings. On the table was a great basket of bright oranges with a handful of ribboned flowers stuck into the top for extra color.

She saw the wooden crate of books which Henry Furlong had selected for her with much heming and hawing, and a basket of needlework topped by a plaited length of silks. She was struck again by the great expense that had been incurred in getting this journey of hers together and grieved that Margaret could not realize how much she appreciated this testament of love.

When the actual moment of parting came, Julie found herself overwhelmed with emotion. How final it was to press her face for this last time against the scented powder of Mistress Furlong's cheek. How marvelously warming to see Henry Furlong struck with a sudden "indisposition" that reddened his eyes and brought his handerchief to his face for a great honking and fluttering that he would not for the world admit had been sentiment. Then there was Mark. Julie strained on tiptoe to wrap her arms about his neck and hold him close. Her tongue was helpless for words to convey her gratitude and tenderness towards him, and she shared the deep sigh that he gave as he drew away and followed her friends down the plank to shore.

In spite of Mark's worried counsel, she stood at the rail and watched her friends until they were in the carriage and the carriage itself was lost among the crowds of moving vehicles.

She was still frozen in that farewell when she realized that she was not alone. A man in the ship's uniform stood a little aside from her, his eyes apologetic on her face. In spite of his sturdiness of build and the rich color of his sun-bronzed face, he looked somehow helpless as she turned to him with brimming eyes.

"Begging your pardon, madame," he said in a broad, up-country tongue that warmed her ears. "I am Jim, Captain Douglas's mate, and I bring you his compliments. He bids me tell you that he would ha' come himself except that a fair wind rises that we must not waste. He bids you welcome to the *Tilbury Belle*."

"Thank you Jim," Julie said, struggling to remove the huskiness of emotion from her voice. "Thank Captain Douglas for me and tell him that I wish him well on this passage."

He nodded with vigor, obviously pleased at her words.

"Likeways he would have me tell you that your companion is below in your stateroom and that when we are at sea, he would be greatly indebted if you both would dine with him in his quarters."

With her acceptance of that invitation, Jim nodded and moved a way a bit where he lingered nervously for a few moments before making his way along the deck to speak to a band of men laboring at the sails. She could feel Jim's urgency that she abandon her post and go below, but the scene was too enthralling to her. Bracing herself against the ship's motion, she watched as the long boats towed the *Tilbury Belle* out into the harbor. Once there, the ship poised lifeless in a mirrored calm.

A faint fluttering began above her in the sails. Then the

loose veils that circled her face began to stir and wave as if they had been endowed with a life of their own. A breeze from the sea came cooling to her cheek, and a tang of salt in her nostrils smelled of adventure. The ship which had been so still began to throb with eagerness, and the sails above her to swell with strength.

The sense of being one with the wind and the pipping gulls and the whipping eagerness of the sails, brought a surge of laughter to her throat. If only Antoine were here. If only he too were making this daring step into a new life where there were no yesterdays, no thief-takers, no regrets. If only . . .

The ship was tugging at its moorings with an almost childish impatience. Then, with screeching winch and loud cries, the men lifted the anchor. Julie clung to the rail with both hands, her legs firmly braced at the *Belle* surged forward like a falcon loosed from a hunter's wrist. And like a freed bird, it lifted into the wind with the sea singing along its sides to ruffle into a lacy wake.

As the last lights of Gravesend dimmed in the distance, Julie found the mate at her side again, dancing nervously from foot to foot. "Truly, madame," he insisted. "It is best that you go below. Night comes."

"I am loathe to leave the sight of the sea," she replied, turning to take his proffered arm. Then she smiled up at him. "The ship will seem like a prison after all that sky."

A look of astonishment crossed his face. "Prison!" he cried aghast. "Oh, no ma'am. A ship is its own world and the freest world that there be, what with its having the broad face of the oceans to itself."

"Its own world," her mind echoed his words. If that were true, perhaps this moving world between England and the colonies would provide her with the healing of time that Margaret had taught her to understand so well.

She could hear Margaret's firm voice and the very words that she had used. "The body itself seeks life," she had explained, "even as the heart seeks hope. Time heals them both, tissue and scars. They need only the chance—time."

Julie looked back over her shoulder at the last fading lights dim along the horizon. Were there enough embers of hope still warm in her heart to fan new hope? She didn't know, she honestly didn't know.

282

In such thoughtful silence, she was led to the stateroom which was to be her own corner of this new world.

"I shall return for you and your companion when the captain is free for a late supper," he told her at the door. "To toast a safe and profitable journey."

"Thank your captain for us," Julie told him. "And assure him that we will be at his pleasure."

She nodded as he held the stateroom door open for her and then quietly shut it after her passage. A single lamp was lit on the low table, and the room seemed dim and shadowy after the star-filled sky. She saw the woman's figure bending over the bed with her back to the door. She raised her hands and threw her veils back and called softly, "Good evening mistress."

Even in that half-light the figure that turned towards her seemed familiar. Then Julie fixed on the girl's face and her breath left her. With dark eyes dancing and smiles wreathing her face, Ellie faced her, hands on hips and challenging as she had been that first time in Newgate.

"Ho there, Sukey, or Julie, or whoever you are going to call yourself this time." Then the jest broke from Ellie's voice and she flew to catch Julie's hand and press her cheeks against it again and again. "Oh Sukey. Oh mistress. Thank God. Thank God."

Clinging to her friend, Julie burst into tears. "Ellie, Ellie my dear. I had no idea. Why wasn't I told?"

The dimple flashed in Ellie's cheek. "It was all Mark Hatter's idea that I should come as a surprise. He thought it might salve a little the grief of leaving England."

Julie sniffled and shook her head. "That Mark. There is no end to his gentleness. Oh Ellie." Her words would not come, and she clasped the girl tightly and hugged her breath away.

Chapter Forty

That hour, which was not half-enough for Ellie and Julie to share their experiences since they parted, was still enough to set both girls to giggling.

Julie was enchanted to find Ellie with the same tart tongue

and vibrant insouciance which had brightened those long weeks in Newgate. But whatever magic had spirited her on board this ship and into Julie's arms (a magic that was concealed under the sober exterior of Mark Hatter) had transformed Ellie's appearance entirely.

The thick, unruly hair which had been a mobcap of tangles was neatly dressed so that it stood high on Ellie's head with a ring of dancing ringlets about her heart-shaped face. Her clothes, while of modest color and design, were fitted to expose a voluptuous young figure that was at once ladylike and provocative.

"Fine feathers made a new bird, yes?" Ellie giggled twirling and prancing and arching her slender back for Julie's admiration. Then she dropped her voice and wrinkled her nose mischieviously. "And I've got underwear even. Who would have thought I would be caught live with underwear? They've lace and some ribbons and are ever so slow to get in and out of. God knows how you fine ladies ever get yourself bedded when there's all that to-do between you and him."

When the mate's rap came at the door. Julie's hand flew to the widow's cap still on her head, and she gasped, "I am noway dressed for dinner."

"Maybe the beast will be dead and the mourning will be only proper," Ellie whispered, having been vastly amused by Mistress Furlong's reasoning in supplying Julie with such dolorous apparel.

Julie giggled then called to Jim. "Only a few moments, sir, if you please."

Ellie wailed with anguish when Julie lifted the cap from her head. "Your hair," she howled. "Your glorious hair."

"That dark-eyed bastard did it," Julie explained. "Quick, let's see what we can do with it."

Ellie deftly caught the mass of shoulder-length curls into a cascade of ringlets atop Julie's head. Then she seized a flower from the bouquet Mistress Furlong had sent.

"Not that," Julie protested, handing the red rose back to her. "I cannot go half-dressed like a Spanish dancer and half as a grieving wife."

"Wet wash," Ellie snorted before turning to fasten the curls into place with a flat bow of black satin ribbon.

What a blaze of light the captain's quarters presented after their own sober stateroom. Crisp, white linen rippled from a small table whose candles sparkled on settings of fine china and a quantity of well-polished plate. Two men rose swiftly at their entry with the mate Jim.

Captain Douglas was a man of middle years with thick, dark hair that sprang back from his face above wings of white hair just above his ears. His eyes were a steely gray, and his touch on Julie's hand as he bent over it to greet her was as cold as an ice bath. Even the rich, sun-stained color of his skin failed to remove a certain somberness from his appearance.

As he bowed over Julie's hand in greeting, his eyes caught hers and held them a long minute, then he sighed. "We have much in common, madame," he said quietly. "Even in addition to the long journey that lies ahead." Then his tone lightened as he turned to his companion. "May I present our supercargo, Mr. Charles Fenner."

Julie's curiosity was sufficiently piqued by the captain's strange comment that she did not at once fix her whole attention on the man at his side. When she did, she was startled to realize that everything about him seemed carefully designed to make him unobtrusive. He wore no wig, and his dark brown hair, lit with reddish lights from the candle's glow, was tastefully arranged, giving him an almost boyishly natural look. His clothing was superbly tailored of fine material in colors that were all quite subdued, a coat of tobacco brown over a cream-colored vest with stockings of the palest yellow. She was instantly impressed to feel that this man, with his warm, shy smile, would be equally at home in the stately London home she had just left as he was here in the captain's quarter with the candles locked firmly into bases and the wine decanter whose broad bottom was weighted against the roll of the sea.

"My compliments, Madame Duvall," he said before turning to Ellie with equal grace. "And to you, Miss Titus."

Julie started with astonishment at the name and saw Ellie's rosy mouth twitch with amusement at her reaction.

Ellie Titus, was it? That little scamp. But Julie at once realized that she had never heard Ellie's last name. Later, when she was to confront the girl with what name she was travelling under, Ellie had bent double with amusement.

285

"You should have seen your face. What a picture!" But she was to turn pensive only a moment later. "Those of us which has no fathers has no name," she reminded Julie. "The ship had a something called a manifest and it needed a name on it. Wot was I to do? I knew you had stopped off using that name since you turned into this Julie Duvall so I just spit it out." Her face darkened. "You don't mind, do you? You told me yourself that he was dead."

"I only wish I had had some warning," Julie assured her. "It is a good name and may you wear it in good health."

Julie was startled to realize what an awkward silence had fallen in the room during her revery. She recovered herself with a quick smile that brought the dimple flashing to her cheek.

"Forgive my lapse of attention," she said with a glance at Captain Douglas. "I am only impressed that anything as lovely as this table could be found aboard a ship of commerce."

"The lovely things aboard this ship are the two of you," the captain countered, gallantly helping Ellie to her seat. Charles Fenner, on Julie's left was holding her own chair for her with a warm smile. "I am sure that Mr. Fenner will agree with me that we are truly blessed to face this perilous voyage with two such charming companions aboard."

"Then there are no other passengers?" Julie asked as the servant bent to her wine glass.

She saw the quick exchange of glances between the captain and Mr. Fenner, but it was the captain who spoke. "There are others on board," he said vaguely, "but no other passengers as you might say."

Ellie, her eyes on the crisp joint of beef that the attendant was slicing, was no help to Julie in keeping the conversation going about the table. So she chattered that light social exchange that she had learned at her father's house while the sumptuous meal was served. Her private astonishment at the cleverness of the servant increased with each roll of the ship which caused the wine to rise from side to side in the glass she held firmly on the table.

During the pleasant meal that followed, Julie was to understand the captain's enigmatic comment on his first greeting her. He was a widower himself, as it turned out. He told a sad and touching tale of his lovely wife Charlotte who had

286

expired giving birth to their only child who had followed her mother in death within a few hours.

"So it is for your late wife that the *Tilbury Belle* is named?" Julie asked.

He nodded, averting his eyes as if to spare her his grief. "I have put my fortunes and my life into the hands of this *Tilbury Belle* even as I committed my heart to Charlotte."

"It is a pitiable story indeed, "Ellie agreed later that night as the two girls sat cross-legged in their cabin while Ellie plaited her hair for the night. "But I've a great naggle of suspicion that any man who tells such a story that well is past hurting from its subject."

"Ellie, you are awful. Can't you ever see an apple without probing at once for where the worm is hidden?"

Ellie shrugged. "Street wise, that's what I am. And man wise over you I would suggest. For instance, what do you really think of that fine-looking Mr. Kenner behaving the way he does? Watching with his half-closed eyes, never speaking until he's spoken to. What's he here for, I want to know if he's not helping to run the ship or filling some job or another? Supercargo indeed, that sounds to me like something that is more than is needed."

Julie laughed merrily. "It's a job, that's all," she said, "And a very good one too. It was as a supercargo that my own father first went to sea before he could afford to buy his own ship. Captains are often up from poor beginnings with little learning except the ways of the sea. They learn to manage men and do those nautical things, but they are not skilled enough to make good trades of the cargo or negotiate with the merchants at other ports."

"He's only a merchant then," Ellis scoffed. "Only a sea-going haggler."

Julie grinned. "You might say that. He is the third son in his family, do you know what that means?"

At Ellie's frown Julie explained. "The first son gets the land and the title, the second goes to military or clergy, so what shall this third son do with his life?"

"There must be something better than dressing up in fine clothes and sitting about listening and never slapping his own clam. That's no way to keep a healthy man out of mischief.

He has that closed face of a man who knows more than he's telling."

"No doubt about that," Julie agreed, hopping into her bed and pulling up the warm comforter that Mistress Furlong had packed among her things. "He was at Oxford in mathematics. I would be surprised if such a man were much for mischief."

Ellie finished her buttons and flopped on her own bed. "Aah," she said with a resigned sigh, "I suppose that if we want mischief on board this ship, I shall have to make it for myself."

"Ellie," Julie rebuked her automatically. Then she felt a ripple of amusement inside her throat. How good it was to be with Ellie again. Somehow Ellie made her feel a child again after such a long time among the older and the mad. Her curiosity about Ellie's words would not be stilled. She raised herself on her elbow and stared across the stateroom at her friend. "What did you have in mind?" she asked.

A sleepy giggle came from the pile of covers across the way. "Something will turn up," Ellie assured her sleepily. "It always does, you know."

Chapter Forty-One

The first month of that sea voyage was a time of such rare peace that afterwards Julie was to look back at it as a kind of a magical interval in the stormy progress of her young life. The slow days were orchestrated by sounds which grew dear by familiarity: the raucous crow of the cock who wakened them at morning from his pen which held the live fowl for the voyage, the steady, rhythmic pacing of the watch on the deck above, the fluttering colloquoy between wind-swollen sail and circling sea birds.

The channel passing was serene, and even though Julie and Ellie hung at the rail like children watching the last point of Land's End fade from view, Julie did not grieve to leave England. Her anguish was only that Antoine grew farther from her by each wave the ship crested.

Julie spent her days in reading, doing needlework in her cabin, and dressing to dine with the captain and Charles Fenner. Once accustomed to her new status, Ellie blossomed into a lively conversationalist whose instant smile and tart tongue brought merriment to them all.

But the restless spirit that she was, she was seldom content to waste hours in the stateroom with Julie. Instead, she was out and about the ship collecting gossip in that same vigorous way she had done at Newgate.

It was she who brought back to Julie the news that the hold was filled with miserable emigrants who were only permitted on deck on the sunniest days and then only a few at a time.

"Like Newgate itself it is," she knit her brows unhappily. "There are babes in arms and crones, young married ones and the fiercest rascals, all tumbled in there together, and God only knows how they survive."

"But who are they? What are they here for?" Julie asked.

"Transport," Ellie explained shortly. "That's wot kind of a kennel I would be rolling in if it were not for you."

"For me?" Julie said astonished. "I had no money. I have none now. It must have been Mark who paid your passage in these quarters."

Ellie's mouth grew slack with astonishment. "He did that for me?" She shook her head firmly. "You have to be wrong. He said it was what you wished for me. He said it was you."

Julie stared at her thoughtfully. "It was what I wanted for you, that you would have a new chance in America and would ask for transport for that reason. But the cost! He told me that it was Margaret's will that paid my passage and laid up my stores."

They stared dumbly at each other for a moment,

Then Julie turned away to conceal her emotion. What was the real secret of all this great affluence? Had it been Margaret, or had it somehow been Mark himself who had arranged for her comfort and safety—and for Ellie's because she wished the girl so well.

"He couldn't have come by this money by some foul means like I would, could he?" Ellie asked darkly. "What a thought to have him end up like those miserable wretches down there, wailing with the roll of the sea and yellow with fever."

True to her old Newgate lectures, Ellie was able to put all

grieving from her mind and go off again on her cheerful meanderings about the ship.

The mate Jim was finally driven to appeal to Julie for help about Ellie.

"A ship is not a place for a sprightly miss like that to be romping about on," he reproached Julie. "There's no end to the dangers here you know—the elements, the men."

Julie raised her clear, golden eyes from her needlework and smiled at him. There was something endearing about his clumsy concern for Ellie. "I will caution her again," she promised him. "But my words are like seeds in the wind to her. She blows them away with laughter."

"I plain fret on her," Jim grumbled, his wide, honest face lined with concern.

"Then be quite cross with her," Julie advised. "Scare her a little."

The mate shook his head and then flushed a deep red. "I tried that, ma'am," he confessed. "She called me a 'great-granny of a worry-pot' and told me not to go throwing boo-geymen at her until she had her sea legs."

Julie laughed merrily in spite of his discomfort. "That's Ellie all right. Now Jim, don't you really feel that she is better than average equipped to watch out for herself?"

"Maybe a little," he admitted grudgingly. "But there is danger on board this ship which is poison passing for comfits."

Julie stared at the door he had closed behind him. Whatever could he mean, speaking in riddles like that? The dangers were there for any eye to see, the ocean itself, the rough men whose eyes followed both Ellie and Julie everywhere, the danger of fevers. She shook her head and decided that his words reflected the hurt pride he felt at having his counsel ignored. She giggled. " 'Great-granny of a worry-pot' indeed. That girl."

Julie was unable to appreciate Jim's high concern for Ellie. It seemed that every time Julie put her nose from the cabin either Jim or the captain was at Ellie's side, paying her pretty compliments or teasing her into some burst of laughter that stopped the hands of the men who labored in the rigging of the ship.

From one of the crew members she had obtained a small stringed instrument that she learned to play. Some of the songs that the crew members taught her to sing in that bright, lilting voice of hers brought waves of scarlet to Julie's own ears, but the men adored her.

"It seems a high compliment to me that Captain Douglas has so much time to visit with you," Julie teased Ellie in the privacy of their room.

Ellie tossed head. "He's a fair flatterer, that man. He does know how to make a piece of street scum like me feel like the grandest lady."

"I hope you don't call yourself that about him," Julie said.

Ellie laughed. "Not on your life." Then she plumped herself forward, her dimple coming and going from the mischief she was making. "He's a great one for questions, always asking me this and that. It seems a pity to waste all those fine questions of his on the dirty truth. So I don't."

"I don't understand," Julie admitted.

"I have just made myself up a fine life to fill his flapping ears with, that's what. I remembered all you talked about those long nights in Newgate, and I just slid your stories under my name, so to speak."

"Ellie," Julie giggled. "How could you?"

"No trouble at all," she said airily. "My tongue was ever better trained for lying than truth. But you should see how sad his eyes get when I tell him of my mother's dying and how gently the servants raised me since my father was lost at sea off merchanting."

First the name Titus, and now her own childhood. But strangely, Julie felt sympathy rather than resentment at Ellie's confession.

"How do you explain this voyage to him?" she asked.

Ellie's sober face was only betrayed by the flash of her eyes. "As a favor to my dear friend," she said in a subdued voice. "I fair broke him to tears with the tale of how grieved you were at the passing of your young, fine husband and your fear of this crossing. He thinks I am a notable friend to undergo the threat of the sea for your sake."

"He must think you have money and property then," Julie warned. "He will be disappointed when he discovers you to be as much of a pauper as myself."

"It will never come to that," Ellie shrugged. "In the meantime, it is ever so merry to watch his eyes narrow with envy when I tell him about the linnets singing in our trees and the fruits of my father's fields."

Julie's attraction to the sea deepened with every day aboard the *Tilbury Belle*. The ship changed in her mind from Jim's image as "it's own world" into something more mythical. She found herself thinking of the ship as a bird whose sky was the endlessly changing face of the sea. Never for two hours running did the sea look back at her the same. Sometimes it smiled under the autumn sun like a great polished sheet of leather, carefully waxed. Sometimes it laughed with curling ripples of glowing foam. And when the moon rode high in the sky, a great silver ladder stretched towards her, making her feel that she could walk in that light into the very face of the moon itself.

With Ellie always off and about with her own mischief, it was Charles Fenner who accompanied Julie on her long, calm walks along the deck. He was so quiet and shy a man that she felt compelled to draw him out. But unlike other quiet men she remembered from her childhood, his words, once set to flowing, were filled with fascination for her.

He explained the working of the sextant and the very new method that had been discovered which enabled a captain to know exactly where he was by use of the sun's meridian.

"How do you come to know all this?" Julie marvelled as he named each star that appeared into the night sky.

Mr. Fenner shrugged. "I have little else to do on these long journeys," he explained. Then Julie noted a strangely intense expression on his face. "These are endless, lonely voyages for me," he finished, his words sounding somehow like a question.

When such awkwardnesses came between them, Julie would distract their talk with a passing bird or cloud that would take his attention from the intimate words that she knew lay just behind his shyness with her. For no sea bird could pass nor any great, lazy sea tortoise swim alongside that would not bring some story or special knowledge to his lips.

When they saw a school of dolphins dancing alongside, leaping wildly for fish, he shared her delighted laughter.

"They are the children of the sea," he told her. "There is a story that once they were men who were changed into this

292

form by an enchantment. In the change they did not lose their joy in each other's company or a man's love of play."

He paused and then added breathlessly, "Even as a grown man who is enchanted by love becomes as playful and joyous again as he was as a child." His hand closed over hers as he spoke, and she was glad to see Ellie, with the mate Jim in tow, turn the corner and draw near them.

"You talk about me and the captain," Ellie teased her later that day. "Here you are supposed to be a proper mourning widow, and that Mr. Fenner is like to drop his heart down the front of your dress with his eagerness."

"He's only a lonely man on a long voyage," Julie protested.

Ellie shook her head. "He's sweet on you and no mistake. But then there is always some fellow or another sweet on you. At least this one won't be kidnapping you on the street or dancing for your sake at Tyburn."

Julie froze, her hairbrush stilled in midair.

"Dancing at Tyburn, What do you mean by that?"

Ellie's glance veered away. "I've been trying to think of how to tell you. That great, blue-eyed highwayman that you watched so many hours from our window."

Julie felt a cold bath of terror move down her body. "And what makes you think he has swung at Tyburn?" she challenged.

"The sentence was set for him that last time I was at court," Ellie told her quietly. "He was sentenced to swing that same session that Mark got my own sentence changed if I would agree to transport."

"They found a third witness then?" Julie asked in a careful, low voice.

Ellie nodded. "It was a straw man, I ween. The gossips at Newgate said he was witnessed against by a man whose wife he had got with child. The bitch bragged that it was he who had done it, and her husband was so wrathful that he made false witness against the big fellow."

All for naught, Julie thought bleakly. All had been for naught. . . .The tears and the pain and the humiliation at the dark stranger's hand, and all had been for naught.

She had thought that the pain in her chest that had come so mysteriously when Antoine was captured would one day

293

leave her. But the testimony that he was indeed dead by this time only made the pain more grievous.

In spite of the great, generous comforter of finest duck down that Mistress Furlong had provided her, Julie lay shivering all that night with an intolerable coldness in the center of her bones.

Chapter Forty-Two

By the time the sea voyage was into its second month, Julie had developed a startling fondness for Charles Fenner's company. She felt about him much as she had in the old days about Giles. He was a joy to look upon, his trim figure always immaculately and tastefully dressed, his brilliant smile blossoming so unexpectedly from such a sober face. His manner with her was so gentle and unassuming that she had to remind herself that they had not been friends for all of her life.

Although he was both too shy and too gallant to force his attentions upon her, she was increasingly conscious of the eager tenderness in his face when he looked at her. After the humilations of her prison and her life with the dark stranger, his tenderness of her feelings came like a precious gift. To have such a deep and honorable affection offered without any promise of return did much to soothe the aching anguish of her mourning for Antoine.

She loved to lead him into gentle reminiscences of his childhood in Sussex, of his father's house, and of his college years when he and his two brothers shared quarters for the last time. Woven into his conversations came only the most discreet references to her "late bereavement" and her "tragic loss", coupled subtly with reaffirmations of the bleak loneliness of his own life.

"But the life of a sailing man is by nature solitary, is it not?" Julie asked, to take his mind a little from the somber picture he drew of his own condition.

"A sailing man, yes," Charles Fenner replied at once, rising as swiftly to her words as a fish to a lure. "But the skills of a sailing merchant like myself would be equally at home in some great colonial port city—Boston or Charles Town."

"Have you then considered abandoning this roving life as a supercargo?" she asked.

He turned and seized both her hands in his. "Not until this voyage, madam," he admitted. "But now I think on little else."

Julie was too quick of mind to miss his implication. But she was also too newly pained from Ellie's assurance of Antoine's death even to entertain his suggestions in her innermost mind. For as much as she looked forward to his gentle smile of welcome and enjoyed the warmth of his hand beneath her elbow on the rolling deck, it was Antoine who visited her in passionate dreams which left her spent and tear-stained on wakening.

The ship had been barely from sight of land before Ellie's curiosity had led her into every barrel and parcel of stores that had been loaded into their stateroom. Among the treasures that she unearthed was a great wooden box of carefully packed bottles of fine red wine. The two girls fell into the nightly habit of long hours of chatter and a glass of wine with a biscuit before tucking away for sleep. Always it was Ellie who was full of lively talk.

"The captain is eager to teach me to read sea maps," she told Julie with a sideways glance and a twinkle.

"And are you eager for such an education?" Julie asked.

Ellie shrugged. "It never hurts a body to know one more thing," she conceded. "But I always note that this urge to become teacher comes upon him when the sea is calm and the men all above with their jigs or their scrimshaw and there is no one about. I have only just managed to slip away from him at the door of his cabin more than once."

"You show a poor scholar when you behave that way," Julie kidded her. "Who knows what fine geography he could teach."

"Fine geography indeed," Ellie giggled. "I can see it now, in that fine carved bunk of his. Mark me, there's a fierce fire blazing under that gray look of his. It ain't the Bristol Channel he'd be lively to enter if he had half the chance."

"Ellie," Julie rebuked her, flushing with embarrassment in spite of herself.

"Be as dainty as you please," Ellie said tartly. "If his hand were as quick on the tiller as it is on my prow we'd be half-way back from Charles Town by now. It's only that he thinks I'm a girl of property that he has not thrown me to the deck before now."

Julie giggled. "Then I gather that he is not to your taste."

Ellie pondered this. "I have been tempted, but there has always been something or another to prevent my being led astray like that—someone coming by or a call for the captain from the deck. A captain is prey to the commands of his mate every minute it seems."

"Just his mate," Julie said pointedly.

Ellie gaped a moment before her mouth spread with a wicked grin. "I had not managed to put that together, mistress," she said with a little praise in the tone. "Can you possibly be as sly as you are beautiful?"

"I live with a good teacher," Julie reminded her. "And perhaps I am growing a little bored with these long days at sea."

"Bored? With that Mr. Fenner on your heels like a hound after a vixen?"

"He is a good man and a gentle one," Ellie conceded.

Julie paused. What did she really mean to say? That he was not Antoine? That much she expected of no man. That he was not Mark Hatter? How unfair to expect anyone to have the warm naïveté of that young apprentice whose memory she carried in her heart like a sun-warmed stone.

"He is not playful," she finally decided aloud. "He does not joke or laugh very much or be bawdy or impetuous. He is Giles Urban over again without the old memories that tied me to Giles."

"Nor would he stray from you even though you were married for two score years or more," Ellie said.

Julie lifted her eyes to her friend with surprise. "You think I should encourage him, Ellie, feeling as I do?"

Ellie wriggled unhappily under her gaze then turned away under the guise of tugging a snarl from her hair.

"There is no answer to that question," she said. "There is only a question to ask back. Will you ever be able to forget the blue-eyed Antoine?"

To actually hear another voice speak his name sent a thrill of shock through Julie. She clasped her bare arms about her chest and sighed. "Never."

"Then I would marry him." Ellie said flatly. Then she

296

leaned forward confidentially. "I would marry the captain himself for the steadiness of his life and the mothering of his children except that I am a fool. If I were you, it would be different. I would marry him in a snitch—less than a snitch. He's your kind, you know. The books and the way with words and his gentleness way inside. If you cannot love him for the memory of that big, blue-eyed stud, then it is likely that no man will ever draw your fancy."

"It wouldn't be fair," Julie shook her head.

"What's fair?" Ellie asked her hotly. "You would make him happy and not suffer yourself. He would love you and protect you and give you fine-blooded babes to raise. He would be amply rewarded by your company. That is not ill use to give any man."

"Even if I yawned a lot?" Julie asked lightly, trying to carry the conversation back towards lightness.

"At least you would have the good breeding to cover your mouth when you yawned, and those yellow eyes of yours would be sparkling at him over your fingers." Ellie laughed. "Me? I'm just not that sort at all. A short life and a merry one, that's what I'm after. Give me a good deal of jam on a single slice rather than a long, dry loaf."

"What then of the smitten mate Jim?" Julie asked softly.

Ellie shook her head darkly. "He is another Mark Hatter, that one. Too decent to bed a girl and walk away whistling. I would only break his heart and then have to live with my grief over being such a bawdy bitch. I have no taste to spoil my own pleasure."

"We are near port," Julie reminded her. "Once there, we shall probably never see those two men again."

The dinners which had been so sumptuous at the start of the voyage had grown less interesting with the depletion of the ship's store. The last of the livestock had been killed from the pen on the deck, and the potatoes had the bitter taste of having been stripped of many eyes.

Captain Douglas, in a note of apology, explained that the very calmness of the sea which had blessed their crossing, had made a drain on the ship's supplies.

"But never mind," he laughed with a warm glance at Ellie. "Only a few days hence and we will be dining like kings in Charles Town. Then this miserable fare will be forgotten."

Charles Fenner laughed softly. "Your captain has just

shown himself to be a very modern man. If he were as super-stitious as most mariners he would never make such a state-ment. To mention the calm sea is said by the unlearned to bring storms to the speaker."

Captain Douglas laughed a little nervously and proposed a toast to the fine beef of the Carolina inns.

"I had thought the sea a little rockier than usual tonight," Julie commented.

"It has been worth ten knots an hour since sundown," the captain agreed. "With luck it will hold with just this strength."

The luck did not hold. By the time they were preparing for bed, Ellie was unable to fill a glass of wine without bracing her elbow against the wall beside her bunk.

"Should we lash ourselves in like we did during the last squall?" she asked Julie with some concern in her voice.

Julie shook her head. "Not I. It reminded me too much of prison. I shall cling to my wall and take my chances."

Sometime in the night, the wind rose until the ship was rocking from side to side in great galloping swings. Julie lay awake listening to the slap of the sails and the creaking of the timbers belabored by the sea. Ellie moaned softly and then again. Julie heard her cry softly and then burst out with a great yell of anguish.

"Jesus, I have sinned," she yowled. Then her familiar, "Ow," and another groan of anguish.

Struggling into her robe, Julie rose to go to her. The ship was rolling with such force that she could not cross the small room without clinging to the wall. Her sea chest, as if gov-erned by an unseen hand, began to follow her across the room only to pause and return docilely to its storing place as the ship changed its angle.

"Holy Jesus," Ellie yelped.

"Come, Ellie, come," Julie pleaded, taking her trembling friend by the shoulder. "It is only a little squall."

"It is my belly and my guts beside," Ellie corrected her, shoving Julie aside. With a great leap, she was out of her bed and halfway across the room.

Maddened by the sickness which had seized her, Ellie raced to the door and pulled it open. A great wall of water came in the open door, throwing her backwards onto Julie,

298

who found herself struggling among the tables and chairs in a swirling pool that half-filled the room.

Through the open door, she could hear the shrouds rattling like doom and the voice of Captain Douglas shouting into the shrieking wind.

The candle was out and Ellie gone, as Julie tried to struggle into her clothes. She heard a man's voice at the door and she bid him enter. With a candle lashed against the wall he explained that he was the ship's carpenter. She did not understand what he meant by "coming to put up deadlights" until she saw the heavy, double wooden shutters he was nailing across the windows to keep out water.

"When it be like this, you're a fish in a barrel in no time," he told her, his voice muffled by his mouthful of nails.

"Have you seen my companion Miss Titus?" she asked the man as readied to leave.

He stared at her dumbly and then laughed. "Madame, there is no one on deck except those which are tied on. There's only the sea out there. The clean sweep of the sea."

The blackness of the room was barely relieved by the single wavering candle he left against her wall. Frantic as to Ellie's fate, she finished dressing. From above came the greatest confusion of sounds. Sails rattled and men shouted at each other wildly against the fierce voice of the gale.

Finally, unable to bear the fear and solitude of that stateroom, Julie wrapped herself in her warm mantle and started towards the deck to prevail upon Ellie to return below.

Once past the weak light of her room's candle, she found herself in a blackness beyond her imaginings. She groped along the wall and felt for the steps. As she gained the deck, she heard a great warning shout and a black wall of water sluiced along the passage throwing her back helplessly to the level from which she had climbed.

From the darkness and pain, she roused only slowly. The weaving of the ship was not diminished, but she was lashed so firmly into a bed that she rolled easily with each attitude of the ship.

When she lifted her hand toward her head, a voice instantly called, "There, there."

"Ellie," she cried out in alarm.

"Lie back," Charles Fenner's voice urged. "If you are all right I will go above and help."

"But Ellie?" Julie cried again.

He leaned so near that she could feel the warmth of his breath against her face. "Don't worry, my dear," he urged. "Lie still and I will do what I can. We all will."

"He will love you and protect you," Ellie had said of Charles Fenner. It was not enough. Where had that wild-headed girl got to in this storm? She struggled at her lashings which only made raw places where the wet ropes bound her in. She settled to listen and watch the candle flame dance and waver from the heaving of the cabin.

Only a few moments later the mate Jim thrust his head in to stare at her wildly. His clothes were sodden and his face a stange blue shade from cold. "Where is she?" he asked fiercely. "Where is Miss Titus?"

"She was ill," Julie explained. "She was going above. I can't find her—"

At her words, Jim gave a great animal cry of pain and disappeared from the room.

Chapter Forty-Three

Ellie's first consciousness of the storm began with nausea. Her stomach insisted on echoing the reeling motion of the *Tilbury Belle* as she battled for survival in the gale that beset her. By the time she was fully awake, she could feel her belly tightening itself like a great fist. She had cried out, half-prayer, half-curse, and Julie, blessed Julie, had fought her way to her side across the pitching room. A clutch of terror had seized Ellie. She knew beyond a shadow's doubt that within seconds her entire dinner and that extra glass of wine she had accepted at the captains's invitation would be thrown all over herself, her mistress, and the already stuffy stateroom.

She remembered throwing Julie aside and making her way to the door to force it open in spite of the pressure that held it from the other side. The water slammed against her chest, throwing her back for just that moment. She clung to the door while water swirled icily about her knees and into the room. She heard Julie's cry of alarm but never looked back. She was choking with nausea as she fought her way towards the deck. Once there, she could relieve the agony in her belly and throat over the railings into the sea.

Ellie never felt the deck beneath her feet. A wave caught her and hurled her along the planks towards the side of the ship that was pitching perilously close to the level of the turbulent waters.

She seized desperately at air and screamed at the limit of her breath. Half-crawling, half-scrambling, she felt her gown caught with a sudden jerk. Then, as suddenly, she was thrown free with half of her gown torn from her body.

As she tumbled helplessly across the deck, her grasping hands caught suddenly at the roughness of rope. With a gasp of relief, she seized the rope with both hands and clung to it with all her strength.

As the storm had risen and the waves had begun to sweep over the tossing ship, the crewmen had leaped to secure her as best they could against the onslaught of the sea. Lashed to one another, they battened down the ship, put up the dead-lights, and struggled with the wind-tormented superstructure. With the first flood of seawater over the deck and into the belly of the ship, the emigrants had struggled up, clinging and wailing, trying to escape the swirling waters below deck. Cursing with fury, the captain realized that these frantic land-lubbers, in their mindless desperation, threatened to lose him control of the ship.

Over their screams of protest, he had ordered the crew to force them back into their quarters and nail it shut against further escape onto the deck.

The bosun, his hands bleeding from the scrape of wet rope, his body aching from the chill of the spray and the ef-fort of his battle against the rigging, felt a sudden pull against him on the rope. Realizing that it was not the sail nor the sea but human hands that blocked his efforts, he struck out at this intruder.

"Get thee off me, you scum," he raged, striking at the form which he could see only dimly in the darkness. The force of his blow was not enough to throw his tormenter free. Instead, he felt himself gripped with terrified desperation as arms slid down his body, pinning his legs together helplessly. He tried to kick the creature free of him, but fear of being swept away gave the clinging arms an unreal strength.

"Ayeeh," he howled. "Hold fast, mate, I've a loonie stuck on me."

"Why wasn't this creature below decks with the others?" he raged to himself as he forced the clawing hands free of his legs. He'd break the bastard's hold and let him find what chance he had on the storm-swept deck. When he managed to get the wriggling body free of his own, he repented. This was no more than a child that gripped him with such desperate terror. Dragging his victim, the mate struggled the few feet that lay between himself and the jolly boat that hung at the stern. Bracing himself, he lifted the struggling emigrant and thrust him into the boat under the tarp before fighting his way against the battering wind back to his post.

Ellie, her strength nearly spent, felt herself being dragged along the deck but was unable to fight free. She felt herself thrown into a curved space where she rolled to a painful stop, half-covered with icy water. She tried to scream and beat with her fists against the canvas cover that closed over her. There was no light anywhere. Even the jagged streaks of lightening that had rent the sky were hidden from her. Whimpering with cold and pain, she sought for escape only to fall back defeated. She curled herself into as small a ball as possible to ward off the dread chill that was numbing her limbs.

From time to time, she stirred to feel the battering of the sea against the ship and brace herself as she was tossed from side to side inside the small boat. The sickness that had driven her from the safety of her cabin returned. She retched to exhaustion, swooned into half-consciousness, only to stir and retch again.

The mate Jim, torn between his concern for the ship's plight and his frantic worry about the girl Ellie, moved, lashed firmly by the waist, from one post to another, shouting orders and giving a hand where needed. Always he asked if anything had been seen of the woman passenger, and always the answer was "nay."

With the coming of morning, the storm seemed to abate. The first light was sickly, barely seen through the sheets of steady, gray rain that swept the ship and joined with the sea's murderous attack on the *Tilbury Belle*. The crew, their hands bloodied to pulp from their labors of the night and drenched and chilled to the skin, surveyed the damage about them with apprehension. Moans of anguish and fervant prayers came indistinctly from the emigrants prisoned in steerage. A wavering, delirious voice rose from among them giving the ship the feel of a sea-borne Bedlam.

The mate, his face like stone, searched the ship with little hope left. Charles Fenner, pressed by Julie's tears, made the descent into steerage and waded among the battered and half-drowned emigrants searching for Ellie Titus.

"She must be here. She has to be on board," he told the mate.

"God knows how many of those poor souls we lost before they were forced back to quarters," Jim reminded him. "Many a man has been swept overboard in such a storm and not missed until the sky has cleared."

"But what can I tell Madame Duvall?" Charles Fenner asked.

"Tell her what a great upheaval there is. Tell her that she must not give up hope until we are free to search the ship more thoroughly."

Charles Fenner stared at the mate, and Jim looked away, his face twisted with anguish.

Through that long day, the exhausted seamen labored to repair the damage of the night's storm. Their faces were gaunt with fatigue as they moved with leaden feet to their tasks, their minds numb with pain and chill.

Captain Douglas, making his circuit of the ship, saw a young seaman in the stern staring about him with a look of glazed terror.

"Fall to," he shouted at the lad. The boy only turned to stare at him, blubbering incoherently.

"Voices," the boy gasped. "A voice from the sky, weeping."

"Jesus," the captain exploded, "It's only the wretches below deck, wailing and screaming."

"From the air," the boy insisted, his eyes white rimmed with terror.

Captain Douglas moved threateningly towards the boy. "God in heaven, you mewling baby. Stop that trembling and lay to." But as he drew near the boy and the jolly boat, he heard the sound himself, a faint, moaning cry that seemed to

303

come from the gray sheets of rain that fell unremittingly on the lurching boat.

Motioning the boy to assist, he leaped to the side of the jolly boat and tore the canvas aside.

The boat was half-filled with water. Ellie, her hair loose like seaweed, floated in delirium in the boat, her bare thighs and legs were blue with cold, and her eyes stared sightlessly into the pelting rain.

"Jesus," the captain cried. He tore his own sodden coat off and lifted the girl down and wrapped her in it. Staggering a little from her sodden weight, he bore the unconscious girl past her own empty stateroom to lay her on the bunk of his own cabin.

He smiled to himself over his silent burden. This would be the turning point, he told himself with satisfaction. The whimsical bitch had wavered back and forth between him and the mate Jim like a weathervane. Every smile she had given the mate had been a torment to him. What use had a country lad like Jim for such a girl as this? But what a great wife she would be to have tucked away in the Carolinas. A nice, round-arsed wife to welcome him home at the end of the voyage. And there would come a handsome dower with her, he wagered. Those landed folk could afford to be generous with an only child like this one.

He would win, he knew he would. She was rough of speech but handled herself like a queen, quite as daintily as her golden-eyed companion whose face would stop a heartbeat but whose eyes suggested more grieving than a man would want to bed with.

A merchant's daughter, he remembered, kicking the door of his cabin closed behind him. A wench whose eyes sparked fire was his tray of meat all right, especially coming with dower like this one.

He could hear her now, heartstruck with gratitude that he had rescued her from the storm. But she was cold, her flesh icy to his touch. He slipped his sodden coat from her and carefully, a garment at a time, began to remove her drenched clothing.

His passion began to rise as he bared the delicate shoulder and the fine, high breasts whose rosy nipples were cold and hard to his touch.

"Aye, they will be warmed," he murmured as he bared her

304

firm white flesh, struggling against the intensity of his own rising need of her.

Gently. He would have to move gently. Softly, he would woo her lest she startle and it all be lost from eagerness. But oh, the prize for the wait, the delicious prize.

The girl stirred softly as he loosed the last of her wet garments from her shapely body. His eyes glittered as he stroked her breast and slid his hand along the thighs that were still ice to his touch.

From above, Captain Douglas heard the voices of his men and the scrape of the cargo still stirring about in the hold. Better than any, he knew the weakened condition of the ship's ropes and what frailties the vessel had brought into that battering gale. The lifeboats he had ordered readied were too few for the human cargo of transports still imprisoned below-decks.

The storm was not over. His nose for the sea told him that this rain-drenched interlude was only the calm that lay before the next battering. If they were to go down, all of them, he would rue this chance not taken. If she were not a rich man's daughter but a slut from the street as she sometimes seemed with her jaunty hips and her devilish glances, he would be on her in a minute, though he died in the rutting.

"Careful," he warned himself as his sweat stood forth on his face and his groin blazed as if with fire.

When he had wrapped her in the driest linen left in the cabin, he stroked her body "to warm her," he reminded himself, "only to warm her." He drew his hand sensually along her small, round belly, about her breasts, and down the graceful length of her arms. He was kneading her wrist, trying to strengthen her fluttering pulse when he saw the mark. He stopped still and then leaned forward to stare in disbelief.

"God in heaven," he cursed. This could be nothing else. He had seen that Newgate mark too many times to make a mistake on it. This was a Newgate bird—no daughter of the landed gentry to bring rich dower into his hands but a Newgate slime who had fed his passions with her tart glances and given him wild, scheming nights with her teasing lies.

"Bitch," he hissed at her as his fine dreams of wedding her for a packet of dowery slid away. "Rotten, stinking jailhouse bitch."

With a curse, he tore at his clothing. By God, she had

305

conned the wrong man. He'll take his pay in a man's way. He threw himself on her and forced entry past that mound of soft curls with a madman's fury.

"Linnets in the hedges, you goddamned whore," he whispered as he stabbed himself inside her belly. "Bitch, bitch, bitch." Aye, what a fool he had made of himself over her. He would revenge himself for that, no matter what else he got.

The freshly rising tumult of the storm outside and his fury fed his passion to frenzy. Although he rutted like a madman, he could not find the release he sought as she lay lifeless between his thighs. Maddened by lust and anger, he sunk his teeth brutally into her shoulder and clawed at her back leaving great, bloody marks where his nails had dug into her chilled flesh.

But the pain and the warmth of his body conspired to revive her. Ellie groped for consciousness only to face the maddened leer of her ravisher only a breath away.

She screamed wildly, and her body stiffened in his grasp. She fought for release, her small, healthy body wriggling to be free of his weight. Her resistance was all that his passion required. With her scream still echoing in the small cabin, he groaned at the surge of his seed pumping into her and fell on her with a dead weight.

She hammered helplessly against his back, a stream of profanity filling the room. She heard an answering voice above the turmoil outside the room.

The captain leaped from her but it was too late. The mate Jim, forcing the lock, stood in the doorway. He stared past Captain Douglas to Ellie, her own blood flowing along her shoulder and her sodden hair fanned on the pillow.

He flew at the captain's throat with a coarse, animal cry. "You devil. You rotten, stinking scum of the seas."

The captain, a man of greater strength and size, caught Jim by the chest and held him at bay. "Hold it, mate," he said, his voice icy with calm. "You can have your own turn when I am gone. She's naught but a rotten street slime and not worth being thrown into brig for."

Stunned by his words, Jim stood frozen for a moment. In that pause, Captain Douglas jerked his clothes together and was past him out the door before the mate recovered his senses.

Torn between shock and compassion, Jim braced himself inside the room, staring at Ellie.

She struggled to cover herself, clutching weakly at the linens of the bed.

"Jim, Jim," she said softly. "He's right, you know. I lied to him, told him I was a lady and with property."

He was at her side in an instant, cradling her in his arms. "Do you think I give a damn where you came from? Do you think I'm blind as well as dumb? Didn't I watch you being brought on board with three strong men keeping you in chains? And didn't I see that Mr. Hatter pay your fare into the hands of the purser before they would cut you free? Wasn't it in my own cabin that I was required to have you lodged until your friend was on board and we were safely at sail out of Gravesend?

"If he were a proper captain at all and caring for his ship as another man would, he would have been on to you at the start as I was. But that one? Never. He was more apt gambling with cards or lying with his wife or he would have known from the start."

"His wife?" Ellie repeated slowly, pulling back from his warmth to stare up into his face. "His dead wife?"

"So he told you that tale too, I should have guessed," Jim spat the words out. "Dead is she? That's a tale he often tells to get the ears of women passengers on this tramp. His wife is as alive as me and twice as canny. The *Tilbury Belle* is her own ship, registered in her own name, and she, great, painted, fat slut that she is, is not apt to let it into that scoundrel's hands. What I couldn't tell his wife about his carrying on—of the wife in Boston, sweet as a morning vine, with babes at the knee, and each wife thinking herself to be the only lover."

"Sweet Holy Jesus," Ellie breathed. Then the laughter came. Jim held her as confused gales of laughter racked her small body and ended finally in an exhausted cough. "Ain't that a fair one? Both of us rascals and neither the wiser."

Her laughter had barely subsided when a great sickening lurch set everything in the cabin to spinning. Ellie clung to Jim, but he took her by the wrists and set her away.

"She's broached to," he whispered as if to himself.

"What does that mean?" she asked, terrified by the sudden drain of color from his face. "What has happened?"

307

He was loose of her and by the door, crawling among the books and furniture as if searching for something.

Even as he spoke, he was tossing garments at her, a woolen shirt and short, dark pants, heavy stockings—all from the captain's chest that was upended at the door. "Get these on," he told her furiously. "As warm as you can dress. The ship is on her side, we must get away from her in time."

Chapter Forty-Four

The frantic words Julie heard called from the deck above made no sense to her. The coarse cry sounded like, "She's broaching to."

There was no time to ponder the phrase before the cabin itself went wholly awry. She seemed to be at the bottom of the world as every article in the supercargo's cabin rose and tumbled towards her as if hurled by unseen hands.

She chafed at her lashings, trying to cover her head with her hands. As swiftly as the shower of articles began, it was over. She lay pinned beneath the table, a chair, fluttering books, and the broken china of a teapot. The boat shivered like a frightened beast.

From above came the wildest sounds of activity, running feet, frantic cries, and a high, thin scream that sliced through her mind like a swift knife.

Nothing made any sense. The door crashed open and Charles Fenner crawled down the wall towards her. He moved like a cat, slicing at her lashings with a short, thick knife.

"What is it?" she cried. "What has happened?"

"The ship is on its side," he explained quickly. "There's no time. Come quickly. Dress warmly. Bring food."

Without giving her time to obey his terse instructions, he seized her and began to tug her along the passageway—along the wall that had suddenly become the floor.

"Ellie," she wailed, pulling back. "I cannot leave Ellie."

"You must save yourself," he said swiftly, thrusting her into her own cabin. He reached for the woolen mantle which lay beside her chair and pressed, "Have you food?"

308

When she shook her head, he sighed.

"God willing there will be ships to sight us this near to land."

With her mantle wrapped about her, he led her towards the deck.

"Quickly, quickly," he urged as they scrambled along the watery wall beside the stairway. Suddenly there came a great groaning of timber and shrieking of wood against wet wood, and the ship gave another massive lurch like the one which had pinned her into her bunk. Julie was flung into Charles Fenner's arms where she clung in terror. He pressed her head against his shoulder as they tumbled about the stairwell.

She felt the deep sigh that seemed to release the tension from his body. "The mast," he sighed. "Thank God, they must have got the mast off. The ship has righted herself."

"Then we will live?" she asked hopefully, raising her eyes to his face. He stared at her with a strangely glazed expression, as if unable to absorb the meaning of her question.

"Julie," he said softly, as if surprised, "Julie Duvall." Her name in his mouth sounded somewhat like a caress. "God, that what I so richly dreamed of would come like this!" A bleak smile crossed his face and his tone was almost bantering.

"Will we live?" he repeated. "Only, my love, if all things go well. If they can fit a jury mast strong enough to carry us to shore, if this poor, battered tub can stay afloat until rescuers come, if the lifeboats are in better condition than they appear to be—any one of these things might keep us alive." His arms tightened about her and his old smile came, like sun on a dark day.

"But, Julie, when this moment is past, I will no longer have the audacity to say to you what I dare to now—here, with your warmth in my arms and the scent of you in my head. Julie, Julie, never have I loved before. Nay, more than that. Never has any man had a love like mine for you. I remind myself that you are newly bereft and I have no right to press a new widow, but it does not stay my dreaming. I love you, Julie. I want you forever. Name the place and I will be merchant there for you. Name the time, today or a hundred years, and I will wait for you. Only be mine, for if you do, then I will have the fullest life every moment that I breathe."

"Charles," Her tongue stumbled on the unfamilar syllables.

How could she reply to him? How could she be honest with his dear face so close to her own? "You are dear to me," she breathed.

His impatience caught at her. "Enough?" he pressed. "Dear enough to accept me as husband?"

Before she could reply, the suddering of the ship threw them awkwardly against the wall, and the passion that filled Charles Fenner overcame him. With a groan, he drew her tighter and sought her lips with his own. His kiss was imperative. When her lips responded to his with the gentle love she had for him, she was conscious that his flesh against her face smelled of the sea and adventure.

At a cry from above, he drew himself away with a start, leaving only his arms loose about her waist. "Oh Julie," he said softly. "Thank you. Thank you with my life. We will be happy. I swear to make you happy."

She had no time to protest as he seized her and hurried her towards the deck of the freshly righted ship.

Bereft of its mast, the ship rocked like a cradle on the heaving sea. Bundles of white sail flopped about the deck which swarmed with frantic people. Bobbing as it was, the deck dipped almost to the green violence of the sea before tilting to duck the other way. There was no space on the deck, and the weeping and screaming emigrants clawed and fought as they hurled themselves towards the lifeboats which bobbed alongside.

Julie searched frantically with her eyes among the mass of people who crowded and clawed and cursed in that wild melee. "Ellie," she cried. "My God, where is Ellie?"

Charles Fenner did not reply. With easy authority, he parted the waves of people and half-pushed, half-dragged her into a crowded lifeboat. The oarsmen were already leaning to their task as his fingers touched hers for the last time. "Ellie," she wailed. "Charles, Ellie."

A second lifeboat was being let down behind them. With a great cry of relief, Julie saw Ellie, with Jim at her side, being helped into the crowded craft.

It was then that the nightmare began. Captain Douglas, his face contorted with fury, seized Jim by the arm and threw him staggering backwards among the frantic people being held back by the crew. Julie could not credit her own eyes. Captain Douglas, his face dark with hatred, pulled Ellie from

310

the boat and threw her across the deck as the lifeboat was freed and the sweep of oars carried it away from the *Tilbury Belle*.

Julie rose in her place and began to scream. Strange hands pulled her down with curses and someone slapped her soundly across the face.

"God," she screamed, "Help her. Help Ellie."

The oarsmen seemed demon inspired. The small craft moved from the *Belle* at a speed that Julie's mind could not accept. Within minutes, she could not distinguish the faces of the people on deck. Within seconds more, she saw what looked like handfuls of toys being tossed away as the desperate emigrants and crew made their last attempt to escape the sinking craft.

There were voices about her, mumbling conversation, and sometimes a soft moan. She was conscious only of the rhythm of the words, not their meaning, as she was concious of the slap of the sea, not what its force might effect on the frail craft she was huddled in.

"I am a Jonah," she told herself, struck with a sudden understanding. Her spirit was all the way dead, she could feel it ashen inside herself. "A Jonah—first Louis, then Titus, Antoine, and now Ellie. What curse do I carry?"

She covered her head with her hands and bent over on her own lap as she had seen Ellie do when she was hurt or afraid. She realized dully that she did not even care whether the oarsmen who grunted so steadily at their task had strength to attain the shore.

PART VI
GAMBLER'S WOMAN
November, 1722–February, 1723

Chapter Forty-Five

A scream wakened her. She trembled to feel the scream still hanging in the air, vibrating about the walls of the small, dark room where she found herself. It might even have been the force of that scream which was fluttering the flame of a single dark candle on the nearby hearth, wavering the flame so that it cast giant, changing shadows on the walls about her.

She tried to raise herself onto her elbows to see better, but there was not enough strength in her arms to support her. She fell back weakly, panting from the exertion. Her body felt suddenly chilled, as if it had been bathed in a swift surge of icy sweat.

"Oh my God," she moaned. "Oh my God, I am alive."

She had not heard him enter. He was only a soldier of darkness against the darkness outside the door. He did not seem to be a large man, yet he filled the doorway completely, even ducking his head a little to pass into the room. The nervous light from the candle was not adequate for her to see the color of his skin or clothes, but it did reveal that everything about him was dark, from the mass of hair pulled back at the nape of his neck to his peculiar leather clothing and the soft dark shoes that enabled him to glide soundlessly into the room.

As he neared, Julie saw a round, black patch covering his left eye. It was held in place by a string that passed about his head. One arm carelessly cradled a gun, while from his free hand, a brace of fowl hung, their heads dragging on the earthen floor beside him.

"Is that bad?" His voice was a little husky and cool in a way that she didn't expect from that dark face.

He was asking her to think. There was no way she could think or face life. She turned her face to the wall so that she need not see him any more.

"I didn't expect to be alive," she explained with her head still turned away from him.

She heard him moving about the room. His feet made only

the softest whisper on the floor. There was a rustling and then the sound that a fire makes when it sparks and crackles to the bait of green wood.

Then he started to hum, a low, rhythmic melody whose words lay just beyond her memory, as her strength lay just beyond her power to move. Her mind groped for sequence, for some series of steps that had brought her to this place.

"The ocean," she finally said aloud. "The boat was going down. We were lashed to the seats."

"How many days?" the man asked in a singularly untroubled tone.

Julie shook her head. "Two, maybe three. After a while I couldn't stay awake and lost track. He died," she added after moment.

"We buried him."

"Who?" she asked, trying to raise herself again. This time she managed to get her head braced up so that she could look across the room instead of only into that strange-patterned ceiling that she seemed to have memorized. How could she know a knothole in a plank of wood that well or feel familiar with a water stain that was shaped like a cat crouched to pounce? Had she looked at that ceiling unknowing for so long a time?

"It was a boy," the man replied. "You were lashed together and he had been long dead. He didn't look more than ten—twelve years old. Skinny little strip."

Unaccountably, the calm voice irritated her. For heavens sake she knew who had died. Matt had died. He had been a cabin boy on the *Tilbury Belle* although she had never known his name until the *Belle* herself was gone. He wasn't a strong child. After the first long night lashed to the plank, his mind had left him. He called sheep, called them by name, and shouted at a dog angrily because the sheep strayed.

He had tried to tear loose of the ropes that bound them together on the plank when a madness seized him at the end. She had been holding his thin wrists to keep his hands from the ropes when he gave a cry of surprise and died.

"I meant who helped you bury Matt," she managed to explain.

"My friend," he replied in that same calm manner. She looked up to see him approaching her. He was holding some-

316

thing carefully in both hands and walking gingerly with his eye on the cup as if he mistrusted it. His brows were heavy under an unfurrowed brow, and the dark moustache that almost concealed his mouth gave him a forbidding look.

When he reached the side of the bunk where she lay, he looked down at her, still sheltering the steaming bowl with both hands.

"All right, lady," his voice was contented. "Can you pull yourself up to drink or should I help you?"

His expression did not change as he watched her struggle to raise herself. Then he nodded without surprise and set the bowl on the floor. He slid a sure arm about her and lifted her into a half-sitting position with a straw pillow cocked under her back to support her weight. Then he reached for the bowl and started it towards her lips.

"What is it?" she asked, reaching for the bowl. A rich, meaty aroma came in the steam, meaty but spicy too, aromatic as if with herbs.

"You better let me do it," he cautioned, bringing the bowl nearer. "It's rabbit soup, you took of it before and seemed to like it."

She might have argued with him but the scent of the food had set her to trembling. She gripped the fur that covered her tightly with her hands to keep herself from grabbing the bowl from him. The soup was blazing hot, but she drew from the bowl greedily, not wanting to stop until the last drop of it had scalded down her throat.

"Easy, lady," he warned, pulling the soup away. "You don't want this rabbit jumping right back up into your lap. Now breathe a little. There's plenty more."

As the fan of warmth spread in her chest, a feeling of vast well-being flowed over her. "I'm Julie," she said. "It is delicious. Can I do it now, sir?"

He frowned. "Josh," he said. "I'm called Josh Simmons." He handed her the bowl. "Don't go gulping like that again. Your belly ain't braced for surprises."

Josh did not move away but sat against her on the side of the bunk watching her drink. She forced herself to swallow the soup more slowly, conscious of his eye on her and his warning.

When she had emptied the bowl, he went to refill it. He

317

brought back with it a piece of flatbread, golden in color with a crisp, nutty flavor.

"Just dip this in the soup and eat it off," he advised. "But take small bites and go slow."

She giggled. "Looks as if I lost my manners in the sea."

"You damned near lost the whole toss," he agreed calmly. "My friend bet me two skins that you'd croak in spite of everything. He's usually right about things."

"So you're two skins richer," Julie said, grateful that this strange, calm man was to profit somehow for his kindness.

He shook his head. "Not so as you'd say," he contradicted her. "I had just bought you off him for five skins before we made that bet."

Julie jerked, almost spilling the hot soup down her front.

"Bought me? What do you mean by that? I'm not a slave to be bought or sold. I'm a free English citizen."

Her voice was suddenly strident in the small room. The first smile she had seen on his face twitched at the corner of his mouth.

"You were found on the beach, weren't you?" he countered. "If you had been a chest full of doubloons or a box of goods or a two-penny knife he would have picked you up and sold you. Hell, he even had to go out into the surf to bring you in. You was flopping out there just lucky to be too far in for the sharks what with your arms hanging off the sides like that."

"I'll pay you back," Julie said boldly.

"I'm sure you will, lady," he said, taking the empty bowl from her hands. "You must be ready to sleep again by now."

Julie was becoming acutely conscious of the amount of food she had taken, of the total lack of privacy in the room, and of her vital needs.

"Not quite," she admitted, dropping her eyes. He stopped halfway across the room and stared back at her with a puzzled frown. Then he realized, "oh." Then after a moment, "of course."

He came back to the bed and leaned over as if to lift her. Come on, lady," he commanded.

Julie bit her lip and glared at him. What did this idiot think he was going to do, carry her out into the brush and hold her while she relieved herself? She would explode first, she decided unhappily.

318

"Can't I go alone?"

He shrugged and stood up, his arms limp at his sides. "Sure you can go alone, lady," he said laconically. "That is, if you can walk that far after laying there screaming in fever for all that time. And if you think you can manage that uneven swamp ground without a shoe to your foot. And if you ain't afraid of bears. That ain't a pussycat hide that you're lying under there."

They stared at each other a long minute and then Julie dropped her eyes. The flickering blaze of the fire and the guttering of that single candle combined into a whimsical light. It was enough to reveal the amusement in his face but no malice. She could find no malice in that dark face at all.

Resigned, she reached her arms up to him. He carried her like a child, only stopping at the door to pull his gun over his shoulder by its long, leathern strap.

When he had set her on the ground outside, he went a little way away from her. He squatted on his heels with the rifle across his knees. He stared off into the woods, humming that same little tune again softly to himself.

She stared about her. Compared to this wilderness, Epping Wood had been a park. The pale moon that floated somewhere behind a froth of fast-moving clouds lent only the most vagrant light to the clearing. In that light she was privy to a nightmare. She was surrounded by giant trees that seemed to reach forever towards the sky. Dark beards trailed from their branches towards the earth, stirring like restless fingers in the moving air. Tangled underbrush coiled off into a deeper blackness. She heard a heavy slip of something sliding heavily into water and a bird shrieked raucously at their invasion of the wild night.

When she called to him, he returned the rifle to his shoulder and carried her back to the bed which was against the far wall. She was conscious of his arms against her bare flesh. The garment she had on seemed to be a shirt. She would judge it to be old from the softness of the fabric. The sleeves were overlong and quite full so that she had to grope to free her hands of them. The tail of the shirt barely reached her upper thigh, and beneath that she was painfully nude.

Her eyes were still wide from terror when he laid her on the bunk and tugged the fur over her again.

"Where are we? What place is this?"

319

"The Spaniards call it Guale," he told her. He pulled a jug from somewhere near the hearth and set it beside him on the floor. She watched him stuff a pipeful of rough-cut tobacco fibers and pull at the stem of the pipe while he held a burning taper to the weed.

The fragrant smoke rose in a blue cloud to hover under the ceiling. She closed her eyes, remembering that same scent from Henry Furlong's pipe. It was a smell of civilization and prettily decorated rooms.

"But who owns it?" she asked.

He turned to her as he laughed. His teeth shone even and white under the darkness of his moustache. A crinkle of flesh almost covered his good eye when he laughed.

"Now the lady has come up with a good question. The king of Spain insists it is his and old King George claims stoutly that it is his, and the Indians hereabouts damned well know it is theirs. Like the wolves and the bears and the alligators, lady, and don't forget them."

She shivered. The exertion and warm food and talk conspired against her. She fought to keep her ever-heavier eyelids from closing in sleep.

"Your friend, Josh. Is he out there?"

He nodded.

"But is he safe?" she asked, feeling a sudden concern for that unknown man who had walked out into the sea to save her—even for a price.

He turned from the fire to stare at her. With his strong, solid body tensed like that, with the firelight catching the rich tones of his hair and reddening them with light, he looked strangely appealing.

"What man is safe?" he asked her by way of an answer.

"I want to thank you," she said, humbled by his tone.

"You will, lady," he told her. "In time you will."

She remained half-concious of Josh across the room from her through the troubled sleep she drifted into. Several times she stirred awake to see, through half-dazed eyes, the pale wreath of blue smoke that seemed to circle the air above her. From beyond the window she heard the cries of alien birds, and once, very near, the howl of some animal.

When the scream came again, she knew it had burst from her own throat. The lifeboat was being borne swiftly away from the *Tilbury Belle* which sagged under the mingled mass

320

of sail and life. She saw the guns of the crew holding back the frantic emigrants. Then she saw the contorted face of Captain Douglas as he seized Ellie from the relative safety of the lifeboat to throw her brutally across the cluttered deck. She wakened moaning to the realization that another warm body was pressed closely against her own. Strong, hard thighs were pressed against her slender legs, and even breath stirred near her face. She struggled wildly, trying to sit up, but Josh's strong arms firmly held her down.

"What are you doing?" she screamed at him, breathing with difficulty from a clamp of terror in her chest. "What are you doing here?"

"I was trying to sleep," Josh's mild voice replied. "Though I will admit that you are among the noisiest bedfellows I have ever endured."

When she tried to sit up again, he released her. With the vague light from the fire the only illumination in the room, she stared down at him furiously.

"How dare you lie with me?" she challenged him.

His white teeth gleamed as he grinned at her wickedly. She tried to edge away and only drew the cover from him, exposing the broad, curled expanse of his naked chest.

She tried to struggle over him but he held her fast.

"Let go of me," she shrieked. "My God. I bet you've been sleeping with me all this time."

"You got a winner, there" he said in a mild tone. "Not that I had much choice since there's only this one bed."

"I can always sleep on the floor," she pointed out.

"I could too if I was that stupid," he commented. He released his grip on her. "Go ahead, lady, have it your way if you want."

He made no effort to make her departure easier. She was forced to crawl over his body, clinging desperately to the short-tailed shirt as she went. Her weakness made her pause to lean a long time against the side of the bed before moving away.

"You must have another blanket," she told him caustically.

"My coat's on that hook over there," he replied.

She crossed the room on trembling legs. She was grateful to get the coat down from its peg so that she could cover her long, slender legs which he was frankly watching.

321

She knelt and spread the coat near the fire, lay down, and pulled half of it over her, using the other half as a pallet.

Her feet felt like ice. I don't care if I freeze, she told herself, trying to control a frantic shivering that had gripped her after leaving the warmth of the bed. The idea of his taking advantage of a sick person like that!

The fire made small fluting sounds as blue jets of flame found new avenues of escape from the heart of the burning log. The leather warmed and softened, and she felt herself relaxing, drifting towards sleep.

He spoke to her quietly, his voice low and sibilant with warning.

"Lady," he said first.

She decided to pretend she didn't hear him.

"Lady," he repeated. His voice was no louder but a tenseness in his control of it alerted her.

"Lady, don't move," the quiet voice went on slowly. "Whatever you do, don't move yourself a single bit."

She froze. She heard the faintest rustle of the bedding and then silence. There was no sound in the room for such a long time that she grew confused. She was trying to get up courage to whisper a question to him when the thunder seemed to explode right at her feet. There was a flash of light and the unmistakeable acrid stench of gunpowder, and she tried desperately to extricate herself from the leather coat.

She was on her feet and trembling. She pulled the fire-warmed coat about herself, but the shock of his gunfire so close to her had ruined all the control she had.

"You savage," she screamed at him "What are you trying to do, kill me? Wouldn't it have been easier just to let me die?"

"There was a serpent," he said in that hatefully calm tone. She heard the click of his gun and the sound of it being reloaded.

"Serpent, hell," she said angrily. "It's just another vile trick to try to lure me back into bed with you."

"Lady," he reproached her with his quiet, disgusted tone. He sighed and threw the bearskin aside and stood up. Julie gasped. Unless she wanted to count his eyepatch, he didn't have a stitch on. She tried to look away, but he moved so swiftly that he seemed to fill the room. His finely muscled body glowed in the firelight as he crossed the room, took a

322

fresh candle, stuck it into his crude holder, and knelt to light it from the fire.

Once the candle was aflame, he hooded its light for a minute before crossing back to where the shot had sounded. He knelt and then stood up, holding a snake the size of a double thickness of nautical rope. The snake, which was almost Josh's height, had some memory of life in it even though its head had been completely shot away. It lashed a little, then writhed limply in his grasp before falling still.

"Coral," he explained. "They're pretty bad poison, those corals. And they got a real social habit of coming in here at night to warm at the fire."

"Then why have the fire for them, you idiot?" she said, feeling herself close to the edge of hysteria.

With his face quite close to hers he spoke softly. "Because I'm such an idiot that I don't want a pretty thing like that in bed with me. I never plan to be the warmest thing in the room with a cold coral snake, lady."

She stared back at him. The strength that had come with her terror deserted her. She realized that Josh was suddenly weaving before her. She clutched at him for support as her legs began to buckle under her. He caught her in his arms and gently restored her to the back of the bed.

Then he slid in behind her and patted her shoulder.

"You ain't been hurt yet, lady," he reminded her.

"Thank you, Josh," she mumbled humbly.

His voice was disgusted as he turned away from her under the bearskin. "This is some kind of a damn-fool test I set for myself, and you might just wish me luck."

"Luck, Josh," she murmured from her half-consciousness.

"And lady," he added slyly, "in the choice between ordinary sleeping noises and them bloodcurdling screams you put out, I'd just as soon you'd saw a little wood."

In spite of herself, Julie giggled.

She had almost drifted wholly into sleep when his voice came again. Clearly he thought she was gone because he was talking to himself with a tone of awed wonder in his voice. "Josh Simmons, you are some kind of a saint. You are a Goddamned, son-of-a-bitching, Foxe's *Book of Martyres* sanctified saint, and ain't you just burning for it?"

Julie stiffened her body and held her breath until she got her fit of giggles under control.

Chapter Forty-Six

In contrast to her first terrified wakening in Josh's cabin, Julie was lured from sleep by a concert of birdsong which was filling the richly coffee-scented air. Breathing the welcome fragrance deeply, she wriggled up to examine the room which had been so terrifying to her the night before.

It was a small room, no larger than a maid's room in her father's house. The walls seemed to be constructed of some rough wood joined together with a rude paste of mud in which stiff grasses were embedded. The single window opened onto a moving sea of green. As she looked, a dart of brilliant color, more a flash of gold and green and scarlet than the shape of a bird at all, flashed past the opening.

She heard Josh coming from the complaint of the birds and the sound of that inevitable humming of his which was growing stronger as he neared the door. She struggled farther up into a sitting position and tightened the bearskin up under her chin.

He kicked the door open to enter with his arms loaded high with sticks for the fire. He smiled at her over his burden. By daylight she could see that his skin was a rich olive tint, browned a little from the sun which had also burnished the thick, dark hair that he held back with a leather thong. She watched him lay the wood by the fire and brush the chips and dirt from his leather tunic with the flat of his hand. He was pleasant to look on, a shapely man with a fine head and a warmth to the smile that showed her again that surprising brightness of teeth.

"Well, if lady didn't decide to wake up now that the day is half-spent."

"I was up half the night," she retorted, catching the jest in his voice. "But I am sorry, Josh."

To her astonishment, a quick anger darkened his face which he turned away from her towards the fire. "I have to tell you, lady, that *sorry* is not my favorite word. Sorry is mighty easy to say if it's just the surface kind; inside sorry has to be acted out."

She stared at him, puzzling his swift change of mood.

"My name is Julie," she reminded him.

He nodded. "I remember, but to me you're Lady. I like the way it feels in my mouth." He repeated it thoughtfully. "Lady."

She giggled. "A mighty fair lady I must be with my hair uncombed and dressed in what I guess is your shirt."

He ignored her comment. "You want your coffee over there or here by the fire?"

How long he had cared for her and waited on her only to be treated as rudely as she had in her night terrors just past. "'Sorry has to be acted out" he had said. "I'd like to have it over there with you, if you would join me," she said quietly.

He tugged a rough stool from under the table and set it by his own. "I had thought of doing just that," he said with a brightness in his voice.

Dragging the bearskin behind her to cover her nakedness, Julie curled on the stool. With the bowl of coffee, he handed her a warmed patty of that same golden bread. He told her it was made of ground maize and showed her how to dip it into a warmed comb of wild honey and twist it quickly into her mouth to avoid getting "sugared up" all over. She ate hungrily, trying to ignore his open examination of her.

"At first glance we thought you was a boy, my friend and I," he told her. "With that cropped head and all, and being skinny as a reed."

When she grinned at him he flushed.

"We figured out right off that we were wrong. How come your hair's like that?"

"It's a long story," she told him.

"There's more time here than most anything else."

"Another day maybe?" she asked, raising her eyes to him with a plea in them.

"Whenever you're ready," he agreed in that calm voice. "But I have puzzled on where you were going. I ain't kidding myself that you were risking life and limb to get here to the marshes and sleep half-naked in a squatter's cabin."

She laughed merrily. "That really wasn't my plan, Josh," she conceded. "But it could have ended a lot worse for me."

His gaze was serious on her face. "Who's Ellie?" he asked.

The bite of crisp bread grew suddenly dry in her throat. She struggled to swallow over the lump that came there. "My friend," she said after a moment. "My great and good friend who was with me on the crossing."

"You always call her before you start screaming," he pointed out.

She stared at the fire. "The captain kept her from being saved. I still have trouble believing what I saw as I left the ship." She raised her eyes to him. "It was the last real memory I had, Josh. The ship had lost its mast and then began taking on water. There weren't enough lifeboats, and what there were, were barely seaworthy, but they were the only chance. I was in one boat and Ellie in the second." She stopped and shook her head. "I saw him. I saw him do it. His face turned like a madman's. He pulled her from the boat and threw her across the deck like—like an animal or something."

"What had she done to him?"

"Nothing," Julie replied, startled at the implication.

"Nothing that you know of," he corrected her. "Men don't go mistreating pretty young girls like that unless they've been brought to hate them. Was she as pretty as you?"

Julie flushed at the unexpected gallantry. "She was marvelous," she said quietly. "Great, lively eyes full of fun and mischief, beautiful hair and skin, and a tongue that would strip off whitewash."

Then after a moment she added. "Thank you for the kind words, Josh. I have to say I don't feel very pretty right now. Just glad to be alive."

"That makes a pair of us," he said, rising to get her more coffee.

"You're a strange man, Josh Simmons," she told him. "I have never met anyone like you in my whole life."

"Same," he said, staring at the fire. "But that figures, you know. Ain't two people ever been made just alike. Gives your life a little meaning."

"What do you do, Josh? How do you live?"

"Like a savage," he grinned at her. Then at her rise of color, he blushed. "I just said that to dig you a little. I do what I want and live like I please, and that takes up just about all of my time. I threw this place together to have a place to squat when I needed to get away, but I can't stand it here all the time. When I get hungry for other men's talk about me, I go north where there are people. I like to gamble and booze it up. Then when I've nothing left to pay my tick I take wares out in Indian country, come back with furs, and do it all over again."

"Is Charles Town north?" she asked.

He studied her reflectively. "I should have bet on that if I'd have thought. You'd look like a Charles Town lady if you was gussied up and dressed for it," Then he nodded. "It's north a pretty far piece from here."

"That's where I was going when the ship got into trouble."

"You got folks there?" His voice die not change.. "A husband maybe?"

She shook her head. "No husband, just an aunt."

"Down low or in the Piedmont?"

She frowned. "I don't understand."

He shrugged. "You'll learn. Anyway it's Charles Town. I might get that far north. I generally do, in fact. I hope your aunt ain't counting the days. When we go, we'll walk."

"But how far is it?"

He shook his head. "I couldn't tell you how many miles, but it is two weeks pushing. With somebody as little and puny as you are, it would probably take three weeks or a month."

"Somehow I'll repay you, Josh," she said, humbled by his calm acceptance of this trek that lay ahead of them.

"I know you will, lady," he said flatly. He had said that before. Why did it sound threatening to her when he said it like that?

"Are you afraid of Indians?" he asked suddenly.

She looked at him startled and shook her head. "I don't know. I've never seen one, only pictures in London."

He laughed. "That's no help. I've seen those pictures too and those aren't the Indians I know."

"Are there Indians around here?" she asked.

He laughed again. "You might say. There are Creeks and Cherokees and God knows how many other kinds who have come to hide in the swamps to keep from being killed off or made slaves of. Along with blacks." She realized that he was watching her carefully. She met his glance and he added, "my friend is a black—the one who sold you to me."

"Is he a slave?" she asked.

"He used to be until he ran away. You'll meet him when you're able to travel a little. I told him you had yellow eyes, and he bet me two skins I was lying to him. I'm going to get back all the skins I paid for you right away at this rate."

She laughed. "You really are a gambling men," she said.

"Look who's talking," he grinned at her. "I'd say it took a pretty good streak of risk taking to crawl back into bed with me last night, wouldn't you say?"

"You have to remember the choice I had," she told him tartly.

He slapped the table as he rose. "Okay, lady. Let's get you rigged into some clothes and moving around. You ain't never going to walk to the Carolinas until we get some muscle on those bones."

She watched him pull a bundle from his shelf and untie it on top of the bed.

"Maybe I was gambling on a pretty long shot when I traded for these," he admitted, "But I figured you might need something more than my old shirt to cover your—" That bright smile flashed at her sidelong, and he spread the garments out. "How do you feel about these?"

Julie stared at the clothing on the bed. Leather. . . .They were all leather, a pale shirt trimmed with quills in an intricate design of brown and gold and a skirt of a darker leather with siken fringe of finely cut leather. She fingered the soft leather gently. "Beautiful. How can they make them so beautiful?"

The skirt was full and loose enough to fall to her ankles, and the shoes were trimmed handsomely across the top with drawstrings of leather.

"They call them moccasins," he told her. "You'll never like a proper shoe after once getting used to these."

"Oh Josh," she said, overcome at his kindness.

He grinned and handed her the last two objects on the pile. "What do you figure these to be?"

They were long rectangles of finely finished leather with thongs tied at one end, long thongs several feet in length.

"They're leggin's," he said. "Like mine. I made them in case you would like to go woodswalking. But only if you wanted to," he added hastily. "It's no matter to me."

She studied the way his own leggings were bound about his well-shaped calves. "For snakes and thorns," he said.

"I'd like to go woodswalking," she told him, nodding.

His grin was instant. "Just tell me when you think you got enough strength up."

He was in the clearing when she finished dressing. He watched with such a controlled face as she walked across to him, that Julie felt strangely disappointed. It was only when she drew near and he was looking down at her that the grin twitched at the corner of his mouth "I'd say that you are the prettiest squaw that ever walked this swamp," he decided aloud. He offered her his arm. "We'll just circle the clearing at first. The air will do you good."

The forest which had seemed so forbidding by night was only strangely beautiful by day. It was a secret place and the great fronds that trailed from the trees added to its aura of mystery. The lean-to that opened onto the narrow clearing was backed against a giant pale tree with roots that rose above the surface of the ground in great tortured knots. A sluggard stream ran behind the tree in back of the dwelling, and the tree roots seemed as comfortable in that depth of water as they did on land.

"Cypress," Josh explained following her glance. Small, bright insects hummed above the stream, and the hidden woods of the swamp seemed to vibrate with life.

"It's beautiful," she said, staring about her. "Josh, it is just strange and beautiful."

She was startled at his hands suddenly upon her arms. She looked up with some alarm as he slid his arms about her waist and stood facing her.

"I can't ever say this to you inside that cabin, Lady," he said quietly. "Not when we are driven together there against the night and the wild. But I got to speak it out sometime and I've chosen now."

He paused and swallowed hard. "You are what is beautiful, Lady." He raised his hands and traced the line of her cheek down her throat. "Everything about you is beautiful to me, those yellow eyes of yours with that smudge of lashes, even that mop hair of yours. For that mouth a man could die."

Then he released her suddenly. She saw a faint trace of sweat across his forehead. It beaded on the leather thong that held his eye patch in place. "You are the most beautiful thing I have ever been this close to. That's what I been waiting to

329

tell you, Lady." Then he took her hand almost roughly and started walking.

"Only go where I say and walk in my steps. The swamp makes death for the unwary. I say you're tired now and could do with a little resting by the fire."

Chapter Forty-Seven

Those first few days, Julie was content to stay near the lean-to, dozing in the sun and eating heartily of the game that Josh brought and prepared for her. She felt her old vitality well within her like a freshet in a spring meadow.

The fourth morning she raised her eyes from her coffee shyly. "You said I should tell you when I felt like going woodswalking," she reminded Josh.

His face lit with pleasure. "Good news, Lady. Remember, I've got a wager to settle. You have to be there to lay the bet."

At the edge of the clearing, he repeated his warning of that first day. "Only where I step," he cautioned. "The marsh is hungry for life."

It seemed to her that they had travelled for a long while through the trackless marsh. Josh moved swiftly and silently in a silent walk that was almost like the movement of a skater. In time, her breath came only with difficulty and her legs felt heavy and leaden.

She tried to keep up, but finally the fatigue struck her so heavily that she stumbled and groped for his arm. "Josh," she called, feeling sudden panic at her weakness.

He turned swiftly and stared at her. "Jesus Christ, what a fool I am. I plumb forgot, Lady." He bent and lifted her into his arms over her protests.

"It's only a little farther. You're no burden at all."

He hadn't said he was sorry. Strange man. *Sorry* for him was in the gentleness with which he carried her and the place he found for her to rest—the knee of a cypress placed so that it was like a chair. She leaned her head back against the tree and smiled at him.

He took a few steps away from her then stopped and

hooded his mouth with both hands. The cry that he uttered was unwordly. If she had not seen the muscles tighten in his neck, she would have sworn that the sound had come from some creature of the marsh, and not in this clearing but several feet away.

They were waiting. She knew that they were waiting for his friend to come, but there was a timeless peace in his relaxed pose that was unreal to her. The place assumed the quality of a dream. The brilliant birds they had startled away with their coming grew accustomed to their presence. One flew to a branch near Josh and cocked his head to peer at Josh curiously. Its plumed head bobbed and its glorious tail waggled as it spoke to Josh.

"*Arrk*?" the tone was a question.

When Julie laughed, he fluttered away with screeches of complaint.

"Handsome little devils, ain't they?" Josh grinned. "Curious too. You aren't much troubled with that, are you, Lady? Most everybody knows me three minutes before they get around to asking how I lost that eye."

"Once before I had a friend with only one eye," Julie told him. "And he lived in the deep woods like you do."

"Men that has been bad hurt by other men like this kind of place," he told her calmly. "Was his eye gouged out like mine was?"

"Gouged out?" Julie gasped, shocked at the thought.

Josh had selected a twig from the tree that overhung his head. He chewed on the end of it and spit splinters away. "It was a fight I lost," he reported calmly. "It was his eye or mine and he had the quickest thumbs."

"My God," Julie said with a shiver.

He grinned at her. "This country ain't London town," he reminded her. "What ever it is, it ain't London Town."

She knew from the alertness of his body that someone was approaching. He drew near her and laid one hand on her shoulder with the other hand cradling his everpresent gun. Then he recognized the mover in the shadows and relaxed, patting her shoulder casually as if to reassure her.

She had expected Josh's friend to have a black skin like the black footmen who had become so stylish an affectation in London. But the man who emerged from the trees bore no resemblance to those fancily dressed men whose faces gleamed like polished coal.

This man was tall, towering over Josh. Clad as he was in a tattered, blue shirt and trousers rent off at the knee, he seemed an aging and beautiful golden statue. He seemed older than time, his head matted with twisted, gray curls and his great beard a shocking gray beneath the warm, golden brown of his wrinkled skin. His eyes were strange, a clouded dark brown that seemed too incredibly dark to belong in that face.

"Lady," Josh nodded. "My friend."

Julie smiled at the man and raised her hand to him.

"How do you do?" she asked, conscious of how affected her greeting sounded to this man in this setting. The man stared silently at her a long moment, then he bowed his head stiffly and took Julie's hand for a brief moment. Then he turned to Josh.

"*Umuntu*," he said quietly and held up two fingers.

Josh laughed and slapped his thigh. "What did I tell you? Yellow as a ripe pear. There's two more skins on your ticket and a compliment besides."

The dark man was smiling too, then he turned wordlessly and disappeared into the woods again.

"What did he say? Where is he going?" Julie asked.

"He's going after the skins," Josh explained. "And he said that you were a real person, not just a white."

Josh examined the skins carefully. They were sleek and pliant from an animal that Julie did not recognize.

While Josh turned the skins in his hands and held them to the light, his friend squatted on his haunches and watched him with those strange, clouded eyes. At Josh's nod, he rose and held out a pouch to Josh.

After a questioning glance, his friend spoke the first English words Julie had heard him speak.

"For Lady," he said.

Josh opened the pouch for her to see its contents. It was filled with small, dark red lumps and in among them gray objects that looked like porous stones.

"Dried mushrooms and wild plums," Josh explained. "A gift to you from my friend."

Julie braced herself against the tree and rose to her feet. She smiled at the old man and held out her hand again.

"Thank you," she said warmly. "Thank you very, very much."

The dark man took her hand soberly and pressed it with a firm grasp. Then he turned away from her and spoke fervantly to Josh for several minutes. She felt Josh's speculative glance on her as his friend spoke. Then the other man saluted her, nodded at Josh, and went back into the forest as silently as he had come.

"Can you walk back home?" Josh asked her.

"I can start," she grinned at him. "No promises."

"Just don't get fat and try this with me, Lady," he warned her, lifting her into his arms to stride off through the marshes.

Back at the lean-to, Josh carefully stored the dried plums and mushrooms in a tin on the shelf. "That's a very fine gift," he explained to her. "He has gathered those fruits and dried them to augment his own diet. There is little to relieve the steady chance of game and fish when the fruit is between season. A compliment to you."

"I am glad he liked me." Julie admitted, still a little bedazzled by the strange, dignified encounter there in those primitive woods.

"Oh, I am not sure you could say that he liked you," Josh corrected her. "He was a diviner among his own people. He gave you credit for being more than just another white, but he also told me that behind your eyes he senses *Batakatsi*."

"Do you know what that means?" she asked, a little disturbed by Josh's tone.

"Not altogether," he admitted. "His system of thought is too different from mine. But the word has something to do with evil. Either that you make evil, like a witch in our understanding, or great evil is wished to you."

He was watching her carefully as he spoke. She raised her eyes to him and shrugged. "I am not a witch," she said firmly. "And as to having evil wished to me. You said it best yourself. 'What man is safe?'"

"Good, Lady," he said thoughtfully. "Very good."

He laid his hand on her shoulder as he spoke. Then she was conscious that his hand had stayed there overlong. She felt the warmth of it through the fine, sheer leather of her shirt. Then she saw tension rise in the whitening of the flesh along his jaw.

He turned from her abruptly and knelt to blow the fire to flame.

"How did you enjoy your first day in the deeper woods?"

"I love it," she admitted. "It doesn't seem that dangerous."

"That is part of its danger," he told her. "You must never venture in there without me. The runaway blacks do not come this close to the edge of the marshes, except for my friend who is wily. But there is a British fort offshore. You would not be safe in the woods alone."

She was unlacing her leggings and stopped suddenly.

"I guess I expected there to be Indians."

Still kneeling by the fire, he turned and grinned at her. "There were Indians, and they got the good look at you that they have been seeking ever since I bartered the clothes for you."

"You're fooling me," she said, a little shivery at the thought that she had been so examined without glimpsing any of their faces.

"Do you want to bet?" he asked eagerly.

She threw a legging at him, and he laughed heartily as it caught him on the ear before falling to the floor.

Chapter Forty-Eight

The weeks that followed brought health back to Julie. Her figure which had melted to flat bone during her exposure at sea and the delirium, filled out to its previous voluptuous beauty. Her breasts strained against the soft leather of the Indian blouse she wore. Her pallor was replaced by warm rose tints that returned to her cheeks and lips. While Josh never lost control of his consuming desire for her, Julie was guiltily conscious of the torment that her nearness brought to his days as well as their nights together on the shared pallet.

When Josh's natural passions threatened to overwhelm his self-imposed control, he grew pointlessly snappish at her or strode off into the woods alone with an angry mutter instead of his usual lighthearted song.

"This is ridiculous," she told him when he had gone a full evening and the next day without speaking gently to her.

334

"Why should you put up with me and me endure your spleen when we have other choices? You said yourself that there was an English fort nearby. There must be someone there who would take the burden of me off your hands."

"Don't be a greater fool than God made you," he snapped back, refilling his pipe and stabbing angrily at the tobacco in it.

"Look who is the fool," she taunted him. "The fort is there for the protection of the citizens. Why not use it to protect yourself from the irritation of my presence? Then there would be one less fool in this cabin."

"Ah, the fort is it?" he said, eyeing her calmly, "And what do you think would happen to you at the fort? How do you think you would be received, Lady. Those are woman-starved men far from home and from the controls of their king. If you came as a lady in a fine carriage pleading for their help, they would still be sore beset to keep from ravishing you. But a woods maiden like you—coming clad in Indian leather?"

"My tongue would tell them quickly enough that I was no squaw but an English citizen like themselves," Julie protested hotly.

"And a Newgate bird," he added quietly. "The mark on your arm would tell them that. Once that was seen, and mark my words, it soon enough would be, you would be fair game—fairer game then they've any of them seen in their lives I wager."

"Wager, wager, wager," she spit at him angrily, realizing what truth lay in his words. "I'll make a wager myself that you never intend to help me get north to my aunt."

"When the mosquitoes come," he said with a laugh. "They are the only creatures under God's sky whose tongue can pull more blood than your own."

But the times of their strife were infrequent. Most of the days, Julie found herself deliciously content, except for a lively restlessness that accompanied her return to strength.

Abandoned to her own resources with Josh gone for a full day of hunting, she decided that a bath in the stream would be an exhilarating change from the warmed pan of water she had been using to keep herself fresh.

She took the rough soap he had given her and went out to the stream that meandered just in back of the trees that supported the lean-to. She had freed herself of her clothing and

335

was slipping herself into the cold water slowly, catching her breath from the shock of it against her warm skin.

To her astonishment, the water began to vibrate about her legs although she herself was not moving. She was puzzling this in her mind when she noticed what appeared to be two round knobs of dark wood moving towards her through the water. She stared fixedly at them, wondering how they floated so swiftly in such a sluggish stream. A wild crashing from the brush startled her into looking up.

Josh's friend, the great golden Negro, was bearing down on her with a tree branch in one hand and an upraised knife in the other. The murderous intentness of his expression terrified her.

She leaped from the water and tried to run, catching her blouse to cover her nakedness. Her instinct was to scream to Josh but she knew he was many hours away in the swamp. She glanced back and slowed her steps. The man had stopped in the center of the stream and was jabbing his knife into the water as if he had gone mad. At his blows, a great churning began and a massive scaled tail rose to lash and whip viciously at him.

Her scream froze in her throat. The lizard that he was battling was like a mythical sea monster, and the fight between the old man and the beast looked to be a fight to the death. Then she saw great fanged jaws, large enough to hold a man, open and snap sharply at its attacker. With swift dexterity, the old man plunged the tree limb down the animal's throat. She heard the wood splinter as the beast snapped his jaws upon it. But with his jaws pried that little bit apart, the old man plunged the knife into the throat. The alligator thrashed mightily and was suddenly stilled. Wordlessly, the old Negro waded tiredly from the stream, his breast heaving with exhaustion.

He picked up Julie's skirt and brought it to her. His face was darkened by fury, and he pointed to the cabin angrily, waiting until she was inside to move from the spot.

She was still curled by the fire trembling with the shock of that scene when Josh slammed into the cabin. His face was pale and his eyes snapped furiously at her. He crossed the room and seized her roughly by the shoulders.

"Fool," he cried. "You child, you idiot child." Then, at her touch, his voice dropped and he pulled her to him. She could

336

feel the violent trembling that shook his body. "Lady, Lady," he said softly. "What would I do if my friend had not been there watching? What would I do?"

"I didn't know," she whispered. "But he was there. How could he get there so quickly?"

He released her to slump in the chair and reach for the jug of rum warming by the hearth. "He's always there," he admitted tiredly. "It is an arrangement we made. When I am to be gone farther than your voice could call, he has stood guard over you out there beyond your seeing. Without that, I would not have dared to leave this clearing. The marsh holds death, Lady. I have told you."

His anger began to renew itself from his words. "I told you plainly, and then you went forth." She could not face his fury again. She knelt before him and looped her arms about his waist. "Oh Josh," She could not inflame him further by telling him how sorry she was so she only repeated his name. "Josh. Josh. I am a fool. I am an idiot child. I am the veriest fool and a great burden to you."

He stared at her, then smiled wryly. His teenth flashed against his dark face in that way she had learned to find most appealing.

He closed his arms about her and rocked her back and forth against himself as if she were a child indeed. "Not as you think, my Lady," he said gently. "You are not the burden that you think you are."

After that day, she pleaded to go forth into the marshes with him. "I like being where you are," she explained. I feel safe."

"Just safe?" he asked watching her face.

"And happy," she added honestly. She giggled at his expression so that the dimple came and went swiftly in her cheek. "I like to hear your song near me," she confessed.

She was seldom far from him after that. The trails she walked with him brought Margaret to her mind. She found many of the herbs and simples in those marshes that were the same that Margaret had taught her to use. She brought back great armsful of what Josh called "weeds" and hung them near the ceiling to dry as Margaret had done.

She finally ceased to rail to him about the trip north. She knew him well enough to realize that he would set out in his own good time and her words only wounded them both.

When she finally saw him sorting his skins and packing them carefully, she felt the time was nearing. When he took smooth leather and punched and sewed a new pair of leggings for them both, she knew the time was nearly at hand.

She found herself brooding about the trip ahead. She was at once eager and apprehensive about her return to civilization after this world they had shared. She did not know her aunt or the manner of household in which she must go as a burden, as a poor relation without property or dower.

She thought of Charles Fenner wistfully. Ellie had said that if she could not love a man so like herself then she would never love anyone again and might as well marry and forget the fine, high thrill she remembered from Antoine.

What would Ellie say to Josh? If I cannot love Josh Simmons, Julie admitted to herself, then my heart is truly dead.

Little by little Josh ceded tasks to her, not because he needed her help but because it pleased her to fill her hours with busyness. He brought her wild onions from the marsh and she learned to use them along with her herbs to prepare a dark, rich stew of wild hare.

"Is there no end to your skills?" he asked when such an experiment came out well. She preened like a vain child at his approval.

She soaked the wild plums that Josh's friend had given her until they were as plump as new. After she cooked them a long time over the fire, their taste was still so bitter that her mouth pulled into an O. She thought to add honey to their juice and a splash of rum from Josh's jug.

"My God, Lady," Josh cried when he gingerly tasted the dish. "You have improved on Spring with your sorcery."

She often took the mushrooms down and turned them in her hands. Josh had said that they too could be restored by soaking them in fresh, spring water. But she could not decide how to fix them.

Mushrooms were part of breakfast at her father's house. She could sit, with the dried, rocklike things in her hand and recall the sound and scent of salted pork sizzling in the pan. The cook always soaked the mushrooms in a large bowl of water to which she had added vinegar. "To chase the ants from the frills," she had explained to Julie. When the pork was brown and crisp, she tossed the mushrooms, dried in a towel, into the hot fat alongside the meat. The mushrooms hissed angrily when they hit the hot grease and let forth a rich, dark juice which was boiled away before the eggs were added. Julie sighed and replaced the mushrooms in the tin. There was no salted meat, and the last egg she had seen was aboard the *Tilbusy Belle* when the red hen in the deck coop laid one to the great delight of the crew.

Even after Josh grew to trust her enough that he did not ask his friend to watch the cabin, he still went almost weekly to see his friend, if indeed his friend did not come first. That strange call would come from the wood and Josh would smile and rise and take his pipe and disappear into the edge of the marsh for an hour or two.

Then his friend went an entire week without either coming or answering the call from their clearing. Often when she glanced at Josh, he would be wearing a puzzled expression that gradually changed to one of concern. Then he ceased humming as he moved about his work.

The second week with no word from his friend brought out the spleen in Josh. He snapped at her without reason and did not listen when she wanted to talk to him. Finally, she turned on him.

"I know you miss your black friend. Why take it out on me? Go and see him. Find out for yourself that he is simply too busy or into some project or other."

"It is too many miles for you," he protested.

"How many miles?" she asked.

"Four hours to go and four to return," he told her. "That is almost morning to sundown. Too far into the swamp for you."

"Then you go alone and I will wait and have food ready for your return."

At his wry glance, she bridled. "I am no child that must have a nurse to watch me. I know to stay safe."

"No foolishness?" he asked. She could hear the temptation tugging in his voice.

"No foolishness," she said firmly. Then she grinned at him. "I will not bathe with alligators nor dump myself into the pulling sand. I shall lock the door and stay inside and behave like a good wife all day."

His face darkened at the word *wife* and he drew away the hand he had laid on her shoulder.

339

But in the end he relented. "I am concerned about him," he admitted. "I shall start at dawn."

He did not even wait for daylight. Julie felt his warmth leave their bed before the light came through the rough window. She wriggled about under the bearskin to sleep some more, both excited and anxious about the long day ahead without Josh.

Without Josh. She turned on her back and stared at the ceiling which she had learned so well during her delirium and these months following. How would it be without Josh?

She had told him at the first that he was unlike any man she had ever known. This was doubly true now that she knew him well. He was rough and gentle at once, like a half-finished coin. Sometimes he deliberately spoke with the crude words of a backwoodsman, and then again he would speak with such words and such thoughts that she knew that the roughness was a deliberate pose. He treated her with the respect a man would show for his own sister, and at the same time he visibly blazed with his unfulfilled desire for her.

She hated to admit, even to herself, that the shared bed had become a strain on her too. He was so dear to her and it had always been her nature to be affectionate. Sometimes in a half-sleep she would start to turn to him, wanting the gentleness of his arms about her. But always she had to draw back for reasons she did not understand.

Small things he said—that talk he had had with himself that first night about being a self-made martyr, his muttering at his own stupidity whenever his natural passions threatened to overwhelm him. She knew that if he would turn to her for physical love she would go gladly into his arms. But something held him away.

Was he, like her dark-eyed master, unable to perform the duties of a man? She shook her head in confusion and rose to heat water for the rough tub he had hacked from a tree trunk and dragged in by the fire for her.

Chapter Forty-Nine

That day seemed to last forever. She bathed luxuriously in her wooden tub, sudsing and singing and finally dozing until the water chilled her and white ridges had soaked into her smooth flesh. She dressed carefully and toyed with her hair until she was really convinced that it must look quite stylish. Josh had no mirror and the only still pool where she had been able to see her face was beyond the clearing. She would keep her promise to stay inside.

She had done everything she could think of against his coming, and the sun was still high in the sky. She had swept the last corner of the room, stamping as she always did to try to smooth away the gouge in the floor that his shot had made the first night when he fired on the coral snake at her feet. She made a row of golden cakes and cooked them to crispness the way he had taught her to do. She had rubbed the flesh of two marsh hens with sage and then simmered them with wild onion until they were tender enough to fall from the bone at her touch.

Then she remembered the mushrooms. After soaking them plump, she sliced them into the brown sauce about the hens.

The cabin smelled delicious from the scent of the meal and the coffee set back to stay hot against Josh's coming. Julie yearned to taste the sauce she had made with the mushrooms but the hens were small. There would be little enough for a man who had walked all day if she took only a little during the meal.

Restlessly, she stirred from the fire to the window and then back. Finally, she took a corn cake and munched on it as she watched the path into the marshes. A pale moon stirred somewhere behind thin clouds, shadowing and silvering the trees by turn. Cries that she did not recognize sounded from beyond the trees, and she startled at every twig snap and leaf drop.

Yet as eagerly as she had watched for Josh's coming, she only knew he was there when he rapped at the door for her to let the bolt so he could come in.

He did not seem the man she knew. His clothing was stained with mud and his face was dark and haggard.

"Josh," she cried, running to him. "What is wrong? What has happened to you?"

He shook his head and went past her to catch the strap of his gun on its hook by the door.

"Dead," he said. His calm voice was dull and colorless. "After all this, he is dead."

"But how?" she asked, seeing that golden man as she had at their first meeting, his air of timeless strength betrayed only by the whiteness of the beard that framed his mouth.

"As he lived," Josh replied. "Alone." Then he straightened himself with an obvious effort. "I must clean up," he told her. "I'll be right back."

"No," she decided suddenly. "Don't go out into the night again. Look, I have water. Lots of heated water. Use my tub."

A grin tugged at his mouth as he looked at her. "Your tub, Lady? What do you think I am, one of your fine London bucks who pampers himself like a whore? You'll be wanting me to press my face with white powder next."

She grinned back at him. "Now come on, Josh," she coaxed. "You are chilled to the bone and wet." She reached up and began to loosen the thongs of his jacket. "Get them off. How did you ever manage to get them so dirty?"

His face was turned away. "Digging a grave."

He was too numbed by grief and exhaustion to resist her. She loosed his garments and he slid into the tub of water as she laid the filthy clothing by the door. Not since that first night when he had come leaping from the bed to show her the coral snake, had she seen him unclothed. His modesty with her now was somehow disarming.

When she brought him the soap, she hesitated and then moistened her hands and made a fine suds to work onto his shoulders. As she pulled the foam along his shoulders and down his back, she felt his muscles like strained rope under her hands.

"That's enough, Lady," he said sternly. "Go about your cooking and I will be ready when you are."

He drank the warmed rum she handed him but sat before his plate dully.

"Eat, Josh," she coaxed, leaning on her elbows and leaning

across the table towards him. "To lose your strength will not help your friend."

He looked at her, at the golden light that shone at him from her eyes, the delicious shaping of her round arms bared by the loose leather sleeve of her blouse. Alive. How ripe and alive she was. He slid his glance away. Coming to her from where he had been was dark into sunlight. He was blinded, and he groped for his food to distract his mind.

The flavor of the dish startled him. "This is delicious, Lady," he said. "How did you get such a taste to simple fare?"

"The mushrooms," she said quietly.

He shook his head. "My friend's last meal was of meat with mushrooms too. I found it rotted in the pan by his dead fire." He paused, eating slowly and talking almost as if she were not there.

"How did death come to him like that? There was not a mark of anything, not snake, not wound. He was in the fullness of great strength still. He was old, grant that he was old, but it was the aging of a great tree that is only more solid with time. His sight had begun to fail when that gray film came before his eyes. He told me himself that one day he expected to see no more, but he could still hunt and fish and gather food."

Julie, her hunger allayed by the bread she had eaten and her stomach taut from the anguish on Josh's face, did not eat. She sat with her coffee cup before her, letting Josh ramble on and on about his dead friend.

"His father had been a king in Africa," he told her. "There were wars between the tribes and my friend and some of the other warriors were taken prisoner. He was sold to the slave traders by black men like himself who were enemies of his people—the Swazi. He never forgave that it was a black man that sold him."

"How long was he a slave?" Julie asked.

"Thirty-five years." Josh's tone was heavy. "Longer by far than my life or yours. Then his wife who was a Swazi like himself but much younger died after bearing a girl child. Since the infant was too young to be of use, the plantation owner sold her for a few shillings to an owner whose slave house contained a woman with child at breast. It was then that he ran away."

"Poor golden man," Julie said.

343

Josh pushed aside the empty plate. "I hope to God I can forget the way he died. His face was contorted as I have seen men in the agony of poisoning. He had thrashed about and made great havoc in that cabin which he always kept as neat as you keep this one." He shook his head.

A slow thread of fear seemed to be drawn across Julies' understanding. "Josh," she said urgently. "Tell me again how he died. You say he looked as if he had been poisoned."

"That was only how he looked," Josh reminded her. "How could that be?"

"And you told me that his eyes had been failing and that he thought he was going blind?"

Josh's tone grew impatient. "I don't know why you want to go over all that again."

But Julie was on her feet, moving swiftly. She tosssed fresh wood on the fire, set water over the flame and tugged her stool over to the opposite wall.

"The mushrooms," she was almost crying. "My God, Josh it was the mushrooms. You said yourself that he had been eating them—his last meal."

"But he had been gathering mushrooms in this marsh and eating them for all these years," he reminded her. She shook her head vigorously without stopping her work. She tore leaves fiercely from the stalks she had pulled from its thong and crammed the leaves into the boiling water.

"Blind, Josh," she shouted at him. "He was going blind. He didn't see the right mushrooms. He picked the poisonous ones by mistake, don't you see? And now you have eaten of them too."

"Lady," his voice was quiet. "Your head has jumped ahead of your sense. Calm down now."

Her hands were trembling so much that she could barely pour the tea into the bowl.

"Drink it," she commanded him. "Please drink it for me. It will make you very sick but it will bring the poison up with the food if you act quickly enough. For God's sake drink."

"This is madness," he said curtly, pushing away the bowl of rank-smelling fluid. "That meal was delicious."

Tears streamed down Julie's face. "For me," she pleaded. "Please, love, drink it for me. Drink it quickly and as hot as it will go down."

He stared at her so intently that time seemed to stop. The
344

endearment she had spoken to him hung in the air between them like a visible sign. Then he reached for the bowl and lifted it to his lips.

With his glance level on her, he spoke softly. "I will drink it for you, Lady, only for you."

When he had drained the bowl, she filled it again. He gagged as the second draft of emetic hit his stomach. She was filling the bowl for the third time when he bolted from his seat, threw the door open, and lunged out into the darkness. When she tried to follow, he motioned her back. She waited in the shadow by the door until his retching was finished. Then he stayed kneeling limply, struggling to rise.

After she helped him to his feet, she bathed his face and wiped his beard with a cool, wet cloth and led him inside.

He tried to help her with his clothes, but his own hands had suddenly become alien to him. She finally tugged him free of them and rolled him in under the bearskin in that spot against the wall where she had lain beside him so many nights.

She sat by the fire until dawn, leaping at his slightest moan and bathing his face to cool the fever that seemed to come and go fitfully, like a moon from behind scattered clouds. With dawn, he grew peaceful and his breathing deep and regular, and she knew the battle was won.

All that day and the next he was too weak to rise. At his insistence, she carried the gun on her arm when she went to the stream for water. He drank a little tea and later some broth, but mostly he slept. Dark phantoms seemed to stir in his dreams, fluttering behind his eyelids as she watched.

On the third morning, he wakened before she did. She opened her eyes to find him staring into her face. His flesh was still pale, but the old tentative smile tugged at his mouth as he gazed at her.

He reached up and ran his finger gently down the line of her cheek. "You don't owe me any more skins, Lady," he said soberly. "You paid them all out with that stinking witch's brew of yours."

Then he frowned. "How do you know so much? Where did the wiseness come that you surprise me with every day?"

"From living," she said thoughtfully. "I have had a strange and various life. Oh Josh, I was so afraid for you."

"Were you, Lady?" he asked with particular intensity.

345

She nodded. "I was desperately afraid for you." Then she wriggled a little to face him better in the bed. She slid her naked arms about his neck and lifted her lips and pressed them to his.

When the shock of her touch moved through him, he shivered and then lay very still. He responded to her kiss with an almost painful, small cry that was buried in her flesh. His kiss was gentle and his hand pressed tentatively on her back as if it doubted his purpose.

All the days of their sharing, his gentleness with her, and the laughter remembered flooded over Julie. She moved closer to him, pressing the round warmth of her breasts against his bare chest. Then she slid her smooth leg in between his thighs, pressing her silken body against the swelling of his desire for her.

"Lady," he moaned as his body moved onto hers. "My lady."

It was not there. That fine, thrilling wonder that flowed along her limbs like fire at Antoine's lovemaking did not come to her. Instead, her body and her heart responded to Josh with the same joyous gentleness that she bore him in their shared time together. When his passion was spent, he tangled his hand gently in her hair and sighed.

"God, how I have dreamed of such in your arms."

He slept and stirred and moved into her again with the same gentle eagerness. The sun streamed across the floor, and the day birds grew riotous before she wakened again.

He was bending before the fire as he had been that first morning. Then he turned and with that familiar, gliding step she had watched from her daze of illness, he came towards her bearing a steaming bowl.

Seeing her eyes on his face, he grinned.

"You had better let me do this," he warned. "It's very hot."

She shifted to sit up, never minding that her breasts rose pale and glowing above the darkness of the fur cover. He held the bowl to her lips and her eyes smiled at him as she drank.

After he set the empty bowl down, he took both her hands and looked down at them. "I have been afraid of you, Lady," he confessed.

"Afraid?" she asked.

He nodded. "From the first, I wanted you like a starvation. From the first day that my friend—that he brought you here lightly in his arm like a broken doll. But I held myself off from you because of an oath I made myself against women."

Her golden eyes studied him seriously.

"To have no woman—ever?" she asked incredulously, conscious of his firm, shapely body so close to her.

He shook his head. "Not quite like that. I swore to have no woman who did not want me as I wanted her. No woman who came to me for land," he spit the word bitterly, "or for money or skins like the whores of Charles Town. I swore to have no woman who did not want me as you did this night past."

"And how was that, Josh?" she asked him, so much hoping that he had understood.

His face was watchful on hers as he replied.

"Because you loved me and were glad I was alive and wanted to share that life with me for that sweet time."

She nodded and smiled at him.

"You do love me, Lady?" he asked softly.

"I love you, Josh," she said, astonished that no twinge of doubt passed in her mind as she spoke.

"As much as Antoine?" he asked, his voice very low.

The stillness in the room was so absolute that the forest outside seemed to flow in through the open window, spilling in sunlight and bird sound and the faint spicy scent of that mint that perfumed the clearing floor.

"Differently," she replied. Then she looked up at him. "What do you know of Antoine?"

He sighed. "That when you dream of terror, you scream and call for help for Ellie; that when you flail with anguish, you cry over and over, 'He is dead. The man who gave me the necklace is dead,'" he paused. "But when the great, silent grief of slow, unending tears comes, you always cry for Antoine."

"I had a long fever," she told him. "Differently, Josh," she said softly. "I loved him differently." Then she lifted her head and guided his lips to her own for both of them to forget.

Chapter Fifty

Her name was Charity. Following Josh's graceful, lean body through the swamp, or feeling his gaze tender on her face, Julie thought about the girl named Charity who was Josh's wife.

"She is fair," Josh said. "She's the most beautiful girl I ever saw before you. Her eyes are that bright blue that a mountain spring comes when the thaw is through, that clear blue you can see through right down to where the last trout hides among the stones. But Charity ain't that easy to see through or understand.

"She smiled, that girl did, from the first, she smiled all the time. She teased me with that smile and the way her eyes clung on and the way she could flip a skirt so that always after, you'd keep watching to see that swelling of firm leg up from a fine turned ankle.

"Yet she seemed so pure with the way she'd squeal if I so much as caught at her hand to hold it."

They were promised when Josh was eighteen and married when he turned twenty, and as Josh put it, there was "delight all around." Her father's lands bordered the Simmons land, and her father had no sons to inherit his holdings. She was young and already sought after, and her father in poor health. He was eager to see her settled into a good life so he could die with an easy conscience. Josh's own father was delighted to see those wide, fruitful acres joined with his own.

Julie listened silently. How this story reminded her of Giles and herself. The difference was that Charity and Josh had actually made it to the altar.

"But not much beyond," Josh told her wryly.

Julie's eyes on his face flustered Josh so that his own glance strayed away. He caressed her hand, trying to find the right words to explain it to Julie.

"I wasn't prepared to learn that I wasn't her first man. She was bare turned sixteen and already she was wise in the sheets. She cried and told me she was sorry." He looked right at Julie with an appeal in his face. "I tell you, Lady, I don't really know how women feel about the bedding business generally, but Charity sure had a mind of her own. She'd make up to me in a hay rick or in any damned place but at home where it was right and proper. I should have figured out right then that she didn't think lovemaking was a thing to be done at home.

"I didn't figure for a while that there were others getting what I was kept away from. Then the sniggers behind my back and the wise glances told me the truth. I was wild for her, but there was always some reason she couldn't be bedded. When I confronted her with the names of the others, it was always the same thing. She cried and said she was sorry and made promises that didn't last until another sundown. She was ice in my bed and fire for any stranger." He glared down at Julie's hand in his own.

"I stood it three years. I couldn't see any babes coming as seldom as she let me close, and if there had been babes who was to know who had fathered them? And every Sabbath, I would look over at her singing hymns with that pale hair shining and swear I was dreaming that such an angel to look at could be so rotten inside."

"So you just left?" Julie asked, incredulous.

"It wasn't quite that simple," he confessed. "When Indian trouble came, I was called out with the others. My patrol was ambushed and my two friends taken by the Indians. They left me for dead, I was that badly wounded. When I came around and was able to drag myself off, I just dragged in the other direction."

"And you never went back or even heard from her?"

A bitter smile distorted Josh's mouth. "I ain't been back but I heard aplenty. I was told that she was a mighty touching young widow all tricked out in black. Then after about a year she married the old man who owned land on the other side of that hill. I also heard he took to the bottle really heavy for an old man like that. They say she leans pretty heavy on the young manager he hired to run the places."

They had worked their way to a certain clearing in the marsh that was Josh's favorite. The smooth, grassy mound was all the way surrounded by a small stream whose face was green from the reflection of overhanging boughs. The massive

349

trees that circled the clearing were droopy with the dark Spanish moss that trailed lazily towards the earth.

"A little later in the season this will bloom all over with flowers," Josh told her. "Come and sit here."

She leaned back against his shoulder and he buried his face in her loose hair. "It's been good, hasn't it, Lady?" he asked.

She caught his hand in hers. "All the way good," she replied.

"You've seen me packing the skins and readying the cabin?"

She nodded.

"We start back to Carolina tomorrow," he said softly. "But only if that's what you want."

"I don't know what I want, Josh," she admitted. "When I'm like this with you, that's what I want. Then other times I feel like I'm always just waiting."

"Waiting for what?"

She shook her head distractedly. "I don't even know. Maybe a proper house and babes and all that."

"I guess you couldn't marry a man who's been declared legally dead," he said quietly.

She shook her head, but inside herself she admitted that she was not being open with him. She could marry him and in this wild free country who would know the difference? Why did she hesitate? Because the life was so strange to her? Because she shared so little with Josh except the memory of pain and later this gentle time? "No," she admitted privately. "It's because of the pain I carry for Antoine. I am married to a dead man and cannot inflict my bigamy on anyone I like as well as I do Josh." She turned to him and pressed her lips to his to make him forget.

He groaned softly as his hands moved expertly over her body. "That's why we came here today, lady," he confessed. "This will be our last time here. This way you'll still be alive in this clearing when I come back alone."

The way they lay entwined after the lovemaking was past gave Julie a view of the sky. The blue of it was like fragments of sea beyond the incredible denseness of the high foliage. When a scarlet parakeet flashed by them screaming, Josh sighed and pulled her to her feet against him. They went all the way home in silence.

350

By the end of their first day of travel Julie was painfully certain that she could never get all the way to Charles Town by foot. Josh made camp while she soaked her feet and legs in a stream. Only his teasing attention kept her awake long enough to eat the food he prepared. After a night of deep sleep cradled in his arms, she started off with him again, ashamed of her weakness enough to hide it from him.

During the long days and nights of that trek, they never saw a living soul, and the only voice was that of an owl that seemed a ghost at each of their campfires. On the third day, Julie glimpsed a light off in the darkness of the trees and saw a slim pillar of smoke fingering skyward.

Josh grinned at her. "We'll reach the inn in an hour," he told her. "With sheets and hot water and food I didn't take off my back."

"Heaven," Julie grinned at him.

"They know me there," he warned. "What shall I tell them?"

"You're the one who turns red and stamps his feet ever time the word *wife* is said out loud," she reminded him.

He bent and touched her forehead with his lips. "Not if the wife was you, Lady. Not if it was you."

Julie stopped dead in her tracks so that he crashed on a minute and had to double back.

"My clothes," she whispered. "I can't go into an inn in these clothes."

"Think they might turn you away as a savage?" He laughed at her. "With those yellow eyes and that face?"

Annoyed by his amusement, she picked up her pace smartly. Encumbered by his packs, he labored to run a few steps and catch her by the arm.

"Come on, Lady," he coaxed. "I already thought about that. I even have our story all worked out. How we got in trouble fording a stream and how we lost all your clothes and had to trade the Indians for dry ones. Okay with you?"

She giggled, having an instant mental picture of some Indian girl marching off in wet English clothes. "Sometimes you make me think of Ellie, Josh. She always said that lying came easier to her than the truth."

"You got to keep the fork in your tongue practiced," he

351

nodded. "That way you'll have it ready when the need comes."

The innkeeper's name was Harris. He was as fat as the hens that scratched in the yard outside his door. His wife, wiping her floury hands on a blue apron, came out right behind him. Her face split in a gap-toothed smile as she saw Julie. She tugged back a wisp of lank hair that was falling across her eyes.

"Lord take us if it isn't Josh Simmons," she hooted. "And look what he's dragged in here. You might have guessed this old swamp fox would win himself the prettiest girl in all the Carolinas."

"And he probably did it with a marked deck of cards," her husband added.

The Carolinas. Julie looked at Josh. His nod of confirmation brought a sudden hard knot to the pit of Julie's stomach, and she felt the smile on her face turn wan.

Mrs. Harris was alert to her paleness and attacked Josh for it. "Josh, you fool, if you ain't just plain tuckered this child out marching her up and down country!" The woman tucked a work-reddened hand around Julie and nudged her forward. Over her shoulder, she bawled at the noisy kitchen beyond.

"Sara, you get some hot water upstairs for Miz Simmons here. What did you say your name was, honey?"

"Julie." The woman turned the name on her tongue thoughtfully. "It suits you just fine, just fine. Josh says that you need some duds to travel on with. Lucky you got with an Indian with leathers that good. Let me see your size there."

Julie flushed at the woman's frank inspection of her body. "The Franks got a girl about your size," she decided aloud. "She's not full grown yet but I bet her clothes will go right onto you."

By the time the girl brought the water, Mrs. Harris could be heard below the stairs dickering with Josh about the price of the clothes and their lodgings and a horse.

A horse. Julie sank into the warm water with a groan of delight. A horse and hot water all at once? She sudsed herself and rinsed and lay in the water humming Josh's little song to herself and half-giggling at the way the resonance of her voice vibrated in the water that held her travel-weary body.

At a little past dawn the next day, they crested the hill beyond the inn and looked at the wide, sunlit, wooded flatland that spread before them. Josh yawned as he guided the horse down the incline. Julie, wedged in between his gear and the bundle of skins, glared down at him.

"I'm glad that you're sleepy," she said crossly. "The idea of sticking me up there in that room while you drank and gambled half the night away."

"Spoken like a proper shrew," he said, poking her in the rump. "You took to this wife business like a wick to hot wax, didn't you? And you abuse me for doing you a good turn. Don't you like your new clothes?"

Julie looked down at herself and smiled. She was pleased. The dress was a simple, flowered calico of a soft blue color with little fans of white ruffled lace at her wrists and along the low neckline. The bonnet was a perfect match. With the aid of Mrs. Harris's mirror, she had been able to twist her growing mop of hair into a knot on top of her head. The mantle had clearly seen better years, but it was warm and the color was good.

"I love them," she told Josh. "I know it must have cost you a bundle of furs to buy such nice things from that girl."

"Seven skins to be exact," he conceded. Something in his tone prompted Julie to look back. A wicked grin met her gaze. "Then there was extra for the bed and board and some more for the beast here."

"Can we afford that?" she asked.

"Not every night," he said with that silly grin still on his face.

"So what is so funny?" she asked, feeling left out.

"That Harris will never learn," he said with a chuckle. "He played faro against me until I had won every one of the skins back from him. Now he has to find something to pay that fellow Frank for those clothes and he's also in the hole for the horse."

"Josh Simmons," she gasped. "I am ashamed of you. How can you keep taking advantage of a man like that? And why does he keep on letting you do it?"

He shook his head.

"You don't understand gamblers, Lady," he explained. "He waits like a vixen at a rabbit hole for me to come back by here. Every time he thinks he is going to clean me out. Every

353

time he loses, and every time he starts thinking about the next time."

Julie giggled.

"Then," he added, "right as I take off, I slip back into the kitchen and slip a nice beaver pelt to his missus and grab her about the middle with a hug so she won't bawl him out for losing to me. It's worked for years."

"Well, I hope all the people you fleece take it that gamely," she said, giggling at his cocky words.

"I only wish they would," he said quietly. "I only wish they would."

There was something so appealing in his quiet words that Julie nudged the horse to make him canter abreast of Josh.

When he glanced up at her, she caught his beard in her hand and held it until she gave him a long lingering kiss on his lips.

When she released him, he staggered back, rubbing his stinging chin. She had kneed the horse, and the dust from its hooves left a cloud in the roadway before him.

"Lady," he said quietly to himself, "if you just don't beat all."

As he moved faster to catch up with Julie and her mount, he felt a heaviness in his chest. Charles Town was getting closer by the mile, and every mile of it weighed on him with a sick feeling of despair.

Chapter Fifty-One

The settlements grew larger as they drew nearer to Charles Town. Julie, plodding along on the mare that Josh had gotten from Harris, stared at the larger houses they saw, the fancier traps, and the rice fields filled with great numbers of laboring black men.

Each night she sat alone in an inn bedroom listening to the sounds of revelry or fighting from the public rooms below. Each night Josh crawled into bed a little before dawn, easing her warm body into his chilled arms. His lovemaking grew more intense, almost frantic. He was so loathe to release her that she slept against him all night with her leg draped across his body and her head nestled against his chest.

"Don't you ever sleep?" she asked, stirred awake to find him staring at her intently.

"I can sleep after I die," he explained dully.

She held her hand to his lips to still such morbid talk. He caught her hand and pressed her palm against his lips, inflaming himself with new desire for her.

Her early concern about his gambling grew more acute with each stop. He always seemed to have friends among the men who crowded the inns, but for every ally, she sensed an enemy, hard eyed and sullen, somewhere in the room.

They were at an inn very near Charles Town when her concern blossomed into actual fear. They had stopped travelling early in the afternoon, and Josh had rested with her in their room before they both went down to have dinner. The public room was filled with men when they entered. A murmur of surprise and approval stirred through the room as Josh led Julie to a small table near the fire. He was holding her chair to seat her when a large, florid man with a thick head of curly gray hair scraped to his feet to approach them.

"Good evening, Major," Josh nodded to the man. "I'd like to present my wife Julie."

"Julie, is it?" the man asked, staring at her rudely. Then he bent over her hand. "Why I do declare your little wife has lost her ring, Josh Simmons."

Julie flushed but Josh seated himself without an untoward glance.

"She sure did," he confirmed calmly. "And her clothes and all the fancy dishes we had and damned near both our lives."

"Indians?" someone asked.

Josh shook his head. "We were fording the Coosawhatchi and I never figured it to have so much current this time of year."

A murmur of concerned sympathy rippled through the room but the Major's expression did not change, nor did he move from Julie's side.

"Damned near made you a widow before you was bare a wife, didn't he?" He smiled at Julie in a way that chilled her blood. "You watch that man, Mistress Julie. The way he deals at cards could make you a widow in the whip of a gun."

355

Julie felt Josh's cautioning nudge on her foot under the table. She smiled up at the man as warmly as she could with her heart thumping so wildly.

"Thank you for your kind warning, Major," she said softly. "I've been led to think that men sometimes change their ways when they settle down with a wife." Dreading his response to her words, she sought wildly for a way to change the topic. Behind him she could see the blaze of the cooking hearth where a great joint of beef was being turned on the spit and a number of fowls were spitting into the grate.

"And since you're here, sir, and a native of these parts, I'd like your opinion about something. Which dish do you prefer here, the roast beef or that fine-looking fowl that our host is preparing?"

After a startled moment, he seemed to swell a little under the approval in Julie's glance. He rocked on his heels thoughtfully. "Well," his tone was hesitant. "While the beef here is as fine as you'll buy in any place about here, I am honest to have a leaning towards the chicken. The way the mistress here stuffs them with onion and that wild sage is like to tear your heart out."

Julie blinded him with a dimpled smile. "Thank you so much, sir. I really appreciate your guidance." Then she turned to Josh. "Can we dine on the stuffed fowl as the Major recommends, dear? He makes it sound irresistible."

Josh's single eyebrow rose only a fraction of an inch, but his look was unmistakeable.

"How can I refuse you anything so sensible?" he asked lightly. He coughed into his handkerchief with the sound of a man who has found something very unwelcome in his throat.

"Thank you for the dimpling little assistance down there," he told her as he joined her in bed later that night. "I had a much easier evening once you got the fuse off that big cannon-mouth."

"Did you cheat him last time you were here?" Julie asked.

Josh made a face. "Lady, what I like about you in how subtle your questions are."

"Well, did you?"

He shouldered her over and slid his arm in under her back. "Well, a lot of rum in a man's belly and the smoke clouding his view makes a man have an unsure grasp on his cards."

After that night, a nervousness followed Julie up to their room where she waited for Josh. She would listen a long time to the tenor of the voices in the room below, terrified that anger and rum would conspire to ignite trouble. She recalled Josh's passing explanation of losing his eye in a tavern brawl and cringed wakeful in their bed until he joined her.

They made less and less progress with every day. With the roads so greatly improved, they should have been making better time, but Josh left later each morning, dallied longer over the noon meal, and was inclined to stop when the sun was still high in the sky. Sensing the anguish behind Josh's unchanging face, she said nothing, only trailed after him whenever his fancy dictated.

Not only did the length of their travelling days change, but even the way they partook of the services of the inns. Instead of taking her into the public room to dine with him, Josh began to act as if he were ashamed of her. He hustled her from her mount and up to a room with as little exposure as possible.

They even dined in their bedroom. Josh ordered the food sent up and took it from the serving girl at the door, setting up the meal between them himself.

"Why all this?" she challenged.

He would not meet her questioning gaze.

"I like to be alone with you," he countered. "I find this pleasanter after a long day's journey."

"Then why do you not spend the whole evening with me instead of going down there to cheat with those ruffians?" she asked tartly.

"Would you prefer the sauce on your meat or your lap, madam?" he asked, jesting with a ladle in his hand. Then he sighed. "You must remember how I told you that Harris waits for me—for a chance to play against me again. All along this route they are waiting."

"But they don't all have a wife in the kitchen who can be bought off for a hug and a beaver pelt," she reminded him. "You have enemies here, Josh. I can feel it in the air."

"The risk of gambling does not all lie in the cards," he said. Then firmly. "We will talk of other things."

She felt that other risk immediately on their last night out before Charles Town. The inn was arranged badly for Josh

357

from the start. There was no back stairs for Josh to use to whisk Julie up into privacy. Instead, they entered a large public room that reeked of the stench of liquor and tobacco. They had no more than put their foot inside the door than a hush fell and Julie found herself staring into a roomful of hostile faces. She shivered and told herself that it was the chill of the gray day that had set her limbs to trembling.

The innkeeper did not greet them himself. He sent a surly girl with an upturned nose and an upper lip too short to cover her stained teeth. Josh blinked at the price she named for their lodging but did not argue with her. When he asked that they have their meal in their room, she was quick to say that such fancy-Dan service was not for the likes of him. Only when he pleaded an illness for Julie, did he get a grudging permission to come down and carry the meal up himself.

The sullen silence in the room only dispelled into grumbling exchanges as Josh led Julie up the stairs past where they could be seen from the staring crowd.

"I don't like this place and I don't like those men down there," Julie pleaded. "Why don't you just stay with me and not do any gaming tonight?"

"I'd love to, Lady," he said, taking her in his arms. He held her very close before releasing her with a sigh. "But they would take it wrong. I tell you, they have been waiting."

"For what? To put a bullet through your head?"

"I will be careful," he promised. "No matter how badly I might be losing, I will be perfectly fair with the cards."

After he left with a final "keep my bed warm," Julie sat a long time staring out the window without even getting undressed. From where she sat, she commanded a view of a small, green area studded with those strange trees that she and Josh had seen so often in their last few days of travel. He called them palmettos but she didn't like them. There was a stiff, unnatural feel to them. Their thrusting trunks and top-heavy foliage seemed hostile to her.

She shivered and turned away to prepare for bed.

With the blue dress carefully folded over the chair, she grew conscious of an extraordinary stillness from the room below. It was wrong, all wrong. There were no peals of hearty laughter, no rise and fall of earnest conversation. She shook her head and bent to loosen her slippers.

The silence broke suddenly. She heard the harsh scrape of

wood against wood as benches and chairs were scraped back. A woman screamed and men's voices rose in angry concert.

She trembled as she drew the blue dress back on and struggled with the buttons with fingers grown icy and awkward. With only a pat at her loosened hair, she let herself out the door as quietly as she could.

She had not needed to be quiet. The din from below would have drowned out her noisiest exit. She crept to the turn of the stairs. From her post in the shadow, she saw that every man in the room was on his feet. Near the door, a crowd of five or six burlies were struggling with Josh. As she watched, they gained control of him. Shouting, they held his fiercely fighting body above their heads and started towards the door.

Miscellaneous shouts came through the din of the room. "Get a rope." "Hang the bastard." The tones of their voices, the stench that filled the air, the pervasive feel of brutishness in the scene made her giddy. Newgate. These men were like the rabble of Newgate whose drunken violence was a fever passed from man to man with no cure but shock.

She clung to the railing to support herself. My God, if she were only Ellie. Ellie had known how to handle rogues such as these. But she was not Ellie, and the roar of the drunken savages bled her strength instead of feeding it.

It must have been hysteria that brought something like a giggle throbbing into her throat. By God, she wasn't Ellie but she had seen Ellie use her womanhood as a weapon. Did she dare? The ghost of Fiona, she thought wryly, as she loosed the buttons of her bodice so that her rosy breasts were half-exposed above the trimming of white ruffling. Her Irish Mother had used those smudged, dark eyes and provocative lips more than once to drive her father to distraction in a war between their wills. She tugged her hair awry so that soft curls tumbled about her face. Creeping back to seize a candle from the bedroom, she left her slippers there, remembering how sensually Josh cradled her fine small foot in his hand.

"Half-whore, half-innocent," she reminded herself as she schooled her steps down the stairs, holding the candle so that its light gleamed across her breast and illumined her eyes which she held wide open as if in astonishment.

She was midway down the stairs when the light of the candle caught someone's eye "It's her," the whisper came, "It's his wife."

She did not betray that she heard him. She only continued to descend with her eyes fixed on Josh, hoping that her expression was one of puzzlement rather than the terror she felt. The group at the door hesitated that one moment that it took for Josh to see her.

"Go back, Lady," he shouted at her angrily.

"But darling," she kept her voice soft. "What is wrong?"

"Your damned bastard husband is stealing us blind," a harsh voice answered.

"String him. Get on with it. String him up," another man urged from the back of the crowd.

"It's my eyes," Josh groaned. "You know how it is with only this one eye."

For the first time, Julie took her eyes from Josh's face. Her tone was one of astonishment as she swept the crowd with her eyes. "But you can't hang a man for half-seeing," she protested. "Can you, gentlemen? Can you really?" She was conscious of how deceitful the softness of her tone was when she was raging with fury and terror inside.

The murmur began at the back of the crowd. "Half-seeing." "Who's to know with only one eye?"

"There's no cure for a one-eyed gambler like a dose of hemp," the harsh voice shouted.

Julie fixed on him now from among the crowd. She started towards him and the other men parted to let her pass. As she neared him, she tried an old trick that she had not used since Mary had been her nurse, a child's trick. Without lifting her hands to her face or sobbing at all, she willed the tears to form in her eyes and pour unheeded down her face to glisten on the roundness of her bare breasts.

"But Josh," she said slowly into his face. "You cannot do that to my Josh—not with our babe's heart beating under my breast this very minute."

A moment of stillness settled in the room. "Hell, let him down," someone said with a tone of defeat.

"Hang him and you'll lay a new burden on the parish," someone warned.

"The rum has got to the lot of you," another voice put in.

As the harsh-voiced man felt his support fall away, he only grew more inflamed. "Listen, you Goddamned hussy," he cried. Then he reached for Julie. As his hand grasped at the flesh of her shoulder, a change came on the room. A wall of

360

men seemed to slide between them. She heard a grunt and a cry as she was pulled away. In the shuffle that followed, Josh was suddenly at her side, groping at his torn coat with his free hand but gripping her arm with a clasp like iron.

"You and the missus better just ride on tonight," the innkeepor said, his eyes greedy on Julie's breasts. "I'll have your mount out by the time you get your stuff down."

"But I owe you," Josh said without loosing his hold on Julie's arm. "Let me settle with you now."

The innkeeper glared at him. "A little peace, you cheating bastard," he said dully. "Just clear out fast and I'll think myself well paid. And if you ever try to put a leg of yours under a table of mine again, Josh Simmons, so help me, I'll string you up myself." His glance slid to Julie. "Babe or no babe," he added fiercely.

They made camp only a few hundreds of yards down the road. "That's the last inn I take you into, Lady," Josh said calmly as he blew the fire to flame.

"What did you expect me to do, lie up there and listen to them stretch your neck?"

Josh groaned and reached for her.

"I don't know what I expected," he admitted. "But I'm pretty damned sure I'm the first man in Carolina to be hauled off a gibbet by his woman's tits."

"You don't have to be vulgar."

He pressed her back against the bed of furs he had laid for them, and his lips moved along her throat towards the offending breasts.

"I know I don't have to, Lady," he said softly. "But somehow I just kind of like to."

Later, when the moon slipped away from them behind the hills to the west, Josh tightened his arms about her.

"Was it true what you said about the babe?" he asked.

She shook her head.

He whistled softly. "You are a full hand of mischief, Lady."

She giggled softly and nuzzled his neck. "You told me yourself how helpful a good lying tongue could be."

He chuckled and then his voice came, uncommonly sober.

"Who would be after you, Lady? Who would be searching for you along this seaboard?"

She sat up abruptly to stare down at him.

361

"What do you mean?" she asked, feeling a flood of something icy and chilling in her chest.

He pulled himself up beside her and looped his arm about her waist. "I don't understand it too well myself, only I started getting the word way back down the road. They tell me there's a madman ranging this area and that he's looking for a yellow-eyed girl named Julie. You must know who it could be."

She sat very stiff. Joseph. It could be Joseph. If she could get to the colonies, so could he. Or the dark-eyed stranger. The thought of her master's fury sent a shiver of apprehension through her.

"I don't know, Josh," she whispered. "I just plain don't know."

He threw her close and soothed her against his breast.

"I got to confess I've been stalling, making my time with you last as long as I could, trying to hide you from anyone who might report on you to that madman, whoever he is. But it's no use. There's not a man in that room tonight who is going to forget those golden eyes of yours," he paused. "Nor the rest of you as far as that goes. I'm beat at this gamble and I cede it."

She stared at him, trying to read his expression in the dark.

"I'm taking you straight to your aunt's house where you will be safe."

"Are you afraid of that madman, Josh?" she asked.

He shook his head with his face half-buried in the fragrance of her hair. "Only for you, Lady. Only for you."

Chapter Fifty-Two

That final day into the outskirts of Charles Town was the hardest day of travel since Josh got the horse from Harris. Julie's bones ached from the gait of the horse long before it was time to stop for lunch.

"It will take all the luck in the world to get you to your aunt's place before dark," Josh told her. "First we have to locate the place, and then we have to get you there."

"Then let me walk a while," Julie said, scrambling off the

beast. "She's been growing bones on her back that were never there before."

"Maybe your own backside is growing tender from wear and tear," Josh suggested with that sidelong glance which always accompanied his off-color remarks. But his grin faded from his mouth as swiftly as it had come.

"Lady, Lady," he said quietly. "What ever am I to do without you?"

"I'll miss you, Josh," she told him. "You know how much I will miss you. How much I love you."

Julie looked up at him beside her. Her eyes dwelled on the thick brightness of his fine hair. She knew the feel of it so well beneath her hand, even as she knew and cherished the scent of his flesh, a smell of out-of-doors and sun and tobacco all blended in. His quick, jesting tongue, the endless gentleness of his lovemaking all pressed in on her bringing a threatening stinging behind her eyes. She loved him. Indeed she did love him and not alone for what he had undergone or done for her but for himself, that unique blending of gallantry and vulgarity, sensitivity and ruthlessness that was Josh Simmons and no one else in the world.

He was silent for a while. "But not like Antoine," he said quietly. "I have to keep remembering that you don't love me as you did Antoine. Sometimes I ask myself if you would ride off to go trading with Indians or squat in the marshes or be a gambler's woman at all the inns if it was Antoine you was with instead of me."

When she did not comment, he asked the question outright.

"What about it, Lady? What if it was Antoine?"

She shook her head. "How could I say what could be, Josh? Antoine is dead." As always, the very words brought a great stab of pain in her chest so that her breath came short. "We aren't ever going to lose what we have had," she reminded him. "We'll always have it, both of us. It can't ever be taken away from us."

"You're right as usual, Lady," he agreed quietly.

"Why do you always call me lady instead of my name?" she asked, after a minute.

He laughed. "It was a kid thing with me, I reckon." He spoke slowly, forgetting to prod the mare. The animal eased her pace and shuffled along lazily as Josh spoke. "When I was just come man, about sixteen, I used to work those fields

363

of my paw's and dream about what could be. How I would have a grand house and acres spreading out green and in that house I would have a lady, a real honest-to-God lady who always smelled clean and was smiling to see me come.

"When you lay there flailing with fever and I was tending you, I made believe that you were her. I was smart enough to bet myself good odds that you would come to life as the foul-mouthed, street-talking scum of Newgate that you should have been with that mark on you and all." He grinned down at her. "Instead, you were my lady come real, and I just liked to call you that."

She caught his arm and hugged it against herself.

"Ours was a grand house," she whispered with her voice thick with tears. "A grand house with acres of green all around."

"Girls must have dreams like that too," he mused. "When they are sixteen and just coming grown. What were your dreams, Lady?"

The scene flashed before her so swiftly and truly that she stumbled in the road. The coach flashed gold and white in the blaze of sun. She caught the glint of sun from the queue of his powdered wig, the swelling of his handsome thighs in those satin breeches with the rosettes at the knee. The full mouth was halfway laughing at her beneath blue eyes that held her own for that one stunning moment that had changed her life. A flush of shame rose in her cheeks at the memory of the passion that had turned her to Giles with lips uplifted.

She shook her head. "That has been too long ago," she lied. "All too long ago to recall." But not to remember, she admitted to herself. It is one thing to remember and something quite different to recall it to Josh.

When they finally stopped on the outskirts of town, Josh laid skins on the green for Julie and tethered the horse to graze while he went off for food. He was gone so long that Julie was dozing with her back against a tree when he startled her awake by standing above her to stare at her.

He was not carrying food. Instead, he reached for her hand and pulled her to her feet almost briskly.

"What's the matter, Josh?" she asked, trying to shake the dreams from her head enough to understand the new, hard lines she saw in his face.

The smile seemed forced. "Only a little switch of plans," he told her. "We are going to eat in style. Come along."

As he led the horse along, Julie sensed a tension in him as well as a new thoughtful concern.

"Are you sure that your aunt's married name is DuBois?" he asked after a bit.

She nodded. "Her husband's name is Yves," she said. "Yves Dubois."

Julie knew Josh too well. He was watching the road with such attention that you would have thought he was expecting to see pieces of eight scattered among the rocks of the road-way.

"What is it, Josh?" she asked. "What is wrong?" Did you ask someone? Is the name unknown here?"

"The name is known," he replied curtly. Then he turned to her with his face dark. "God damn it, Lady. I don't see how you can expect me to turn you over to some wild Frenchman like that without a backward look. Who knows what will become of you in this place?"

"Wild Frenchman," she teased. "He is my aunt's husband. They have been married ever so long. He must be in his forties by now, if not his fifties. And it is to his wife, not him, that I am going."

"It feels wrong," he told her sullenly. "I asked the merchant if he knew such a name. A stillness fell in that shop. I swear to you, lady, that you could have heard a feather fall. When I looked around, the place was ringed with staring eyes, and they all looked away before they met my gaze."

Julie searched her mind for what she knew of her uncle. But it had been so long and she had been only a child. "A fanatic," that was the expression her father had used, "a wild, religious fanatic." But her own father would have been classified like that by some. Hadn't he exiled himself after Louis revoked the Edict of Nantes rather than betray his own religious beliefs?

"But he must have told you something," Julie protested. "That merchant couldn't have just stood and stared at you."

"Oh, he told me something all right. He told me what road to take and how long it would take on horseback. But his face was closed like a mask, Lady, and there was no blood in his lips when he spoke of that place. It feels wrong," he added sullenly.

"It is not as if we were in the middle of the wilderness out there," she reassured him, nodding towards the hills whose dark shape lay at the other end of the city to the west. "I could not be so terribly stranded with a great city this near."

"Well, I am going to look that place over before I leave you there," he announced stubbornly.

"I am sure that my aunt would be happy to make you welcome if she has room," Julie told him quietly, with her hand on his arm.

As he looked at her, his expression softened. Without taking his gaze from her, he mused aloud. "Why do I keep remembering my friend's warning about you, Lady? That Swazi word for evil that he used. I have been a fool not to understand what it meant long before now. The evil is against you, Lady. It comes from the way you look, the way you affect a man's passions. I fear for you."

She leaned against him lightly. "Josh, Josh," she chided him. "How I will miss you. How dear you are to me." She nuzzled the leather of his coat. "Don't you know that the dread you feel is a part of any love? Fear lives in the center of love. You see a villain in every man and an alligator in every stream I cross because you love me. Don't you know that I see a murderer in every gambler you have beaten and a savage in every Indian you trade with? It is the same—a part of any love."

His look was swift, almost suspicious on her face but then he relaxed a little. "There's truth in what you say," he told her, "but little comfort."

Josh stopped before a private house. The woman who opened the door was obviously expecting them. She welcomed Julie with a softly blurred accent that brought a smile to Julie's lips.

"I am sorry that you are feeling unwell," she said, urging Julie in. "Do come and sit until I have the lunch ready for you."

Julie tried to glare at Josh without Mrs. MacRae seeing her glance. What did he think he was up to with this new trick? He was overdoing it, eating his meal with slow appreciative bites, lingering over his third cup of tea like a man with a new life spread out before him. He visited with Mrs. MacRae about the crops and the coming of spring and whether the malaria would be so severe in the rice fields again this year.

366

He finally rose, gave another great effussion of compliments to his hostess, and turned to Julie.

"I have arranged with Mrs. MacRae that you can rest here for a few hours. You will still get to your aunt's by evening. Now you must rest easily, my dear."

Not to be put off, Julie stubbornly followed him out to where he was untieing the horse. "What in hell is going on here, Josh Simmons?" she challenged him. "What are you doing while you fob me off on that nice lady in there?"

He caught her chin in his hand and looked tenderly into her face.

"I decided I could not do it," he told her bluntly. "I could not take you to that place of your aunt's until I had been there to scout it for myself. If I find it suitable for you, fine. If not, we will make other arrangements."

"But Josh," she protested.

He grinned at her. "I figure I get my way about once a month with you, Lady," he drawled. "Just for convenience, why don't we say that it's my turn today?"

She giggled and realized that he had been unable to release her. When he spoke again, his voice was broken and strained. "I got this one dream of caring for you. Let me do what I can while I can."

She dropped her eyes to hide the rush of tears. She winked hard and looked up. "Later then, Josh?" she asked.

He drew her close and kissed her tenderly full on her lips.

"Later, Lady," he said.

She watched as he disappeared down the road, and she thought she had never seen Josh's step so plodding and heavy.

Chapter Fifty-Three

"It's as much for her good as mine," Josh told the horse angrily. "Life is a stinking bitch." But he smiled as he waved back to Julie until she was only a faint smudge of blue against the sunlit white of Mrs. MacRae's front porch.

The bastard was still following. It was no wonder that he lost every time they met across a table. The trader had two hands of thumbs and a wide place in his head where no

367

juices ran. But he could hate. Josh had felt the man's hate follow him since he had first seen him in the seafood shop before noon. Once he had seen that face full of hate he knew he had to get Julie away from himself, get her into some safe place that if there was a shoot-out, she would not fall as prize to the wrong survivor.

By angling his head just right, Josh could watch the man slip from one tree to another in an ox-clumsy attempt to keep himself hidden from his quarry. Josh laid his gun across the top of the pack and plodded on. "We'll see if he's got legs as strong as his hate," Josh told the mare. The man wouldn't dare start anything on a public road like this, not in Charles Town which prided itself on being clean and Christian in spite of its fancy whores and gaming pits. It was one thing to kill a man in a tavern brawl, something else to gun him down on a public road.

He had been lucky to find this Mrs. MacRae who was eking out her widow's share by taking in roomers. He was lucky that the man had seen him leave so that the filthy old scam wouldn't be hanging around where his Lady was.

The road he had to follow went west of town into the green hills beyond. Now and then a horseman passed or a waggon of timber. Lucky, for the traffic kept his stealthy follower that few careful yards behind. Then it seemed that the distance between them was greater. Then it came that Josh could not see him at all, even watching for long minutes at a stretch. Josh shrugged and grinned, "Man enough to ambush me but not man enough to climb for it." It was well enough that his enemy had fallen away because the road off into the Dubois place should be coming up right away.

Josh could not decide at once whether the darkness had fallen suddenly or whether the wall of trees that enclosed the narrow rough road was too dense to admit the light. But there was a threatening quality to the uneven passage that made him lash the horse to quicken its pace.

The road through the woods seemed to stretch on without end. An owl called from the dimness, his warning passed on to be repeated again and again like an eery, echoed question. Josh cursed himself for having lost his way. The merchant had betrayed him. He was being led into the impenetrable wilderness.

Then, just at the depth of his despair, a turn of the road exposed a drive leading off into a grove of live oak trees.

Tethering his horse in the woods. Josh moved carefully along the drive until the house came into view. The plantation had been neatly laid out. Even from this distance Josh could see quarters for what looked like at least a hundred slaves. He picked out the mill and a number of small buildings whose function he couldn't guess, a forge for sure would be among them, a smoke house, and the other equipment to run an operation of this size and value. He was a man of property, this Yves DuBois but the look of the house was unsettling.

It was at least two stories in height, two long wings that flared out from a center section faced with brick. Its roof line was uneven, staggering towards the late afternoon sky like a series of double stone steps. The roof over it all was prickley with chimneys, and from one of them a drift of smoke rose to fuse into the blue of the upper air. A massive, live oak tree almost hide the front of the house, and the Spanish moss that trailed from it stirred as if alive in the breeze of afternoon. It was his native fear for her welfare, he told himself. There was nothing wrong with the place. The fear that Julie said lived at the center of love was working on him.

Josh plodded back for his horse and led it up the drive that swung in a great circle before the low, vine-covered porch.

From the alarm in the young, Negro man's face, Josh judged that few unexpected callers came to that door. Flustered and wide-eyed, the young man shot off to relay his wish to speak to Madame DuBois, leaving Josh to stand in the wide front hall, his ears tuned to the rustling and whisperings behind the closed doors that encircled him.

The woman who descended the stair towards him was taller than his lady. Her face was innocent of paint or adornment but still bore traces of a great beauty. Her dark eyes were intent on his face under a thick crown of braided, white hair. The stuff of her dark dress rustled as she neared Josh and stood very still, her hands clasped together tensely to stare into his face.

"You wished to see me?" she asked from an expressionless face.

Josh nodded. "I bring you word from your niece, Julie Duvall."

369

Her face did not change, but he saw her hand grope blindly for support in the bannister of the stair.

"Juliette?" she breathed. "Juliette Duvall? What have you heard of her? What has become of her?"

"She is well," Josh reassured her swiftly. "She is even now in Charles Town. I am sorry that I bring such shock to you madame."

The woman shook her head. "A shock, perhaps," she conceded, "but such a wonderful one. I have been able to hear nothing from her since shortly after her father's—my brother Etienne's—death. In Charles Town?" Her tone was incredulous.

"She was coming to you by sea," Josh explained. "The ship fell afoul of a storm. She is only this day arrived north from the wilderness to seek you out."

"Juliette," the woman breathed, and a gentle smile touched her mouth. "Blessed child. Thank God." Then her face gained animation. "But where is she? Did you not bring her with you? I must see the child of my favored brother."

"She has no home in this world," Josh said bluntly. "She is without protection except for you."

The woman's face turned expressionless again. But her voice vibrated with anguish. "God help her," Madame DuBois intoned bleakly. "God help her."

The great doubt Josh felt settled back on him, but her sudden flurry of activity startled his fears away as quickly as they had come. The woman turned and issued swift orders to the Negroes who seemed suddenly everywhere, the young man scuttling off to equip a trap, and a slender, young girl bringing a cap and mantle to her mistress's side.

"I cannot thank you sufficiently for the marvelous message you have brought to me today," she told Josh. "I do not even know your name or where to find Juliette in Charles Town."

"Josh Simmons," he said swiftly, then filled in where Julie was staying and how to find the house of widow MacRae. "And I have a message I would like you to deliver to your niece for me," he added.

"Most certainly, Mr. Simmons," she said, her eyes watchful on his face. "What would you have me to tell Juliette for you?"

Juliette. Already she was slipping away from him into this

370

new name, this new life. Was she still his own or was she the Juliette spoken so flutingly on this sad woman's tongue?

Josh's words stumbled from his lips. "Give her my fullest wishes," he said lamely, "for good fortune in life, for great joy in life."

Unaccountably the woman reached out and laid her gloved hand on his.

"I sense a great friend in you," she said quietly.

Josh could only nod, not trusting his tongue.

At Josh's insistence the trap left first. He felt the eyes of the slaves following him and his horse down the long drive and onto the narrower drive that led on towards the road. When he was well past the view of the house, he drew the horse back into the privacy of the trees and tethered it there.

Darkness had wholly fallen when the trap rattled off the road turned into the drive and drew near where he waited. Twin torches flanked the driver's seat. Their wavering light through windows of horn gave him only a moment's glimpse into the interior of the carriage.

His lady's head was like a flower balanced on the straight slenderness of her neck. She was staring straight ahead into the darkness, and her mouth was soft with that mingled pain and puzzlement that he had brought to it too many times ever to forget. A loss like flame seared over him pinning him to the spot. Then, with a lurch and a rattle, the torches disappeared into the darkness of the lane.

"Fool. Fool. Fool," he screamed into the echoing woods. When his eyes lost the dazzle of what had passed, he untied the horse and started back to Charles Town and whatever waited for him there.

PART VII
THE WIZARD IN THE GLEN
February, 1723-Mid-May, 1723

Chapter Fifty-Four

It seemed to Julie that everywhere she turned in her aunt's house, a dark slave face stared back at her. She had never known a Negro until she met Josh's friend. Was it the memory of him that made his Swazi word for evil return to her mind with such persistence? A nameless fear had shivered along her spine from the moment she stepped into the shadow of the imposing house.

Batakatsi. The word kept coming back to her mind. How had Josh defined it? He had said it was evil wished or evil contained.

She shook her head restlessly. At least she knew that this apprehension had nothing to do with her Aunt Anne-Louise.

Julie smiled at the memory of their meeting. She had become fretful from Josh's long absence. She had rested at Mrs. Mac-Rae's insistence. Then she had risen and drunk tea with her hostess, trying diligently to keep her mind on the woman's happy chatter. It was reasonable enough that Mrs. MacRae would be lonely and hungry for female company. She had been left widowed after her husband was killed in an Indian uprising. In spite of her hostess's heartbreaking story, Julie found her attention wandering as she watched the door and listened for Josh's return. Her mood swung from anger to concern and then back to anger.

His precipitous departure had confused her at the time. "Later," he had said. How much later did he mean? Why should she be left waiting through a long afternoon when her aunt's home was only a short drive away?

She paid no attention to the sound of the carriage in the street. She was only interested in the road-weary horse that Josh would be leading.

She paid little attention when Mrs. MacRae rose to respond to the rap of her door. She was totally startled as the tall, elegant woman rushed into the room, seized Julie in her arms, and began to weep with delight.

Even Mrs. MacRae was brought to tears as Julie and her aunt faced each other for the first time.

"Your eyes," Julie said, with a catch in her throat. "They are so like my own father's eyes."

The older woman smiled. "And you, my dear, are the image of your lovely mother. Are you like her, my dear, with her fresh wit and renegade will, or are you like my brother?"

Julie's smile brought the dimple flashing into her cheek. "I do not know myself yet, madame," she admitted. "Thus far in my life I have only been what life demanded of me, not able to ask what I am really like."

The two women exchanged an understanding glance.

"God willing that will change for you, my dear," Mrs. Mac-Rae said. "For most of us it is the long history of our years."

At her aunt's entry, a tall, strongly built Negro man had posted himself just outside the door. At her aunt's brisk movement towards the door, Julie saw him stiffen to attention. "I must be gone with this precious child before the night deepens," Anne-Louise DuBois said regretfully. "I cannot thank you enough for your kindness to her. I must be in debt to you for your hospitality."

Mrs. MacRae shook her head. "It was all arranged," she explained quickly. "Her young friend Mr. Simmons paid all the allowances in advance."

Julie tried to hide the pain she felt. So he had planned to leave her thus all the while, without a farewell.

As silently as he had waited, the tall Negro helped them both into their seats before taking the reins to the conveyance himself. Julie noted that her aunt never spoke to him or met his eyes. Instead, it was as if he were a useful shadow that she did not need to acknowledge, indeed, did not wish to admit was there.

Only after they were heading west from Charles Town did her aunt mention Josh.

"I feel so remiss about your young friend," she mused. "I was so delighted to hear that you were safe and so astonished that you were near, that I did not even think to offer him the comforts of my home. Will he return that I may thank him more appropriately?"

Unable to face Josh's departure yet in her own mind, Julie only shook her head.

Her aunt's curious glance slid away swiftly. With great tact, she turned their talk to other topics, to her memories of

Julie's father before they were separated to seek asylum in different lands. Julie was grateful that her aunt did not even inquire of her brother Simon. It would be awkward to report his long stay in debtor's prison and the mean circumstances under which his wife and family lived.

The sense of evil that prickled along Julie's spine came with her first glimpse of the house. The weak light of late afternoon failed to penetrate the narrow drive that crawled between massive trees. The house seemed to leap at her at the last turn of the drive. The tapers already lit in the downstairs windows seemed more like a row of hostile eyes staring from darkness than any symbol of welcome.

Even her aunt seemed as affected as they neared the house. Julie felt the slightest shudder move along the arm that was affectionately linked with her own. "My husband is absent from home for a few days," she reported in an abnormally level tone. "Tonight we will have a quiet celebration of your arrival, just you and the children and myself."

The children. Julie knew there was a son, a boy of about her own age, but through the lost years she had heard no more of her aunt's family.

"I fear you will find me terribly ignorant about your family," Julie admitted. "I am eager to meet my cousins."

The expression on her aunt's face as she turned to reply confused Julie. But the trap drew to a stop by the vine-covered porch and her aunt remained silent.

The black driver held the door as they dismounted, and her aunt turned with a startled look. "You have nothing you wish Perry to take to your room?"

Julie smiled at her and spread her hands. "I have only what you see," she said. "All else was lost with the *Tilbury Belle*."

Her aunt flushed. "Of course, my dear. How foolish of me. Come Juliette, welcome to your new home."

As a young Negro man in a white coat opened the front door for them, Julie glanced back into the darkness of the trees that hid the road beyond. Only the faintest shading of color separated the hill from the darkening sky. Josh was out there, Josh with his single eye fixed on the road that led to the savage wilderness.

I have made a mistake, she realized with sudden panic.

377

I have made a cruel and heartbreaking mistake. I should be out there with Josh.

When she stumbled, crossing the threshold to her aunt's house, her aunt commented that she must be overfatigued from her travels. Julie herself hoped it was not an omen.

The house teemed with servants like the fallen logs of the marshes had teemed with laboring ants. A young girl appeared from nowhere to escort Julie to the room her aunt had hastily prepared for her. As she entered the upstairs bedroom, another girl, appearing to be freshly out of her teens, gave the freshly made bed a final pat and backed away into the hall, grinning with nervousness.

Julie stared about at the room which was to be her new home. The air was strangely stale although the room was immaculately clean. She did not recognize the wood of which the furniture had been formed, but it glowed a soft red in the light from the candle the maid had left burning. Braided woolen rugs covered the polished floor, and the hangings that ran the length of the room behind the bed were of the same woven blue stuff that trimmed the single window.

Julie stood very still, trying to control the sense of panic that had only worsened since entering the house. She was startled from her revery by a rap on the door and a soft voice announcing, "Hot water."

The sturdy young woman who entered bore two steaming pails of water which she took to the metal tub that stood in the far corner of the room.

"Mistress sent you bath before supper," she explained in her rich, soft voice. "You want me to help wash?"

"No," Julie said quickly. Then added. "I do not wish to delay the family meal."

"Your leisure, miss," the girl reassured her. "Your own leisure."

As swiftly as she could, Julie bathed, put back on the road-weary, blue dress, and arranged her hair before the large mirror that was hung above the mirror at the foot of her bed.

She sighed as she rose to leave the sanctuary of the room. "Now what?" she asked herself, and was appalled at the apprehension she felt.

Tapers fluttered in wall sconces along the hall and down the stairway. Julie paused to listen. Silence. Where were the children? Where were the sounds of life that one would expect in a house so filled with servants. Not servants, but slaves, she reminded herself, unused to this phenomenon. Old memories tugged at her emotions. Her father's house, as old and solidly built as it was, had been unable to muffle the sounds of life. To listen on a stair like this would have been to hear the changing rhythm of voices muffled behind doors, the clatter of the scullery and always, off somewhere, a peal of laughter from some giddy maid.

From the turn of the stair, she could see her aunt standing in the center of the entrance hall. She seemed lost in thought. Her slender figure was very erect, but her head, with its glowing crown of white hair, was bent as if in deep revery—or grief.

"Tante Anne-Louise?" Julie called softly, not wishing to startle her aunt.

Her aunt's head rose instantly and she smiled warmly as she came and caught Julie's hand.

"Come, my dear," she said. "Come and meet the children."

Three young figures leaped to their feet as Julie entered the sitting room with their mother.

Her aunt's voice was warm and coaxing, "Here she is, my dears." She paused. "Your very own cousin Juliette whom I have told you of— Juliette, my children."

Julie guessed their ages to range from about ten to sixteen, one boy and two girls standing stiffly in a line like soldiers for inspection. Their almost identical dark eyes stared at her from expressionless faces. They were plain, Julie realized with astonishment. How could they be so dull and plain with such a vibrant, beautiful mother?

"My daughters," her aunt spoke on, "Yvonne and Cecilia." Yvonne, who was apparently the baby of the family, set one neat foot forward, and held out her hand. Her dark dress, cut high to the neck like her mother's, exposed a ruffle of pale petticoat as she bowed.

"I am happy to meet you, Cousin Juliette," the child recited with a flatness that belied her words.

Her sister, a slender girl of about sixteen, similarly dressed, repeated Yvonne's performance with the same stiffness.

Pierre simply bowed from the waist without meeting her eyes and repeated her name in a dull tone.

Anne-Louise's bright tone was startling in contrast to the

379

dullness of her children. *"Allons,"* she said brightly. "Let us have supper."

The long dining table was far too long for the five of them. As the girls slid into their chairs, Julie saw each glance towards the empty chair that loomed over them at the head of the table.

The burden of conversation fell entirely on Julie and her aunt. What strange, sullen young people they were, Julie thought with astonishment. Each attempt their mother made to draw them forth yielded only the minimal response, "Yes, maman," or "No, maman."

Julie's own efforts were equally unsuccessful.

"But I am Julie," she finally told Cecilia, smiling warmly at the girl. "I am your cousin."

"Yes, mademoiselle," the girl replied in the same disinterested tone as before, with her eyes on her plate to avoid meeting Julie's glance.

The only interest the young people showed in their conversation was more discomfiting to Julie than their apathy had been.

Exhausted from her attempts to keep a pleasant interchange going, Julie turned to her aunt with a question.

"Did I remember wrongly, Tante, or do you also have a son of about my age?"

An almost visible tension stirred along the table. The eyes of all the young people turned to their mother's face, waiting for her response. Her aunt's head seemed to become immobile on her slender neck. During what seemed an interminable pause, her aunt toyed with a portion of food that rested on her plate. Then in a voice so calm that it suggested inner turbulence by its very monotony, she spoke.

"My son Jacques is no longer of this household."

Julie, who had cringed in the aftermath of her question, felt her aunt's words lie heavily on the air in the room. She had not said that he was dead. She had not said that he was gone from home. By simply stating that he was no longer of the household, she managed to raise strange, difficult questions in Julie's mind.

The mild, sweet wine that she had drunk throughout the meal began to spin in her head. She felt vastly grateful when her aunt laid her napkin by her plate and rose.

Although it was very early, Julie very soon pleaded tiredness from journeying and asked to be excused for the night.

Her aunt, the warm, lovely smile on her lips, kissed Julie tenderly. "I was about to suggest that myself, dear," she admitted. Without a glance at the three young people who sat quietly in the sitting room as if waiting for release, she added, "I fear we are not the most lightsome company you might have."

Before Julie could protest her words, her aunt went on. "Since you have suffered the loss of your wardrobe, I have taken the liberty of supplying you with some articles to use until new clothing can be made for you. You will find them in the chests and cupboards of your room. Oh yes, and the girl who will attend you here is Mandy."

Her aunt had been more than generous. A lovely nightdress of soft white linen trimmed with lace was laid neatly across the foot of the bed. The girl Mandy shifted her weight unhappily from one foot to the other as Julie insisted on undressing herself.

"You may go, Mandy," Julie told her. "I will want nothing more tonight."

The girl's dark eyes shone with fear. "I am supposed to serve you."

Julie grinned at her. "While I sleep? Come, child, run along and sleep yourself."

"I sleep on your rug," Mandy suggested.

"For heavens sake, child," Julie teased her. "You would wake up with your bones blue in the morning. Do go and have some rest so you will be as pretty tomorrow as you are today."

The girl grinned and tucked her head and let herself out of the room.

Alone in the room at last, Julie went to the window which overlooked part of the courtyard where their carriage had stopped and a broad stretch of cleared lawn. Only after great effort was she able to loosen the sash and throw the window open. Leaning on her elbows, she stared out into the night. Here and there clusters of stars seemed huddled together as if for comfort. Somewhere out there was Josh. She wanted his warm arms about her, wanted to hear his teasing, level voice close to her ear. My God, what was she doing in this strange silent house?

All these people were near, her aunt, the children, all those servants she had seen in the house. Yet not a single human sound was carried to her on the night air. Instead she heard only the lonely call of a wolf which rose and fell and then faded into silence.

It was a dream. She knew it was a dream by the eery silence in which she watched it happen, by the dampness of her sheets from that cold sweat of terror that comes with nightmares.

It began with a curious, musky odor like flower petals that had been dried with spices. She trembled with some nameless terror and dreamed that she had been wakened.

It took her several moments to realize where she was, to recognize the dark hangings of the bed, the chest and table that stood along the wall. Her aunt's house, she was at Tante Anne-Louise's house. She relaxed at the thought and drifted in a dreamlike peace until her eyes strayed to the mirror at the foot of her bed.

The glass reflected an alien shape. She braced herself to sit up and stare more intently. There was a formed darkness against the glass. Her eyes slowly distinguished the black face of a woman staring back at her through half-closed eyes. Her hair was hidden under something hard and patterned, her naked breasts shone like bulbs of ebony. Her chest was draped with strings of baubles that lay loosely on her shining flesh. Her eyes held Julie's in a dark, implacable stare.

Julie's instinct was to scream. But as always, her scream froze silent in her throat. Then, as she caught her breath to call out for help, the figure in the glass grew dimmer until suddenly it was gone.

Strain as she might, Julie could not see anything in the glass of the mirror except the bedposts of her bed and the drapes that hung behind it which moved uneasily in the night air.

But the window she had left open had been closed and the musky, spicy scent hung in her head like smoke.

Chapter Fifty-Five

Anne-Louise DuBois slept hardly at all that first night that her niece Juliette spent under her roof. She lay staring at the ceiling rebuking herself for her own stupidity. The joy of hearing that Etienne's daughter was safe and that she was as near as Charles Town had blown the wit from her mind.

Finally, she threw aside the covers and rose from the bed she had once shared with her husband and to which she now came alone. With her arms crossed tightly over her breasts to ward off the ominous chill, she paced the room, crossing and recrossing it in swift nervous steps.

Where had her mind been? Why had she not been more devious? She could have sent a message to the child—even visited her. She could have made arrangements for Juliette to stay with that gentle Scots widow until she found a more suitable sanctuary for her, some gentle home from which she might meet the other young people of the city. The eligible young men of Charles Town would most certainly fall over each other to court a girl of such remarkable grace and beauty. But no, she had thoughtlessly brought her into this prison that paraded as a home, under the fiendish control of Julie's uncle.

"Fool," she upbraided herself, "thoughtless, selfish fool."

What could she do to rectify this dread mistake she had made? How could she manage to protect this lovely young girl from Yves's madness?

She shook her head in despair. She could warn Juliette, using the gentlest terms possible to keep the girl from being thrown into helpless terror. She could spend the precious time with the child in teaching her all she dared about how to handle the monster who was her supposed protector.

One thing was certain, she promised herself. She would not let Juliette be destroyed by Yves DuBois as her own son Jacques had been.

The other children? She would worry about them in their own time. The way they had turned against her after Jacques's trouble gave their father great satisfaction. As long as

383

they enjoyed his approval, they were safe from him. She was better able to deal with their rejection of her than the sight of seeing them driven to desperation as Jacques had been.

Thank God that Yves was away on a slave-buying trip. At last she would have a little bit of time with Juliette alone—time to win her confidence, and hopefully, to teach her that she must handle her uncle in only a certain way.

Julie's doubts about her Aunt Anne-Louise began at once. She felt a swift affection for the older woman and was charmed by her aunt's gentle manners and obvious attempts to make Julie feel welcome and cherished. But behind her aunt's words, half-hidden in those smoky, dark eyes, Julie glimpsed a desperation that seemed unbelievable in a woman who appeared so secure in the midst of her affluent family.

From the talk of servants in her father's house and from her work among the sick at Margaret's side, Julie had learned to accept that women of middle years were prey to a passing madness that fevered their nights and tormented them into strange behavior by day.

Julie seized on this possibility to explain to herself the extraordinary tension that lay coiled behind her aunt's gracious manner and endowed all her words with a double meaning.

The plantation which had seemed so ominous in darkness became a bustling, sunlit village by day. A legion of different works went on all at once. The house was being polished by white-kerchifed maids, while the cook house down the brick path literally breathed steam and the scent of baking bread. She heard the vibration of saws and hammering from the carpentry shop in the settlement of smaller buildings behind the great house. Over the songs of the birds and the cries of barnyard fowl sounded the musical resonance of hammer on anvil from the forge whose blazing furnace belched smoke into the still air.

"Not a village but a world," her aunt corrected Julie with a smile. "Monde DuBois is what it is called." There was pride in her voice. "We began with fifty acres of standing trees and five slaves. It has grown to all this."

"A world of wood," Julie translated quietly. Then she grinned, remembering the meaning of the name DuBois. "Or World of the Du Bois, which is it?"

"Both and neither," her aunt replied enigmatically.

Over the breakfast cakes which were served with preserved peaches and honey and hot coffee, her aunt chattered about the coming day.

"You must have a fitting," she said at once. "Hannah does our sewing. She is clever with a needle, having learned it from her mistress in the islands."

Julie grinned at her. "You cannot imagine how little I understand of your lives here. What islands are those?"

"The West Indies," her aunt replied. "We have few Africans here, that is to say, slaves brought directly from Africa. Most of our people are from the islands where their families have been in bondage for generations."

"Is this to be preferred?" Julie asked, finding it hard to discuss people as if they were articles to be compared and bought and sold like chattel.

"They are different," her aunt said. "They have all learned to speak French or English which is helpful. There are other things about them that are much less attractive." Her voice broke off as if her own words had plunged her into deep thought.

Then she looked up with a smile. "As I started to tell you, I have instructed Hannah to fit you for clothing whenever you are ready to stand for her."

Julie was overwhelmed anew by her aunt's graciousness to her.

"I feel so bad about coming and making myself a burden on you," she told her aunt quietly. "I would have taken any other reasonable course that was open."

Her aunt's hand was swiftly on Julie's own. Those great, dark eyes which tugged at Julie's heart with memories of her father grew suddenly moist.

"I love you coming here," Anne-Louise said softly. "I love your good, bright company. I want you here——" Then a look of pain crossed her face swiftly. "I only hope that you can find happiness here. Your uncle, my husband—is a different man."

That sense of evil came again, chilling Julie's flesh.

"I know little of my uncle either," Julie confessed. "I only remember my father saying that he was a man of great faith."

Her aunt's expression grew suddenly sardonic. Her tone when she spoke was crisp, almost scathing. "Come now, my

385

dear," she chided Juliette. "You forget that your father was my brother and I was very close to him in spite of the great difference between our ages. Your words do not sound like anything that Etienne would have said of Yves." She glanced about and a twitch of a grin came to her mouth. "How about religious fanatic? Or God-driven idiot? He hated Yves and did all in his power to prevent my marriage to him. Would to God he had been given more power for that task." She sighed and the energy drained from her words. 'He was right of course. I only thank God that he has not lived to see how right he was and to suffer from that rightness."

What could she say? Julie silently absorbed her aunt's despair, as the serving girl removed their plates and poured fresh coffee before disappearing as silently as she had come.

Her aunt watched the girl's retreating before turning to Julie and whispering bitterly. "You see? She has left the door a little way open behind her. That appears to be carelessness, but it is actually stealth. In this house, someone will listen to every word we speak and report them to their master."

Then with a sudden, lightsome tone she laid her napkin aside. "Ah, Juliette," she said in a tone designed to be heard clearly from the next room. "It is far too lovely for us to stay indoors. Let me show you around this wooded world before we settle to our day."

With her aunt's light shawl pulled about her shoulders, Julie followed Anne-Louise out of the house and down the stairs onto the wide lawn. Julie was startled to realize that a man's figure was in the vines that pressed against the window of the room they had just left. Perry. She remembered that when he had driven them home from Mrs. MacRae's, her aunt had called him Perry.

Her aunt paused and looked back at the man. Julie could not have imagined that the glance that passed between them was raw hostility. Then Anne-Louise smiled bitterly.

"My niece and I are going to walk about the grounds. We will not leave the plantation."

The man nodded and stopped his work to stare after them intently. Julie could feel his gaze on their backs until they were out of sight of the porch.

Her aunt had been right. The plantation was more like a world in miniature than a village. They visited the granary and the forge, the carpentry shop where two sturdy young

386

men were assembling barrels from fragrant white wood. Julie's mind was staggered at the many activities going on simultaneously: the candle shop redolent of juniper, the wash house steaming with strong lye soap, the herd of grumbling hogs protesting the sharp stick of the small Negro boy driving them.

"Our principal sources of income are from the hogs and dried beef and indigo," her aunt told her. Then she smiled that wry way. "This is all to prepare you in case your uncle will probe you on what we have talked about. It is always best to have ready answers."

Turning away from the busy row of shops, her aunt started towards the woods which circled the plantation grounds. Julie, following, was suddenly startled to hear children's voices, many children's voices, some in childlike contention and some riotous in play. She stopped and listened curiously.

"The nursery," her aunt explained, nodding towards a sturdy building a few yards away. "The slave children are tended there while their mothers work."

"Babies too?" Julie asked, as the wail of an infant rose above the other voices.

"The mothers come from the field or their work to nurse them," her aunt explained. Then Annne-Louise's eyes darkened. "They are beautiful, with lovely curly hair and great trusting eyes, too young to carry the fear or hatred that comes later, still free of the spirits that will haunt their lives—the master's whip, Tonton Macoute—" Her voice trailed off as she turned to a path that led off into the woods.

Julie looked back thoughtfully. She noticed a trail of smoke rising lazily from the chimney of a sturdy house behind the nursery. A bunch of bright feathers adorned the closed door, but Julie saw a dark movement at the window that told her that someone had been watching them. "Another nursery?" she asked her aunt.

Her aunt's face turned pale, and Julie could see her struggle with herself before she could summon an answer. Then she only shook her head and tugged at Julie's arm. "Come, I will show you the cemetery we have carved from the woods."

How many had died. Julie stared at the fenced burial ground marked by square, painted boards bearing only a name and a year.

387

"These are the slaves," her aunt explained, walking on. "Over here are our own people."

A massive, white stone stood at the head of the second fenced plot. It was handsomely lettered with the name *DuBois* in flowering letters. Beneath the name was engraved a strange design that portrayed a cross being licked by flames. In and about the tongues was woven a serpentine figure that more than anything else reminded Julie of a great writhing snake.

Small stones were lined beneath the towering centotaph. Julie silently read the names and dates that recorded the brief lives of what had apparently been her aunt's other children.

"Phillipe, Etienne—" her aunt recited the names quietly. "He had been named for your father. Caroline, Mignonette and Jacques."

"Jacques," Julie repeated involuntarily. That had been the name of the cousin who was her own age. And the birth date on the headstone was right. The final date had not been added.

"The grave is empty," her aunt said in a careful tone. "His father has had the grave dug and the stone waiting."

As the shiver passed through Julie, her aunt took her hand.

"I did not bring you here by accident or to grieve you," she said in a hurried, tense voice. "I brought you here because this is the one place they will not follow and spy on me. I needed to tell you, my dear, that if my actions are strange, it is because I am not free to act as I would prefer."

She paused only briefly to turn away from the headstones. She did not face Julie as she spoke on in a low, sibilant whisper.

"I need to warn you before your uncle's return. Do not be deceived by your uncle's civil manner. Do not be seduced if he elects to be charming for you. He is a madman. He is all the things your father warned me and more. He is like the serpent that he worships. He will slide into your mind and read your very thoughts to turn against you in punishment. Be wary of him, Juliette, for behind that calm face lies great disorder. And for the love of God do not cross him nor give him cause to be angry at you. In this world he is all things— God, judge, and executioner."

Julie stood stunned. Before she could speak, her aunt slipped a friendly arm through Julie's. It was as if her fierce

388

words had been a sudden wind that had swept through her only to leave without memory of its passing. "These woods about us are infinitely beautiful with the coming of spring. There will be bright flowers everywhere, and the nuts and berries will adorn our table all through the year."

Julie allowed herself to be led along woodenly, her mind still echoing her aunt's warning. "They are wild and beautiful woods," her aunt repeated. "Stretching from here to some strange and unknown sea. But in the spring they smell of the gardens of home."

The days following that first walk with her aunt were serene and peaceful days. Too peaceful, Julie thought ruefully. Without distraction, her mind kept turning backward, always backward to the lives she had lost through death or denial. How could this strange place evoke such haunted memories?

When the birds fluted in the vines about the porch, Julie heard in their tones the spring birds of Epping Wood and half-dreamed that she could turn to see Titus swinging down the path towards her in his awkward, rolling gait, his face twisted into a smile. The silken night sky blooming slowly with its clustering of stars recalled such nights whose darkness she had watched eagerly, knowing it would bring Antoine to her pillow. Even the days brought those waking dreams. The green woods that seemed to flow forever into the west drew her eyes like a magnet. Where was Josh? Josh of the calm voice, the wounded heart. That lilting tune he had whistled or hummed would come to her own lips involuntarily, bringing a flood of tears behind her eyes.

"What tune is that which is always on your lips, Juliette?" her aunt asked.

"I do not have a name for it," Julie confessed. "But my friend carried it always on his lips and he seems to have left it with me."

Her aunt shook her head. "I would rather guess that he still has it too. When it comes to you it is because he is somewhere thinking of you."

"What a nice thought," Julie told her, hoping that it was true.

The seamstress Hannah was a large-boned heavy woman with a delicious low laugh and nimble fingers. She measured Julie and pinned and fitted two dark dresses, strangely designed, with the same high necklines and long, full sleeves

389

that comprised the costume of Anne-Louise and her daughters.

Her aunt, watching, remarked wryly. "Your uncle has very fixed ideas on the proper, modest raiment for women."

Julie made several shy attempts to make friends with her young cousins. Pierre, whom Anne-Louise explained was studying with a tutor in Charles Town in preparation for going back to France for his advanced education, seemed mostly at his books. When he did leave the house, he walked swiftly through the grounds as if on some unpleasant errand. He was a scowling young man whose riding crop never left his hand. When she could not elicit more from him than a surly greeting, she abandoned the cause.

But as unpleasant as he was, his sisters were no more prepossessing. They seemed always to be closeted away in their rooms together or walking about unsmiling followed by two neat Negro maids who stayed only a few feet behind.

The girl Mandy would have followed Julie with the same shadowy insistence if Julie had not protested at once.

"For heavens sake, go about your business, child," she told the girl with a smile. "If I want anything, I shall just call for you."

The girl looked frightened and hung her head.

"I do what I must do," she told Julie.

"You would get into trouble?" Julie asked.

The girl nodded slowly. Julie sighed and smiled at her. "Very well, but watch that I do not turn swiftly and squash you like a bug beneath my heel."

The jest was not lost on Mandy who chuckled and grinned back at her. "I be careful," she assured her. In those few brief days, a warmth sprang up between Julie and the girl.

Julie enjoyed teaching her things—to write her name, to sew a simple seam. In exchange, Mandy told Julie strange tales of the animals of her own country, of the wise hare and the clever spider Anansi who had once been a man himself, an officer of the God of that place.

A little after twilight on the fifth day, the tempo of the entire plantation changed. After one of those exhausting evening meals with her aunt and the silent children, Julie was curled in her room doing some needlework. Mandy was beside her on the floor, plying her own needle with unaccustomed hands.

At first, Julie could not imagine the source of the sound. It was if a strange rhythmic cadence were coming from the woods beyond the clearing. She went to the window to stare out into the gathering darkness. Then she saw a wavering light and then another flicker through the trees as the sound grew louder.

Torches. Torches were being carried up the low drive that tunneled through the trees. Mandy, at her side, stared at the lights silently.

"What is that, Mandy" Julie asked. "What is coming?"

"It's the coffle," she said quietly. "See? Now you can see."

A caravan of people emerged from the cover of the trees. It was headed by a dark horse bearing a man in dark clothing with only a flash of white at the throat.

"The master," Mandy whispered. It was too dark and the distance too far for Julie to see his face, but he rode regally, and she felt a clutch of fear at the thought of finally meeting this strangely reported man face-to-face.

Behind him, she saw a double line of dark figures, both men and women, dragging chains heavily along the rutted drive. The torches, whose light had attracted her attention, were carried by two tall, unchained black men who followed the others. In his other hand, each man bore a long, curled whip.

"New slaves," Mandy explained.

They watched silently while a smith came running to loose the chains from the weary slaves. Her uncle, still mounted on his horse, watched the proceedings with his back to the house so that Julie's curiosity only deepened. He sat a horse regally, she must cede him that. He was a larger man than she had imagined, the width of his coat betraying a portly frame beneath his head of dark hair.

When he finally turned to glance towards the house, Mandy leaped backwards with such celerity that Julie did the same, discovering that her heart was beating wildly.

She was grateful that no tap came at her door, summoning her to meet her host. When she went to bed, she was actually happy to know that Mandy was just outside in the hall on her small pallet.

But that night, for the first time since her arrival, the strange, flowery, spicy scent filled her head, wakening her in

391

terror. She stared at the mirror at the foot of her bed a long time, but only her own terrified face stared back. But the smell hung in the room until the breeze of dawn.

Chapter Fifty-Six

"I wish Hannah had been able to finish just one of your new dresses before your uncle got home," Julie's aunt fussed nervously with the ruffle at the bodice of Julie's blue dress, then smoothed back her niece's rebellious curls with a gentle hand.

"For goodness sake, tante," Julie smiled at her. "You are giving me the terrors."

Her aunt bit her lip. "I'm sorry, dear," Then she raised those smoky eyes to Julie's face imploringly. "It's only that things just must go off well between you."

The rest of the family waited in the library. The children turned to stare coldly as Julie entered at her aunt's side. Their father was at a desk with his back to the room. He was much larger than she had expected, even from seeing him astride his horse the evening before. Somehow she had cast him in her mind in the mold of the dark stranger, tall and cadaverous with beetling brows and a stern visage.

The man who turned to face them had softer coloring. His hair was a deep brown only slightly tinged with glints of silver just above his ears. His long, oval face with the wide-set, pale brown eyes was heavy with flesh. It was the face of a dissolute man even though the full, sensual lips were drawn down firmly into a stern expression. His cheeks flamed with color, and the inner parts of his lips showed a startling red surface when he spoke. Julie was startled at the softness of his tone.

"So you are Juliette Duvall, daughter of my brother-in-law Etienne."

Julie nodded, irresolute as to whether she should bow or offer her hand to this man. Since his own stance was unmoving, she did neither.

"That is right, Monsieur DuBois."

A humorless smile came to his lips. "Monsieur DuBois, is

392

it? Don't you think that when you have come to my house in my absence, pleading for shelter and food, throwing yourself upon my charity with the lame excuse of a blood link with my wife, that you might more properly address me as Uncle Yves?"

Julie heard her aunt's small exhalation of breath and felt her own blood rush to her cheeks with shame. She dropped her eyes. "Yes, Uncle Yves," she said, unable to keep a tremor of emotion from her voice.

Seemingly satisfied with her meek answer, he turned to his older daughter. "Let us test your education, Cecilia. Observe the wantonness with which your mother's relative displays her body before the eyes of us all. Does a proverb from the Holy Writ come to your mind in this connection?"

Cecilia, without lifting her eyes to her father's face, recited dully, "As a jewel in a swine's snout, so is a fair woman without discretion."

Julie felt her nails digging into her palms as Cecilia turned to look at her with an air of quiet triumph.

"I regret that my costume offends you, sir," Julie said between clenched teeth. "I lost all my own wardrobe in the sinking of the ship and have only this one dress which was obtained from a generous farmer's daughter."

"Hannah is already at work preparing clothes for Juliette," his wife put in quietly.

Yves DuBois let his glance stray from his wife's face to Juliette. Then he shrugged.

"It is good to hear that one problem is being solved." He waved Julie towards a chair. "You may as well sit down while you tell us the story of the adventures that brought you to my home."

"It's simple enough," Julie began. "I left England on the *Tilbury Belle*." He stopped her with an uplifted hand.

"You will begain when you left your father's house," he ordered.

Julie flushed again, furious that her own skin and voice kept betraying her storm of emotions.

"I was dispossessed of my inheritance when my Uncle Simon lost the estate and its proceeds by bad investments."

He stirred restlessly. "On with it, we have not all day for this recitation."

Between clenched teeth, Julie forced herself to continue.

"After some months in his house, I went to London where I stayed with the sister of my old governess until embarking for this country on the *Tilbury Belle*."

"And this is all that you wish to tell us?" he challenged her.

"You indicated that you did not have time for a complete account," she reminded him.

He sprang to his feet. "Account! I have time for any true account. It is for wild stories like the one you just told that I have no time. I have unending patience for the truth."

He whirled on her, staring at her intently with those pale, widely set eyes. "Can I give you my account of your adventures, Juliette Duvall?"

Without waiting for her reply, he began pacing back and forth, speaking pedantically, letting each sentence sink into the understanding of the listeners.

"When your uncle's earnest attempts to increase your estate resulted in certain reverses, he graciously invited you to share his own home. You repaid this generosity by luring from his household his son Louis." His voice dropped dramatically as he leaned towards her. "This Louis who was a sickly child at best, was the only threat in the world to you, Juliette Duvall. He alone of that household carried the Duvall blood and would, by English law, be enabled to inherit what could be redeemed of your father's estate."

Julie gasped, shaking her head wildly.

"You lured this child from his home in the dead of winter, left him murdered in a field, and disappeared into London to avoid being tried for this heinous crime. Where you lived in that sinful city and what nature of life you led is only conjecture, but seeing you come into a decent home dressed like a saucy harlot, brought here under the protection of an uncouth Indian trader and gambler gives us many clues to the level of immorality to which you have sunk."

Fighting for control, furious and shamed and near tears all at the same time, Julie glanced towards her aunt in hope of some support. To her astonishment, her aunt sat quietly, her hands on her lap, her face devoid of expression.

So that was how it was to be. She was alone against this monster. Her aunt's warning came to her. "Do not cross him," her aunt had whispered in the burying ground. "He is a serpent. He is God, judge, and executioner."

"I am waiting," he said. "Surely you have a more fanciful and self-serving version of this history."

Julie looked at the man. Whatever she said he would twist her words and turn them back on her like a weapon. The cold skill of disciplined control that she had learned at Newgate and later with the dark stranger returned to her, stiffening her spine under the blue dress. She held his pale eyes with her own and her voice was serene.

"I did not kill Louis." She fell silent.

He stared at her and the color rose even higher in his face. His lips seemed to tremble, and then, as if conscious of the loathing she felt for him, he turned away. He went back to pacing the room. His movements were agile for a man of his bulk, his step light on the floor. For what seemed an interminable time, the room was silent except for his manic pacing.

Then he stopped. He trained his eyes on the ceiling of the room and pressed his fingertips together thoughtfully.

"I have thought carefully of what possible place could be found for such as you within this household. By the right of your blood you might expect to be treated as a member of the family, but the life you have led makes this impossible. I cannot have my own carefully nurtured children exposed to your corrupting company.

"If you had skills, other than those of the street, you could be useful as a governess or a helpmate to your aunt, but I doubt if such is the case. We have trained and docile slaves to do the necessary labor of the house, so that use is closed to you.

"I understand that your aunt, without consulting me, has taken the liberty of releasing the slave Amanda from her ordinary tasks to serve you. This coddling is at an end. You see, Juliette Duvall, there is really no place for you here. But ingrate and murderess and possible adulteress that you are, I am still obliged to extend you charity. This I will do and no more.

"You will make your presence as inconspicuous as possible. You will keep yourself totally apart from our view until your half-nakedness is covered. And after that, how you entertain yourself is your own concern as long as you do not have anything to do with the ordinary life of this family."

His glance flicked over the other members of his family.

395

"That is all," he said with finality. Then he resumed his writing at his desk, his broad back turned upon them all.

Julie was stunned. She felt her aunt's hand on her arm. Julie let herself be led woodenly across the hall and up the stairs to her room.

Mandy was gone.

All her freedom of movement was gone. It seemed that even her Aunt Anne-Louise was gone as three full days passed with only the slaves bringing her meals or hot water for her bath. At last Hannah came, her face closed of expression. She watched as Julie had the final fittings of the dreary dresses and the nightwear and underclothing that Anne-Louise had ordered.

Her room became a closed cell to her. As she had at Newgate, she sought the window as her only touchpoint with the real world outside. Her mood swung wildly from fury to self-pity to helpless grief. Still only the maids came with fresh trays and clean linen and Julie moved about her prison to be out of their way.

Her first visitor was her Uncle Yves himself.

At the rap on her door, she presumed that another slave had come on a housekeeping errand. She called a listless, "Enter," without changing her position in the chair.

The door opened and closed. When she heard no further movement she looked about. Her uncle stood inside the door, looking more massive than ever in that small room.

When she saw who it was, she leaped hastily to her feet. "I am sorry, sir," she said swiftly. "I did not know it was you."

"And how differently would the greeting have been if you had known?" he asked in a soft voice. Suddenly he was smiling and his voice teasing.

She realized he was looking at her, really looking at her, as a man does a woman, and she felt herself color with shame. His eyes moved from her face, lingered at the fullness of her bosom, and travelled almost tenderly down the line of her figure to her slender ankles.

When she did not answer, but only stared back coldly at him, he let himself down on the edge of her bed. "I have thought over my instructions to you, Juliette Duvall, and find I was hasty. Idleness such as I proposed will bend you to the devil's will. It is unrealistic to expect one of your youth and

396

fiery nature to remain idle. What useful skills do you have, mademoiselle?"

She hated him. How could she manage to hate him even more when his voice was soft than when he was harshly brutal as he had been that first day.

"I have certain skills with herbs and healing," she said quietly, standing by her chair as far away from him as possible.

"Witchcraft?" he asked quietly.

Her eyes widened in astonishment. "Oh no, sir," she protested, "only simple cures."

He smiled. "Any other skills?"

She was remembering her aunt's words. He will take your thoughts and twist them. "No, sir," she shook her head.

"You are too modest," he chided her. His voice grew even milder. "Come closer to me, child."

She walked towards him, her heart battering like a prisoned bird in her chest. She feared to go towards him as much as she feared to disobey him. When she was quite near, she grew suddenly giddy. A strange scent came from this smiling mountain of a man. The spicy, flowery scent that had haunted her nightmare hung about his flesh. She gasped, fighting for breath untainted by that strange sweetness.

"Why do you fear me?" he asked.

She would not answer. She need not answer for he would read her thoughts without her words. She only kept her eyes averted that he would not see the hatred there along with the fear.

His hand was suddenly tight on her arm. She was conscious of his great strength even though his grip was not tight.

"You fear me because you know me to be a high priest, a high priest to a powerful God." His voice was persuasive and so soft that Julie could hear the rhythm of her own heartbeat as an accompaniment to his words. "I can command the dead and bring them out of the waters. I can set the souls of the dead to fury and use that fury for my own ends. I am your master, Juliette Duvall, and that is why you fear me."

Master. That was not a word he should use to her. Quickly, like a series of rapid images, there flashed before her eyes the images of abuse that had come when men chose to be masters. Joseph slobbering against her neck, the violence

397

of the thief-taker ravaging her body, and the blows of the dark stranger.

As she stared at him, she saw his eyes narrow as if with greed, she saw his tongue slide quickly along the raw inner edge of his lips, she felt his hand move from her arm and stir along her shoulder. The rhythm of his breathing changed, and he panted, reddening from the thrust of his growing passion as he groped for her.

She did not move from his grasp. She did not scream. With the cold fury of her unforgotten discipline she spoke to him.

"No," she said quietly. "You will not master me. Not you, ever. Do what indignity to me that you will, but I belong to a greater strength than yours. Humiliate me, ravish me if you will, but you will not master me. Not in this life."

His heavy jaw slacked at her words. His hands cupping her breasts froze in place, and a cold sweat seemed to burst from the surface of his flesh. He leaped to his feet and threw her away from him across the room.

His eyes were dilated as if with belladonna. His words came with difficulty from his terror-constricted throat.

"Devil," he cried in a fierce whisper. "Spawn of the devil. You have been sent to master *me*." He shook his head violently. "No. No. No. I am the priest. You will not reach me with your carnal trickery."

She lay where he had thrown her, watching his terror guide him from the room backwards, as if he feared to make himself vulnerable by taking his eyes from her. Then he groped the door open and was gone, his feet rapid and heavy along the hall like a man pursued.

When she knew he was well gone, she rose and sank weakly into her chair. Mad. The man was wildly, impossibly mad. She heard a flurry of sound from below. Perry was leading a black horse into the clearing. She saw the big Negro give his master a leg-up. She saw the stallion rear and dance before Yves brought him to control with a lash of the whip. Then the horse wheeled, and bore his master off towards the woods with a frantic whinnying. She buried her head on the windowsill and wept.

She did not know how long she lay there before the soft hand was laid on her shoulder.

"Dear child," her aunt whispered. "Dear, helpless child. I would help you if I could, but there is no one."

398

Julie raised her tearstained face to her aunt. "But what can I do, tante? I do not even know what I said to enrage him like that."

Her aunt sighed. "His mind is a dark place unlit by reason. You must stay out of his sight. In a way he has made it easier for you by your not having meals with us or working with the children. This way you will not be such a thorn in his flesh."

"How can he hate me so when I have done nothing to him?" Julie asked quietly.

"He is possessed by many demons," her aunt replied. "And not the least of them is lust."

Anne-Louise left Julie's room with a sick heart. It was easy enough to guess what Yves had gone for, what evil hunger had driven him to the girl. But what had Julie said to strike terror into her uncle's heart? She had seen his face as he plunged away from the girl's room. He feared her. He feared her as much as he desired her.

Even before Anne-Louise reached her own room, she heard the low insistent drumming of the voodoo music begin. She pulled her shawl about her shoulders closer.

How could she warn Julie of the brutal nature of the God her uncle had learned to worship? How could this fresh, lovely girl understand the unthinkable cult that dealt with the desecrated bones of the dead, with human dung and the sacrifices that were made to drive spirits from the frantic worshippers.

Oh God, if she could only reach that strange young trader who had brought Juliette to Charles Town. She had seen his love for Julie in the anguish of his face as she left.

Anyone, anyplace would be better for Juliette than this place.

Chapter Fifty-Seven

Yves DuBois did not come to her room again. For this Julie was thankful. But her aunt's admonition to stay out of his sight proved to be a hopeless task. It did not seem to matter where she went or at what hour of the day, he would appear as if from nowhere, his pale eyes studying her from a distance or his level voice challenging her.

"What mischief are you into this day, mistress?" he asked in a deadly serious tone.

"No mischief, sir," she would reply, dropping her eyes to conceal her loathing from him.

"Look at me," he commanded hoarsely, seizing her wrist.

When she raised her golden eyes to his, he stared fixedly at her a moment before flushing with painful color and throwing her arm away fiercely.

Since he seemed able to appear anywhere she went, she concentrated on knowing where he was that she might avoid contact with him.

When, with rare luck and careful management, Julie was able to go a few days without being confronted by her uncle, she grew almost lighthearted. Who could resist a spring that came like a carpet of flowers being unrolled under the fragrant, bird-filled trees? "I am like Ellie in Newgate," she told herself, "singing in the shadow of the gallows." But how strange it was that although it was Josh's song that came to her lips, it was Antoine who brought tears to her eyes when a scent of spring earth or a surprise clump of violets took her swiftly and brutally back to Epping Wood.

Since the affairs of the plantation often took her uncle from its grounds on trips of several days length, Julie looked forward eagerly to those times. In his absence, she and her aunt would resume their old relationship, except for the meals which Julie still ate alone in her own room.

Little by little, Anne-Louise related the story of Yves's dread descent from religious fervor to superstitious madness.

"The day can be named," she told Julie. "I can recall the exact day when his destruction in the sight of both man and God was begun."

Her aunt's lap was filled with freshly gathered wild flowers that she had picked along the path that led to the burying ground. As Anne-Louise talked, her fingers nervously plaited the stems of wild daisies into a braid of rigid green, like the woven leather whips that the drivers wielded over the backs of the field slaves.

"It was a little over ten years ago," she said. "I was heavy with Yvonne who was less than a month from term. Yves had gone to buy slaves from a West Indies shipment that had been widely advertised in Charles Town.

"His arrangement with the slave dealer had been made in advance. He had bartered many hundreds of pounds worth of pork and hides for which he expected to bring back four or five strong slaves for the field work."

She paused and frowned into the forest. "It was so strange, Juliette. At twilight we were all expecting the coffle to come clanking up the drive the way they do, in that steady rhythm and the humming they make when they march together. Instead, he came up the drive with his helpers following and a single slave at his side.

"At his side," she repeated incredulously. "An unchained woman walked at his side alongside his horse. She seemed ordinary enough at first glance, a young woman clad in a light, country cut of dress and barefoot because it was summer. She had that erect carriage that they all have from bearing great weights on their heads from infancy.

"Her name was Tomala—is Tomala," Anne-Louise corrected herself, staring at Julie intensely. "As mad as this may sound Tomala had bewitched him. She did it somehow from the slave block. It was almost as if she were bringing him back here. He did not put her in with the other slaves but housed her in the nursery until he had a separate house built for her."

Her voice dropped. "He has not visited my bed since that night. Her wish becomes his will."

"Is he in love with her, a black woman?" Julie asked aghast.

"Love?" Her laugh was brittle. "She possesses him. There were no drums until Tomala came. Now there are drums and beastly orgies in the woods in a special place where serpents are tended." She glanced about the graveyard.

"In the old days the slaves tended these graves, mowed the wild grass and planted flowers and kept the stones straight. Now they will not come near. Someone called Baron Samedi lives in this place." She shook her head. "There was no Baron Samedi until Tomala came. She has filled the minds of the young with *loup-garoo*, a monster that comes by night to suck the blood of children, and Tonton Macoute, a travelling sorcerer whose bags are filled with magic charms, the bones of the dead, and talismans.

"Do you remember how wide-eyed and terrified the house-boy was the night you came? When your friend Josh had come out of the woods with his horse laden with bags, the poor lad thought it was Tonton Macoute and nearly died of pure terror."

"And an educated man like Uncle Yves believes all this?" Julie asked incredulous.

Anne-Louise rose, letting the flowers tumble from her lap onto the ground about her feet. She tossed away the chain she had woven. It writhed like a snake among the flowers.

"How is belief born?" she asked Julie. "On the evidence of the senses or the desires of the heart? I myself have seen these people sicken and die because of the *Obeah*. This is the bad medicine of the witch doctors. I have seen them writhe in pain because a doll made in their image with a single hair of their heads woven in was pierced by needles or thrown into the fire." She shrugged. "Yet I do not believe. But as for the heart wanting to believe, Yves DuBois is not one to deny a voice that proclaims him priest—all knowing, all powerful. Tomala spoke into what he already desired to believe—that he is different from other men, grander and immortal."

"Then why does he act as if he fears me?" Julie asked.

Her aunt looked at her searchingly. "If I were a better student of voodoo I might understand that. As it is, it only terrifies me."

"Tante Anne-Louise," Julie asked softly. "What if I should run away?"

Julie saw her aunt's body stiffen. Then she shook her lovely white head. "Where would you go, my love?" she asked gently. "To Charles Town? You could not hide from him in Charles Town. We are small pockets of humanity pinned onto the endless cloth of a savage country. How could you live? How could you protect yourself?"

"You must know, Juliette, that I have cherished the same dream. Jacques entertained that dream and acted upon it." Her face twisted with pain. "His father has had agents out searching for him since the day he left. Their instructions are to bring him back, alive or dead. You know how that will end. You have seen the welcome that his father has prepared for him."

Julie shuddered, unable to look back at the open grave

402

half-filled with spring rain, the headstone with the birthday engraved and the death date left blank.

"You are doing well," her aunt assured her. "His mind fixes on what his eye falls upon. By avoiding him, you are saving yourself."

But when she had told the girl good-bye at the door of her room, Anne-Louise thought back over their talk. She had told Juliette that she was doing well. She did not herself believe the words. There was a wildness in Yves eyes when they fell upon the girl that terrified her. And the fear. If Yves truly feared Juliette, there was no way to save her.

And Julie herself had been thinking of running away. Anne-Louise had thought of little else for the girl in the weeks since Yves had created the great scene in the child's room. She had not conceived that he would turn on the girl with such cruelty. But where could she get help?

She stopped stock-still in the hall staring at a pattern in the rug. It was such a frail hope that she scarcely dared to entertain it. But it was a thought. A thought that might breed hope.

Chapter Fifty-Eight

In the ten years since the coming of Tomala to the plantation, Anne-Louise's only contact with the people of Charles Town had been on her infrequent trips to buy such womanly supplies as a man would be at a loss to select. Even then, she would only go along when Pierre was scheduled to be with his tutor. And always, Perry stayed with her, standing just outside a shop or waiting a few steps behind, guarding her. From what? Yves must surely know that she would not abandon her children even to seek a life for herself. She was powerless and he knew it, yet he demeaned her by setting the great hostile Negro to guard her every move.

But the limits of Perry's authority over her were set only by the master. With Yves gone, she might make a strange request and get away with it because no specific order had been made to the contrary.

She dressed with trembling fingers, keeping an ear to the

schedule of the house. When she heard Pierre leave his room to go down to the carriage, she followed him. Perry rose from his work when she came out onto the porch.

"I am making a social call in Charles Town this afternoon while Pierre takes his lesson," she told him coldly. "Perhaps you will wish to drive the trap for us instead of Ben."

The Negro frowned but did not reply. Instead he turned and approached the trap. The usual driver dismounted quickly and handed the reins to Perry.

After Perry had dropped Pierre at his tutor's quarters, she directed him to the home of Mrs. MacRae.

The Scotswoman greeted her with fluttering cries of delight, set the pot to boil, and showed her into a favored chair. "I have thought so much of your lovely niece and your own visit here," Mrs. MacRae said with great earnestness. "Such a lovely girl, such gentle company."

To Anne-Louise's delight, Perry seemed perfectly content to stay outside the house. He leaned against a post of the porch, dozing in the sun, providing her the opportunity to get past the first social amenities into the true reason for her visit.

"I never saw Josh Simmons before that day," Mrs. Mac-Rae replied to Anne-Louise's probing. She lifted the pot with both hands to refill her guest's cup. "He was the most appealing young man in spite of his rough appearance." She grinned at her guest. "And your niece! I must confess that I have never seen a lovelier girl, nor one with such striking coloring."

Anne-Louise smiled in agreement. "She is the picture of her lovely Irish mother." She paused. "Except for those eyes—those strange, lovely, golden eyes."

Anne-Louise had felt her spirits plunge when Mrs. MacRae had revealed her small knowledge of Josh Simmons. Her hope in coming to see the woman was that the Scotswoman could somehow get her into contact with Josh, to let him know that Juliette needed help, that she must be rescued. With that hope destroyed, Anne-Louise felt strangely limp and carried on her conversation with Mrs. MacRae with only the practiced skill of her early upbringing, smiling on demand and speaking gently but not caring, not really caring at all.

But Mrs. MacRae was indeed a talker. Her mind was still on Juliette's rare beauty and her tone, as she spoke on, was

404

one of almost excited confidence. "Those eyes of hers gave me quite a start when I first saw her," Mrs. MacRae confessed. "I had never seen a truly golden-eyed person before, or even heard of one until just a few weeks before she came."

Anne-Louise looked up with a revival of interest. "Was this other person a man or a woman?" she asked.

Mrs. MacRae smiled at her. "Oh, I didn't *see* another such person," she said. "I only heard of one."

She paused and selected another shortbread cake from the box that Anne-Louise had brought her. "It was so lovely of you to bring these cakes to me, Mrs. DuBois. They are delicious. But it was not at all necessary. I was delighted to share my home with your niece that day and I was amply paid."

"You were telling me about the other golden-eyed person you had heard of," Anne-Louise prodded, as her hostess's voice trailed off.

"It was an intriguing story," Mrs. MacRae said thoughtfully. "It seems that a great searching is on in all the colonies for a dark-haired, golden-eyed girl from Middlesex."

The name of the county struck Anne-Louise almost like a blow beneath her belt. She paused with the teacup halfway to her lips. Etienne's home had been in Middlesex County, Juliette was a dark-haired, golden-eyed girl from Middlesex.

"Who is making this search?" she asked, as levelly as she could.

Mrs. MacRae shook her head. "No one seems to know. But one of the storekeeper's wives told me that among her customers is a fine lady of great property who is highly interested in the search."

"A lady," Anne-Louise repeated aloud.

"Fascinating, isn't it?" Mrs. MacRae asked, leaning forward a little with her eyes sparkling. Then she laughed at herself. "What a gossip I am. But I spend so much time alone, and a mystery like that comes rarely in a quiet life."

Anne-Louise smiled at her hostess and touched her hand affectionately. "Oh, come now, Mrs. MacRae. We are all women together. Let us admit that we love a story, a strange tale like this! To outgrow her love of a little gossip, a woman would have to be past speaking or hearing."

"I am certainly not at that point," Mrs. MacRae laughed.

"Nor am I," Anne-Louise said brightly. "In fact, I am fascinated. I would love to find out who this woman is and why she is so interested in the search for someone with coloring like my niece."

"I shall make a point of inquiring for you," Mrs. MacRae promised. "In fact, I love having a reason to do so besides my own idle curiosity."

Perry rose and glanced towards the door. It was time for Pierre to be picked up from his tutor. Anne-Louise also rose and took her hostess's hands in her own.

"This has been such a lovely treat," she said, smiling. "Do tell me that I can come again soon and you will have some more news for me of that exciting search."

Mrs. MacRae giggled like a young girl. "Indeed, waste no time. I shall burst with all the news I can find until you come back to me. The girl is well, of course?" she added, "Well and happy in this new land?"

Anne-Louise caught her breath. She dare not reveal the desperation that lay behind her visit lest the woman think her mad and lose interest in the search. But she could hint.

"She is well," she said slowly and sighed. "But she is not happy. How I would love to see the child happier than she is."

After their affectionate parting, Anne-Louise sat silent in the carriage on the way home. Did she dare to hope that the person behind the search for the golden-eyed girl might be someone bearing good news for Julie? She did not believe the stories that Simon's wife had written to Yves about the child; she could not accept that Juliette had been anything but a girl sadly maligned by odious people. Perhaps some of her father's estate had been redeemed and she would have a suitable dowry. Perhaps some old friend from their life in Middlesex was concerned for the child.

Any small hope was worth exploring.

Chapter Fifty-Nine

Julie continued to chafe at the inactivity of her life. As neither a member of the family nor yet a servant, she was left to find what amusement she could. She tried to persuade

Hannah to let her help with the endless stream of dresses and shirts and nightwear that emerged from the small, untidy sewing room.

"It's not fit," the woman protested so unhappily that Julie gave up trying to persuade her.

She yearned to enter the nursery. Surely an extra pair of hands could be used there. But she dared not. Since she had fallen from the grace of the master, none of the slaves would meet her eye even in the nearest passing.

Finally she resigned herself to idleness and set a small routine for her days. Mornings she spent in her room doing needlework or reading. After lunch, she napped and bathed, and when the afternoon sun began to slide behind the trees, she walked for an hour or so along the trails in the woods that surrounded the plantation clearing. Sometimes she took the path that led to the burying ground. On other days she chose the wide, cluttered trails that led back to the logging sites deep in the forest. These paths were kept clear by the logs that the slaves dragged in from the felling site.

She learned where the wild grapes tendrilled towards promised fruit and watched the pale clusters of blossoms which would be blackberries in their season. She even found a special way to slip from the house by the rear door so that she could take a careful path to the woods without being in easy view of her uncle's study.

That afternoon in early April she realized that her stealth had been in vain. She had made her way into the cover of the great trees and was humming Josh's song to herself as she wandered down a familiar trail. She whirled in alarm when she heard a twig snap and a footfall on the bark-strewn path behind her. Yves Dubois was following her a few yards back.

"Good afternoon, sir," she said, her heart thumping.

"Good afternoon to you," he said quietly. "I decided it was my duty to see what tryst you keep daily in these woods." He came towards her slowly, never taking his eyes from her face. "Have you some enraptured, savage lover hidden among the trees, mistress?"

She flushed and would have pulled away but he was too swift for her. His hand seized her wrist, and he tucked her arm in under his own against the soft flesh of his waist. He kept moving, tugging her along beside him.

"You wished to walk, let us walk," he said.

"I wish to go back," she protested. "I have taken my walk and now I wish to return to the house."

He shook his head. "I am taking my walk now," he said harshly. "And you will walk with me."

She tightened her lips and stared straight ahead, keeping pace with him to prevent being dragged.

"You must be lonely for the lights and music of London," he observed. "A lovely creature like you. You must miss the coddling and caresses, the pretty compliments on your well-formed body and your tempting face. Have you considered seducing your young cousin Pierre as you did young Louis? Perhaps you could lure him into the nested evil between your thighs as you did that other dear boy." His voice purred with sweetness.

When she did not reply, he turned on her, jerking her to a stop. His voice rose, growing almost shrill.

"Or is it only me that you plan to tease to destruction?"

Julie bit her lips. "I have no designs on any man." She kept her voice as calm as possible. "Please, sir, I would like to go back now."

"You will go back when I say and not before," he warned her. "Now we will walk and talk of the eternal damnation that awaits you for your sins and for your alliance with the devil."

Julie kept her eyes on the path and stayed silent. What could she do but provoke his madness further?

"Do you deny that you are damned?" he asked, his voice rising in anger. When she still did not reply, he whirled her about to face him and shook her hard. "Answer me. You are damned, aren't you? You are in league with the devil, aren't you?"

Her fear and anger made her reckless. "Only God knows that," she told him harshly.

"God," he howled, his eyes wide with fury. "You dare to mention God to me. You hussy, you temptress." He gripped her upper arms with a force that sent pain coursing along her arms and into her shoulders.

"I have seen the devil working through you," he hissed at her. "I have seen your careful campaign against my priestly defenses. I have seen you swinging your skirts in that sensual way across the grasses into the dim woods, beckoning, always beckoning. I have heard the song you hum and felt it enter

408

into my own head so that its rhythm haunts me even when you are silent." His voice dropped ominously. "I have listened at your door as you slept, monitored your breathing, and heard the soft sighs calling to me with your carnal longing."

She stared at him aghast.

He sneered at her almost triumphantly. "You had thought me a fool, hadn't you? Did you think me too stupid to understand your aim? It is to possess me," he shook her fiercely again. "Answer me, it is to possess me, to draw me into that well of vice that is your body. To possess me." His voice rose to a shriek.

She shook her head helplessly at his accusations, but the slightest movement of her body only served to inflame him further.

"You have tried to bewitch me," he said in a low tone. "You have woven spells in the vines of my own woods to ensnare me, but I have eluded you. You have not won over me. I am master of your master. And of you." He paused and gazed maniacally into her eyes.

"You live or die by my will, slut," he said with satisfaction. "I could take that slender neck of yours in my hands this moment—" His eyes were on her throat as he released her arms and raised his hands, curled in the air, towards her.

She panicked. She slid away from his grasping hands and began to run. His laughter followed her.

"Run, harlot, run," he shouted after her. "Run and see what profit you make of it."

She turned to look back at him. Darkness was filling the wood. He stood where she had left him smiling indulgently. Beyond her lay the dense woods which stretched, as her aunt had said, to some unknown sea. Between that peril and his certain madness what choice could she make?

She did not wait to see his astonishment but turned and plunged down the path into the darkness.

He cursed as he came after her. Her chest ached from her frantic pace, but still that great lumbering creature drew near enough to seize her arm. Then, with a swift movement, he caught her with his leg and tripped her so that she fell headlong at his feet.

"Slime," he screamed at her. "Dirty, rotten slime."

He leaned over her in the darkness. She could feel his breath against her face. Then, as she watched, his face was

409

contorted as if with terror, and he stepped back rapidly, struggling to maintain his balance. He yowled with a cry like an animal before turning to plunge back towards the house with a drunken reeling gait.

She knew what had been in his mind. But he had won over his driving lust. How? What power did he have to outwit the frantic lust she had seen in his face. She shook her head. Whatever it was, thank you for it. She shuddered at the thought of his great fleshy hands on her. She had survived him again but only because his will was stronger than his passion. What was she to do? What in the name of God could she do to survive this man, to be free of him?

Chapter Sixty

Julie somehow reached the safety of her own room without encountering anyone. She closed her door behind her and leaned against it a long time, breathless with relief. Without even brushing the twigs and soil from her clothes she stretched out, face down, on her bed. From below, she could hear the soft clatter of dishes as the evening meal was being served. The smell of roasted meat and vegetables that usually whetted her appetite somehow sickened her.

The rap at the door announced that her own evening meal had been brought.

"I am not hungry," she told the slave who stood in the doorway with the napkin-covered tray.

"The master says you must eat," the girl replied, not meeting her eyes.

Julie shrugged. "All right, you may set it there."

The girl shook her head. "The master says I am to stay with you while you eat."

"Such touching concern." Resigned, Julie swung her feet off the bed and went to her basin to wash her hands while the girl arranged the food on the table by the window.

Julie sat before the table listlessly. "I will eat it, don't worry," she told the girl who stood stolidly just inside the door.

"He say that I stay and watch you eat it," the girl explained.

Julie shook her head in wonder. The wind of that man's madness blew all ways at once.

The melon soup was colorful with bits of bright scallion and cubes of sautéed bacon decorating the broth. Julie cut her meat and forced the bites down past the lump of anguish in her throat. The salad of mixed greens, dressed with spices and oils, blazed on her tongue.

But it was the tea that tasted really dreadful.

"Ach," Julie said after the first sip. "Whatever is this stuff?"

"Spring tea," the girl explained. "It is to keep off ague. We all drink it."

"You can all have it," Julie said, pushing the cup away.

The girl's expression grew pained. "If you don't eat and drink all on the tray, I am to go get the master," she warned.

Julie sighed and swallowed the bitter stuff in great, fast gulps. "Now am I through?" she asked crossly.

"Not my doing," the girl reminded her softly as she left with the tray.

Julie locked the door after her. The exertion of the encounter with Yves DuBois had left her drained and exhausted. Donning the lightest gown she had, she stretched out on the bed, hoping that the cool night air that swayed the curtains at her open window would stop the strange drumming in her head.

It was a dream and yet not a dream. Julie's consciousness registered the deepening of night, the last of the birdsong stilling and the first faint stars that shone beyond the window. The pounding of her heart seemed to grow louder and yet duller and be coming from somewhere outside her body. Drums. What had her aunt said about the drums? Never had they been so insistent and never had they seemed to beat at one with the steady throbbing of her own pulse.

Was it the outdoor air that bore that spicy fragrance into the room or was it her imagination? Julie strained to rise, to explore the strangeness in the dark room. A heaviness in her limbs weighed her down.

Battling against her terrible lassitude, she glanced towards the mirror. Something was moving in the glass. She stared at it fixedly, trying to get her heavy eyes to focus on that strange, moving shape. An orb about the size of a man's doubled fist seemed to be moving in the glass of the mirror. It glowed like copper and was brightly ornamented with colored beads and a chain that looked like tiny bones. Each time it moved, she felt as much as heard a faint hushed rattle in the air of the room.

"No," Julie whispered aloud to herself. "No." She was not seeing that toy in the darkened glass. She was dreaming. She was not being seized with the madness that obsessed her uncle. It was a dream. *"No,"* she screamed suddenly, roused by the quickening rhythm of the orb which was forcing her own heart to beat faster.

It was as if the sound of her voice broke a spell. The orb disappeared, leaving only the reflection of her bedpost and the curtains behind the bed moving. Moving?

There was somebody there.

With a moan of terror, Julie slid from her place and groped for the side of the bed, feeling for the floor with her bare foot.

She felt her gown being pulled up about her knees in her desperate effort to escape the bed. At the moment that she felt the reassuring hardness of the floor beneath both her feet, she was seized roughly and thrown back onto the mattress. She tried to cry out but her strength was inadequate. Rough hands seized her gown and jerked it up, looping it about her head like a shroud.

She was conscious of faintly damp human flesh against her own and the scrape of something cold and ropelike against her breasts. As she fought silently, this unseen creature threw his great weight upon her body and clawed her legs apart for a thrusting entry.

She cried aloud at the pain of this brutish rutting and clawed wildly at her attacker. Then she felt the weight of his body limp upon her, crushing her breathing. He was still arching in a strange aftermath of ecstasy when she recognized her uncle's voice through the folds of her gown.

"Bitch," he hissed. "Pawn of the devil, you have drawn me to this." He groaned heavily. "But you have not won. You have not won."

Julie could not speak. She was fighting even for the breath of life beneath his great weight. She prayed that he would stir, giving her the smallest chance to fill her pained lungs

412

Then, unexpectedly, his body stiffened against her own as if he were turned to stone.

A voice spoke softly in the room. It was a low and melodious voice with a faint haunting accent. It was a calm voice and seemed to come from a great distance and yet fill the room like the spicy fragrance.

"She has won," the voice said quietly.

"No, Tomala, no," Yves DuBois shouted. "Say no."

"She has won," the woman repeated calmly. "The spells you have sent against this spirit have brought back a shock in return. Else why would you have succumbed to this?"

Frantic for breath, Julie fought herself free of the folds of her gown as her uncle's body left hers. Gasping, Julie gulped the welcome air as her uncle rose and stood by the side of her bed. Except for the rope of tiny bones that was draped about his neck and chest, his great, flabby body was unclothed. His flesh shone with moisture like the soft underbelly of a freshly caught fish.

He seemed unconscious of her presence. He stared past her towards the head of her bed. As crazily as her eyes were behaving, as wildly as the drums kept beating in her mind, Julie was able to see the figure of a tall, handsome Negro woman in the mirror facing the bed. Her fine, shapely body was covered only by a loose, flowered skirt tied below her navel so that the rounded beauty of her hips and belly were not concealed. One arm rested on her hip while the other held the drape aside with an upraised hand. Her fine, high breasts gleaming with darkness in the room were draped with beads and talismans.

"*Baka*," she said ominously.

At the word, Julie saw her uncle bury his face in his hands and begin to sob like a child.

The woman moved into the room in a sinuous glide. With her graceful head erect, she stared at him with dark, shining eyes intent on his face. When she reached him, she clasped him to her naked breasts as if he were indeed a child.

"*Baka*," she insisted, still in a warning tone. Julie saw her strong arm stroke his back, and Tomala added, "but the *Baka* is easily fed."

Her uncle's sobbing stopped. He raised his head and stared searchingly at Tomala, then at Julie. A strange elation seemed to fill him.

413

"Ah," he cried. "Ah." Then he seized the Negress's hands and pressed them to his lips again and again. "The *Baka* is always hungry. You are right, Tomala, the *Baka* is easily fed."

As if disinterested in the terrified girl crouched on the bed, the woman walked to the window and looked out.

"The blood moon is coming soon," she said quietly. The scent of that spicy fragrance moved in the air as she walked past the bed, lifted the curtain, and was gone.

Only when the tremble of her passing had left the curtained wall did her uncle turn to look down at Julie. He shook his head with an expression that suggested pity.

"Poor, stupid vessel," he said. "You do not even know what spirit has used you to search me out." His tone grew plaintive.

"I have summoned all the magic that I knew against you, and still you were strengthened to possess me." He shook his head. "Now my own magic will serve against me unless you are sacrificed."

He leaned over and coolly drew his hand along the line of her bruised hip, as if savoring the feel of her pained flesh.

"Cherish your hours," he said. "The blood moon comes soon."

Julie, her whole body trembling, watched him bend to lift something from the floor. It was the orb she had seen in the mirror, the orb of a rattlelike object such as one would make for a child from a dried gourd. Without another glance at her, he passed her bed, lifted the curtain, and stepped into whatever blackness was hidden behind that wall. She heard the faint squeak of wood against wood and then silence.

It had to be a dream. It would have been a dream except that when the first faint rays of morning came through the window, Julie saw the loose, bright beads lying on the floor along with a length of small interlocking bones like the skeleton of a snake.

Racked by the pain of her assault, and still too drugged to do more than clutch her torn gown about her chilled body, she lay in a stupor as morning came brightly into the room.

Chapter Sixty-One

So rarely had Yves entered her bedchamber in these past ten years, that when Anne-Louise recognized his voice at her door, she laid down her brush to stare with puzzlement.

She flushed to realize that she was still in her dressing gown and somehow embarrassed that its soft folds exposed the lines of her body to this man who had been the father of her children.

"Come in," she said when she caught her breath from the surprise.

Only her long apprenticeship at concealing her true feelings kept a gasp of dismay from her lips. The Yves who stood in the doorway looked ages older than the same man she had dined with the night before.

"Come in," she urged in her customary controlled voice. "Be welcome." She waved him to a chair.

His face was haggard and unshaven. Across his right cheek ran a deep claw mark which gleamed with freshly dried blood. Although his shirt and trousers were immaculate, they had been carelessly donned, giving him an unaccustomed look of slothfulness.

"I have come to speak to you about your niece," he said, still standing just inside the door.

Anne-Louise gripped the edge of the dressing table. This was a twin to the scene she had labored to erase from her memory for the years just past. That other morning he had stood stiffly in the same place and said, "I have come to speak to you about your son."

To cover her trembling, she lifted the brush and turned away from him towards the mirror, drawing the brush slowly through the mass of her long, pale hair.

"She is not to leave her room without my permission," he said quietly. "And I will give no such permission."

Knowing that it would avail her nothing to ask questions, she continued to brush her hair while she waited.

"Her meals will be taken to her room as usual," he went

on. "But no one is to speak to her or have contact with her except the slaves."

She turned to look at him without allowing her expression to change.

"She is my brother's child," she reminded him.

"She is a creature saturated with evil," he said fiercely. "She is possessed of fiends and must not be let free in this house again."

She turned back to her mirror so that he might not be alerted to the design behind her words. "What if she grow frantic with loneliness and tries to destroy herself?"

She knew that she did not imagine his small start of surprise at this thought. Pressing her advantage, she said again, "After all, I am her father's sister."

He shrugged. "Very well, you may see her," he amended. "But only you and only one brief visit a day lest her evil spirits corrupt you even further."

When he was gone from the room, Anne-Louise finished dressing swiftly. With icy hands, she waited impatiently at the window watching his stallion being brought forth. She watched him mount and saw the beast disappear down the drive before hastening to Julie's room.

Even though she rapped many times softly, she could hear no answering call. Finally, she tried the knob and found it locked. She bent and called the girl's name through the key hole.

Yvonne, curious at the noise, came from her room to stand staring at her mother.

"I cannot waken your cousin," Anne-Louise told the child. "She must be sleeping like a baby."

"Polly said she must be dead," the child reported haughtily. "She brought her breakfast and banged and banged and could get no answer."

Anne-Louise stared at the child thoughtfully before turning to run swiftly downstairs to her husband's study. She paused at the door. It was a room she loathed and would never enter. Yves spent so much time closed up in the room that it air always carried a faint smell of Tomala's body, that spicy primitive odor that was too powerful a reminder of the agony that the black woman had brought into Anne-Louise's life.

She found the keys in the top dresser where he always threw them when coming in from his work. She lifted th heavy ring and searched among them. With the key between her fingers, she mounted the stairs and thrust it into the lock of Julie's door. At first she could not get it to go in. Then she heard the faint click as she dislodged the inside key and it dropped on the floor.

After a single glance at Juliette, she locked the door behind her. The child was curled in a strange position in the bed. Her lovely face was whiter than the sheet it rested against. The great mass of rich hair was tangled about her, as she slept shallowly with her lips a little agape as if she were too weak to draw proper air. A glance about the room confirmed Anne-Louise's worst fears.

"Merde!" she uttered fiercely, absorbing the fragments of the cursed voodoo rattle, the rumpled bed and torn nightdress, and the heavy scent of spilled sperm mingled with the cursed scent of Tomala.

"Batârd," she cursed softly, crossing to the bed. She pulled aside the heavy curtain behind the bed and cursed again. That miserable secret stair. Why had she been so quick to humor his ridiculous ideas? "An easy way to get to the children's room if they should need us," he had said.

"The bastard. The miserable, lusting, God-driven bastard."

Bending over Julie, she checked the child's pulse. After a quick intake of breath, she pulled the cover over the girl gently and left the room, locking it behind her.

After ordering the cook to brew strong coffee and a stop in her own bedroom, she returned to Julie's side.

With Julie's limp head against her arm, Anne-Louise held the strong salts to her niece's nose. Julie's head twisted wildly and then she gasped awake, coughing and with streaming eyes.

"Easy, my love," Anne-Louise told her. "Be easy. I have a drink coming for you."

Julie's eyes widened with fear. "Not tea," she protested. "Not any more of that bitter tea."

Anne-Louise's eyes narrowed in understanding. So that is how he brought it off. He had drugged her with one of those hideous native potions that Tomala made in her fine house out by the woods.

"This is coffee," Anne-Louise assured her. "My own brew. The maid will be along with it any minute."

With her face gently washed by her aunt, and with a few

sips of the scalding coffee down her throat, Julie showed signs of reviving. Her aunt, watching the color return to Julie's lovely face, finally asked, "What happened here last night?"

Julie lifted her golden eyes to her aunt and then they slid away. How could she reply? How could she tell this dear relative that her husband had come in the night with his heathen toys and raped her?

Julie shook her head distractedly. "At first I thought it was a dream."

"You were drugged," her aunt said shortly.

Julie's voice kept stumbling in the telling and a flush of scarlet rose in her cheeks at the memory of her uncle's great, hideous body pressed tightly against her own. Anne-Louise's face was stoical.

"Tomala," she said thoughtfully. "Then Tomala too was here."

When Julie nodded, her aunt sat very still for a long time, then she sighed. "I should have known. But even if I had thought he could be such a beast, what could I have done?"

"I don't understand," Julie told her. "He is convinced that I am the pawn of some spirit and I have been sent to destroy him."

Anne-Louise nodded. "The old voodoo belief. From what you have told me I guess that he has worked all his primitive magic against his lusting for you and failed. When his passion overcame him, he drugged you, thinking in that twisted mind that by possessing you he could both satisfy his lust and control you. Then Tomala came."

"Does her coming make a difference?" Julie asked. "She terrified him by mentioning *Baka*. What is *Baka*?"

Her aunt nodded sadly. "It matters because Tomala wants no one to have control over him but herself. I cannot pretend to understand all that wild ritual of theirs, but I do know that *Baka* is an evil spirit—a very evil spirit."

"And he is always hungry," Julie added, watching her aunt's face.

Anne-Louise turned away. She could not let the child see the despair in her face. The blood moon was only a few weeks distant. What would it profit Julie to know that a *Baka* could be fed only by the living sacrifice?

"I am a prisoner in this room," Julie told her. "If what I

418

remember was not a dream, I shall be a prisoner in this room until I am sacrificed on the night of the blood moon."

"Don't even let your mind accept that," Anne-Louise said with tears in her eyes. "I will do all in the world to help you. But do not despair, my love, do not despair."

As she closed the door behind her, Anne-Louise wished she were able to follow her own good counsel. She was halfway down the stairs when she paused and stayed a long time in thought.

Would there be enough time? Would Mrs. MacRae be able to find the woman's name and get some information from her? Would that person seeking the golden-eyed girl care enough to brave a band of armed and fanatical Negroes serving a priest they feared?

She was still standing there, twisting her hands together absently when Pierre passed her on the stairs.

"Where are you off to?" she asked, noting that he was wearing his dress coat and good, new breeches.

"It is my day for the tutor," he replied with disdain in his voice as if she were a fool for asking.

She managed a bright laugh. "I guess I had forgotten what day of the week it was. I wonder if I have time to prepare myself to go along."

Her son shrugged. "If Perry is free to go with you," he said mockingly.

She stiffened her stance and stared at the boy. He was the devil's own seed, that one. "Perry has nothing better to do than to be where I am," she said sweetly.

Chapter Sixty-Two

Julie, confined to her second-story prison, unable to face in her mind the constant threat of the door behind the blue-draped wall, numbly watched the days pass. She was conscious of the peaceful routine of the house, the regular passage of the maids, the muffled domestic sounds. How could such normalcy exist about her while her own heart was torn by storms of rage and terror?

Even her Aunt Anne-Louise seemed impervious to the anguish of her predicament. She came daily only to sit and chat almost idly of the garden or the weather. Julie, watching her with eyes that were steadily more hostile, sensed a strange excitement in her aunt. It was almost as if Anne-Louise's tedious conversation was a screen thrown up between them to hide her own real thoughts. A glistening brightness to her aunt's eyes, the animation of her speech made Julie wonder if some perverse madness in her aunt did not find relish in the horror that came closer with each day.

The flowers her aunt brought faded in the bowl and were replaced by new offerings. "My God," Julie cried to herself, "all things measure time, and all the measurements end in death."

The woman who cleaned the room daily was called Rody. Like the other slaves who brought the food or the hot water for her bath, Rody would not meet her eyes. Yet Julie felt that in some unrealized way the woman was her friend. The other slaves wore a uniform look of dull terror while they were in the room. It was as if they felt that her approaching ordeal was a disease that they would contract from the air in the room. How much did they know of her predicament, she wondered. She longed to see Mandy once again. She had been Mandy's friend during that brief time they had together. She comforted herself that Mandy would not have looked away from her with that paleness about the lips that the others wore.

One day as Rody was cleaning the room, Julie turned from her window to see the girl dabbing vigorously at the corner of the ceiling with a cloth held on the end of her mop.

"What are you doing?" Julie asked.

"Anansi," the girl answered, prodding at the wall.

Curious, Julie went and drew the girl's mop away. Then she remembered. Mandy had told her this story during their time together. And sure enough, in the smallest corner of the ceiling crouched a tiny, black spider. How pitiful and beseiged it looked, trapped like herself in a small corner of a threatening world.

"Leave it be," Julie told Rody.

"But it is Anansi," the girl protested. "Your people despise and fear Anansi."

"Anansi was once human like us," Julie told her. "I do not fear or despise him. Leave him be. He is my brother."

After that, Rody was clearly terrified of Julie, watching with fearful eyes this woman who was protector of the creature who festooned the ceiling with ropes of webbing that caught the dust and trailed silk in the air. Julie saw her terror but she didn't care. She cared about nothing but the changes of the moon that she watched from her window.

She had been an idle fancier of the moon all her life. She remembered returning from the village or an errand with her father when the early moon rose above Middlesex. His warm body had been firm against her back as she rested against him. Sometimes, she had watched it rise from behind the great yews along their drive, fancying that it was a brighter child who climbed those trees to free itself into the sky. She had watched the slim moon crescent above Epping Wood and had lain in Antoine's arms when its rays made a path of light across their tangled limbs, and there had been that moon-born ladder of light she had watched from the railing of the *Tilbury Belle*. But now of a sudden, there was no idleness in her attention to that ominous brightness. The changing moon was as closely linked to her existence as the drawing of her own breath.

The first night of her prisonment, she had seen it rise as a slender melon slice with a witchlike profile facing north. It shrunk in the nights to follow until it disappeared altogether, leaving the sky to the brilliance of stars who came earlier and brighter without its light to challenge them.

She decided that it was a measure of herself growing mad that she toyed with the hope that it would never come again. She tried to imagine what consternation would come if the moon disappeared from the world, like a comet gone forever to become only a tale told by old grannies to young children.

But return it did and with its face turned the other way. Now it was a giant fingernail paring curved to her left. Her childhood Latin lessons came back to her mind; the very word *left* meant sinister.

With the return of the moon, the drums which had fallen silent began to pulse again. Like a hapless prey who cannot remove its gaze from the eye of its enemy, Julie stared into the woods watching the glint of torches as the drums rose and fell at the vagary of the wind.

Julie's were not the only eyes that watched the lunar changes with growing dread. But Anne-Louise still had that

421

one slim thread of hope that sustained her. She found her palms moist as she moved about the household and chanced to pass her husband unexpectedly. She felt tremors of fear when she saw his eyes rest speculatively on her face. He could know nothing, but what had he guessed? Her desperate efforts to appear even more calm than usual lent her movements an awkwardness that she knew his shrewd eyes did not miss.

She needed to make only one more trip to Charles Town and visit with Mrs. MacRae to make this hope turn into a possible solution for Juliette. Mrs. MacRae's delicate search had yielded the name of the woman who was actively seeking the golden-eyed girl. It had also yielded the astonishing fact that the girl being sought was known by the name Julie.

The only reason that Anne-Louise had not at once prevailed on Mrs. MacRae to appeal to the woman to make some effort to free Julie from her uncle was that Mrs. MacRae had, at the same time, been told that a madman was behind the search, a man of great strength and ruthlessness who had stormed through the colonies in his search. Anne-Louise remembered the tale of Julie's supposed murdering of young Louis and was afraid. Yves had not yet had his fatal encounter with Julie. Anyone, anything that would release Julie from her approaching fate could only be better. Anne-Louise memorized the words she would say to Mrs. MacRae. She tried to prepare herself for the appeal that she must make that would reveal to this gentle woman the horror of her own life.

One more trip was all she needed, and then she could only pray that whoever sought Julie wanted her badly enough to confront the crazed, voodoo-driven Negroes under Yves's control.

On the night before Pierre's next appointment with his tutor, Anne-Louise grew conscious of her husband's eyes studying her during dinner.

"Is there something?" she asked, raising her gaze to his.

He chewed his food deliberately, his pale eyes thoughtful on her. "Nothing of any importance," he said. "But I did want to mention that you do not need to accompany Pierre to Charles Town on another of these little jaunts that Perry tells me you have enjoyed during my absence."

How did he know? My God, how had he guessed that this errand meant more than her own life to her at this point?

She braced her arm against the table to control the sudden trembling that seized her. Forcing herself to remain expressionless, she took another serving of food on her plate even though the few bites she had swallowed lay like a stone below her belt.

She cut the fruit carefully, separating the stone from the flesh and laying it aside.

"Have you no comment?" he asked finally.

She raised her eyes to his. "What comment did you have in mind?"

"I had thought perhaps that you had made plans to visit this new friend of yours—this Scotswoman," he said, his expression still watchful.

She shrugged. "So I had, but it is easy enough to send a note of apology. And I only had one important errand other than having tea with her."

"What errand is that?" he asked.

She smiled. "Woman's things—matching thread for sewing and selecting some silks to finish a pattern."

"Surely these things can wait," he suggested acidly.

"The silk can for sure," she agreed easily. "And as for the sewing thread, it will do no harm to let Hannah stay idle for a few days. She works very hard and probably needs some rest."

"We do not keep slaves for resting," he said.

She shrugged. "Nor do we have a seamstress who can join cloth without thread." Her look was level on his.

"It occurs to me that your management of this household grows less efficient by the day."

"I am sorry that it seems so to you," she said quietly. "I simply forget how fast Hannah's needle flies."

"Surely the mistress of a great house does not need to paddle about town on such mean errands. Couldn't one of the slaves pick up those things for you?"

She stared at him thoughtfully, her heart racing. "Perry?" she asked innocently.

"God in heaven, woman," he exploded. "You would take a strong man from his work to run some piddling female errand for spools of thread? Send one of that pack of lazy housemaids. That Amanda who does nothing but shuffle backwards and stare when I pass her."

Anne-Louise managed a soft laugh. "She is shy and awkward but she is learning. She would probably do as well as any."

"I will write a pass for her," he said gruffly. You have your list together by the time Pierre is due to leave. She could take your apologies along to that widow too I guess."

She nodded and pressed the bell beneath the table. "Perhaps your master would like more coffee," she suggested when the slave appeared beside her. She did not accept any more in her own cup lest Yves see the trembling of her hands.

The next morning, her visit to Juliette set a great strain on her. How she yearned to tell the girl of the desperate plans she was making. Yet she dare not. Not only did the curtained wall hold some threat of their being spied upon, but it would be unfair to raise Juliette's hope for a reprieve which now seemed suddenly less likely to materialize. Her mind kept straying to what she must do before it was time for Pierre to leave. She glanced up, realizing that Juliette was singularly silent, her great golden eyes cool and curious on her face. Anne-Louise rose awkwardly and took the girl's unresponsive hands in her own. "Do not despair, my dear," she said softly. "Please try not to despair."

Juliette's cheek was cool against her own. She made no reply, only turned her face away as if in rejection.

By the time the trap was brought to the door, Mandy was waiting in the shadow of the porch. Her face and hands were polished from scrubbing, and her hair was carefully plaited into a legion of tiny pigtails. Over her dress she wore an apron so white that it was blinding against her dark skin.

As Pierre came out of the house, Yves followed him. Mandy's arms tightened perceptibly against her sides at his approach.

"Do you know what you are to do?" Yves asked the girl.

She nodded vigorously and patted her pocket.

At his frown, she would have reached for it but he was too quick for her. He grabbed her by the arm and pulled out not one note but two. He read the detailed list with the samples of colors carefully tacked to the edge. Then he unwrapped the second note with a fierce look at Anne-Louise.

She watched him read the message, once and then again, and turn the paper over to examine it. "Have you been given any other mesage?" he asked roughly.

The slave's eyes were white rimmed as she nodded at him.

"What message?" he asked.

"Mistress say to tell her—" The girl paused, stammering from fear.

Yves hand was cruel on her arm. "Your mistress said to a say what?"

The words came out all at once. "She say tell lady she hope she be able to come again soon."

Yves's grip on the girl relaxed so that she staggered backwards against the trap. "Very well," he growled, turning away. "You be sure to be at the tutor's on the hour or you'll taste the whip. Do you understand?"

She was still nodding vigorously as she scrambled onto the trap beside the driver.

"Half-wit," he muttered as the trap clattered down the drive.

"If she had a whole wit you would have scared it out of her," Anne-Louise commented mildly.

"You have given me little reason to trust you," he said starting for the door.

"What could I do if I wished?" she asked blandly.

He cursed and slammed the door behind him.

Julie felt some small guilt as her aunt left her room that morning with a small pinch of hurt about her mouth. It didn't matter. What could possibly matter? Her aunt had chattered like a magpie saying nothing, her mind obviously in some other place. Her aunt had abandoned her; it was as simple as that. Her words and gestures were as affectionate as ever, but in her heart her aunt had withdrawn from her, unable to face what was happening. How could she expect other than this, remembering the coolness with which she had told her of Jacques's absence. "He is no longer of this household."

It simply didn't matter. There was a day left, possibly two or three, but the moon was swelling nightly in the sky like some loathsome thing inflated with disease, growing closer to that full, glowing circle that would be the blood moon.

"What are you like?" her aunt had asked her that first day hands. She had tried, in her flight from her uncle's house; The answer she had given had surprised even herself. Only when the words had sprung from her lips did she realize that indeed she had never taken her life firmly into her own hands. She had tried, in her flight from her uncle's house, when she had made a choice against betraying Antoine; she had even made a positive and dreadfully wrong choice not to stay with Josh. But all these choices had been forced on her by the traps in which she had fallen. And not the least of these traps had been her hopeless devotion to Antoine. And there was no Antoine. Antoine had died before the *Tilbury Belle* had left Gravesend. She envied him.

The bloated moon heaved over the trees and laid a pattern of light on the stoned drive beneath her window. She stared at that pathway and her golden eyes narrowed. She envied him and it was time to claim her life as her own.

It would be so easy from this place. Simply to leap out might not do the job. There was always the chance that she would survive the fall on the stones below and only add fresh pain to what she was enduring. But there was Antoine's way. She rummaged in the chest and found the old gown that Anne-Louise had provided her on her arrival. She tested the fabric with her hands and found the hemming too strong. When she clipped the hem with her embroidery scissors the soft fabric tore along its length into long strong strips.

Three of the strips plaited made a sturdy rope. For once, the moon rose without her help. Her fingers worked steadily until the rope was the height of a man and as strong as a plaited rein. On this she would dance as Antoine had done. No bells from Saint Sepulchre, only the drums of the voodoo and the cry of night birds from the endless woods.

Very early, when she had yet to lay her eyes on her monster uncle, her aunt Anne-Louise had warned her that this man could crawl into her mind and read her thoughts. When she had heard those words, Julie thought them the deranged words of a woman frantic with the loss of her prime. With the plan of her own self-destruction full in her mind, Julie lay with the plaited rope hidden beneath her body waiting for the deep of night, praying that her aunt had been wrong.

It was only because she was waiting so intently that she heard the faint screech of the door to the hidden stairway slide open. She was instantly on her feet and across the room to conceal herself in the darkness by the door. The door itself was now useless to her, being locked from the outside and her own key gone.

Only as the spicy scent assailed her did she remember the rope that she had left behind her. The gibbous moon, swelling towards its fullness, layered the room with light. She watched Tomala glide silently into that light, her bare breasts gleaming. She saw the flash of the woman's long, fine legs as her skirt parted as she walked. She saw her lean and lift the braided rope from the bed and turn it curiously in the light.

"Your bird plans flight," she said quietly. "She would steal your offering from under your nose."

Only then did Julie's eyes make out her uncle's great body in the shadows of the curtained wall. She cringed against the door. If she could see him, how much easier would he be able to see her, clad as she was in the filmy white gown Hannah had made for her.

His answer was a low, throaty curse as he moved swiftly across the moonlight and caught her by the arm. Her struggle only netted bruised flesh as he held her tightly against the wall while Tomala ripped the clothes from her with strong sure hands.

"Chains," he ordered, and Tomala slipped from the room. In the black woman's absence Julie's uncle held her against the wall, his moist flesh sickening against her. "Slut," he kept repeating. "You thought to escape me, didn't you, slut? And leave me damned for all eternity. But I knew—I knew."

They chained her to the bedpost, arms outspread and legs wide apart like a beast for slaughter. "Oh God," she moaned quietly as the chains cut into the flesh of her ankles.

"You dare to call God," he whispered fiercely. Then he leaned over her, his great, white belly a mass quivering above her, his flesh whiter than the snake bones that swayed in the air, brushing her breasts. Then he spat full in her face. She felt his hot spittle ooze down her cheek and gather in a sickening pool at her throat.

Anne-Louise came with morning. At the first sight of her niece she staggered towards a chair, her face covered by her hands, seized with a despair past tears.

"Why?" she asked in a whisper more powerful than a scream. "Why? Why? Why?"

427

"I planned to kill myself," Julie said numbly. "Somehow he knew."

Then Anne-Louise's tears came. With her head bent on the side of that loathsome bed, she cried until there were no tears left. He was a demon. He had read the child's mind even as he had caught the scent of her conspiracy with Mrs. MacRae before she could bring it to fruit. With Juliette chained like a beast to this bed, there was no hope left, no hope at all. The careful message that she had drilled into Mandy's terrified mind had been to no avail. All hope was gone.

She felt a movement on the bed. Juliette's hand was trying to reach out to her, to comfort her. She took the girl's delicately formed hand and pressed it against her wet cheek.

There was one day, one single day more before the blood moon would rise, full and round and deadly.

Chapter Sixty-Three

It had been late winter when Josh had left her at Mrs. Mac-Rae's. The moon that rose was the full moon of May—Yves DuBois's blood moon.

She had gone from the freedom of the plantation, a cherished guest at her aunt's side, to a chained prisoner whose whole view of the world was a mirror, a stretch of wall, and a window, tightly closed, whose curtain hung spiritless at its sides.

The air in the room was still fouled by the scent of Tomala which lingered through that long day. There was not even enough movement in the air of the room to stir the dust-laden strands of Anansi's abandoned webs. From under the light coverlet with which her aunt had covered her nakedness, Julie watched the blue day fade to streaks of stranded color. Fused color was drawn across her line of sky like scarves trailed by a careless dancer.

Was it her imagination that each night the moon rose later, as if reluctant to begin its heaving journey across that same arc of sky?

The house held that same ominous stillness that had disturbed Julie on the first night of her arrival at this place. But

428

still the world went on outside this house. She heard the muffled hooves of horses on the drive below and what sounded like the trap being driven away. Once, faintly, she heard the plaintive call of a whippoorwill from a tree near the house.

She heard the drums begin before she even saw the moon. They began in a low insistent cadence. Their slow, steady pulsing brought a line of moisture across her upper lip.

Then she saw it, the curved arc of rose rising above the jagged roof of the forest. She had to strain her neck painfully to watch, but she could not draw her eyes from that perfect orb that flowed slowly up into the sky until its last edge broke from the tops of the trees and it hung, paling and shadowed on the horizon.

"Quickly," she prayed silently. "Let it be done quickly."

In spite of the quickening pulse of the drums, Julie felt a strange lassitude flow over her. It was over. If not over completely, it was so near done that no anguish, no flailing against her fate would serve any purpose. She let her head drop back and closed her eyes.

She heard muffled steps coming nearer. She did not stir as she heard the faint sound of the door behind the tapestried wall being pushed aside. She heard her uncle's voice, low and hoarse.

"She has to be alive."

A cold draft struck her as her covering was jerked away. She felt her uncle's thick hand drawn across her flesh, over her breasts and down the line of her belly to linger a moment on its warmth.

His voice vibrated with relief. "She lives. The chains, Perry."

Her gasp was involuntary. She could not open her eyes to the humiliation of the men working over her, loosing the chains from the aching flesh of her ankles and wrists. She caught her lip between her teeth to hold back a cry as someone seized her raw wrist and dragged her to her feet. Only when something coarse that smelled of smoke and earth was wrapped about her did she open her eyes.

Her uncle, with his arms crossed on his belly, stood at the window watching her. It was Perry whose hands braced her as she swayed unsteadily on her feet. When she caught at the rough cape and struggled to close it about her nakedness, her uncle chuckled softly at her discomfiture.

"Get hold of yourself, wench. Nobody means to carry you."

The stairway secreted within the walls was spiral. Weakened by her confinement, Julie could barely negotiate the narrow stairs one at a time. They seemed to descend forever, past narrow doors like the one she had first been thrust through, and finally into a passage whose ceiling was so low that Perry walked in a crouch to avoid striking his head on the raw timber of its roof.

The passage smelled of earth. The timbers which supported it were stained with age. When it came to an end suddenly, Perry raised his hands and forced open a trapdoor in its roof. A flood of clean, cold outdoor air poured in about Julie as the big Negro sprang out and reached down to seize her by the wrists and pull her up after him. When her uncle, grunting, scrambled out after her, he clapped an evil-smelling hood over her head, shutting out the varying shades of the night wood and the moon, now riding high above the trees.

Her brief glimpse of her surroundings had shown her a clearing like many she had walked through. She sensed they were west and a little north of the plantation house, but she knew this judgment came more from the nearness of the drums than by any real sense of direction.

The trail she was shoved along was rough. Her bare feet recoiled from the prickle of pine needles, but this was no logging trail. It was narrower and uncluttered with the fragments of torn limbs that marked those trails.

They were nearing the drums. In among the rises and fallings of that rhythm, Julie could hear voices, chanting and moaning and making strange hollow sounds like animal cries.

Only the relentless hands of her uncle kept her moving along that trail. Her feet seemed to have acquired a wilful stubbornness of their own, refusing to carry her towards the rising sound of the drums. Finally, his voice raw with irritation, Yves DuBois snapped an order at Perry who seized her and dragged her along the path.

The intensity of sound about her was overwhelming. The drums seemed to be beating inside her own skin, and the cries and moans of many voices seemed closer than her own breath. Her heart was fluttering so wildly in her breast that

430

she fought for air, feeling that her consciousness was a physical thing that she must grip with her mind or be lost.

In a single instant, the hood was pulled from her head and the drums stopped. Fire. She was so near the giant fire that her naked flesh turned rose in its light. It rose in scarlet tongues above the trees that circled the clearing. A sea of black faces circled her. Their eyes shone with light and their half-naked bodies glistened as they stood immobile watching the pillars of flame lick up the giant tree.

She did not at once see Tomala among so many. But within a moment, the drum began again, a slow, single roll of sound that was sinuous and low. Then Tomala emerged from behind the great flaming tree. She walked with that same easy grace, one slender foot and ankle set before the other, knees a little bent so that with each step the long, brightly-colored skirt she wore separated, revealing her well-shaped, mahogany-colored leg bare to the hip.

One arm was upraised and the other fondling something at her hip. A long, faint sigh rose from the watching faces as Tomala moved slowly in perfect time to the rhythm of the drums.

As she neared, her eyes fixed on Julie's own, Julie could not drag her own gaze from that cold, terrifying face. Then a faint sound sent a ripple of fear along Julie's spine, and she realized that the object Tomala was caressing was a giant serpent. The creature was twined about her body, its head held aloft by her jewelled arm. The body of the snake was as thick as a man's arm. It writhed about Tomala's swaying body, turning its flat head from side to side, the quick, split thread of its tongue darting in and out beneath gleaming, leaden eyes.

"No," Julie screamed. "No. No. No." She recoiled, but Perry's hands held her fast.

As if her scream were a signal, the drums changed to a rapid tempo and the circle of bodies about her began to move. Julie flailed against Perry's grip on her as the dancers moved about and against her. Their faces were contorted with some obscene ecstasy, their heads were thrown forward and back as if they were not even connected to their moving bodies, and she felt the smooth oiliness of their flesh press and slide against her own. The hiss of the serpents that they bore sounded in the air all about her.

"No. No. No," she continued to scream, feeling the helplessness of hysteria pounding in her chest and head.

It seemed impossible that the drums could beat faster. Yet they did, steadily whipping the dancer's bodies into wild contortions in time to their beat. Only one figure failed to respond to the furious demands of that music. He smiled as he moved towards her on solid, slow steps. The dancers parted to make an open path for him. Her uncle, his great, pale body wreathed with beads and feathered ornaments, those evil bones in great chains, his head crowned with a towering, bright turban of feathers and bright stones. He moved towards her smiling the most vicious grin she had ever seen on a human face. His eyes were intent on her own, and his thick lips curled in derision and triumph. The smoke of the fire seemed drawn to him, circling his head, fusing her view of his face so that only his eyes held hers.

Then a movement at his waist broke the spell. About his belly was looped a great, colorful snake whose scales were patterned in diamonds of mingled colors.

For a mad moment, she conceived that for him, the serpent, with its broad, flat head erect and swaying, was his own manhood. His eyes blazed with lust as he thrust the belly forward at her, the snake's quick tongue licking for her flesh.

She strained backwards from Perry's grip on her. She felt the pain of her own screaming against the frenzy of the drums and the wailing of savage cries about her. The very earth beneath her feet seemed suddenly alive with a new and violent rhythm.

Something touched her with the swift pain of a needle thrust against her belly. A fan of pain spread from that place, and the flames and her uncle's triumphant face began to blur in her sight. She fought to hold onto her failing consciousness as her legs failed beneath her and she felt herself falling.

But even as she fell, her eyes still wide and screams tearing from her throat, she had a mad vision that her mind discounted even as she observed it. She saw her uncle's lascivious face grow slack with astonishment and then fear. The moans and cries of the dancers turned to anguished screams like her own. And there were horses, great, round flanks of dark horses whose hooves stamped on the fleeing communicants. Their riders were hooded, and the loose, full robes that they wore shipped in the air as they swung over the fleeing, howling Negroes who fled madly from their swinging clubs.

There was blood everywhere, scarlet in the light of the forgotten fire. She saw her uncle grasp at the snake that encircled him. She saw his hands struggle to wrest the snake from about his body. She saw the flat head of the snake whip up from between her uncle's thighs and strike, again and again, at the broad, white chest above his heart. Then the snake, freed from his grasp, fell into the darkness. As she felt its cold folds pass swiftly over her own body, all consciousness left.

PART VIII
THE BURNISHED ANGEL
Mid-May, 1723-July, 1723

Chapter Sixty-Four

If she could only keep her body still, she felt that the unrelenting drumbeat of pain in her head might lessen. But her body arched painfully, and her arms and legs flailed and twitched of their own volition, driving quick stabs of agony through her fevered brain. Perhaps it was the pain itself that hung between herself and the real world. There were people there. She narrowed her eyes at their shadowy shapes, but the blur hid them from being realized in her mind. They spoke and moved about, but the words and the sounds of their passing were muffled by that same fevered veil.

Because of the pain and the nausea that rose in her throat, she fought whatever ministrations they attempted. She flailed against their restraining hands and tightened her lips, jerking her head from side to side against the cold fluid that they forced between her teeth to spill and run down the fevered flesh of her breasts. But they were stronger than she, and she felt the bitterness of their fluid taken into her body in great, painful gulps, and in time she slept.

Dimly, she knew that same pattern was repeated again and again: that she was given coolness in her throat, and that sleep came and sleep passed, and that the flames that seemed to consume her flesh abated, leaving only weakness.

Her hearing returned first. A tapestry of birdsong grew even louder than the frantic, irregular beating of her own heart. It registered in her mind that these were small birds, that swift kind of small bird that twitched in the bushes of the gardens at her father's house. Then the cooling draft of air moved across her face, and she found it to be scented faintly of flowers. And she heard laughter.

Julie opened her eyes in astonishment. When had she last heard laughter like that, a small child giggling with merriment and then the bark of a playful dog?

Her vision was still hazy. By narrowing her eyes and studying a single spot for a long time, she was able to see that a window was opened on a dark blue sky. White curtains billowed and fell limp again from the vagaries of the breeze. As if strengthened by her will, her eyes grew stronger as they explored the room where she lay. It was a large, pale room with delicate appointments in gold against the cream walls. The petals of the slender iris by her bed were the same deep blue as the sky beyond the long window.

Impossible. Suddenly, pressed between the peace and elegance of her surroundings and her own eyes came the face of her uncle contorted in pain as a serpent's head struck again and again at the broad, white plain of his chest.

She covered her eyes to block out that phantom and fought back a scream. She lay a long time with her eyes closed, leaning on the comfortable darkness inside her lids.

Dimly, she heard a door open and knew she was no longer alone. She pulled her hands from her eyes and opened them with apprehension.

She could not focus on him at once, but after a moment she realized that the figure in the door was a child. The boy looked to be about eight or ten. He had thick, caramel-colored hair that waved carelessly about a thoughtful face. He was staring at her from eyes so richly colored that they made her think at once of something warm and spicy to eat. Under his knee pants, his rounded calves betrayed an appealing sturdiness, and there was a streak of dirt along the ruffled edge of his collar.

When he smiled suddenly, she was instantly convinced that it was his laughter which she had heard during her slow wakening. When he spoke, she was even more certain.

"You feel better now, mademoiselle?" he asked. He was just tall enough to stand at the side of her bed and stare directly into her face. As he did so, his generous mouth widened in a sudden grin that sparkled with delight.

"Buttercups," he said in a tone of discovery. "How come you have eyes the same as buttercups?"

She laughed weakly and grinned back at him. More than anything, she wanted to reach out and touch him, but she was too afraid that he might be startled away.

"And how come your eyes are the color of ginger cakes?" she asked in return.

He laughed. "Ginger cakes. Like ginger cakes with tea." Then he leaned closer. "Are you too hot?" He frowned with concern. "You have sweat on your face." Unselfconsciously he pulled his shirt loose from his pants and wiped the line of moisture from her forehead. "There," he said with satisfaction. "That's a lot better." He did not repair his clothing but left his shirttail hanging out in a smeared point over his dark pants.

"Thank you, my dear," she said softly. "That is much better."

"My name is Charles," he corrected her. "After my grandfather whose name is Charles too."

He pronounced the name in the French manner, softly, like a child being hushed.

"How do you do," she said soberly. "My name is Julie."

"I know," he said. Then his face brightened. "Is it all right for me to run again in the hall now? Sally said that I couldn't run in the house when death hung over it."

A gasp from the door caused Charles to whirl about quickly.

"She was awake," he said defensively, "I didn't hurt her at all."

The tall, black woman crossed the room quietly. The concern on her face was softened by her smile at the child. "I know you would not hurt her, Master Charles," she said gently. "It is only that mademoiselle has been very sick for a long time and you must not exhaust her."

"She likes me," he told her firmly. Then he paused and frowned. "You do like ginger cakes, don't you?"

Julie laughed softly. "I adore ginger cakes."

"You see, Master Charles? You have a new friend who likes you. Now trot along and let your new friend grow strong enough to rise from this bed."

"*A bientôt*," he promised from the door. His feet pounded down the hall and Julie laughed softly.

"You are better," the woman said with satisfaction. She laid a silken hand on Julie's forehead and then laid it a moment on her throat beneath the tangled hair. She nodded. "The fever is gone. You can see again and hear our voices?"

Julie nodded. "But I don't know where I am or how I came here. Who is that lovely child, and who are you?"

"You are at the Bontemps plantation," the woman answered levelly, turning away to the dresser. She returned with a basin and a soft cloth. "Here, let me cleanse your face. I am called Sally. And Master Charles is indeed a lovely child." She deftly wiped Julie's face and drew the warm cloth along her throat. "Where is your pain?"

"Everywhere," Julie confessed. When Sally carefully lifted her arm to push back the full sleeve of her nightdress, Julie cried out involuntarily.

"I am sorry," Sally said quietly. "I must look at your wound."

Julie watched the woman's face as she unbuttoned the front of the nightdress clear to Julie's waist. She stared closely at Julie's waist where the worst pain was and then straightened, apparently satisfied with what she saw.

"What is it?" Julie asked, unable to see what the woman had examined.

Sally's face darkened. "The bite of a serpent," she said quietly. "It is in a bad place but the redness is going away." Her hands moved swiftly to Julie's buttons.

"But what happened? How did I come here?" Julie pressed.

"You tire yourself with much talking," Sally told her firmly. "That same venom from the serpent that made you blind and unable to hear makes it hard to keep food down. Do you think you could eat now?"

"I feel like trying," Julie admitted. "And I flame with thirst."

"It will only be a few moments," Sally promised her as she let herself out.

Alone in the room, Julie listened to the sounds of the house. Someone was playing a stringed instrument far off. The melody rose and fell plaintively with the wind. She heard Charles calling outside along with the bark of a dog and that burst of rippling laughter again.

Before Julie's exhausted mind would face the questions that Sally had left unanswered, the woman had returned with broth and warmed bread and a pot of sweet, rich tea which sent Julie into drowsiness with the cup still at her lips.

When she awakened again, it was morning.

The woman standing at the window had her back to Julie. At first it seemed that another phantom had come to her. That tall, fashionably dressed figure seemed completely out of place in this rough world. Her elegant dress was of a deep, rich green with panniers of a paler shade. A carefully curled, white wig crowned her slender neck. On the hand which

440

rested lightly on the chair back, Julie caught the glint of light from an emerald-set ring.

Julie must have gasped without knowing it for the woman turned at once.

"Good morning and welcome, Julie Duvall," she said, smiling as she crossed the room. Her voice was low and throaty, almost deep enough to be a man's voice. Although she was clearly a beautiful woman, there was a difference to the lineaments of her face that struck Julie at once. There was a certain lift to the corner of her eyes and a twist to her lips that suggested . . . It did, Julie told herself defensively. . . . That face suggested mischief. How could this woman attired as if for the finest society of London, and wigged as for a fancy ball, manage to present a face as impish as a rowdy child?

"Good morning, madame," Julie said, trying to struggle up in the bed. The woman shook her head reprovingly.

"Here," she said. "Let me help you."

Deftly, she braced Julie's body while tugging the lace-trimmed pillows up behind her back.

"There," she said, stepping back to admire her handiwork. "It is better now. Tell me how you are. Is the pain gone? Can you see me clearly?"

"Yes, yes," Julie stammered. Then she tried, "Mistress—" she began.

A low, throaty chuckle interrupted her, and the woman shook her head. Her dark blue eyes almost disappeared into the dark brush of her lashes when she laughed. "I know what comes to your tongue, my dear. You are dying to know how you came here and why you are here and what is next and all those busy questions. Sally told me that you had asked many questions on your moment of waking. But we must take things in their proper order. And the next thing is breakfast."

Julie watched her step to the door, speak to someone in the hall, and return to draw a chair near the side of her bed.

"There," she said happily, plumping herself down in the chair. "I have waited to have breakfast with you. I do so hate to eat alone and Charles—" She made a grimace.

"I have met Charles," Julie told her. "He is a love."

She glowed at Julie's words. "Thank you, my dear. But he

441

is also exhausting. An exhausting love. It is much nicer that we have our first meal together alone."

"I am Sophie Bontemps and I had you kidnapped."

Julie felt her eyes fly wide at the woman's words. But Sophie Bontemps grinned puckishly, enjoying her surprise.

"But how? Why?" Julie asked when she caught her breath.

Her hostess shrugged. "With the help of many others, I must admit. Your aunt, Anne-Louise DuBois, and her friend, that nice little Scotswoman named MacRae reached me with word of your dreadful plight. My own slaves knew of the dread things that went on at Monde DuBois or I would have thought the whole story was a mad fabrication." She grinned happily like a child reciting the tale of an escapade.

"We all worked together and broke up the party." She grinned wickedly for a second before a shadow of regret crossed her face. "My people were not so quick as they wished, or you would not have been struck by that serpent and brought so near death."

Julie's hand moved towards the painful place beneath her gown and Sophie nodded.

"Ben thinks it was a copperhead, a very venomous snake, but it could have been what they call here a rattler too. In any case, it was my man Ben who slit you with a knife that he might draw the venom out before it chilled your blood. He had to have you free of your uncle's place before he could minister to you and it was almost too long.

"You will wear that star-shaped scar to your grave," she added regretfully after a moment.

"To a much later grave," Julie reminded her softly.

"As to why I kidnapped you," she leaned forward and winked at Julie. "Let us say that it entertained me. There is little enough amusement in these colonies, you will find. But this was exciting. Especially since it turned out so well."

Her words, the mischievous angle of her head, that roguish wink, flooded Julie with memories of that scene in *Tilbury Belle*. Ellie, her fine eyes dancing, crying. "Aach, I suppose that if we want mischief on board this ship, I shall have to make it for myself!"

Ellie. Sophie Bontemps reminded her of Ellie. Julie grinned, the dimple flashing in her cheek. She was going to like Sophie Bontemps a lot. No matter what mysterious hidden motives lay behind the woman's quick words, she was going to like her a great deal.

When the breakfast arrived, Sophie lifted the cover from the tray with the eagerness of a child. Then her face fell.

"Spartan fare," she sighed. Then she smiled. "What we do not eat today will be there for us to enjoy tomorrow. Sally says that you must have nothing to inflame your blood after a snake bite. So here are croissants with eggs and not a sign of meat." Then she giggled softly. "Look at this, she even sent a dull-colored marmalade, as if the exciting reds of a currant jelly might inflame your blood."

Julie's appetite astonished them both. Sophie declared that she too, was inspired to hunger by it, and a second tray of delicately browned croissants was brought. The pastry was devoured before Julie let herself back onto her pillows with a groan.

Sophie's chatter had suffered not at all from the interference of the meal. Julie learned that the plantation was devoted almost entirely to rice and that the heat and the agues from the water drove them inside the walls of Charles Town to a second home in summer. She was told that Charles was eight and already cleverer with Latin than his mother. He was a "terror" with his fencing foil but could not do sums.

In among the light talk, Julie was apprised that Sophie had sent a message of condolence to Anne-Louise on the death of Yves. It had been reported officially as death by snakebite.

"I took the liberty of adding your name to my note of sympathy," Sophie added. "I wanted her to know that you were well and in friendly hands but unable to visit her in her time of stress."

"But I should return," Julie said hastily, feeling a dark dread stir in her at the thought. "I must not take advantage of your hospitality when my own aunt's house is now—" her voice trailed off.

"Safe for you with that mad monster dead?" Sophie finished lightly. She shook her head. "Your aunt has much to do to straighten out the affairs of that great plantation. While she has good help now, I cannot think she needs an extra person who is in need of good nursing."

She patted the bed. "Just relax, my dear Julie. Enjoy your rest because it will not last long. Within a week I have a little dinner party planned here. You must be up and ready to flirt like a proper young lady. I do hope you are not out of practice at flirting," she added with a mock frown.

As sleepy as the heavy meal had made her, Julie still giggled.

At the door Sophie paused and looked back.

"Did I tell you that your aunt's oldest son, Jacques, has returned to help her put the affairs of her plantation in order?"

Julie sat up swiftly in amazement. "Jacques!" she cried. "He is back? But how? When?"

Sophie's bright eyes held Julie's in a suddenly serious look. "Surely you, of all people Julie, have learned that the hunted is the great student of the hunter. Jacques has been too long a fugitive from his father's madness. He has been near for a long time, waiting and watching his enemy for the sake of his mother and the other children. And you in the end."

"Then he is well and there with Tante Anne-Louise," Julie said with a happy sigh.

"Not altogether well," Sophie demurred. "In fact, even as you did not escape unscathed, he is still recovering from burns he received when his mantle caught fire in the clearing that night of your rescue."

Julie stared at her. Sophie nodded happily.

"He was with my men, Julie. He had the privilege of leading them into that hidden clearing. It was he who lifted you from the coils of the serpent—but not quickly enough."

"My God," Julie said softly, feeling her strength desert her as she sank back against her pillows.

Sophie spread her hands in self-reproach. "Look at me. Standing here chattering while you need rest. Sally will be terribly incensed at me, and I will not even blame her. Rest well, my dear. And if that Charles comes to pester you, threaten him with a lesson in numbers. He will be gone like an arrow from a bow."

Julie heard her low chuckle in the hall and the light, swift steps down the stairs.

Chapter Sixty-Five

Julie had been a week with Sophie Bontemps, and the night of the promised dinner party was at hand.

From the window of her room, Julie watched the light change on the flooded rice fields that seemed to stretch forever through the marshes beyond Sophie's yard and garden. The last of the slaves were making their way between the flooded beds towards their quarters whose chimneys smoked from the fires of their evening meals. If it had not been for the dimpling of young rice plants, the fields would have been like great watery mirrors catching the last of the day's light.

She was excited. She ran her hands down the bodice and over the full, flowing skirt of the blue dress that Sophie had ordered a slave to adjust for her, since there was not time for a new gown to be made.

"How do you breathe with no more waist than that?" Sophie had kidded her as the dress was being pinned in to fit snugly to Julie's body. "Don't tell, me," Sophie laughed. "I have just noticed ample room for air to move in other places."

Julie flushed as she grinned back at her. The excellent meals and the tender care she had received had restored not only her strength but filled out her form so that her breasts rose invitingly above the low, ribboned neckline of her gown.

"You are simply delectable," Sophie decided aloud. "I must admit that I am happy not to have a cherished swain at his party. I would not wish to vie for his attention against our charms."

Julie caught the quick, sidelong glance that the Negress grinning at the hem shot at her mistress, but no word passed.

In those days following her return to consciousness, Julie had watched Sophie Bontemps with fascination. This was a woman who never let down at all. Without ever indicating the least haste or exhaustion or loss of merry humor, Sophie ran the affairs of this great plantation, mothered her rowdy son, and still had time to be a gracious hostess to Julie herself.

Perhaps it was Sophie's perfect grooming that astonished

her the most. Although whole days passed with only the slaves, her plantation manager, and herself being about, Sophie still spent every minute of each day pressed and trimmed and wigged as if to be ready for a surprise visit from the king himself.

Sometimes when Sophie pulled herself away from her desk in the well-equipped little library just off the living room, she would catch Julie romping with Charles and his dog Lapin on the lawn. With her own curls all atumble and her cheeks glowing from sun and laughter, Julie felt like some urchin child next to her immaculate hostess.

As hesitant as she was to pry into the affairs of her gracious hostess, Julie still could not restrain her curiosity about Sophie Bontemps. When several days had passed with no word or sight of a master for this great house, Julie finally summoned her courage to put her question to the maid Sally.

"Is there a Monsieur Bontemps?" she asked directly.

"Not here," Sally said with a closed face. "He was lost in the war—the Indian war."

Like Mrs. MacRae's husband had been, Julie thought.

"When was this war, Sally?" she asked.

Sally rolled her eyes upwards in thought. "Master Charles was just a babe in arms then, maybe about one year. The Yamasee made war on all the people. The women and children finally mostly ran away to the north to be safe."

"Madame Bontemps too?" Julie asked. How strange to think of Sophie anywhere but in her own lovely home.

Sally, tugging at the tangles of Julie's hair, nodded.

"She went all right, and took Master Charles and Miss Henriette too."

Henriette. Julie knew the child Henriette Beauchamp. Charles had brought the child to meet Julie very soon after Julie was able to get up.

"This is my sister-friend," he announced, shoving the little girl towards Julie. "She is my friend like a sister."

Henriette was shy and small for her age, no larger than Charles himself, although he told Julie that she was two years older.

Henriette had curtsied and blushed before raising her eyes to Julie disarmingly. "What color are my eyes?" she asked in a small, frightened voice.

"She's jealous because mine are ginger cakes," Charles explained.

Julie looked at the girl's blue eyes warily. She simply could not disappoint this appealing child, yet what possible thing could she say that would sound good and funny enough to make Charles and her laugh?

"Blueberry tarts," she announced finally. "Henriette's eyes are like blueberry tarts. Without the clotted cream, of course."

The children had been enchanted. Charles had dragged Henriette off at once to report to anyone who would listen that his sister-friend had "blueberry tart eyes. Without the cream, of course," he added faithfully.

"Henriette's mama died when she was being born," Sally explained. "Very nice lady, very pretty lady they say. But it ain't easy for a man to run a big plantation and raise up a girl child like Henriette all by himself. Mistress take over that girl a lot right from the start she come here. But that was before—"

"Before what?" Julie asked.

Sally's face darkened ever so slightly. "Before Mr. Beauchamps have his sister come from France to live there. Now she keeps Henriette home a lot more. Her name is Marguerite—but she goes by name Rita."

From the tone of Sally's voice, Julie inferred that Sally either did not like the girl or disapproved of the name she affected.

"Then it is eight years that Madame Bontemps's husband is dead." Julie mused aloud.

"Oh, no say that," Sally rebuked her in a startled voice. 'Mistress say that her husband is not dead. She say he was taken prisoner by Indians and will one day come back. That s why she won't listen when fine men want to talk her into marriage. That's why she dress all the time for company, so that she be ready when he come walking down that road home."

"Eight years," Julie breathed in amazement. Then she sighed, a sudden surge of new understanding for her hostess flooding her heart. Oh, to have even that last, small edge of hope. If she could even dream that somewhere Antoine still lived. She checked her thoughts sternly, finding herself near

tears. "It is amazing that she can run such a great place a
this, a woman alone like that."

"She has good slaves," Sally said quietly. "She treat u
good and we be good for her. Then Mister Beauchamps hel;
her make plans and do the selling and those things a woma
have a hard time to do."

"She is lucky to have a neighbor like him," Julie comment
ed.

"He's lucky to have neighbor like her to help him rais
little girl baby," Sally corrected her.

Now she was to meet Henriette's father, this Henr
Beauchamps who was such a good neighbor to Sophie tha
she had even taken his child to safety along with her own
There were other guests, the attorney who handled the lega
affairs of the plantation for Sophie, a man named Buchana
whose wife Sophie referred to as "Sairy."

Julie felt her heart trip unevenly under the bodice of th
blue dress. A party. When had she last been to a party wit
her hair piled high and the scent of perfume clinging to he
flesh? She felt insecure and even a little afraid as she stare
into the mirrored rice fields which were darkening against th
night. She watched the patrols move along the outer reache
of the fields and wondered idly why Sophie, whom Sally sai
was such a good slave master, would need guards about he
plantation.

Sophie must have guessed how much support Julie neede
to face the evening. She tapped at the door as she called o:
in a bright tone.

"For heavens sake, let me in quickly, Julie, or I shall mak
a great mess in the hall."

As she flung open the door, Julie found Sophie in the ha
with a great quantity of white flowers poised gingerly on he
outstretched arms.

"Wild roses," Sophie explained. "I must get them off me
once. They stab like bandits."

After dumping them in a pile on the dressing table, sh
popped a finger in her mouth and made a face. "Damne
little beasts, they stabbed me bloody."

Julie giggled. Sometimes her elegant hostess was startling
like Ellie in her language as well as her humor.

Sophie was fishing among the flowers and chattering o
"Usually they bloom pink, you know, but this one bus

comes white every year, and luckily they are in full flower. Turn around, dear."

In spite of the thorns which elicited more than one muttered curse from Sophie, she deftly wove a crown of the snowy blossoms in among Julie's dark, massed curls. Then she stepped back and sighed.

"An angel. A veritable angel."

"They are beautiful," Julie leaned to the mirror. Then she sighed. "Oh you are so good to me, Sophie. I confess I do not understand why you are so kind to me."

"We love you, you little goose," Sophie teased her.

We. That would be herself and Charles.

"Oh, I love you and Charles too," Julie told her quickly. "But it seems to me that I should take myself off to my aunt's home and remove the burden of myself from your household."

"Burden" Sophie laughed merrily. "Believe me, if all burdens were such as you, we would all chose to be martyrs. Believe me, Julie, it is not time for you to return to Monde Dubois. Have trust in me." Her voice grew coaxing. "Write your aunt another little note and I shall send it along. She knows herself that you are better off here for a time. You are happy here, aren't you,"

"Oh my goodness yes," Julie assured her. "But I feel so deeply in your debt—so humble at your generosity to me."

"Humble," Sophie echoed with a squeak. "Humility is for Puritans and Quakers and those stiff people of Boston. Be happy and have fun."

Julie, watching Sophie's face in the mirror, saw a strange and painful change in her expression.

"You know about my husband Paul," she said quietly.

"I have been told that he was lost in the Yamassee war," Julie replied carefully.

"I thank whoever told you," Sophie said softly. "After all these years, I am not able to say the words easily myself. I am sure that people wonder that I entertain, have parties like this one tonight. I have to, Julie. I have to keep myself alive and young and attractive for when he comes home. He will come back, you know," she said fiercely. "And when he comes, I must be as he remembered me. It frightens me a little. By his being gone I am changed—no more the protected wife, much sheltered, much pampered. The loneliness I

449

can do nothing about. But grieving publicly is a luxury that would destroy the Sophie he left."

Julie nodded thoughtfully. A sense of waiting hung in the air.

"You must know what I mean," Sophie said quietly. "Surely there is one man you love above all others and your dreams must be full of how it must be when the two of you are together again at last."

Julie thought for that dizzying moment that she must be still suffering from the venom of the serpent. The mirror fused giddily before her eyes, and she felt the weakness of sudden tears well behind her eyelids. She raised her fingertips to her eyes to halt the flow. She shook her head, conscious that Sophie was watching, waiting for her reply.

"The only man I have ever truly loved is dead," Julie said finally, in a choked and husky voice.

The moment of pained silence hung between them.

"What a fool I am to speak of such serious topics when this is an evening to be festive," Sophie said crossly. "Come, love, forgive my tactlessness and let us go down."

She linked her arm with Julie's and grinned at her.

"See how foolhardy I am? To walk beside a young girl of such beauty, I must have slept with the moon on my face and be wholly mad." Her laughter seemed to tumble down the stairs before them, setting the bright mood of the waiting guests.

As beautiful as it was, the party had a strangeness to it that kept catching in Julie's mind like a half-heard whisper.

They were twelve at the table whose tapers glittered in silver holders between masses of banked flowers. The rich terrapin soup was followed by a fine, chilled fish garnished as in life, and the entré of roasted meat was succulent in its bed of carefully prepared young vegetables.

Henri Beauchamps, on Julie's left, could not have been more charming or gallant or effusively flattering. Yet Julie was all the time conscious that his eye wandered hungrily to Sophie's face as she divided her attention between two young attorneys who flanked her at the table.

Julie was grateful when the last course was finished and the strong, black coffee was served in the drawing room. Henri Beauchamps's sister Rita was finally coaxed to play on the spinet, and one of the young attorneys produced a violin and a packet of music which belied his astonishment at being asked to perform.

Finding herself by Sairy Buchanan, the older attorney's wife, Julie turned to her with a smile.

"This is a lovely place, isn't it?" she asked for want of a common topic to begin with.

Sairy's face dropped with astonishment, "My goodness child, you have an English accent."

"I suppose so," Julie said, surprised by her reaction.

"I don't know why I just presumed that you would be French too," the woman said hastily. Then, as if she had committed a social error which she regretted, she chattered on. "So many are French in the Carolinas you know. So many French." Julie was still wondering at her words as the woman turned and gave such total attention to the music that Julie finally wandered away, feeling that she had been forgotten.

The evening continued to produce one strange conversation after another. Julie had the uncomfortable feeling that these people knew much about her while knowing nothing at all. No one asked if she liked the colony—a normal question for a newcomer. No one asked her plans or mentioned her hostess to her. It seemed that a mutual conspiracy confined their speech to small banalities of no substance.

Julie confined herself to watching the other guests. Henri Beauchamps's sister Rita was the sparkling center of the attention of the two young lawyers, while Henri himself watched Sophie, with painful devotion apparent in his face. Julie was startled to see Rita Beauchamps separate herself from her admirers to approach Julie with a sly smile.

The girl could be no more than seventeen, yet she handled her lovely body like an arrogant queen as she came to poise herself on a chair by Julie.

"How excited and half-afraid you must be," she said to Julie in a half-rushed, whispery voice.

Julie puzzled the words swiftly, then smiled. "At meeting all these strangers?" she asked. "Yes, of course, but I really love meeting new people."

The girl studied her with level eyes. "You are braver than I," she said suddenly.

What a strange girl. "Haven't you just recently come from France yourself?" Julie asked.

451

An instant scowl marred the girl's face. "I did not come," she corrected Julie. "I was sent. That is quite another thing."

Then, as if annoyed at their conversation, she leaped to her feet and looked about. "Well, we must make do with what we have, I suppose," she said in a vague, distracted voice.

With that, she walked across the room and slid her arm intimately through the arm of the young attorney who was visiting with his friend. At his startled smile, Rita smiled up into his face.

"Have you seen this garden by moonlight?" Julie heard her ask. "If not, I would be delighted to show it to you."

Julie followed her with her eyes. What a strange and restless young woman. She had not understood her words at all. Why should such a bold young woman consider her brave? She must certainly have had something in her mind aside from the terrors of meeting Charles Town society.

But Julie did not misunderstand the way the girl led the young man apart nor the look of high concern in Henri Beauchamp's eyes as he watched his sister's skirt sway through the open doors and onto the darkness of the verandah beyond.

Chapter Sixty-Six

The rice plants thrived in the fetid waters of the marshes, changing the face of the swamp to a pale, soft green like the young oat fields of England. Charles's friend Henriette escaped to visit at every opportunity, so the house and verandah rang with their laughter and the excited barking of the dog Lapin.

Julie tried to take each careless day as it came, but her mind was torn with conflict. That tension that is born of waiting continued to spiral inside her. Her mind told her that she should firmly insist on returning to Monde DuBois. After all, it was now wholly her aunt's home, and hadn't it been to join her aunt that she had undertaken this long, arduous pilgrimage from the very first night that she and Louis had crept out into the storm to start for London?

Yet the very thought of Monde DuBois brought a rising of

her skin, the scent of Tomala's flesh to her head, the dark swaying memory of serpents.

Her notes to Anne-Louise were promptly answered by loving letters. Her aunt spoke of the health of the children, of Jacques's rapid healing from his burns, and of her tender devotion and good wishes for Julie. But never did her aunt even mention her return to Monde DuBois.

Yet why was she here? Why did her aunt not urge her return? Every detail of her days reassured here role as a treasured guest of a great house, yet she felt that mysterious tension building, always building. She learned to watch for well-hidden patrols that guarded the plantation boundaries at night; she was slyly conscious that she herself was never far from the Negro Ben's watchful eye.

She wondered bitterly if her own mind had been so twisted by her experiences that she smelled peril in even so gentle a situation as this.

Sophie worked at her accounts in the library or made trips to Charles Town and back as busily as a man of affairs. But still she had time for Julie and for the constant visits of Henri Beauchamps and his sister Rita.

While the children played and Henri and Sophie conferred on the business of the plantation, Julie was left to entertain Rita.

Not since her early childhood had Juile spent any time with a girl of her own class. She found the girl fascinating. Rita's reckless tongue and careless but conscious vanity made her sparkling company. Tossing her fine hair, with her lovely body always seeming in restless movement, she was so tremendously alive that Julie was drawn to her in spite of the shallowness of the girl's chatter.

Gossip and jewels, fine clothing and romantic intrigue obsessed Rita, and she often complained to Julie that she was, as she put it, "bored out of her wig" at this dull provincial place.

"Maybe you could talk Madame Bontemps into letting us go to Charles Town together," Rita suggested. "It is certainly no Paris, but there are nice things to look at and buy." Then she grinned. "It is fun just to parade along the streets to admire and be admired."

"You are a flirt, Rita Beauchamps," Julie teased her. "An out-and-out coquette."

453

Rita shrugged and laughed. "Who denies it? But then you must remember that *my* heart is not taken." Her arch glance gave her words some second level of meaning that Julie would have asked her about if she'd had time. But as so often, their talk was interrupted by Charles and Henriette who tumbled into the room to absorb all their attention.

"Well, if she won't let you go to Charles Town, she must at least let you come and call on us," Rita said petulantly, as her brother called her to leave with him. "It is such a little way that you could walk it in a few minutes." She drew Julie to the verandah. "See there, those chimneys behind the trees are our house. You only follow the road past two fields, through a small, wooded place and *voilà!*"

She grinned and tightened her shoulders with pleasure at the thought. "We could try some different makeups. I even have some patches." She eyed Julie's mass of curls. "We could design new things to do with our hair and you could try on my clothes."

Julie laughed. "I have to admit that sounds like it might be fun."

Henri Beauchamps who had joined them on the verandah caught her last words.

"What kind of 'fun' is Rita suggesting now, Julie?"

"Girl fun," Julie replied, smiling. "She was inviting me to run over to your house to play dress-up with her."

To Julie's astonishment, Henri shot his sister such a glance of stern reproof that Rita tossed her head rebelliously and looked away from him. Then his anger passed as he turned to Sophie, his expression thoughtful.

"I would be delighted to send a man over to accompany Julie to our home anytime it is convenient for her to come."

"Oh heavens," Sophie said lightly. "Ben would be ready to take her whenever she wished."

Behind her brother's back, Rita rolled her eyes skyward with a shrug. "Past two fields and a grove of trees," she had said. It was clear that Rita was disgusted about this great fuss about who would accompany her guest.

"Come soon," she pleaded, her hand on Julie's arm. "Come tomorrow," she decided, as if it were all settled.

Not only Ben but Charles accompanied Julie to Rita's home that first time. Julie gasped at the magnificence of Rita's wardrobe. And it was like being a child again to primp

454

and dress and undress in the handsome clothes while Rita chattered like a magpie with excitement.

"You really are smashingly beautiful," Rita said when Julie had donned a gown of rich, dark red velvet. "That makes you terribly easy to hate, you know."

Julie turned to stare at her. "What a dreadful thing to say, Rita. Do you really hate me?"

"Not exactly," Rita said candidly. "I would probably like you better if you were afflicted with moles or had an eye that wandered off towards your ear, but I really don't hate you. But if we ever set our caps for the same man, I would loathe you instantly and with great passion."

"Don't hold your breath for that day," Julie laughed. She slipped off the heavy gown and placed it on its hanger. "The thought of marriage is very far from my mind right now."

Rita's mouth dropped and she stared at Julie as if stunned. "Then what in the name of God is on your mind?" she asked in a perplexed tone.

Julie turned her golden eyes on the girl thoughtfully. Rita was always so overexcited about everything, but it seemed that she was more incensed than usual at Julie's remark. Yet how could she answer the girl when she did not herself know where her mind was. She was grateful that a tap at the door brought the message that it was time for mademoiselle to return to her home.

Julie was glad to escape having to answer the question, but the question itself hung in her mind against her will.

The business of the plantation seemed to pick up by the day. Sophie herself was like a small, immaculate whirlwind, spinning from one task to another, overseeing the tending of the vegetable garden, directing cooking and cleaning and the crop care with growing momentum. Her low throaty voice, always warm with laughter, could be heard everywhere about the place.

"Is it always this busy and exciting in spring?" Julie asked sally as Sally helped the sewing woman pin heavy bands of lace on a full petticoat that Sophie ordered made for Julie. The camisole was already finished, a tiny bodice fitted with insets of lace with fine, pale ribbons that tightened it along the curve of Julie's high, full breasts.

Julie felt Sally's eyes lift to hers, but when she looked down, Sally's eyes were on her work again.

"Spring very busy time everywhere," Sally said blandly.

"But all the cleaning and trimming and cooking," Julie insisted.

"Can't clean with winter on," Sally reminded her. "Nobody ever trims a wintering tree."

"I wonder if it is this busy at my aunt's house," Julie wondered aloud.

She felt the skirt jerk under Sally's hand and she looked down. Sally's face was tense with what looked like fright.

"You're not thinking of going there," Sally asked sternly.

"Why shouldn't I?" Julie asked.

Sally shook her head and went back to the needle. "The mistress knows best," she said sullenly, as if Julie had asked her to speak some forbidden word.

"If you mean all that *obeah* and the voodoo business, those things are all over there," Julie said, suddenly needing to have the air cleansed between them.

Sally shook her head. "Nothing ever over that quick. Big tree take a long time to grow, big tree take a long time to rot down."

The girl's words troubled Julie. She shook her head, groping for a comparison of her own. "Evil like that is like fire. When it is stamped out, it is gone."

Sally raised her eyes to hold Julie's. "Then the fire hides under the leaves and crawls away to break out and burn again when the stamper has looked away."

Julie was more troubled by her words than she wished to admit. But why should she argue with Sally about it? It was over. Sophie herself had said that Jacques had sold away the bad slaves and he was there to guard the place as master.

Julie's visits back and forth to Rita's house became a bright part of her life. Usually Charles went with her to play with Henriette, and always Ben tagged along and waited silently for their time to return. Then Charles, against his mother's distinct orders, waded in the marsh on a chill evening and became terribly feverish from the cold that followed. The extra nursing of the child became just one more burden on Sophie who would not let Julie get near the child.

"I could read to him, play games," Julie protested.

"And be piled up in bed sniffling like a fountain yourself," Sophie laughed. "He got this cold for himself and he can jus

456

keep it to himself and not pass it about like a tray of comfits. You keep yourself and Lapin happy, and you will be doing me the greatest favor of all."

And truly, the dog missed his master painfully. He lay at the door whining as soon as the sun was full up and dogged every step Julie took when she came outdoors. That afternoon that Rita came flying over with a new present that had come from an aunt in Paris, he sat between their chairs on the lawn so that Julie had to lean over him to see the purse properly.

"It is lovely," Julie said, turning the finely beaded bag in her hands.

"And that isn't all," Rita said. "Look inside."

The tiny metal box inside the purse was hand lacquered with a bright, dancing shepherdess.

"For rouge," Rita sparkled. "I am going to fill it and carry it tonight. I shall dress my face like the king's own mistress does and be the belle of Charles Town." She grimaced. "This is all talk, of course, because it is only a dull dinner party by some of Henri's dull friends, but I can feel better about it if my face is rouged."

"And you will surely be the loveliest one there," Julie said quite honestly.

"I wish I could look as breathtaking as you did that first night I saw you," Rita said thoughtfully. "You had done something extraordinary with your hair."

"Sophie did it," Julie explained. "She wound it with fresh flowers."

"How marvelous. But what is in season now that I could use in my own?"

"Oh, let's look," Julie cried leaping up and almost tripping over Lapin. "I shall get a cutter and be sure that it is all right with Sophie for us to pick them."

Armed with Sophie's approval and a sturdy knife from the kitchen, they cut a fragrant bouquet of lilac and some small, white daisies with golden faces.

Rita watched with excitement as Julie trimmed the stems and wove the flowers into a circlet that just caught like a crown on Rita's head.

Rita planted a quick kiss on Julie's cheek. "Now I must run or I shall not have time to bathe. Thank you so much, I shall be the belle of Charles Town indeed, thanks to you!"

The streaks of sunset had started across the sky as Julie walked with Rita to the edge of the lawn where the road began. Julie was conscious of Ben, standing by the door watching her and Lapin. She also saw him turn and go on into the house as she and Lapin made their way back to the verandah, where she had left the knife and the waste from the bouquet.

Julie idly gathered the stems and discarded leaves. As she bent to gather them from the grass, she saw the glint of metal in among the green. Rita's new rouge purse.

"Too bad," she told Lapin, turning the trinket in her hands. "She wanted so much to use it tonight."

She glanced west to where the smoke from the Beauchamps chimney was trailing a pale genie into the darkening sky.

"This is silly," she told Lapin. "The two of us can run it over to Rita and be back before we are even missed."

Without even returning the knife to the kitchen, Julie started across the green lawn with Lapin at her side. As they reached the road, she tucked the knife into her belt and discarded her handful of flower debris into the ditch by the roadside, then she set off at a laughing run down the road with Lapin racing delightedly at her side.

She had passed that way so many times in her visiting that she barely glanced at the fields as they passed them. When the shadows of the woods darkened her path, she slowed her steps, not wanting to fall headlong on the uneven, damp earth of the path. She walked with her hand resting lightly on Lapin's back. His tongue and his tail both swayed from side to side like two pendulums on a living clock.

They were only a few yards into the wood when Julie felt the dog's body tense under her hand. A ridge of hair along his back rose like bristles grown suddenly stiff. At almost the same moment, she heard a low, warning growl gather in his throat. He slowed his steps, pressing his warm side against her and staring into the woods on the left of the road.

"It is an animal of some kind," she reassured herself, picking up her speed. "Come, Lapin," she urged. "Come, run." In spite of her own reassurances, her heart began to race, and she was suddenly chill with fear.

Lapin did not obey. Instead, he stopped still in the road,

bracing his front legs, his head swung low as if to ward off attack.

"Lapin," she shouted in fear and anger. "Lapin, come."

He only growled more ferociously and stood his ground. When his cry changed to a frantic barking, panic seized her. Clutching the metal box tightly, she began to run, leaving the big, stupid animal to bark his head off there in the middle of the woods. There was nothing in the woods, she promised herself as she fled along the ruts. It was only a few yards, only a few yards more before the turn of the road and the woods were through and she would be safe.

She saw the figure from the corner of her eye. It was as if a massive tree had separated itself from the woods and started to move towards her. At the same moment, she heard the hoofbeats of a horse very near. My God. She must choose between that figure in the woods and the oncoming rider who would not see her for the bend of the road. She swerved away, her fear only made worse by the frantic barking of Lapin growing nearer from behind her.

One instant he was in the dark of the trees, and the next his hand was over her face and his arm like a vise about her chest. She heard him rumble something like a curse as she scratched and clawed at him and sunk her teeth into the fat butt of his hand. He tightened his grip, fastening her left arm tight against her body as he began to drag her backwards into the shelter of the trees. She fought and screamed, hearing the horseman grow nearer, hoping that her assailant could not drag her into the concealing darkness before the rider turned the bed in the road.

Lapin had leaped into the fray. Teeth bared, the animal lunged and leaped and dived against the kicking legs of the man who held her. She heard the sharp howl of the dog's voice in pain as he was kicked away only to lunge into the attack again.

She felt with her pinned left hand for the knife she had tucked into her belt. One inch at a time, she groped for it until she felt the warm comfort of its wooden handle slip into her grasp. As she turned the blade carefully, she realized that if her single blow missed, she would bury the blade in her own chest. But in spite of Lapin's noble efforts, she was being dragged from the road and she dared not hesitate.

Tightening her body with all her strength, she drove the

459

knife into the arm that prisoned her. She felt the warm stickiness of blood flow over her hand and down the shaft of the knife and onto her own chest. He screamed at the wound and for an instant his damaged arm loosed its hold. The instant was all she required. Dropping to the ground, she seized her skirts and scrambled for the road shouting, "Lapin, Lapin."

She heard her pursuer behind her, cursing at Lapin, his progress impeded by the attacking dog. With his gutteral voice terrifyingly near, she broke from the brush and tumbled onto the road.

She saw the startled eyes of the horse as she stumbled into his path. She saw him rise, and the curve of his rounded hooves poised in the air above her head. She heard the rider's frantic curse as he struggled with his frightened mount. She dived across the road to escape the fall of the steed's hooves. Even as she rolled into the nettles of the ditch on the other side, she heard a man's voice screaming, the whinny of the horse, and a horrified shout.

In the stillness that followed, a damp, stiff warmth moved over her face, and a whimpering came against her head. She reached up and caught Lapin in his arms, sobbing and holding to him while he bathed her face with his great hot tongue.

Her head was swimming dizzily as she pulled herself up to stare at the scene in the darkened road. The rider dismounted and knelt over the man's body crumpled in the road. The rider's back was to her as he rolled the body over. She tightened her fists against her mouth to hold back her screams. Perry. My God. The man in the road who had been waiting to waylay her was Perry. His broad, black face had been sliced open by the hooves of the horse. The eye that was left stared dully at the sky, but the leg crumpled under his broken body still jerked with life.

Lapin, at her side, whimpered and pressed himself more tightly against her.

She watched the rider rise, draw a handkerchief from his coat, and wipe Perry's blood from his hand. The horse, its hooves still scarlet, cropped quietly on the roadside grass.

She trembled as she saw the tall man in the road turn in the darkness and start towards her.

"Well, miss," he began, his tone acid.

Then he froze, staring down at her.

The eyes. The clear, brilliant blue eyes. The fine, high arch of brows and the full mouth suddenly slack in an astonished face.

He began to sway in her sight, to circle like a great wheel spinning about her.

It could not be. Not in this life, not on this road in this far place. Yet the tears rushed from behind her eyes shutting off what view she had of him. She raised her arms, struggling to reach this image that her wounded mind had conjured for her.

"Antoine," she cried, calling out to him from the dizzying darkness. "Antoine." Then there was only darkness.

Chapter Sixty-Seven

Sophie Bontemps, her palms moist with excitement, struggled to keep her voice calm. The light had long faded from the room, and the candle's light fluttered on the pages of Charles's favorite story book.

A moist sniffle from the bed distracted her. She handed him a kerchief without lifting her eyes from the page. She struggled with the words which she knew by heart at any ordinary time.

"Maman," he complained. "You are leaving parts out."

"You must forgive me, Charles," she sighed. "I have much on my mind tonight."

His dry, hacking cough reminded her that she must have the maid bind his chest with freshly oiled cloths before he slept.

She carefully recited the words to the story to Charles while her mind swung wildly away. It was time. She had half-expected him the day before, but surely he had to arrive this day. Had he encountered some trouble on the road? She had chafed at one delay after another since the night of the blood moon. Her first messenger had gone and returned without locating him. Even when he was found, he was so many days travel away that she had counted them in her mind a hundred times, praying that a quicker route could be found.

He must hurry. The girl was not stupid. She was sensible that some mystery stirred in the air. She was sensible that she was guarded. How long could she keep this lively spirit from escaping a confinement that she did not understand? Yet he had insisted that she not be told, that it was his privilege to face her without advance warning.

The concern bred by her thoughts trembled in Sophie's voice so that her son raised his eyes to her face with a frown. It was fear, she admitted to herself. Face it, Sophie, you are afraid. He was so sure. He was so rock-solid positive that this beautiful child with the golden eyes was as impassioned to be reunited with him as he was to have her again. "We are destined," he had told her over and again. "It is in our stars."

Sophie herself was not so sure. How much can a life sustain without changing a person completely? This was her own constant fear about Paul—that one or the other of them would have changed past their mutual love. And as for Julie!

The girl had most certainly been dragged through hell at Monde DuBois, and what adventures had she had before that? Anne-Louise had told Mrs. MacRae of the shipwreck in Julie's crossing. Mrs. MacRae herself had described the young Indian trader who had brought Julie to her door. "Clad in country clothing like a rare flower in a weed field," Mrs. MacRae had said.

Sophie had tried to draw the girl out, to get some clue to what quiet person lay hidden beyond those jewelled eyes. She had found strange gifts of skill and knowledge and a gentleness that seemed to have no place of stopping. But where was the girl's heart?

"Surely you have a true love," she had suggested to Julie only to have the girl fight back her tears and speak quietly "Dead," she had said. Dead.

"Maman," Charles's voice was soft. "You can stop if you want to. I know that story already anyway."

"Oh, Charles," she bent to press her face against his cheek "Do forgive me, love. I am not myself tonight."

"Is *mon oncle* coming home?" he asked quietly.

After an astonished look, she laughed merrily. "You little fox, how did you know that?"

"You always get very excited when he comes home," he explained. He shifted up in the bed. "Will he come to see me?"

462

She shook her head. "Not until that sniffling and snorting is all through, you little beast," she smiled at him. "Would you want your uncle to ride all the way from Boston town just to catch a sickness from a bad little boy like you?"

"You like me," he reminded her.

"I love you," she corrected him. "But now I must go and see that all is ready for your dinner."

"And Julie's too?" he asked.

"And Julie's too," she replied, stroking his thick tawny hair back from his forehead.

Sophie hastened to Julie's room. This had been a terrible day altogether. Would she ever learn to be graceful at waiting? It was bad enough that Charles's cold was little better, but a dozen things had gone wrong in the fields and in the kitchen to take up her time and attention. It had been a lucky stroke that that silly little Rita Beauchamps had come for flowers. It had been amusement for Julie for an hour. But in truth it made Sophie nervous to have the girl about. Henri insisted that he had sworn the girl to secrecy about her brother's coming, but Sophie had no confidence in the girl's careless tongue.

She tapped at Julie's door which opened at her first touch. Sally stared out at her, "She ain't here," Sally explained. "I got her things ready and have been waiting."

Sophie's eyes flicked about the room, at the finished petticoat and camisole laid out on the bed, the steam from the cooling bath breathing into the air.

"But it's full dark," Sophie protested. "Are you sure?"

At Sally's shrug, Sophie cried, "Aaach," and turned to race down the stairs as swiftly as she could on her high-heeled slippers. "Ben," she began shouting before she reached the hall. "Ben. Where is Ben?"

The fragrance in the kitchen was overpowering. The spice of the shellfish and the crisp, garlicked scent of the roasted pork mingled as Sophie stood in the door. One glance at the ashen face of the cook made Sophie reach blindly for the side of the door, her breath suddenly gone.

The cook's eyes were wide on Sophie. "He's out looking for Miss Julie and that dog. That just disappeared into thin air."

"When?" Sophie gasped, still clinging to the frame of the door for support.

"Just as the light left," the woman told her. "Maybe a hour, maybe more."

Once on the verandah, Sophie stopped to catch her breath as she stared about the yard. The night throbbed with sound. A chorus of spring peepers sounded from the marshes with the bullfrog's deep tones as accent. A whippoorwill fluted from the grove against the faint, rhythmic strumming of music from the cluster of slave's quarters nearest the house.

"Lapin," she called. "Julie, Ben." She felt her voice die on the air. What had she done? What had gone wrong?

Even as her eyes explored the darkness, she glimpsed something moving along the road by the rice field. As she raced towards the road, her eyes picked out the straggling figures, a man striding ahead, carrying a burden in his arms. Behind him followed a horse with Ben by its side. Across the back of the horse was draped the body of a man, his hands trailing in the dirt of the road. In and about them wove Lapin, circling back and forth in that excited way he did.

As she approached, she saw her brother's face set like stone. He lifted his feet and thrust them down woodenly like a man in a trance. Julie's eyes were closed. The soft curve of her breast and the pale fabric of her bodice were thick with half-dried blood. Her face, against the white shirt, was paler than its fabric.

Sophie felt herself growing giddy, her knees buckling beneath her. Then she gritted her teeth and turned to run towards the house, only stopping to take her slippers in her hand that they not impede her.

"Hot water to mademoiselle's room," she shouted into the kitchen. "Sheets and linen and all the hot water you can find."

Antoine stopped indecisive in the hall, his eyes dull on his sister's face.

"Upstairs," she ordered. "The white room upstairs."

The key to the liquor cabinet would not fit. Sophie cursed and thrust it again and again at the tiny slot before she could get it to enter. She chose the bottle with trembling hands. Halfway up the stairs, she heard Antoine's firm voice call loudly.

"Out," he shouted. "All of you. Out."

Her maids, their eyes wide with terror, clustered in the hall

464

outside Julie's closed door. Sophie swept past them with a reassuring nod.

Julie seemed no larger than a child there on the smooth bed. Antoine was grasping at her bodice with awkward, blood-stained hands.

"Here," Sophie ordered, shoving him aside.

"If she should die," he said to her between clenched teeth. "Oh, God in heaven, if she should die."

When Sophie's deft hands had stripped the girl's torso bare, she stopped stunned. Although the blood had seeped through the fabric of the dress to stain her flesh, Sophie could find no wound on the smooth skin.

"Water," Sophie said swiftly to Antoine. "Bring me a cloth with water."

He obeyed so awkwardly that a stream of drops trailed across the floor and dampened Sophie's gown. Carefully, Sophie wiped the stains of the blood from Julie's flesh then raised her eyes to her brother's.

"Why is she like this then?" he pressed.

"Shock," Sophie decided aloud. "It is not so wondrous, considering what she has been through. Here, lift her."

As Antoine slid her arm about Julie and lifted her head and shoulders, Sophie poured brandy with still-trembling hands. When the few drops passed Julie's lips, the girl gasped, and her great golden eyes opened on Sophie's face.

"Sophie," she whispered urgently. "A dream—a horrible dream that Perry was waiting." Her voice rose, and the flesh of her face paled again. "There were horse's hooves and blood, and I dreamed—" Her lips seemed unable to say what fluttered behind them. "My God, Sophie, I dreamed—" Her eyes shone like topaz on Sophie's face as she clutched at her friend's arm.

Antoine drew silently from the shadow beyond the bed to lean towards her his hand resting lightly on his sister's shoulder.

"Did you dream it was I, Julie?" he asked softly.

Sophie watched the transformation of the girl's face. What did she expect? A scream? That the girl lapse again into that shock she had so recently been drawn from? She expected anything but what happened.

Unconscious of the bareness of her breast and arms in the glowing light, oblivious of all except the face that smiled

465

down into hers, Julie's lips parted in an expression of joyous disbelief. That dimple whose barest shadow Sophie had glimpsed in the weeks past deepened by the girl's mouth as she devoured Antoine's face with her eyes.

"You." It was more an exhalation than a word. "You. It is you." Then with a cry that was half-sob, half-laughter, Julie raised her arms to Antoine. As he caught her against his breast, he buried his face in her hair like a child.

Sophie found her face streaming with hot and painful tears as she let herself out of the room. In the hallway, a cluster of frightened slaves waited. She shook her head and managed a damp smile for them.

"Mademoiselle is fine," she assured them. "Someone run tell the cook to hold the dinner indefinitely."

Chapter Sixty-Eight

Julie clung to Antoine, not caring that the fastenings of his shirt dug roughly into her breast. She burrowed her face into his neck, breathing that singular scent of his flesh that was dearer to her than any perfume.

"My love. My love," she kept repeating against his skin.

He loosened her arms to set her away from him. "How can I have all of you at once?" he complained. "All at once, Julie, in one great completeness, to feel you against me, to see you and hear your voice, to taste your lips—all at once."

Her parted lips lifted to his, stilling his question. That torrent of passion which had slept in her like an underground river when she was apart from him rose to her lips in undiminished power. She caught his tongue between her teeth and guided it between her lips eagerly.

"Julie. My God, my God, we can't. You can't."

As his own hand groped to loosen his clothing, she slid her hand under his shirt and then along the line of his belly in an eager caress as her lips clung to his.

Only when she felt the warmth of his seed fan within her own body, did her smooth, eager limbs loose their hold on him. He groaned as he lay with her body a willing captive of his own. Then he felt the faint vibration start deep inside her.

It was like a half-forgotten melody whose single notes tease the memory until the whole of the tune bursts forth in delighted recognition. Her laughter, that same vibration of delight that began deep in her small body and rose to explode into merriment as she nuzzled his neck, rose in Antoine too.

"You wench," he cried, clinging to her and fighting his own joyous response. "What hell you have put me through! You disappeared like the pale mist of morning. Then you are reported to be dead and then alive. I have searched for you like a madman from one stinking end of this savage country to another. I pour my passion into that precious body, and you burst into laughter."

She gripped his shoulders with her hands and pushed him away so she could see into his face. "A madman," she repeated. Those had been Josh's words, "'A madman seeking a girl such as you!"

"Oh, God, Antoine," she cried and began to laugh again, this time even more merrily.

Antoine was strangely affronted, but she could not help it. She clung to him, exploding with giggles until he shook her by the shoulders. "My God, woman, are you out of your own mind? What if I had said that I died for you? Would you then be so convulsed with merriment that we would have to pitch you into icy water like a crazed beast?"

"Oh, Antoine, Antoine," she gasped. "You do not understand. But it is over. Now it is all over and we are together. For indeed I was told that you had died. I have mourned you with each breath I have drawn since. And all this time I have been fleeing, I have been fleeing from you. Admit it now that there is a great irony in it. They told me that a madman was searching for such a girl as I. How was I to know whose fury I was flying from? And I fled, Antoine. I fled into horror and almost into death—from you."

When she coaxed him with her smile, he bent his head to hers.

"You are right. It is over and we will never be apart again for the length of our lives. You will marry me, Julie—"

When he saw the gentle shaking of her head, he paused aghast.

"Come, woman," he said hoarsely. "This is no time for idle games. You will marry me though a million men lie between

467

us. You are mine, Julie. If there is a husband between us, he is marked as dead that I may claim his fresh widow."

At her strange expression, he grew only more insistent.

"You will wed me willingly or you will wed me in chains, Julie, but you are mine." He seized her arm with such force that she cried out from pain.

As he loosed her, she slid away from him, rubbing her wrist with the palm of her hand.

"I will wed you, Antoine Riviere, if it pleases you to take part in such a farce as that. But I have been wed to you such a long time already. From the betrothal in our shared glance while I was yet a child, from that first night when you seized me from Joseph's fury in that snowy field. A thousand weddings or a thousand thousand weddings would not make me more married than I have been since the day I first saw you."

He studied her and his face turned sober. "You are right, my love, there is no doubt of that. But the small detail of a legal wedding will no doubt delight my sister. Let us say that we do it for her and for our sons that they not come into the world as bastards in the eyes of men."

His words set a sudden child on her heart. "Our sons." How often had she pondered the thought of children? She and Antoine had shared their love so freely. Those long nights with Josh. And there had been the seed of her ravishers, the thief-taker in Epping, her uncle. Why had no child come? Could she be barren?

That would be the final irony of all. That she and Antoine would not bear the sons who already joyed him though they were unborn. The shiver that the thought sent along her back edged her back into Antoine's arms, her own arms pressed about his waist.

He moved away from her touch. "My God, Julie. You do not know what the feel of your flesh against me does to me after all this time. Do not flame me into desire again while we have a whole household already set on its ears with our dalliance."

He began to button his shirt, smiling down at her. "There are other hungers, you know. We must at least keep up enough strength for lovemaking."

She giggled and crossed the room towards her cupboard. He watched her pass with the rosiness of his caresses still coloring her flesh. He smiled with the rich delight of possession on his lips. Then, as she turned towards him, her arms raised to slip on her fresh camisole, he frowned at her.

"Come here, love," he urged her. "What mark is this?" He laid a careful finger on the star-shaped mark between her waist and her breast.

"It is from Ben's knife," she told him. "He cut me there that he might draw the venom of the poisonous serpent from me to save my life."

He groaned and pulled her close. There in his arms the old serpent of her own flaming jealousy rose and swayed in her mind again. She held out her arm that he might also see the Newgate mark on her flesh.

"And that one I got in Newgate when I was prisoned. The same Newgate where I watched from a high window as you embraced a slender girl with hair the color of burnished copper."

His face was slack a moment and then, unaccountably, his eyes began to sparkle with that same light of mischief that Julie had cherished so much in Sophie's eyes.

"Clearly we have much catching up to do, madame." he said lightly. "But I do suggest that you cover that tempting ass of yours lest this night's dinner never get served."

He was barely able to get his words out for laughter. She could still hear his vibrant chuckle as he reached the bottom of the stairs and called out to Sohpie.

She wanted to cry and shout at him and curse him all at once. What was so damned hilarious about his inconstancy when he had been so punished for his loyalty? She fumed as she caught her hair up in a single swift movement, winding a ribbon about it so that it tendrilled down her back and upon her half-bared shoulders. Her eyes were still snapping with irritation as she descended the stair.

Sophie was lighting the dinner candles herself. A sly smile tugged at her lips as she glanced over her shoulder at Julie.

"Ah, there is our late bird." She waved her hand at the table of cooled roast and cheeses set out with her own fine bread and a tart of red cherries.

"When it seemed that your reunion might not be quickly consummated, I sent the slaves all away. It seemed appropriate that we share an intimate dinner together—the three of us."

Antoine, his mouth still tight with that roguish grin, held Julie's chair with a great show of gallantry.

"Since we are to dine in such delightful intimacy, sister, may I ask one more intimacy of you?"

Sophie raised her eyes to him in question.

"Would you do us the honor of dining with us au naturelle?" At his sister's astonished glance, he went on quickly. "It is not your clothing that I want you to remove but that damned affected wig."

Sophie lifted her hands to the elaborate coiffure with a pout. "This is not a 'damned affected wig.' It is admirably stylish, the very rage of Paris this season."

He leaned towards her coaxingly. "Please, sister."

Confused, Julie watched Sophie's initial resistence crumple as she gave an amused shrug. As Sophie passed from the lights of the table into the darkness of the hall where a long mirror hung, Antoine stared about at the table, avoiding Julie's eyes.

When the door to the hall reopened, Julie turned.

Her hands flew to her mouth with a cry. Sophie, with her hair about her shoulders, stood in the doorway almost shyly. To Julie, who had never seen her except in the formal wig, it was a transformation. Cascades of dark hair tumbled down Sophie's back, framing her face with deep-curved waves that made her look more child than woman.

"Sophie," Julie breathed. "How beautiful you are."

"Is that all you can say, Julie?" Antoine prodded slyly. "Come nearer, Sophie my dear—here into the light."

At Sophie's approach, Antoine lifted a candle from its holder to hold above his sister's head. Julie gasped.

"My God," she cried. "Antoine, forgive me. Forgive me." She was up and around the table in a moment, clasping Sophie in a tight hug. "Oh Sophie, My God. My God."

Sophie, her brows arched with amusement, looked from Antoine, who was helpless with laughter, to Julie, who was hugging her breath away.

"You see why I affect a wig, dear friends," she said archly in her deep, warm voice. "The very sight of magnificence such as mine sends even my dearest friends into excesses of madness. Now for God's sake let me in on the joke."

"Newgate," Antoine explained. "This doll was watching us from a high window in Newgate. She saw the warmth of our

470

reunion, saw our heads bent in tender talk. She accused me of inconstancy with a girl who had hair like burnished copper."

Sophie stared at Julie with wide eyes. "Oh my love," she said swiftly. "How ugly for you." Then she pursed her lips and smiled. "But I do adore the way you described it. Burnished copper. I must remember the exact words. That is by far the most delicious description my hair has ever had."

"Better than carrot top?" Antoine asked slyly, filling her wineglass with a grin.

She darted her tongue out at him with a grimace.

"To those who he hates, God sends little brothers," she told Julie with a grin.

Her face grew suddenly serious as she lifted her glass so that the candlelight fragmented the glow of the red wine.

"I would propose a toast to that bright particular star which brought you two together in the beginning and has kept you safe for each other."

As the wine passed her lips, Julie looked over at Antoine with wonder. The delight was still there. That demon brightness that had shone from his eyes that first day in Middlesex still sent a giddiness through her. "A bright and particular star" Sophie called it. Even as she finished the wine of the toast, Julie's heart ached for Sophie who was clinging to her long-desperate hope of being united with her own lover and husband.

"So many years, so many perils," Julie mused. "Antoine, I have this great empty place in my understanding, a hundred questions." She dimpled in apology. "I do now confess that my raging jealousy was misplaced, but many things I do not understand. You were there, Sophie, at Newgate. How did that come to be?"

"When I learned of his charges and his poor chances of escaping the gallows, I dared not give my mission into careless hands. I went to England myself to arrange for him to be freed for transporting." She grinned. "I thought to buy his freedom from all bonds, but it was impossible. I found him totally enslaved to a girl with golden eyes. The hardest part of it all was to persuade him to leave England without you. Can you imagine our high delight when we learned that you were here in the colonies and we had only to find you?"

471

"That would be my next question," Julie laughed. "How ever did you find of my rescue from the raft?"

"We only presumed on that," Antoine admitted, "but we had great hopes after hearing of your departure from the *Tilbury Belle*."

"And Antoine was not ever going to give up."

Sophie was laughing softly, and Antoine laid his napkin down with a thump. "That wench of a sister of mine will never rest until I tell her how we found that you had most probably been saved."

"He got it full in the face," Sophie giggled.

Antoine nodded. "Just like that. A wench spat in my face. A lithesome little tart she was too, with a great enamored sailor in tow. She saw me from afar and switched her little ass across a street to run me down. I was watching her as every red-blooded man in town was doing, that fine little body twitching along double time through the crowd. Then the little bitch walked directly up to me, reared herself onto tiptoe, and spat full in my face."

"She did," Sophie affirmed, collapsing into giggles. "It was the funniest thing I had seen for years. He was too astonished to move. He only stood rooted there like a great oaf, blinking through the spittle with his mouth hanging open."

"Oh, but then I went after her," Antoine explained. "When I caught her by the wrist she clawed me like a cat, kicking and screaming. She called me every foul name that a good London whore can scrape from the kennel of that city before I calmed her down."

Julie listened in confusion as Sophie choked her laughter into a cough.

"At last she confessed the reason for her fury at me," Antoine explained. "It seems that according to her, the finest lady ever born in Christendom was like to have been hung for my sake. 'I'd know you anywhere, you bloated cock. My Julie would have died for you, you scabrous prick.' It was that kind of a conversation."

That could be no one else. "Ellie," she breathed with delight.

"The same," Antoine confirmed. "Ellie was somehow drawn from that wreck to come to new and lusty life here in the colonies. It was she and her tale of your safe escape in the rowboat set me upon this long, crazed search that has ended here tonight."

Julie did not try to restrain the tears of joy that sprang from her eyes. She let them flow unheeded down her cheeks and onto her bare throat. The wine and the joy that was even a headier brew conspired against her. She felt a strange giddiness that changed the flames of the candles to blurred rainbows.

"A bright particular star," Sophie had called it.

She was conscious of Antoine's rising and Sophie's throaty voice murmuring. Ellie lived. And the arms that lifted her from her chair were Antoine's. She looped her own arms about his neck and buried her head against him as he mounted the stairs with her in his arms.

Chapter Sixty-Nine

Sophie, with her elaborate wig back in place, tilted the dark stream of coffee into Antoine's cup. Sunlight patterned across the breakfast table. From the lawn outside came the peal of Charles's laughter followed by Lapin's excited barking. When the maid's steps ceased to sound in the hall, Sophie leaned towards her brother.

"Toni," she said in a firm, determined tone. "'We must discuss sleeping arrangements."

Julie, feeling the sudden rush of color to her cheeks, kept her eyes carefully on her plate.

"Why madame," Antoine said with raised eyebrows. "Have I been remiss as a guest? Have I failed to inform you that my sleeping accommodations here are the finest that I have ever enjoyed in my wide travels? Not the finest hotels of Paris, no, truly, not the palace of the king himself could compare—"

"Stop it, you fool," his sister giggled. "You know damned well what I mean. My household is all agog that my brother not only cannot keep his eyes or his hands from Mademoiselle Julie, but that he also wakens each morning in her arms."

He shook his head sympathetically. "Jealousy, madame. It is jealousy that is plaguing them. You must convey my regrets to them that they will simply have to settle with what they have. I am far too satisfied with my current bed partner to do any shopping around among them."

"Discretion," Sophie pleaded helplessly. "A little discretion is all I am asking of you. There will be a wedding, a great, flower-decked wedding with Julie trailing white lace as a proper bride should do. Do you want scandal to carry her train?"

"Scandal can bring her whole family. Gossip, nit-picking, slander, let them all come. The only true members of that wedding party will be my bride, myself, and my beloved sister whose untiring intrigue has made our marriage possible."

Sophie took a sip of the scalding coffee. When she spoke, her tone was gentled.

"Very well, Toni," she agreed. "It was just a suggestion."

"What you must understand, Sophie," he told her. "Is something that Julie herself pointed out to me. Our marriage is older than we are. By God, we are convinced that it was set in the stars while we were both seeds in our father's pouches. We are married, Sophie, as we have been since our eyes first met. I never intend to drift into sleep nor rise from it again without Julie in my arms."

"Then by God, wake up earlier, you miserable stud," Sophie laughed at him. "At least you don't have to keep Sally standing in the hall with pails of hot water for Julie's bath until the morning is half-spent."

"I always wished I had a brother," Julie put in softly. "As I listen to the two of you, I am not all that certain that I could handle it."

Sophie grinned at her. "Brothers can be special or brothers can be a real bore." She exchanged a quick glance with Antoine. "I have two brothers, as you may know. Emile—" She shrugged and fanned her hands a little. "Emile I can easier leave than take, but this brother here. He is the one soul in the world who cared enough to help me find my life with the man I loved."

"I don't understand," Julie told her.

"Few people do and few people would, I fear," Sophie said quietly, "Toni's plans were so wildly audacious that I myself did not believe he could bring them off."

Antoine rose and laid his napkin beside his plate. "With your permission, sister, I will go and tumble that nephew of mine about for a bit." He leaned and tilted Julie's face up for his kiss. "You see," he whispered. "I have heard this story and she will say much more complimentary things about me if I am not in the room."

Julie giggled as her eyes followed him to the door. Then she leaned forward, "I am fascinated to hear your story."

Sophie toyed with her silver as she began to talk, her low voice vibrant with emotion.

"You see, Paul and I have loved each other since we were children. He is hotheaded and given to wild pleasures, but I have loved him no less for that. My father never really approved of him but could not deny our betrothal because Paul's family is too highly placed and well connected for him to be able to state any objection.

"We had been betrothed for several years and had grown almost to the age for marriage when Paul fell on hard times." She raised her eyes in a bid for Julie's understanding. "He was jailed for gambling debts. This so disgraced his family that they renounced him and would have left him to rot away his life in prison. My own father formally revoked our betrothal and began arrangements for me to marry a hideous old man of high station."

She raised her eyes to Julie's. "I would have killed myself before being bedded by that old man. It was Antoine who saved me from that choice. He became thief, stealing from our own father enough gold to pay off Paul's debts, and to get him released from prison. He became smuggler. Along with Titus, he managed to get us both out of France and into this new world with money enough to start our new life. Now is that a brother?"

It didn't matter that Julie was speechless because Sophie spoke on swiftly.

"Being the man he is, Antoine would not launch his life until he had repaid every franc that he had taken from our father. So he and Titus fled to England together. Now the story must start to make some sense to you. He installed Titus as a gamekeeper in Epping and hired himself out as a footman. From that he went to gambler, and then to highwayman, all to accumulate the money to repay his debt."

Julie hated herself for her own pettiness but the ruby cirlet was there, in her mind. "And how did Mignon fit into all this?" she asked.

A shadow crossed Sophie's face. "Ah, poor Mignon LeFevre. There but for the gallantry of my brother might be the story of my own life. She was given in marriage to a nobleman twice her age even as I would have been. She bided many years with him, enduring suffering and abuse. She had fled to England with her lover when she and Antoine met. It was Mignon who guided Toni in his career as gambler."

"And her lover, tell me about him." Julie pressed.

Sophie shook her head. "I never even knew his name, only that he was an impetuous and passionate man. When he returned to London after an exile and suspected Mignon of inconstancy with Antoine, he murdered her brutally. Toni fled from the scene and after that took to the road from Epping."

Julie nodded to herself. "And Mignon's last gift to Antoine must have been a pouch of gold and a ruby circlet." Even after so long a time, the shame and humiliation of that summer trembled in Julie's voice.

Julie had never really tried to tell that story before. She found that her words stumbled a little even for a listener as sympathetic as Sophie.

"It was Antoine they wanted all the time," Julie explained. "Not me, but Antoine. And they had him. He was there in Newgate on another charge, and they never were able to put it together. Because I had the necklace, they knew that I could lead them to the man who killed Mignon. But he didn't kill her, you know. It was her lover who killed her and sought Antoine brutally because of his vengeance." She shook her head. "When the courts failed to open my lips on where I had gotten the circlet, he bribed them and spirited me away." Unconsciously, she lifted a hand to her throat. "He loved her. He loved Mignon with such passionate fury that his life held no other aim but to punish the man he thought had seduced her."

Absorbed as she was in the difficulty of telling her tale, Julie did not notice that Sophie had lifted her eyes to stare past her to the door that opened onto the verandah. Julie did not know he had returned until Antoine's hands slid along her bared shoulders.

"This is a story I have only heard second hand—through Ellie," he said quietly. "I was afraid to ask you myself, Julie, fearful that I was not strong enough to stomach what really befell you after my flight.

"I went back to find the doors of the cabin flapping in the wind but no life there. I had freed my horse in the woods to throw them off my track, and not even that stallion was left for me to find. There was no life, no life at all.

"Later in taverns along the road I heard whispered tales of a great deformed dwarf and witch-eyed girl who had risen in the smoke from that hearth fire while the thief-takers were scouring the woods. Nowhere. You and Titus were nowhere."

Julie raised her hands to hold Antoine's tight against her flesh. She did not try to dry the tears that came suddenly to her eyes.

"I buried Titus myself," she told him.

"But where?" Antoine asked. "How,"

Somehow she smiled. "I think about him a lot, Antoine. He sleeps in the priest's hole behind the wooden wall of that cottage. He is curled there like a child among the withered ghosts of his own apple harvest. I tell myself that someday, when the stories have been forgotten, his bones will be found. He will be given a proper burial and people will wonder about that bent form, no taller than a child, who slept all those years in Epping."

"And now Ellie wears his name," Sophie said with an air of triumph. "My God, why does it bring so much pure delight to me for that saucy wench with the tongue of a sailor to carry Titus's name to this new land? I am entranced by it."

"She got it her favorite way," Julie laughed. "She stole it from me. She always said that stealing came more natural to her than having things 'come proper.' "

In the laughter that followed, Antoine pulled Julie to her feet against him.

"Sister, could we have a basket of food and a good stout horse? My dreams have included a picnic by a wild river with this delicious wench pressed into the grass beneath me."

Julie gouged him with her elbow rather more sharply than he enjoyed for which she got a sharp pinch in return.

Sophie's frown dampened their playfulness.

"There is one man dead already from the fevered madness of Monde DuBois," she reminded him. "While Ben tells me that Perry, the man whom your horse dispatched so untidily, was the most dangerous of the lot, who knows?"

Julie stared at her. "Then that is why I have been so carefully guarded here? My God, it never occured to me! And that must also be why I have not seen Tanta Anne-Louise all this time."

Sophie nodded. "It was cruel but necessary. Your cousin Jacques gathered together the worst of the fevered cultists and chained them and sold them away. Perry escaped, as did the slut Tomala. We feared for you, knowing the vengeance that they bore against you for your uncle's death.

"We dared not let your face be shown at Charles Town nor let a message go direct from this plantation to that one lest they be led here. Mrs. MacRae has always been the go-between for your letters even. We will probably never know how long he waited in those woods for his opportunity to strike at you."

"Thank God for Lapin," Julie said, feeling a sudden weakness along her limbs. "And for the timely arrival of this long-awaited madman here."

"We will take no chances with secluded places yet," Antoine promised aloud. "But with Ben along I shall parade my bride in Charles Town this afternoon. When the world sees what treasure I have been seeking for these many months they will no longer call me a madman."

Chapter Seventy

And indeed, it seemed to Julie that she was to meet every soul in Charles Town in the days to come. Antoine's arrival at his sister's plantation provided the signal for a round of social events that kept Julie whirling. There were teas, dinner parties, musicals, and dances, and always an "open house" on the verandah of Sophie's plantation on late sunny afternoons.

Not since she was a child in her father's house with her mother still well and her father's laughter booming in the rooms could Julie remember such a season of partying. Even in those days when her happiness had bubbled to overflowing her maid Mary was wont to caution her with dour words.

"There are worms even in paradise," she reminded Julie.

Mary's words came back to Julie when the plantation was bright with friendly people.

478

Rita Beauchamps, her eyes sparkling with envy, fell on Julie with a shriek. "My God, if I had known what Sophie's brother was like, I would have torn out my own eyes and replaced them with yellow glass. Such a man. I would be proud to stand by him at any Parisian party. How did this come about? Tell me the tale?"

Julie frowned in thought. As much as she enjoyed being with Rita, she was wary of a tongue that swung so freely. "What do you know? How much have you been told?" Julie asked her warily.

"Just what everyone knows," Rita shrugged. "That Madame Bontemps's brother had lost his affianced through a terrible disaster at sea. That he heard she had been saved and was searching her through the colonies like a madman, not meaning to rest until she was found. I never met him before, you know. He came and went from here swiftly, like a fugitive with no time for anyone. How did you know him? Where did you meet?"

"North of London," Julie told her quietly. "When I was yet still a child—ten years ago."

Rita's eyes shone. "A fairy tale," she decided. "It is like a fairy tale romance. But it raises my hopes that there is indeed more hope in life than to be bartered into marriage for a square of land and a fine name that does not warm a bed."

Julie was perhaps the most overjoyed when she saw, among Sophie's guests, a friend whom she considered her very own. She clapped Mrs. MacRae to her breast with a great hug of recognition.

The little Scotswoman, dressed with painful care of the meeting in linen that screamed of bleach and starch, watched, with her tongue already flapping, Julie pour her tea.

And their conversation went just as it had on their other meeting, with Mrs. MacRae chattering on endlessly while Julie nodded and smiled. But this time Julie's attention was wholly riveted on the story that her guest was burning to tell. How proud she was of the conspiracy that she and Anne-Louise had plotted together. How she herself, Maggie MacRae, had been the go-between who learned the details of the search for the golden-eyed girl, how Anne-Louise had hesitated because of the story that a "madman" was somehow involved.

"She almost hesitated too long," Mrs. MacRae said in a

dramatically lowered voice. "By the time she realized that any escape was better than what faced you, that husband had grown suspicious of her visits to me. She sent this child, a lovely Negro child with pigtails all over her round head. Can you believe my astonishment as that child danced from one foot to another and recited, word for word a message that your clever aunt had made her memorize? Such a clever girl, now what was she called?"

"Mandy," Julie guessed aloud. "It had to be Mandy."

Mrs. MacRae nodded vigorously. "That's right, it sounds exactly right. And all the time, working there on the water-tongue, your cousin Jacques was waiting and watching. And front in a shipyard, wearing a great bush of a beard to hide his face and pretending not to understand a word of our he came forth in just the pinch of time, too, he did."

Jacques and Mandy, Anne-Louise and Mrs. MacRae. "I am rich in friends," Julie told her friend.

The woman's eyes flew open in astonishment. "Oh my dear no," she protested. "It is I who have been blessed. Such an adventure to have had a part in. You cannot imagine what nice little gatherings I have been asked to—all so that the dear ladies can hear this romantic tale, of your rescue and your being found by your lost love."

There are no worms in this paradise, Julie kept telling herself. And yet there were small things.

In spite of Sophie's resigned protests, no night passed that Antoine did not waken with his arms about Julie. And never did she move in a group that his arm was not sheltering her or his eyes on her from across the room.

But he was not always smiling.

She would have named his surliness as jealousy but hi pride would not accept the word.

"Jealous, hell!" he exploded. "Am I to smile idiotically while a fat old fart of a rice planter slobbers down the fron of your dress? It makes me sick, just sick."

"He means nothing," Julie soothed him. "Men of that age behave thus because they have energy to do nothing more."

"Well, let him drop his spittle on someone else's wife," he muttered crossly. "I have a thumb ready for every eyeball in this town that hangs out for you."

She giggled but could not completely condemn his flamin fury. She found herself similarly roused when she noted him in conversation or leaning over the hand of one of the Charles Town belles, smiling at her silly prattle.

"This will pass," she promised herself. "It will be better when we are married all legally the way Sophie is planning for us to be."

There was also the nagging concern about Anne-Louise. Once Antoine had returned, the messages from Monde DuBois changed to much more than the simple greetings she had received before.

You do understand, my dear, that my mourning has kept me from your this long time. I cannot leave this place nor cease my mourning until I have found peace in my own heart for the evilness I have sheltered in me.

But now you would come to me. You must know how eagerly we wait for your return to see for ourselves that you are as happy and well as you are reported by our mutual friends.

Julie crumpled the letter in her lap, shaking her head. "I can't do it," she admitted to herself. "It is not fear nor lack of strength. I simply will not force myself to go back to that place lest the evil of it infect my mind. To go down that narrow tunnel of black trees, into that hollow-eyed house whose face hides the secret stairway and the room that was my prison. I cannot go. I will not go."

So she penned gentle notes in return and sent them by messenger, thanking her aunt for her words of good will and sending her own dearest love. Of a visit to Monde DuBois, she said nothing.

Lively arguments rose daily between Sophie and Antoine. Their exchanges sparkled with false intensity and ribald wit.

Sophie, who had revealed herself as a total romantic, was pressing for the plans of the wedding to be made, a day to be set. She wished the gown to be in preparation in the sewing room upstairs, to start writing invitations at the polished desk of her library.

"What a party it will be," she coaxed Antoine. "The garden riotous with flowers and every slave adorned in costume. Small garlands of ivy on the attendents, and Julie herself—"

"I'll be damned if our marriage will be turned into a

481

pleasure-garden fete," he protested. "This is a marriage not a public spectacle. These are lives we are joining, not the binding of social ties."

"Oh very well," Sophie sighed. "At least name a day and date for this bleak little Puritan ceremony to take place."

Mollified by her final retreat, Antoine turned to Julie. "I have no date in mind, my love. Have you?"

Maybe it was because the same flowers were blooming in Sophie's garden, maybe the same sweet summer scents in the air. In any case, the day had been full in her mind, and when Antoine put the question to her Julie replied promptly.

"The fourteenth of July."

They both stared at her.

"The fourteenth of July. Why that is—" Sophie was actually spluttering. "But my dear, that is no time at all. Let me see, what day of the week will it be?"

"I have no idea," Julie admitted.

Antoine roared with laughter as he reached for her hand. "You wild fey creature. You name a day that you drew from under your hat just like that, not knowing even what day of the week it is, not caring that there would barely be time to bake a cake for you to slice."

"I did not pull that date out of my hat," Julie protested. "It was on the fourteenth of July that I first saw you, Antoine. In Middlesex. Ten years ago."

"My God," Antoine slapped his head. "The lord protect me from a woman with a memory like that! How have you remembered? How can you be sure?"

He could not know of the terrors of that night. He had not heard her mother Fiona screaming with the pain of her dying. "I have remembered," Julie told him soberly. "I am sure."

Julie felt Sophie's eyes thoughtful on her. "It can be arranged, my dear." She said quietly. "It will be done and without the elegance that you deserve, but it can be arranged."

"This haste will not put too great a burden on you, will it Sophie?" Antoine asked with sudden solicitude.

Sophie grinned at him. "I would not tell you if it did, you idiot," she told him. "And you know it."

That afternoon, like so many others, found the three of them circulating among Sophie's friends who had stopped by to meet Julie and have tea and cakes with her and Antoine

Julie, concentrating on trying to remember the names of so many strangers met all at once, gave only the briefest notice to the lone figure of a man crossing the lawn towards Sophie.

But from that single glance, she found herself frozen in shock.

Some unintelligible apology fell from her lips as she abandoned the guest at her side and walked, as if in a dream, across the verandah to where Sophie stood with the man.

He raised his eyes to Julie and smiled. Julie sobbed and quickened her steps towards him, her eyes clinging helplessly to his face. His smile widened warmly at her approach.

She heard Sophie's low voice but the words were unnecessary. Jacques DuBois. This could be none else than her own cousin whom she had never met. But by what magic had her father's face leaped from the grave, across a generation and this wide sea to smile at her from a stranger's face?

"Juliette," she heard him say. *"Cousine."*

Belatedly conscious of the staring guests, Julie would have offered her hand to him in an ordinary social gesture but he was too quick for her. He leaned forward at her approach, caught both her hands and drew her into his arms for a warm embrace.

"Juliette," he kept repeating. "Juliette."

A self-conscious burst of chatter from the verandah drowned out their ensuing conversation from the other guests. Without even glancing at him, Julie was conscious of stiffness in Antoine's stride as he approached her and her cousin.

Sophie, also sensitive to Antoine's mood, broke in hastily.

"My brother and I are so happy to welcome you to this house, Monsieur DuBois. We have been so pleased to know that you were with your mother during this difficult time." Her words flowed easily, but she was deftly leading the two men and Julie away from the other guests as she spoke.

"Without your great service on my cousin's behalf, there would be no joy at Monde DuBois," he reminded her in a low voice. "For this we find ourselves eternally in your debt."

Julie was painfully torn between the two men. She ached at the rage and jealousy in Antoine's face, yet she could not resist the warm smile of her cousin. My God, he was her father again in life. The same tall, spare form, the angle of his head in speech, the warm, deep tone of his voice.

"To see you is to have my father with me once more," Julie told him quietly.

He smiled at her. "So my mother is wont to say. And she has talked of little but you in these weeks past, cousin. Of your strength and courage," he paused, "and your loveliness."

Sophie with an alarmed glance at her brother, seized Jacques by the arm. "Come, my friend, I want you to meet our friends, have tea."

"I will happily do so at another time," he said, "But at this moment I have a message from Juliette's aunt that I am pledged to deliver. This seems an admirable time to convey it."

A solemnity in his tone set a sudden stillness on them all. Julie felt her fingers tighten on Antoine's arm involuntarily.

Jacques's smoky eyes, so like her father's, held her own gaze as he spoke. His voice was low and quite firm. "My mother sends her dearest love to you as always, Juliette. And to you, sir," he nodded at Antoine. "Her heartfelt congratulations and best wishes on your coming marriage into this family. Juliette, she wishes me to say that she is eagerly awaiting your long-delayed return to the home of your family from which she will be happy to see you wed to this man of your choice."

Julie was conscious of Sophie's sudden intake of breath, and she felt the jerk of Antoine's arm against her own.

Into that stunned silence Jacques spoke again quietly. "Surely this comes to no one's surprise that my mother is eager for the return of this child to our hearth after so much has befallen her."

Incredibly enough, Sophie's tongue, whose calmness and ready words had seemed capable of all challenges, was suddenly struck dumb. Even though Antoine's breath felt suddenly shallow and strange at her side, neither did he speak. It was only after a long, awkward silence that he spoke her name, like a question.

"Julie?"

Julie felt time grow suddenly soft and shapeless about her. What must have been a minute stretched loosely to hold within its pulsing the weight of time past and the threat of coming years.

She saw herself in the misery of her uncle's house, scheming to escape, dreaming of the refuge that lay with her aunt in the Carolina colony, she saw Mark's sacrifices and the machinations of the Furlongs, Josh's long trek through the wilderness with her at his side, all to reunite her with her own family, to make her a child of the heart of Anne-Louise DuBois.

At that quiet moment, when she was conscious of the hum of summer insects about her, of low laughter from the tea table, and of these three precious people waiting, she knew she must make the decision that would define her to the world and to herself. She must make it even though someone be terribly hurt. Even if it meant cutting away her own past and threatening Antoine's understanding of her. There was no time to frame those important words. They must be said boldly, without artifice, for she had no time.

Sliding her arm from Antoine's grasp she stepped toward Jacques who had earned her love and allegiance at her first glance. She raised her golden eyes to him, pleading.

"You must listen to me with your whole heart, cousin, remembering what trials both you and I have survived separately. My love for your mother is deep and sincere. My gratitude for her welcome to me and her efforts in my behalf is boundless.

"But Jacques, I am not a child of hers or any house. I have been too long a wandering fugitive, separated from the people of my blood, surviving by the gentleness of friends and strangers. Try to make her understand, Jacques, that I do not reject her nor the blood of the Duvalls. It is simply that I am no one's child. I am my own woman and I choose to marry from this house, not as a child being given, but as a woman giving herself—freely and by choice.

"I will see her in time, Jacques. I shall say these things again to her when I am healed enough to enter those walls again. But I will not come as a child of the house nor as Antoine Riviere's wife, but as myself who is married to Antoine Riviere. Do you understand?"

He nodded, his head bent. "I do understand and I must say that this is neither more nor less than I expected of you having heard so much of you from my mother. You owe us nothing. We owe you much."

He raised his eyes to Sophie and Antoine. "May I say to you that I envy you the love and loyalty of this woman?"

After leaning briefly over Sophie's hand and her own, Jacques turned and made his way across the lawn to the waiting trap. Only as his slender figure receded did Julie realize that he walked with a painful limp.

"Julie," Sophie breathed turning to take her in her arms. "Oh thank you, thank you, Julie."

Julie leaned against the fragrance of Sophie's shoulder until she felt Antoine gently pull her away.

"I am sure that you need to return to your guests, sister," Antoine told Sophie. "I would appreciate your making an apology to them for Julie and myself."

Chapter Seventy-One

And truly, Julie was relieved to have Antoine's supporting arm about her as he led her up the stairs into the coolness of her bedroom whose curtains had been drawn against the afternoon sun.

Once inside the door, he lifted her and laid her on the bed with her head on the ruffled pillow.

She smiled wanly at him. Where had her strength and vitality gone? Had it really been that hard to speak to Jacques what lay in her mind?

"I can't conceive of what came over me," she told Antoine. "Please forgive me being such a weakling."

"Those were hard words that you said to your cousin," Antoine said quietly, sitting beside her on the bed. He lifted her hand and turned it idly in his own. "They were not words I ever expected to hear a woman speak. Hard words, and hard to say." He fell silent before raising his eyes to her defensively. "I was ready to challenge that man."

"I know it, Antoine," Julie said tiredly.

"But he is in love with you," Antoine argued truculently, his voice rising with anger. "He looked at you across that lawn; you smiled and he was smitten."

"My God, Antoine. He is my cousin. We come from the same blood."

"And hot, sweet blood it is too," he said quickly. "Do you think I did not see the way you leaped into his arms like a

486

common strumpet when your eyes first met? Do you think I missed his compliments, your eager, fawning smiles?"

She stared at him in disbelief. How could he do this? How could he let his miserable jealousy goad him into an attack on her when she had just made a commitment to him that had terrified her even as she spoke the words?

Fool. He was behaving like a fool.

She tried to rise but a dizziness held her back. "Oh go away," she said tiredly. "Just go away until you can cleanse your mind of your filthy thoughts."

With her head turned from him she did not at once realize the fury of his silence. When he seized her wrist, his grip brought a quick cry to her lips. "Don't ever do that, Julie." His tone was threatening. "Don't ever try to send me away from you."

She stared at him in astonishment. That look in his face, the warning in his voice were too hatefully familiar to her. A shiver trembled along her spine. There is a beast in man, she realized with sudden horror. There is a beast in man that must master what it possesses. So Antoine too, harbored this same beast, and jealousy was its food.

"I will not go through that again," she promised herself silently. Though I lose Antoine, though I lose all, I will not again be enslaved by any master.

She struggled up against the pillows, her eyes narrowed on his face. "Don't ever speak to me like that, Antoine Riviere, not ever again." Her voice was soft and low but in no way gentle. "Your words to me are as uncivil as your intent. I did indeed leap into the arms of my cousin Jacques, and I would do it again and may perhaps do it again. He is my only close relative within this generation. He is the only man alive who fully comprehends the experience I went through at his father's house. He is also the living, breathing image of my father whose memory still glows in my heart like a remembered hearth fire."

His look of astonishment was quickly replaced by a scowl.

"You have a tart tongue for such a gentle face," he said harshly. "Has my rose grown thorns in our time apart?"

"Not so much as your memory has chosen to pick and choose what it recalled of me," she replied. "I did not take such scathing, demeaning remarks from you when I had my

487

friend Titus at my side. Now that I am my own woman I intend to be no different from what I am."

She knew that his fury was born of love and astonishment, but this knowledge made it no easier to bear. Her own palms had grown slick with the fine sweat of fear. He would not strike her. She was sure that he would not wound her physically, but some sixth sense warned her that she dare not lose this small battle lest a long war go with it.

He rose and stood above her beside the bed, looking down at her.

"You call yourself a changed woman. Tell me what has so educated you, madame. I have pondered greatly on this all the time I sought you. It is burned into my memory that it was I who first introduced you to the flaming pleasures of the flesh. Who have your teachers been since then? Who has changed you from a dimpled girl to a sharp-tongued shrew?"

He towered above her. This was a child's game, to try to intimidate her with his greater size and strength. She fumed at the ruthlessness of his words. Power is a game that two can play, she told herself furiously. Our tools are different, that is all.

Sliding off the bed away from him, she stood and tugged at the fastening of her dress, and then her undergarments until they lay in a silken pool about her ankles. She slid her arms in under her hair and loosed it, throwing it back from her face to curl about her shoulders and back.

"Are you asking me how many men have possessed me since you?" she asked quietly.

The same dim light that played rosily across her smooth flesh showed a fine sheen of sweat on his face.

"God damn it, Julie. What kind of a question is that to ask? What kind of a strumpet's trick is it to bare your body and stand there like a wanton whore while I am trying to talk to you?"

"Since you were asking me about my whoring, it seemed appropriate," she said quietly. "That question has rankled behind your eyes since I first wakened from the shock of our meeting. I have felt it roughen our lovemaking and turn an edge of irritation when I have exchanged words with any man, even my own blood cousin. We need it out."

"Jesus, Julie," he pleaded, reaching for her. "Lay off. I am not ready to hear this from you."

488

She backed off from him. "You will never be ready, Antoine," she predicted. "Yet you will never rest until you know. If you cannot live with the truth of me, then we might well save a doomed marriage now."

He turned away from her to stare at the closed curtains with his arms folded across his chest.

"Clearly this is a long and tortuous list," he said acidly. "Are you sure we have started early enough in the day that you may adequately whip my heart with your confessions?"

"On the contrary," she said softly. "Two."

But he had indeed been drawing his own scorecard, she realized. He turned to her with fury contorting his face.

"Two!" he screamed at her. "What of the fancy pants attorney that Ellie told me set you up in such grand style in Newgate? And the prentice whose hopeless passion for you caused him to rescue you from Mignon's lover and pay your passage to America? And the grubby Indian trader who kept you hidden somewhere all those months? And that demented uncle of yours?"

"Three," she said thoughtfully. "My God, I had forgotten Giles Urban."

He turned to her and seized her arms again, livid with rage. *"Forgotten!* As God is my judge, Julie, I will kill you for tricks like that. I will not mean to, but my body will move swifter than my head. Forgotten! If I must have the truth, let me have it all at once and be done with it."

He had not wanted to touch her. She felt him struggle to pull away from her touch. She realized his failure as his hands slid about her, light against the coolness of her flesh.

She raised her eyes to him. "I had forgotten about Giles. That is how much he meant to me, Antoine. I laid with him. It was truly a whore's work. I accpted food and drink and shelter from him. I let him protect me from the filth and the disease and the dangers of the common rooms at Newgate. For this I paid him with my body's favors, not my heart's but my body's.

"You see, Antoine, at that point, I was still eager to live. Anything that I could do to stay alive until I was united with you again was worth the price."

He bowed his head a minute and then nodded. "That's enough then. I understand that with the others you were prisoned and unable to defend yourself. I am man enough myself to know that a woman entrapped is subject to assault—how well I know it."

"And so it was with my uncle," she said quietly. "Mignon's lover, as much as he wished to be otherwise, had grown impotent at her death. He punished me as much for his own impotence as my silence."

He took her hands and lifted them to his lips.

"Forgive me my doubts," he asked quietly.

She was no more immune to his nearness than he to hers. She could smell the fresh scent of his hair. His hands against her own brought memories of too many caresses. She could lift her lips to his and it would be over, all over. She shook her head. If she did not resist this temptation, who knew what deception she might be forced to next?

"It is I who am confessing," she reminded him. "And I do not ask forgiveness but understanding."

"What are you trying to tell me now?"

"The third man was Josh Simmons." She saw the white line come along his cheek as his jaw tightened.

"You were in his power," he said dully.

"I was, but he took no advantage of me," she told him slowly.

His glance was a question.

"He suffered greatly in denying himself the luxury of assaulting me. He nursed me to life, he shared all he had with me, he brought me from a wounded, terrified object, praying for death, to the full status of a woman loved and respected and—yes, enjoyed for herself. For that I gave him my favors freely, of my own accord. My love if you will."

His voice rose perilously in disbelief. "You seduced him? A one-eyed Indian trader?"

"And given the same circumstances I would do so again," she said recklessly. "Only this time I would do it sooner, that he suffer less."

This was a fury she had not seen. He threw her hands away from his. He backed off from her, his flesh darkening so that his brilliant eyes seemed to own their own threatening light. "Bitch," he hissed at her. "I can accept you as victim, I can accept your being ravished for the sake of your life, but for you to seduce that man, to deliberately lie with him and then say to me with your own lips that you have ever been

490

wife to me. Oh Jesus Christ that I should have sold my soul for such a worthless strumpet."

The draft from the slammed door chilled her from head to foot. She stood a long time staring after him before numbly crossing to the cupboard, donning a gown, and groping her way into the bed. Where were her tears? Where they should have been came only a dry, hopeless pain.

"I had to do it," she whispered to herself. "Sooner or later, I had to do it."

She stirred as the light tapping sounded at the door. She could tell it was twilight by the pattern of the birdsong through the window. The faint musical strumming told her that the slaves's day was through, and she knew that lights glistened from their quarters behind the stables.

Sally would be there to help her dress for dinner. Sally would simply have to report that she was not feeling well enough to join them this night. She called, "Come," listlessly without turning her head.

At the clink of glasses, she turned to glance at the door. Antoine was inside the room, carrying a tray with a silver cover on it.

"Did you rest well?" he asked, pushing the door shut behind him with his foot.

She did not answer. She only watched him cross the room, his face knit in concentration as he balanced the big tray. Her heart pressed against her throat, and still he did not speak to her again nor meet her gaze. With one hand, he pushed aside the objects on the table to make room. Then he set the tray down, carefully level all the way. The waiting was suddenly more than she could bear.

"Is your fury suddenly spent?" Julie asked him. "Or have you thought of new foul names to define me with?" she eyed him warily.

He shook his head and looked at her quite soberly.

"You were the victim of the froth of my passion, Julie," he said. "I am man. It is in our nature to pick and choose before a full board. We always ask that our fowl be roasted the brownest and that fruit be sweet only for our tongue.

"You are too honest a woman, Julie. Any other woman would have given me what I wished in sweet words and swallowed the truth, praying that it never pop from her mouth by chance.

"I had indeed forgotten what a prickly tongue you once gave me when I vented my spleen on you. I had chosen to remember only your beauty and sweetness, your playful mind and your constant affectionate nature.

"How strange it is. I can see you with your arm about young Charles and your hand in affection on the dog Lapin. I cherish that giving affection of yours. How could I ask that it be stoppered as if with a cork when we were apart? Can you ask a plum to be rosy only if you are watching it?"

He shook his head. "I will not lie that the truth is easy to swallow. I will carry that Josh in my heart with a brooding fury for all of my days. But it is the fury of envy, not hatred against you. I hate him because you cherished him that much, not because you were being yourself in his company."

"You are making me cry," Julie confessed softly. "I was afraid."

"I am sure I will do that many more times, my dear," Antoine told her. "But it will never be because I wish to pain you. It will rather be that I am man and raddled with imperfections.

"And never be afraid of losing me," he added after a minute. "That is a job you are simply too much a woman to do."

"Now." He lifted the top from the tray so that a fragrance of spiced shrimp and peppers escaped into the room.

"Oh," she cried, "I am ravenous."

"And ravishing too, I might add," he said, serving her plate and bringing it to the bed.

"I can get up, for heavens sake," Julie protested.

"Not this time," he argued. "Now hold that while I bring the wine."

It dawned on her that there was a different lilt to his voice, that his mouth twitched suspiciously like mischief.

"What are you up to?" she asked with a challenge.

His eyebrows rose in exaggerated insult. "I? Madame, what can you possibly mean." With one of Sophie's embroidered towels across his lap, he was wrestling with the wine cork.

"I mean this seems very festive, dining in my room. That looks to be a special wine too."

"We do everything in style," he said patiently, leaning over

492

to fill her glass and then his. "Everything," he repeated, leaning over to press his lips on her half-exposed breast.

She giggled but he shook his head.

"Glass up there. We have a toast," he ordered briskly.

With his own glass against hers, he suddenly frowned. "Now what was that damned expression that Sophie came up with that first night—something about a star?"

"A bright particular star," Julie reminded him. "It's from Shakespere."

"Whatever," he shrugged, holding his glass against hers. "A toast then, to the sons of the 'bright particular star.'"

The glass was halfway to her lips when his words registered on her. That quick thud of terror came again. Their love had survived so much, their long separation, his forced knowledge of her infidelity with Josh. But would it survive the coming years if he were disappointed in this dream that he mentioned oftener and oftener as their wedding date neared?

"You do not like the toast?" he asked.

"I like it," she sighed and drained the glass.

"Do you know what day this is?" he asked slyly.

She shook her head.

"It is the seventh of July."

"The seventh," she breathed, amazed. "I have lost all count."

"Sophie and I decided that you had when you set our wedding day only one week hence."

"Oh, I am sorry," she cried. "I cannnot do that to Sophie. We must tell her."

He shook his head. "On the contrary, it will be barely soon enough." He laughed merrily. "Sophie will at once begin to circulate some gossip to explain our early and quiet marriage. She will explain that you preferred it in deference to your aunt's mourning. How shy you are in this new place. So on and so forth. Then there will be only the six of us there."

"Six?" she asked, trying to count them out.

His eyes were dancing at her. "You and I, of course. Then the minister who will mumble all the necessary words. Then there will be Sophie and Charles."

"But that is only five."

He slid his hand under the cover and cupped it over her warm belly. "And our friend here."

493

At her astonished expression, he burst into a roar of laughter.

"It seems that you have lost track of more things than the days, my sweet. It was that wench Sally who first dared to speak to Sophie of it. It seemed she quickly noticed how sleepy you had grown of late, how slowly you came to feel lively in the mornings, having a distaste for food until the day was well begun—even the way your fine breasts seemed to leap from the bosom of a dress that had fitted quite decently only a few weeks before."

Julie felt her breath stop in her throat. She leaned towards him, her golden eyes glinting with excitement.

"You wouldn't tease me, Antoine. That would be cruel. Are you sure?"

"The two of them are sure, and that is enough for me."

She clambered from the bed to clasp him in her arms.

"A child," she cried. "A child of our very own." Then she paused. "But oh, Antoine, what if it not be a son but a girl child instead? Will you be dreadfully disappointed?"

"Not at all," he shrugged. "I only said there would be sons. I did not direct their order. If some minx of a girl wants to come first, we will be happy to greet the little beast. But whatever comes, it already has a name."

"How can that be?" Julie asked.

"Because I have already chosen it," he said blithely.

He drew her close and slid his hand inside her gown to rest his finger on the star-shaped scar that Ben's knife had left there above her waist. "The name is Etoile."

She looked at him, puzzled.

"Star," he translated slowly. "Now tell me that it does not have a fine ring, Etoile Riviere. For our star, Julie, our bright and particular star."

Then his hand slid past the star, along her waist, over the roundness of her belly, and between the silken flesh of her thighs. She clung to him as he laid her back gently onto the bed.

"You must take very excellent care of yourself," he whispered as he freed her of her gown and loosed his own clothing. "You must sleep a lot, eat properly, and avoid excitement."

He slid his arms under her body drawing her close.

"Tomorrow," he told her. "Tomorrow we will start doing all those sensible things."

494

Chapter One

The matched grays that drew the carriage down the Ashley River road towards Charles Town moved along at a dignified pace, maneuvering the deep curves with an easy, if ponderous, grace. Even if the carriage had not contained three women and a small child on that summer morning of 1726, the pace would still have been well chosen. For although Charles Town had grown apace and many travellers passed along this way, the road remained a rough country lane whose sudden turns could reveal unexpected peril.

Both the man and his mount who followed the carriage gave a startling contrast to the staidness of the carriage's pace. For one thing, both man and horse were of astonishing size. The black stallion, his wide nostrils flaring, strained against his reins with the same look of furious impatience that darkened his rider's face.

Antoine Riviere was wigless with his thick hair tied at the nape of his neck and his coat across the pommel of his dancing mount. His shirt was laid open at the throat against the heat, and its fine fabric showed a pattern of sweat on his broad back. The scowl on his face was as dark as his sun-bleached hair was pale as he struggled with his mount.

"Another damned muggy day," he muttered to his horse. "A man could swim in this cursed air."

Glancing over his shoulder, he stared into the west at a bank of gray clouds forming along the horizon. There could be rain. God willing there would be rain to sweeten the air before nightfall.

Now and then the trees, in full leaf with summer, parted to show the broad face of the river glinting with sunlight. Young mockingbirds being forced to flight by their parent birds clung to their branches with desperate claws, screaming in terror.

What a bastard day this one was turning out to be, Antoine raged inwardly. It was bad enough to have to spend a day away from his wife Julie when she was so near to her time with their coming child. There was nothing he could do

497

about that. His sister Sophie, along with her maid, needed to ready the town house for the summer move, and one day was as good as another for that task. But to leave Julie at the plantation as he had, with tears still fresh on her face and harsh words hanging between them, set him to writhing.

The anguish of the long argument between them flooded back on him, filling him with despair. It was true enough, as Julie said, that he and Julie herself owed their very lives to his sister Sophie. It was also true that leaving a beautiful young woman alone to manage a huge plantation made no sense, but God's blood, a man had a right to set forth on his own.

It was Sophie's insane stubbornness that was setting all their teeth on edge. How could she believe that her husband Paul, lost these many years since the last Indian war, could possibly be still alive to return to her? Yet she primped for him daily as a bride would do and refused the sensible offer of a good marriage to wait for a man long gone, if not long dead.

Only because Antoine pressed Sophie to marry did Julie ever raise her voice and will against him. Only because he loved that willful wench and their daughter so much did guilt boil in his gut as it did this morning.

At last the walls of Charles Town were in sight. As the carriage slowed for the gate, Antoine kicked the stallion alongside where his sister Sophie raised her face to him at the window.

"After I see you safely inside the gate, I'm going back to the plantation for a quick trip. I'll be back in an hour or two."

"No hurry," Sophie assured him. "We plan to stay in town until late afternoon." A sudden twinkle came in her clear eyes, and Antoine knew that some mischievous, probably ribald, thought had come to her mind. Whatever it was, she banished it, dropping her eyes from his to repeat dully, "No hurry."

The stallion stamped with impatience as Antoine waited to see the city gates close securely behind the carriage.

Pain. A sudden stab of pain came at his sister's stiff way with him. How could he and Sophie have conspired together and laughed together for so many years and still have managed to sour to a formal coldness over this matter of her re-

498

fusal to forget Paul Bontemps and marry? She was mad on this one point, purely mad.

Paul Bontemps had long ago rotted to mulch in the midden of an Indian camp somewhere in this wilderness. But as long as Sophie fought this hard truth, Antoine himself was honor bound to be the master of her household, even though it meant he could not embark on his own life with his growing family.

With the city gates behind him, Antoine gave the stallion his head. Crouched on his mount's neck with his body low against the lashing of overhanging branches, Antoine clasped the beast between his thighs. Julie. He would at least make peace with Julie before setting out for his day in Charles Town. Once that was done, the day would turn fair.

Once at the plantation, Antoine took the stallion to the stableyard to be sponged of his lather and crossed the green with eager steps to seek out his wife. As he reached the verandah, he stopped with a quick intake of breath. He had almost passed her in his haste to reach the house. What a fool he was. He should have guessed that the heat of the day would not keep her in. This was never a woman to be trapped inside of walls as long as there were doors that opened out.

He approached the chaise silently to stare down at her asleep.

Would that face ever cease to startle him with its purity of line, its gentle molding? The golden eyes which had ensnared him at his first glimpse of her moved in dream beneath closed lids. Her ripe, perfect mouth stirred in a vagrant smile as some image of the dream pleased her.

He smiled back at her unconsciously. This child of a woman with the mass of black curls framing her heart-shaped face looked pure and unused, virginal in spite of the great belly on which her fine hands rested lightly.

How could she have come so unstained through the years just past? Their quarrel of the morning had freshly reminded him of the incredible horrors that her short life had held.

She had been a child on her father's estate when he first saw her and a penniless, helpless prey of a brutal assailant when he had first lifted her into his arms. She had gone from a falsely accused prisoner in Newgate Prison to be shipwrecked and sheltered by a primitive Indian trader, and finally into the ruthless hands of her maddened uncle. But still her beauty and humour, and God help him, her spirit were unscathed.

Her words of the morning echoed in his mind.

"How dare you try to force me to make Sophie abandon her faithfulness to Paul?" she had confronted him, her eyes blazing. "You ask me to do that. Me, who happily went through hell waiting for you. What would you have done if I had wedded when I was so certainly told that you were dead."

"I would have widowed you and taken what was rightfully mine," he told her angrily. "But this is different. My God, Julie, this has been going on for years. Look at her son Charles. He was but a child of two when the Yamassee struck the settlement. Now he is grown and off to France for his education and still she waits."

At her stubborn glance, his voice softened.

"What about us?" he asked gently, laying his hand on the great belly which held their second child. "What about you and our child Etoile and this one coming? Do we not deserve a life of our own? To be apart from this place to build a home and a life of our own? All my work here, no matter how well I am paid, is labor in another man's vineyard. I need to build an estate of my own, for you and our children."

"I want that too," she replied softly, lifting her face to his. "But I cannot seize our own happiness by forcing Sophie into another man's bed while she still believes that Paul may return."

The scent of her skin close to him stirred in his head. The helplessness of desire drew him to her irresistibly. His passion for her was a deep, whirling pool that drew him from reason at the touch of her flesh on his. He drew back, gripping his control with clenched teeth. "Jesus," he stormed at her. "How can a man call himself a man when he is so entrapped by women?" He was still struggling to contain his emotions as she pulled herself to her feet and started towards the door.

"Entrapped," she repeated quietly. "Is that how you see yourself?" As she flung open the door he saw the sudden glint of tears on her cheeks. "There. The trap is sprung. Walk out that door. Go and make your fortune in the wide world like

500

a third son in a fairy tale. Your life is your own. Be free of us women."

"Oh yes," he said acidly. "Just walk away, is it? And what of you and my daughter Etoile? And that one?" He nodded towards her swelling body.

"An escaped prisoner does not concern himself about the welfare of his jailer," she reminded him quietly.

Fury boiled in him. Why did she not dissolve into helpless tears and start bleating like other women in anger? What a stubborn, independent bitch she could be. He forced his own voice to coldness.

"I realize, madame, that you have managed to enslave half of the men in this miserable colony with your 'innocent' flirtations. I realize that your cousin Jacques DuBois would give his fortune and his life for those same charms that have so thorough entrapped me. Is this your plan? To run to your cousin for sanctuary knowing that his lust glitters for you even while you are great with another man's child?"

Even as he spoke he knew that her anger would rise to match his words, but he could not stem his torrent of insult. He wanted her, God, how he wanted her, and the passion he could not still with her body turned to acid on his tongue. He braced himself for her fury. It did not come.

She stood quietly, her small body curiously graceful, balancing the weight of her swollen belly. Her golden eyes were calm and a little quizzical as they met his gaze.

"If you do not choose to walk, then I intend to," she said quietly. Before he could catch his breath and reach out for her, she had passed through the door and closed it against his outstretched hands.

The tears that had still shone on her cheeks that morning were gone as she lay sleeping. He watched the faint movement of the child beneath the mound of flowered skirt that concealed her body and smiled with tenderness for that restless unborn child.

Leaning, he lifted a straying curl from her cheek. "Forgive me, Julie," he whispered. Then cursing himself silently for the lust that stirred in him at the touch of that silken strand across his finger, he turned and entered the house.

At his sister's desk, he found ink and a quill and scratched the note hastily.

"Julie, my love," he wrote. "I came back to you. As I al-

501

ways do. As I always will. Your own." He did not need to scratch the great flowing initial. She would know.

He slipped the folded note into the open basket of needlework that stood by her lounge chair. She could not fail to see it at once and even if she did, it would fall out if the basket were lifted.

She would be wakened soon enough he thought, as he called for the horse to be saddled anew. The darkness in the west was clearly rising to a storm that would be at his back as he thundered down the river road to Charles Town for the day.

Chapter Two

The hoofbeat of the stallion were long gone from the air before Julie stirred awake, startled as she often was, by the strength of the child within her. She did not at once open her eyes but lay quietly, savoring the scents and the sounds that filled the air about her.

"Blind," she thought with a smile. "I could be blind and dropped in this place and know at once where I was." She smiled contentedly with her lids still closed against the shimmering radiance of the Carolina sun rising towards noonday. Not that the sun could reach her lounge chair that Antoine had carried to the verandah for her.

She ran her fingers along the smooth, upholstered arm of the chair, conscious of the satin pillow in the nape of her neck so that she could lie back idly just like this, listening to the calls of the mockingbirds. The fragrance from the summer flowers in Sophie's garden was so heavy in the air that Julie felt it cling to her skin like a carefully applied perfume.

How spoiled she was, pampered both by Antoine and by her sister-in-law Sophie. How could she let herself be driven to such cold fury by Antoine when she loved him with a passion that caught her heart in her throat at the thought of him? She shook her head. I must not do that, she cautioned herself. I must not think of the angry storms between us. I must not let his thoughtless words upset me. Not now, with the child within me needing only joy and strength from me in this time of waiting.

Waiting. Her hand stirred on the roundness of her belly. She opened her eyes and giggled at the flowered mountain that rose before her. The child within was a son. It had to be a son this time for Antoine. Not that any man could love a child more distractedly than Antoine did their small daughter Etoile. But a man needed a son, and Julie was secretly sure that the life that stirred uneasily against her ribs or thumped secret messages during the fretful night was a son who would come from his dark world to become a man of great power and size, even as Antoine was.

With the satisfied smile still on her lips, she let her clear, golden eyes stray about the garden, studying one mass of carefully tailored bloom after another. In spite of Antoine's fevered haste to be gone from his sister's home and onto a plantation of his own, Julie herself felt no such pressure to hurry. With her daughter Etoile only two and the new baby coming, they were better off where they were for a time.

And how sweet it was to be indolent like this. She was so rarely alone that she cherished the quiet. There was needlework for Etoile in the basket at her side. She could ring the small bell on the table and a maid would bring her a tall, cooled glass of the cherry cider whose tartness she so adored.

"You would have to sit up straight to drink it, you slattern," she laughed to herself. She would simply lie here beneath her child and think of Sophie, who had taken her maid and Etoile and the child's nurse Maggie MacRae off to Charles Town. There would be movement enough when the town house on Tradd Street was ready for their coming and she must leave this garden, this mockingbird's song.

She was startled to full wakefulness at the figure of a slender Negro girl approaching the verandah steps with a hesitant look on her face.

"Mandy," she cried with delight, struggling upright in the chaise. "Why it is indeed you, child. And whatever brings you here? Nothing is wrong at Monde DuBois, tell me there is nothing wrong."

The girl ducked her head and grinned with delight at the greeting. "All well," she assured Julie. "Your aunt, the mistress, is still off hobbing and nobbing with her Philadelphy friends. Mister Jacques say I must bring you a message."

"On such a hot day," Julie said, taking the folded note from the girl's outstretched hand. Whatever could her cousin Jacques want? Surely there was no trouble at the plantation. Since his father's death, Jacques himself had run Monde DuBois, and the place had the name of being one of the best run properties in the area.

She was conscious of Mandy's steady eyes on her as she held the paper in her hand.

"You feeling fine now?" the girl asked gently in her soft, hesitant voice.

Julie smiled at the girl, delighted to realize how the young slave had flowered under Jacques's management of the plantation. Mandy's stick-thin body had filled out, and her face had lost the shadow of terror that Julie remembered from the old days when Mandy had been her only friend in her uncle's house. A band of shining sweat stood out on the bridge of the girl's nose, and her richly colored cheeks glowed from heat.

"I could not be better, thank you, Mandy," Julie told her. Then briskly. "While I see what my cousin has to say, you trot in there and tell the cook to give you all the cold water you can drink and then have some of that cherry cider chilling in the well. Tell her I want you to have some nutcakes to go with it."

Mandy hesitated.

"That's really what I want you to tell her," Julie insisted. "Now scat so I can read this."

Her smiled faded as she unfolded the crisp sheet of paper. She would know Jacques's handwriting anywhere. Antoine's unremitting jealousy of her cousin made writing their principle means of communication. Antoine had never specifically forbidden her to have any contact with Jacques DuBois, but it was only because he dared not. Jacques and his mother and her family were her only blood relatives in all the colonies and he knew she would stubbornly fight any attempt to cut her off from them. But his resentment of Jacques, the way his face darkened at the very mention of his name kept her contacts with her family at Monde DuBois at an absolute minimum.

She read her cousin's message through twice without stopping. The second time she frowned with disbelief at Jacques' words. Whatever was he thinking of? He was asking her to come to Monde DuBois for some curious, unnamed reason

504

He knew how near she was to the time of the baby's birth. Surely he knew that bouncing about on rude colonial roads even in the best of carriages was hardly what a woman heavy with child should be doing. Yet, there it was, in his flowing hand whose letters were only formed more hastily than usual as if they rose from some urgent need. Jacques better than anyone knew how furious Antoine would be at the very thought of her travelling to Monde DuBois in the best of times and for the best of reasons. She shook her head in disbelief and read the note again, frowning earnestly as if her expression would clarify the meaning of the words.

Ma belle cousine,
    Something of possible great urgency has come to my attention. It is not some simple problem that I can send to you by word of mouth. You must come and hear it for yourself. You will only need to be here for an hour. This could be vital to you, my dear Juliette. I have sent my easiest carriage with the steadiest driver. He will take the best of care of you. Only an hour, my dear. Your life could be changed.

An hour that could change her life, how could that be? She seized the bell at her side and rang it vigorously. A maid popped from the kitchen almost instantly.

"Is Mandy having a bite to eat?" Julie asked.

At the girl's nod, Julie lifted her hand. "Would you help me up please? I want to speak to her."

"I can send her right out," the girl protested even as she gave her hand to Julie.

Julie shook her head. "I have to get up anyway," she said, her mind spinning with questions about Jacques's note.

Mandy leaped to her feet, brushing crumbs from her mouth as Julie entered the kitchen house.

"What did my cousin say when he gave you this?" she asked.

"Just that it was only for your eyes and that I should wait." A little tremor of fear stammered her words.

"And the carriage is out there waiting in the road?"

The girl nodded at Julie, her eyes white rimmed as she stared back.

505

"And you have no idea what this is all about?" Julie pressed.

The girl shifted her weight from one foot to another, and her eyes slid away.

"Mandy," Julie coaxed softly.

Julie was startled at the sudden moisture in Mandy's eyes. "I really don't know, Miss Julie. If I was to make you my guesses, I be very bad unfair to Mister Jacques."

Julie measured the girl with her eyes. Mandy's loyalty to Jacques was stiffening her already straight spine. How could she coax Mandy to unfairness to a master who had brought her from a stammering, terrified child to this healthy young woman? Julie sighed.

"Finish your cider and we will go."

"Go!" the cook exploded behind Mandy. "You don't real-life say you going to go anyplace out in the heat of this day. You got no lunch in you even. You can't go racketing off all that way for this chile or anybody."

"An hour," Julie told her firmly. "My relative needs to consult with me on a matter which will only take an hour. I will be back and resting in my chair before the others are fin-isehd at the house on Tradd Street."

"The sun has touched you." the woman grunted, suddenly turning on Mandy. "What do you mean, child?" she challenged the girl fiercely. "What you mean coming in here and dragging Miz Julie out in the blaze with no lunch in her and she buried under all that baby?"

Mandy stepped back quickly as if she feared a blow from the older woman.

Julie laid her hand on Mandy's shoulder and shook her head.

"Nobody's dragging me," she said softly. "I am going to Monde DuBois for an hour and then return. But I need my shawl for the coolness of my aunt's house after my rest outside."

Julie and Mandy grinned wickedly at each other as the cook stamped off grumbling to get the shawl.

Chapter Three

Insisting that Mandy sit inside the carriage with her to be out of the sun, Julie drew the curtains shut, preferring the stuffy air of the enclosed space to the blaze of heat.

Julie forced herself to make perfunctory inquiries about the rest of the DuBois family, the younger cousins, and what news came of her aunt's stay in Philadelphia. But her mind was not on Mandy's soft answers and almost at once she lapsed into silence as she puzzled Jacques's strange note.

Whatever he was talking about had to be important, she kept reassuring herself of that. The very fact that she was there in the carriage swaying along the road to Monde DuBois represented a dangerous gamble for herself. Only something of critical importance would keep Antoine from wild fury when he discovered that she had left the peace and safety of the plantation this day. And Jacques knew this. He had to be conscious of the risk she was taking in response to his summons.

The very thought of Jacques melted her heart in a way that Antoine could not understand. How like her own dead father this cousin of her was. From their first meeting shortly before her marriage to Antoine, she had found herself drawn irresistibly to this tall, slender man whose smokey eyes dwelt on her with the same tenderness that her father's had. At first Jacques had been graceful about ignoring Antoine's furious jealousy, but that passed with time.

"I'm not a man of stone," Jacques had protested to her crossly. "I find your husband's attitude insulting. If that big stud of yours must constantly accuse me of lusting after his wife, of being the viper in his marriage bed, then I will damn well go for the game as well as the name. And he calls the truth fairly, I must admit, except that what he names as lust I now as love."

She had tried to still his tirade to no avail.

"Love, Julie," he repeated soberly. "Your happiness is the most important thing in this world to me. I am helpless at your very word, your every move. When the day comes that you have had enough of his jealous tirades, come to me. Or better yet, don't bother coming. Call, raise an eyebrow, and I will be there for you. Forever."

Knowing Jacques's feeling was a burden whenever they were together. She was always acutely conscious of his eyes dwelling on her. She saw the great effort it took for him to avoid physical contact with her, a quick drawing back of hand after touching, the briefly, cousinly kiss that failed to touch her cheek. If their eyes happened to meet, she always felt her own heart pounding from the passion in his eyes. Yet she did not love Jacques, not in the way she did Antoine, whose brilliant eyes and teasing mouth had been imprinted in her heart at her first glance of him so long ago when she was a child in Middlesex and he was a footman on a gold and white coach thundering towards London.

She sighed and pulled the curtain back to stare at the passing scene. The blaze of the sun was muted by a frail cover of cloud borne across the sky by a swift wind. Perhaps the trip back home would be cooler. There might even be rain.

She had barely dropped the curtain again before the swaying of the carriage signalled a turn. Julie knew without looking that the carriage was passing along the tree-tunneled drive that led to the great house at Monde DuBois. Dark memories of her brief life in this place flooded over her, and she shivered as she thrust the image of her mad uncle's face from her mind.

An hour, Jacques had said. She need stay no more than an hour in this house in which evil memories hung like an eternal shadow.

Jacques was quick to the carriage to help her alight. The pressure of his hand on her arm was tender and his face cool as she lifted her cheek for his kiss.

"This mysterious business had better be important," she warned him with a smile.

"You mean that you'll catch hell if it isn't, don't you?" he challenged her. "You don't have to put up with that violent temper, Julie, you know that."

She raised her finger to his lips. "Stop that talk or I shall return on the instant. Now what is this urgent business you wrote of?" She forgot between meetings how he towered over her, even as his uncle, her father, had. Her heart turned a

508

she looked up at that fine angle of jaw and her father's smokey eyes smiling from his young face.

"I am greatly relieved that you came," he said, his face suddenly sober. "This could mean everything or nothing—" He paused with a perplexed look. "My God, Julie, I just don't know but I couldn't risk not trying."

"Jacques," she said. "What in the world? You grow more confused and confusing by the moment."

He shook his head and slid his arm behind her. "Come in, my dear. There is at least no reason that you should stand out here in the heat."

Once inside the hall, with the maid gone and with her shawl around her, Jacques took both her hands in his. His eyes were very sober on her face. "You have a friend here, Julie. I am giving you this notice that you not be shocked when you enter that room. You have a friend here that I thought best that you meet and talk to alone."

Her golden eyes studied his face and a tremor of dread stirred along her spine at his words.

"In the parlor, Julie," he said hoarsely. "Go on in. I pray God that this meeting be worth your trip today."

He turned and strode away down the hall, leaving her standing outside the closed parlor door of Monde DuBois.

She stared at the door with apprehension. What mysterious friend was this? She felt her heart racing wildly. What a fool she was to be beseiged with terrors when the mystery could be solved by the turn of a brass doorknob.

At first the room looked ghostly from the dust covers that Tante Anne-Louise must have had put on before leaving for her trip. The drapes had been drawn against the sun, plunging the room into dimness.

Julie stared into the half-light, recognizing the shapes of familiar chairs, the delicate desk which no one ever used, the piano gleaming from polish in spite of the absence of its owner. Then a movement against the drape caught her eye, and as she stepped forward a little, her lips parted in disbelief.

He was standing in the shadow behind her uncle's chair, immobile, his single eye watching her with that thoughtful expression that she had so long ago learned to cherish so dearly.

He was so perfectly as she remembered him that for one shattering moment she believed herself to be dreaming. Time

509

and the curtained room slid away from her, and she was on a pallet in a rough lean-to in the swampland of Guale. He had come as a soldier of darkness into a dimly lit room, the mass of dark hair pulled back against the nap of his neck, the leather clothing and the black patch over his left eye, and the surprising brush of moustache above the unsmiling mouth. Only that time, his arm had cradled a gun, and a brace of freshly killed fowl had hung at his side.

She felt her legs go weak beneath her, and she groped for the support of a chair back. In that swift, silent tread that she remembered so well, he was instantly at her side. Her mind was suddenly filled with the bright tune that had always been on his lips. But he wasn't humming, he was speaking to her in that low, calm voice that was dearer than any song to her ears.

"Lady," he said softly. "Easy there, Lady."

How could she be easy? She felt the joy begin like an explosion deep inside her chest. Tears came in and about with helpless laughter. As he caught her in his arms, the feel of his strong, sturdy body against her only made the tears flow freer.

"Josh," she cried. "Oh my God, it is you, Josh. My love my dear, dear Josh."

The past swept in on her. She remembered the first time he had buried his face in her hair as he was doing now. She remembered the fine feel of his hard, strong legs pressed against her own and the precious scent of his flesh against her face.

What was she doing? Josh had walked out of her past and swept away all that she had become. Her husband Antoine her lovely daughter Etoile, even the child rebelliously kicking under her heart had dissolved in the shimmering memory of Josh's scent in her head, the rich mingled leather and wood smoke smell that tightened her arms about him.

It was Josh himself who stirred away. He brought a line from somewhere and wiped her face solemnly, looking at her not at all, only careful at the task like a man mopping up a social error. Then he grinned that swift, bright way into her face.

"Lady," he said softly. "It has been a long sleep between dreams."

A long sleep between dreams. Indeed, standing there still
510

the loose circle of his arms, their life together had been a dream, a gentle dream in a life more often visited with nightmares.

Josh's arms were swift about her again. "Lady, it was what dressing her in Indian leather and bringing her tortuous miles through the wild country to reunite her with her family. Josh honoring her as no man else ever had by letting her make her love a gift rather than forced tribute. Josh leaving her at Maggie MacRae's without even the raised hand of farewell.

"You left me, Josh," she said quietly. "You left me at MacRae's without even telling me good-bye. Oh Jesus." She groped for the chair back again. She must not let the memories flood in on her like that. She must fight back the thought of the horrors that had followed her arrival at her uncle's house, this house which was now Jacques's.

Josh's arms were swift about her again. "Lady, it was what you wanted. It was all you ever wanted, remember? It was your choosing, Lady, not mine."

She nodded. "You are right of course. And I have lived through it and you have lived through it and—"

His words broke in. "And the man you told me you would always love lived through it too, remember? You were so sure that he was long dead even then."

"I was sure, Josh," she nodded. "And now we all live."

"Some of us live more fully than others," he reminded her in that calm, soft voice.

She dropped her eyes. "And all of my life is owed to you, Josh. If you had not cared for me after the shipwreck, God only knows."

He caught both her hands in his and his single eye grew sober. "We will have only a moment before your cousin returns, Lady. But I have one thing you must hear. It is I that need to thank you for my life—my real life. It was with you, and it stays with me as long as my mind is alive."

Her lips were parted in protest when Jacques opened the door into the hall. The slave behind him bore a tray covered by white linen.

"I have brought tea for you, Juliett, and something a little stronger for Josh and myself. Remember that you have only an hour. Josh has a story I want you to hear, *ma cousine*. You must decide for yourself if it is a story that might change your life."

511